About the Author

PJ O'Driscoll is the author of *These Kids Today*. He was born in Melbourne, Victoria in 1976, and was raised in both Sydney, New South Wales and Perth, Western Australia. He is a movie buff who enjoys a good story and scare and likes to know what makes people tick. This is the follow up to his debut novel, and sequel, *These Adults Today*.

These Adults Today

PJ O'Driscoll

These Adults Today

Olympia Publishers
London

www.olympiapublishers.com
OLYMPIA PAPERBACK EDITION

A CIP catalogue record for this title is
available from the British Library.

ISBN: 978-1-78830-857-1

This is a work of fiction.
Names, characters, places and incidents originate from the writer's imagination.
Any resemblance to actual persons, living or dead, is purely coincidental.

First Published in 2020

Olympia Publishers
Tallis House
2 Tallis Street
London
EC4Y 0AB

Printed in Great Britain

Dedication

I remember those days as a kid, in the weeks leading up to starting the new school year when I went to the store to buy stationery. I always held the thickest book in my hands, casually flicking through the pages, and would think to myself that one day I would be holding a novel that I had written in my hands. Man, I was a nerd. A nerd with a love for horror movies and losing myself in my writing. This novel is dedicated to my family.

Chapter One...

We open from the darkness like the set of some scary Hollywood movie. But this wasn't a movie. It was nothing more than life, continued. It was the early hours of the morning, somewhere before sunrise and a mild, cool breeze rushed through the city.

The curtains to the master bedroom were pulled almost to a close, but just open enough to allow the neon lights of the city to creep inside and splash across the walls. The bedroom lights were switched off and the figure of a large man somewhere in his early fifties was lying on top of the king-size bed, his body entwined in the bed sheets. He was showing signs of waking up, slowly moving and waking from his slumber from the night before. He turned over onto his chest and belly, the right-hand side of his face partially buried into the soft, white duck-feather pillow. His left hand, extended outwards, towards the nightstand, past the lamp and paperback novel and reading glasses, towards his cell phone.

The screen of the cell phone came to life with a push of a button. The glare of the light revealed the man to be Robert Prescott. His eyes closed quickly, if just for the moment, adjusting to the light. His eyes soon opened, again. The time on the cell phone was four-eighteen in the morning. There were no missed messages or phone calls. Robert dropped his cell phone back onto the nightstand.

Robert began to toss and turn under the bed sheets and cover. And although his eyes were closed, his mind was racing. It was the start of a new week. It was Monday. Robert pulled at the bed cover until it reached his chest and shoulders before burying his left arm under the pillow as if to prop his head a little higher. He opened his eyes now. The bedroom was still dark, with the neon lights against the bedroom walls. Robert propped himself up a little further now, sitting up in bed, against the bedhead. The bed cover fell to his waistline, exposing his chest and portly belly. The pillows were used to support his lower back. He leaned over and grabbed his cell phone again, disconnecting it from its charger and switched on the lampshade.

Robert Prescott was alone in bed. It had been a little over four years since the events in which he lost his family: his daughter, Carrie, his ex-wife, Anne. And all because of his youngest child, his son, Ben. The years that followed the tragic events hadn't been so generous, nor kind to Robert. He had stacked on the weight, gaining the pounds, and becoming chubbier around the belly, arms and face, than he cared to admit. But he grew to live with it, nonetheless. He was also bearded, now. The flecks of salt and pepper in his beard made him look distinguished. Robert surveyed the bedroom, taking in the silence of the room and the remainder of his apartment. His thoughts raced around, coming back to the life he once had, and the life he once shared with Peter Harmon, a love and a life once lived which he had now lost. Robert wiped the sleep from his eyes, a little. He reached out for his paperback novel and reading glasses. He flicked through the drugstore paperback novel aimlessly, before quickly losing interest and tossed it across to the other side of the king-size bed.

He kept his reading glasses on, as he turned his interest back to his cell phone. The screen came to life, again.

The morning had progressed. It was almost six now, and Robert had climbed out of bed. The wooden floorboards felt so cool to the touch. Robert wiggled his toes a little and stretched to work out the muscles in his lower back. The silhouette of the large man revealed himself to be naked. His once defined chest was now no more. His torso had passed the point of belly and was on its way to being a gut. Robert stood there a moment. The floorboards cracked under the pressure of the weight of his frame as he adjusted himself before walking into the en-suite. The light switch flickered on and the room came to life. The en-suite was immaculate. The white tiles were cleaned and polished and everything was in its place.

Robert walked in a little further, and turned towards the vanity. He leaned into the mirror, taking a look at his tired reflection. His hands ran through his beard as he moved his head left and right. A hint of a smile surfaced to his lips. The beard was growing well, but it needed a trim. Robert pulled away from the vanity and headed over to the shower. The frosted glass door opened. The water began to run, and Robert stepped inside, closing the glass door behind him. He stood in the shower with his back to the warm water as he reached for a bar of soap and washed all over, including his chest and arms. Robert closed his eyes and let the water consume him. It felt ever so inviting.

The frosted glass door opened again, and Robert stepped out of the shower. The water continued to a slow drip; his wet feet touching the tile below, careful not to slip. Robert walked over to the vanity and leaned into the mirror, once more. And with one almighty, strong move, he wiped the steam from the mirror to look at his reflection, again. There was a smile on his lips, more than just a hint. He felt awake and refreshed, for the first time in a long while.

The lights in the kitchen and living room were now switched on. The apartment was coming to life for another day. Robert busied himself in the kitchen, making breakfast. It was two slices of toast with chunky peanut butter, a coffee with milk and two sugars and an apple. Robert knew that he had allowed the weight gain to go beyond where he was happy and was in a place to finally get back into shape. The volume on the television set was down low. It was more like white noise in the background. Robert was dressed for the day. He was in a pair of jeans and a navy-blue polo shirt, which felt a little snug in places. Robert tended to pull at the shirt, now and then.

Robert took his breakfast into the living room and sat on the couch, in front of the coffee table, and caught the rest of the morning news. There was a story about a young girl, no older than ten, who suffered a heart attack whilst riding a water slide at a theme park. Robert grabbed the TV remote and switched off the television set. He finished his breakfast and returned the empty plate to the kitchen sink before making his second cup of coffee for the morning. The kettle boiled and the water poured. Robert took his freshly made cup of coffee into his office. He sat at his desk, behind his computer and waited for it to boot up. He played with his cell phone whilst he waited.

The computer came to life. Robert was quick to take the mouse and navigate to an existing file on the desktop screen. He clicked on the folder and navigated to a video file, clicking again. The video began to play. The setting looked all too familiar. It was his very own bedroom. The curtains were pulled to a tight close. The lights were switched on. And there were voices of six, maybe seven men, all in their forties and fifties, talking and laughing, and they were all naked. A young man, no older than twenty-two, was lying on the king-size bed, whilst the other, older men, stood in single file, all awaiting their turn with him. Robert was second in line. He looked over his left shoulder, laughing with the man behind him, whilst stroking his manhood, getting excited, and waiting for the man in front of him to finish his business.

The man in front was built like a steroid-induced brick house. He was bald with large defined, muscular arms, pectoral muscles and a paunch belly. He finished his business, as the young man lay there on the bed, his eyes rolling into the back of his head, barely conscious. The mountain of a man stepped to one side and walked out of camera shot. Robert was glued to the video. He watched himself step up to the end of his king-size bed and the young man. He was excited.

"Are you ready to…" Robert could hear himself say on the video.

It was at this point, he switched the video off. The memories of the night before came flooding back. He felt embarrassed about what came next.

Robert looked at the video file and the folder. He felt angry now. It wasn't just the one video.

There were multiple over the years that he had collected. All of similar themes. Robert clicked on the file and dragged it onto the trash can icon. A small grey box appeared on the screen asking Robert if he wanted to permanently delete the folder from his computer. He confirmed and hit the yes button. Robert was quick to step away from his computer. He switched it off, grabbed his cell phone and walked out of his office, leaving his coffee cup on his desk. His pace picked up a little, almost jogging now through the apartment, as much as his portly frame would carry him. He made his way down the hallway, past the kitchen and living room, and towards the small wooden table by the front door, to collect his belongings, his wallet and keys. Robert opened the front door, stepped out of his apartment and locked the door behind him.

Peter Harmon was no longer a boy. He was a man now. Bigger. Stronger. His arms were much more defined, as was his chest. His legs were still the size of a rugby player. He was in the East Village, completing his morning jog, in and amongst the other pedestrians. He was dressed in a pair of grey sweat pants and an old, fading black t-shirt. His face was a shade of pink and his forehead and chest were drenched in sweat as he jogged towards home, whilst listening to his music collection on his headphones.

Peter reached the entrance of his building. He climbed the stairs in leaps and bounds as he made his way indoors, after searching for his keys. He walked across the foyer and rode the elevator to the third floor. The elevator soon arrived on the third floor. Grabbing the keys from his pocket, he walked the corridor and made his way into his apartment, closing the door behind him.

The apartment in the East Village was not as opulent as that of the one he had once shared with Robert Prescott on the Upper East Side. Far from it. It was a one-bedroom, one-bathroom apartment with enough space for its laundry. The living room was designed with an exposed brick wall as a feature whilst the rest of the room was painted stark white. There was a coffee table in the middle of the room with a chocolate brown three-seater couch and a television set in the corner. It was simple. It was a home. And it was what Peter wanted, and could afford. The living room was adorned with framed photographs of happier times with new friends, on his own, and one as a child with his father over the Christmas season.

Peter bypassed the rest of the apartment. He dumped his keys and wallet into the small ceramic bowl he kept by the front door. Peter took off his headphones as he made his way deeper into his apartment, and made his way to his bedroom. He kicked off his shoes and stripped from his damp clothes, leaving them on the bedroom floor, at the end of the bed.

The bedroom was not as opulent either as the one he once shared with Robert. It didn't have a fancy view of the city. It didn't have a view of the park. It was fitted out with the bare basics; hardwood floors, a queen-size bed in the middle of the room, a set of drawers, and a very small wardrobe, which housed his work and casual clothes. Peter turned and made his way out of the bedroom, walking down the corridor and toward the bathroom shower. He kept his cell phone in his left hand as he walked. He had an app which counted his steps for the day. There was a missed text message. It was from Robert. Peter signed into his cell phone and opened the message.

See you tonight.

It read.

A smile surfaced to Peter's lips, as brief as it was.

Peter dropped his cell phone on the vanity by the side of the shower, pulled on the white cotton-like curtain back and stepped into the shower, under the warm water. The curtain pulled to a close behind him as the plastic rings along the rod above clustered together.

Robert sat quietly on a crowded bus, minding his own business. He sat toward the back and next to a window. He watched the city pass by, its traffic and its people. He sat there quietly, turning his cell phone over and over in his hands, almost nervous. He pressed a button on the side of the device and the screen came to life. There were no missed calls nor text messages.

The bus ride continued. Robert travelled from the Upper East Side and over to the west side of town to attend a meeting. The town car service was now no more. Bruce had passed away of an apparent heart attack, a little on two years now, so said his wife. Robert had sent flowers and attended the funeral.

The meeting was an anonymous support group for those experiencing grief and loss. In the years since Ben, and everything that he did, Robert couldn't bring himself to grow past the blood-stained memory. The gunshot wound in his chest was a constant, daily reminder of what happened, and what Ben couldn't bring himself to be. Himself. Robert had lost his job, a good chunk of his fortune, and of course, Peter. He dabbled in anonymous sex, from time to time.

Robert arrived. He stood outside the front of a local Presbyterian church before wandering inside. There were a handful of others, all there for the same thing. For support and to be heard or just listen. The others stood in small groups, some drinking coffee from takeaway cups. And there were others, standing outside finishing off a cigarette. Robert stood there, looking at the red brick building as the two large wooden doors were pushed open at the top of the cement staircase. The day was overcast, and the clouds were grey. Robert made his way up to the top of the cement staircase, passing the others and stepped inside the building.

The church stood tall and was grand in all its glory. It stood on the street corner, a pinnacle of the neighbourhood for well over one hundred years. The pews had been refurbished over the years and looked almost brand new with a bit of elbow grease and polish. Robert crept forward, moving further, deeper inside the church. A group of chairs were positioned into one large circle. Robert looked around at the others attending the meeting. Some were taking to their seats, with a coffee in a takeaway cup and a small pastry. The manager, the one who was officiating the meeting, stood inside the circle. He had held onto a pen and a clipboard. His eyes darted around the church, doing a quick headcount, before making his way outside to count the stragglers. The manager walked towards the outer edge of the circle, passing some of the other attendees. He walked with confidence with his clipboard. He and Robert made eye contact and gestured to each other politely.

The manager walked past Robert briskly. He was a tall, bear of a man. He stood at six feet with a muscular frame and a neatly trimmed beard. He wore a white polo shirt, with beige slacks and dark brown loafers. His chest was built and defined.

"Good morning, everyone!" the manager called. His voice was deep and echoed throughout the church. "It is so nice to see you all here today. How about we make our way inside and take a seat? Feel free to make yourself a coffee. It is instant. And grab yourself a pastry and let's get underway."

Robert got caught up in a group of people making their way in from the outside. He walked over to the table and poured himself a coffee in a takeaway cup and grabbed himself a glazed doughnut. It was his third coffee for the morning. He was going to have to nurse this one, or he would be bouncing off the walls. Robert found his seat. He sat three chairs to the right of the manager. The seats to his left and right of him were vacant. The rest of the group made themselves comfortable.

"Welcome one and all," the manager started, "in case this is the first time you are joining us here today, my name is Mark Brewster. I run this local chapter for people who have experienced loss and/or finding it difficult to cope, not only with the loss of a loved one, or a friend, but also getting through the day to day. You can talk. You can listen. There are a few ground rules before we begin. All I ask of you is that, for those who have a cell phone, please either turn them off or set them to vibrate. If you are not talking, then I simply ask you to listen. There will be no talking over one another. And, under no circumstances, will there be physical altercations. Zero tolerance."

Mark made himself comfortable in his chair.

"I do see some new faces joining us this morning," Mark continued. "Would there be anyone who would like to kick things off and get us started?"

The room went silent.

"I hate the sound of my voice," Mark continued again, with the hint of a chuckle. The comment was met with some laughter from the audience.

Robert looked around the room. He could feel his heart starting to pound. His palms went cold and sweaty.

Mark looked around at all the eyes on him sitting around in a large circle. He clapped his hands together once. It was hard and deep. The sound echoed through the church, some.

"Okay." Mark smiled. "I will tell you a little bit about myself and how I got here." There was a pause. The audience looked on.

"My name is Mark."

"Hello, Mark," the audience answered in unison. Mark cleared his throat a little.

"When I was fourteen years old, I was like a lot of kids in my neighbourhood," he started, "I came from a lower-middle-class family. And to help out, I got myself a paper route before and after school and on weekends. I rode my bike up and down the neighbourhood. That was until one day. On one day, I came across a house. It had been there for years. I never noticed it until that *one* day. I had passed that house countless times before. Until one day, the owner of the house was sitting out on his porch. One day, he decided to step off that porch and it changed my life. He invited me into his front yard as I handed him his paper. I said no, and he grabbed me by my left wrist, almost breaking it, and dragged me off my bike and took me inside his home. He locked the front door and sexually abused me for hours. I eventually woke, hours later, and found him unconscious on the couch in his living room as porn played on the television."

There was a pause. The audience, including Robert, were quiet. There was a sombre tone in the air.

"I didn't say a word," Mark continued, "not even to my parents. I told them that I got into a fight with a neighbourhood kid. In the years that followed, I developed a habit for alcohol and random sex with older kids in school. We would play together during gym, and afterwards in the shower block. Sometimes it would be with a teacher, sometimes not. But, I finally hit rock bottom, when I found myself in a hotel room with four businessmen two weeks after my sixteenth birthday. It wasn't the smartest of decisions. I got drunk and they passed me around like a game of musical chairs. I was raped multiple times."

There was another pause. Mark stood up from his chair, in front of the other attendees, in silence. He smiled, eventually, and confidently. "And today, I smile. I take it one day at a time. We are all going to fall and have our bad days, but I take it all one day at a time, and learn to step out of the shadows and into the sunlight."

The speech was met with a small round of applause. "Who is next?"

Robert smiled, feeling a little more confident. He raised his left hand, slowly above his shoulder. Mark acknowledged Robert with a smile and a nod, before taking to his chair, again.

"My name is Robert," he started.

"Hello, Robert," the audience, including Mark now, replied in unison.

Robert repositioned himself in his chair, moving ever so slightly forward. His hands were together, rubbing them warm and a little nervously.

"Today is a good day," Robert started. "I am here, and I am breathing. So, today is a good day," he repeated, under his breath and forcing a smile. "And today, I have a date. With someone… someone special to me." Robert nodded his head slowly. "No names. I understand. We had been seeing each other for a number of years until…" Robert paused. "Until recently, we re-opened the lines of communication with a text message here and there. It's nothing serious, mind you. But it's a big step forward for me."

"Thank you, Robert," Mark responded with a warm smile. "Would you care to share anything further with us today?"

Robert paused a moment thinking, feeling a little nervous.

"You are safe here," Mark continued.

Robert drew in a deep breath. "Okay," he answered, rubbing his hands together feverishly. "Almost four years ago, I lost my daughter and my ex-wife…" Robert paused again. "It was my son… He murdered them." Robert's voice began to break a little. "He butchered them. Their blood…" Robert was quick to wipe the tears from his eyes with the back of his left hand. Another forced smile. "Well, let's just say, after that, I found it difficult to cope. I fell into a very dark place in my life. I lost my job. My friends. My…" Another forced smile. "But today we are talking. And this is a good sign. It is."

Robert grabbed his coffee and took a deep sip to help ease his nerves.

"I used to be fit. I used to box in my spare time. Now, look at me." Robert grabbed as much of his belly with his left hand as he could. "I love soft drinks and doughnuts these days, maybe a little too much."

Robert laughed at his own joke. The audience, including Mark, followed.

-

Peter left home, dressed smart casual for work. He wore a plain dark blue button-down shirt with black trousers and matching shoes. He carried his bag over his left shoulder, with the strap across his chest. He walked out of his building with his headphones plugged into his ears, listening to his music. Peter made his way via the subway from the East Village to Midtown Manhattan on the West Side.

In the years that followed the blood-soaked events that were Ben Prescott, Peter Harmon had graduated from university with a degree in English Literature. He wrote and published a memoir, which was a flash in the pan for a good fifteen minutes, then disappeared from sight. The telephones stopped calling for interviews and Peter found his normality. His relationship with Robert was a casualty in the process. Peter was now single and writing the movie sessions and crossword puzzles of a local newspaper. That was his college education.

Peter made it to work. He stood in front of the skyscraper, which appeared to stretch on forever and a day, up high into dark and greying clouds, which hovered over the city. He watched the other employees march toward the building, like worker ants, ready to tackle another day in the trenches.

"Welcome to Monday," Peter whispered to himself, staring high up at the skyscraper.

Peter walked through a set of the revolving doors at the front of the building. He searched his bag for his security access pass. The security staff were on call and behind the desk, doing their rounds. Peter walked over to the elevators and waited for the next one that would take him to the fifteenth floor. He made it to the office on time and stepped off the elevator, walked past reception with the help of his security pass and made his way deep inside the office. There were rows and rows of desks. There were employees sitting in front of computer screens and typing away, whilst answering their telephones. It was a madhouse. And it was only Monday morning.

Peter arrived and dropped his bag on his desk, in front of his computer screen. He leaned down and switched the computer on. He opened his bag and retrieved his water bottle and reading glasses whilst removing his headphones. Peter looked around the office. There were a few team members he knew that were already busy at work. They ignored him. Peter looked over toward the corner office. The blinds were marginally open. His boss, Mr Thomas Walsh, was busy at work, making wild hand gestures whilst pacing his office, talking to someone on the phone.

Mr Thomas Walsh was a large hulk of a man. He was one of the editorial managers for the newspaper. Thomas had recently turned fifty, just four months ago. The office surprised him with a cake and presents. He kept a strong, fit build. His used his spare time in the gymnasium, lifting weights, running for miles on a treadmill and swimming endless laps of a heated swimming pool. Thomas shaved his head. He sported a neatly trimmed dark brown beard and stood tall at a little over five feet ten inches.

The morning had progressed. Peter was sitting in front of his computer screen, reading glasses on, and his water bottle half-filled, typing away on his keyboard. And all the while, his colleagues surrounding him, the other worker ants, traded in their weekend antics and office gossip. Peter looked up from his computer screen from time to time to survey the corner office. The elevator doors to the fifteenth floor opened again. It was Thomas Walsh standing alone on the elevator. He stepped out and into the office and moved rather quickly across the floor, toward his corner office. Thomas was impeccably dressed in a crisp white, long-sleeved shirt that hugged his torso in all the right places, and black jacket, tie and trousers, with matching shoes, by Tom Ford.

Peter look around at the other worker ants, again. The stories of weekend antics and office gossip quickly disappeared, and the sound of fingers typing away on keyboards, printing paper and answering inbound telephone calls took its place.

"Good morning, Peter," Thomas Walsh said, just above a whisper, creeping up from behind and placing his right hand on top of Peter's left shoulder.

Peter was a little startled, turning round in his chair.

"Good morning, sir," Peter answered, looking up at his boss.

"I need to see you in my office." Thomas Walsh smiled. "Give me a few minutes and I will call you in, okay?"

"Um…" Peter mumbled, "of course."

And just like that, he gave Peter's left shoulder a friendly squeeze, his hand pumping twice, before leaving him behind and disappearing into his office as his door closed behind him. Peter swung in his chair, again, to face his computer screen and resumed typing. But not before catching the glimpses of his other colleagues, staring back in interest. Peter shrugged his shoulders, confused. His mind was racing. What had he done wrong?

The telephone began to ring. Peter shifted his eyes away from his computer screen, momentarily, and looked at the caller ID. It was Thomas Walsh. Peter diverted his eyes to the corner office. He could see him sitting behind his desk, staring back with his desk phone planted to his right ear. Thomas was no longer wearing his jacket.

"Peter speaking," he muttered just above a whisper.

"I'll see you now," Thomas replied, his voice professional.

"Yes, sir."

The telephone line disconnected. Peter removed his reading glasses, laying them by his keyboard, stood up and stepped away from his desk and made his way across the office floor. He leaned into the door somewhat and could hear his breathing. He was nervous. Peter knocked on the door in quick succession. *Knock. Knock. Knock.*

"Come in," the deep, yet professional voice called.

Peter pushed down on the door handle, pushed the door open and walked inside, closing the door behind him.

The office was almost sterile and cold. Except for the mess of files which lay scattered across the surface of Thomas' desk and an open cupboard door which housed his jacket. The tall, hulking man was quick to jump out of his chair and walk around from his desk to meet Peter. He walked across the office rather quickly, barely giving him space to walk from the office door. He pounced on him, almost like a predator in search of prey. The curtains were open, marginally.

Thomas was quick to push Peter backwards, just a step or two, mind you, with his left hand, and pressed against his pectoral muscles, and leaned in, as Peter and his boss hid behind the closed door.

"I enjoyed last night," Thomas said just above a whisper, as if sharing a secret, as a smile surfaced to his lips.

He was close enough to lean in and kiss him.

"You did?" Peter asked, matching his smile.

"When can I see you again?"

Thomas was eager.

"You're seeing me right now."

"You know what I mean," Thomas chuckled. "You. Me. The two of us. Dinner. Then back to your place."

"Oh, that." Peter nodded. "I'd like that."

A glimpse of a shadow walked past the office window, past the curtains, and along the office floor. Peter caught it in the corner of his right eye. Thomas had his back to it. Peter felt nervous as if an inappropriate office affair had just been exposed. Peter smiled politely and broke from the embrace and walked further into the office. Thomas was left feeling a little confused, catching on momentarily, as he turned in his tracks, watching Peter take one of the two seats in front of his desk. Thomas played along.

"I've heard many good things about you," Thomas said, raising his voice a little, and its tone returning professional.

"You have?" Peter asked as he watched his boss return to his chair behind the desk. Thomas shifted his head to the left a little, taking in a glimpse of the other worker ants in the office. They were safe. The two exchanged smiles.

"I enjoyed last night," Thomas repeated himself, as he leaned into his desk, just above a whisper. "I woke up this morning and I could smell you all over me."

"You did?"

"Uh-huh. I like that." Thomas answered with a coy smile.

"You do?"

"I do."

Thomas smiled. He leaned into his desk a little more, repositioning himself in his chair, a little more. "I could take you here and now. I want you so bad."

"I like the sound of that," Peter answered, just above a whisper.

"Fuck!" Thomas whispered. "You turn me on. When can I see you again?"

"How about you let me know and we will see what we can do." Peter smiled, playfully.

A knock at the office door interrupted their private conversation. It swung open swiftly. And there, standing in the entrance, was a big-boned girl, somewhere in her later fifties with curly grey, shoulder-length hair.

"You can guarantee that," Thomas answered with a smile, his tone of voice returning professional, once more. His eyes strayed from Peter for a moment, and moved to the big-boned girl standing in the entrance of his office.

"Good morning, Deborah."

Peter turned in his chair a little to see one of the other editorial managers standing behind him.

"Good morning, Thomas," Deborah replied, as she made her way inside, taking the seat next to Peter, with multiple manila files bundled in her arms.

"Yes!" Thomas answered, remembering. "We have our quarter results meeting." Thomas diverted his eyes back to Peter.

"Thank you for your input, Peter. We will take this up again shortly."

"Of course." Peter stood from his chair. "I'll let you both get back to work."

"Thank you, Peter," replied Deborah.

Thomas looked at Peter and didn't say a word. His eyes said *sorry* and *we will pick up our conversation later*. Peter excused himself from the office and closed the door behind him before returning to his desk.

22

The morning progressed further. It was somewhere past first coffee break but before lunch.

Thomas was still in a meeting with Deborah, and now, a third colleague. Their conversation bounced back and forth. Peter was busy typing away on his keyboard and answering telephone calls. His cell phone sat next to his water bottle. It vibrated and caught Peter's attention. He stopped typing, if just for a moment, and looked at his cell phone. The screen came to life. It was a text message.

I hope you are having a great day so far and am looking forward to seeing you tonight.

The message was from Robert.

It made Peter smile.

The cell phone began to vibrate, again. It was a second text message. It was a picture message. It was a picture of Robert, back in the gym, sweating it out, with a smile on his face, and his boxing gloves on. Peter took his eyes from his cell phone and looked at Thomas in his office. In a fleeting moment, their eyes caught each other. A glimpse of a smile. Peter returned to his cell phone.

I miss you. See you tonight.

Peter was quick to type and hit the send button.

He placed his cell phone back down on his desk and returned to his keyboard, typing away, drawing the attention of some of the other work colleagues.

Peter left his desk and retreated to the men's restroom for a few moments. He walked inside the restroom, pushing the door open with his left foot, not wanting to use his hand to touch the wet and unsanitary door handle. Peter could see drops of water clinging, ready to drop to the floor below at a moment's notice. The restroom was empty. The doors leading into the stalls were all pushed open. The floors were tiled white, matching the paint on the walls and ceiling. A large vanity, with four washbasins, stretched from one side of the room to the other. Peter walked to the end basin, farthest from the door. He looked at his reflection in the mirror, for just a moment. His eyes were immediately drawn to the scar above his right eyebrow.

The faucet began to run. The warm water poured hard into the basin below. Peter leaned forward a little, ready to catch the water in his hands.

He splashed the water onto his face. It startled him a little, only at first, as he caught his breath in his chest. His mouth was wide open. Peter stood up and looked at his reflection, again. The water dripped down his face and over his shirt, a little.

The water didn't wash away the scar. It couldn't, nor the memory. Four years ago, was another time and another place. The memories of the last four years were stowed away, and he found himself not wanting to remember, yet unable to forget. Peter turned to the right a little and grabbed a paper towel to dry down his face. He closed his eyes tightly. The image of Ben Prescott came flooding back. Peter opened his eyes in horror, almost gasping, unable to breathe. He could feel his heartbeat pounding in his chest. Ben Prescott stood there, behind Peter, in the reflection of the restroom mirror, clutching that creepy clown mask tightly in his right hand, by his waistline.

"Oh my God!" a voice called out, unexpected.

It startled Peter. The image of Ben Prescott quickly vanishing.

"You are going to be my new best friend. Promise," the voice continued.

Peter looked in the reflection of the mirror to see a short man, shorter than himself, anyway, neatly dressed in a tight, white long-sleeved shirt, which hugged his chest well, which was tucked into just-as- tight black trousers. His hair was manicured to an inch of its life. The man was somewhere in his early to mid-twenties.

"I'm sorry," Peter responded, catching his breath. "Excuse me. Who are you?"

"I'm Stuart Miller."

"Nice to meet you. I'm P—" Peter answered, dropping the paper towel in the waste paper basket below.

"I know." Stuart smiled. "We all know. So, what's your story? Give me the deets. What's your damage? Single? Married? It's complicated?"

"My damage?" Peter answered, just above a whisper. It's definitely complicated." Peter laughed, a little.

The run-in with the office gossip had come and gone. He was harmless and flirtatious at best. Peter stepped away from his computer and walked out of the office. It was lunch. Peter made his way out of the building and across the road to a sandwich store he found himself going two to three times a week. The sandwich store was well known for its large and over-the-top sandwiches and their creative fillings. It was always quite popular. Fridays were chaos. Peter made his way into the store, walked up to the counter, having waited a good ten minutes in the queue, placed his order and grabbed the first available table he could find.

Peter had ordered a meatball sub which came with all the fixings, including melted cheese, lettuce, pickles and a large helping of barbeque sauce. It looked like a bomb had gone off on a plate.

But it was just as delicious as it was messy. A medium-size soda sat to the left side of the plate. Peter balanced his time doing his best to neatly make his way through his sandwich, and not create a barbeque sauce mess across his face, whilst consumed with logging into his social media accounts on his cell phone.

He looked up, taking his soda in his free hand, to see Thomas walk into the store, flanked by two office plebs on either side of him. One was hanging onto every word Thomas had to say, whilst the other was feeding him what he wanted to hear, as if to make him happy or stroke his ego.

Thomas glanced at Peter and the two exchanged pleasantries with a brief smile and a nod of the head. Peter took a sip of his drink and returned to his cell phone and sandwich.

Thomas and one of the office plebs grabbed a nearby table, two over to the left from Peter, whilst the second pleb was sent to the counter to make their orders. The pleb was happy to do it. Peter could overhear Thomas talk about office politics.

"I like the man, but…" Thomas started. The remaining pleb listened in.

"The problem with the team is…" Thomas continued, on another tangent.

Peter had his head buried in his cell phone. There was another text message from Robert. And one from Thomas.

Help! Save me!

The message from Thomas read.

Peter smiled, chuckling to himself, a little. He looked up from his cell phone to see Thomas looking back at him. He was smiling back at Peter, his eyes happy to see a familiar face in the crowd, not paying attention to the one office pleb rambling on. Peter nodded with a smile surfacing to his lips. He returned to his cell phone.

Peter returned to his sandwich, mess and all. He dusted himself off, cleaning himself up a little, and took one last sip from his soda, to finish it off. He stood from his chair, collected his belongings, and walked out of the cafe, before dumping his remaining rubbish in a nearby trash can.

"We get in first and hit hard," Peter could overhear one office pleb say to Thomas.

Thomas was too consumed with Peter to listen, or to even care. The second office pleb had returned to their table, carrying three sandwiches and three sodas on a food tray, careful not to drop them on the floor. It was a real balancing act. All this whilst Peter and Thomas made eye contact, only briefly, before the boss returned his attention to the office pleb and Peter walked out of the cafe, fumbling for his cell phone from his trouser pocket, before walking out onto the sidewalk amongst the rest of the human traffic.

I wish I could help.

Peter typed and hit the send button.

Thomas could feel his cell phone in his trouser pocket vibrate. He smiled, somewhat.

The end of the workday was fast approaching. It was the end of another Monday for another work week. Peter was sitting at his desk, in the process of signing off from his computer for the evening. It was coming up on six o'clock. Peter looked around the office. The other teammates had gone home for the evening. There were still a handful of other employees across the floor, still at work, including Thomas who was sitting at his desk, Peter could see, peering through the blinds in his office. Thomas was leaning against the back of his chair, his hands joined behind his head, and reading something from his computer screen.

Peter stood up from his desk. He leaned down and picked up his bag, placing it on his desk, a moment. Thomas looked away from his computer screen and could see Peter call it quits for the evening. The door leading into his office sprang open. Thomas appeared as he made his way over to Peter's desk.

"Burning the candle at both ends, huh?" Thomas asked as he walked towards Peter. "I like it. Keep it up!"

"Thank you." Peter smiled. "Just finishing up on a few things and making a head start on tomorrow."

The two exchanged a smile. Thomas looked around the office, for just a moment, making sure the other employees weren't paying attention.

"It was great seeing you at lunch today," Thomas said, just above a whisper as he leaned in toward Peter.

"You noticed that, huh?" Peter answered a little sly.

"I noticed, yeah." Thomas smiled. "You have been on my mind all day. I want to see you again."

Thomas looked more human, standing there in front of Peter. He was no longer a boss in an office. There was no jacket. No tie. His shirt was neatly tucked into his trousers, but the top two buttons were undone, exposing a hairy chest beneath. Peter couldn't help but look. Thomas noticed. And he liked it.

"You have my number," Peter answered simply, "use it."

Peter reached for his bag on his desk. The strap went over his head and rested on his left shoulder and across his chest. Thomas noticed. He watched on. He could see Peter's shirt move a little at the front, exposing a little of his belly beneath. Thomas looked up and across the office. There were only a handful of employees across the floor left, all busy at work, some talking on the phone, others with their backs turned away. And, it was in that moment, Thomas reached out and grabbed Peter by his belt buckle. He pulled him in close and kissed him briefly on the lips. No one paid attention. No one cared, not the other employees, anyway.

"I've been wanting to do that since I saw you at lunchtime," Thomas said, just above a whisper and a smile on his lips.

"Good," Peter answered, unable to hide his smile, and also looking over his shoulder, out at the other employees, before returning his attention to Thomas. "I shall see you tomorrow." There was another smile.

Peter had his bag and his belongings. He was good for the evening. He tucked in his shirt, making himself look a little more presentable, and turned on Thomas and slowly walked away from his desk and over to the elevator. Thomas followed, walking briskly across the office floor, toward the elevator. Peter soon arrived and pressed the button on the wall and waited for his elevator. He turned and faced Thomas, again.

"A personal escort," Peter smiled, "I'm impressed."

"Well," Thomas started, "'it's all about care. I want to make sure you get home safely." Peter looked at Thomas.

"What have you got planned for this evening? A hot date?" Thomas asked before he could say a word.

"Just visiting a friend." Peter nodded, reassuringly.

"Good." Thomas nodded. "Does he like you? You know, like the way I like you?

"He is just a friend," Peter repeated, reassuring Thomas again.

"Good. Because I like you."

The bell above the elevator chimed. The doors opened.

Peter was quick to make his way inside the elevator. He turned and look at Thomas before the doors closed on them.

"I like you, too." Peter smiled. "See you tomorrow." The elevator doors closed.

Thomas turned on the elevator. He had a smile on his face, which stretched from ear to ear as he returned to his office.

Peter made his way out of the elevator and walked out of the building for the evening as he made his way to the Upper East Side. He tracked down a cab that waited in a nearby rank outside the office. He climbed into the backseat of the first available one he could find and gave the driver the address. The cab pulled out into the traffic. Peter sat back and peered outside the window, watching the city pass him by as he hugged his bag across his chest that sat in his lap. The memories of sitting in the back seat of a town car with Robert came flooding back, just momentarily, with Bruce behind the wheel. Peter felt his cell phone vibrate in his trouser pocket. He was quick to retrieve it. It was another text message from Thomas. Peter logged into his phone and opened it. It was a picture of Thomas. He was sitting behind his desk. He looked happy and relaxed. His business shirt still unbuttoned. There was a smile on his face. And there was a caption to the photograph.

You make me so happy.

The message read. Peter smiled.

The feelings are mutual.

Peter typed and hit the send button.

The cab pulled out in front of Robert's building. Peter paid his fare to the driver and climbed out of the car, his bag strapped across his chest tightly. The engine of the cab continued to run. It pulled out into the traffic, in search of another charge. Peter stood there, looking up at the building. The lights were all switched on. It looked like Christmas. Peter could feel his chest racing. He was nervous and excited all rolled into one. He was excited to see his friend, again. He was excited, as it felt like a first date all over again. His mind was all over the place.

Peter held onto his bag, holding it close to his chest. He dodged the other pedestrians and made his way inside the building, past the doorman, across the foyer and into another elevator. The building had seen some minor renovations since the last time he had been in the building. The elevator moved fast, arriving quickly on Robert's floor. Peter could hear the chime. The doors parted and he stepped out onto the floor. The minor renovations weren't so minor after all. The floor had a minor face lift, a nip and a tuck, here and there. There were new light fixtures, paint and wallpaper. Peter could feel his heartbeat racing and his hands grew sweaty as he walked along the floor, toward the apartment. He arrived. Peter stood in front of the apartment door, for just a moment, to gather his thoughts. It was the first time in a very long time. Peter held his breath a little and leaned in and knocked on the front door.

Knock. Knock. Knock.

The inside of the apartment was alive for the evening. The lights were all switched on. The television played softly in the background. Robert was in the kitchen, busying himself, cooking dinner for the evening. He stood over a newly purchased wok, cooking green chicken curry and steamed rice. Robert noticed the knock at the door. He looked up from the wok. A smile came to his lips. He grabbed the tea towel from his right shoulder and dusted off his hands before leaving the kitchen behind him, and walked through the apartment.

"One second!" Robert called out.

The front door to the apartment eventually opened. Robert smiled. He could see Peter standing in the doorway, dressed for work. Peter smiled back, still feeling a little nervous. Robert was dressed casually for the evening. He sported a dark blue polo shirt and jeans. His feet were bare.

"It's you," Robert said, just above a whisper, and so happy to see

Peter, again.

"Hello," Peter answered.

"Hi," Robert whispered. "Where are my manners?" he continued, shaking his head, a little. "Don't just stand there. Please, come on in."

Peter continued to smile and nodded. He walked into the apartment and Robert closed the door behind him.

Peter was inside the apartment. He walked in a little and surveyed the living room and the hallway leading to the master bedroom and into the kitchen. There was a new coat of paint on the walls. The living room was a shade of grey with a stark-white outline. The shade of grey fell somewhere on the darker side. Peter put his bag on the ground, near the table by the front door. He did it like second nature as if he were home. Robert turned to Peter and greeted him with a strong hug. Peter could feel his arms around him, squeezing in on him, a little tighter. It felt like old times, like good times. Robert still smelt the same; of a hard day's work and Old Spice. Peter closed his eyes and smiled, if just for a moment.

"It's great to see you," Robert said, just above a whisper. "It's good to see you, too," Peter answered.

Robert was the first to pull away from the embrace. The two looked at each other and smiled. "Dinner smells delicious." Peter was the first to jump in.

"I'm glad you like. A little favourite. Green chicken curry and steamed rice." Robert walked on ahead, and back into the kitchen. Peter followed.

The evening progressed. Peter had slipped off his shoes and socks and left them by his bag by the table at the front door of the apartment. Peter and Robert were in the kitchen, chatting away. It was like they were getting to know each other, after all this time. It felt comfortable. They traded laughs. Peter nursed a bottle of water as he watched Robert in the kitchen cooking away. He was a new man. Robert was also drinking water this evening. He had stopped drinking alcohol altogether.

"I like what you have done with this place," Peter said, looking around the apartment.

"Thank you," Robert replied, with a smile. "I've made a few changes over the last few months."

The hallway was adorned with framed photographs. The frames were all matching, and all painted black. The photographs themselves were of Robert, spanning over the years, from his childhood, his teen years, to young adulthood, his marriage. The photographs included his daughter, Carrie. The photographs of Robert were taken during much happier times in his life. It was good to see Robert smile, again. It had been almost four years.

The evening progressed. And dinner had been served in the living room. It was where Robert and Peter had their most fun, and felt most relaxed. And that was what this evening was all about. The coffee table in the middle of the living room, which sat in between two couches, was cleared and was set as a dining table, set for two. Robert and Peter sat opposite one another, enjoying good conversation and great food. They shared a few laughs and reconnected. The time was getting on as they lost themselves in deep conversation. The food was almost eaten.

"I don't know how you do it," Peter said, with a hint of a smile. "But you cook a mean chicken curry. I am stuffed. I don't think I'll eat again."

Peter leaned back from the coffee table, resting on the floor, and staring up at the ceiling, with a hint of a chuckle. He raised his left hand and rubbed his belly, a little.

Robert looked on. It brought a smile to his face. The memories of a past relationship.

"You're more than welcome. I have missed this. You. Us. Being together." Robert chuckled. "I remember rubbing your belly when you had too much to eat."

"Nothing has changed," Peter laughed.

Robert climbed to his knees from the opposite side of the coffee table and made his way over toward Peter. He collapsed on the floor, almost imitating Peter, as he stroked his belly, having had too much to eat. The two were lying on the floor next to each other, laughing and talking and staring up at the ceiling, reminiscing about times gone by.

"Thank you for this evening," Robert said, just above a whisper as he turned to face Peter.

"Anytime. You know that."

"Anytime," Robert whispered to himself, nodding.

Robert held his breath for just a moment and climbed to his knees, then his feet. He helped Peter to his feet, too. The two cleared the plates, cutlery and glassware from the coffee table and headed toward the kitchen. Robert ran the faucet and dumped the plates in the sink, followed by the cutlery. He kept the glassware separate. Peter stood behind Robert and fed him each plate, each piece of cutlery and both glasses. Robert turned and retrieved them. He placed the last glass on the side counter. He looked down at the sink, as if thinking for a moment, then sprung from his moment of solitude and leaned in and kissed Peter on the lips. It was a friendly gesture, nothing passionate or romantic, mind you. Robert pulled back looking at Peter, searching his eyes for some form of response. Something. Peter smiled. He wasn't startled. It felt nice, actually. Peter leaned in and returned the kiss.

"Well, will you look at the time," Robert said, almost nervously.

Peter grabbed his cell phone from his trouser pocket and pressed a button. The screen came to life. The time on the cell phone was a little after half-past nine. There was also a missed text message from Thomas. It made Peter smile, knowing he was thinking of him.

"Look at that," Peter replied.

"You know I have a spare room if you would like to crash the night." "Thank you." Peter smiled, warmly. "Another time, I'm sure."

"Of course. Absolutely."

"I must make a move." Peter nodded, staring at Robert.

Peter leaned and kissed Robert again, although briefly. "You're most welcome."

The evening progressed further. Peter made his way from Robert's apartment, down the elevator, across the foyer and waited near the curb for a passing cab. Robert followed Peter downstairs, making sure he got safely into a cab to make his way home. Peter stepped out from the curb and waved his left arm around to hail down a driver. He caught the attention of one driver. It all seemed so very quick. The cab pulled in from the traffic and stood near the curb, it's engine still running.

"This is it. You, I guess," Robert said confidently.

"Thank you again for dinner." Peter smiled.

"Let's do this again. Soon. Please."

"I'd love to." Robert smiled.

Peter climbed into the back of the cab waiting for him, pulling the door to a close behind him. Peter sat forward in his seat, motioning toward the driver, something. The driver, a hulk of a man, with chocolate-brown hair and a neatly trimmed beard and bulging biceps, which almost tore the sleeves of his K-Mart print t-shirt, sat patiently for his next order. The window in the back seat of the cab rolled down. Peter leaned out, as much as he could, anyway, and smiled and waved at Robert, one last time. The two exchanged pleasantries, and Peter watched Robert make his way back into his building, through the door, past the doorman, and into the foyer. He lost him after that. Peter returned to the driver in front of him, repeating his address. The driver pulled out from the curb and made its way into the evening traffic.

Peter was quick to retrieve his cell phone from his trouser pocket. The battery power was low. Only fourteen per cent remaining. There was a reminder notification to hook the phone back up to its charger. Peter dismissed it. He opened his message from Thomas. It was a picture message. It was a picture of Thomas sitting up in bed, by his nightstand. He was wearing an old college t-shirt, that he could see, his reading glasses and a smile.

I'm just catching up on some Colbert from last night. I hope you're having a fun time tonight.

The message read.

I'm just on my way home now. See you tomorrow. Sleep well.

Peter typed, hitting the send button.

Robert was fast asleep. It was somewhere o'clock in the early hours of Tuesday morning. The living room in the apartment was cleaned. The kitchen was spotless. And the lights about the apartment were switched off. It was a cool evening. The hallway was empty and quiet, as the bedroom door leading into the master bedroom was wide open. Robert was asleep on top of the bed, entwined in the sheets and cover. His cell phone was hooked up to its charger on the nightstand, next to a paperback novel and his reading glasses.

Robert tossed and turned, back and forth, on top of his king-size bed, and his speech was slurred. It was like night terrors. It was a nightmare. The image of the clown mask returned. It stood silently at the end of the bed, overlooking Robert. The image of that mask stepping out from the darkness. It was him. His right hand, bound in a black leather glove, rose slowly, higher, reaching the mask, itself. The image pulled back on the mask, removing it, exposing the face beneath. It was Ben Prescott, standing at the end of his father's bed, looking back at him. His tone of skin has shades of blue, the veins were black and dead.

"Look what you did to me," Ben whispered, slowly removing his left hand from his stomach, to reveal a catastrophic bullet wound. There was blood. A lot of blood.

It stained the shirt, dripping to the floor below. "Come home to us," Ben whispered again.

Robert awoke from his nightmare, screaming. He was covered in a cold sweat. He looked around the bedroom. There was no one and nothing there, except the neon lights of the city, just beyond the window of the master bedroom. Robert ran his right hand over his eyes, wiping away the sleep.

"Fucking sleeping tablets!" Robert whispered to himself.

Robert leaned forward a little, over to the nightstand and switched on the lamp. A warm glow of light sprayed across the walls of the bedroom. He looked around the bedroom, again. And again. There was no one around. He kicked at the bed cover a little and climbed to the side of the bed. He sat there a moment, his feet touching the hardwood floors beneath. It was relaxing and cool to the touch. Robert stood up from the side of the bed. The weight of his frame propelled him forward, a little until he found his balance. He was naked, standing there beside his bed. Robert adjusted himself, a little, before walking out of the bedroom and deep into the en-suite.

The lights in the en-suite flickered on. The room was bright. The walls were coated in new stark-white paint, almost matching the tiled floor below. Robert walked over to the bathroom. He leaned down, deep into the tub and drew himself a bath. The faucet switched on, as the water poured hard and the temperature rose quickly. Robert held his hand under the faucet, catching some of the water in his right hand. It splashed and was hot to the touch. Robert cooled the water, some. The bathtub was filling with water quite rapidly now. Robert turned on the bathtub, only momentarily, and walked out of the en-suite. He made his way through the master bedroom, down the hallway, and into the kitchen. The lights remained switched off. Robert returned to the bathtub just moments later.

The bathtub was almost full now. It felt so warm and inviting. The water was quick to consume Robert's naked body, as he slowly and carefully, lowered himself in. He felt relaxed and at peace, at last. Robert tilted his head back a little, making himself a little more comfortable, before sinking below the surface of the water. He held his breath tightly and opened his eyes. He could hear his heart beating in his ears. Robert remained under the water for a few seconds, maybe five or six, before reaching the surface of the water again, gasping for air. Robert laughed heartily, resting his back on the bathtub, again. He lay there resting, staring up at the ceiling a moment.

Robert looked around the en-suite. That smile of his, it was still there. He leaned to the right of the tub a little and reached down to the tiled floor, below. There was a flash of silver, something bright. Robert grabbed a small silver-coated toaster oven that sat plugged into a nearby power socket. That smile was still there, on the surface of his lips, as tears began to well in his eyes. He held that toaster oven tightly to his chest and sunk deep beneath the surface of the water, again. A flash of light sparked throughout the room as a charge of electricity filled the bathtub and blew the light socket in the en-suite and across the apartment.

The elevator on Robert's floor opened. And there, standing on the elevator, was a woman, no older than forty-five. She was a short woman, with a big build, and black, stringy, curly hair. She was dressed in a nondescript black t-shirt and grey sweat pants. The woman was carrying a selection of cleaning products and a yellow, plastic bucket. The doors to the elevator closed behind the woman as she made her way down the hallway. She reached for her keys in her sweatpants pocket. The keys jiggled a little, as she placed the bucket and cleaning products on the floor, between her feet, for just a moment. The key inserted into the lock and turned. The door unlocked and was pushed open.

"Mr Prescott!" the woman called out. There was no answer.

The lights in the apartment were switched off. It was dark inside.

The woman placed her set of keys on the table by the front door and placed the bucket and cleaning goods on the floor. A wallet and set of keys were on the table. They belonged to Robert. The woman raised her left arm and flicked on the power switch. There was still no power. The woman tried again but to no avail. She was a little annoyed.

"Mr Prescott!" the woman called again, "you have no power!" And again, there was no response. She shrugged.

The woman made her way deeper into the apartment. The door leading into the master bedroom was wide open. So was the door leading into the office. The woman made her way down the hallway, slowly, and did her best not to make too much noise, so as not to disturb anyone.

"Mr Prescott" the woman whispered, as she approached the master bedroom and peered inside. The king-size bed was a mess and, the room was empty. The curtains were drawn, allowing for very little light inside.

Robert Prescott had known the woman for almost two years now. It was Celia Helvig, the cleaning lady. Celia had seen Robert in times of need before, more than she cared to remember. Celia was there when Robert was too drunk to climb out of bed, almost choking on his own vomit. Or when she found him bruised and beaten after a wild night of anonymous sex with strangers. She had taken him to the emergency room then.

Celia stood in the entrance of the master bedroom for just a moment longer, looking around the room, and wandering where to start. She walked into the bedroom and over to the curtains. She pulled them back, as far as they would go, to make the most of the light from outside. Her small, dumpy stature stood as tall as she could on tiptoes to pull back the heavy curtains. She was almost out of breath. Celia turned around to find the door leading into the en-suite wide open. The light from outside helped a little, but not much. She walked closer, and again, careful not to draw unwanted attention.

"Hello?" she whispered. There was no response.

Celia stood in the en-suite entrance. A blood-curdling scream escaped her lungs and past her lips. She screamed again. Her eyes welling with tears. And there in front of her, was the bathtub. The water was cold, and the level was low. Robert was facing up, not really floating in the low water level of the bathtub. He was naked. His hands, arms, feet and legs had suffered catastrophic burns. There were areas of the skin that were black in colour, horribly burnt and peeled back. The skin had blistered and torn, exposing the veins and some of the muscle beneath. His blood vessels in his eyes had ruptured. The colour of his skin around his eyes was almost purple. Robert Prescott was dead.

Chapter Two...

It was the early hours of Tuesday morning and Peter was back in the office, again. He was dressed neatly for work this morning, just like every other day, and attending a meeting with his colleagues. Thomas stood in front of a whiteboard with graphs, charts, facts and figures, giving a presentation to his team. He was running through the benefits of a new formatting process. The younger staff members, most of them, anyway, remained silent. Some were eager to raise their hands and ask questions, whilst the older staff members threw in their two cents' worth and complained about the change.

Peter sat at the end of the table, farthest away from Thomas. He remained silent, listening to Thomas talk on and on about new office procedures. It was a very boring stuff. He watched Thomas stand in front of his team, pacing from left to right, pointing at the board with a coloured marker.

Thomas was dressed in a fresh white long-sleeved shirt. It was crisp and new. Today, he wasn't wearing a tie but opted to unbutton the top of his shirt, giving a mild hint of his sculptured and furry chest beneath. The shirt itself hugged his torso and arms tightly. Thomas caught Peter's glances.

The conversation continued on about new procedures and cutting down on work time when Peter felt his cell phone vibrate in his trouser pocket. It caught the attention of some of his colleagues, the ones sitting close enough to hear it. Peter retrieved his cell phone and looked at the screen. It was an unknown caller. So many thoughts ran through his mind. Peter motioned toward Thomas, grabbing his attention a moment, and seeking his approval to take the call. Thomas gave a quick nod of his head, and Peter walked out of the office, and across the hallway to an empty, adjacent office. The walls were made of clear glass and the office was furnished identically to others like it.

"Hello?" Peter asked, pacing the empty office.

"Is this Peter Harmon I am speaking with?" a female voice asked on the opposite end of the line. Her voice was mature and straight to the point.

"Yes," Peter replied, a little concerned, "who is this?"

The mature, female voice belonged to that of Senior Detective Nancy Hudson. She advised Peter that Robert Prescott had been found unresponsive in his apartment at a little after nine-thirty that morning. His mind wandered after that. It was a blur. There were specific words he heard and picked up on: Robert Prescott. Bathtub. Burnt. Electrocution. Deceased. Peter collapsed to the office floor. He was in tears, sobbing and screaming. That is all that he remembered.

Peter arrived home from work early that day. It was like a grown-up version of leaving school early, for whatever reason. Peter climbed out of the back seat of a cab, alone in the front of his building. He passed the driver whatever money he had in his wallet at the time. It seemed to be enough, plus tip. Peter didn't count it. He couldn't bring himself to do it. His mind was racing.

The back door to the cab slammed shut. The driver seemed happy enough. Peter walked toward his building, up the cement staircase and buzzed himself inside. His eyes were hidden behind large black sunglasses, and the strap of his bag was firmly wrapped around his chest. He rode the elevator to the third floor and made his way to his apartment. Peter retrieved his front door keys from his bag, and fought with the key chain, struggling to find the right key. The lock in the front door jiggled a little and Peter made his way inside, as the front door closed behind him.

Peter collapsed to the floor. His legs gave out from underneath him. His hulking frame lay in an agony of the emotions churning up in him. Ben. Anne. Carrie. And now Robert. The events that transpired almost four years ago came flooding back to the forefront of Peter's memories. That hideous clown mask. He couldn't forget that clown mask. He was sobbing, again. It didn't take too long before Peter climbed to his feet, and pulled himself off the floor. He left his bag and his sunglasses on the hardwood floor. He was in a hazy state of mind. Peter walked from the front door, across the living room, down the hallway and to his bedroom, pulling at his clothes, unbuttoning his shirt, removing his belt and, kicking off his shoes and socks and climbing out of his trousers, leaving them all in a trail behind him.

"Not here," Peter whispered to himself, just above a mutter. He closed his eyes and shook his head.

Peter left his bedroom and backtracked to the hallway, and made his way to the bathroom.

The door pushed open and the light switch flickered on. The lights were almost neon. The room seemed so bright. Peter rubbed his eyes a little and made his way inside, leaning into the bathtub. The faucet was leaking a little. *Drip. Drip. Drip.* Peter closed his eyes tightly and shook his head. He opened his eyes, again, and drew himself a bath. The water was hot, and it poured out loudly and rough, splashing almost everywhere against the deep walls of the tub. He stood in front of the tub, watching the water levels increase steadily, as he stood there, in nothing but his boxer shorts.

It took a few minutes, but the tub was almost full now. Peter leaned in and switched off the faucet. He stood there, looking down at the water, thinking. He was thinking of Robert and the pain he must have suffered. He thought of Ben and everything he had done. He shook his head, again.

His eyes dragged away from the tub and looked out of the bathroom, past the open door and into the hallway. The hallway was dark, and the lights were switched off. He heard the sound of the wooden floorboards creaking, bending under pressure.

"Hello?" Peter called out. There was no answer.

Peter felt his breath catch in his chest; he tightened his fists, a little. He walked to the entrance of the bathroom and peered into the hallway. He looked left and right. There was no one there. That same sound. The hardwood floors bending, cracking under pressure. Peter could feel his heart racing and retreated back into the bathroom, slowly. He turned and faced the tub, climbing in, submerging himself in the warm water, forgetting to remove his boxer shorts. He made himself comfortable, leaning his back against one side of the tub, before sinking under the surface of the water.

Peter lay on the floor of the tub, under the water. He lay there for a moment, for as long as he could hold his breath, anyway. He opened his eyes and his vision was blurry, as he stared up at the ceiling, and could hear the sound of his heartbeat racing in his ears. Peter raised his hands to the sides of his head, covering his ears, closed his eyes and released a blood-curdling scream.

The morning progressed into the early evening. Peter awoke slowly, lying on top of his bed in a plain white t-shirt and dark-red cotton boxer shorts. The curtains were pulled closed and the lights in the bedroom were switched off. The room was dark. His cell phone was attached to a charger on the nightstand. Peter reached out for it, past a half-full glass of water and a bottle of sleeping pills and past the latest autobiography he was reading. Peter cleared his throat a little as he pressed a button on the side of the cell phone. The screen came to life, again. It was almost seven in the evening now. There was a missed text message from Thomas. Peter rubbed his eyes, a little, adjusting to the light. His vision was still a little blurry.

Give me a call, anytime, day or night. Let me know how you're doing, or if you need anything. T.

The message read.

Peter disconnected the cell phone from the charger and rolled onto his back onto the bed, staring up at the ceiling for a moment.

Peter climbed to the side of the bed, by the nightstand. He placed his feet on the hardwood floor and wriggled his toes a little. He grabbed his cell phone and climbed off the bed, walking from the bedroom and making his way back to the living room. Peter switched the lights on inside the apartment as he made his way through. The apartment felt like it was coming back to life. Peter shook his hands by his side, vigorously, for a second or two, before reaching for the TV remote on the

table. He pointed the remote at the television and switched it on. And there, in front of him, was the evening news. A female TV reporter, somewhere in her mid-to late-forties, appeared ambitious and out to make a name for herself.

"… and the body of one-time Wall Street financier, Robert Prescott, was found in the early hours of this morning. All signs, right now, point to suicide. Robert Prescott made a name for himself and hit the headlines, not four years ago, when his only son, Benjamin, a college student, here in the city, went on a deadly rampage, killing a total of—"

Peter pointed the TV remote at the television set and switched it off. He was angry, standing there in the middle of his living room, fighting to hold back the tears welling in his eyes.

"Fuck!" Peter whispered angrily.

Peter tightened his grip on his cell phone. He dialled a number and placed it to the side of his left ear. The phone call was connecting.

"Hey, you," a familiar voice answered. It was Thomas.

"I just needed to hear a friendly voice," Peter answered, pacing the living room.

"Understood. How are you doing?

"I'm… doing… I'm sorry about work too, by the way."

"No. Not at all. You have nothing to worry about," Thomas answered, his tone of voice calm and reassuring.

"Thank you." Peter tried to smile. "I just feel like it's happening all over again, you know? The reporters on TV. I hate all those *that's him* looks."

"Would you like me to come round? We could stay in and watch a movie. I can order a pizza."

"That sounds… perfect. Thank you."

"I'm on my way."

The phone line disconnected.

The evening progressed further. It was now somewhere in the early hours of Wednesday morning. And both Peter and Thomas had fallen asleep on the couch in front of the television set which was still on with the volume down low. And there were two open pizza boxes spread across the coffee table. There were slices of uneaten pizza, with pepperoni and sausage and capsicum. The glow of the television screen sprayed across the living room walls.

The next few days were spent at home. Peter didn't go into work. He skipped it. He had enough time accrued to take some personal leave. And he didn't travel too far from his apartment. He walked back and forth, to and from a local grocery store. The people in the street recognised him, as the TV reporter from a couple of nights ago extended her story on Robert Prescott and his family. There were pictures of Peter all over the news. And not just from four years ago. But also, his childhood in Hillsboro. Thomas kept in touch, sending text messages throughout the day, and checking in on him with a call, here and there.

The days were spent watching trash TV and thinking about what to wear to Robert's funeral.

Peter received a call not twenty-four hours after learning of his death from Robert's law firm, inviting him to the funeral. The evenings, when he couldn't sleep, were spent in a nearby neighbourhood gym, lifting weights and running endless miles on a treadmill, listening to his music. His mind raced. There was no coming back from this now. There were no answers. Only questions. One main question: *Why?* It tore Peter to shreds. His cell phone also racked up many calls and text messages. There were some from Thomas, of course, but also the local media, and the female reporter who was out to make a name for herself. Peter was the one surviving link to Robert Prescott and his family. Peter hadn't felt this way in years. Not since the bloody aftermath that was Ben Prescott.

It was somewhere in the early morning, just shy of sunrise. Thomas had decided to take some personal leave from the office, too. He spent his time helping out and supporting Peter where he could. He'd packed a small bag and spent the past two nights in Peter's apartment. Thomas tossed and turned a little, slowly waking up in bed, as he lay next to Peter. He moved over, onto his back. His mind was awake. He raised his left hand to rub and remove the sleep from his eyes. Thomas peeled back the bed cover, which was raised high over his chest to keep himself warm, and climbed to the side of the bed. He sat up a moment and looked down over his left shoulder, down at Peter.

He was fast asleep.

The floorboards were cool to the touch. Thomas' toes wriggled vigorously for a moment before he stood up from the bed and walked across the bedroom to retrieve a simple white cotton t- shirt and a pair of black jockey shorts he'd left there the previous night. Thomas was naked. He climbed into his clothes he had so casually slung on the floor from the night before and tiptoed his way out of the bedroom, down the hallway and into the kitchen.

The apartment was still dark and cool. The lights to the kitchen flickered on. Thomas stood there a moment, in the entrance of the kitchen, as his eyes adjusted to the light. He made his way in and immediately walked over to the cupboard and reached for two coffee cups and placed them on the counter. Peter had a thing for coffee cups and their design. One of the cups was a New York Yankees cap. Peter loved the dark blues and stark white. The other coffee cup had more sentimental value. It was from his university days. Peter had purchased the coffee cup from his university gift shop in his junior year and kept it ever since. Thomas reached for the kettle next and filled it with water. The kettle soon boiled as Thomas prepared two cups of coffee. He worked his way through the kitchen quite comfortably, knowing where things were located, as if he had been living there for more than the last two days.

It only took a couple of minutes, and Thomas held two freshly made, and incredibly hot, cups of coffee in either hand, as he made his way out of the kitchen, leaving the light switched on, for just a moment, as he went back to the bedroom, careful not to spill a drop or burn himself. He stood in the entrance of the doorway, for just a moment, and a little surprised. The hulking frame of a man stood there to see Peter sitting up in bed with his cell phone in his hands, face-down and typing away furiously. The lamp on his nightstand was switched on.

"Good morning," Thomas said, just above a whisper and with a smile on his face, as he made his way deeper into the bedroom. "You're awake."

"Good morning," Peter answered, as he raised his eyes up and off his cell phone. "Uh-huh. I had a question about the funeral. I wanted to message the lawyer before I forgot."

"Of course," Thomas smiled reassuringly.

Thomas made his way across the floor of the bedroom and over to Peter's side of the bed, first. He put his cup of coffee on the nightstand, leaning in a little.

"Be careful," Thomas smiled, "'it's hot."

"Thank you." Peter said, watching the process.

Thomas returned to his side of the bed, placing his cup of coffee on the nightstand before climbing back into bed, under the cover and next to Peter.

"Thank you for this," Peter said, making eye contact with Thomas as he moved his cell phone back to the nightstand. "Not just for the coffee. But *all* of this. The taking time off, out of the office, to be with me. It means a lot. It does."

Peter nodded, a little.

"I couldn't think of a place I'd rather be right now." Thomas smiled reassuringly.

The cups of coffee took a back seat. They sat there and cooled down. They sat there until the milk grew still and formed that skin across the surface of the coffee. Thomas leaned in, cuddling closer, kissing. Thomas and his hulking frame climbed onto the top of Peter, almost consuming him, as the two kissed deeply and passionately, as their hands explored one another under the lamp on the nightstand.

The television set in the living room was switched on. The volume just north of low. The morning news played on in the background. It was the day of Robert's funeral. The service was held at the McIntyre Memorial Chapel, located on the West Side. It was on West 79th Street. Peter and Thomas were sitting down at the kitchen table, which was also the dining table, eating breakfast.

The menu this morning consisted of scrambled eggs with toast and a selection of fresh fruits and freshly squeezed orange juice. Thomas was a master in the kitchen, compared to Peter anyway. Thomas sat opposite Peter in the same white t-shirt and black jockey shorts, with his cell phone in his hand, checking work emails. Peter drifted between his breakfast and watching the morning news.

The morning went on. The plates, glasses and cutlery from breakfast were washed and stowed away in the kitchen. Peter sat on the couch watching television, as Thomas was the first one to hit the shower. He stood under the hot water with his head tilted back a little, his eyes closed tightly, as he rubbed the bar of soap all over himself. He soon emerged from the shower and walked down the hallway, toward the bedroom, with a damp towel wrapped slanted and loosely around his waist. There was a trail of water which followed him. Thomas reached the bedroom and made his way in. Peter was laying on the bed, playing with his cell phone. He dropped it, face-down on the bed, as he saw Thomas make his way inside. Peter watched on curiously. The two made eye contact. Thomas smiled a little, somewhere between playfully and seductively. He dropped the towel from his waistline and walked naked over to his bag. He leaned in and grabbed himself some fresh underwear and black socks for the day. Peter chuckled, a little. Again, the two caught each other's eyes.

Thomas stood at the end of the bed as if almost putting on a show as he got dressed for the funeral. He kept it simple and elegant for the occasion. He climbed into a crisp, white long-sleeved shirt. He pulled on the shirt and started to button it up, from the top to bottom, as he stood in front of Peter in just a pair of red jockey shorts. The shirt buttoned, one button shy of reaching the neck.

"How do I look?" Thomas asked, again with that coy smile as he made his way to sit on the side of the bed, next to Peter to pull on his socks.

"You look great." Peter smiled. "I'd fuck you."

"If I'd let you."

There was that coy smile, again followed by a chuckle.

The morning progressed further. It was almost nine o'clock now. Robert's service was scheduled to commence at ten forty-five. Thomas was in the living room, sitting in front of the television set. He wasn't paying attention to it. His black jacket, by Tom Ford, sat over the top of one of the chairs around the kitchen table. He was face-down in his cell phone, following up and replying to work emails as Peter got himself ready for the day. Peter soon appeared from the hallway and made his way into the living room, dressed almost identical to Thomas, in black trousers and a white shirt. Peter also wore a simple, black tie.

"How do *I* look?" Peter asked, standing in the middle of the living room, in front of Thomas sitting on the couch.

Thomas looked up from his cell phone. He looked at Peter a moment before answering as if to take in the view of the young, broken man who stood before him, doing his best to appear strong and confident.

"You look," Thomas answered, just above a whisper and climbing off the couch to walk towards Peter, "you look incredible."

There was that smile, again. Thomas leaned in and gave Peter a quick kiss on the lips, before leaning in and wrapping his arms around the young man firmly, so brave to put on a strong front, but knew he was crumbling on the inside.

"I got you," Thomas whispered in Peter's right ear.

The McIntyre Memorial Chapel was a large and elegant red brick building located on West 79th Street. Its architecture was grand in its appeal as the interior design was ornate and also recently renovated.

Peter and Thomas reached the building and they climbed out the back seat of a yellow cab. Thomas handed the driver a handful of dollar bills. The driver nodded and accepted the fare plus tip. Peter was the first to climb out of the backseat of the yellow cab and he slammed the car door shut behind him. He stood there on the curb, looking up at the memorial chapel in his suit as his eyes were hidden behind his large, black sunglasses. Thomas was quick to join him as he climbed out and ran around the back of the cab to join him, standing on the curb. Thomas also wore sunglasses with his suit. The frames were also black, but smaller and more refined in their design.

"Shit!" Peter whispered to himself, muttering under his breath.

"Are you ready?" Thomas asked, turning his neck slightly to the left, looking at the young man beside him.

"A good time as any, I guess," Peter smiled, feeling nervous.

That tough exterior was trying to shine through. It didn't. Not really. Peter felt like he was going to break at a moment's notice. Thomas stood by Peter's side, watching him take the first step towards the building, and move slowly up the large cement staircase.

The walk up the cement staircase felt long and arduous. Peter kept his head down, not wanting to make eye contact with people standing in several groups on the staircase, outside the building. A tall, but rather stocky-framed twenty-something was the first to rush towards Peter and Thomas. He charged at them as if this were a celebrity sighting. The twenty-something knew Peter as a local celebrity victim that flashed across the local news, rather than someone who just lost someone very dear to them.

"Hey," the twenty-something said, a little nervously and behind a nervous smile, "if there is anything we can do, you just let us know."

"Yeah. Thanks. We will." Thomas answered quite bluntly and to the point. Thomas pushed past the kid, as he walked past him.

"Good morning, Peter. How are you holding up?"

Peter looked up from the cement staircase, with his eyes still hidden behind his sunglasses and smiled. The voice sounded familiar. It was Joseph Rubinstein, Robert's lawyer acting on behalf of his estate, and the one who invited him to the funeral.

"Good morning, Joseph. I'm… holding up. Thank you." Peter forced a smile.

"I wanted to express my deepest condolences before the service."

"Of course. Thank you." Peter nodded.

"We will talk. And of course, if there is anything further you need, you just let me know."

"I will." Peter smiled, again.

Joseph Rubinstein was somewhere in his mid- to late-fifties. He stood in front of Peter and Thomas, standing higher up on the cement staircase, and made brief eye contact with Thomas, as if to be polite. He stood there standing in a suit, black in colour, including tie and shoes. All by Armani. A white crisp long-sleeved shirt was worn underneath the open jacket. Joseph was a short man, almost stocky in build with a shaven head, with two, maybe three days stubble. He wore bifocals. Joseph Rubinstein had all the mannerisms of a friendly TV sitcom dad; that is, outside the courtroom.

The crowd began to disperse. Peter and Thomas slowly made their way to the top of the grand cement staircase and walked inside the building, through two large wooden French double doors. The members from the law office stood together and whispered amongst themselves. Peter caught the eye of some of the staff members, junior office clerks, low on the totem pole, getting those *that's him* looks. Peter remained stone-faced. Thomas leaned in and whispered something in his ear as if to cheer him up. There were other guests. Peter didn't know who they were.

The main foyer inside the McIntyre Memorial Chapel was grand and opulent. The walls were painted cream in colour with large framed photographs of the corporate staff members on display, including the founder and CEO. There was a framed print which described the chapel's early and humble beginnings and where they wanted to see themselves in the future. The floor was a dark, rich red carpet with gold accents. The air conditioning was running throughout the building. The temperature was a few degrees lower than it was outside.

A middle-aged woman, somewhere in her early to mid-forties was the first to greet Peter and Thomas, followed by Joseph Rubinstein. She was a little taller than Peter, with a slender build. She looked like she spent her downtime swimming endless laps in a swimming pool. Her long, dark locks were sleek, and pulled into a ponytail, and away from her face. She smiled and extended her left hand to greet Peter.

"Good morning," she said warmly. Peter smiled.

The two exchanged a few words, and, of course, she offered her deepest sympathies at this time. The representative wore a name badge on her black cotton, poly-blend jacket. It read, *Andrea.*

Andrea ushered the guests quickly and swiftly, through the main foyer, led by Peter, Thomas and Joseph. They walked in near silence through the room, taking a left at one corner and down a large hallway. Peter looked at the walls and took in the opulence of it all. The walls were adorned with further framed photographs. The group made their way into the first memorial chapel on the right. There was a designated area which catered with small, bite-size sandwiches of various fillings, pastries and coffee, tea, various juices and water for refreshments. The chapel catered to eighty guests in total. The walls were painted in a cream colour with elegant lighting features around the room. Peter stood still for just a moment, taking in the room itself. It got the attention of Andrea and Thomas.

"Are you okay?" Thomas asked, leaning in and just above a whisper. Peter looked at Thomas for a moment. He smiled. Eventually.

"Of course." Peter forced a smile. "It's just so real. I mean, this is it, you know? Goodbye." Thomas rested one hand on Peter's back as if to help usher him inside the chapel. They walked to the front row and took to their seats, with Andrea's assistance. Thomas sat to Peter's left. Joseph Rubinstein sat to his right.

The chapel itself was personalised with photographs of Robert, taken during happier times in his life. There were also keepsakes and mementos around the room. A closed casket lay at the front of the chapel and one large photograph, stood tall within the frame of a wooden easel. The photograph was taken almost four years ago. Peter remembered the night. It was taken from his fiftieth birthday celebrations. Peter looked over his shoulder and around the room. He looked at the other guests, making their way inside. Still, he knew none of them.

The priest was the last to enter the chapel. His large, round, ball-like shape walked briskly down the aisle, with a near bounce in his step. The priest was somewhere close to sixty in age with a greying beard and a short-manicured haircut with flecks of grey in his blonde hair. He took to his post in front of the seated guests and was quick to introduce himself.

"Good morning everyone," the priest started. "I am Father Henry

Moore." His voice was deep and strong.

Father Moore wore a white alb, a floor-length robe made of linen with tapered sleeves. He dusted himself off a little, lowered his eyes to the podium and started to talk. He talked glowingly of Robert's successful financial career, his now-deceased ex-wife, Anne, and daughter, Carrie, but omitted mentioning his son, Benjamin. He also glossed over the tragic events of the last four years, including Robert's struggle with sobriety and his addiction to alcohol, prescribed medicines and anonymous sex. Or his depression. It was if he were talking of a different man, in different time and place. Peter had to wonder, was this the watered-down, made-for-TV version of one man's life?

Peter sat there in the front row, his eyes still behind his black sunglasses, staring back at the priest. He didn't know Robert at all. Peter wanted to stand there and shout it out, for everyone to hear.

Thomas removed his sunglasses and moved his eyes onto Peter. Peter didn't look back. Thomas stretched his right hand out, taking Peter by the left hand and giving it a gentle squeeze, letting him know he was there and thinking of him.

The service was over. Father Moore mingled with the higher-ups from the law firm, whilst others approached the closed casket to share their final thoughts and prayers with Robert quietly. Peter and Thomas sat in the front row and talked amongst themselves a moment. It was then that Peter stood from the almost uncomfortable wooden pew and left Thomas behind, while he approached the closed casket. It drew the attention of some of the guests. They stared and whispered amongst themselves. The casket was black with a shiny gloss. Peter was next in line to approach the closed casket. He stood there, in front of the casket, looking up at the photograph on the easel. He stretched his left hand outwards, resting it on top of the casket for a moment. The memories of Robert's fiftieth birthday party came flooding back. A smile was quick to surface to his lips. Peter chuckled, somewhat to himself a little, whilst holding back his tears.

The guests dined on bite-size sandwiches and pastries and sipped from their throw-away coffee cups. Peter hobnobbed with members from Robert's law firm, including Joseph, as they paid their condolences and organised a time that suited everyone for the reading of the will. Peter was reaching his limit now. He had a smile plastered across his lips, his voice was a little hoarse, from the mild and repetitive conversation and crying, all whilst doing his best to maintain a professional outlook and play the role of a grieving loved one. Thomas stood by closely, almost like a bodyguard, and did his best to provide support.

"Are you okay?" Thomas asked, as he leaned and whispered gently in Peter's left ear. Peter looked up at Thomas a moment and glanced at him.

"Get me out of here," he whispered.

"You got it." Thomas smiled politely.

Another office junior, low on the office totem pole, approached Peter and Thomas, to offer his condolences. He didn't know the man. He knew nothing of Robert Prescott but the office talk of his combined net worth. Totem Pole had a nervous smile plastered across his thin, lizard-like lips as if it were all a dare from an office colleague to approach a local celebrity victim and survivor. Thomas was quick to step in between the two men, as if acting like a bodyguard, again.

"Thank you," Thomas said, quietly, as if just above a whisper. "You got a business card?"

"No." Totem Pole answered, as if let down.

"Good." Thomas paused a moment, still with a smile, and his eyes hidden behind his sunglasses. "Now, fuck off! Back the fuck up and give this man some space to breathe, okay?"

Totem Pole was in shock. "Of course. Of course." He fumbled with his words, nervously. "Yes, sir. I just wanted…."

"I know what you wanted. You wanted shit! Your attempt at playing the grieving and supportive nobody is both desperate and obvious."

Totem Pole was embarrassed. He turned and scurried away, amongst his other office workers. Some looked on.

"I'm impressed." Peter smiled, his eyes no longer hidden behind his sunglasses.

"Stick with me, and I'll take you places." Thomas smiled, reassuringly, whilst extending his right hand out, as if to take Peter's. "How about we get out of here?"

"I'd love that." Peter smiled, again.

"I was hoping you'd say that. Come on."

Peter and Thomas walked out of the chapel, leaving behind Joseph, the law firm, and the remaining guests. And leaving behind Robert Prescott, the man. The memories, he would carry with him for the rest of his life. Peter was happy with that. They walked down the hallway, across the foyer and out to the front of the grand red brick building, in and amongst the other pedestrians.

Peter and Thomas made their way from the McIntyre Memorial Chapel and headed back to the apartment, first. They changed out of their suits and into something more casual, jeans and t-shirts, as they ventured out of the apartment and explored the city as if acting like total tourists in their town. They started in Times Square, taking in the large grandeur of it all, and all the flashing, neon lights. The fanfare and spectacle of it all, making their way into department stores to bypass the large pedestrian crowds. They grabbed a bite for lunch in a small, out-of-the-way burger joint on the Lower East Side before making their way to Central Park.

The day progressed onwards, into the late evening. Peter spent the night at Thomas' apartment. The bedroom seemed spacious and the ceilings high. It maybe had something to do with the fact that Thomas' bed was nothing more than a king-size mattress laying on top of a thin wooden base, close to the floor. It wasn't your traditional bed. It lay in the middle of the room with a nightstand on either side of the bed. The lampshades from outdoors shone brightly, as the light sprayed across the bedroom walls. The curtains were pulled wide open, and the doors leading out to the balcony were pulled to a close.

Thomas and Peter were lying on top of the bed. It was in the early hours of the morning, somewhere past three. The bed cover was stripped from the bed and laying on the floor. The two men were naked and entwined in the crisp, white sheets, kissing passionately. The cordless telephone in the living room began to ring. The tone seems to almost echo off the walls of the apartment in the quiet of the night. *Ring. Ring. Ring.*

"Who the fuck is calling at this time of night?" Thomas asked, a little annoyed, as he raised his head from his pillow.

"Maybe it's important."

"Fuck it! It can go to voice…"

The answering machine took the call. There was a caller's voice. It was male, somewhere in his early-to-mid-twenties.

51

"I can't stop thinking of you," said the voice, "I can still smell you in my clothes. When can we fuck… again?"

Thomas was quick to climb to his feet and run naked, out of the bedroom and out into the living room to answer the telephone.

"Hey, how you doing? Why are you calling me so late?" Thomas asked, a little out of breath.

"I couldn't stop thinking about us."

Thomas fumbled with the answering machine for a moment in the dark, to take the caller off speakerphone.

Peter appeared in the entrance of the living room, partially dressed and leaning against one side of the wall, in a simple white t-shirt a black cotton boxer shorts.

"I guess it was important," Peter mumbled, just above a whisper. "You weren't meant to hear that," Thomas answered, apologetically. "Obviously."

"It was a one-time mistake," Thomas replied, disconnecting the call and walking toward Peter. "I promise. He doesn't mean anything."

"That's what they all say." Peter's voice was deflated, not angry. Just disappointed. He was just too tired to fight back. "He didn't mean anything to you. But was just that important enough to fuck and get your rocks off, right? I get it."

In the days that followed Robert's funeral, Peter found himself back where it all started, in Robert's apartment on the Upper East Side. The front door was locked. Joseph Rubinstein had the keys and jiggled the lock a little, opening the door wide enough to let them both inside. The apartment looked different, somehow. The curtains were pulled opened to allow the light in. The walls were all painted white. The apartment was also empty. The furniture and all the belongings were gone. Peter didn't know where exactly. He stepped inside the apartment as Joseph walked around, leaving him to his own devices. Peter stood near where the table and bowl *used* to be. He looked down the hallway, and there, in front of him, was the master bedroom. The door was pulled to a close. The other doors in the hallway were left open, to allow for more light.

The office, one spare bedroom that had been converted into a walk-in wardrobe, and a spare bedroom for guests. Peter closed his eyes for just a moment and lowered his head as he thought of Robert. He opened his eyes and made his way into the living room. Joseph was out of sight.

Peter stood in the living room, making his way over to the large windows, peering over the view of the city. He turned around and looked at the living room as if feeling he were almost from the outside looking in. He stood there reminiscing of the relationship he once had, both the good and the bad times, just long enough before he broke down in tears. He could feel his heartbeat racing, his hands grow sweaty and the tears well in his eyes.

The apartment was the last stop after the reading of the will. Robert left the majority of his remaining bank balance to various charities across the city. But enough money for Peter to set himself up in life, maybe buy a home and the rest, to do whatever he decided to choose. The sale proceeds from the apartment in the city would go to outstanding lawyers' fees and charities.

The sound of a vibrating cell phone came from Peter's trouser pocket, breaking the silence in the apartment and his train of thought. Peter reached into his left trouser pocket and retrieved the cell phone. The front of the screen had come to life. The caller *Unknown.* Peter sighed a little before placing the cell phone to his left ear to answer the call.

"Hello?" Peter answered.

"Hello." the deep and dark, yet familiar voice replied.

Peter was caught off guard, a moment. He caught his breath in his throat, a moment. "Remember me?" the voice continued.

Peter was angry, yet careful not to draw attention from Joseph. He turned to face the view of the city in front of him, again.

"It's not you," Peter whispered, "it can't be. You're *dead.*"

"Do you think that this is over, do you?" the voice yelled back. "You always think you're so fucking special, don't you? This is over when I say it is, and not a moment before!" the voice screamed before breaking into laughter.

Peter remained silent. His facial expression, stern, as if trying to decipher the voice. Nothing. A smile soon surfaced to his lips.

"But you're forgetting one major plot hole…"

"Yeah? What's that?"

I fucking *killed* Ben Prescott. So, who are you, huh? Some D-grade, Walmart, straight-to-video version…?"

"Really? That's what you think?" the voice asked, almost politely. "Well, I'm very much fucking real and alive. I think I have enough time to slash and cut you deep before the cops arrive," the voice continued, angrily.

"You have to find me first, motherfucker!"

"I already did."

Peter turned his back on the view of the city, his mouth opened in horror.

"Yeah?" he asked, tears welling in his eyes. "Well, I call your bluff!"

Peter was quick to run across the living room floor and to the apartment door. He opened it and peered into the hallway, looking left and right, and left and right, again. There was no one there.

"I'm closer than you think. See you soon," the voice laughed.

The phone line disconnected.

Joseph appeared from the kitchen. Peter turned around to face him. He was visibly shocked and shaken.

"Is everything okay?" Joseph asked, concerned.

Peter was unresponsive. He stood there angrily, with tears welling in his eyes.

Chapter Three...

Thomas removed what personal belongings he had out of the apartment by the following morning. He stuffed them into an over-sized sports bag and left Peter in the apartment, alone. The night had been spent slinging words, hurtful words, and accusations, back and forth. Thomas made it very clear that for the better half of the last year, he had been fucking around. There was no working on weekends. His gym buddies got together, once or twice a month, for the specific purpose of picking up young twinks with low self-esteem at the gym. They paid them just enough attention, just enough, to make them feel special and wanted, taking the weak ones they desired from their group, leaving them vulnerable, and nothing more than easy prey. Thomas and his friends took turns in taking them home to have their pack-sordid way with them.

It was Saturday morning and the house was empty. Well, almost. Peter was in his bedroom, on his knees, and keeping himself busy, placing personal belongings into large brown boxes — there was a separate box for t-shirts, casuals, a box for work shirts, all neatly folded, as best they could. And a box for old shoes, both work and casual. And for everything else that he didn't want to keep, that held an unwanted memory, there was a box set aside for Goodwill. The sides of the box were marked in black marker, with big letters — G O O D W I L L. Thomas had already taken what he wanted from the apartment and was ready to move on.

In the days that followed the demise of what he thought was a healthy and trusting relationship, Peter found himself tying up the loose ends of life in New York City. *His* life in New York City. He cleaned out his apartment and terminated his lease, he handed in his resignation and received another call from the clown mask. It was very casual, as far as conversations go. *How have you been? I'm going to take a hunting knife and slit you from throat to groin and expose you for the whore that you are, don't you know?* That sort of thing. Peter spent his final full day in New York City, being a total tourist in a city he once called home. He visited the obvious hot spots, such as the Statue of Liberty and the Empire State Building. He also took in the local attractions, which brought back the memories of Robert and Ben; Riley's for a soda and some cheese fries. It was still pulling in a decent crowd. The layout of the diner was still the same. The only real difference was a fresh coat of paint on the walls. The mum-and-dad video store was now out of business. Laurie had passed away a little over a year ago now, and since then, Jim had given up on the business. It was now a *Baby Gap*.

Peter found himself on the West Side. He was standing on West 34th Street; he passed the pedestrians and made his way inside the Empire State Building. It was chaos inside. It was like going through airport security. The crowds of people were herded into a long queue which snaked it's way left and right and left and right, again. And that of course, was after passing through a metal detector. Peter had to hand over his backpack and pass it through an x-ray machine. The backpack came out the other end of the machine and slid across a smooth, metal bench, pushed along quickly by some beefy security guard.

The security guard was somewhere in his early thirties. His dark, navy blue shirt clung to his round, ball-shaped figure, with the hint of a white t-shirt underneath. His belt around his waist began to buckle, protruding outwards, and upside down, pushed by the girth of his stomach. The security guard didn't make eye contact with Peter, or anyone for that matter. He grunted a little and moved onto the next bag that was waiting in the queue. It was all a game to him. It was called *Keep The Customers Happy And Keep Your Job*.

Peter grabbed his backpack and made his way to the end of the long snake-like queue. The head of the snake, the front of the queue, moved in groups of up to six people at a time, as a staff member ushered them into waiting elevators. The doors closed and the people were shot into the air, high above the city skyline. It took the better part of half an hour before Peter reached the elevator. He joined a small family; father, mother, and two screaming toddlers. Peter felt the father's pain and the two exchanged pleasantries, with a nod and a smile. The doors to the elevator closed. The parents took to their kids and made sure they were comfortable. The elevator rose quickly into the air. It arrived onto the eighty-sixth floor within seconds.

Peter stepped out of the elevator. He was greeted by a small, narrow hallway and countless tourists, and another staff member quickly ushering them out and pointing them in the right direction. He made his way down the hallway and past the tourists, before making his way onto the observation deck of the Empire State Building and the famous skyline that lay before him. Peter made his way around the balcony and found a quiet place to himself. He slowly, and cautiously, stepped closer to the edge of the observation deck, as far as he could go, anyway. He could feel his heartbeat racing, his palms getting sweaty and his knees turn to jelly. And there, in front of him, was a sea of cement skyscrapers, one taller and bigger than the next. The sky was clear, and the sun was out.

"Thank you, Robert," Peter whispered to himself, with a hint of a smile that surfaced to his lips. "Goodbye."

Peter spent another twenty minutes or so walking laps of the observation deck, taking in the views of the city, taking photographs with his cell phone before he made his way back inside, down the elevator and out of the building.

The weather began to change as the afternoon progressed into the early hours of the evening as dark, ominous clouds rolled across the city, bringing with it mild rain and lightning. Peter was back in his apartment for the night. *His* last night. The apartment itself was bare. There was a couch in the living room and a hardwood coffee table. The television set was switched on. The living room was also going to be the bedroom for the evening. The remaining rooms in the apartment were stripped bare. The furniture, including the television set, came with the lease.

The lights in the apartment were switched on, providing warm atmospheric glow about the apartment as the rain from outdoors hit the window frames. Peter was in the living room, standing by the window, watching the rainfall as a crack of lightning lit up the skies. He took his eyes off the kids running home, running anywhere, out of the rain, in the street below and looked up at the sky. A second crack of lightning hit. This one was harder and more ferocious. Peter took a step back from the window and fell deeper into the living room. A large size pizza box was open, and inside, a partially eaten pepperoni pizza with sausage and green capsicum and a couple of soda cans decorated the outside of the box. The local nightly news was playing on the television set, and there, a story about something was playing.

Peter walked about the apartment, very casually. He was dressed in a simple white cotton t-shirt and grey sweat pants for the night. He walked from the kitchen and back into the living room, again, with some paper towels to dab the oil from the surface of the pizza, and a freshly open can of soda, that made that loud popping sound with the pull of the tab. Peter reached the coffee table and leaned down and dropped the paper towels and can of soda by the open pizza box. It was then that the cell phone, sitting on the coffee table, came to life as it began to ring. *Ring. Ring. Ring.* It was an *Unknown Caller*. Peter closed his eyes a moment and shook his head, catching his breath in his throat, a little.

"Hello?" Peter answered, quite shortly, as he stood tall from the coffee table.

"Hello," the dark and familiar voice replied.

"What do you want?"

"I want you. I've always wanted you. I watched you from afar and—"

"Who the fuck is this?" Peter shouted angrily, interrupting.

"You'll find out soon enough and not a moment before. In the meantime, I want to play a game."

"No!"

"You fight. I may let you live. You run. They die!" the voice began to laugh, almost heinously.

"Who?"

Peter pulled the cell phone from his ear and looked at the screen on his cell phone, for a moment. It didn't take long before he composed himself, regaining his confidence.

"You want me, huh?" he asked.

"Uh-huh." the voice answered. "I'm on the other side of this phone call, right now. I'm in your head. I'm in every waking moment. You can't leave me alone."

"Fuck you!"

"You'll see me very soon." The phone line disconnected.

It was the start of a new day. A long day ahead. The storm from last night passed, leaving the clouds over the city overcast and the weather, humid. Peter was awake, had showered, polished off a cold slice of pizza for breakfast, before throwing the box in the trash, and was now standing outside the front of what was once his apartment building. The footpath was filled with other pedestrians, all going about their day-to-day lives. Peter stood on the curb doing his best to hail down a passing cab. A yellow cab soon rushed out of the traffic and to the side of the curb and came to a halt. Peter chased after the yellow cab, running along the footpath, carrying his sports bag over his left shoulder. He raced around to the driver's side and leaned in.

"JFK?" Peter asked.

"You, Peter?" the driver replied.

"Yeah," he answered, with a hint of a smile.

"Get in."

The boot of the yellow cab was quick to pop open. Peter ran to the back and threw his sports bag into the boot before slamming it shut and climbing into the backseat, behind the driver. The yellow cab pulled out from the curb and into the traffic.

Peter made himself comfortable in the back seat as he peered out the window, watching the world pass him by. His eyes pulled away from the excitement of the city and looked around the inside of the cab. The cab was neat in appearance. But there was the slight hint of Old Spice and freshly brewed take-away coffee, coming from the driver.

The driver of the yellow taxicab was somewhere in his mid- to late-forties. His back was turned to Peter, but from what he could tell, the driver had thick, curly chocolate brown hair, which was in need of a trim. He wore a blue and white polo shirt with horizontal stripes and denim jeans. His photo ID sat on top of the dashboard. The driver's name was Joe.

"So, what takes you out to JFK?" Joe asked with a genuine interest and a thick Bostonian accent.

"A new chapter." Peter smiled, as he looked at Joe in the rear-view mirror a moment before answering.

"I get it. I do." Joe nodded. "There are times when I think to myself, I am done with this city. But how could you not? Look at it! It's fucking beautiful! There is always *something* happening."

Peter smiled at Joe and nodded. He turned his eyes away from the rear-view mirror and peered out the window, again. The traffic was in near gridlock.

Joe and his yellow cab pulled into the short-term drop-off area outside the front of JFK airport. It was crowded, to say the least. There were passengers and people walking in every direction. Joe turned around in his seat, using one arm to hug the chair, to turn ever so slightly, to look back at his passenger. Peter grabbed his wallet from his trouser pocket and gave Joe money for the fare and a little more as a tip, for the conversation.

"Hey man," Joe smiled. "Great tip! Thanks a lot. You have a great flight, you hear?"

"Thank you." Peter nodded, with a hint of a smile.

He climbed out and retrieved his sports bag which he slung over his left shoulder and slammed the boot shut, giving Joe the thumbs-up to let him know it was good to drive away. He stepped onto the curb, before making his way past the other pedestrians and inside the departure terminal.

The flight out of New York City to Chicago was done in just under three hours, and change. The flight was rather full. There was a little turbulence as the plane took off from the runway and made 'its way high above the overcast clouds. Peter buried his head into a couple of celebrity trash magazines to entertain himself during the flight. He had an aisle seat, just in front of the wing. It was better than focusing on option number two. A screaming youngster, no older than four or five, a few seats in front, who wouldn't listen to his parents, who were doing their best to keep him quiet, bribing him with video games and candy.

The plane touched down at O'Hare safely. Peter, along with all the other guests onboard the flight, made their way off the plane and made their way through the airport to baggage claim. Peter retrieved his sports bag before making his way over to the car rental office. The service was fast and polite. Four staff members were standing behind the counter, some waiting to serve, whilst others were busy with customers.

Peter made his way out of the terminal and followed the instructions to pick up his car rental. It was a Hyundai Kona and black in colour. He walked towards the parked car, pointed the clicker and unlocked the car, the back door on the passenger side first. The sports bag was thrown, sliding across the back seat of the car. Peter opened the driver's side door and climbed inside, making himself comfortable, before slamming the car door behind him. The key was inserted into the ignition and the engine roared to life. Peter placed his foot on the accelerator cautiously and made his way out of the car park and out into the traffic.

The city was becoming a distant picture, growing smaller and smaller in the rear-view mirror with each passing mile. The music blared from the radio as Peter tapped his left hand to the beat of the music on the inside of the door. The window was down, and the breeze blew through the car.

Peter was done with all the hustle and bustle of the big city. It was just too painful, with too many memories.

Hillsboro was a sleepy little town. The people knew each other and gossiped behind each other's backs. The local police department dealt with one, maybe two, homicides a year. The drive looked so familiar, the roads and street signs hadn't changed in the past four years. Not much, anyway. Peter's eyes were firmly on the road ahead. His thoughts started to wander, just like they had done in the office.

Peter thought of his father. The memories, both the good and the bad, came flooding back. He chuckled to himself, a little. A smile surfaced to his lips and the tears welled in his eyes, too. He laughed at the thought of his father, of the time he chased a neighbourhood dog out of the front yard, only to run into an oak tree in his flip flops and bounce backwards, getting himself tangled in a tree swing. And how he had cried himself to sleep, the night of his father's funeral, well after the guests had left the church service and family gathering afterwards. He thought of his mother, also both in the good and the bad. The bad outweighed the good, unfortunately. Peter shook his head quickly. He also thought of his high school years, of the time his mathematics teacher, senior year, who whispered answers to him during an exam. And the friends he hung out with.

"What am I doing?" Peter asked himself under his breath.

He shook his head again, and turned the volume on his radio up further and found himself singing to the music blaring on the radio as he cruised the open road.

Peter arrived in Hillsboro. It took him almost as long as his flight, completing the drive in just under three hours. He found himself coming off the main interstate and driving through the country roads, some were winding, and others were mountainous, with views of forests for as far as the eye could see. The music from the radio cut out, losing reception, from time to time, as the sports utility vehicle headed deep into the forests.

Hillsboro, apart from its tragic and bloodstained past, did look picturesque. A sign on the side of the road, planted on the outskirts of town, appeared almost new, with a happy family, complete with a young father, mother, and their two children, laughing and having fun. The caption on the sign read, *Welcome to Hillsboro.* Peter glanced at the sign a moment, as his car drove past, just under the speed limit. The population was thirteen thousand, eight hundred and fifty-two.

The local roads took the sports utility vehicle and Peter, deep inside Hillsboro, arriving in the heart of the town, pulling up to the street lights around the town square. The lights turned red, for what felt like a good couple of minutes. It gave Peter the chance to look around town. There were high school students, running and having fun, some laughing and playing jokes on their friends. An elderly couple was sitting on a bench feeding the local birds. It was quite a postcard moment. A hint of a smile surfaced to Peter's lips. The storefronts looked almost identical to the time that had brought him back to town for his grandfather's funeral. There was the hardware store, newsagents, a local diner, a movie theatre and a handful of take-away joints.

The traffic lights turned green and the sports utility vehicle moved forward, slowly and with caution, looking for a place to park. Peter flicked on the left indicator, looked in his rear-view mirror for any traffic behind him, and safely pulled into a nearby parking spot, just inches away from the local hardware store. The engine to the car rental died. Peter climbed out of the sports utility vehicle, slamming the door behind him, and stretched his legs a little. Peter pressed the button on the clicker, again. The car alarm switched on. Some of the local high school students looked at the car as they crossed the road. Peter didn't pay any attention. He made the slow walk past his car, leaving it behind him, past the other store fronts of the town square. Peter took another look around, as if with fresh eyes. He still felt a little uneasy and walked with caution. After all, he represented the bloodstained history, of a story the local town wanted to bury, wanted to forget and leave in the past, once and for all.

The local real estate business was located next door to a take-away joint. Peter was dropping by to pick up the keys to his rental, before finding his forever home. A local elderly woman, walked from the opposite direction, in a flowing, flowery maxi dress and a neatly coiffed bob with almost silver-white highlights, as she walked briskly with a cane. She made eye contact with Peter, for just a moment, and smiled a little. Polite. The smile quickly vanished, her eyes soon filled with hatred. Peter looked back at the elderly woman a moment longer, before turning again and looking forward, toward the real estate office.

"I know who you are," the elderly woman called out, "what are you doing here?" It was enough for Peter to turn around and look back, again.

"Excuse me?"

"You heard me," she replied, clearing her throat a little.

"I don't understand."

"Your family was nothing more than a dirty little secret in this town. People want to forget! What are you doing here?" she screamed, almost charging at him, with her cane raised a little, shaking under the stress.

Peter didn't fight back. Not with an elderly woman. He raised his hands, using his forearms to protect himself from the cane, as she swung from left to right and left to right, again. The scene drew the attention of some local high school students, some taking out their cell phones and recording the fight to upload onto social media later. It also drew the attention of one of the office workers inside the real estate office. She was a tall, beautiful woman with long, straight blonde hair, pulled back into a sleek ponytail and neatly dressed. She would have been somewhere in her late thirties.

"Mrs Baeyer!" the real estate agent yelled, grabbing the attention of both the elderly woman and Peter.

The real estate agent and Mrs Baeyer made eye contact. Not a single, further word was uttered. The cane came down. Mrs Baeyer nodded, pulled herself together, feeling somewhat embarrassed, and turned and scurried away. Peter was left feeling confused.

"Please, come inside." the real estate agent called, in a more friendly tone.

Peter looked at the woman with the blonde hair. He walked towards her, as she ushered him inside the office.

It didn't take too long before Peter was out of the real estate office and had collected the keys to his rental home. He dropped by a local grocery store and picked up a few provisions to store in the refrigerator and make himself feel more at home, before he was back behind the wheel of his car, again. The back seat was stacked with his sports bag and groceries. The car engine roared to life, once more. Peter looked into the rear-view mirror, again, and cautiously pulled into the traffic once more.

The sports utility vehicle turned onto Raleigh Crescent. It looked picturesque. There were beautiful weatherboard homes, some single storey and others, two, with rows of trees planted on either side of the road. There were families and children about the street, all minding their own business going about and enjoying their day. The car rental pulled outside 482 Raleigh Crescent.

The engine died. Peter opened the side door and climbed out. He slammed the door shut, walking around the front of the vehicle and up onto the pavement. And there, in front of him, was the house. It was a beautiful home. A plush two-storey weatherboard house, complete with a neatly manicured front lawn, two large oak trees, planted opposite one another, and a porch which overlooked the view of the street.

The afternoon progressed into evening, almost. The sun was beginning to set over Hillsboro for another day, and some of the local children were playing in the street. There were kids on bikes, whilst others were chasing a large green rubber ball, that they kicked about amongst themselves.

The children soon disappeared as they were called inside for dinner.

The lights inside the house were switched on. The house was alive, again. There was music playing from the stereo in the living room. Peter was upstairs, putting the finishing touches on putting his clothes away. The house came furnished with all that was needed. There was furniture in the living room, there were four bedrooms, each neatly presented with clean, fresh linens. White goods. A television set. The property was turn-key ready. It was a place to stay for the time being.

The home was to come, down the track a little, and in time. Peter was dressed in a simple white t-shirt and blue jeans and was barefoot as he walked about the house. He could hear the music playing from downstairs, moving to the beat of the music, in his own, weird way. It wasn't before long, that he made his way downstairs, into the kitchen, and grabbed himself a can of soda from the refrigerator and put another takeaway pizza in the oven to warm up. The exercise regime would begin again tomorrow, he decided. But tonight, it was time to relax and unwind. The music coming from the stereo was now switched off. The television was now switched on. The local news was playing.

Peter made his way into the living room, with a can of soda in one hand and a plate with two slices of pizza in the other. It was a thin crust meat lover's delight with extra pepperoni. Peter sat down on the couch closest to the coffee table, and in front of the television set. He took a sip from the can of soda before his cell phone on the armrest of the couch began to ring. *Ring. Ring. Ring.*

Peter looked at the screen of the cell phone as it came to life. *Unknown Caller,* again. "Hello?" Peter answered, a little cautiously.

"Welcome home, Peter," the dark, yet familiar voice answered.

Peter closed his eyes a moment. He opened them, again, as he climbed off the couch and walked across the living room and to the front door. The front door was pushed open. There was no one there. Peter stepped out onto the porch, to take in a view of the street. Kids were playing in the street, a family walking past, the mother pushing a pram with a toddler inside, and she turned and made eye contact with Peter.

"Can you see me right now?" Peter asked, with the same amount of caution.

"You came home." the voice answered. "To the town you once left behind and the bloodstained memory you left on the people in your wake. Do you think people forgive and forget? I don't think so!"

"Enough of this shit, already!" Peter demanded. "You want me, motherfucker? Come and get me!"

"You'd like that, wouldn't you? It sure would make life easier. Peter snaps his fingers and the world bends to your demands? I don't think so. You might have fooled people in the big city, but the people here, well they know different. They know the real you. I told you I wanted to play a game. Welcome home, Peter. There is going to be blood spilt on this town once again, and it's all your fault!"

The phone line disconnected.

Peter stood on the porch a moment longer, still getting those *that's him* stares as the local people whispered and gossip.

"It's all your fault!" a local woman called out.

Peter stood there. His face solemn, before turning to walk back inside his house. The front door shut quickly.

Peter awoke in the early hours of the following morning. He was still getting used to a new bed. He laid there, in the middle, and rolled over onto his right shoulder to grab his cell phone from the nightstand. The screen came to life with a push of a button. The time was four thirty-two in the morning. Peter dropped his cell phone back down on the nightstand before collapsing onto his back again and rubbing the sleep from his eyes. He lay in the middle of the bed, again, staring up at the ceiling fan above him. It was switched off. He had one arm propped under his pillow, with another hand resting on his chest. Peter was awake now.

The kitchen. It was alive for the start of another day. The kettle was boiling. There was bread in the toaster and there were scrambled eggs in the frying pan. Peter was out of bed and dressed in a simple grey t-shirt and navy blue sweat pants. The television set in the living room was switched on. The usual morning programming was interrupted with breaking news. It caught Peter's attention as the loud music introduction quickly played. Peter moved the frying pan off the top of the stove top. The scene from the breaking news was that of a local wooded area, a park nearby. And in the background, there were a string of police officers and a detective combing the area.

"The identity of the girl is yet to be established," started the TV reporter, "but, police are investigating what appears to be the brutal and visceral murder of a young woman, no older than twenty-five. She was found hanging from a tree, in a wooded area, near the local quarry, with what appears to be knife wounds from throat to the pubic region, the skin was torn and pulled open, exposing the insides; whilst she was wearing what appears to be a clown mask. The same one used years ago in the Sidney Green-Harmon case. Police are yet to report, but sources say this is the most gruesome murder scene since…."

The TV reporter was somewhere in his mid- to late-forties, suit and tie and had a swimmer's build.

Peter was quick to grab the TV remote from the couch and pointed it at the television set, turning it off. He was angry. There were tears welling in his eyes. The cell phone in Peter's other hand began to ring. *Ring. Ring. Ring.* The screen came to life, again. *Unknown Caller.*

The phone call opened with the sound of that same heinous laughter from that same dark and familiar voice.

"Welcome home, Peter. I told you that there would be blood. Are you enjoying the game so far? We've only just started."

"That poor girl," Peter answered, just above a whisper. The laughter continued.

The phone line disconnected.

There was a heavy knock at the front door. *Pound. Pound. Pound.* Peter took his eyes off his cell phone and looked towards the front door of the house from the living room, as he could see the shadow of a heavyset man in police uniform standing on the porch. There was more pounding coming from the front door. *Pound. Pound. Pound.* Peter walked across the living room and answered the door. There, on the other side, standing on the porch, was a deputy police officer, dressed in uniform, flanked by junior officers standing to his left and right.

The deputy standing on the front porch was a bear of a man. He stood at six feet and was somewhere in his late twenties, a little older than Peter Harmon. The man had dirty blonde hair with a neatly trimmed beard. He looked like he spent most of his spare time in the gym. His uniform shirt and trousers clung tightly to his body. The shirt was unbuttoned from the neck, one, maybe two buttons were undone, exposing a white t-shirt underneath.

"Andrew?" Peter whispered, shocked.

"It's Deputy Preston today, Peter."

"Officers," Peter answered, acknowledging the junior officers with a head tilt. "What can I do for you today, Deputy Preston?"

"I heard you were back in town."

"News travels fast."

Andrew Preston looked past Peter, over his right shoulder, and into the foyer, as he stood in the doorway of his house, looking around, if only briefly.

"This is you, huh? Nice digs." With a hint of a smile.

"It's only temporary whilst I look for something a little more permanent. Wait! How did you know I…?"

"This town, Petey." Andrew smiled, again. "People talk. You've been a hot topic of conversation everywhere. Personally, it's good to have you home."

"But renting a home isn't a crime, is it?"

"No." Andrew smiled, giggling a little.

"But murder is!" one junior officer interrupted. Peter was in shock. And angry.

"Step down!" Andrew ordered. "The girl...on the news. I'm sure you've seen the news this morning?"

"Of course. And you think *I* had something to do with this?"

"Personally, if it were me, I would say no way. Not my high school buddy. But I have a boss, and he is inquisitive. He wants me to bring you in for questioning. That is all." Andrew shrugged his shoulders, a little. "At best, you'll be home again inside the hour."

"I see."

Peter locked the front door of his house, but not before grabbing his wallet, house keys, and cell phone, and putting on a pair of sneakers. The house was secure. Peter walked towards the squad car that was parked out in the street, in front of the two-storey Victorian house. There were people in the street, in their gardens, peering, watching on, as some of the neighbours pretended to busy themselves with this and that.

Peter soon arrived at the Hillsboro Police Department. The station was busy. There was a handful of reporters, some from television networks, and others from newspapers, all trying their best to get the lead on the latest, breaking story. Peter sat in the back seat of the squad car, with Andrew sitting next to him. The two junior officers sat up front, one of them behind the wheel. The squad car drove past the front of the station, driving around the block, and pulling into the back, to avoid the awaiting circus.

Mr Harmon was ushered into the station quite quickly. Andrew led the way, from the car park, inside the station and into the interview room. Peter sat at a table in a cool room with brick walls, fluorescent lighting hanging from the ceiling, a basic office table, with two sets of two chairs on either side and a two-sided mirror on the north wall of the room. The room was sterile. Peter couldn't help but look at the two-sided mirror a moment and wonder who was standing on the other side, staring back at him, if anyone. He had seen enough movies and television to know how it worked. He had lived through this. The two junior officers left the interview room. One of them slid a cup of water towards Peter, whilst the other handed Deputy Preston and his senior colleague, Detective Wallace Quinn — a clean-shaven man in his early fifties, with an athletic build — a thick manila folder.

The folder hit the table with a little thud and was pushed along the surface. Peter looked at it. He could see newspaper clippings and articles with his name on them. He could see pictures of his mother and father, and Robert, Ben and the rest of the Prescott family. Peter felt more than a little concerned.

"Thank you," Detective Quinn answered, pulling the manila file in close to himself, keeping his right hand on it for a moment. "That will be all."

Detective Quinn turned in his chair a fraction. The rubber stoppers on the bottom of the chair squeaked against the surface of the floor, as he watched the junior officers leave the room, looking past Deputy Preston. The door leading into the interview room was pulled to a gentle close. Peter and Andrew maintained their eye contact.

"We are seeing a lot of you, aren't we?"

"Pardon me?" Peter answered, confused.

I know about you," Detective Quinn nodded, a little. "Your childhood. Your return to Hillsboro for your grandfather's funeral almost four years ago. And last night."

"Wait! What? Do you think I had something to do with this? Are you fucking with me?" Peter made himself comfortable in his chair a little more, leaning forward into the table, maintaining eye contact with Detective Quinn now.

"All I am saying is, you turn up and people start dying. Why is that do you think?"

"Fff..." Peter answered, ready to drop another expletive, before regaining his composure.

"Is my line of questioning getting under your skin?"

Peter stopped. He smiled, leaning into the table, again.

"Tell me, Detective. There is a killer on the loose in your small country town, why are you bothering me with this shit? I have lived through this, okay. Remember? I want nothing to do with this... I just want..."

"Well, if it isn't you, then who is it?"

"I don't know." Peter shrugged. "*You're* the detective. You figure it out."

"Someone knows you're back in Hillsboro, Peter. And they are sitting back and watching, enjoying every moment." Deputy Preston interrupted, his tone of voice deepening.

Peter looked at Andrew, a little surprised. "You know I'm back in town?"

No one answered.

"What are you saying? You think *I'm* the killer?"

Peter stopped a moment. He looked at the deputy, his high school friend. He looked at the detective. "I just know you know I'm back in town. I also know the detective knows I'm back in town."

"Enough of this!" Detective Quinn shouted, "the whole damn town knows you're back, Peter Harmon. Carry on, Deputy."

"Someone knows you're back in town. He. She. Or whoever this is, is getting a real hard-on about having you back in their lives."

"What do you want me to do, Deputy? Climb under a rock? Disappear? I'm sorry. I can't do that. You sort this shit of a mess out. Are you charging me with anything?"

The deputy and the detective looked at each other for a moment.

"One more question," Detective Quinn started. "Why come back to Hillsboro? After everything you lived through, why now?"

Peter leaned in further to the table, maintaining fierce eye contact with the detective. "Why not?"

The interrogation was finally over. Detective Quinn grabbed the manila folder and held it tightly to his chest, pushed backwards in his chair, stood up and walked out of the room. He wasn't particularly forthcoming but offered a polite farewell. Then, he grunted a little and disappeared into the corridor, leaving the door behind him open. Peter could see into the corridor, and all the other police officers on duty, all going about their day to day lives in the office.

Deputy Andrew Preston continued to sit opposite Peter. He rocked in his chair a little, running his hands across the surface of the table. He raised his eyes off the table, looking at his friend, Peter.

"Let's get you out of here," he said, just above a whisper.

Andrew stood from his chair first. His uniform continued to cling to his muscular body, just like it did as he stood on the front porch. The only difference was the buttons on the shirt, particularly the lower ones, around his stomach, stretched a little, exposing his white t-shirt underneath. Andrew waited patiently for Peter to stand. Peter was the first one to move, walking away from the table.

Andrew followed. The two took an immediate right, into the corridor, and headed toward the front of the police station.

"You know," Andrew started, "we don't have to do this."

"Do what?" Peter answered, not looking back at the deputy, or his friend, as the two walked the corridor and into the heart of the station.

"You know *exactly* what. This. Heading out the front of the station, knowing full well there is a squad car waiting for you out the back, waiting to take you home."

"But I'm not guilty. Innocent people don't run. I'm not running."

"Understood." Andrew rolled his eyes a little in frustration.

Peter and Andrew reached the heart of the police station. The office was full and running to capacity. Police officers were sitting at their desks, typing away at their computer screens, and talking on their phones. Local townspeople were being processed for questioning.

"Are you sure you want to do this?" Andrew asked again, grabbing Peter by the right arm, stopping him in his tracks a little.

Peter stopped and looked at the deputy, almost giving him the eyeball once over. "I have nothing to hide."

"Okay, then. Let's go."

The deputy took the lead. He stepped in front of Peter and led the way out of the front of the police station, to be met by a frenzy of local media awaiting a photo opportunity or first interview with the town's most infamous son. The front doors pushed open and the lights and cameras started to flash. The voices were yelling over one another, all trying their best to get Peter's attention. Peter kept his head down and quiet. Andrew grabbed Peter's left hand tightly and lead him through the crowd of media, and to the waiting squad car parked at the front of the station. A microphone was waved in front of Andrew and Peter.

"How does it feel to be home, Peter?" yelled one female reporter. Peter remained silent.

"How does it feel to come home to this?" shouted another reporter. "People have a right to know!" Andrew continued to work as his bodyguard, as he used his brute strength to push past the media. One of the junior officers stood by the squad car, ready to open the front door for Andrew as they approached.

"You got to give us something!" yelled a third reporter.

"We are investigating the matter. That is all you need to know!" shouted Deputy Preston. Andrew and Peter reached the squad car, past the frenzied media. Andrew climbed inside, behind the steering wheel. Peter climbed into the back seat. The junior officer was dismissed.

The engine of the squad car came to life, not exactly roaring to life, but it made an impact, and it pulled out from the curb and into the local traffic, making its way to the end of the street, and turning left. The fanfare of the media was well and truly over. Deputy Preston looked over his shoulder, past the back seat, and there was no one there, no one chasing them. Deputy Preston returned to his seated position in the car. He made eye contact with Peter in the rear-view mirror.

Peter looked back.

"I'm sorry back there," Peter said, just above a whisper. "The questions and all. I hate that I implied…"

"Understood." Andrew nodded, with a hint of a smile.

He was no longer the local deputy. He was a high school buddy.

"I understand. If I were in the same situation, I think I would say the same thing."

"Your boss is a real hard-ass, you know that?"

Andrew chuckled.

"I've heard him called worse." Andrew chuckled again.

The drive from the police station continued in near silence for a few minutes. Peter sat in the back of the squad car, peering out the window and watching the local life of Hillsboro pass him by. There was police chatter on the CB radio. Andrew picked up the radio and talked, now and then, doing his job.

"This is never going to end, is it?" Peter asked, his tone of voice a little more serious now. Andrew cleared his throat, a little.

"What do you mean?"

"That poor girl."

"We will catch him. Her. Whoever. All you need to do is keep your mind focused on something else. We," Andrew heard himself talk and paused a moment. He cleared his throat, again. "I got this. Remember that."

"Focus on something else? Yeah? How do I do that?"

The two friends maintained eye contact in the rear-view mirror. Andrew winked at Peter and smiled, flashing his teeth, a little. Peter chuckled.

"That's it!" Andrew answered. "There it is. I have missed that laugh of yours. Don't worry about the bullshit. Don't. It's good to have you home."

Chapter Four...

Peter woke up early the following morning. He had trouble sleeping. It was a little before five and not quite sunrise. The morning fog had rolled in from the outer woodlands overnight. Peter was dressed in a plain, no-brand grey t-shirt, and navy-blue sweatpants. He was out for his morning jog. His first in Hillsboro. His face had a pinkish hue and his hair and shirt were drenched in sweat, as his breathing became restricted throughout the run. Peter wanted to clear his head over the detective's questioning, as well as help burn off the pizza he'd had for dinner, two nights in a row.

The morning jog lasted a good forty minutes to an hour. Peter jogged the nearby streets, exploring the neighbourhood, taking a left then right, and left then right, again. He turned off Menhaden Street and pulled onto his home street. The street seemed so peaceful so early in the morning. There were no kids on bikes or playing sports. The trees were calm and still. Peter reached his home and ran across the front yard, between the oak trees and up onto the front door. He collapsed on the front porch, staring up at the ceiling, a moment. He had his left arm resting over his stomach, as he felt the burn across the muscles of his stomach and course through his veins. Peter was panting, out of breath. He searched for his door keys as he eventually climbed to his feet and made his way inside. The front door closed as the lights in the foyer switched on.

Peter was still out of breath. He was hunched over, just a little, as he took the keys from the front door and placed them in the ceramic bowl on the table, nearby. He grabbed his cell phone from his other pocket and hit a button on the side of the device. The screen came to life. There was a missed text message. Peter opened it as he climbed the staircase.

Let's catch up.

The message started.

A boy's night out.

Drinks after work this week at The Watering Hole. What do you say?

The message was from Andrew.

That sounds great. Let me know when you're free.

Peter typed and hit the send button.

Peter reached the second-floor landing at the top of the staircase. His right hand raised against the wall, in search of the light switch. The lights in the hallway switched on. The hardwood floor looked so elegant against the cream walls and stark white framing. Peter took a right turn and made his way down the hallway and stepped into the bathroom, with a push of the door and the flick of the light switch. The lighting was fluorescent. The bathroom had a single wash basin, toilet and shower. The shower was in the far-left corner of the room. It stood tall with a circular, glass-like tube design that had a sliding glass door. Peter stripped from his sweaty clothes, leaving them on the white tiled floor, and placed his cell phone by the wash basin.

The hot water was quick to run from the faucet. The steam rose high and splashed against the clear glass. Peter stepped inside the shower, sliding the door to a close behind him. The water touched his chest and splashed across his face. The warm water felt so inviting. Peter closed his eyes and stepped further under the shower. He was quickly consumed by the water. Peter reached for a fresh bar of soap and lathered himself all over.

Peter was in a world of his own. He drove into town and found himself in the hardware store. He was no handyman, not really. The only real experience he had was searching the Internet for how-to videos. How to paint a wall. How to hang pictures without getting electrocuted. That sort of thing. Peter walked the aisles, up and down, minding his own business. There were a handful of customers, the majority of them, burly, flannel-clad men, men who worked the local quarry, discussing and comparing chainsaws and this season's snow tyres. Peter continued to walk up and down the aisles, in search of what he thought he needed.

An elderly woman stood at the counter. She was small in stature, hunched forward, a little, and wore a light brown coat over a plain white dress which hugged her tiny frame. There were a couple of bags of nails, two, maybe three, spread across the glass counter. She was talking with the man behind the counter, on which was the best one to use, but most importantly, which was the best value. The man behind the counter soon lost all interest. The man found himself quiet, listening to the woman drone on and on. The conversation was now nothing more than white noise. The man kept his eyes on Peter, walking aimlessly up and down the aisles.

"If you'll excuse me a moment," the man behind the counter said, just above a whisper.

"Pardon me?" the elderly woman responded, mid-sentence. "Well, I never...."

The elderly woman watched on as the man walked out from behind the counter and made his way down the farthest aisle. A young girl, no older than eighteen, with shoulder-length mousey-brown hair, left the conversation about snow tyres with the flannel-clad men and assisted the elderly woman in need, wearing a warm and comforting smile.

The man appeared at the end of the aisle, watching Peter. He stood there, a bear of a man, somewhere in his later forties to early fifties. He was dressed in faded blue jeans, and a dark blue open flannel long-sleeved shirt with a plain black t-shirt underneath and matching black leather boots. The man was intrigued. A smile surfaced to his lips, watching on as he stepped closer and closer towards Peter. The man was around six feet tall, muscular and a little north of two hundred and forty pounds. His jet-black hair was short on top, neatly coiffed and brushed back, and shaved, almost bald on the back and sides. And sported a neatly trimmed beard.

Peter stopped in his tracks and looked at the hammers. They were all of different sizes and prices. He didn't know which one to choose. He reached out for the largest one he could find. It felt heavy. Peter put it back up on the shelf, trying his best not to make too much of a noise and draw any unwanted attention. When a strong-looking, muscular hand reached out and took the hammer from Peter. Peter quickly blinked his eyes and turned to face the man. The man was smiling.

"You don't know what you're looking for, do you?" the man asked, just above a whisper. His cheeks were a little red, as if embarrassed, as he smiled at the young man in front of him.

"Excuse me?"

"I've been watching you since you came in the store," the man continued.

The expression on his face immediately changed. The smile was gone, and instead, confusion. He realised what he had just said as if he were some stalker.

"I'm sorry." the man smiled again, placing his hand on his chest, a moment. "I can help you. I own this store," he continued quickly. "What are you after?"

Peter looked at the man a moment, studying the expression on his face, his body language as if he knew him from somewhere.

"I…" Peter started, feeling a little embarrassed. "I recently moved into a house in town and noticed a leak in the pipes under the kitchen sink." Peter paused a moment. "I don't know what I need." He chuckled, a little.

"That's okay. I can help."

"Thank you."

The two men walked up and down the aisles.

"My name is Mike. Walters. Mike Walters. It's nice to meet you." Mike said, extending his right hand out to shake.

"Peter. Harmon. My name is Peter Harmon."

"Yes, you are," Mike whispered, under his breath.

"Pardon me?"

"I'm sorry. That sounded very creepy of me. I'm sorry. You're Peter Harmon. I knew your father. We worked the quarry together for a number of years. Your father always spoke so highly of you. I met you once, a very long time ago. You were like nine or ten, at a family barbeque."

Peter searched Mike's face for some sort of recognition.

"You knew my father?" Peter whispered to himself, still searching for that recognition. "It's nice to meet you again."

"What are you doing in town?"

"I live here now. Well, searching for a place. I rented a place on Raleigh."

"That's a nice part of town."

"New York was just too… New York. I needed to get away."

"I understand that." Mike nodded. "Life happens when we make plans. It is good to see a friendly face back in town."

"Enough about me," replied Peter. "How are you? What are you up to?"

"Me?" asked Mike, surprised. "I'm just me. I get up and come to work. Go home and do it all over again the following day." Mike laughed a little.

He stared at Peter, again.

"As I live and breathe, I can't believe I am standing in front of Peter Harmon. I have missed you so much. Welcome home."

The two continued to walk the aisles, as Mike assisted Peter with his shopping list of needed tools. They traded in family stories as they reconnected. Mike recalled childhood memories from Peter's past, the happier ones, that is. He also filled him in on his dating life or lack thereof. Mike told Peter of his partner, Jason, passing away seven years ago of a heart attack. Peter touched on his relationship with Robert, the happier times, of course, and the mess that was Thomas. They shared a laugh and traded phone numbers.

"What are you doing tonight?" Mike asked, as he helped carry some of the tools Peter was after. "I want to take you out for drinks, maybe a bite to eat, and catch up."

"I thought that's what we were doing now?" Peter asked, as he looked confused, a little before a smile surfaced to his lips. "I would like that."

Peter closed his eyes and flinched. "What's wrong?" Mike asked, concerned.

"I just remembered," Peter answered. "I'm catching up with an old high school buddy tonight at The Watering Hole. Do you know the place?"

"You're going there?"

"Uh-huh. What's wrong?"

"It can get a little rowdy at times. Weekends, especially. But the food is good. And beer. You can't go wrong with the beer."

"If you aren't doing anything later, you should swing by and say hi. I'll be there around seven. It would be nice to see a familiar and kind face."

"Seven, it is." Mike smiled. "I'd like that."

The tour of the hardware store was over. The flannel-clad men were still talking amongst themselves. The conversation had moved on from snow tyres and was now discussing their favourite power tools, and why. The young girl behind the counter re-joined the conversation and made cups of coffee for the three men. Mike returned behind the counter and walked over to the cash register. And there, in front of him, was a pile of tools, out on display. There was a hammer, a spanner, batteries, and a new torch, to name a few. Mike rang the items up on the register and offered a friendly discount, then helped Peter carry his newly purchased tools out to his car parked outside the store.

The police station was busy, again. The officers were at their desks working away. Detective Quinn was in his office, the door closed. He was pacing in front of his desk and had cleared the clutter that once hung on his wall and replaced it with a more family-friendly photograph of the girl that was found in the woods, hanging from a tree. Her name was Casey Rabe, a twenty-three-year-old, single mother, who had worked as a waitress at a nearby diner. A manila file, with Casey's details, paperwork, photographs — including explicit photographs, outlining the way she was murdered — was sitting on the detective's desk. Casey wasn't just murdered. It wasn't a lover's tiff gone horribly wrong. She was butchered. Someone knew what they were doing, and they liked it.

Andrew was sitting at his desk. His shift was over for the afternoon. He signed off and logged out of his computer. He stood from his chair and tucked it into his desk, before walking across the office, past his colleagues, and local townspeople brought in for questioning. He leaned in and knocked on the detective's office door.

"Come in!" Detective Quinn called out.

The office door opened, a little. Andrew and his muscular build leaned in.

"I'm heading out and calling it quits for the day. Is there anything I can help you with before I go?"

"All good here. You go home and get some rest. You deserve it. Good job, today. If I hear anything, I'll give you a call."

"Thank you, Boss."

Andrew retreated from the office door, closing it behind him. He left the detective to his work and walked further down the corridor toward the men's locker room.

The door to the men's locker room pushed open, almost silently. The brick walls were painted an almost army green as neon lights hung from the ceiling. There were male police officers, standing around their lockers, some chatting amongst friends, whilst others were in various states of dress, some starting their shifts, whilst others were finishing. Andrew walked into the locker room, waving at a few friends whilst he made his way to his locker. It was several rows down, in the middle somewhere.

Andrew reached his locker. He stood there a moment, twisting the lock, punching in his locker combination, lifted the handle and opened his locker. Some of his clothes were hanging in front of him, along with some more of his personal belongings, a watch, a cell phone, a stick of deodorant. Andrew collapsed onto the bench in front of his locker and sat down a moment. His uniform shirt clung to his broad, muscular chest. He began to slowly unbutton. And, underneath, he wore a white cotton wife beater. His chest, exposed. It was muscular and defined, and hairy. Very hairy.

The bear of a man stood up from the bench. He crumpled his uniform shirt up into a ball and sniffed it. His face scrunched up tightly. The shirt was in need of a wash. Andrew grabbed his sports bag, unzipped it and stuffed the shirt deep inside. He left his wife beater on and leaned into his locker and grabbed an old baseball t-shirt. The t-shirt stretched as he pulled it on. Andrew tugged at it a little to get it feeling more comfortable. He started next on unbuttoning the top of his uniform pants. He climbed out of them, exposing the black cotton jockey shorts he wore underneath, and neatly hung the pants inside his locker. He swapped the uniform pants for a pair of blue denim jeans and was quick to pull them on. He pulled up the zip and popped the button, and with another stretch of the t-shirt, Andrew grabbed his cell phone and slid on his watch, and slammed the locker door to a close. He grabbed his sports bag and made his way out of the locker room and out of the station, toward his truck which was parked in the staff parking lot.

Andrew made it out to the parking lot. He unlocked the driver's side door and climbed inside, slamming the door to a close. The window was quick to unwind. The sports bag sat next to him in the truck, on the front passenger seat. Andrew turned a little in his seat, unzipping the sports bag some and searched for his cell phone. He found it. He signed in and navigated to Peter's number.

I just finished work. I'm on my way around.

Andrew typed and hit the sent button.

Andrew dropped the cell phone back in the sports bag and turned again to switch on the ignition. The motor roared to life. Andrew looked in the rear-view mirror for any further traffic and reversed out of his parking spot, out of the parking lot of the police station and pulled out onto the road. He was heading for Peter.

The truck pulled up outside the front of Peter's home a mere ten to fifteen minutes later. The truck, itself, pulled into the curb as it came to a slow halt. The key in the ignition turned and the engine died. Andrew sat in his truck a moment longer. He took off his seat belt and leaned over, grabbing his cell phone and keys. The driver's side door of the truck pushed open, as Andrew rocked his bulking frame from side to side a little to climb out of his truck. He leaned against the door, closing it. Andrew pocketed his cell phone and keys in his jeans and walked up onto the sidewalk.

He stood there standing alone, staring up at the two-storey weatherboard Victorian home. A smile surfaced to his lips a little before he made his way toward the house. He followed the cobble-stoned path up to the front porch.

The weight of his hulking frame pushed down the wooden porch as he took his first steps. The wooden steps bent a little, under the pressure, cracking a little. His feet ran up the stairs and up to the porch, and to the front door. Andrew stood there a moment. He tidied himself up a little, picking at his baseball t-shirt some, and leaned in and knocked on the door. *Knock. Knock. Knock.* It was in quick succession. Three times. The weight of each knock was heavy and hard. Peter was in the kitchen when he heard the knock. The cupboards under the sink were wide open. An old, ratty-looking beach towel lay on the floor, and a newly purchased set of tools sat in a painted navy-blue toolbox. Peter climbed to his feet and dusted himself off as he made his way to the front door.

"One second!" he called out.

Peter walked briskly through the foyer of the house and answered the front door. He leaned in and opened it. And there, standing in front of him, was Andrew Preston. His friend from high school and deputy of the local police station. The two friends exchanged smiles. Peter stepped to one side and invited his friend inside. Andrew took his first steps inside the house. He was in awe of the place.

"Your home is amazing," Andrew said, just above a whisper.

"This place?" Peter chuckled, "'it's only temporary until I find a place of my own. Please, come inside."

Andrew followed Peter deeper inside the house. They left the foyer and made their way into the kitchen.

"The place came fully furnished," Peter continued, "but it also came with a leaking pipe under the sink in the kitchen. I have been spending this afternoon trying to fix the fucking thing."

Andrew chuckled, a little.

He walked into the kitchen and saw the mess on the floor.

"You were always terrible with tools in high school." Andrew chuckled, again. "I can fix this in no time."

"Really?" Peter answered, a little excited.

"Does a bear shit in the woods?"

The two friends laughed a little more.

"Get me a beer and a spanner." Andrew continued.

Andrew walked closer to the kitchen sink to inspect the damage. He leaned in, quickly sticking his head under the sink. He pulled out to see Peter in front of the refrigerator pulling out two ice-cold bottles of beer. The refrigerator door closed softly. Andrew stood in front of his friend, in the middle of the kitchen, and pulled at his baseball t-shirt, again. He tugged at it some more, before pulling it off. He stood there, his hulking frame, in his white cotton wife beater, blue jeans and black leather boots. He held his baseball t-shirt in his hands a moment, before exchanging it with Peter for one ice-cold beer.

"Here. Take this." Andrew said, tossing his t-shirt to his friend as he took a deep sip from the bottle of beer. "I'm going to need your hand."

Andrew turned and placed the bottle of beer on top of the kitchen counter. He climbed down onto his hands and knees before making himself comfortable on his back, laying on the kitchen floor, looking up at Peter, with his knees bent, pointed to the ceiling.

"It's dark as shit under here." Andrew continued. "I'm going to need some light. I'm going to need you to point the torch at my hands whilst I work on these pipes. You think you can handle that?"

"Hold your torch for you?" Peter asked, with a hint of a smile.

"You wish you could hold *my* torch." Andrew winked and followed with a smile.

Andrew prepared himself for work. He sat up from the towel on the kitchen floor and looked through the blue toolbox. He grabbed what tools he needed, including the torch. He tested the torch first, flicking it on and off before passing it to Peter.

"We are good to go." Andrew smiled as he cautiously lowered back onto the towel, on the kitchen floor, careful not to bang his head.

"Get that torch up!" Andrew called. "Give me some light. That's it. Shine it there. You got it. You got that big torch." Andrew laughed.

Andrew got to work on the leaking pipes. He loosened some bolts, cleaned the edges, and tightened them back up again. It was a rather quick job.

"There. All sorted." Andrew announced.

"Yeah? All good?" asked Peter.

"All good," replied Andrew. "I got you, Petey."

"Thank you."

"No worries at all. Buy me a beer this evening and we will call it even."

"Deal."

Andrew wiggled his way out from under the kitchen sink. He moved his large frame from left to right and left to right, again, before he was out from under the sink and looking up at Peter, again. The light to the torch switched off.

"Don't just stand there." Andrew smiled. "Help me up."

Andrew extended his right hand out. Peter took it and helped lift him up.

Peter pulled at Andrew's right hand. His friend's hulking frame pulled forward until he was in a sitting position. Andrew turned, rolling almost, onto his hands and knees, before climbing up onto his feet. He dusted his hands off, wiping them on his wife beater and turned and grabbed his bottle of beer. The bottle was still cold. Andrew took another deep sip, leaning back a little.

"Fucking done!" Andrew announced, followed by a beer belch. Peter laughed.

The early afternoon progressed. The two friends left the kitchen behind and made their way out onto the porch. It was a warm afternoon. The sun was out, even though winter was only weeks away. The two friends reconnected, sitting on the porch, taking in a view of the street and the truck. They swapped high school stories and reminisced about how they met. Andrew was almost eighteen months older than Peter. He had been left behind, having to repeat his junior year. Andrew and Peter were assigned together as chemistry partners and were friends ever since. They saw each other through exams and failed relationships, hung out on weekends, and ditched school together. They opted for a Friday off school to make their way into Chicago and wander around during their senior year. Their parents found out and were grounded for two weeks.

Andrew sat opposite Peter on the front porch, leaning in closer to his friend as he nursed the remains of his second beer. He was still dressed in his wife-beater, feeling the remains of the afternoon sun focus on his back. It felt good.

"You remember what it was like to grow up here in Hillsboro." Andrew started, his voice taking an almost serious tone, just above a whisper.

"How could I forget?" Peter shrugged.

"I hated high school," Andrew said flatly. "I hated that place more than life itself. It was my 'dad's fault. It always was. Nothing was ever good enough for him. I'd come home with a B paper, he wanted an A." Andrew laughed to himself, a moment. "There I was struggling to make him happy, and there he was. My dad. A part-time truck driver for that damn quarry and a full-time raging alcoholic. My dad would beat me if I wouldn't…"

A concerned look fell upon Peter's face.

Andrew forced himself to smile. And took another sip of his beer. It was empty now. He shook the bottle a little from side to side, to indicate he was receptive to another. "But you, Petey, you were the star. You made it out of this town. You made it all the way to the big, flashing neon lights of New York City."

"Yeah," Peter answered, just above a whisper. "And look how that turned out, huh." he shrugged. "And now I am back in Hillsboro trying to piece together some form of normality. I don't even have a fucking job!" Peter laughed, taking a gulp from his beer.

"Yeah? What's with that, you fucking deadbeat!" Andrew laughed. The two friends laughed at each other.

The laughter soon stopped. Andrew locked eyes with Peter. He stared at him a moment longer. "You're home. With me. Where you belong." Andrew said, just above a whisper, and leaning forward, he squeezed Peter's right knee. He smiled. "I need another fucking beer!"

The afternoon progressed. The sun was beginning to set on another day. Peter and Andrew left the house and walked from the front porch to the garage on the side of the house. The garage door began to rise, and Peter and Andrew made their way inside the sports utility vehicle. Andrew had already downed three beers and Peter opted to drive for the evening. The truck remained parked outside the front of the house.

The Watering Hole was located on the outskirts of Hillsboro, down a long narrow road with many twists and turns, close to the quarry and forest. The sports utility vehicle pulled off the side of the road and made its way into the parking lot. There was plenty of space this evening. It wasn't the weekend. It was only Tuesday. There were three, maybe four trucks parked on the side of the bar, along with a handful of cars. Peter soon found a place to park. The engine to the car died. Andrew looked at him and smiled.

"We are going to have fun tonight, buddy!" Andrew muttered, a little tipsy. Peter looked at his friend and forced a smile.

"Great!"

Andrew leaned in and squeezed his friend's knee a second time.

The two friends climbed out of the sports utility vehicle and slammed the doors shut. Peter hit the button on the clicker and the alarm was set. They made their way inside the bar. The Watering Hole had the exterior of a wood cabin, located somewhere out in the middle of nowhere by a lake somewhere. There were neon signs attached, promoting their world-famous spicy chicken wings and cheap beer, Tuesdays.

The bar itself was filled with patrons, all lining up, waiting to order their next drink. There wasn't a free chair in front of the bar. There was music playing on the jukebox. Some country number. It felt a world away from New York City. People were smoking. And there were people playing darts and watching sports on the television sets hanging from the ceiling. Peter made his way to the bar, through the crowd of people.

Andrew followed. The patrons were talking amongst themselves. There were four staff members behind the bar, all serving the patrons, and making drinks.

"Hey! What do I have to do to get a little service around here?" Andrew shouted, his left hand hitting the bar.

The announcement was met with booing from some of the other patrons. They knew who Andrew was.

"We see you!" a bar woman answered.

The bar woman was somewhere in her early forties. She wore a simple white cotton t-shirt, blue jeans and boots. Her red hair pulled back into a ponytail. "Find a seat. I'll be with you soon."

"Thanks, Darlene. My good buddy is back. I want to show him a good time tonight."

"Welcome to Hillsboro, a friend of Andrew," said Darlene.

"Thank you," replied Peter, smiling.

A couple of the other patrons looked on. It was a married couple. Both in their late forties and both had a little too much to drink for the evening, already. The wife sat on the stool at the bar whilst feeding on the bowl of nuts on offer. Her husband stood behind her as if standing there, to protect her from the crowd. He looked in Andrew's direction before his eyes fell on Peter. His expression changed. His eyes glared as his brain searched, trying to place him, to remember him from somewhere, anywhere.

"Hey!" the drunken husband called out.

Peter heard him but didn't answer, hoping he would disappear.

"Hey, you! Kid!" the drunken husband called again. "I'm sure I know you from somewhere."

"I get that," Peter answered, acknowledging his rants. "I must have one of those faces."

The drunk husband continued to look at him, studying his face, as he tried to remain balanced.

"I know you." he continued. "You're that kid! The one with all those murders and shit! I'm surprised to see you. I thought you'd be all fucked up and shit!"

Peter looked at the drunken husband, now getting the attention of his drunken wife. Peter looked guilty as if caught doing something he shouldn't.

"Hey!" a deep voice called out. It was Andrew. "You leave my good friend alone. You hear me?" Andrew stared down the drunken husband and wife. The drunken husband looked back at Andrew, beaten. "Now, apologise to the man."

The drunken husband and wife looked at Peter, then back at Andrew. "Do it!" Andrew shouted.

"It's unnecessary. Please." Peter responded. "I got your back, Petey."

"Fuck this!" the drunken husband declared. "We're out of here. I know better bars than this. Let's go! We're outta here."

The drunken wife dumps what was left of her beer and left it on the bar before getting up from her chair and walking off with her husband.

The two friends hung around the bar a little more, no more than five or so minutes before they were eventually served. Peter ordered Andrew his favourite beer. Peter ordered the same, with a pitcher of water to follow. Andrew took his pint of beer and the pitcher of water to the table they had reserved for the evening. Peter was still at the bar. He put the change from a twenty dollar note in his wallet, grabbed his beer and made his way through the bar, towards Andrew.

The table reserved for the evening was located in the restaurant of the bar, near the stage.

The bar hosted live bands on the weekends. Tonight, was a little quieter. Andrew was already at the table. He took to his seat, drinking from his pint of beer. The pitcher of water was left alone. Two others were sitting at the table. They were Emily Olsen and Jayne Scott, both friends from high school.

Emily Olsen was tall and thin. She stood at almost five feet ten inches with a petite build and long blonde hair. Her hair was tied neatly into a bun that sat just below the top of her head. Her ears were pierced with simple gold studs and she was dressed in a simple white blouse and blue jeans plus a pair of black running shoes. Emily had ordered lemonade with a hit of vodka. She sat opposite Andrew and was front row to his antics. Emily had been front row to Andrew's antics for the last four years. They were in an on-again, off-again relationship. At the moment, they were off again.

Then, there was Jayne Scott. She was also dressed in blue jeans and a simple black, long-sleeved sweater to stay warm for the evening. She wore simple white running sneakers. Jayne had wildly curly brown hair with streaks of red, all tied back in a simple ponytail. Jayne was five feet eight inches and was drinking a glass of Coca-Cola for the evening. Jayne worked as a cashier at a local grocery store in town. She was single and had her list of men. And conquered them all.

"Hey, you! Welcome home, stranger!" Emily announced proudly, as she stood from her chair to welcome Peter to the table.

Peter smiled politely.

"Thank you, thank you," Peter answered with a smile.

"It is so nice to see you again." said Jayne, standing from her chair and leaning in to give him a kiss hello.

"My good buddy is home!" Andrew announced with a chug of his beer.

Peter took to his seat, and sat next to Emily, opposite Jayne and Andrew, but not before kissing Emily hello on the side of her right cheek. Emily had such a warm smile.

Peter had been best friends with Emily throughout junior and senior year in high school. They had shared homeroom, along with maths and English literature. Emily was the first person, outside of his direct family, whom he had told was gay. Emily admitted she knew for quite a while and the reason she didn't want to say anything was that he wanted to wait until he was ready to admit it himself. Emily confided in Peter with her secret crushes and they were each other's back-up dates to the senior prom. The theme of the night was enchantment under the sea. It was horrible.

The night progressed. The four friends had reunited over cheap beer and hard liquors, as well as a selection of cheesy fries, pizzas and nachos. The swapped high school stories and caught up on their day-to-day lives in Hillsboro. It had been years since they all reunited like this. Jayne was in awe of Peter. She was so proud of him for escaping Hillsboro and making a life for himself in New York City.

"New York City must be so exciting. I mean, big city, beautiful people," said Jayne.

"It had its moments." Peter smiled, feeling somewhat forced and polite.

.The rest of the table was in awe of Peter. He was the one who escaped a country, quarry town and made a life, *any* life for himself.

"But it wasn't meant to be," Peter continued.

Peter looked around the table and saw his friend's expression. Andrew and Emily seemed the most genuinely hurt, but happy to have their friend closer to home.

"Can we please change the subject?" Peter asked, raising his voice a little after taking a sip from his beer. "Tell me. What's going on here? What have I missed? What's happening?"

Andrew was the first to cheer the return of his best friend. He was also inebriated, raising his hands, and charging his glass. His baseball shirt raised a little, exposing his furry belly underneath.

Andrew collapsed in his chair and regaled the group with stories from work about his colleagues. The ones he liked. The ones he hated. And the ones he despised. Jayne was hanging off every word he dribbled, as his drunken state was becoming more and more obvious as the night progressed. The two laughed at the same jokes and made a little too much eye contact, for Emily's liking, that is. Emily and Andrew exchanged looks as if she were telling him to stop drinking and to eat more than just a handful of cheesy fries.

Emily turned to the right in her chair and made brief eye contact with Peter, as the two friends were sitting front row seats to the Andrew and Jayne show. Emily was pissed. But she took the high road and plastered on a smile she could muster, under the circumstances.

"I see it." Peter leaned in and whispered.

"You do? It's not just me?"

Peter shook his head.

Peter stood up from the table and dusted himself off a little. He needed to stretch his legs and go to the bathroom. He was reaching his limit on cheesy fries and the idea of more pizza was going to make him vomit.

"I'm doing one more round," Peter announced. "Who's in?"

"One last beer for the road never hurt anyone," Andrew replied, almost begging in his drunken stupor.

"I'm cutting you off. I love you. But, no! A soda for you. Ladies?"

"Nothing for me," answered Emily, politely.

"I'm good," replied Jayne, as she covered the top of her wine glass with her left hand and smiled.

"Okay. I'll be back."

Peter left his friends sitting around the table. The plates of food had been picked at, throughout the evening. The only thing left was a few fries and a lot of cold, melted cheese. Peter made his way to the bathroom, before returning to the bar. It was a lot quieter now, compared to when they first arrived. Peter was at the bar and placed his order, two sodas. Andrew had work in the morning. And Peter was the designated driver for the evening. Peter looked up and across the bar. And there, sitting on a stool and nursing the leftovers of a beer, was Mike Walters. The two exchanged a glance and a wave. Mike smiled and grabbed his glass and made his way around the bar towards Peter.

"Hey, you," said Mike, standing in front of Peter with his glass of beer. "You came." Peter smiled.

"Well," Mike smiled. "It was a tough day. A drink is a nice way to finish off a busy workday. And I remember you said you might be here, so I thought I would take a gamble."

"I'm glad you did. It's great to see you. Do you care to join us?"

Mike looked over at the table a moment. He could see Andrew sitting at the table, his back to him, his arms waving around as if telling some wildly imaginative story. Emily and Jayne were engrossed. They were laughing. He looked back at Peter. There was another smile.

"Another time."

"Are you sure?"

"I'm sure." Mike smiled, nodding a little. "You join your friends. Catch up. Have fun. I'll give you a call tomorrow. We can catch up another time."

"Sure. That would be great. I'd like that."

"Me too."

The evening eventually came to an end. Emily was the first to bow out for the evening. She stood from her chair, also dusted herself down, collected her belongings and leaned in and kissed Peter on the side of the head, almost messing his hair.

"It is wonderful to have you home again, Peter. Let's arrange a lunch in the week," she said, almost in her nerdish high school demeanour.

"Of course," Peter replied, "I'd love to. Goodnight, Jayne, Emily."

Emily collected her wallet and her cell phone and her car keys into one neat bundle and left the table. Peter watched her leave. She made eye contact with Andrew, who sat there, just barely clinging to the right side of sober. His baseball shirt was dirty from the food.

"Shit!" Andrew whispered under his breath, as he watched Emily walk away without saying a word. "Excuse me whilst I go put out another fire."

Andrew stumbled to his feet and followed Emily out of the bar and into the car park, leaving Peter and Jayne to entertain themselves.

Andrew raced from the bar and out into the car park. He found Emily and chased after her.

He ran up behind her, his right hand on her right shoulder, almost pushing her forward, some. Emily was startled, a little. She turned around, knowing who she was facing.

"What do you want?" Emily asked bluntly. "You don't think I see what you're up to?"

"I'm sorry for the way I acted this evening. It was the beer. I was a dick! I don't know what else to say."

"You don't?" Emily asked, confused and laughing to herself a little. "I am talking about Jayne! I see the way you look at her and the way she hangs on your every word. I'm not stupid, you know!"

"No one said you were. And Jayne! Nothing is going on, I swear."

"Fuck you!" Emily replied bluntly. "Until you get your head sorted, and you decide what you want, then give me a call. But, until then, we're done!"

Emily stormed off. She left Andrew behind, as she searched for the alarm clicker for her car in her bag. She found it, pressing the button. Emily reached her dark red bug and climbed inside, slamming the door closed. Andrew was left standing there, feeling somewhat confused, but more so, drunk. He wanted to vomit.

The front door to The Watering Hole was pushed open. Peter emerged from the door, in search of his friend. Jayne was still in the bar, collecting her personal belongings and taking her time as she walked across the floor of the bar. Peter could see Andrew in the parking lot, almost past the floodlights. The night shadow consuming the top half of his frame. Andrew was feeling depressed, his head lowered, facing the gravel, and smelling of alcohol.

"How are you doing?" Peter asked, his tone of voice quiet and almost gentle. There was no response.

"That bad, huh?" Peter answered his own question. "Look. You're in no position to drive. I'll take you home. You can come to pick up your truck at my place in the morning."

"It wouldn't be the first time I've left my truck somewhere."

"Let's go."

Peter and Andrew made the slow walk across the parking lot, under the floodlights back to the sports utility vehicle. Peter unlocked the car and opened the front, side passenger door for Andrew and helped him climb inside. The door slammed shut once he was comfortable and the belt clicked in. Peter ran around to the other side of the truck. He climbed inside, up behind the wheel, got himself comfortable and the engine roared to life. Peter looked at Andrew a moment. His head was down and to the left, fast asleep. He was worried he was going to vomit at any moment. Peter applied his foot on the accelerator and drove out of the parking lot, and into the traffic. The drive back to Andrew's home was done in near silence, except for the few, incoherent grunts Andrew made about Emily and the radio played in the background. It was a radio show. The guests called in and admitted to their deepest, darkest secrets. It was borderline, soft core porn. Peter changed the channel, in search of something easier to listen to.

The drive to Andrew's didn't take too long. Peter had pulled into his driveway within the space of twenty minutes, give or take.

"We're home," Peter said, just above a whisper and shaking his friend awake, a little. Andrew came to, slowly.

"Here. Let me help."

Peter climbed out of the sports utility vehicle and ran round to Andrew's side of the car. He opened the door and leaned in, unlocking the seat belt. It took a few moments to get Andrew, and his towering, large frame out of the car, and onto his feet. They stumbled forward until he found his balance and made the start of walking towards the front of the house.

The cool night air was starting to affect Andrew. He was coming to, realising where he was, barely. Andrew fumbled, looking for his keys in his pocket. He dropped them. Peter was the first to swoop down and pick them up off the porch. Peter fumbled with the keys himself, struggling with the light and keeping an eye on his friend until he unlocked the front door and the two made it inside the house. The front door slammed shut. The lights switched on. Peter searched the house for Andrew's bedroom. It was the last room at the end of the hallway. Peter got Andrew inside the bedroom. Andrew collapsed onto the bed, laying on his back. Peter helped remove his shoes and pushed him onto his right side, so he wouldn't choke on his vomit.

"Goodnight, buddy," Peter whispered to himself, a little out of breath.

Peter left his friend to sleep in his bed. He could hear him snoring away. He made his way down the hallway. The light wasn't the best, but he could make out the framed photographs which hung on the wall. They were of Andrew and Emily during happier times. There were photographs of them smiling, laughing, at friend's weddings, bowling, on picnics. Peter wondered what went so wrong.

The morning arrived. Andrew was awoken to the sound of his alarm clock on his nightstand. It was six in the morning. Andrew was still dressed in the clothes from the night before, his dirtied baseball shirt, which twisted and hugged his large chest, his jeans and a pair of socks. Andrew didn't remember removing his shoes last night, or how he got home for that matter. Andrew hit the alarm clock heavily. The alarm discontinued. Andrew climbed out of bed sometime shortly after the alarm started to scream, maybe twenty minutes or so. He was out of bed. The clothes he had worn the night before were a tangled mess on the bedroom floor.

Andrew was in the shower. The hot water ran fast. He stood under the shower, his eyes closed, and head tilted back a little, and scrubbed his body, all over, with a bar of soap. The dirty blonde hairy chest was nothing more than sudsy, white soap. The hot water in the shower felt so inviting, but his head still felt like it was pounding. It was Wednesday morning. And work was the last place he wanted to be.

Andrew stepped out of the shower. His naked body stood dripping with water and the remaining suds of soap, as he reached for a towel and dried himself down. He was quick to wrap the towel around his waist and walked back to the bedroom. He grabbed his cell phone off the charger on the nightstand and signed into his phone. Andrew navigated to his text history.

Wake up! I'm coming to pick up my truck. See you soon.

Andrew typed and hit the send button.

Andrew walked from his bedroom, partially dressed for work. His shirt was unbuttoned, his torso was exposed. He walked into the kitchen, flipped the switch on the kettle, waiting for the water to boil. Andrew walked over to the refrigerator. He grabbed two eggs and a glass from above the kitchen counter. And a bottle of Tabasco from the pantry. Andrew was quick to crack two eggs into a glass with a dash of Tabasco.

"Fuck!" he shouted.

The taste was disgusting. But it was his go-to for a quick hangover cure.

Chapter Five...

The kitchen was alive first thing in the morning. The kettle was boiling, and oil was bubbling away in the fry pan. The kitchen was filled with the aroma of scrambled eggs and crispy bacon, like the setting of some out of the way, country cafe. Two slices of toast popped from the toaster and a freshly made glass of squeezed orange juice sat on top of the kitchen counter. The television set in the living room was also switched on. The volume was down low. It was the local news. It was nothing more than white noise in the background. Peter stood in the middle of the kitchen, in his boxer shorts, putting the final touches to his breakfast when a heavy knock came from the front door.

Knock. Knock. Knock.

Peter lifted his eyes from the kettle for a moment. The frying pan was now sitting in the kitchen sink and the scrambled eggs and bacon were neatly presented on top of the toast on a single plate. There was a second knock at the door.

Knock. Knock. Knock.

Peter shifted his eyes to the front door. He left his breakfast behind on the kitchen counter and walked towards the front door.

"One second!" he called out.

Peter could make out the shadow of the heavily built frame on the other side of the frosted glass. He leaned in and opened the front door. And there, standing in front of him, was Andrew.

"Morning," Andrew said with a nod, and just above a whisper, as if he had just woken up.

"You look like..." Peter responded.

"I know how I look. How I feel, that's another fucking story."

"Come in. I have coffee."

"You're a lifesaver, know that?"

Peter turned and made his way back inside the house. Andrew followed, closing the front door behind him.

Andrew was dressed in his police uniform, for another day ahead of him. It moulded to his muscular frame quite tightly this morning. The two top buttons on his shirt were undone, exposing some of his hairy chest beneath. Andrew followed Peter inside the house, through the foyer, down the hallway a little, and into the kitchen. He spotted the keys to his truck on the kitchen counter and was quick to grab them. Peter attended to the kettle. He flicked the switch and the water started to boil within seconds. Andrew looked around the kitchen. He held his keys tightly in his right hand and walked up behind Peter, leaned in a little picking at the scrambled eggs on toast, like a hungry bird. Peter could feel the warmth of his towering frame behind him. It felt good, for the first thing in the morning. But, of course, he would never say.

"That's delicious," Andrew mumbled, as he swallowed some of the scrambled eggs. "You read my mind."

"Help yourself," Peter answered.

"Thank you. Who would have thought it would be a good idea to go out for drinks in the week?" Andrew shrugged. "I'd kill for a day off work. I feel like shit this morning."

Peter tended to the kettle, and within the space of a couple of minutes, the coffee was poured. Black with a little milk and two sugars. Andrew sipped his coffee slowly, careful not to burn the roof of his mouth. He was quick to gobble the rest once it got to a more satisfactory room temperature. "Thank you for breakfast and looking after my truck," said Andrew, politely.

"Anytime."

"Don't say it unless you don't mean it. You may just have me at your front door for breakfast before work every morning. What will the neighbours say?"

Andrew and Peter chuckled.

The morning progressed. Andrew had finished breakfast and collected his keys to his truck and made his way to the station for work. Peter was still at home. He had cooked some more scrambled eggs, showered, dressed in a simple t-shirt and jeans, barefoot, and was now upstairs in one of the bedrooms he had converted to a personal office. Peter sat at his desk, in front of his laptop computer, in front of an almost blank screen. The only thing that appeared on the screen was the word "resume" in big, black, bold type. There was another cup of coffee, freshly poured, sitting to the right of his keyboard. The cell phone began to ring, breaking the silence and his concentration. *Ring. Ring. Ring.* Peter was startled. The screen of the cell phone came to life. *Unknown Caller.*

"Hello?" Peter answered cautiously.

"Hello," a deep voice answered.

It took Peter a moment to register and recognise the voice. A smile surfaced to his lips. It was Mike. "How was last night?" Mike asked, politely.

"It was…" Peter paused, a moment, thinking of a word to best describe meeting up with his high school friends he hadn't seen in years, and watched his best friend fall into a drunken stupor. "Like that, huh?" Mike asked, as his voice lightened, chuckling a little.

"Like that." Peter nodded. "It was nice to reconnect."

"I'm sure it was. So, how does it feel to be living back in Hillsboro?"

"It's strange," Peter answered, sitting back in his chair, looking around his office. "I'm still finding myself and running into memories. Does that make sense?"

Peter felt a little confused by his own response.

"Perfect sense." Mike chuckled. "You're still finding your feet. Anyone in your situation would be feeling the same."

"I guess."

The conversation progressed. Mike felt out the conversation and asked Peter out. It wasn't a date, mind you. Nothing official. It was simply one friend asking out another for lunch, in the early afternoon. Peter was quick to accept. He told Mike he was tired of looking at a blank computer screen, trying his best to re-write his resume for the umpteenth time. Peter gave up and left his laptop computer behind. He stood up from behind his desk, grabbed his coffee cup and walked out of the office, down the hallway, and downstairs. Peter passed a small, framed photograph of him and Robert, a black-and-white photograph, taken in happier times. The two were laughing. Peter felt the pangs of guilt from his conversation with Mike. The guilty feeling lasted as long as it took to get to the kitchen. The coffee cup sat in the kitchen sink, empty. The contents tipped down the sink.

Peter walked out of the kitchen, shaking his hands by his sides, vigorously, as if a cold shiver ran the course of his veins. The cell phone in his pocket began to ring, again. Peter stopped what he was doing and stood still in the entrance of the kitchen. A smile surfaced to his lips, again.

"Hello," the deep and dark, yet familiar, voice answered first. The smile vanished from his lips.

"What do you want?" Peter asked, just above a whisper.

"I told you I wanted to play a game. And now we can. You came home to Hillsboro and you brought me three of your closest friends. Now, we can get started!" The voice grew angry.

"No! They have nothing to do with this. Come for me," Peter begged.

"They have everything to do with this!" The phone line disconnected.

The sound of glass smashing echoed throughout the quiet of the house. It was loud and intrusive, and coming from the living room. Peter turned and raced down the hallway, towards the front of the house. He reached the foyer and the entrance of the living room. The glass window was now no more. Mostly. The glass itself had shattered and splintered, with large shards of glass broken into pieces, which sprayed across the living room floor, on the couch and coffee table and television set. A large rock, almost the size of a football, give or take a few inches, sat on the living room carpet. Peter stood there, angry and in shock. He could see some of the neighbours out on the street, going about their business. A young mother looked on in horror, pushing her pram faster, escaping the scene.

It didn't take long for the sound of a police squad car wailing in the background. The sound grew louder and louder as it approached. There were multiple sirens.

"Are you fucking kidding me with this shit?" Peter whispered under his breath as he looked on to the front of his yard from the living room.

There were two squad cars. They pulled into the street on a fast turn, racing down the road a little before pulling into the driveway.

Peter stood there in his living room, with sneakers on his feet, and a broom in his left hand, looking down at the front yard. He could see Detective Quinn and Deputy Preston emerge from one of the cars. And two junior officers climbed out of another. It was a show, especially to the rest of the neighbourhood. The neighbours slowly emerged from their front doors and wandered into the street. There was a heavy knock at the front door, again. Peter could see the officers, including Andrew, standing on the front porch. He dropped the broom and walked to the front door to answer it.

"Can I help you?" Peter asked, almost sarcastically.

Detective Quinn stood there, closest to the front door as if leading his officers into another crime scene. Deputy Andrew Preston stood to his right and a little behind. Peter made eye contact with Andrew first. He noticed the two buttons on his shirt, from earlier this morning, were now buttoned up. And was wearing a tie.

"A local neighbour heard a noise and called the station," Andrew replied, calmly.

"Really? Over a smashed window?"

"They didn't know what was going on." Detective Quinn jumped in. "And I suppose you want to come in an investigate?"

"That would be protocol," Detective Quinn answered, almost flatly. "And ask a few questions."

"Well, then," Peter answered, just as flat, and angry. "I guess you should all come on in." Detective Quinn lead the way inside. He walked into the foyer, past Peter, observing, looking around the house. Deputy Preston followed, then the junior officers.

The junior officers made their way into the living room to inspect the damage. Deputy Preston gave charge. Detective Quinn, dressed in a coal-grey suit with a white shirt and black leather lace-ups, stood behind, waiting to talk with Peter in private. His suit wasn't cheap. It cost just enough on a detective's salary. It looked affordable. Peter made eye contact with Andrew as he walked by. The two friends did not exchange words.

"I'm sure it was just some local kids having fun, Detective." Peter started. "I have seen some kids out in the street, well after sunset these past few days. They probably just wanted to give me a scare. You know how parents are these days. They feed their kids stories, urban legends, and kids get interested. Nothing more." Peter shrugged.

The crowd in the front yard, out on the street, was growing larger now. "Have you been receiving further phone calls?" Detective Quinn asked.

"No," Peter answered quickly, as his eyes drew toward the detective. "No, I haven't." Peter shrugged.

That was a lie.

Detective Quinn studied the foyer of the house. He noticed the framed photographs hanging on the wall.

"You'd tell me if you were receiving more calls, wouldn't you? I'm here to help you, Peter. To protect you. I'm doing my job here."

"Of course," Peter answered, like a kid in trouble looking at their parent.

"Then, why does my gut tell me that you're lying to me? You know, that girl we found in the woods? She had a name and a family. I believe that *all* of this is related. Somehow. And I believe you know it, too. All of this can go away. All you need to do is help me connect the dots. I want to help you, Peter. And her. Help me."

"I don't know what to tell you, Detective." Peter smiled grimly.

"Then, I guess we shouldn't be here," Detective Quinn sighed. Peter looked at the detective directly.

Detective Quinn left Peter behind, standing at the bottom of the staircase. He walked across the foyer and into the living room to inspect the damage for himself. The junior officers were in the room, helping to tidy up, some. Deputy Preston surveyed the room, carefully watching where he stepped, noting some of the damage.

"We're done here." Detective Quinn announced. "Let's clear out." "But Detective…" Deputy Preston answered.

"Peter Harmon says it was just some local kids, out having fun. We don't know what they look like, we have no further leads to work on."

Deputy Preston shifted his eyes away from Detective Quinn and looked at Peter, as he appeared in the entrance of the living room, surveying the damage.

"If you change your mind, or if you can think of anything else, you have my number." Detective Quinn said, as he turned and walked out of the room, and headed for the front door. "Don't be afraid to use it."

The two junior officers were next to follow through. They had placed what shards of glass they picked up off the floor and placed it into a trash can they found in the kitchen. The trash can was almost full. They followed the detective out the front door. Peter could hear their heavy feet walk off the front porch. Deputy Preston remained behind. He made eye contact with Peter, again. They stared at each other for a long moment.

"Kids? Really?" Deputy Preston asked, unconvinced. "I'm here to help you, Petey. Let me in. Please?"

Peter stared back at Deputy Preston. But it wasn't the deputy he was looking back at, not now. It was his best friend from high school, Andrew. Peter blinked, holding back tears in his eyes.

"As I said," Peter replied, clearing his throat, "it was probably just kids having fun." Peter coughed. Deputy Preston leaned in toward Peter, a little.

"You do know, that if the detective doesn't buy your story, he will be back within twenty-four hours with a warrant to search your phone records. *I* don't buy your story, Petey. Let *me* help you. Let me do something."

Peter opened his mouth as if to say something, but no words escaped his lips.

"I'll be in touch," Deputy Preston continued, "if I were you, I'd clear up that mess and secure that glass window, asap."

Deputy Preston walked past Peter, but not before leaning in a little more, and tapping him on the right shoulder, briefly. Peter closed his eyes tightly, a moment.

"There is nothing to see here!" Deputy Preston called out to the neighbours who stood out in front of the house, by the squad cars. "Show is over! Go home, now!"

Peter opened his eyes and cleared his throat, again. He walked out, just past the front door, standing on the front porch, himself. He watched the people in the neighbourhood stand there, and stare back. He felt like a goldfish in a bowl, on show. Deputy Andrew Preston and the junior officers were helping with clearing the crowds, as they began to break up and disperse. Detective Quinn stood by his squad car, on the front passenger side, standing, staring back at Peter and the two-storey, Victorian home. He nodded his head, a little before climbing back inside his squad car, slamming the door to a close behind him. The squad cars came to life, again. Deputy Andrew Preston was behind the steering wheel and was the first to leave the scene. The junior officers followed.

The morning bled into the early hours of the afternoon. The living room in the front of the house was cleared, as much as it could. Peter put in a phone call to the real estate office who put forward a request for the glass to be replaced. A nondescript white van pulled up in front of the Victorian home. And there, inside, were two glaziers, there to fix the damage. Peter left the two workmen to their own devices. There was one glazier, somewhere in his early fifties. He was of Greek heritage, with black hair, salt and pepper on the sides of the temple, a muscular build with an evident fascination for the gymnasium, sporting faded denim jeans and a simple grey t-shirt. His arms were solid and defined and he sported a neatly trimmed beard and a thick moustache. His co-worker was young. He was somewhere in his early twenties. An apprentice. He followed orders and kept to himself.

Another vehicle pulled up in front of the Victorian house. It was a truck. It parked behind the white, nondescript van, giving enough room to access the back of the van. The key in the ignition of the truck turned and the engine died. It was Mike. He sat behind the steering wheel of his truck in jeans and a white polo shirt. It was tucked into the waist of his jeans. His chest and arms filled out the polo shirt quite well. Mike turned to the right a little, leaning forward some, and looking up at the house. He could see the glaziers hard at work, reaching the final stages of completing the fixes on the living room window.

"Oh shit!" Mike whispered, under his breath.

He was quick to grab his personal belongings, his wallet and his cell phone, along with some take out for lunch, in a large, brown paper bag, and climbed out of his truck. The driver's side door slammed shut.

Mike raced toward the front door of the house. He clutched the take out bag, tighter in his right hand. He knocked on the front door, quite heavy and looked around, making eye contact with the older glazier, giving him the once over, and sizing him up. He turned and faced the front door, hearing the sound of footsteps racing toward the front door, and the blurry image of a body approaching, through the frosted glass. The look of concern disappeared. Mike smiled as the door opened.

"Hey, you," said Mike.

"Hi." Peter smiled back. "Shit! What happened here?"

"Kids, I'm guessing." Peter closed his eyes tightly, for just a second. "Please, come on in." Peter stood to one side of the front door, allowing

Mike inside the house.

"Thank you." Mike nodded. "Since we missed our lunch date, I thought I would bring lunch to you. Have you eaten?"

"No."

"Good thing I'm here to take care of you."

Mike walked past Peter and made his way inside. Peter closed the front door, staring through the frosted glass, a moment. He turned to face Mike standing in the foyer of the house, staring up at the photographs on the wall, and the grand staircase.

The glaziers had finished up on the work in the living room. It looked brand new. Peter and the older glazier had exchanged words and had given him a copy of his business card, before following his apprentice back to the van parked out in the street and driving away. Peter closed the front door and returned to the kitchen. Mike was inside, preparing lunch. He brought two large sandwiches, one steak and salad, the other chicken and salad, with potato chips to share. Peter grabbed two beers from the refrigerator. They took their lunch and set up, what looked like a picnic in the front living room. The two sat opposite each other over the coffee table. They talked and laughed, reminiscing about a lifetime ago. Mike took a bite out of his steak and salad sandwich, leaning forward a little, careful not to make too much of a mess. He laughed as he felt the contents of the sandwich across his face. Peter was quick to hand Mike a paper towel. Mike accepted and cleaned himself up.

"Thank you for lunch," said Peter, smiling. "How much do I owe?"

Mike's right hand extended out, across the coffee table, and reached for another paper towel, their fingers touched a moment. It was long enough for Mike to notice. He looked at Peter and smiled. "I got this." Mike nodded.

"No," Peter replied. "I got money. I can afford to pay for my lunch."

"I'm sure you can." Mike smiled, politely. "But not today. I got this. My treat." Peter smiled.

"Well, thank you," Peter replied politely. "My treat next time."

"Deal." Mike smiled, again.

The coffee table had been cleared away and lunch was over. Peter and Mike were upstairs.

Peter was giving him the twenty-five-cent tour of the house. Peter had taken the lead and was walking along the hallway. Mike was following. Mike extended his left hand, grabbing Peter's. He squeezed his hand, applying pressure to the smallest finger, squeezing it twice. Peter held Mike's hand. A smile surfaced to his lips, surprised by it all. Mike pushed Peter forward, against the wall. Peter couldn't hide his smile and laughed, somewhat. The two made eye contact. Mike was the first to lean in and kiss Peter, deep. It was slow and romantic. Mike pulled back, still maintaining eye contact. Peter was stunned for a moment. Another smile surfaced to his lips. Peter leaned in and kissed back. Mike pulled away, again.

"Wait!" he said, just above a whisper. "Wait a minute! I have to ask you something."

"Of course," replied Peter, a little concerned. "What is it?"

"Your friend, Andrew. You like him, yes?"

"Not like that." Peter chuckled, a little. "He is a friend from high school. Nothing more." Mike smiled, feeling somewhat relieved.

"Good," he whispered, again. "Because I like you."

"You do?" Peter asked, feeling a little surprised.

"You know it." Mike smiled, again.

The sun began to set over Hillsboro for the end of another day. The house was more or less empty. It was quiet, nonetheless. Mike left shortly after lunch to head back to work for the rest of the day. The light in the office and the laptop computer was switched off. The television was also switched off, too. Peter was laying on the couch in the living room. The sun was now setting for another evening. His cell phone sat on the coffee table by the side of the couch. Peter was fast drifting off to sleep. The shade of the sun sprayed across the living room floor reduced, the room growing darker as Peter fell asleep.

It was somewhere in the early two-thousands. An interior, spacious living room. There are balloons and streamers all over the room. There is uneaten food, party foods, sausage rolls dipped in sauces and fairy bread and sodas on the coffee table. And there are unwrapped presents on the floor, neatly stowed in the corner of the room. All signs pointed to a birthday party in progress. A pair of small blue sneakers with white rubber tips and double-tied shoelaces come into the picture. They run across the living room floor. There is the sound of giggles and a shortness of breath. The feet run along the living room floor and into the kitchen.

Peter's father and mother were bickering, standing in the middle of the kitchen. The father was the first to notice a little boy standing to the left of him, in the entrance of the kitchen. They stopped bickering, turned and smiled, and pretended that they were happy. The father leaned in and down toward the young boy, the smile only grew larger. He was dressed in a tight, navy blue polo shirt and just as tight white shorts. The father was a bear of a man. He spent his spare time in the gymnasium and sported a neatly trimmed beard.

"Why don't you go and be a good little boy and go play in the back yard?" the father smiled.

The back yard. It was empty, almost. There were tables and chairs and an assortment of decorations for a seven-year old's birthday party. A table was made up in the backyard for a dozen guests. The table itself was a mess. There was food, including cake, which had been cut up into slices, and cans of soda, everywhere. Swings were hanging from trees in the back yard for the guests to play on. And there was a pinata, beaten and hanging from another tree. And, just beyond the empty table, an image of an elderly man, slightly hunched forward, as if hiding something, with his back facing the young boy, was facing the far corner fence.

The small blue sneakers were quick to run across the freshly cut blades of grass and toward the elderly gentleman, as fast as his little feet could carry him. The voice of the young boy called out, but to no answer. The boy reaches out, extending his arms forward, a smile surfaced to his lips, eagerly in anticipation. The young boy reached out to the elderly man, and tugged at his shirt, some. The elderly man turned around to face the young boy. It was Grandfather. His mouth opens in horror, he is startled, some, and he has been dribbling from the mouth. And, there, in front of him, a faded black leather belt is wrapped tightly around his right arm. The skin is red and sore. The veins are enlarged and inflamed. Grandfather stood there, his jeans were unbuttoned at the top, the zip lowered, and he had exposed himself, in the throes of self-gratification....

Peter awoke from the couch, covered in a sweat, and screaming. He was quick to catch his breath, familiarising himself with his surroundings. The living room was dark now. The lights were switched off, so was the television set. The hint of a glow came from the street lamps outdoors.

Peter wiped his eyes and stretched across the couch and grabbed his cell phone off the coffee table. He pressed the button on the side of his cell phone. The screen came to life.

The time was seven fifty-three in the evening. There was one missed phone call from Mike. And there was a text message from Andrew.

"Thank you for today. I had a great time. Call me. Anytime. It would be nice to hear your voice again." The voice mail from Mike played. Peter smiled.

Peter climbed off the couch. He walked over to the entrance of the living room and switched on the light. He walked to the kitchen and turned on another light, too. He went over to the refrigerator, opened the door, and leaned in, grabbing a bottle of beer. He popped the lid and took a deep sip. It felt so cold going down his throat and the taste was so good. Peter leaned against the refrigerator door, closing it behind him. He was still startled a little from his nightmare. Peter walked across the kitchen, and placed the bottle of beer on the counter, by the sink. He looked down at the bottom of the sink, a moment, closed his eyes and shook his hands by his side quickly. Peter noticed his cell phone notification signal flashing. It was the missed text message.

"I'm just checking in on you, Petey. Call me." The message from Andrew read.

Andrew was behind the wheel of his truck. He had pulled into the driveway of his home. It was a little after eight in the evening. The lamps in the street were spaciously spread throughout the neighbourhood. The truck pulled in close to the garage. The garage door was pulled to a close. The truck stopped and the engine died. Andrew sat there a moment and rubbed his eyes a little. He was tired. It had been another rough day, dealing with Detective Quinn, and his hard-on for his friend, Peter Harmon, and some untraceable ghost. He was also patching up his relationship with Emily.

They were now talking to each other, after a series of text messages, back and forth. They had agreed to go to lunch tomorrow, to talk and go from there.

A local neighbourhood dog, a golden retriever, ran across the street, barking. It grabbed Andrew's attention. He sat up straight in his truck, looking into the rear-view mirror, adjusting it, a little. He heard the bark of the dog, and saw, what appeared to be an elderly, female golden retriever. It ran fast and hid in the darkness of the bushes of a house across the road.

"Damn dog!" Andrew whispered to himself.

Andrew adjusted the rear-view mirror, again. To the way it once was. He then shifted the weight of his frame, from side to side, a little, pushed the driver's side door open, and climbed to his feet, out of the truck. Andrew pulled at his uniform trousers, adjusting himself, a little. His uniform shirt was messy. Andrew turned his head to the left a little and peered into the street from his driveway. The road was empty now, and quiet. There was no sign of the golden retriever. Andrew left his truck behind and walked along the footpath from the garage, along the front of the house, and up to the porch of his home. Andrew searched the right-side pocket of his uniform trousers for the keys to the front door.

"Fucking keys!" Andrew whispered, under his breath, again. "Where's the fucking light?" Andrew pulled out his cell phone and switched on the torch app, in a bid to assist finding the right key.

The key jiggled a little, before finding 'its way into the lock. It turned, and the front door was open. Andrew walked inside his home. His right hand lifted, a little, searching the wall for the light switch. He found it. The switch flicked on. The front room of the house lit up, leaving a warm atmosphere about the house. Andrew closed the door behind him and locked it. He peered through the glass. The tree swing across the street had a gentle breeze to it, lightly swinging back and forth, back and forth, again. Andrew shrugged his shoulders and made his way inside the house.

The house looked the same way he left it earlier in the morning. The lights in the house switched on as Andrew made his way, deeper and deeper inside the house. Andrew was in the hallway of the front of the house. He walked further down, reaching his bedroom. The door was still open. He walked inside and flicked on the light. And, there, by the door, was a large set of wooden drawers. Andrew reached for his wallet and cell phone in his trouser pockets. He placed them on top of the set of drawers. Andrew clicked a button on his cell phone. The screen came to life. There was a missed call from Emily.

Andrew stood at the end of his queen-size bed as he kicked off his shoes and unbuttoned his uniform shirt, exposing his hairy chest and stomach below. The cell phone sat on top of the set of drawers as the voice mail from Emily played.

"It's just me," Emily said. *"I hope you had a great day at work, and I look forward to seeing you at lunch tomorrow."*

The voice mail ended.

Beep. Beep.

The police uniform shirt dropped to the bedroom floor below. Andrew was now dressed in just his trousers. The belt had unbuckled. The top of the trousers had popped open, a little. Andrew grabbed his cell phone, again, as he walked out of his bedroom, taking a left, and walking down the hallway, toward the kitchen. The lights in the kitchen switched on. Andrew headed straight for the refrigerator. He leaned in, opened the door and grabbed himself a bottle of beer. The lid popped open and Andrew stood there a moment, his head tilted back a little, gulping the beer. The cell phone in his trouser pocket began to vibrate. Andrew noticed. He stopped drinking his beer, a moment, and retrieved his cell phone from his pocket. It was a text message. From Jayne. Andrew looked at his cell phone, quite curiously. A hint of a smile surfaced to his lips, a little. Andrew opened the message. He could feel his heartbeat racing a little, with excitement.

It was good to see you at The Watering Hole. When can we meet up again?

The message read.

A second message came through. This time, it was a picture message. Still from Jayne. She was sitting seductively in a chair, her legs crossed, back pushed forward a little, in a large white blouse, the buttons undone, a little, not all the way, mind you. It simply gave the idea of seduction with the hint of a right breast.

"That's what I am talking about," Andrew whispered to himself, staring at the picture. "Give Daddy some sugar. Fuck!"

Andrew stared at the picture a moment longer. He licked the surface of his lips, biting the lower one, just a little.

When are you thinking?

Andrew typed and hit the send button and placed his cell phone back in his trouser pocket.

Andrew grabbed his bottle of beer and walked out of the kitchen. He walked further down the hallway, and into the front room of the house. A computer sat on top of a desk in the far-left corner of the room, close to the entrance of the living room. Andrew leaned into the computer and switched it on. The computer booted up. It took a couple of minutes. Andrew sat at on the swivel chair in front of the desk and taking another deep sip from his beer, again. He swivelled in his chair a little, dressed only in his uniform trousers, his muscular and tanned chest, exposed. The computer booted up and Andrew navigated to a popular porn site. He placed the bottle of the beer on the table with his right hand and lowered his left hand in and under the waistband of his trousers and underwear. Andrew was jerking off before calling it a night.

Andrew was just about to get into it further, leaning back in his chair, about to relax, as an eerie sound came from the front porch. The sound itself was like that of wooden beams bending under pressure and fingernails scratching down a chalkboard. Andrew was startled. He quickly pulled his left hand out from under the waistband of his underwear. He spun in his swivel chair, sitting upright, facing the entrance of the living room and the front door of the house.

Andrew climbed to his feet. He pulled his trousers up, feeling comfortable on his hips, securing the zip and top button, and walked over to the front door slowly. He peered through the peephole. The light on the front porch flickered on. But there was no one there.

"Fucking dog!" Andrew whispered under his breath, again.

Andrew looked down to the hardwood floor. He lifted his head, again, before opening the front door.

The light on the front porch was still switched on. Andrew stepped outside, past the front door, and onto the porch. His right foot took the lead and stepped onto the weather-beaten wooden floorboards, which bent under the pressure, a little. Andrew stood there a moment, resting his hands on his hips. He felt his cell phone in his trouser pocket vibrate. He didn't tend to it.

"Hello?" Andrew called out. There was no response.

Andrew looked out onto the street. There was no one there. He closed his eyes, for just a moment, and shook his head, left and right. He stepped almost cautiously, as he made his way back into his home. The front door closed behind him, and the light on the front porch switched off. And, there, stepping out from the darkness, in the front yard, stood an image. It was the clown mask. It was that *same* mask. The eyes were painted wildly in a dark blue, from left to right, like a drawing outside the lines. The nose and lips were red, crimson. It stood there dressed in a black hoodie, which rested atop of the mask. The image also wore black leather gloves, trousers and boots, fading into the darkness of the night. The image stood there, unnoticed, before running toward the front of the house. They moved in leaps and bounds towards the front porch, climbing it in seconds, taking two or three steps.

The front door to Andrew's home was pushed open wildly, it slammed forward, hitting the wall behind. The clown mask stood there, in the entrance of the home, just a moment, before making their way inside. Andrew stood in the hallway at the front of the home, occupied with his cell phone, with another message from Jayne. The clown mask ran inside the house, catching up with Andrew in a matter of seconds. Their leather-bound hands, extending forward, and grabbing on tightly to his right shoulder and the waistband of his uniform trousers. The clown mask pushed Andrew, and his hulking, muscular frame forward, down onto the hardwood floor. Andrew fell forward, hitting his head on the corner of the wall, leading into the entrance of the living room, rendering him almost unconscious. Andrew rolled onto his back, startled and out of breath. His right hand raised a little, covering the bloody wound on top of his forehead.

"What the fuck?" he screamed.

There was no response. Not yet anyway.

Andrew's vision was blurry for a moment. He blinked his eyes tightly. The blood from his head wound clouded his vision in his right eye, some. Andrew did his best to climb to his feet, to protect himself and fight back. The clown mask stood over him, knocking him down, as he kicked him about the stomach and torso with his left foot, in a wild frenzy. The cell phone escaped Andrew's hands. It slid across the floor of the hallway, out of reach.

"Who the fuck are you?" Andrew screamed, scared and out of breath.

The clown mask stood there silently, as their head tilted a little, down and to the right. The gleam of a hunting knife appeared from behind the clown mask's back, gripped tightly in their left hand. The blade was long, with jagged, sharp edges, appearing brand new.

Andrew extended his right arm outwards, as a way of protecting himself. The blade of the hunting knife came down with such force, slicing the skin, tearing the veins beneath. The blood poured heavily from the wound and dripped onto the hardwood floor beneath. Andrew screamed in horror. The blade of the hunting knife attacked a second time, slicing at Andrew's torso, on the side of his belly. The bloody wound was minor, compared to that of his forearm. Andrew screamed, again. The clown mask took a slow step forward, standing over 'its latest prey. The blade of the hunting knife was stained with blood.

"What are you waiting for, huh?" Andrew yelled. "Go ahead, kill me. If you have the guts!"

"You think that this is all because of you?" The clown mask responded, almost calmly. "You think that you're the star?"

The clown mask shook their head from side to side, slowly.

"You tell Peter Harmon this is all because of him. You tell him heads are going to roll! Welcome to the game, Andrew."

"What game?"

"You know what *game*. You're the message for Peter. See you again soon, Andrew."

The clown mask turned and ran out the front of the house, past the front door, off the front porch, and escaped into the darkness of the front yard. Gone.

Andrew lay on the hardwood floor, his eyes staring up at the ceiling, his body beaten, mutilated and bloody. He hugged his right forearm, doing his best to apply pressure to the bloody wound. He screamed again, loudly and angry.

"Fuck!"

Chapter Six...

The sound of ambulance and police sirens wailed in the background. They grew louder and stronger, with each passing moment. Andrew continued to lay on the hardwood floor, in the foyer of his home, clutching at his wounds, doing his best to stop the blood. It was a mess. A crowd of people in the neighbourhood stood in the front yard, watching on helplessly as the scene played out. His body was growing weaker by the minute.

The ambulance was the first to arrive on the scene. It parked in the driveway. The engine died. And two officers quickly wheeled a stretcher to the front of the house. A police squad car also arrived. It was Detective Quinn and a junior officer. They were quick to do their best in controlling the crowds and taping off the front yard. Andrew didn't remember much. It was all a blur. The voices talking. It was a blur. He could see Detective Quinn running alongside one of the ambulance officers as he drifted in and out of consciousness.

The doors to the back of the ambulance slammed shut. Andrew was laying on the collapsed stretcher, staring up at the inside roof of the ambulance in nothing but his uniform trousers, as his bloodied wounds were exposed under the neon light. He looked around, feeling dazed and confused. A breathing apparatus was strapped firmly to his face. Andrew could see an ambulance officer, female, somewhere in her mid- to late-thirties, checking his vitals. Someone else was driving the ambulance at a gaining speed. The sirens continued to wail.

"Back to bed!" the junior police officer yelled out. "The show is over! Go home, now!"

The crowd of people in the neighbourhood began to disperse now. The show was over.

There was nothing to see. But it didn't stop the neighbours from whispering amongst themselves. Detective Quinn was already in the squad car. He was sitting in the front passenger seat, going through his notes and photographs he took from the crime scene. The junior officer turned his back on the neighbours and made his way back to the squad car. He opened the door and climbed inside. The door slammed shut and the engine ignited.

"The hospital," Detective Quinn ordered, "now!"

"Yes, sir."

The squad car pulled out from the side curb, out onto the street, and drove quickly to the end of the road, before making a right turn and disappearing into the darkness of the night. The siren of the police car echoed in the quiet of the night, growing stronger and louder as it made its way toward the hospital.

Peter sat patiently in the waiting room. Emily sat nervously next to him. She was the first point of contact, the person to call in case of an emergency for Andrew. Emily was quick to call Peter for support. Peter sat quietly, a moment, sitting back in his chair, his arms folded across his chest, watching the medical staff, race about the floor, in and out of Andrew's room. Andrew was screaming, cussing, as his body flinched with tremendous pain, as the doctor in charge finished up on the stitches along his torso, and a nurse worked on his forearm. The curtain surrounding the bed was pulled to a close. Almost. There were stains of blood on the bed sheets.

"Who would even *do* such a thing?" Emily asked, just above a whisper. It was evident that she had been crying. Her voice was a little hoarse.

"I don't know," Peter answered, shrugging his shoulders a little and whispering back, turning his head a little, to face his friend.

Emily had her face buried in her hands. "What was he even doing there?" Emily asked.

"He *lives* there," Peter answered.

"No!" Emily answered, raising her voice a little more. Her voice clearer and stronger, as she pulled her head out of her hands. "I mean, *who* is doing this? It's like the police are fucking clueless!" Peter didn't answer. He didn't know. His guess was as good as hers.

Peter continued to watch the police officers on duty patrolling the hospital corridor. The police officers were male and female, and of different ages, shapes and backgrounds. The stretcher which Andrew was brought in on, from the ambulance, was parked in the corridor. The bed sheets were stained with blood. The doctor and nurse who had attended to the stitches walked out of the room, along with Detective Quinn. The doctor whispered something to the detective. Detective Quinn was still sporting that horrible grey suit and tired, white shirt. Emily watched on. She climbed to her feet and was the first to walk from her chair and toward the detective. They exchanged a few words.

"If you can think of anything else, please give me a call," Detective Quinn said to Emily, handing her one of his business cards.

"Thank you," Emily answered, "I will."

Emily passed the detective and the doctor and walked immediately into the emergency room. She grabbed a nearby chair and sat next to Andrew, her nervous hands reaching out for his.

"Did you find what you were looking for, Detective?" Peter asked, almost sarcastically, as he sat in his chair in the waiting room.

"Not yet," Detective Quinn answered, approaching Peter.

"What's the body count now?"

Detective Quinn didn't answer. He was furious.

"You're doing a bang-up job, Detective," continued Peter.

"Okay, then. I'll bite," Detective Quinn responded. "Where were you tonight?"

"Detective?" Peter paused a moment. "I was at home. That was until my friend called me and wanted a ride into the hospital after hearing her boyfriend was attacked this evening. Where were you?"

Detective Quinn laughed, a little.

"You think *I* had something to do with this?"

"I don't know. You're the detective. You are supposed to be piecing this puzzle together. You're supposed to be solving this thing. Then again, there is nothing scarier than a man with a knife, who just... snaps."

"I'm on the right side of the law. You can guarantee that. I'm doing my job here!" Detective Quinn snapped back. "I'll be in touch. How about you go and check in on your friend and see how he is doing."

"Yes, Detective."

Peter and Detective Quinn stared at each other a moment. Detective Quinn made the last of his notes, as he scribbled something into his notepad, before placing his pen and notepad in the inside pocket of his jacket. Peter stood up from his chair and walked past the detective and stood patiently in the emergency room entrance, watching Andrew and Emily together, a moment.

Andrew was propped up in his hospital bed. The bed cover was pulled up to his waist and folded over. He was now sporting a hospital gown. It was very loose-fitting. The back of it was left undone. Peter could see his right forearm bandaged tightly and the side of his torso. There was white bandage peeking out from under the hospital gown. Peter stood there silently, a moment. His face was angry. He was doing everything he could to hold back his tears. Emily and Andrew were whispering to each other.

"Hey, you," Andrew said, just above a whisper, as he pulled his eyes off Emily and looked at his best friend standing in the emergency room entrance.

"Hey," Peter answered, clearing his throat a little and forcing a smile. "How are you doing?"

"Sore!"

"I bet."

Peter pulled himself off the side of the emergency room door and walked inside.

"I'm going to grab myself a coffee. I'll let you boys chat, a little." Emily smiled, feeling a little more relaxed as she walked out of the room, turning left at the door and walking down the corridor.

Peter watched her leave, before he made his way deeper into the room, and grabbing Emily's chair.

"Look at you, huh?" Peter continued. "Pulling a stunt like this. You went and got yourself hurt." Andrew rolled his eyes, a little. He coughed, a bit. His body flinched at the pain.

"This is the part where you tell me that this is all a prank," replied Andrew. "Because he, she, or whoever the fuck is doing this, is a strong motherfucker! They blindsided me."

"It's not a prank," Peter answered, just above a whisper, shaking his head. "Look at you. You got hurt. You could have died this evening."

"I don't think that was their intention. They said I was a message, a calling card for *you*. This time. They said heads were going to roll."

"Did you tell Quinn this?" Peter asked, concerned. "Did you say anything to Emily?"

"Are you nuts? Fuck, no!"

Peter rubbed his eyes, a little. "I am so sorry. This is *my* fault."

"It's not your fault, Petey," Andrew replied, shaking his head and stretching his left hand out a little to comfort his friend. "Just remember, when I am out of here, and feeling better, you are buying me a beer!"

"Deal!" Peter forced another smile. "But, in the meantime, I want you to rest up. Do as the nurses tell you."

"Yes, Boss!" Andrew replied with a smile, trying to break the tense situation with a chuckle. The pain in his forearm and torso coursed through his body. His face flinched, a little.

Peter looked on, concerned.

Emily returned with coffee in hand. She watched her man and their best friend talk a little before making her way in further and breaking up the brotherhood.

"Emily," Peter said, looking over his shoulder. "Look after your man, okay? Make sure he does what the doctors and nurses tell him."

"Of course," Emily answered, smiling.

Emily took another sip of her coffee as she made her way into the room. "This is the part where I bail and leave you guys alone." Peter smiled.

Peter stood to his feet and gave Emily back her chair. He turned and started to walk out of the room. "Hey!" Andrew called out, just above a whisper.

Peter turned and faced his friend, as he stood there, at the end of the bed. "Hey," Peter answered, smiling a little.

"Thank you for dropping by and bringing Emily."

"Of course." Peter nodded. "Any time."

"Thank you, Peter." smiled Emily.

"Welcome home, Petey." Andrew smiled. "Yeah. Nice. Ain't it?"

Peter chuckled a little.

"I'll check in on you two, later. Rest up."

Peter walked out of the emergency room, leaving his friend and his partner behind for the evening. He stood in the entrance to the door a moment, looking around, before taking a left turn and walking down the corridor. The nurses were busy at work, manning the nurse's station. Peter walked the corridor, rubbing his eyes a little, as he made his way to the elevator. Doctors were walking the corridor, to the nurse's station, returning patient's files, and grabbing the next, as they did their rounds.

Peter pressed the button and called for the next available elevator. He waited patiently, a moment, standing there, waiting for the doors to open. The light above the elevator switched on, followed by a soft bell. There was, standing in front of him, a married couple, somewhere in the late forties, walking off the elevator. They ignored Peter and went about their business, as their two teenage children followed. Peter stepped to one side and gave them room to move, before he made his way onto the elevator. The doors were quick to close behind him.

The doors to the elevator opened again, within seconds. It arrived at the car park. The car park was near on empty. Peter could see people off in the distance, out of earshot. He searched his trouser pockets, looking for the keys to his car. A concerned look fell upon his face, searching, remembering where he parked his car. Peter pressed the button on the clicker of his alarm, a couple of times. He could see the lights on the sports utility vehicle flash on and off, in the corner of his left eye. A smile surfaced to his lips. The near silence of the car park was broken with the chime of a ringing cell phone. *Ring. Ring. Ring.* Peter searched his other trouser pocket. He looked at the screen come to life. *Unknown Caller.*

"Hello," Peter answered cautiously.

There was a laugh, a heinous laugh, over the phone line. "You brought me three new people to play with."

"What do you want?" Peter asked angrily.

The clown mask laughed, again.

"I enjoyed playing with your friend tonight. I could play with him, again. Correction. I *will* play with him again, until I am finished with him, discarding him like nothing more than a rag doll."

"Fuck you!"

"Always the potty mouth. Did your mother like you talking like that? I bet she didn't." Peter disconnected the phone line, angry.

The cell phone rang, again. *Ring. Ring.*

"You hang up on me again, and you'll feel the blade of my hunting knife slice your eyelids open before I stab you in the chest."

"What the fuck do you want?"

"I told you," the clown mask responded, quite calmly, "I want to play. That's all I ever wanted. In the meantime, sit back and enjoy the show. I'll kill you. But not before I'm ready."

The phone line disconnected again.

Peter arrived at his car. His heartbeat was racing wildly, and the palms of his hands and his back were covered in sweat. Peter opened the driver's side door and climbed inside the car, slamming it shut.

Peter dropped his cell phone onto the front passenger seat, next to him. His hands tightened around the steering wheel, as his fists turned white and red. Peter pulled at the steering wheel angrily, rocking back and forth.

"Don't lose it now!" Peter whispered to himself, holding back his tears.

Peter's hands slipped a little and hit the horn. The car horn echoed loudly in the car park for a moment. Peter looked around, searching, looking for anyone. There was no one.

Peter drove home from the hospital. He pulled out of the car park and into the traffic. It was a quiet drive on the way home, this evening. The music played on the radio, gently, in between people calling up and requesting songs.

Peter awoke the following morning. After a late night, he slept in a little. He was always used to waking early, around five or six. The time was just coming up to eight. Peter was slow waking up this morning. He turned in his bed, laying on his back, and wiped the sleep from his eyes. Peter stretched over to the nightstand and took the cell phone from the charger. There was a text message from Mike.

Good morning, I hope you slept well and have a great start to your day. I will give you a call later this morning.

The message from Mike read. Peter smiled, some.

Good morning.

Peter typed and hit the send button. It was short and to the point.

The bed cover pushed back, a little. Peter climbed out of bed and turned, placing his feet on the hardwood floor. It was so cool to the touch this morning. Peter sat there a moment longer, slowly waking up. He was naked. Peter climbed to his feet and walked across the bedroom floor, down the hallway, and into the bathroom. The door closed behind him. The sound of water rushing from the shower started to race. Peter stood in front of the shower, his arm under the water, testing the temperature, before stepping under the water altogether and sliding the glass door to a close behind him.

The morning progressed into the early afternoon. Peter left the house and drove into town. The sports utility vehicle was parked in the town square. Mike kept to his word and called later in the morning and arranged for a catch-up and to do lunch in town. Peter sat opposite Mike in the local diner. It wasn't so much a date, although all the nervous anticipation was there. It was just two friends catching up for lunch, even though neither would admit it, yet. Peter ordered the chicken and salad sandwich with fries and a chocolate shake. Mike ordered a cheeseburger, double meat patties and fries with a soda. The two talked and a shared a few laughs. Mike leaned into his side of the table and talked about how work was busy, now that they were leading up to winter, and how he wanted to invite Peter over for a home-cooked meal, sometime. Peter agreed. He nodded his head and couldn't hide his smile. Peter talked about his run-ins with Detective Quinn, Mike didn't like that.

The lunchtime catch-up was over. Mike had returned to work, with a promise that he would call again, this evening. Peter found himself walking the corridor of the hospital, again. He walked the same corridor he did last night, towards the nurse's station. It was a busy afternoon in the hospital. Doctors were doing their rounds, with med students following their every move, like shadows. Peter almost reached the nurses' station when he stopped in his tracks and peered through the window. The curtain was partially opened and could see Andrew sitting up in bed. He was wearing a plain, white baseball t-shirt with navy blue sleeves. The t-shirt clung to his muscular build and highlighted the bandages which wrapped firmly around his torso. Peter could also see the bandage around his right arm. The bed cover was pulled back to his waist, keeping his legs warm. Andrew was in the process of an interview with Detective Quinn, who stood at the end of the bed, asking his deputy question after question. A junior officer stood to the right of the bed, with his back to the window, directing a camcorder on a tripod, recording the interview. Peter looked at Andrew's face. He was deep in thought. Peter stood there a moment longer, unnoticed before he turned his back on the hospital room, and the nurse's station, and walked the corridor. His steps grew faster, and his feet grew heavier, with each passing step. He reached the elevator and leaned in and pressed the call button. His index finger of his left hand pressed the button three times in quick succession.

"Hey there, you," a friendly voice called. "Peter!"

Peter turned his back on the elevator, and there in front of him, with another take-away cup of coffee in her right hand, was Emily.

"Emily!" Peter answered, surprised. "I didn't know. I didn't know you were here."

"I'm taking a few days off, making sure that big lug in there follows doctor's orders and is on the mend." Emily nodded.

"Of course."

"Have you seen Andrew yet?"

"Me? No." Peter shook his head. "I saw he was busy with Detective Quinn. I didn't want to interrupt."

"They turned up like an hour ago." Emily nodded, again. "He thought he would try again and ask Andrew some questions from last night. Maybe he forgot something. Or remembered. I don't know." Emily paused a moment and looked at Peter. "I'm glad I ran into you, by the way." A smile surfaced to her lips. "I have been meaning to call you. You know, since our night at The Watering Hole. I have been meaning to organise a time to meet up, maybe do lunch in town?"

"I'd like that." Peter nodded.

"Good. Great!" Emily answered, as the answer immediately cheered her up. "How does sometime next week sound, say Monday?"

"Monday?" Peter thought to himself. "Monday sounds great."

"Andrew should be discharged in the next day or two. You should come round and see him. I know he would like that. Me, too. Between you and me, I could do with a break. It would be nice to have another adult around the house."

"Absolutely." Peter nodded, again. "You just let me know when."

"I will."

"I'll leave you to it. With Quinn and all, you don't need another body around taking time from you and Andrew. Enjoy. Tell Andrew I said hello."

"I will. And thank you."

"Anytime."

Emily leaned in and kissed Peter on the cheek and gave him a quick hug as she juggled her cup of coffee.

Another elevator arrived. The bell above the door began to chime, again. "Well, this is me." Peter smiled. "I'll see you soon."

"Bye, Peter."

Peter stepped on the elevator and turned to face Emily. The two friends smiled and waved at each other, a moment before the doors to the elevator closed.

Peter left the hospital and drove back into town. The sports utility vehicle parked in the town square, just outside the local movie theatre. The engine died. Peter climbed out of the car and walked back, towards the hardware store. But, not before popping into the diner and ordering two coffees to go. There was one for himself and the other for Mike.

The door leading into the hardware store was pushed open slowly and with caution. The winds were beginning to arc up a little, and the weather was cold and damp. Peter carried the two cups of coffee into the hardware store, careful not to spill a drop, and careful not to burn himself. Peter pushed the door open with his left foot. He gave the door a little oomph, and the bell above the door began to chime. There were a few customers in the store. Mike was busy working, talking to a customer. Peter couldn't tell what they were talking about. He was too far away, and couldn't read lips. Peter walked down an aisle, towards the counter and cash register, and Mike. There were chainsaws on the left and lawnmowers on the right. Peter watched Mike take cash from a customer, place it in the cash register, and give her change. The cash register slammed shut.

"Hey, you." Peter smiled.

"Peter, hi," Mike answered with a smile, and genuinely surprised. "It's great to see you. I hope one of those coffees are for me. It is freezing today."

"You know it."

Peter slid the cup of coffee across the glass counter. Mike extended his right hand and grabbed the takeaway cup. His fingers wrapped around Peter's, for just a moment. There was a pause and another smile.

"You read my mind. Thank you."

"Anytime." Peter smiled. "So, how's your day?" Mike smiled.

The afternoon turned to night. The weather was still a little rough. The rain fell harder, so did the gusts of wind. Peter drove carefully, taking the twists and bends of the country road. He was on his way to visit Andrew, at home, who had been discharged later that afternoon. Emily called and invited him round. The drive took no more than fifteen minutes, weather permitted.

The sports utility vehicle was parked out the front of Andrew's home. The engine died. Peter grabbed his keys, his cell phone and his wallet and ran towards the front porch in the light rain. Peter dusted himself off, making himself look a little more presentable before he knocked on the front door. *Knock. Knock. Knock.* It took a moment before the door answered. And there, standing in front of him, was Emily. She was dressed casually in denim blue jeans and a simple white t-shirt.

"You made it!" Emily smiled.

"At last," Peter answered.

"Please. Come on in." Emily stepped to one side.

"The patient is sitting on the couch in front of the TV in the living room." Peter laughed.

The front door to the house closed behind him.

The lights in the living room were dim. Andrew grabbed the remote off the couch, sitting next to him, and pointed it at the TV to adjust the volume. The volume on the television was now down low.

"It's great to see you, Petey." Andrew smiled, as he looked out of the living room, and into the kitchen, watching Emily busy herself with placing a few nibbles and drinks together.

Andrew was sitting on the couch in a pair of black shorts and another one of his baseball t-shirts. He was propped up on the couch, unable to move a great deal. Peter sat opposite Andrew on the couch. They sat face to face.

"I heard Quinn spoke to you," said Andrew, just above a whisper, as if he didn't want Emily overhearing their conversation.

"Yeah," Peter answered, matching his whisper, "it was the same, you know? How are you? How have you been? Where were you last night? You know, the usual." Peter shrugged.

"Fuck him!" answered Andrew bluntly. "But, seriously, be careful. That motherfucker is strong. They went to town on my stomach and forearm."

Peter remained silent. His face was solemn.

"You rest up." he forced a smile. "You already got hurt. Don't go being a hero, Andrew."

Emily stood in front of the kitchen counter, over a tray of cheap nibbles, cubed cheese, crackers, dips and other bits and pieces, with three bottles of beer, from a six-pack she purchased from the supermarket earlier in the day. She looked up from her culinary treat and peered into the living room, intermittently, to check up on Andrew. Emily could see him and Peter, sitting on the couch, deep in conversation.

"We've been through a lot over the years," said Andrew.

"We have." Peter nodded, slowly. "How are you holding up?"

"I'm doing…" Andrew slowly nodded, "a little tender and sore, but I will get there." "It's going to be like that for a few days yet."

Emily walked into the living room, holding a tray of nibbles, and balancing the three bottles of beer on the tray. Peter smiled at Emily and nodded.

"Thank you," Peter said, just above a whisper, taking a small handful of nibbles, and leaving the beer behind. "But I got to go. I'll leave you guys alone."

"Thank you for popping round and helping out," smiled Emily.

"My pleasure. If there is anything you need, day or night, you know where I am."

"Thank you, Petey," Andrew responded. "I'll call you tomorrow."

"Sure."

Peter stood up from the couch.

"Wait!" Andrew called.

"What?"

"Can you give us a minute?" Andrew asked, looking at Emily.

"Of course." Emily nodded. "Goodnight, Peter."

Emily leaned in and kissed Peter on the right cheek, before turning and making her way out of the room. Andrew watched Emily walk out of the living room, disappearing deeper inside the house.

"How do you handle all of this?" he asked, just above a whisper. "What?"

"This," Andrew answered, "your life, I mean. The police…The

murders." Peter smiled. He felt a little taken aback by such a forthright question.

"I try and focus on the people and the things I care about. It helps." Peter shrugged his shoulders.

Peter climbed into his sports utility vehicle and slammed the car door to a close. He turned and looked in the back seat of the truck. It was clean and tidy. There was nothing there. Peter turned, again. This time, facing the front of the vehicle. He looked into the rear-view mirror, adjusting it a little before igniting the engine. The engine rattled a little as the truck stood still a moment longer. Peter reached out for his cell phone that sat on the front passenger seat. The screen came to life. There was a text message from Mike. Peter looked into the rear-view mirror one more time and made his way out from the curb and into the traffic.

A few nights later. The time was a little after seven in the evening. The sports utility vehicle was parked outside a single-storey weatherboard home with a porch out the front, and garage on the right side of the house. The lights in the front living room were switched on, and could be seen from outdoors. There was an almost glow from the front living room. Peter took Mike up on his offer for a home-cooked meal.

The dimmer lights in the dining room were lowered, giving off a romantic atmosphere. The dining table was set for two. The plates were left on the table. The food, or most, thereof, had already been eaten. The menu for this evening was steak on the barbeque, greens and mashed potato with a hint of wasabi.

The television set in the living room was switched on. The volume was down low, but the room was empty. There was a movie playing on the television, a horror movie. It was about a serial killer stalking some girl with big breasts who was running upstairs searching for a place to hide. The light in the hallway was switched off. But the door leading into the master bedroom was wide open. The lights in the room were also switched off. The curtains were pulled open a fraction, allowing in some of the light from the streetlamps outside. Mike was kissing Peter slow and hard, their tongues almost fighting each another. His hands searched Peter. They started on the side of his face, before lowering down and wrapping around him. Mike pushed Peter backwards, onto the bed behind him. They bounced on the mattress a little, casually chuckling, before their lips found one another, again. They fumbled at their clothes, struggling to remove them.

The hours progressed. It was now somewhere in the early hours of the following morning.

Peter was fast asleep in Mike's bed. The bed cover had folded back on its self, to his waist, exposing his naked chest. Mike lay beside him. He was the big spoon. Mike was also bare-chested, the bed cover raised as high as his waist, as he wrapped his arms around Peter, holding him close to his chest.

Andrew was taking a few extra days personal leave from work as he got over the pain of his knife wounds to his torso and forearm. Detective Quinn had been in contact regularly, every other day. The bandage around the torso had come off now, and the stitches were scheduled to come out in the next day or two. Andrew was at home. He was in the kitchen, grabbing himself a soda from the refrigerator. The door to the refrigerator closed, as he held the can of soda in his right hand, and his cell phone in his left. Andrew walked from the kitchen and turned into the hallway. The can of soda popped open as he dialled a number into his cell phone and hit the call button.

"Hey, you," Andrew started, "what are you up to?"

"What did you have in mind?" Peter asked.

"Emily is back at work and has left me home alone. I'm bored. Feel like going for a drive?"

The weather was beginning to clear now. It didn't take long for Peter to drive over to Andrew's home; no more than fifteen minutes. Peter had picked up his best friend and the two were back on the road. The music on the radio was playing. The windows were wound down. Andrew enjoyed the breeze as the sports utility vehicle cruised up and down the country hills, passing the trees. The drive took them a little north of the town square. About twenty minutes' north.

The sports utility vehicle was parked outside the local high school. Of course, it looked a little different now, compared to when Andrew and Peter were seniors. There were new buildings added to the school grounds and a fence around the perimeter of the estate. The engine to the sports utility vehicle was dead. Andrew and Peter sat on top of the bonnet of the car, looking up at the school. Andrew looked angry and sombre as he sipped a can of beer.

"You remember what it was like growing up in this town. You escaped. Why would you even want to come back?" Andrew asked, taking a deep sip from his beer.

"How can I forget? I know exactly what it was like. But I also know what it's like out there. Nothing. And no one is perfect." Peter answered, just above a whisper and lowering his head, as if ashamed and embarrassed of his past.

Andrew looked at Peter.

"I hated high school," Andrew responded. "But you got me. You make life just... so."

A smile surfaced to Andrew's lips. He leaned over a little, as much as he could, anyway, and squeezed Peter's left kneecap a little. The two friends looked at each other. Peter also smiled. "Thank you," he whispered.

"I envied you, you know that?" said Andrew. "Growing up, you always seemed to have a perfect life. Your father. Your stepmother. Your sister. That house. What did I have? I had my... dad. A part-time quarry man and a full-time raging alcoholic. You know, my dad would beat me if I wouldn't..." Andrew forced another smile. "But you, you were the star. You escaped this town and made it to the flashing neon lights of New York City. Well done, Petey. I'm so proud of you."

"Yeah? And how did that turn out?" Peter shrugged with a hint of a smile. "Let's get out of here. I've had enough reminiscing for one day."

The afternoon progressed. Andrew was back at home, wandering around his house. The television in the living room was switched on, so, too, was his computer. The lights in the kitchen were switched on. Andrew paced from room to room of the house, bored, walking up and down the hallway. He carried his cell phone in his right hand, twirling it about, back and forth, back and forth, again. Andrew paused. He stood in the hallway and navigated to the last conversation he had with Jayne. His thumb crawled the screen upwards, back to the last picture of Jayne. He stared at it a moment. The thoughts he was having. Andrew bit his lower lip, a little and sighed.

Let's catch up in a day or two. After I get my stitches out.

Andrew typed and hit the send button.

He walked to the end of the hallway and turned into the kitchen to grab himself another beer from the refrigerator.

The cell phone vibrated a few minutes later.

Andrew looked down the neck of his beer bottle at his cell phone. It was another message from Jayne. He opened the message.

Deal.

It read.

Andrew found himself sitting on the side of a hospital bed in the emergency room of Hillsboro County Hospital. He was sitting there in black jeans and boots. They hugged his thick, muscular legs well. Emily sat close by, in the corner of the room, holding Andrew's t-shirt. She held it tightly in her hands, as she watched the nurse cut and pull on the stitches in his torso. Andrew flinched. His face screwed up. The two made eye contact.

Emily was the first to smile. It was her way of showing support. The balled-up t-shirt in her hands still felt warm. Maybe it was her, maybe it was Andrew. She lifted it a little, covering her smile, some, and smelt the t-shirt. She closed her eyes for a moment, before resting it back down on her lap.

"All done," said the nurse, looking up at Andrew. "Thank you." Andrew smiled.

The Roadside was a motel located on the outskirts of Hillsboro. It was a small, almost rundown kind of place on the side of the road. It was a popular motel for local families, men and women on business trips, finding a place to crash for the night, as they drove through town. It was also popular for the extra-marital affair, now and again. The Roadside was a single-storey motel. It catered for twelve rooms. The doors leading into each motel room were painted a bright red. The doors were weather-beaten and needed a fresh coat of paint. And there were three vending machines: one for snacks, one for drinks, and one for ice. Andrew's truck was parked outside room number eight.

Jayne agreed to meet with Andrew at seven in the morning. She arrived a little early and checked in under pseudonym of Veronica Sawyer. It didn't mean anything in particular. She was simply covering her tracks. Jayne was in the motel room, already. She was dressed in a simple t-shirt and jeans. Her feet were bare as she lay on the double-size bed with a blood-red cover that fit the shape of the mattress tightly. The TV was switched on. The local news was playing.

Andrew sat in his truck. The engine was dead. He sat there, in the car park, outside room number eight. He was dressed in a plain white t-shirt, pale blue jeans and black boots. He was on his way to work. His shift didn't start until nine. His large, muscular frame tilted from side to side a little until he climbed out of his truck and slammed the door behind him. Andrew was quick to walk from his truck to the room. He knocked on the door three times, in quick succession.

The motel room door opened. And, there, standing in front of him, was Jayne. Andrew was welcomed with a smile. She was so eager to see him, again. Just the two of them. No friends hanging off their words, no on-off partners. Just the two of them.

"You made it," Jayne said, unable to contain her smile.

"Of course," Andrew replied. "I always come when I say I will." Jayne giggled a little and stepped to one side, allowing Andrew inside. The motel room door closed behind him.

The curtains were almost pulled to a close. But there was enough light to show the room. The television set continued to play. Jayne decorated the room with some snacks and cans of soda from the vending machine. There was also a bucket of ice. Andrew pulled Jayne close to him. They stood at the end of the double-size bed, and he kissed her deeply. His tongue made its way in, finding Jayne's. He pulled back and looked down at her. Their eyes connected. Jayne kissed Andrew back, with force and passion. Her tongue found his. The breathing became heavy. The two pulled at each other's clothes before they stood in front of each other naked.

"You want me?" Jayne asked, almost seductively.

"You know I do," Andrew responded, just above a whisper.

"Then, why are you just standing there? Show me!"

Andrew pounced on Jayne. He kissed her again, slow and deep. His mouth moved all over her, down her neck and over her breasts. His tongue played with her nipples, licking them, sucking on them, devouring them, biting them. Jayne writhed with pleasure. Her head tilted back, a little, burying into the pillow. Andrew turned Jayne around. Her back was facing him now. He stood over her, towering almost.

Andrew pushed Jayne onto the bed. She fell forward, onto her chest, using her hands to break her fall. Andrew took a step forward. He leaned down and grabbed Jayne by the hips, pulling her in close to him, almost with force. Jayne could feel Andrew's manhood grow by the moment with excitement. He pulled her close again, his manhood finding 'its way inside her with each thrust. The two moaned.

"Fuck me!" Jayne shouted. "Take me."

Lovemaking lasted several minutes. Maybe, nine or ten. It wasn't lovemaking, though. It wasn't sex. It was sport fucking, at best. A little naughty something, something on the side to tantalise and share a dirty, little secret. It was fun. Andrew collapsed on top of Jayne. His arms wrapped around her, holding her close. Their breathing was tired and restricted. He leaned in and kissed Jayne slowly and passionately for a moment before she climbed out from underneath Andrew and climbed to the side of the bed. She ran across the room and closed the door to the bathroom behind her. The water from the shower was quick to run. Andrew rolled over onto his back, laughing a little, as he wiped himself down with a hand towel, watching the TV.

The water from the shower continued to run. Andrew climbed over to the furthest side of the bed. His arm reached out to the nightstand and grabbed a can of soda that sat in the bucket of ice.

The can opened, making that hissing sound. The bubbles raised, and Andrew took a deep sip. He turned and saw Jayne standing in the doorway to the bathroom. She stood there, refreshed. Her hair wasn't wet, not really. It was tied back into a bun. A white cotton towel wrapped firmly around her body. She made eye contact with Andrew a moment as she walked across the floor and pulled on her clothes. Andrew was next to climb off the bed and take a shower. He let the hot water run a moment before stepping into the shower. Andrew grabbed the container of liquid soap and scrubbed his body, all over. The soap raced over his chest, his belly, his arms and legs, all over.

Jayne sat at the cheap vanity in the hotel room, by the side of the bed, applying the last of her make-up. She stared at herself for a moment whilst the water in the shower ran. Jayne applied her lipstick. The lipstick was a hard beige in colour. She admired her reflection.

"I'm a lady," Jayne whispered to herself. "I. Am. A. Lady. I am." Jayne smiled to herself.

The door to the bathroom soon opened, again. And Andrew stood there, with a towel around his waist. His muscular, furry body was damp from the shower, and the sweat from the lack of air conditioning in the hotel room. The scar across his torso looked prominent. He dropped the towel from around his waist and walked naked across the room, and over to the pile of clothes he left tossed on the floor. Andrew pulled on his underwear and jeans first. He sat on the end of the bed, struggling a little to put on his socks, as his wet feet clung to the cotton.

"If we are going to do this again, there are a couple of things I have to say." Andrew started, just above a whisper as he pulled on his socks and leaned back on the bed, a little, to relax. "You got to find a better place than this. The Roadside? The air in this place is for shit! I'm sweating fucking bullets here! And next, I want you to dress up for me. Put on a dress. Something nice. Make an effort. Something."

"You'd like that?" Jayne asked, as she stood up from the chair in front of the vanity and walked over toward Andrew, standing in front of him, her best to look seductive.

"You know I would."

"Anything for you, baby."

"Good."

Andrew grabbed his t-shirt, climbed into it, tugging on it a little to make himself feel a little more comfortable and climbed off the bed. He stood up and leaned in to kiss Jayne goodbye, giving her a quick peck on the lips. He was the first to walk out of the room, without saying anything further, leaving her alone. The motel room door to number eight was pulled to a close behind him. Jayne rushed to the window and watched him as he walked across the car park and climbed into his truck. The engine ignited and pulled out of The Roadside Motel.

The day progressed on. It was somewhere in the late afternoon. Andrew had his cell phone on him, all day. He hadn't heard from Jayne. Not since this morning. Andrew got a text message from Peter. It was nothing serious. Just a 'hey, how are you?' And there was a missed call from Emily. Either Andrew was busy at the time and didn't notice the call, or he felt guilty after his morning shenanigans with Jayne, but the guilt held him back. Andrew was sitting at his desk, typing away on his keyboard, finishing his paperwork. Detective Quinn had closed himself off in his office, reading through files, again.

Chapter Seven...

Exterior. Night. A two-storey Victorian, weatherboard home was alive as the sunset upon Hillsboro for another day. The weather was calm. The leaves on the large oak trees rustled a little in the cool night breeze. The street lamps had flickered on. The street itself was quiet and vacant.

Near vacant.

The living room had a real lived in feel to it, as the walls were adorned with framed photographs which stretched the course of a near lifetime of Mrs Baeyer. The earliest memories of a young girl growing up in Hillsboro with her mother and father. The only child who grew into an awkward and gawky beanpole of a teen, to her confident mid-twenties, where she found love with a travelling salesman. The photographs spanned the courtship of their relationship, to their eventual wedding day, their marriage. Mr Baeyer passed away in his sleep in his early sixties after suffering from a life-threatening stroke.

The television set in the living room was switched on, the volume down low as a TV drama was playing. It was about a doctor or police officer. Something. A collapsible table with kitchen tray sat in front of the couch with a tall glass of water and ice cubes sat alone. Mrs Baeyer was alone in the kitchen, dressed in a flowery maxi-dress. She made her way from the kitchen and back into the living room with a cup of tea and a handful of sweet cookies which sat on top of a plate. Mrs Baeyer took her time walking back into the living room, careful not to spill a drop and burn herself.

The cup of tea and the sweet cookies finally reached the table as Mrs Baeyer made herself comfortable on the couch, getting back into watching her stories. She leaned forward a little, careful to take a sip from her cup. Her tongue ran over her lower lip, deciding which cookie to eat first. Mrs Baeyer took the shortbread. The sugar and butter tasted so inviting with a cup of tea. She leaned forward, again, resting her cup back on the tray. It was then that a dark shadow ran across the window of the side of the house. It moved at an electric speed. It was nothing more than a blur. The shadow cast on the wall as the television played, unnoticed. A heavy pounding, hitting the front door followed. *Pound. Pound. Pound.* Mrs Baeyer looked over her left shoulder, out past the living room, and into the foyer of the home. She was clearly frustrated by such an interruption. Another heavy knock followed. *Knock. Knock. Knock.*

"You have got to be kidding me with this," she mumbled under her breath to herself, "who could this be at this hour?"

Knock. Knock.

It repeated.

"One moment!" she called.

Mrs Baeyer inched herself forward off the couch, moving the table a little and made her way out of the living room and to the front door.

The light on the front porch was switched on. Mrs Baeyer leaned forward and looked through the peephole. There was no one there. She pulled away from the front door, feeling irritated, that same expression surfaced to her lips, from moments ago. Her eyes lifted from off the floor, and looked again. She looked left. It was a blur. She looked down and fumbled with the keys in the lock. The front door pulled open. And, there, standing in front of her, was no one at all. The gently evening breeze blew past her as she stood at her front door on the porch of her home.

"Hello?" she called. There was no answer.

"Fuck this!" she mumbled under her breath.

Mrs Baeyer turned her back on the porch and made her way back inside the foyer, slowly.

She waddled forward. The image of the clown mask appeared silently, out from the darkness behind her, at the bottom of the stairs of her porch. The light in the foyer highlighted the white paint on the mask, as well as the black and blue in the eyes. The clown mask stepped forward, again. The sound of the wooden beams of the porch bent and cracked under the pressure. The clown mask moved fast on their feet, sprinting forward, and was quick to catch the elderly lady. It grabbed her, on the right shoulder and the scruff of the neck, as the leather-gloved hands extended outwards, pinching deeper into her fragile skin, almost leaving a bruise. The clown mask pushed her forward, throwing her violently. Mrs Baeyer fell forward, losing her balance, tumbling forward, and banging her head heavily on the hardwood floors. She lifted her head from the floor, slowly, and in a daze, as blood began to pour heavily from a wound on top of the right side of her forehead.

The front door to the two-storey Victorian home swung to a close behind them. The clown mask stood there quietly, watching Mrs Baeyer sprawled across the floor in front of them, watching her hands trembling with fear. She was out of breath and very rattled. Mrs Baeyer ran her tongue over her lips a moment, doing her best to regain her breath, before letting out a blood-curdling scream. She got onto her hands and knees, as fast as she could, before turning around to face her assailant. She stared back at the mask.

"Who the fuck, do you think you are?" she asked, out of breath.

The clown mask stepped forward, inching closer and closer, tilting its head, a little as they tightened their left fist. The glove struck first. It moved fast and violently, hitting Mrs Baeyer on the side of the temple, just in front of her right ear, pushing her backwards, making her lose her balance and rendering her unconscious.

The lights in the living room were still switched on. The curtains were now pulled to a close.

The television set continued to play as the volume was placed on mute. The table in front of the couch was gone. Instead, Mrs Baeyer was taped securely at the wrists and ankles, and gagged around her mouth, too. She was sitting on the couch in her living room. Her hair was ratty and dishevelled. The right side of her temple was red and bruised and horribly beaten. And a bloody wound covered the left corner of her forehead. Mrs Baeyer was struggling to remain conscious, as she inspected her surrounds. Her eyes darted around the room. The image of the clown mask stood in front of her. A large, sharp hunting knife with jagged edges, which almost gleamed under the living room lights, waved in front of Mrs Baeyer, left and right, left and right, and left and right, again, as the image stepped a little closer, now. Her heart began to race wildly. Mrs Baeyer could feel it in her chest. Her eyes welled with tears, and her breathing was muffled.

The hunting knife pulled away, just like it first appeared, very slowly. The clown mask placed the hunting knife on top of the coffee table and walked in front of the couch, now sitting on top of the coffee table, too, in front of Mrs Baeyer, leaning in forward, a little, coming inches away from her, almost eye to eye. The clown mask reached for the hunting knife, again, with their right hand, the blade scraping the surface of the coffee table. The blade of the hunting knife raised, again. The tears. The muffled screaming. The panic began to set in, again.

"Mrs Baeyer," the deep, yet familiar voice behind the mask started, "you would have to be the answer to the question nobody in this town bothered to ask."

Mrs Baeyer continued to cry.

"You're always… just there, aren't you? Sticking your nose in where it doesn't belong. You think you're fucking perfect, don't you? Like this town owes you a favour or something."

The clown mask leaned in, a little more, running the hunting knife across the surface of the tape over the lips of her mouth.

"This town owes you nothing. You're shit! This town would carry on without you, and not a body would care."

The clown mask stood up from the coffee table. Mrs Baeyer's eyes remained on the assailant, watching their every move. Her eyes lifted just a fraction. The image stood tall and made their way around to the back of the couch, now standing behind Mrs Baeyer

"It's people like you, Mrs Baeyer, that town's like this should do without. It's people like you that deserve to be out of the picture."

"No!" Mrs Baeyer mumbled, with tears in her eyes.

"It's all for the greater good, believe me."

The clown mask lowered their left hand, bound in a leather glove. It ran over the top of Mrs Baeyer's dishevelled hair so gently. Mrs Baeyer flinched at the touch as tears ran down her face. Her nose was blocked, her breathing becoming restricted.

"It's time to say goodnight," the voice whispered, leaning into her left ear. The voice alone carried a balance of unspeakable horror. The tone of their voice taking its victims into the realms of horror so very easily.

"No!" Mrs Baeyer screamed behind the tape, pleading.

The clown mask grabbed at Mrs Baeyer tightly, pouncing on her, wrapping their arms around her head and neck in almost a bear hug. The motion was fast and exacting. And in one twisting motion, the bones in her neck snapped. The fragile and aged bones moved back and forth in a fast motion. Mrs Baeyer slumped into the couch, her fragile frame twitching with convulsions, before winding down like a child's toy running on dying batteries. The clown mask stood behind the couch, looking down at Mrs Baeyer, their head tilting.

The floor of the living room was now clear. The coffee table moved out of the way, to allow for further flooring. A large, single plastic sheet lay above the beige carpeted floor. Mrs Baeyer is deceased. She is laying face up on the plastic sheet, staring up at the ceiling. The television set is now switched off. It was like watching a scene from a horror movie. The image of the clown hovered above the Mrs Baeyer. The mask tilted left and right, a little, staring down at the deceased body. The large hunting knife appeared again. The blade itself slithered over the deceased body, starting at the gagged mouth, and down over the chest, past the stomach.

The sharp, jagged edges of the hunting knife were hard at work. It slid from left to right, left to right, and left to right, again, sliding back and forth, slicing and tearing at the thin, fragile flesh around Mrs Baeyer's neck. The hunting knife sliced through the flesh quite easily at first. The blood poured from the wound and out onto the plastic sheet beneath. The blade of the hunting knife continued to slide back and forth. The clown mask applied further pressure now until the blade sliced, reaching the base of the skull beneath. And what followed, can only be described as a horrifying noise. The base of the skull cracked, popping from the top of the spine. The clown mask stopped a moment, dropping the hunting knife onto the plastic sheet, on top of the blood.

The clown mask shifted the body, moving it some, propping it up, a little. It raised the body, into an almost sitting position, lifting from the armpits. The blood continued to pour, draining from the corpse. The hunting knife lay on top of the plastic sheeting, the blade itself stained in blood. The clown mask got themselves into position, wrapping their arms around Mrs Baeyer from behind, her chest and neck, slowly moving, like a coiling snake around 'its latest prey. And, with two of three fast and exacting twists, the base of the skull cracked further.

Mrs Baeyer was decapitated.

Chapter Eight...

The sun began to rise over Hillsboro for the start of another day. The trash was still collected at a little after six in the morning. The council truck turned and pulled into the neighbourhood, breaking the morning silence with all its stops and starts. The trash collectors ran along the side of the truck, collecting and disposing of the neighbourhood trash. An ambulance was parked out in the driveway of Mrs Baeyer's home. There were multiple squad cars parked outside the front yard, too. The squad cars parked in a single file, stretching, down the neighbourhood, a little. The scene itself drew the crowd of the local neighbours. And there was yellow police tape blocking off access to the front of the house.

Deputy Preston received a call from the station just after five-thirty this morning. The cell phone began to ring. *Ring. Ring. Ring.* The call woke him up. His right arm stretched across the bed, over to his nightstand and grabbed his cell phone.

"Hello?" he answered, just above a whisper.

"We have another one," Detective Quinn answered, flatly.

"Shit! Where?" Andrew answered, rubbing the sleep from his eyes.

Andrew climbed out of bed, kicking the bed cover back, some, and climbed to his feet. He splashed water on his face and put a brush through his hair, climbed into his uniform, and had just enough time to make himself a takeaway coffee, before finding himself behind the wheel of his truck, and making his way to 1430 Belmont Avenue, the home of one Mrs Dorothy Baeyer

The only access permitted inside the home were members of the Hillsboro Police Department, ambulance officers and the coroner. There were at least five, maybe six, junior officers patrolling the front of the yard, controlling the neighbourhood crowd now. The crowd was rife with whispers and speculation, gossip and hearsay. The family name *Harmon* bounced around the crowd.

Deputy Preston was already inside the house. He stood almost in the entrance to the front door, by the porch. The front door was wide open. The inside foyer was busy with police officers collecting evidence, one taking photographs from multiple angles. And there were some police officers, one, maybe two, who couldn't stomach the scene. They politely made their way out of the front of the house, passing the deputy on the way out, one holding their stomach, the other, covering their mouth. Deputy Preston eyed the officers as they made their way out onto the front porch.

"Take it easy, fellas. Go grab some fresh air," he said.

"Yes, sir," answered one officer.

Deputy Preston turned his head and made his way deeper inside the house. He walked past the foyer, and took the first left, into the living room. The living room was busy with other officers, other warm bodies, including Detective Quinn. He was in the far-right corner whispering to another officer. Deputy Preston surveyed the room, as he made his way in, watching carefully where he stood. The carpet on the floor was stained with blood. The plastic sheet was gone. A corpse, the decapitated body, of one Mrs Dorothy Baeyer, remained seated on the couch, facing the television set. The television set was still switched on, the volume down low.

The body of Mrs Dorothy Baeyer remained bound with duct tape at the ankles and wrists. The maxi dress she wore was soaked, stained in blood. Her head, which most officer's speculated, and couldn't confirm until the arrival of the coroner, sat next to the body on the couch. The head itself, was bound and the face covered by a clown mask. Deputy Preston could feel his stomach turn, a little.

Detective Quinn made eye contact with his deputy. He left the police officer he was chatting to and made his way across the living room, to meet with Deputy Preston, as he clutched a pen and notepad.

"This is it, huh?" Deputy Preston asked, just above a whisper.

"A local kid phoned it in this morning when he was delivering the newspaper. He must have peered through the living room window or something."

"Shit! Any idea who?"

"Not yet." Detective Quinn shook his head. "We will know more just as soon as we have investigated the scene. I want officers out front talking to the crowd. Someone must have seen something. Heard something."

"Yes, sir."

Deputy Preston left Detective Quinn to go over the living room and the remainder of the house with his officers, as he walked out the front of the house, and out onto the porch. Deputy Preston touched his stomach, feeling it do somersaults. He stepped out onto the porch and took a deep breath, his with his hands on his hips, tilting his head back a little. The morning air was crisp and a little cool. The crowd from the neighbourhood, standing on the opposite side of the yellow police tape, was growing in size.

"Shit!" Deputy Preston whispered again, under his breath.

His tall, hulking frame took one step forward, the weight on his right foot leaned into the wooden beams of the front porch, stretching, cracking a little.

The grass on the front yard was cold and covered in a dew from the night before. Deputy Preston was quick to walk across the lawn, shouting instructions at the junior officers to control the crowd. His eyes were now hidden behind his aviator sunglasses. The image only projecting a more authoritative image of himself to his subordinates. Deputy Preston soon reached the yellow police tape. Peter and Mike were standing on the other side of the tape, in the front row, just inches away from Deputy Preston. They watched the commotion play out.

"What are you doing here?" Deputy Preston asked, almost angrily, as he removed his sunglasses. "You shouldn't be here. If Detective—"

"Who is it?" Peter interrupted.

"You know I can't say."

"You've seen it again, haven't you?"

"What?"

"The mask." Peter could feel his heartbeat starting to race and his palms grew sweaty. It was the first time since Robert that he felt this way.

"There was a mask, yes," Deputy Preston answered, flatly.

"Who is doing this?" Peter asked concerned, as Mike watched the conversation between the two friends fold out. "He? She? What the fuck is going on?"

Deputy Preston shifted his eyes from Peter a moment and peered out at the rest of the crowd. A smile surfaced to his lips, a little, purely out of frustration, hoping that the rest of the crowd didn't overhear them speak. He turned his head quickly, back to Peter. "Go," he whispered. "Get out of here, Petey. Please."

"What?" Peter asked, searching his friend's eyes for some sort of answer, something he wasn't telling him.

"I don't want you seeing this."

"Let's get you out of here." Mike interrupted, putting his left arm around Peter's shoulder as if to steer him away from the scene.

Andrew and Mike made eye contact. It was as if they were eyeballing one another, sizing each other up, as if playing a game as to who knew Peter Harmon the best.

"You better listen to your boyfriend, here," said Deputy Preston. "Fuck you!" answered Mike, angrily, and just above a whisper.

"The two of you can compare dick sizes later!" answered Peter, almost distraught.

"Go!" Deputy Preston said, again. "I will call you later when I know more."

"I have lived through this, remember? A mutilated body found inside a house. A weapon of choice is usually a hunting a knife. And a mask. A creepy looking clown mask. Am I close?"

Andrew almost charged at Peter, stepping in closer toward his friend, the police tape holding them apart, as his chest flared forward.

"It's good to have you home, Petey, it is. But, please, let me do my job. I'll call you later. I promise."

"Of course," Peter answered, staring at his friend.

Mike stepped in. His left arm extended and rested on Peter's shoulder, again. He steered him away from the front of the house, and through the crowd, and past the local hangers-on, all wanting to see what happened and any evidence of some gruesome crime scene. Peter and Mike got several looks from the crowd, nothing more.

"Not again." Deputy Preston muttered to himself as he stood there, watching on, seeing his best friend disappear into the crowd of on-lookers.

"Sir, you need to look at this." A junior officer interrupted Deputy Preston.

Her words brought him back to reality. He blinked his eyes several times and looked in her direction.

"What is it, officer?"

Deputy Preston followed the female officer back up to the house, onto the porch, and into the living room. The coroner had arrived. The living room was alive with the investigation. Detective Quinn stood in the corner of the living room, again, near the entrance to the kitchen, speaking with the coroner.

"I don't want my men and women here as long as they need to be here." Detective Quinn told the coroner. "And most importantly, Dorothy Baeyer I want her taken to the morgue as soon as humanly possible. No one deserves this, not even Dorothy."

"Yes, sir. I'll have this tied up shortly."

"Get to work."

The coroner was somewhere in his early fifties. He was a short and stocky man. His black hair was greying at the temples and thinning on top. He was almost clean-shaven, although there was a growth of almost three days stubble. The coroner sported grey trousers and black shoes, a white, long-sleeved business shirt, which he wore open buttoned, without a tie, which hugged his portly belly, and a navy-blue jacket with the word 'Coroner' written on his back in bright yellow lettering. His hands were covered with blue disposable rubber gloves.

A police officer was still taking photographs, on direction from the coroner. They whispered amongst themselves, and the coroner pointed to Dorothy Baeyer, and various points around the living room. One of the junior officers was unable to stomach the sight or the smells any longer, and raced from the living room, through the kitchen and out the back door, into the yard to vomit.

"Go and check on him," Deputy Preston told another junior officer, "make sure he is okay."

"Yes, Deputy," answered the officer.

Andrew watched the junior officer take off after the one in the back yard. His eyes diverted back to the crime scene. He watched on as two ambulance officers were careful to remove Dorothy Baeyer from the couch and place her onto a stretcher that was waiting for her nearby. A white bedsheet was quick to cover her up and hide her identity from prying onlookers outside. Her head was removed from the crime scene separately. And secured.

Deputy Preston made his way across the living room, meeting Detective Quinn in the corner, by the kitchen. The two made eye contact.

"What are you thinking?" Deputy Preston asked, just above a whisper.

"It's the same MO," Detective Quinn answered, flatly. "The same person. It's not like they just kill their victims, that would be too easy."

"They are making a point. Putting them on display. Showing dominance." Detective Quinn turned his head a little to the left, looking at the deputy.

"You're right."

"A hunting knife was used," Deputy Preston continued. "You can see by the lacerations around the neck. The flesh is not finely sliced. Someone hacked at Mrs Baeyer violently, with hatred, and they enjoyed it."

"Fuck!" Detective Quinn whispered frustratedly under his breath, as if not to draw attention. "I want Peter Harmon in the interrogation room within the hour."

"Yes, sir."

Deputy Preston was now sitting behind the wheel of his truck. He sat there quietly a moment, watching the junior officers hard at work, controlling and removing the crowds that awaited outside. He was alone. And frustrated. Andrew tightened the grip he had around his steering wheel, shaking at it violently, screaming.

"Fucking Petey!" he shouted, frustrated.

Andrew looked down at the front passenger seat. His cell phone was sitting there, face up. He grabbed and dialled a number, waiting patiently for the call to connect. The engine to the truck ignited. Andrew was careful to make his out from the side of the curb and into traffic, past the on- lookers, standing on the side of the road. Andrew drove his truck slowly to the end of the road, before switching on his indicator, and turning right.

The morning progressed. Deputy Preston was now behind the wheel of a standard-issue squad car. The weather looked bleak outside. The clouds were showing a shade of grey, with a hint of rain. Peter sat in the back seat of the squad car, silent. He was looking out at the world passing him by. Andrew was busy concentrating on the traffic in front of him.

"Take him round back," a male voice over the radio said, breaking the silence.

"Yes, sir," Andrew answered, picking up the radio.

"Take him around back and avoid the crowds. It's a circus," the voice repeated.

The squad car was reaching the Hillsboro Police Station. There was more than a handful of representatives of the local media, both newspaper and television, standing out front, ready to pounce with their questions. Peter watched the crowd a moment, before looking forward and catching his friend's eyes looking back at him from the rear-view mirror. The cameras from the media outside the police station began to flash wildly. The two friend's eyes met. Andrew had sympathy for his best friend. A hint of a smile surfaced to his lips.

"You got this, buddy," Andrew whispered under his breath. Peter remained silent.

The squad car made its way past the media frenzy and pulled into the car park behind the police station. The engine soon died.

"Are you ready for this?" Andrew asked his friend.

"Do I have a choice?" Peter answered, quietly. "Let's go."

Deputy Preston rocked his hulking frame in the driver's seat of the squad car. He opened the side door and climbed out. He walked the side of the vehicle and opened the door for his friend. He stood there, watching Peter climb out of the squad car. The door slammed shut behind him.

"I have nothing to hide," Peter whispered, staring at his friend. "Let's do this."

Peter Harmon lead the way. He made his way from the squad car and inside the police station, as his friend and deputy of the town, followed on. Neon lights were hanging from the ceiling inside the police station, and other officers were looking on, shooting Peter *that's him* looks, as if he were the catch of the day. Peter walked quietly and confidently. Deputy Preston was walking behind him, making eye contact with his friends and colleagues. Two other junior officers were walking behind Deputy Preston.

The media were camped outside the front of the police station. The crowd was growing. The front doors to the police station pushed open. And, there, on display, almost, was Detective Quinn. He was dressed in another grey suit, neatly dressed in a white business shirt and navy-blue tie, and black loafers. He walked with confidence, toward the awaiting podium with microphone, and awaiting audience, with members of the media. Detective Quinn adjusted the microphone a little. The light bulbs from the cameras began to flash wildly and in quick succession. Deputy Preston was on duty, there to help calm the audience, some. It didn't work, not much.

"Is this thing switched on?" Detective Quinn asked, tapping on the head of the microphone.

A rather disturbing echo bounced around the front of the police station, leaving members of the audience feeling dishevelled. It was quick to quieten the members of the media. Deputy Preston watched on in silence, his eyes hidden behind his aviator sunglasses.

"The Hillsboro Police Department can confirm that a body was found earlier this morning. I can confirm the identity of the deceased, was one Mrs Dorothy Baeyer. She was eighty-three years old, and lived alone." The members of the media were listening on, intently. "With the recent activities in this town, first the finding of Jayne Doe, Dorothy Baeyer, and an attack on our very own, Deputy Andrew Preston, I am now calling for a city-wide curfew, starting at nine this evening. The police department is actively looking into all angles. No one is ruled out. There will be no further questions at this time."

The media went into another frenzy. The light bulbs began to flash, again. There was a sea of microphones, all of them moving, jolting forward, in front of the detective, the reporters asking their questions, one over the other. Detective Quinn left the podium and walked back into the station, Deputy Preston followed. The junior officers were left behind to calm and disperse the crowd safely.

The door leading into the interrogation room was pushed open, almost wildly. The two junior officers that sat opposite Peter Harmon, keeping him company, turned and watched the detective and the deputy enter the room. Detective Quinn's arms were wrapped around multiple manila files, all with Peter's name on it, held close to his chest.

"You're excused. Both of you." Detective Quinn said, just above a whisper as he entered the room. The manila files were dropped onto the surface of the desk.

"Yes, sir," answered the junior officers in almost unison.

The two junior officers got up from their chairs and left the room, with one of them closing the door behind them. Deputy Preston watched them leave. Detective Quinn took to the first empty seat. He sat down and dragged it closer toward the table, making himself comfortable. His attention was on the manila files, sorting them into a neater mess. Deputy Preston grabbed the seat next to the detective, sitting opposite his best friend.

"I have a serial killer on the loose in this town with no fucking clue who is behind this," Detective Quinn started. His tone of voice was fragile, almost ready to snap at a moment's notice.

"A serial killer is incorrect," Peter answered, just above a whisper. The response grabbed the police officer's attention.

"By definition alone," Peter continued, "a person would need to rack up at least three bodies. By the last count, you only have two."

"Don't play smart with me, Peter," answered Detective Quinn. Andrew continued, looking at his friend, intrigued.

"I need an answer to this, all of this." Detective Quinn continued. "And I think you can help me with this."

"I have lived through this, remember?" Peter answered. "And if you think I offed Mrs Baeyer, then you're incorrect. I didn't know her from a bar of soap. Yes, I ran into her a few days ago when I arrived in town. But that's it. That's where the similarities end. We exchanged words. Granted, hers were a little more heated than mine. But the last time I checked, being subjected to an old lady screaming at a stranger is not a criminal offence."

A pause fell over the interrogation room. All eyes were on Peter Harmon. "Let's cut the shit, shall we?" Peter continued.

"What are you saying right now, Peter?" Deputy Preston asked, his eyes looking at his best friend. "If there is a copycat killer out there, patterning themselves off my… mother, off my family, then it is someone local. Someone who knows their history. They have a love of the macabre. They know their way around a knife. A butcher's knife. A hunting knife. Look there. Someone is hiding in plain sight. Review your photographs. If the killer is loving every moment, then you'll find them there. They should appear at every crime scene, right? Taking it in and enjoying every moment." Peter diverted his eyes back to Detective Quinn.

"That is all I have got. So, until you find me standing over a dead body with a knife in one hand and a mask on my head, I gather I am still a free man, am I right?"

"Yes," Deputy Preston answered, clearing his throat a little.

Peter stood up from behind the table. Detective Quinn kept his eyes on Peter.

"The next time you drag me down here, Detective, I advise you better have proof. Otherwise, you'd better lawyer up. You're going to need it. Two strikes and one more, you're out."

Detective Quinn sat there, quietly, a moment, feeling angry and embarrassed.

"Deputy Preston, make sure an officer gives Peter Harmon a ride home. If we have any further questions, we will be in contact."

"Yes, sir."

Peter was the first to walk out of the interrogation room. Deputy Preston stood up from his chair, making eye contact with Detective Quinn. No words were exchanged. Detective Quinn remained seated, looking through the manila files.

The morning progressed into the early hours of the afternoon. Peter was in his sports utility vehicle. He pulled into a gravel car park, just outside a small, rustic cafe, just outside the heart of Hillsboro. It was about a twenty-minute drive north. The local stores nearby had already had their homemade curfew signs made up and hanging in the front windows. *Closing at 9.00 p.m.!* the signs read. *Curfew.* The engine to the sports utility vehicle died. Peter pushed the side door open and climbed out. He stood there a moment, taking in the sights of the cafe, stretching his legs, and looking at the other cars parked close by. The driver's side door slammed shut. Peter walked towards the cafe, as he pressed the button on the clicker, locking the alarm on the car.

Peter walked in through the front door of the cafe. It was rather busy. It was filled with patrons, all eating and talking amongst himself. For a moment, it reminded him of Riley's in New York City. Just for a moment. Peter could see Emily sitting alone, out on the balcony. She was sitting there in a simple white blouse and blue jeans. A single glass of champagne sat in front of her. The glass was a little less than half full, already. Emily stood from her chair and waved at Peter as if flagging him down. The two friends connected eyes and smiled and waved at each other. Peter made his way out onto the balcony and took to his seat opposite Emily.

"Hello," said Emily, happy to see her high school friend, "how was the traffic?"

"Not too bad." Peter nodded, a little, "I'm so happy to see you. After the morning, I've had."

"Oh, really?" Emily asked, playing dumb. She knew. Andrew had told her everything.

"Fucking Detective Quinn. Apparently, he doesn't have a clue and I'm his poster child." Peter shrugged his shoulders. "I'm hungry. What's good here?"

Peter grabbed one of the menus that stood tall in the middle of the table, squashed between the salt and pepper shakers. His eyes perused it for a moment.

It took a few minutes, but a waiter, somewhere in his early thirties, approached the table. He wore blue jeans and simple black, short-sleeved cotton t-shirt with the name of the cafe in fine embroidery on the top right of the chest and in large print on the back. The waiter was bearded, muscular, and wore white tennis shoes. Emily was immediately drawn to the waiter. The two shared a smile.

"Good afternoon," said the waiter, as if introducing himself. "Welcome to The Wild Bird Cafe. How can I help you today?"

"I'll have my usual." Emily smiled. "This place does the best Cesar salad," she said to Peter. Peter was still eyeballing the menu.

"Um," he said, just above a whisper, trying to finalise his order, "I'll take the pulled pork sandwich and fries."

"Excellent choice." The waiter smiled. "And drinks?"

"A soda is fine. Thank you," answered Peter.

"I'm good. Thank you," answered Emily.

"Certainly. Your orders will be out shortly."

The waiter cleared the menus from the table and disappeared inside the cafe, leaving the two to themselves.

Emily eyeballed the waiter as he left. She was quick to re-focus her attention back on her friend.

"You were saying," she continued, "Detective Quinn?"

"Yes," Peter answered, just above a whisper, so not to draw too much attention. "Clueless. Fucking clueless."

"Don't worry about him. You're safe. That's the most important thing." "I'm just tired of the bullshit. The stares."

"Well, I'll tell you. The food here is to die." Peter looked at his friend, Emily.

"I can't believe you," he whispered again. Emily was taken aback, a little.

"You grew up so beautiful since high school."

"I know," she laughed, jokingly.

Peter looked around the cafe, taking in a view of the place as if surveying the property and its patrons.

"I have never been here before. It must have opened whilst I was in New York."

"It's been around for a good four or five years, now," she nodded. "I come here once a month. It's nice to get out of the house and away from the town square. I feel like some of the local people stare and gossip, you know?"

Peter smiled.

"When I was living in New York, I would go to a shooting range once a month."

"Really?" Emily asked, inquisitive.

"With everything that happened over the years, I like to keep trained."

"There are a few people in this town whose brains I wouldn't mind blowing out. Jayne for one." Emily laughed, as she took a sip from her champagne.

Peter looked at her friend quietly, with a hint of a smile.

The waiter appeared through the door leading out onto the balcony, with Emily and Peter's food orders. He bussed them to the table rather quickly.

The night fell upon Hillsboro. It began to rain, again. The winter season was growing closer and closer by the day. The weather was beginning to worsen. Peter was at home for the evening.

The lights in the living room were switched on. The volume on the television set was on low. Mike was spending the night. He was dressed casually and relaxed for the evening, in a simple white cotton t-shirt which hugged his frame well, and a pair of navy-blue boxer shorts. He was sporting his reading glasses, as he had his head buried in a paperback novel. He was in a world of his own. The cell phone on the coffee table began to ring. *Ring. Ring. Ring.* It grabbed Peter's attention. And Mike's. Mike lifted his head off his novel and looked at Peter.

"I'll get it," Peter answered, just above a whisper, as he leaned forward off the couch and grabbed the cell phone.

"Hello," he answered, as he stood from the couch.

"Welcome home, Peter," answered the familiar, dark voice. It was the clown mask. "Are you enjoying the show?"

Peter walked across the living room. He turned and faced Mike. He was consumed with his novel. Peter left the living room and walked down the hallway, toward the back of the house, switching on the lights as he made his way through the house.

"What do you want?" Peter whispered angrily.

"You've been home less than a week and already there is a body count," the voice laughed. "I told you I wanted to play a game. I'm so close I could reach out and cut you. It's delicious."

"What do you want?" Peter repeated, being a more annoyed version of himself than before.

"A young, innocent girl had to die to get your attention. And now local busybody, Mrs Baeyer. Mrs. Baeyer? What the fuck? She was an old busy body who *deserved* to die. This town won't miss her. In fact, I bet the people of this town are glad she's dead. I told you I wanted to play a game. They were—"

"You piece of shit!" Peter interrupted. "You're nothing more than a D-grade, Walmart straight-to- video version release on this town. Do you think you're a copycat? Do you think your special? That you knew my mother? That you know me? You're shit! You're no one. You're nothing."

"Be very careful, Peter. You can't save everyone. All you can do is watch! Enjoy the game." The phone line disconnected.

Peter retraced his steps, down the hallway and back into the living room to check on Mike. He was there. Still sitting on the couch with his head buried in his paperback novel. "You okay? Who was that?" Mike asked as he looked up.

"Fine," Peter answered, just above a whisper.

The same little sneakers, navy blue in colour, with white rubber tops with double-bowed laces, began to run down a wooden staircase, in the cellar of a house, somewhere. The light in the room was dim at best. The sneakers reached the bottom of the staircase. A young boy's hand reached out and touched the bottom of the banister. It's Peter. He is no older than eight, give or take. He turns left to see a single light bulb, exposed and hanging from the ceiling. The light bulb is switched on. And, there, in front of him, were Grandfather and Mother. They had their back's turned to Peter, for a moment. Grandfather was the first one to turn around. He turned his head and looked down.

"What do you want, kid?" Grandfather shouted.

Peter looked on shocked and horrified. He was nervous and could feel his heartbeat racing, ready, at a moment's notice, to pee his pants.

Grandfather stepped aside, a little. Peter could see another young boy, just a few inches beyond him. He was dressed simply in a pair of green shorts and sneakers. The same sneakers. The young boy's chest was naked and exposed and was tied to the wooden chair, bound and gagged. A white cotton cloth had been torn into strips and was tied tightly around his mouth, to keep him from making too much noise. There were tears in the boy's eyes. Peter took a step closer from the bottom of the banister. The young boy was Peter, himself. Grandfather stood there in faded denim jeans and a wife beater, barefoot and his faded, leather belt doubled over on itself, used as a strap, and ready to flog. Peter continued to cry. The tears welled in his eyes as he now peed himself. The urine ran from his pants and down both legs, dripping onto the dirt floor, beneath, turning to urine-stench mud. Peter's mother stood next to her father, watching it all play out. She held her son's t-shirt tightly in her hands, as she twisted it, further and further.

"No one likes a bed wetter!" Grandfather screamed.

The mother giggled a little, covering her mouth with both hands.

Grandfather gripped his leather belt tightly, raising it high above his shoulder in his right hand. It came down with such anger, hitting Peter on his left shoulder and back. The leather belt was quick to leave welts.

The flesh itself, tore, causing the wound to bleed. Peter opened his mouth in shock and horror as his eyes were quick to well with tears. His back felt like it was on fire. He was ready to scream.

The curtains in the bedroom were almost pulled to a close. Peter awoke from another nightmare. He was gasping for air as he clutched his chest tightly. His body was shaking and drenched in a cold sweat. Peter was struggling to breathe. He lay on the bed, staring up at the ceiling, a moment, before turning on his side, a little. Mike was fast asleep, snoring away, some, undisturbed.

Peter pushed back the bed cover, some. He climbed to the side of the bed. His feet felt so cool and relaxing to the touch on the bedroom floor as his toes wiggled, a little. Peter was dressed in just a pair of black cotton boxer shorts. He tiptoed out of the bedroom, careful not to make too much noise, and walked down the hallway, down the staircase and into the kitchen. The light in the kitchen flickered on, as he made his way towards the refrigerator. The door pulled open and he leaned in to inspect the contents. Peter grabbed the carton of orange juice. He opened the carton and took a deep sip. The juice cooled his throat.

"What are you doing up so late?" asked Mike, just above a whisper.

Peter was startled. He swallowed the juice in his mouth and placed the carton back in the refrigerator, closing the door. He turned around to see Mike standing in the entrance to the kitchen, just off the hallway from the foyer. He was naked. Peter could see the scar Mike got at the age of twenty when he had his appendix removed.

"I couldn't sleep," Peter answered, just above a whisper.

"What's wrong?" Mike walked into the kitchen, towards Peter. "Maybe this town is right."

"What do you mean?"

"I mean, maybe I shouldn't have returned."

"No!" Mike answered, sternly, raising his voice a little. "Don't listen to them." He shook his head.

"That poor, innocent girl. The attack on Andrew. And now, Mrs Baeyer."

"Don't listen to those people. You are just as much a part of this town as they are, more so. Never give them the satisfaction. Stay and fight. Stay for yourself. Stay for... me."

Peter stared at Mike a moment before a smile surfaced to his lips. Mike returned the smile and leaned in and gave him a strong hug.

Peter and Mike returned to the bedroom. Mike lead the way, taking Peter by the hand. The lights in the house switched off as they walked towards the bedroom. Peter was the first to climb into bed. He pulled the bed cover up, over his shoulders, but not before checking his cell phone on the nightstand. There was a missed text message from Andrew. It remained unread, until the morning, anyway.

Chapter Nine…

The alarm on Peter's cell phone began to chime. It was five-thirty in the morning. Peter awoke and rubbed the sleep from his eyes, some. He turned over in the bed and saw Mike lying next to him, fast asleep. Peter turned his back to Mike and reached out for his cell phone on the nightstand, and switched the alarm off. Peter turned and faced Mike, again. He was still asleep. The unanswered text message from Andrew was still waiting for him. It came in eight hours ago. Peter rubbed his eyes, again, before navigating to his text message history and opened the message.

We need to talk. When can I see you again?

The message read.

I'll be at the gym at six o'clock.

Peter typed and hit the send button.

Peter climbed out of bed and tiptoed across the bedroom floor, again, careful not to wake Mike. He got himself dressed and pulled on a pair of sweat pants, sneakers, and a navy-blue t-shirt and matching hoodie. Peter zipped the hoodie, up over his chest, before he made his way out of the bedroom, looking over his shoulder, one last time, watching Mike sleep. He walked down the hallway, down the staircase, and into the kitchen to make a cup of coffee before making his way to the gymnasium. Peter grabbed his wallet and keys in the bowl by the front door and made his way to his sports utility vehicle. The front door closed behind him.

It was chilly this morning. The front yard was covered in dew as the fog rolled in. Peter made it to his car, climbed in, and slammed the driver's side door closed, before reaching for his cell phone. He navigated to his text history.

I'm just heading to the gym. I'll see you when I get home.

Peter typed and hit the send button, sending the message to Mike.

Mike was lying in bed. He had turned now, facing his side of the nightstand. The bed cover had peeled back a little, exposing his muscular, hairy biceps and chest. His cell phone was in the pocket of his denim jeans he wore the day before. He left his charger at home. His cell phone vibrated, one message received. Mike continued to sleep.

The engine of the sports utility vehicle came to life. Peter looked in the rear-view mirror and quickly over his shoulder, checking for clearance. The street was quiet this morning. The sports utility vehicle crept out from the driveway and out into the traffic, before increasing in speed, making its way to the end of the road, stopping at the street sign before taking a right.

It didn't take fifteen minutes before Peter pulled into the car park of the local gymnasium. Andrew had already arrived. He sat behind his steering wheel and kept himself warm, as the radio quietly played in the background. Peter pulled his sports utility vehicle in next to Andrew. The engine was rattling as the two friends turned and looked at each other. The engine quickly died, and Peter grabbed his personal belongings from the front passenger seat and climbed out of his car.

Andrew was next to climb out of his truck. He also grabbed his personal belongings, a small sports bag, and shift his hulking frame from the seat of the truck. He stood tall and slammed the door shut. He stood there, looking back at his friend in grey sweat pants and white cotton sweatshirt. His grey hoodie was unzipped, exposing his muscular chest beneath.

"Good morning," said Andrew.

"Morning," replied Peter. "How are you doing?"

"I could say the same thing." Andrew was the first to smile.

"You're the one who invited me to the gym. I'm gonna whip your ass." "You think you can, huh?" Peter laughed.

"I know I can." Andrew laughed in return, flexing his muscles a little.

The two friends walked from their vehicles and made their way inside. They shared a laugh and talked amongst themselves.

The gymnasium was busy this morning, filled with 'its regular clientele, all of whom were looking to maintain a healthy lifestyle and bulk up. The door to the men's changing room pushed open. Andrew lead the way. The walls were brick with a thin coat of white paint. The lockers were navy green in colour, with rows of wooden benches in front of them, and neon lights which hung from the ceiling. Peter was given locker number 1428, and Andrew, 1436. The two friends sat opposite each other, after opening their lockers. They opened their sports bags and changed into their gear. It was the first time they had seen each other partially naked since high school. Peter changed into a pair of navy-blue shorts with a white, cotton tank top Andrew, grey shorts, with black, cotton tank top.

"This is new," Peter said, noticing a tattoo on Andrew's right bicep.

"No," Andrew answered, looking down at the tattoo, itself. "Not really. I got it coming up on two years now."

The tattoo was of a ripped flesh design, with what looked like fur and bear claws escaping underneath.

"Looks good."

"Thanks."

Andrew turned his back on his friend a moment, and slammed his locker door shut. He turned, again. His shoulders appeared more relaxed as if they slumped down, as if a weight had been lifted from his shoulders. Andrew was avoiding making eye contact, and staring at his sneakers.

"Listen." Andrew started. "I got to tell you something."

"What?" Peter answered, a little surprised.

"This story is blowing up. It's like a wildfire. It's gone everywhere. The media has picked it up and are running with it. 'A local serial killer haunts the small country town' angle."

Peter looked at his friend, a moment as concern fell over him. "You don't think I don't know this, already?"

"This is not your high school buddy telling you some urban legend. This is your local deputy telling you this story is serious. *This* is serious! There is a killer out there patterning themselves after your mother and grandfather."

Peter was quiet, again. Angry and a little embarrassed. He looked over his shoulder a moment, hoping no one had overheard the conversation.

"It's like déjà vu, you know? The police. The media. The murders. How long is curfew in place?" "Until next weekend, at the very least."

"Quinn?"

"Uh-huh." Andrew nodded.

"So, who is behind this?"

"Your guess is as good as mine." Andrew shrugged. "Quinn says he has some suspects. But, from now on, wherever you'll be, I'll be. I'll be your PD protection." Andrew chuckled a little.

Peter continued to look concerned. "What?" Andrew asked, a little confused.

"You said yourself, this is serious. You've already got hurt once. I'd hate to see it happen again. Or worse."

"Petey," Andrew smiled. "We got this. We do. You just have to ride it out. I'll be here to the end credits. Promise. We will catch this guy, this girl, whoever!" Andrew smiled.

"This isn't a movie. It's life. Period."

Peter forced a smile. He turned and slammed his locker door shut. "Now, let's get sweaty!" Andrew chuckled, more half-heartedly.

The two friends walked out of the men's change room, each carrying a fresh, white, cotton towel.

There was always a cross selection of people, all going about their own business, using the equipment. There were the local high school athletes, office workers before they started their day, and strong men. The kind with the ripped muscles, six-pack, and hairy chests who wore tank tops and shorts. They listened to their music from their headphones and took private selfies in the gymnasium mirrors for social media posts. A progression picture. Or a thirst trap for one of their many social media followers.

Andrew and Peter made their way across the floor of the gymnasium and over to the punching bags by the boxing ring. Peter was spotting Andrew. The boxing ring was being used by a muscle strong man and his trainer. Andrew strapped on the boxing gloves before throwing punches and jabs, as Peter stood behind the bag, his face partially hidden behind the red leather bag.

"Don't forget to breathe," Peter said, from behind the bag.

Andrew punched at the bag harder and faster, and wilder until he was exhausted, dripping with sweat and ready to collapse. Peter held the punching bag in place, as much as he could, anyway. Andrew broke down. He pulled at the boxing gloves and threw them on the ground. The gloves bounced a little.

"I'll breathe when they catch the killer. But, until then..." Andrew whispered, out of breath, and taking one last punch with his bare fists. "Fuck!"

The hour in the gymnasium seemed to pass by so quickly. Peter was in the men's change room, again. He was alone, standing in front of his assigned locker. The door was open as he stood there, with a towel wrapped loosely around his waist. Peter was getting dressed, back into the clothes he wore, leaving his house. Peter sat in front of his open locker on the bench, slipping on his sneakers when he paused a moment. He lifted his head a little, to the ceiling. Peter was listening carefully, for anything, for anyone. Something. There was nothing. A strange noise so early in the morning could have been anything. Peter shrugged his shoulders and carried on getting dressed. He stood up, picked up his sports bag and other personal belongings, before slamming the locker door shut, one last time.

Andrew was in the shower block. He walked along the tiled floor, his clothes damp from his workout, which clung to his hulking frame. His towel hung over his right shoulder as he made his way to a vacant cubicle. He pushed the door open and peered inside before making his way in. The door leading into the shower cubicle was painted navy green, just like the lockers. Andrew hung his towel on the hook on the back of the door and pulled at his clothes, quickly stripping. He turned and faced the shower. A slow drop of water dripped from the shower head. Andrew noticed. *Drip. Drip.*

Drip. He stared at it a moment, before he shook his head and stepped under the shower.

The water in the shower started to run. Andrew turned his back on the water. It felt so good against his back. Warm. He tilted his head back a little and closed his eyes. Andrew grabbed the bottle of liquid soap, catching it in his hands, and spread it across his hulking chest. The soap reached his stomach, his arms, all over.

The morning had progressed. The dew on the front lawn and the fog was beginning to burn off. The sports utility vehicle pulled up outside the front of the house. Peter was home. The engine died. Peter turned in his seat, a little, and reached for his personal belongings before climbing out of the truck. He peered through the front passenger window and looked up at the house. It looked the same. The street was coming to life now, too. A local neighbour taking their golden retriever for a walk. The dog, itself, walked alongside its owner, holding the purple lead in its mouth. The golden retriever was well behaved. Peter grabbed his personal belongings from the front passenger seat before climbing out of his truck and slamming the door to a close behind him. He ran up towards the house, onto the porch and through the front door.

"Hello?" Peter called out, as he stood in the foyer, closing the front door behind him.

There was no response. There was, however, the sound of the television coming from the living room. The volume was on medium. It was the morning news.

Peter walked deeper inside the house. He walked down the hallway, passing the living room. There was no one there. He saw the television and continued to walk on towards the kitchen. Mike was in the kitchen. He was busying himself with making breakfast. Mike was dressed in the same clothes from the day before but looked as though he already had a shower. His hair was wet and slicked back a little, with a comb.

"Good morning," Mike said, as a smile surfaced to his lips as he turned around. "How was the gym?"

"Great. Busy." Peter answered, with the same smile. "The kitchen smells great.

"I hope you don't mind."

"Not at all. I'm starving."

"Great. Grab a seat. Breakfast will be ready shortly."

Peter walked over to the small dining table by the kitchen and watched Mike hard at work. "Since you hit the gym this morning, I thought I would make a breakfast of champions. We have some bacon, scrambled eggs, toast, juice."

"It sounds perfect." Peter smiled.

Mike walked out of the kitchen, holding two plates, one in each hand. Each plate served a breakfast of champions. The only difference was that Mike's breakfast came with mushrooms. Peter hated mushrooms. He stored them, just in case of an emergency, such as this. The kitchen table was already set. There were knives and forks, condiments, glasses of orange juice and cups of coffee.

Mike served Peter first.

"Thank you," Peter answered. "Dig in!"

Mike sat opposite Peter at the table. He looked at him and smiled. "It's good to have you home. What have you got planned for today?"

"I have a few things I thought I would follow up on," Peter answered, as he started in on slicing his bacon into smaller, bite-size pieces. "You?"

"Work," Mike answered. "I'll be in the store until around midday. I thought maybe, after, if you are free, we catch a movie tonight before curfew, what do you say?"

"That sounds great. I'd like that."

"Me, too." Mike smiled, again. "I'll pick you up after work?"

"Great."

The morning progressed. The fog had burned off now as the sun was out, and the clouds raced across the sky. However, there was still a bit of a chill in the air. It was enough for Peter to wear his hoodie from the gym, earlier this morning, along with a pair of jeans, t-shirt and sneakers. Peter left the house and got inside his truck. Peter sat behind the steering wheel, in search of a radio station, looking for music he liked. He did. It was an early track from the boy band, New Kids on the Block. Peter had seen them play live in concert a few years back. The engine to the truck came to life. Peter looked in his rear-view mirror, again, and pulled into the traffic. The truck raced to the end of the street, before turning left.

Peter drove through Hillsboro. The music on the radio changed now. Peter didn't know who it was. It was just noise. These kids today. The sports utility vehicle raced the suburban streets, and hugged the mountainous roads, left and right, left and right, again, as it passed through the forest. Peter was mindful to stay to the local speed limit. He didn't want a ticket. It would be yet another reason for Detective Quinn to be sniffing around.

The sports utility vehicle finally arrived. Peter had been driving for close on half an hour now. The vehicle parked in front of a two-storey, weatherboard home. It looked so familiar. Peter turned a little, reaching across to the front passenger seat, grabbing his cell phone, and peering up at the house through the window. Peter could feel his heartbeat racing and his palms grow sweaty, again. He cleared his throat a little before climbing out of the truck. The driver's side door slammed shut. Peter stood there, in front of the house, in the empty road a moment, looking upwards, before making his way onto the curb. He had arrived, continuing to stare up at the house. Peter was standing outside what was once his grandfather's home. It was the first time in almost four years, since the sale of the house. It brought back so many memories. They all just seem to come flooding back. Peter caught his breath in his chest, a moment, before taking his first steps closer to the house.

The two-storey house had some minor renovations since it had sold, nothing special, mind you. There was a fresh coat of white paint and a newly, restored front porch. Peter swallowed hard. He recalled some of his childhood memories, again. They were nightmares. Peter rubbed his hands together roughly, a moment, and made his way up to the front porch, through the front gate. The front yard was neatly manicured and well maintained. He stood on the porch a moment and looked around, a little. There were three deck chairs on the porch and a small table in the middle. Peter stepped closer to the front door and knocked heavily on the door. *Knock. Knock. Knock.* There was no turning back now. Peter stood there a moment and could hear the sound of footsteps walking towards the front door.

The front door opened. And, there, standing on the opposite side of the wooden door with white paint and glass accents, was a young girl, no older than seventeen. She had long, stringy chocolate-brown hair. She was barefoot. That was one of the first things Peter had noticed, and the fact, that she appeared so incredibly shy and tepid, as she hid behind the door, only poking half her head from behind the door, and her left foot. The girl appeared to be wearing a long, flowing, flowery maxi dress. It was white with sunflowers printed in a piling heap towards the bottom of the dress as if a wind gust had picked them up and dropped them.

"Hey, there," the girl said, in an almost southern-twang accent, "can I help you?"

"Hey," Peter answered. "I used to live in this house." Peter took a gulp, whilst trying to remain confident.

"No foolin'?" the girl answered. "Did you want to come in and have a look around? My parents are home. They could show you."

The girl opened the front door further, exposing her full figure, and her flowery maxi dress. Peter looked past the young girl. The inside of the foyer of the home was different. The paint was removed. There was wallpaper, now. It was yellow with green vertical stripes and gold trim.

"I'm sorry," Peter answered. "I shouldn't impose. I have wasted your time. I'm so sorry about that." Peter took a step backwards, a little. The young girl noticed his shoes. A hint of a smile surfaced to her lips as if she were turned on by the man's fear.

"I know you," the girl continued. "You're that Harmon boy, aren't you? We found photographs in the cellar."

Peter felt his palms. They were sweaty, even more so. He turned his back on the girl and walked off the front porch, and into daylight, in the front yard.

"Well, if you change your mind. You know where I am."

The tone of the girl's voice began to change now, becoming almost evil, as she began to laugh uncontrollably. Peter ran to the gate in the front yard. He passed it and reached his truck, as his hands fumbled for his keys in his pocket.

Peter climbed inside his sports utility vehicle, slamming the door to a close behind him. The engine roared to life, once more. He placed his foot on the accelerator and raced to the end of the street. The window in the driver's door was down. The cool air helped calm his nerves as he raced to the end of the street. The music on the radio continued to play. It was just more noise.

The day continued. Peter was still behind the steering wheel of his truck. He drove around town. He first stopped at a local fast-food pick-up joint for a burger and a chocolate shake, before making his way towards familiar territory. A smile crept to the surface of his lips as he recalled the happier memories.

The sports utility vehicle pulled into the car park of the Hillsboro Cemetery. Peter finished his lunch and left the wrapper of the burger and the remains of the chocolate shake in the front passenger seat. He climbed out of his truck, setting the alarm as he walked the open, green fields. Peter had his cell phone, gripped tightly in his right hand for security. It was his go-to in nervous moments. His hoodie hugged his chest tight and kept him warm in the early afternoon cool breeze. Peter reached the burial plot. It took a little over five minutes to walk. A smile surfaced to his face, again. Peter leaned in and lowered to his knees, clearing some of the debris from the headstone. His fingers of his left hand ran over the lettering in the headstone. It brought back so many memories, feeling connected. His hand covered his father's first name, and there, in front of him, was his surname. *Harmon. Father. Husband. 2013.* Peter removed his left hand from his father's headstone and sat on the cool grass with his legs crossed, getting himself comfortable.

"I miss you, Dad." Peter started, clearing his throat, some. "I have moved back to Hillsboro and reconnected with my friends, and there is someone I'm seeing. It's new. We are finding our feet. But I don't know if me being here is a good thing." Peter paused a moment. "It's happening again. The murders. I wish I knew who Mum was and her connection with Grandfather. Why were they so secretive? Each time I think about them, I don't know…"

Peter slumped forward, lowering his head.

The morning had progressed into the early hours of the afternoon, and Peter found himself back at home after having driven around Hillsboro, with a series of childhood memories, all unfolding, which came flooding back. The time was just before two-thirty. The television set was switched on. It was nothing more than noise to fill the house as if to give the impression that there was more than just one person at home. An episode of *Bewitched* played. Peter made his way down the staircase. He was neatly dressed for his date with Mike. He wore a navy blue, three-quarter length jacket with a simple white t-shirt underneath, denim jeans and black boots. Peter's left hand slid almost effortlessly down the banister. There was a heavy knock at the door. *Knock. Knock.*

Peter looked up and saw the image of a large shadow through the frosted glass accents in the front door. He reached the bottom of the staircase, ducking into the living room, a moment, to switch off the television before answering the door.

The front door opened. And there, standing on the front porch, was Mike. Peter smiled. Mike had thought the same. He ducked home, showered and changed before the date. He stood there, on the front porch, casual, yet neat. He wore black jeans with matching boots and a classic, simple black t-shirt which promoted the sci-fi classic, *Star Wars*, in small, white type. On top of the t-shirt, he wore a simple cotton, long-sleeved white shirt, left unbuttoned and rolled up at the sleeves.

"You look great." Peter smiled.

"Really? In this?"

"Absolutely."

"Well, thank you. So, do you. Very distinguished. Very New York." Mike smiled. "Are you ready to go?"

"Sure. What did you have in mind?"

Peter grabbed his keys and wallet in the bowl by the front door. He walked out onto the front porch, before turning, closing and locking the front door behind him.

"There is a Wes Craven marathon playing at The Limited tonight. I thought, if you were up to it, of course, we could check out the original *A Nightmare on Elm Street.*"

"You like that, huh? All that blood, gore and horror?" Mike looked stunned.

"Relax," Peter laughed, as he extended his left hand out to calm Mike. "It's one of my favourite movies of all time. I haven't seen it in years. Thank you. I'd like that."

"Great. For a second there, I thought you were giving me a heart attack or something."

"No. Not at all."

Great. Let's go."

Mike waited for Peter, for a moment. He stood on the front porch and watched, making sure his date had everything he needed for the night. Peter checked his jacket pockets. House keys.

Wallet. Cell phone. Check. Mike lead the way, off the front porch, across the front yard, past the gate and out onto the curb, where his truck was waiting. Peter followed right behind. Mike was the first to reach the truck. He was quick to run around to the driver's side of the vehicle, unlock the door, climb in, and lean across to unlock the passenger door. Peter turned and looked up at the house, one last time, before climbing inside the truck. The door slammed shut. Mike already put on his seat belt and placed the key into the ignition. Peter adjusted the seat belt a little before pulling it over his chest.

"You good?" Mike asked, with a hint of a smile. "All good!" Peter smiled.

"Great! It's going to be a fun night. Well, afternoon." Mike laughed.

The truck pulled out from the curb and into traffic. It raced to the end of the street before turning right.

The Limited was a little busy for a weekday afternoon. With curfew and all, the residents of Hillsboro tried to fit in all their chores and daily activities before nine in the evening. Mike and Peter had queued for tickets, then walked over to the candy store to purchase a large popcorn to share and twin medium sodas. There were a few whispers from local teens and single mothers. Peter did his best to ignore all the *that's him* stares. Mike was a separate character, all together. He played the role of over-protective boyfriend to a T. Peter felt safe. For the first time in a very long while.

Peter and Mike walked out of the theatre as the credits began to roll. Peter hadn't felt so switched on after a horror movie in a long time. It still got to him, every time. He loved it. The time was coming on a little past six in the evening. The two walked over to a nearby diner and dined on burger and fries. It was quick and simple food, all before curfew.

The date was coming to an end for the evening. Mike gave Peter a lift home in his truck. The truck, itself, pulled up in front of Peter's home. The sun was beginning to set upon Hillsboro for another evening. The engine to the truck didn't die, exactly, but more a low rumble. Peter looked up at the house through the window, a moment, before returning his gaze upon Mike.

"So, traditionally, this is that awkward part of the date where one person asks the other if they want to come inside for a cup of coffee that will inevitably lead to sex, which will inevitably lead to that one sleeping over for the night. So, would you like to sleepover?" Peter asked, with hope in his voice.

Mike leaned in and kissed Peter on the lips, a moment. He pulled back, a little. A smile surfaced to his lips.

"As much as I would love to, and believe me, I would love that so much, I can't. Not tonight. I have an early start tomorrow."

"Of course." Peter nodded. "That's what they all say. I've heard that excuse before." Peter nodded, again.

"No. Seriously," Mike answered, his tone of voice dropped as worry fell upon his face. "I have a plumber coming round in the morning. He said he would be round between seven-thirty and eight, which means any time of the day. I am getting my laundry re-modelled. You should come over sometime and see."

"I'd like that."

"You would?"

"Of course."

"Okay, then. Tomorrow night."

Mike leaned in and kissed Peter, again. It lasted longer this time. "Goodnight," said Peter, just above a whisper.

"Goodnight," replied Mike, smiling a little.

Peter turned a little, undoing his seat belt, opened the door and climbed out onto the curb. He stood there a moment and turned round to face Mike, one last time for the evening, through the open window, as he closed the front passenger door behind him. The two made eye contact and smiled. Mike raised a hand and waved a little. Peter stood there and watched Mike, and his truck, pull out from the curb and race to the end of the street. He then turned and made his way across the front yard, up to the porch and the front door.

The lights in the house switched on as Peter made his way deeper and deeper inside the house. The wallet and the keys were placed in the bowl on the table by the front door. Peter made his way into the kitchen. The lights flickered on as he made his way toward the refrigerator. The door opened and Peter leaned in. He grabbed a bottle of beer, opened the twist top, and sat on top of the kitchen counter, as his legs dangled. Peter took off his three-quarter length jacket and dumped it on the counter, next to his bottle of beer, then searched for his cell phone in his trouser pocket. Peter pressed a button on the side of the cell phone. The screen came to life. There were two text messages, one from Emily and one from Andrew. Peter decided to read them in the morning. He grabbed his bottle of beer and slid off the kitchen counter, his boots and feet making a deep thud-like noise as his bulging, muscular frame hit the floor, before walking back into the hallway, taking a left, and walking to the front of the house, and making his way up to the top of the staircase. The lights in the house switched on in front of him and switched off behind him as he made his way through the house.

Peter made it to the end of the hallway on the second floor. He pushed open his bedroom door and switched on the light. The room was neatly made. The curtains were open. Peter made his way inside, switching on the lamp on his nightstand on his side of the bed, before turning around and switching off the ceiling light. Peter returned and placed his beer on the nightstand and his cell phone on the charger, before standing by the side of his bed, and slowly stripping naked, and climbing into bed for the evening, pulling the bed cover over the top of him, resting at his shoulders. The lamp on the nightstand switched off.

Chapter Ten...

The little navy-blue sneakers with the white rubber tops returned. It was Peter. He was breathing. There was heavy breathing. And in slow motion. It was like sitting back and watching a scene from a movie or TV show, as something dramatic, something horrifying was in the process of unfolding. Peter was in the back yard, again. The very same back yard where his birthday party had taken place. He was running out of the house, out into the open, out into the sunshine, and gaining speed.

The heavy breathing was becoming restricted now. The back yard was green and bare. The grass was neatly trimmed, as if it were mowed, just days ago. Peter raced out into the open, drawn to the far, right corner of the back yard. And there, in front of him, only metres away, were two adult bodies, standing, with their backs turned, their faces hidden.

"What is it?" a young Peter called out. "Can I see?" There was no response.

It was Grandfather and Mother. They stood there in the corner of the back yard, hunched forward, ever so slightly, looking down at the ground. Peter reached out to his mother and grandfather, as his left hand lifted, ready to tug at their clothing. Grandfather led the way. His torso shifted moving slightly. And, again, like watching a scene from a scary Hollywood movie. Grandfather moved fast. Very fast. It was as if sitting back and watching a movie or a nightmare on fast forward, the image breaking, pix-elating, in that brief moment. Then, all of a sudden, stops, returning to nothing more than their life.

Grandfather and Mother stood there, silent, as their faces hid behind clown masks. The masks looked like something they had made themselves. The base of the mask was stark-white. The eyes were painted a dark navy blue, with a touch of black. The painting itself was child-like. The lines were painted horizontal, across the mask, wildly outside the lines, from ear to ear, as if scratched on, scratching at the surface of the mask, itself. The nose and the lips were painted in the same design, crimson red in colour.

The sound of the restricted breathing began to ease now. Grandfather and Mother kept their faces hidden behind their masks, as they pulled large sticks from behind their backs. The sticks were thick and large with jagged, sharp edges. The end of the sticks were drenched in blood and dripping. Grandfather and Mother stepped apart as if to reveal some hidden secret. And there, in front of Peter, was a German Shepherd. It was huddled in the corner of the yard, in the foetal position up against the fence. The dog was scared, whimpering endlessly. She had been beaten and stabbed repeatedly with sticks. The German Shepherd was pregnant. Was. Her stomach sliced open, with 'its unborn young, exposed, bloodied, and dying. Mother was next to make a move. She handed the bloodied stick to Peter.

"Go on," Mother whispered, from behind the mask. "Give it ago. Make Mama proud."

Mother pulled at the mask, revealing her face beneath. Her hair was dishevelled, her eyes wide open with maniacal excitement.

Peter woke up screaming from his nightmare. His bare chest drenched in sweat. He clutched at his chest and the bed cover tightly. His grip loosened a little as his eyes floated around the room, staring up at the ceiling.

"Shit!" he whispered under his breath.

Peter tossed and turned in his bed until he reached for his cell phone on the nightstand. He clicked the button on the side and the screen came to life, again. The time was three fifty-five in the morning. There was now a third text message. One from Mike. Peter dropped the cell phone back on the nightstand, and collapsed onto the bed, staring at the ceiling, again. Peter raised his arms and used his left forearm to cover his face. Peter was terrified.

The minutes passed and Peter pushed back the bed cover with both feet, faster and faster until his body was exposed. The temperature quickly dropped. Peter felt cool in the early night air. He sat up and crawled to the side of the bed, before climbing to his feet and walked out of the bedroom, down the hallway a piece, until he reached the bathroom. The ceiling light flickered on. The bathroom door was pushed to a close. Peter walked toward the vanity. He leaned in and ran the faucet. The cold water was quick to run. Peter leaned in, again, cupping his hands together and catching the water. It splashed everywhere. Peter splashed the cold water on his face. His breathing became a little restricted, as he stood up and looked at his reflection in the mirror. The beads of water dripped from his face and down his chest.

"I hate this fucking shit!" he whispered to himself.

Peter turned on his reflection in the mirror and walked out of the bathroom. The scar on his back was visible. He walked across the white tiled floor, opened the door and switched off the bathroom light, before returning to bed and falling asleep once more.

The time was a little after six now. The fog had returned, again. So did the dew on the front lawn. Peter walked across the front lawn of his house until he reached the curb. He was dressed in grey sweat pants and matching hoodie, which was zipped high, to the neck to help stay warm, as much as possible, anyway. Peter plugged his headphones into each ear and switched on his iPod, ready to listen to his music collection. He stretched a little, before making a start on his morning run.

The neighbourhood was grey and damp this morning. The fog continued down, along the street. The clouds were heavy and grey and looked as though it was about to rain at a moment's notice. Peter held his breath in his chest as he ran, it became more and more restricted with each step taken. His sneakers were navy blue with white rubber tops and the laces double knotted. The cool morning air felt damp on the clothes and cool against the skin. Peter could feel the sweat on his forehead and feel it drip down his back, underneath his hoodie. He was reaching the stop sign at the end of another street, almost three miles from home, now. Peter was making good time. He had been out on the roads for almost half an hour now.

The street was empty. The roads were wet, and the front lawns were icy. The houses on the street were slowly waking up to another day. The glow of the lights from different windows, gave the street an almost Christmas feel to it. Peter had adjusted the zipper on his hoodie now. It had lowered a little, to cool his chest down, some. Peter reached the stop sign. He put his hands out in front of himself and tapped the silver pole. He stopped a moment, jumping up and down in one spot, so as not to lose his momentum and maintain his heartbeat. He looked around at the connecting streets, determining the next route to take. Peter looked left to right, then left to right again, and crossed the road, making his way down the hill. He took to the left side of the road, following a gravel pathway along the forest side of the hill.

Peter was in his own, little world, running and listening to his music. He kept to the side of the road, as a sports utility vehicle, black in colour, with blacked-out windows, appeared at the top of the hill. The indicator flicked on, indicating left. It turned on the street slowly, making 'its way down the hill, following Peter. The halogen lights switched on. The engine roared to life. The vehicle began to garner speed now, catching up to Peter. The sports utility vehicle swooped into the side of the road, just inches away from Peter. It caught him unaware. Peter was surprised and terrified. He clutched his chest as he ran, running further into the side of the road to escape the truck. Peter pulled his headphones from his ears as the music continued to play.

"What the fuck?" he turned and yelled at the driver. There was no response.

The sports utility vehicle pulled into the middle of the road, again, hugging the road markings. Peter stood there, still, staring, watching the truck, as he caught his breath.

"What the?" Peter muttered under his breath.

The sports utility vehicle turned around, after making a three-point turn, and started the incline up the mountainous hill. Peter continued to watch on. He looked for any sign of the driver's identity. Nothing. The windows were blacked out. There were no number plates. There were no distinguishing features. The sports utility vehicle continued to make its slow incline up the hill, and round the bend, out of sight. Peter continued to watch on. He shook his head, a moment, before concentrating on his run. He plugged his headphones back into his ears, dusted himself down, and continued with the run, down the hill.

Peter was finding his form, again. He was gaining speed in his run, concentrating on his breathing as the music continued to play in his headphones. The sports utility vehicle appeared, again. The halogen lights were switched off. It was on a slow cruise down the mountainous hill, moving in closer and closer, towards its prey, unnoticed. The speed of the vehicle increased now, pulling in closer and closer to the side of the road.

The sports utility vehicle accelerated again, before taking one final swoop on the side of the road. The sports utility vehicle raced past, knocking Peter forward, pushing him off the side of the road, into the gravel and the rest of the debris. Peter was tossed like a rag doll. He fell forward, grazing and cutting his hands and arms in the debris, hitting his head. Peter was unconscious. The sports utility vehicle sped off, down the winding hill, into the fog, and out of sight. Peter lay on the side of the road. His clothes were dirty. His flesh torn, exposed and bleeding.

The neon lights hung from the ceiling of Hillsboro County Hospital. They appear almost blurry and to shoot by in quick succession, one after the other. Peter was struggling to remain conscious. His eyes were rolling into the back of his head. An oxygen mask was strapped to his face. Peter tried to remove it, but it was his arms, they were just too weak. He was pushed down a hospital corridor, on top of a stretcher at a rather high speed. There were nurses on duty, stabilising the patient and recording vitals. The stretcher was being pushed by an ambulance officer whilst the other one on duty was re-calling the patient's vitals to the doctor on call.

Mike was the first to appear. He burst through the doors of the emergency room and ran down the hospital corridor at an almost break-neck speed. His eyes darted left to right in search of Peter. His heartbeat was racing, in almost near panic. Emily was sitting in the waiting room, just outside the emergency room with a celebrity gossip magazine folded over on her lap, just as she did with Andrew, not too long ago. The hospital corridor echoed, almost, with the sound of heavy, black leather boots running at a speed. Emily looked up from her magazine on her lap and watched the image of a hulking man run the corridor.

"Mike?" she called.

The hulking frame of the early fifty-something, was like that of aeroplane touching down on the tarmac after landing. His feet almost buckled from underneath him as his heavy frame was finding its way to slow down.

"What?" Mike answered, a little out of breath. "I got a call about Peter Harmon. What is going on here?"

Emily looked at Mike with sympathy in her eyes. She forced a smile as she walked toward the hulking man. He was sweating and out of breath, a little. She reached out and took his hands in hers.

"Peter is being seen at the moment. He's fine. A few scratches and some stitches, but he will pull through. Come, sit down with me." There was that smile, again.

"I'm sorry. I don't know… Who are you?"

"I'm Emily Olsen. A friend of Peter's. We went to high school together."

"Of course. You guys caught up at The Watering Hole the other night."

"That's right." she nodded. "The doctor and nurses are in with him at the moment. And the police. Come, sit down. They won't be too much longer."

"The police?" Mike asked, confused. "Just what the hell happened this morning?"

Mike turned his back on Emily and walked across the corridor. The door was open, and he could see Deputy Preston, through the partially open curtain, standing at the end of the bed. The curtain was pulled to a near-close, for privacy. Deputy Preston appeared to be observing the nurse tending to Peter's bloody wounds. Peter had regained consciousness. He was weak, but still, awake. Deputy Preston looked out into the corridor and saw Mike standing there, facing him. He said nothing. Mike's face was filled with worry and anger.

"You gave us all quite a scare back there." the nurse said with a warm smile and reassuring voice, as she finished applying the bandage to Peter's right side of his forehead.

The light above the hospital bed was switched on, just inches from Peter's eyes. It was a distraction. "What happened?" he asked, just above a whisper, and more than a little confused.

"We were hoping you could tell us," Deputy Preston said, standing at the end of the bed, holding a small notepad, ready to jot down any information.

Deputy Preston was neatly dressed in his uniform. His tone of voice was stern and authoritative. "I don't remember much. All I remember is jogging down Quarry Lake Road."

"The ambulance found you off the side of the road, near some trees and further debris. The way they had found you, suggests you were run off the road, possibly by a large vehicle."

Peter stared back at his best friend. He was speechless.

"I am finished here." the nurse smiled again. "You get some rest, you hear?"

"Yes." Peter nodded slowly, as his eyes diverted to the nurse for a moment.

Peter watched the nurse stand from the chair by the side of his bed. The nurse herself was somewhere in her late thirties, with a large build, and stringy, curly blonde hair with minimal make-up. She smiled at Peter again, and then nodded toward Deputy Preston, as she made her way out of the emergency room and into the corridor, pushing a small trolley which sported bloodied bandages and wiring used for the stitches and other instruments. She passed Mike standing at the entrance of the room, careful to excuse herself, and the trolley, so as not to bump into him. Peter lay in bed with a bandage wrapped around a good portion of the right side of his forehead and his hands, too. Mike watched the nurse leave the room and make her way partially down the corridor, before he raced into the room, and grabbed the chair by the side of the bed, once occupied by the nurse. Peter made eye contact with Mike. His face dropped, a little, as if ready to hold back his tears.

"Mike!" Peter whispered, just under his breath. "What are you doing here?"

"What do you mean, what am I doing here?" Mike answered, just above a whisper, with concern in his voice. "I got a call from the hospital. What the hell happened to you?"

Peter diverted his eyes from Mike a moment and looked to his best friend.

"Mike, I'm gonna have to ask you to step out of the room whilst I finish my investigation," Deputy Preston said, looking down at him.

"Yeah?" Mike answered, with a sarcastic tone to his voice and smile on his face, as he turned in his chair to face the deputy. "And I'm going to ask you to eat my hairy ass! I'm not going anywhere. Period!"

"Mike, please?" Peter asked.

Mike turned and made eye contact with Peter, again.

"It's just a few questions. The deputy won't be long. I promise. You can wait out there, in the waiting room. I'm not going anywhere." Peter smiled.

The concern on his face was gone now. Mike smiled, in return.

"Are you sure?"

"I'm sure."

There was a brief pause. "Okay, then," Mike answered.

He stood up from his chair. The rubber stoppers scratched on the surface of the smooth floor, beneath. He turned and walked out of the emergency room, but not before making eye contact with Deputy Preston, again. He sized him up, playing the role of the over-protective boyfriend.

Mike had left Peter to Deputy Preston and sat a couple of chairs over from Emily. He sat forward in his chair, with his hands clutched between his legs. Deputy Preston followed Mike to the open door and pushed it to a close, as he looked out into the waiting room, at Mike and Emily, for a brief moment. He stepped backwards, deeper into the room, taking to the chair by the side of the bed. Deputy Preston tugged at his uniform shirt a little, as it hugged his frame and adjusted himself more comfortably. The curtain around the bed was now pulled to a close.

"I am fine." Peter started, forcing a smile. "Really, I am. Granted, a little shaken, but I am fine."

"You call this fine?" Deputy Preston asked.

"It's a couple of scratches and some stitches. That's it. I have lived through worse."

"That may be, but…"

"But?" Peter asked, confused.

Deputy Preston looked at his best friend. "What…? What?"

"Forget that Deputy Preston is here on duty tonight. Fuck that! I am speaking to you as my best friend, here. The killer struck at you. Whoever is doing this, has found you."

"They have already found me. I have been receiving calls from the killer since I arrived."

"I just don't want to see you get hurt, again. I'm doing my job here. I'm fulfilling my end of the bargain. I don't want to see you get hurt. I'm trying to fucking protect you, Petey."

"What are you going to do? Wrap me in cotton wool? I can't do that."

"You rest up." Andrew started, having bitten his lower lip out of frustration. "When you get discharged, I'll have a squad car parked outside the front of your house, twenty-four, seven."

"I know you mean well, I do. But do you really think that is going to help? Whoever this is, has already got to me. If anything, having a police car parked outside my house is only going to draw them in closer. Taunt them."

"Okay, then," Andrew answered flatly. "When you are discharged out of here, you spend a few nights at my place. Just a couple of days, until you are feeling better and are on your feet. I mean, psychos can't kill what they can't find, yeah?"

Peter looked at Andrew, concerned.

"What?" Andrew asked. "I just don't' want to see you get hurt. Get some sleep. You look tired. I'll be around later to check up on you, see if you remember anything further, okay?"

"Okay." Peter forced a smile.

Deputy Preston turned and walked out of the hospital room, past the curtains, opening the door, and out into the corridor. Mike looked up from the floor, sitting in the waiting room. Andrew walked over, toward Emily. He maintained eye contact with Mike as if sizing him up, again. "Will you two quit eyeballing each other?" Emily said, just above a whisper, as if not to draw attention to herself or to her friend lying in a hospital bed, just metres away. "I can see you both care for Peter. We all do. But give it a rest, please. It's not a dick-measuring contest."

Emily stood up from her chair and walked toward Andrew, reaching out for his hands, as if to drag him away.

"Mike, it was a pleasure to meet you. You have my number. If you need to talk, give me a call sometime, okay?"

"Thank you."

"Honey," Emily said, looking Andrew in the eyes, "let's go, okay?"
"Sure," Andrew nodded, "let Peter rest for a bit."

Peter had spent the next two days in the hospital, recuperating. And, during that time, Mike spent as much time as he could with him. Deputy Preston had kept to his word, and returned the following day, with Detective Quinn, with another list of questions. Mike had taken some time off work to spend with Peter. As Peter slept, he had his paperback novels to keep him company.

"This wasn't exactly the way I pictured the two of us spending some quality time together." Mike chuckled, a little. He sat in a chair by the side of the bed and under the windowsill.

"Yeah? The food is fantastic." Peter laughed. Mike laughed, too.

"Well, when you get out of here, you can spend a couple of nights at my place. I don't want you on your own whilst your recuperating."

"It's a few scratches and some stitches. I'm fine."

"To you, maybe. I just want to keep you close. Is there anything wrong with that?"

"No," Peter answered, just above a whisper as he shook his head.

"Good!" Mike smiled.

He leaned in and kissed Peter on the lips, a moment.

It was now day three. Peter was still in the hospital. He had been wheeled out of the emergency room and taken to his own room. The bandages around his hands were still in place, as was the bandage covering the right side of his forehead. Peter looked around the room, tired and a little dazed. The painkillers were working a treat. The television set was switched off. And Andrew was sitting in the corner of the room, thumbing his way through a magazine.

"Hey, you," Peter said, feeling a little groggy.

Andrew looked up from the magazine and placed it to one side. He was dressed in uniform. "Hey there, welcome back to the land of the living. How are you feeling?"

"A little sore. But, getting better. Where's Mike?" Peter looked around the room, again.

"He left," Andrew answered, almost bluntly. "He said he had something to deal with at the store. He will be back soon, I'm sure. You got me now. I hope that's okay?"

Peter smiled, adjusting his comfort in bed.

"Can I get you anything?" Andrew asked, almost in a panic as he sprung from his chair. "Water," Peter answered, just above a whisper.

Andrew wheeled the table toward Peter and poured him a cup of water. He even placed a straw in the cup and directed it toward Peter. Andrew sat back down in his chair as he watched his best friend drink from the cup, with minor difficulties. Peter finished with the water and rested back in his bed, a little. He looked around the room and saw an officer posted at the front door, standing in the corridor.

"What's going on?" Peter asked, his throat now clear. "It's official Hillsboro PD business, I'm afraid, Petey."

"Yeah? What happened?" Peter felt sore, closing his eyes again, for just a moment.

"You did," Andrew answered, almost surprisingly. "You were run down on the side of Quarry Lake Road. Any ideas who?"

"I can't remember. A black truck with tinted windows." Peter shrugged. "It could have been anyone. You know how this town feels about me."

"Have you received any further phone calls?"

"Not recently. How about you?"

"We're not here for me." Andrew smiled briefly.

"Then you have heard from them. What did they say?"

"I didn't say that."

"You didn't have to."

Andrew cleared his throat. He tugged at his uniform shirt, again, feeling a little nervous, almost. "Back to work and answer my questions."

Peter was in the hospital for another two nights before being discharged. Mike returned to the hospital, bright and early that morning. He swung by Peter's home and picked up some fresh clothes and a gym bag to carry the dirty clothes and all other personal belongings. Peter was feeling better, not one hundred per cent, yet, but well on the way. The bandages around his hands remained. The bandage around the right side of his forehead was still there. Peter was dressed and sitting on the side of the bed, quietly talking with the doctor on call.

An orderly soon appeared at the entrance of the open door leading into Peter's room. He was somewhere in his early forties with black hair, salt and pepper on the side. He had a bit of a portly belly and was clean-shaven, and still looked distinguished. He stood there, with a wheelchair in front of him.

"Your chariot awaits, Mr Harmon." said the orderly, with a hint of a smile. The orderly entered the room, pushing the wheelchair by the side of the bed.

"Thank you." Peter smiled.

"I'll leave you two to it," said the doctor. "I have everything I need.

And you have your check-up appointment next week to take a look at those stitches on your forehead. I will see you then. Take care, Mr Harmon."

The doctor grabbed Peter's chart and other paperwork in a manila file, held it to his chest and walked out of the room and out into the corridor.

"I got you from here, Mr Harmon." the orderly smiled.

Peter climbed off the side of the bed and sat himself down in the wheelchair, with minor assistance from the orderly. Mike looked on, as he clutched the gym bag.

"Are you ready, Mr Harmon?" asked the orderly.

"Yes, please. Let's go home."

The orderly pushed the wheelchair forward. It reached the entrance of the open door and turned right into the corridor. Mike followed from behind. He picked up his pace and was walking alongside Peter and the orderly.

The day had progressed into the evening. Peter had been discharged from the hospital and was spending the night at Mike's place. The house itself was a single storey, weatherboard home with a porch which seems to stretch almost the entire width and length of the house. The lawn on the front yard was a deep, dark green in colour. The grass was thick and neatly manicured. With a large oak tree out the front, just like some of the other houses in the neighbourhood. It provided shade during the summer season whilst gardening.

The night air was almost still. A slow breeze fell over Hillsboro as the leaves in the trees gave a gentle rustle. From the street, the front of the house had an almost glowing quality to it. The lights in the front of the house, including the living room, were switched on. Mike had given Peter the whole twenty-five-cent tour upon his arrival. It started with the front door closing and Mike pulling Peter in close for a long, slow welcome home kiss. Peter smiled.

"Welcome!" Mike said, just above a whisper.

Mike had packed Peter's gym bag with enough clothes to last him a couple of days. Peter was resting in the living room, lying on the couch, in front of the television. Mike was in his master bedroom, sorting and hanging Peter's clothes. The network news aired on the television set as

Peter started to drift off to sleep. He didn't hear the hard thud of Mike's boots walk from the bedroom, down the hallway and into the living room. Mike entered the room, standing there, silent, over the top of the couch, peering down at Peter, his face filled with concern.

Peter had been awake for almost two hours now. Dinner had been served and eaten and the table had been cleared and the plates washed and stacked away. There was music softly playing from the stereo in the living room. The two retired to the living room for the evening. Mike was stretched out on the couch this time, with his reading glasses on, reading a paperback novel. Peter sat on a recliner on the opposite side of the living room.

Peter was losing his concentration. His mind bounced between the television set and Mike stretched out on the couch. The hint of a smile surfaced to his lips, a little.

"Everything okay?" Mike asked, as he lowered his paperback novel and looked over the rims of his reading glasses.

"Of course." he smiled. "You just reminded me of… another time. It's not important." Mike looked at Peter longingly before going back to his novel.

The truth was the memory of Robert Prescott came flooding back. It was one of the things they would do after dinner, spend time together in the living room, ask each other about their day, before calling it quits for the evening and going to bed.

It was then his eyes diverted out of the living room and toward the front door, toward the front porch. Peter climbed out of the recliner, walked across the living room and out toward the front door. Mike dropped his novel, and looked over the rims of his glasses, again.

"What's going on?" Mike called out.

"Nothing!" Peter replied.

Peter stood at the front door of the house. The light on the porch was switched on. There was nothing but a bright blur through the frosted glass window.

"It's nothing," Peter whispered to himself, under his breath.

Peter raised his left hand and placed it on the door handle. The gold-plated metal was cool to the touch. He held his breath in his chest, tightly, and pushed down nervously. The door pushed opened. A gentle breeze was first to come through the door. Peter sighed, feeling a heavy weight lift from his shoulders, and the hint of a smile surfacing to his lips. Peter took a step outside the house, out onto the front porch, leading with his left foot. The wooden floorboards cracked under the pressure, a little. He stood there, silent, peering out into the darkness of the front yard, his eyes squinting, a little. There was nothing there, not that he could see, anyway. It was nothing more than the gentle breeze of the evening air. Peter looked around the porch.

"What is it?" Mike asked, startling Peter a little, from behind.

Peter looked over his left shoulder, turning around, some. He could see Mike standing at the front door in his navy blue sweat pants and a simple, plain white t-shirt. He was still wearing his reading glasses. Peter liked that.

"I heard a noise," Peter answered, just above a whisper.

"And let me guess, you thought you'd come out and investigate?"

"I found this," Peter answered, walking along the front porch, picking up a dreamcatcher from the wooden floorboards. "It must have fallen or something."

"It's always doing that. I got to fix that." Mike answered, rolling his eyes, a little. "Pass it over." Peter handed Mike the dreamcatcher and placed it on the small wooden table by the deck chairs. "Leave it," Mike said. "It's cold out here. Come inside."

Peter turned and took one last look out in the front yard, peering into the darkness of the evening. Still, nothing.

"Of course," he smiled, "'let's go."

Peter walked through the front door as Mike put his right arm around him, over one shoulder, guiding him inside before he locked the front door for the evening.

Peter and Mike were fast asleep, now. The bed cover was pulled a little high, just above the waist, at least for Mike. He was lying on his back, fast asleep, snoring away, some. Peter was lying in the bed next to him by the windowsill. The time on the alarm clock was twelve thirteen in the morning. The breeze from outside started to pick up a little. The wind whistled as it hit the window pane. A couple of dead leaves hit the window, then disappeared, pushed away by the wind. Peter tossed and turned in the bed. He woke up, feeling uncomfortable. The bandage around his head felt itchy. Peter turned and looked at Mike. He was still fast asleep, unfazed by the weather.

His cell phone was connected to his charger on his side of the nightstand and his reading glasses sat on top of his paperback novel.

Peter pushed back the bed cover and climbed to his feet. He was dressed in a pair of white cotton boxer shorts and an old simple grey, no brand t-shirt. It was comfortable and fit well in all the right places. Peter tiptoed across the beige carpet of the master bedroom and made his way to the open door. He walked down the hallway, exploring the house. The wooden floorboards cracked under the pressure in the quiet of the night. The walls of the hallway were decorated with framed photographs of Mike and his friends, during happier times, some in colour, and others in black and white. He passed the bathroom, and his office, and came up to a closed door on the right. Peter stopped in his tracks. He had never seen this room before. His hand lowered again, onto the door handle. He twisted it a little, and pushed it open. The room was used to store clutter. There were clothes hanging in the wardrobe and shoes on the floor. And an ironing board in the corner of the room. Peter stepped inside. The door closed behind him. He walked across the room and into the wardrobe. The light in the room was switched off. The street lamp from the window outside shed some much-needed light. It sprayed across the far wall of the room, edging its way inside the wardrobe, a little.

Peter stepped inside the wardrobe some more. His left hand gently glided over the hanging shirts, his mind was immediately intrigued by Mike's questionable fashion sense. A smile surfaced to his lips. He looked up. And there, above him, were rows and rows of shoe boxes.

"Hello, Imelda," Peter whispered to himself, with a hint of a chuckle.

Peter raised his left hand a little higher, reaching for a shoe box, any random shoe box. There were so many. He grabbed at one and pulled it down.

The shoe box felt a little heavier and bulkier than it should. Peter made some space for himself and sat on the beige carpeted flooring of the wardrobe and removed the lid of the shoe box. And, there, in front of him, were countless photographs and newspaper articles, clipped and saved, collected over time, about Peter, his father, mother, and the murders.

"What the fuck?" Peter whispered to himself, under his breath, feeling his heart start to pound in his chest.

Peter fished through the newspaper articles. They covered the murder of Peter's father and his then wife, as well as their child. They covered the arrest of Peter's mother. And a story on Grandfather. Peter's eyes widened in horror, capturing his breath in his chest, again. He sat there, legs crossed, pushing the shoe box away, a little.

A heavy thud came from somewhere in the back of the house. It repeated. Then, a third time.

And a fourth. Peter looked over his shoulder, toward the closed door. It was the heavy thud of feet walking down the hallway. Peter fumbled with the lid of the shoe box, carefully trying to make it fit, again. He climbed to his feet and stacked the shoe box on top of another, careful to make it balance. The door to the bedroom swung open. Peter stepped backwards, hugging the wall, out of sight and holding his breath. His right hand covered his nose and mouth, tightly. The bedroom door swung to a close.

"Fuck!" Peter whispered under his breath.

Peter was quick to make his way out of the spare room, carefully, quietly opening the door. He peered left and right, up and down the hallway. There was no one there. The door leading into the master bedroom was wide open. Peter tiptoed across the hallway and into the kitchen, leaving the bedroom door open. He raced towards the refrigerator and opened the door. He leaned in and grabbed a bottle of the orange juice. He opened it and took a deep sip, to help calm his nerves, some.

"Here you are!" Mike whispered, standing in the entrance of the kitchen.

Peter swallowed the juice rather hard and wiped his lips the back of his right hand. "I couldn't sleep."

"Come back to bed." he smiled.

Peter forced a smile. He placed the orange juice back in the refrigerator and closed the door. The light from the refrigerator caught Mike standing in the entrance of the kitchen. He stood there naked. Peter could see the scar left behind after his appendix operation.

Mike waited for Peter to join him. They walked from the kitchen to the master bedroom together, almost side by side. They reached the master bedroom and climbed into bed. Mike snuggled up to Peter, wrapping his large, muscular arms around him, resting on his chest. His legs tangled in his.

"Goodnight," Mike whispered, leaning in for another kiss. Mike closed his eyes.

Peter lay there on the bed, staring up at the ceiling. His eyes were wide open, his mind racing.

The winter season made its presence known the following morning. It started out with patches of grey clouds racing across the morning sky. The wind was starting to arc up. The rain began to fall. It was the official start to winter. There were no severe weather warnings issued for the town of Hillsboro.

Peter had been awake for almost an hour now, give or take. Mike soon followed. Peter started his morning lying in bed and catching up on his social media from his cell phone before climbing out of bed and making his way to the bathroom. It was an awkward process, with the bandages, and all. The cell phone remained in the master bedroom, sitting on the nightstand, linked to its charger. Peter stood in front of the washbasin, standing there looking at his reflection in the bathroom mirror, a moment. A white, cotton towel wrapped firmly around his waist. There were beads of water that dripped down his chest and back. Peter had brushed his teeth. The door to the bathroom pushed open, almost silently. Mike stood in the bathroom doorway, still playing the role of the ever-protective boyfriend. His eyes caught Peter in the reflection of the bathroom mirror.

Peter could see him standing there, in nothing more than a simple, white t-shirt and blue and black jockey shorts. Mike was the first to smile.

"What's on your mind?" he asked, just above a whisper. Peter turned and smiled at Mike in the doorway.

"Just thinking, is all," he answered.

"Yeah?"

"I mean, this is my life. I can't escape this. The looks. The stares. I know what people in this town think of me."

"Fuck that! And fuck them! You don't need their bullshit! Learn to look past them. They can't hurt you if you don't let them in. Don't let them in."

"I wish I had your confidence, I really do."

"You do. You're a fighter. You're a survivor. It comes instinctively for you. It's there when you need it. Just like me. Just like everyone."

"When I was a kid, like seven or eight, I saw my mother and grandfather kill a pregnant German Shepherd. Just because." Peter shrugged, lowering his eyesight, embarrassed. "When I was nine, my father and his new wife took full custody of me. I was ten years old when my grandfather decided to break into my house one night to make his way into my bedroom. I awoke to the sound of him screaming at me, and feeling his thumbs pressing down hard into my eye sockets. He wanted to kill me. My father heard me screaming and raced into my bedroom and took a baseball bat to the left side of my grandfather's head."

"Shit!" Mike answered just above a whisper, almost unable to stomach such a thought.

Mike stepped into the bathroom, standing behind Peter, his arms wrapped around his shoulders, and staring at his reflection, making eye contact, in the bathroom mirror.

"That is my life." Peter forced himself to smile.

"No." Mike answered. "That *was* your life. You're here with me now." Another forced smile from Peter in the bathroom mirror.

Chapter Eleven...

The house was silent. Almost, anyway. There was the sound of a clock faintly ticking away, which hung on the living room wall. Peter was alone in Mike's house. He sat at the dining table in a t-shirt and jeans, his feet were bare, touching the cool beige carpet below. Mike had been called into the hardware store. There was an emergency. The water pipes had burst overnight. The young girl who worked behind the counter arrived to work to find the mess.

A glass of water sat atop of a coaster on the table. And next to it, a bottle of painkillers the doctor in the hospital prescribed for headaches and migraines. Peter popped the white cap from the orange bottle and poured himself a couple of pills, catching them in his left hand. The instructions on the bottle read to take before or after food. Peter threw the two pills to the back of his mouth and chased it with a hard swallow of water from the glass. His head tilted back and forth in quick succession. The glass of water returned to the coaster on the table.

The surface of the dining table was scattered with newspaper articles. There were clippings and photographs of Peter as a teenager as well as the rest of the Harmon-Green family. There were also photographs of the clown mask, which had been collected as evidence over the years. Peter sat at the dining table in near silence, staring down at the bloodstained family history out on display in front of him. He could feel his heartbeat racing in his chest as his left hand stretched out, reaching for his cell phone. He logged in and went through his text history and brought up the conversations he'd had with Andrew.

I need to see you.

Peter typed and hit the send button. He put the cell phone down, sliding it across the surface of dining table, a little. Peter took another deep sip from his glass of water, finishing it off now, before putting the glass down on the coaster, again. He swallowed hard, again. The cell phone began to chime and vibrate, a second. Peter leaned into the table and reached for his cell phone. The screen came to life. There was a message from Andrew.

Where? And when?

The message read. It was short and to the point.

His mind raced. The clock hanging on the wall in the living room continued to tick away. *Tick. Tick. Tick.*

The morning progressed. The engine in Andrew's truck was dead. Andrew, himself, was sitting behind the steering wheel of his truck, his hands at ten and two, dressed in his police uniform. The shirt clung tightly to his muscular frame. Both hands dropped from the steering wheel, landing in his lap. They cupped together, his thumbs twirling round, faster and faster, as if nervous on a first date. Andrew drove from the police station to Mike's place to pick up Peter, then over to a local park, opposite the high school.

The truck sat silently in the almost empty car park. There were a few other cars parked, no more than five or six. Andrew turned his head and looked at his best friend. Peter sat in the front passenger seat of the truck, staring out the front window, in an almost dream-like state, watching the kids in the park play grass-roots baseball, and parents taking their new-borns for a stroll in the fresh air. The clouds were starting to clear now.

"I'm here. *We're* here." Andrew said, just above a whisper. "Do you care to tell me what this is all about and why we are in a park, across the road from our old high school?"

Peter blinked his eyes in quick succession.

"Have the police checked out Mike?" Peter asked, just above a whisper, turning to his head to face his best friend.

"Mike Walters?" Andrew asked, surprised. "It doesn't matter what I think of him, but in general, he is a stand-up kind of guy. He runs his own business. He employs local kids. Why do you ask?"

"So many questions," replied Peter.

"I'm a cop. It's my job."

"I woke up in the middle of the night," Peter continued, in that same tone of voice, shrugging his shoulders, a little. "I got out of bed, and before I knew it, I was snooping. The curiosity got the better of me, and I found myself in the closet of a spare room and found countless shoe boxes, just filled with photographs of me and my family when I was a kid. He had newspaper articles, you know, about the murders."

"Shit!" Andrew answered under his breath. "You think Mike may be the killer?" Peter slouched forward in the truck, his mind racing.

"As I said, I just want to know why he has *those* photographs at *that* time in my life. I know Mike was a family friend, I know that. But who collects shoe boxes full of old photographs and newspaper articles? It's just… creepy."

"Serial killers are typically single white males, approximately thirty to fifty years in age. They cannot manage their anger and take it out in violent, destructive ways, either with strangers or people they know. The latter. They kind of get off on that. It is creepy. It's creepy as fuck! Do you want me to put an officer on him?"

"You know, if this were a horror movie, this would be the part where the hapless lead would say yes, not go out and investigate some strange noise in the dark which would inevitably get themselves killed." Peter stopped in his tracks. He took a deep breath and smiled. "What am I saying?" he asked, chuckling a little. "This isn't a movie. It is real life. No. Just forget everything I said, okay?"

"If that is what you want?" Andrew asked, more as a best friend, then the deputy of the town, as he leaned in, a little. He looked at Peter and took a deep sigh. "Since we are sharing and all, can you keep a secret? Between you and me, I am fucking Jayne Scott. As much as I love Emily, and I do, there is just something about Jayne I just can't leave alone."

Peter wasn't surprised.

The engine to the truck roared to life once more. Andrew looked over his shoulder, then in the rear-view mirror before reversing from his parking spot and making his way out into the traffic. The truck drove on, almost racing to the end of the street. Andrew gave Peter a lift back to Mike's house before making his way back to the station. Andrew rolled his window down, a little, enjoying the cool breeze, some. It didn't take long, less than ten minutes, before the truck pulled up outside the front of Mike Walter's home.

"Thank you for today," said Peter. "I just needed to get it off my chest, you know? Put a stop to all the what-ifs and questions in my head."

"Of course," Andrew answered. "Anytime. You know that Petey." Peter let out a deep sigh. A smile surfaced to his lips.

"I'm sure there is an obvious reason, right?"

"I'm sure there is." Andrew forced a smile, reassuring his best friend, as much as he could. "Thanks."

Peter climbed out of the truck and stepped out onto the curb, before turning to take one, last look at his best friend before closing the truck door.

"Talk to you soon." Andrew smiled.

"Talk soon," replied Peter.

Peter turned his back on his friend and walked briskly into the front yard and up to the porch. Andrew leaned to the side a little, peering through the passenger window, watching his friend make his way inside the house. The smile on his lips quickly dissipated, as concern consumed him.

"Mike Walters," he whispered under his breath.

Andrew turned and faced the road in front of him. He applied pressure to the accelerator and took off from the curb. The truck raced to the end of the street as the horn echoed throughout the street two, maybe three times.

The front door to the house was now closed. Peter walked deeper inside, down the hallway, a little, and toward the kitchen. The silence was broken with the ringtone of a cell phone. Peter searched his pocket and checked the caller ID. It was Mike. Peter looked at his ringing cell phone a moment longer more before answering.

"Hello?" Peter answered, clearing his throat a little.

"Hey!" a cheerful voice answered.

Peter smiled a little.

"What are you up to?"

"You know me. I'm just resting and taking it easy." Peter answered, walking into the kitchen. "I'm sitting on your front porch and watching the world drive by."

That was a lie.

"How's work?" Peter asked.

"A fucking nightmare! My stock is ruined. Damn water pipes! I'm gonna be out of business for at least a couple of days, maybe more, whilst I clean up this mess."

"What can I do to help?"

"How good are you with a wet-dry vac?"

"I'll come in. I'll be there just as soon as I can."

"You're in no position to drive."

"I'll order a cab. See you soon."

"Bye."

The phone line disconnected.

The lights along the town square turn green. A taxi cab drove into the square and pulled up outside the hardware store, within the space of half an hour. Peter was sitting in the back seat. He peered outside the window, taking in the sights of the local town and its people. There were people, of all different ages, and backgrounds, going about their daily lives before curfew hit for another day.

The driver of the taxi cab turned around. He placed his right arm at the top of the faded brown pleather chairs, hugging it tightly, to turn his portly frame to see his passenger sitting in the back seat of his cab. The engine remained running. There was a low, rattling hum to it. The driver himself, was somewhere in his early to mid-fifties, from what Peter could tell, anyway. His hair was black in colour, neatly managed, but thinning on top with maybe two days stubble about his chin and cheeks. He had green eyes and a nice smile.

"Okay," the driver started, sounding very upbeat, "'that'll be nine bucks and seventy-five cents."

"Of course," Peter answered, politely.

He dug his left hand into his jean pocket and pulled out his wallet. He looked through it quickly and handed the driver a twenty dollar note.

"Here you go."

"Thanks," the driver nodded, smiling. "Nice tip! You have a great day now."

Peter opened the back-passenger door to the taxi cab and climbed out of the vehicle. He stood there a moment and closed the door, before it drove off down the street a little, to the next set of traffic lights. Peter stepped up onto the curb, just outside the hardware store. Peter looked around the town square. There was a closed sign on the front door to the hardware store. A teenage kid, no older than sixteen, dressed in denim jeans and an oversized hoodie and sneakers, purposely bumped into Peter, trying his best to scare him.

"Boo!" he shouted. "Seen any creepy masks lately?"

"Freak!" his friend followed.

The friend of the teenage boy laughed.

"Fuck you!" Peter shouted at the kid and his friend, whilst flipping him the bird. "Fuck you, both!" Peter stood there, making eye contact with both kids, a moment, before returning his focus on the hardware store. He still copped several looks from passers-by, a single mother pushing her infant in a pram, and an elderly married couple, going about their daily lives. Peter looked back at them, not backing down. Peter rolled his eyes at the single mother and bypassed her as he made his way into the hardware store.

The bell above the door inside the hardware store began to chime.

"Sorry! We're closed!" Mike yelled out from behind the counter, clearing debris from the floor.

"Oh really?" Peter answered.

Mike lifted his eyes off the debris on the floor a moment and made contact with Peter. His face was delighted. He smiled. It was genuine.

"Wow!" Peter started, as he looked around the store. "The pipes did a real number on this place, didn't they?"

"Damn right."

Peter looked around the hardware store. The lights were switched off. Mike used torches around the store for make-shift light. The aisles were flooded with water. Peter watched where he stepped, making his way to the glass counter, careful not to flood his feet with cold water. There was a wet- dry vac plugged in and already hard at work, cleaning the floor behind the counter.

"Look at this place," Peter said, just above a whisper.

"You made it." Mike smiled. "There's a face I'm happy to see."

Mike left the wet-dry vac a moment and walked out from behind the counter toward Peter. "How you doing?" he asked, as his eyes shifted to the bandage wrapped around his forehead, a moment.

"Fine," Peter answered. "What about here, more importantly?"

"I could use another set of hands if you're up to it?"

A smile surfaced to his lips.

The days passed by. Mike decided on a return to work sale, a little something to entice his customers back into the store. The big reveal was due in two days. Peter helped out where he could, as much as he could. It kept him busy and his mind off things.

Peter was back in hospital. He was sitting on the side of a bed, in the emergency room. His leg dangled, a little, back and forth, his feet almost touching the floor, as a large lamp stood tall, above his head, the light focusing on the wound. The curtains were pulled to a close for privacy, as a doctor stood in front of Peter, inspecting the bandage wrapped around his forehead. The doctor was a short man, almost as tall as Peter, himself. He was of Italian heritage, somewhere in his early fifties. He sported a salt-and-pepper goatee and buzz cut. When he wasn't walking the hospital corridors on duty, and doing his rounds, he was in the gymnasium lifting weights. His arms were solid and defined, and his chest, muscular, not that you could see much through his navy-blue shirt and white coat.

"Let's take a look, shall we?" the doctor asked, just above a whisper, as he removed the clamp which held the bandage together.

"Sure."

Peter diverted his eyes on the staff ID, pinned to the doctor's coat. *Dr Jim Goulas.*

Dr Jim Goulas turned a little, placing the small clamp on a metal tray which stood close by. *Clink.* The sound of metal scratching against another metal surface. The tray was adorned with fresh bandages, gauze, scissors, etc. A student nurse, a young twenty-something, with curly, mousey brown, shoulder length hair and prescription glasses stood nearby, watching Dr Goulas at work and interacting with his patient.

The bandage unwound from the forehead, over and over, again, until it was removed completely. It was discarded and placed on the metal tray, along with the clip. There was a piece of gauze placed over the wound, specially cut to fit the size, itself. Dr Goulas used tweezers to remove the gauze from the forehead. It required some tugging, as the blood from the wound coagulated and dried. The gauze was stained with blood and placed on the metal tray. The wound looked red and inflamed under the lamplight. Dr Goulas counted eight, maybe ten stitches. The stitches looked fresh and neat.

"I think the stitches are coming along just nicely," Dr Goulas said, nodding a little. "I think we leave the stitches in for another week, at least, before taking them out. I'll have my office call you in the week and arrange an appointment, okay?"

Peter nodded his head, gently.

"I don't think you need the bandage. It's important to keep the wound dry, let the air get to it. You don't want infection setting in."

"Yes, sir."

"Good boy." Dr Goulas chuckled, a little.

Peter was out of the emergency room shortly thereafter. Dr Goulas exchanged pleasantries with his patient before leaving the student nurse behind to clear up the mess. Peter climbed off the bed, left the room, and walked the hospital corridor. The stitches felt exposed under the neon lights, and for a brief, fleeting moment, he felt invincible, like nothing could push or keep him down. Peter reached the end of the corridor, by the nurse's station, near the waiting room. Andrew was sitting, waiting patiently, with a magazine in his hands. He tossed it on the table as he looked up.

"Look at you, huh!" Andrew said, standing from his chair, and dressed in civilian clothing. "Those stitches look pretty bad-ass!"

"You think?" Peter asked.

"Hell yeah!"

"Great!" Peter smiled. "Let's get out of here."

"Let's get you home."

"I'm not glass, Andrew. I'm not going to break."

"No one said you were," Andrew responded, just above a whisper, with a hint of a smile surfacing to his lips.

"Good," Peter forced a smile, back.

The morning progressed into the afternoon. Andrew and Peter had left the hospital and dropped by a local diner for a drink and a snack, before going their separate ways; Andrew returned to work and Peter filled his afternoon at the shooting range.

The room had limited lighting. There were small, cube-shaped neon lights hanging from the ceiling, protected within wire cages. Peter stood within the confines of his designated cubicle, his eyes hidden behind shock-absorbing glasses and wearing headphones to protect his ears. He stepped closer towards the bench in front of him, taking, gripping the pistol in his hands. It felt cool to the touch, yet strikingly familiar. The room echoed with the sound of bullets. The firing range was filled to capacity, with local people firing arrange of guns from pistols to much more heavier firearms, used for accuracy and stopping power. Peter shifted in his stance, a moment, feeling a little nervous, before picking up his firearm, again.

"Just breathe," he whispered to himself.

The gun itself was a Glock 19. Its retail price was just north of five hundred dollars. It fired nine-millimetre rounds highly effective and efficient and was accurate. His hands cupped the handle of the gun. His fingers falling into place around the trigger. Peter was very conscious of his breathing. He stood there, in position, staring out at the paper target in front of him. The black and white image staring back. Peter maintained focus and squeezed the trigger softly. The gun fired, over and over again, until the chamber was empty.

Peter took another step forward, inside the cubicle. He placed the Glock 19 on the table in front of him, and turned slightly, hitting a green button inside the cubicle. The paper target came racing in, toward Peter, filled with holes. Some were good, others, not so. Peter inspected the bullet wounds on the target.

"Fuck you!" he whispered under his breath to himself. "Whoever you are."

The days passed. It had been almost a week now since Peter was initially discharged from the hospital. Mike was sitting behind the steering wheel of his truck. It pulled up in front of Peter's home. The engine died with the twist of the key in the ignition.

"Are you sure?" Mike asked, just above a whisper. "You know you're more than welcome to stay at my place as long as you want."

"Thank you." Peter nodded, looking back at Mike. "But I got to do this. If I don't do this now, I never will. It's kind of like getting back on a bike, you know?"

"Understood." Mike nodded. "You have my number."

"I do," Peter answered, as a smile surfaced to his lips. "I'll call you."

"Okay, then." Mike smiled. "I look forward to it."

Peter turned in the truck, a little, releasing the seat belt from around his torso. He pushed the door open and climbed out onto the curb with his sports bag. The front passenger door to the truck slammed shut. Peter leaned in, popping his head through the open window, a little. Another smile surfaced to his lips.

"Thank you for letting me crash at your place. Thank you for everything."

"Anytime." Mike smiled.

Peter turned his back on Mike sitting inside his truck and made his way toward the house. He stopped by the letterbox and retrieved the mail. There was nothing too important, just some flyers and a local newspaper. Mike leaned forward a little more, inside his truck, watching Peter walk across the front yard, up onto the porch, and make his way inside the house. Peter turned and waved from the front door before disappearing inside. The engine to the truck came to life, again. Mike placed his foot on the accelerator, pulled out from the curb and raced to the end of the street.

The afternoon progressed into the early evening. The sun was setting upon the town of Hillsboro for another evening. It was the first night home since the accident. The lights in the house were switched on. So was the television, for added noise. Peter ordered take-out for dinner, too tired to cook for himself. The menu consisted of sweet-and-sour pork and special fried rice from the local Chinese restaurant in town. He sat in the living room, on the couch, watching the television. There was an encore episode of *The Late Show with Stephen Colbert*. His monologues at the top of the show were always on point and made Peter laugh. His political digs were just what the doctor ordered.

The television set in the living room was still playing. It was a gentle noise in the background now. Peter was upstairs, wandering around the house. The doors in the hallway were open, exposing each room. The lights were switched on. He stood in the entrance of the master bedroom. The sports bag was empty and on the floor at the end of the bed. The clothes were in the hamper in the laundry, ready to be washed tomorrow. The sound of his cell phone began to ring and vibrate in his pocket. It broke the silence of the second storey of the house. Peter pulled it from his trouser pocket. The screen of the device had come to life, and there, in front of him, were missed text messages from Andrew, Emily, Mike, and Jayne, all welcoming him home. A smile surfaced to his lips and feeling a little baffled by a message from Jayne of all people. It was true. They were friends in high school. But, never close. She was the type of friend who was just there, by association. She was like the garnish on a plate you get when you order a burger and fries. You never asked for it, but there it was, nonetheless.

Welcome home, Petey. You know where I am if you need anything, big or small, day or night.

The message from Andrew read. Peter smiled.

The other messages were left to later.

The night was cold. A small winter breeze made 'its way down the street, rustling the leaves, a little. Winter was here. A squad car parked silently outside Peter's home. It was a little something Detective Quinn arranged since Peter's attack last week. For Deputy Preston, it gave him peace of mind. For Detective Quinn, it was keeping an eye on a possible suspect, and for Peter, it was an annoyance and breach of privacy. Peter made his way downstairs and to the front door. He stood in the foyer of the house, peering out into the street, looking at the squad car. The night air was chilly. Peter was quick to close the door again. The police officers on duty saw Peter stand at the front door before it closed. They turned their heads and resumed their duty.

"I love horror movies," said one police officer. "There is just something about a guy or a girl, who, one day has had enough and just… snaps. It happens. More than you know. It's wild."

"This town has seen more than 'its fair share of horror over the years. It's time to pick another genre," replied the senior officer.

The police officer sitting in the front passenger seat was young. He was just out of high school, just out of the academy, and posted in Hillsboro. He stood tall at almost five feet ten inches with short, cropped chocolate brown hair. His frame was thin and sported Coke bottle-like black, thick-framed glasses. The senior officer sat behind the steering wheel and was in his late forties. He sported salt and pepper throughout his hair and was clean shaven. His uniform clung to his muscular frame.

"It's time to put it all to rest," the senior officer continued. "Let Peter Harmon rest. Let the people of Hillsboro rest, once and for all and find some form of normalcy again."

"Just think!" the junior officer, said, full of enthusiasm, "if ever they made a movie of this town, who do you think would play you?"

"I'm no one," the senior officer answered, uninterested, "'we're no one. We are police officers doing our job, simple. We're not movie stars or a character in a film. This is real life. Let it go."

"Well," the junior officer said, with a smile brimming from ear to ear. "I see you as a Sam Rockwell type, myself. A big, teddy bear, if Sam Rockwell piled on the muscle and the chub."

The senior officer turned his head, a little, shooting his subordinate a cold, frosty look, as cold as the temperature outside the squad car.

The evening progressed into the early hours of the morning. The lights of the two-storey Victorian home were switched off. Peter was fast asleep in bed. The bed cover was pulled high, to his rib cage, as he slept on his back, comfortable, next to the nightstand. The cell phone was connected to its charger on the nightstand. The time was two thirty-eight in the morning. The wind had died down, a little.

The squad car was still parked outside the front of the house. The engine was dead. The two police officers had fallen asleep on duty, and the image of the clown mask appeared from out of the darkness, out from under the tall, billowing branches of an oak tree. The image stood there, a moment, looking at the squad car. It turned 'its head and looked up at the two-storey Victorian home. The clown mask moved fast and with precision, up to the front porch, toward the front door of the house.

The light in the kitchen flickered on. A middle-aged woman with an athletic build, somewhere in her late forties, and feeling tired and sleepy, dressed in grey sweat pants and a simple white t-shirt, made her way into the kitchen. Her long, black hair was tied into a bun, which sat loosely on the base of her skull. The woman reached for a tall, empty glass in the cupboard above her. The cold water began to run. The tall glass caught the water. The woman lifted the glass and took a sip. Just a little, something to wet the lips and throat. The water in the sink switched off.

The woman peered through the living room and past the window, onto the porch. She walked quickly to the living room window, with her glass of water still in her right hand. She looked out past the porch and the front yard, and out into the street. The leaves of the oak tree continued to rustle, some. The woman could see the two police officers on duty, awake.

"That damn Harmon family," she muttered under her breath.

The image of the clown mask appeared in the kitchen, unnoticed.

Silent. It stood there, looking out into the living room, watching, with a large, sharp kitchen knife gripped in their left hand, which was bound in leather. The woman was quick to turn around, feeling unnerved, somewhat. But the clown mask was faster. There was no one there. The sound of a screaming toddler broke the silence of the early hours of the morning.

"Shit!" the woman whispered, looking up at the ceiling of the living room. "Wait there. I'm coming, darling."

The woman raced from the living room and into the foyer of the home. She placed a hand on the banister, ready to run to the top of the staircase, in leaps and bounds. The sound of a crying toddler continued. The woman was climbing the staircase, taking two, maybe three steps, as a leather glove reached out, reached forward, grabbing the woman from the left shoulder, pulling her backwards, a little. The woman gasped as she lost her balance, as she fell backwards. The blade of the kitchen knife was sharp and moved at almost electric speed. The blade sliced at the skin of the woman's throat, tearing the tendons and muscles beneath. The blood poured heavily and quickly.

The glass shattered at her feet on the floor as the water spilt everywhere. The woman clutched at her throat tightly, gasping for air, suffocating with each passing breath. She had fallen down the staircase, staring up at the ceiling, staring up at the intruder, the clown mask, who was standing above her.

The clown mask looked down at the woman. The mask, tilting a little, watching. The woman continued to gasp for air, fighting for life, and quickly losing. Her grip around her neck was showing signs of weakening as her body went into convulsions. The blood continued to pour from the wound and through her fingers as it dripped to the floor beneath. The convulsions continued, also growing weaker. The clown mask tilted some more, appearing intrigued. The woman now released her grip from around her throat. Her hands fell to her sides. She was growing weaker and weaker by the moment, with each passing blink of the eyes. Finally, the woman was dead.

The clown mask stood over the deceased body and the bottom of the staircase. The sound of a toddler screaming from upstairs continued. The clown mask looked up from the deceased body, up the staircase, up at the second storey of the home. The clown mask was quick to move, running, from the foyer, down the staircase, and out the back of the house, leaving behind a lifeless, bloody corpse.

"Did you hear something?" the young police officer asked, looking over his shoulder up at the house.

"What?" the senior officer asked. "I don't know. A baby screaming."

"It happens. Babies wake up screaming in the middle of the night." "Shouldn't we go check it out or something?"

The senior officer looked at his subordinate with that same frosty stare, a moment. A silence soon followed, only seconds later.

"See? Nothing. The parents put the kid to sleep. Besides, we're police officers, not babysitters."

"You're right," the younger officer nodded.

The morning broke over the town of Hillsboro once more. The squad car that was parked outside Peter's home was still there. The neighbourhood had turned into a circus. The house next door was a crime scene. The front door leading into the house was open. The front porch was littered with police officers. The coroner on duty had arrived and was on his hands and knees at the base of the staircase. He was concentrating, quietly working away, with the help of his assistant.

"Another day, another murder," whispered the coroner to himself.

The woman remained at the bottom of the staircase, as her lifeless, bloody corpse, stared up at the ceiling of her home. Her greying eyes and blue skin were hidden behind another clown mask. The front of the house, the front yard, was taped off from the public. People were crowding in the street, watching on, some in terror, some intrigued, whilst others were delighted, amongst the squad cars and ambulance waiting in the street.

Detective Quinn was dressed in another grey suit. He raced from his squad car. He raced from the curb, across the front yard, up to the porch and the front door. The traffic was busy.

Officers were making their way in and out of the house. Deputy Preston was on duty, following the detective. They arrived in the same squad car. Detective Quinn stood on the front porch, just inches away from the front door, a moment. He turned and looked across the porch. He could see Peter Harmon standing only yards away, just next door, standing on *his* front porch, staring back, with a coffee cup, nestled in his hands, as if to keep himself warm. He took a sip from the coffee, staring back at the detective.

"Before we leave, I want an officer on Mr Harmon's door. I want to know everything. Where he was last night. What he was doing. *Who* he was doing! God damn it! Everything! Including his fucking jock size! Do I make myself clear?" shouted Detective Quinn.

"Of course, sir," Deputy Preston answered, just above a whisper.

Detective Quinn made his way in through the front door of the house and into the foyer. The living room was the first room to the right. His eyes lifted, a little, up the staircase. A female officer walked briskly down the staircase, carrying a toddler, no older than eighteen months old.

"You are fucking kidding me with this shit!" Detective Quinn muttered under his breath. "That poor child."

The detective kept his eyes on the toddler as the female officer walked out of the house with the baby in her arms, cradling it gently, trying to keep it calm.

"I'll talk to the officer," Deputy Preston said, following the female officer.

Detective Quinn said nothing. He shifted his eyes back to the bottom of the staircase. He could see the commotion carrying on.

"What have we got here?" he asked the coroner.

"Detective," the coroner answered, their tone of voice professional. "A single, white female. Her name was Eleanor Padbury. Age. Forty. She was the neighbour of, er, um, Peter Harmon." His voice trailed off.

"Of course!" Detective Quinn answered, angrily. "You don't think I don't know that? I mean, what the *fuck* happened?"

"Her throat was slashed. Her body was found this morning. A neighbour heard a baby crying and called the police."

"A call? Who called?" Detective Quinn asked, intrigued, looking at the officer.

"Um… Peter Harmon, sir. I have been here for almost half an hour. I place her death, Eleanor's death, between two and four this morning."

"Boyfriend? Girlfriend? Husband? Wife?"

"No, sir. Eleanor was single."

"Where are the two officers we had on duty outside last night?" Detective Quinn shouted, hoping one of his officers paid him the slightest of attention.

A few eyes looked his way.

"Where are they? Are you telling me they didn't see a fucking thing all night? Get me the officers on duty!"

"Yes, sir." answered the closest officer.

The police officer walked briskly past the detective, leaving him with the coroner.

There was another police officer taking photographs of the crime scene. A stretcher was wheeled into the front of the house. Detective Quinn kept his eyes on it, a moment, as two ambulance officers made their way into the room, moving Eleanor Padbury onto the stretcher, and covering her deceased body with a single white bed sheet. There were other police officers on duty covering the living room and the rest of the house.

"Detective," the coroner said, just above a whisper as he walked across the room.

"Bill, what have we got?"

"Same killer."

"How?"

"Whoever this is left an identical mask to that of Dorothy Baeyer's crime scene and the young girl in the park. This wasn't just some random act of violence gone wrong. Whoever this is, whoever is behind this, has a story to tell."

"Fuck!" Detective Quinn muttered, just above a whisper.

"Whoever this is. They're smart. They made their way in and out without disturbing anything. I'll have my report on your desk within twenty-four hours."

"Thank you, Bill. Good job."

The coroner walked past Detective Quinn, patting him on the left shoulder as he walked past.

Deputy Preston made his way through the front door and into the living room. His eyes scoured the room. Detective Quinn was standing over the crime scene talking with the photographer. Deputy Preston made his way in further.

"We have Officers Woods and Knight in the kitchen for you now, Detective," Deputy Preston said, just above a whisper as he leaned in, not wanting to disturb the photographer.

"Thank you, Andrew."

Detective Quinn made his way down the corridor and into the kitchen. He dodged the oncoming traffic of the other officers, as Deputy Preston followed.

The detective stood in the entrance to the kitchen. The two officers on duty from the night before, stood before him, in civilian attire, t-shirt and jeans. The younger officer, Officer Woods, appeared sheepish and nervous. Detective Quinn was the first to notice. He looked to Officer Knight, the bearish, Sam Rockwell type.

"What have you got to say?" Detective Quinn asked calmly.

"It was a quiet night," Officer Knight answered. "We didn't see anything. We heard a baby screaming. It stopped. We thought the parents woke and put the baby to sleep." He shrugged.

"That's it?"

"That's it."

"Get out of my sight. Both of you."

The two officers walked out of the kitchen, past the detective and the deputy. Deputy Preston walked past Detective Quinn, standing in front of him now. The two made eye contact. Their faces were sombre.

"That makes three," Detective Quinn said, softly. "We officially have a serial killer on our hands. Just like Peter said."

"What would you like to do?"

"Nothing yet," the detective answered with a sigh, followed by a hint of a smile.

Deputy Preston was thrown, a little.

"I don't want to spook the locals," Detective Quinn continued. "The curfew remains in place until we find this son of a bitch!"

"Yes, sir."

It had been three days now since the discovery of Eleanor Padbury, at the base of her staircase, her throat slashed, and her face hidden behind a clown mask. The squad cars had gone. So, too, the ambulance. And the crowd of people in the street returned to their daily lives. The house remained locked. The curtains in the front living room were pulled to a close. There was a local newspaper thrown into the front yard. It had been sitting there now for almost two days.

There was a knock at the door. Not heavy, not like Mike or Andrew, say. This was repetitive and petite, almost. Peter walked to the front door. The image, unknown to him, appeared, through the frosted glass. The front door swung open. And, there, standing in front of him, was a woman, in her early to mid-fifties, black, long, fine hair, tied back into a slick ponytail. She was dressed casually, in denim jeans, slim cut, with what appeared to be riding boots and a thick, navy blue puffer, winter jacket to keep warm. Winter had arrived.

"Hello?" Peter asked, politely, yet concerned.

"My name is Rebecca Hudson. We spoke on the phone. I'm from Channel Seven News."

"Of course. I know who you are." Peter answered, a little uninterested.

"I'm here to talk about your father. Your mother. This town."

"I'm sorry," Peter answered, just as uninterested as before. "I can't do this. I won't sell out the memory of my father for you to sell a story and win the ratings against a competing network. But, to say, there are no new insights into my mother and my family. People know the truth. They know what happened."

"And now, the murders?" Rebecca asked, intrigued.

"Time's up, Ms Hudson. I'm sorry."

Peter took a step backwards and slammed the front door shut.

Rebecca Hudson stood there on the front porch, angry, her shoulders slouching forward.

Peter walked from the front door, deeper into the house. He climbed the staircase, in leaps and bounds. He reached the second floor, a little out of breath. He turned to see the image through the glass of the front door gone. His cell phone began to ring. Peter retrieved it from his trouser pocket. Caller Unknown.

"Hello, Peter," the deep and familiar voice said.

"Now what?"

"I was so close to you the other night. I could have broken in and slashed your throat whilst you slept."

Peter was angry. There were tears welling in his eyes.

"But I'm afraid poor Eleanor Padbury. Her role got cut. A little cameo and a real crowd-pleaser for you and your neighbours whilst the police investigated the scene. I slashed her throat just to watch her bleed out in front of me as her kid screamed for its mother, upstairs."

"This isn't a fucking movie!"

"You'll die when I want you to, Peter, and not a moment before. In the meantime, enjoy the suffering!"

The phone line disconnected. "Fuck!" Peter shouted in frustration.

Peter was back in the hospital, again. He was sitting on the side of a bed in the emergency room, with the curtains drawn for privacy with a large lamp shining on his head wound, again. Dr Jim Goulas was in the same position, wearing the same white coat, standing in front of Peter, almost over the top of him, as he tended to the stitches in his forehead. The first stitch was picked at with a fine pair of small scissors. Dr Goulas turned and dropped the small scissors on the metal tray behind him. Another medical student was hovering close by, watching the procedure. Dr Goulas picked up a scalpel, next. He was deep in concentration. The blade of the scalpel moved in close, for finer inspection.

"This won't hurt a bit." Dr Goulas said, just above a whisper.

"Yeah?" Peter asked, flinching a little, feeling the cold of the blade against his skin, tugging at the wound, and tightening his left fist as it grabbed at the bed sheet, screwing it into a tight, little ball.

"There we go." Dr Goulas smiled. "All done. How do you feel now?

"Great," Peter answered, shortly, as he caught his reflection in the mirror Dr Goulas held in front of him. Peter leaned in for a closer inspection. His fingers of his left hand ran over the scar, a moment. The memory of the scars on his back came flooding back. He closed his eyes tightly.

Peter was home now. The evening was setting in on another night over Hillsboro. The lights in the house were switched on. Peter was in his bedroom, getting dressed for the evening ahead of him. It was an invitation to dinner at Andrew's home, care of Emily and Andrew. He stood by the side of his bed in black cotton boxer shorts as he pulled on a pair of denim jeans, one leg at a time, before pulling on a long-sleeved, black cotton button-down shirt. It was then, a heavy knock at the front door, pounded. *Knock. Knock. Knock.* Peter diverted his eyes. He stood there, at the end of his bed, midway, buttoning his shirt, staring down the hallway. There was another knock. *Knock.* Peter raced out of the bedroom, down the hallway, and the staircase, with his hand firmly on the banister. The shirt was tucked at the front only, leaving the rest of the shirt to fall naturally. A blurry image appeared through the frosted glass in the door. Peter leaned in and opened the door.

"Hey, you," Peter said, just above a whisper, with a hint of a smile on his face.

"Don't you look good this evening," Mike answered, smiling back.

"This old thing?" Peter asked, jokingly. "Where are my manners? Please, come on in."

Peter stepped to one side and let Mike walk through the front door. He came into the house, walking into the foyer, as Peter closed the front door behind him.

"I'm almost ready."

"Don't rush on my count. I like what I see."

Mike turned and smiled. He stood there, in front of Peter in a navy blue, long-sleeved shirt with black jeans and boots, neatly dressed.

"Look at you." Peter smiled.

Mike stepped in close to Peter, leaning in and kissing him deeply.

"Hey, you," Mike said, just above a whisper, and a smile brimming from ear to ear. Peter looked at Mike a moment, he couldn't hide his smile.

"I'm running late. I'm sorry. I'll be ready in five, I promise."

Peter climbed the staircase. His hand firmly on the banister, once again. Mike followed him to the bedroom.

It was Andrew's turn now. He walked from the hallway and into his bedroom with a damp white cotton towel wrapped loosely around his waist. It was on an angle, showing a little more side muffin and butt cheek than he normally would, but Andrew was in a hurry. His hair was wet.

Andrew dropped the damp towel to the bedroom floor and walked naked across the floor to the set of drawers pushed up against the wall at the end of his bed. He pulled open the drawer, second from the top, and pulled out a pair of underwear and climbed into his boxer-briefs. He adjusted himself, a little, making himself feel a little more comfortable.

Emily appeared in the doorway of the bedroom. She stood there silent, a moment, watching her other half, in his underwear, deciding what he will wear for the evening.

"Keep it simple," she said, grabbing Andrew's attention. "A shirt and jeans."

The two caught each other's eyes and smiled. Emily walked into the bedroom, confidently. "You look amazing," Andrew answered, just above a whisper.

There was soft music playing from the living room that made 'its way down the hallway and into the bedroom.

Emily walked into the bedroom, sporting a bright-white dress with a high neckline. The dress clung to her petite frame well. And as the eyes dropped further and further down the dress, the lining of the skirt was filled with what looked like shadows of birds, in a large flock, wild in movement, in dark grey.

"I need your help with this dress," Emily said. "Can you zip me up?"

"This is new?" Andrew asked, still above a whisper, standing in front of her in his underwear. "I like it."

"It was on sale."

"Come here."

Emily stepped in closer, turning her back a little, for help on the zip. Andrew leaned in and kissed the back of her neck. It startled Emily. A smile surfaced to her lips. It was a nice surprise. But a surprise, nonetheless. She tilted her head back, a little.

"That zip is going in the wrong direction." Emily laughed.

"We have time," Andrew whispered in her left ear. "Besides, I like what I see."

"You do?"

"Yeah."

"Keep it in your pants, big boy. Our guests will be here any minute."

Andrew took control. He zipped the back of the dress up quickly, turning Emily a little, before leaning in and kissing her deeply and passionately. He pushed her up against the bedroom wall. His kiss lowered down, past her lips, to her neck, lower. Andrew was on his knees. Emily tilted her head back a little further, closing her eyes tightly.

"I guess we have a few minutes," she whispered with pleasure.

The doorbell soon rang. *Ring. Ring.* Andrew raced from the kitchen, with a cold bottle of beer in his hands, and walked to the front door. He leaned in and opened it. And, there, standing in front of him, under the light bulb on the front porch, were Peter and Mike.

"Hello, fellas," Andrew said with a smile. "Please, come on in." Andrew stepped to one side to allow his guests inside his home.

Peter smiled at his best friend as he walked into his house, carrying a bottle of red wine. Mike followed. He forced a smile and shook Andrew's right hand, politely.

The guests stepped inside the house. Andrew closed the front door.

The evening was underway. The two couples followed the rules of etiquette when it came to double dating. Each partner eventually strayed from the heard of the pack and hung out with a member of the other couple. Mike stood by the refrigerator, watching Emily dance around the kitchen, putting the final touches to tonight's menu. It was quite simple. It was home-made burgers, thick-cut fries and salad. Whilst Peter and Andrew were in the living room, sitting on the couch, quietly talking amongst themselves, in a world of their own. The music from the stereo was now switched off. The lighting in the living room was quite sombre. The lights in the ceiling were switched off. However, the two large lamp lights, standing opposite each other, on the far sides of the room, were switched on.

Emily took her time with dinner. It was all a balancing act. And she did it incredibly. Emily worked on preparing dinner, in between enjoying her conversation with Mike, whilst peering into the living room, from time to time, checking in on Andrew and Peter. She was a real marvel. A glass of red wine kept her entertained, giving her a little buzz. Mike nursed his bottle of beer in his hands.

"I admire Peter," Emily said, peering in the living room, then looking over her right shoulder, back at Mike. "I can see why he likes you. You guys make a great couple."

"Thank you," Mike answered, with a smile, after taking another sip from his beer.

"I can't believe how much he has been through over the years. You're one lucky man."

"I can only imagine what it must have been like for him," Mike answered, just above a whisper. "But I do love him. He is a strong man."

The dinner double-date had come to an end for the evening. The food was fun, as was the conversation and evening, in general. The three high school friends shared some laughs and traded some stories, whilst Andrew got to know Mike a little more. They weren't best of friends, but they tolerated each other, for the sake of their partners. The conversation touched on Andrew's impending birthday, and what should be planned. The best the four minds could come up with was dinner out at The Watering Hole, only this time, rent it out, and keep it a private function. Invite only. The four agreed.

Mike drove Peter home for the evening. He spent the night at Peter's. The two were fast asleep in bed. The bed cover was pulled back, a little. Mike was exposed. He was naked under the bed cover. He slept on his left shoulder, almost cuddling up to Peter. His right leg lay on top of the bed cover, to help cool the rest of his body. The muscles in Mike's back were bulging and defined, some. The hint of his butt cheek was exposed from the bed cover. Peter was fast asleep. He was lying on his back, his chest exposed, sleeping away.

The light in the living room was switched off. There was a shade of light coming in from the porch, lighting the room, some. It was enough to outline a young boy, no older than seven or eight, standing in the middle of the room, staring down at a handful of young bodies lying unconscious on the floor. There were marks, which were red in colour, around their necks, outlining the shape of fingers and hands around their necks. A single sneeze, followed by a small, chuckle from another, broke the silence and filled the room. It was nothing more than a game. A childhood game on a sleepover. The living room floor was littered with children in sleeping bags, some sleeping away, others playing games and telling jokes. It was just children having fun. A young Peter looked down, over the other children. It was nothing more than pretend. A game. A sleepover.

Peter awoke from the nightmare, gasping for breath; his hands clung to his chest tightly, his body drenched in sweat. It took a moment for him to catch his breath again. He turned his head a little to the right, and there, staring back at him, fast asleep, and snoring away, was Mike, unnoticed.

Chapter Twelve...

It had been several days now since the dinner party at Andrew's home. Peter followed up the dinner invite with a phone call, both to Andrew and Emily, thanking them for their hospitality, conversation and good food. The phone call to Emily inevitably turned to Andrew and organising his birthday party. Emily, herself, was back at work and juggling her time between making her boss happy, and locking down a location for her partner's birthday, as well as working on an invite list.

Peter. Mike. And Emily were a given. And, yes, Jayne, too. Emily couldn't think of a reason why they never hung out, just the two of them. But it was safe not to rock the boat. There were also friends from the station. Peter cringed at the very thought.

Peter made his way into town. The pantry was in dire need of stocking up; the refrigerator too, for that matter. Peter walked into the grocery store, grabbed the nearest cart and started making his way aimlessly up and down each aisle.

"Excuse me!" a voice called out. "Excuse me!" it repeated.

Peter looked around, blinking his eyes a few times, looking around. "Hi, Peter," the familiar voice called.

It was Jayne.

"Jayne, hi," Peter answered, forcing a smile. "I'm sorry, I didn't hear you. Own world, you know?" Jayne chuckled a little.

"What can I do for you?"

"I won't take up too much of your time. I just got to ask. Call me, nosy." Another chuckle, mixed with nervous anticipation. "I just have to know. Why did you come back to Hillsboro? You know, with all the murders and all."

Peter was stunned by such a question. It rendered him speechless, a moment. His eyes widened in horror at such a question.

"Don't you think you should have stayed away?"

"What concern is it of yours?"

Jayne chuckled nervously. She retreated into herself a little, a little sheepishly. Peter pushed his cart forward, taking a single step toward Jayne. She locked eyes on him. Peter reached out and grabbed her by the wrist. His grip tightened, a little.

"I want to know, Jayne?

The expression on his face was one of anger.

"You hunt me down in a grocery store and harass me with questions about my personal life. I have a right to know, don't you think?"

Jayne pulled her wrist from his grip. She flashed a forced smile, albeit briefly.

"The people of Hillsboro don't need reminding of your bloodstained history." she shrugged.

"Fuck you!" Peter whispered, viciously.

"Excuse me?" she asked, shocked.

"Don't play the innocent, Jayne. It doesn't suit you. There is a reason I don't talk to you. You never changed since high school. Always the bitch! Always having to stick your nose in where it doesn't belong. You cunt!"

Jayne's eyes and mouth opened in horror. "Well...." she began.

Peter turned his back on Jayne, pushing his cart forward, down the aisle, some more. He paused a moment, and turned back, looking over his left shoulder at her.

"If there is a serial killer out there, patterning themselves after my mother, that would put you in the line of fire, wouldn't it?"

"Was that a threat?"

"Seriously, Jayne, have a nice day," Peter answered, just above a whisper.

Peter turned, again, pushing his cart as he walked to the end of the aisle, leaving Jayne standing there, all alone.

The bags from the grocery store were littered on the kitchen floor, spread around the refrigerator, with nothing packed away. Brown paper bags were sitting inside plastic bags, filled with wrapped cold meats and other items. A low hum echoed from somewhere inside the house. It was a single-storey dwelling with three bedrooms and one bathroom. A cheap rental property on the outskirts of Hillsboro. The television set in the living room was switched off. The kitchen table was immaculate. The hallway was long and dark, as all but one of the doors was pulled to a close. The door at the end of the hallway, the one leading into the master bedroom was wide open. The low humming was becoming much clearer now. It wasn't so much a hum, but more the moaning, the heavy breathing, the panting of making love. It was wild and intense. It was forbidden and a secret. It was Jayne and Andrew.

The bedroom floor was littered with clothes. A white, floral sundress and women's underwear. And, a pair of denim jeans, jockey shorts and a black polo shirt and boots. Andrew was fucking Jayne, again. They were in the throes of passion, enjoying every lasting moment. Jayne was straddling Andrew. His fingers running down the arch of her back, his nails almost clawing into her, leaving behind red marks, stretching several inches down her back. Her head tilted back, her eyes closed. The two almost ready to climax at a moment's notice. It wasn't love. It was sport fucking, at best. Andrew reached his climax. His large hands moved from the arch of Jayne's back and down her chest, over her breasts.

"Get off me," he said, just above a whisper, and lifting his left leg a little. "I need a shower." Jayne climbed off the top of Andrew and on top of the bed, quick to pull the sheets and cover over the top of her naked, petite frame. Andrew crawled to the side of the bed, pulling off his condom and throwing it in the waste paper basket by the nightstand.

Andrew stood in front of the bed, in front of Jayne, his body covered in sweat. "I'm taking a shower," he repeated.

Andrew turned his back on Jayne. He walked out of the master bedroom, down the hallway a little, reaching the second door on the right, pushing it open and leaning in to switch on the light, before walking into the bathroom. The door closed behind him and the water from the shower was quick to run. The water under the shower was hot. The steam rose to the bathroom ceiling. Andrew stood under the hot water, his head tilted back, his eyes closed, his hands racing over his chest and torso, and all over his body, washing himself down with a bar of soap. Andrew turned and faced the water. He raised his hand above his shoulders, a moment, leaning against the wall.

Jayne remained in the master bedroom, lying on the bed. The bed covers kicked back, a little, and she climbed to the side of the bed. She climbed to her feet and retrieved her dress from the bedroom floor. She slipped into it quickly, including her underwear. Jayne stood tall and pulled her hair back into a rather messy ponytail. She looked down at the floor, again, picking Andrew's clothes from the floor and laying them neatly at the end of the bed. She took pride in his clothes. It was love, on her part, anyway. His cell phone from the back pocket, from his pair of denim jeans, fell to the floor.

"Shit!" Jayne whispered to herself, in frustration. She leaned down and picked it up off the floor.

The screen of the cell phone came to life. There appeared to be a missed call and a few text messages, from various people, including Peter, Emily and Detective Quinn. But it was the cover screen of the cell phone that got Jayne's attention. It was a picture of Emily, smiling. A black-and-white picture. A photograph taken of the two of them on a recent camping trip. There were trees and wildlife in the background. Jayne looked at the picture intently.

"What are you doing?" Andrew asked, surprised, standing in the bedroom doorway with a towel around his waist.

"It was your phone. It fell out of your pocket when I picked it up off the floor." Jayne answered, concerned and feeling a little hurt.

"Don't ever touch my stuff like that, again. Period!" Jayne was startled.

"It could have been work. It could have been Emily," Andrew smiled, a little, trying to defuse the situation. He stepped into the bedroom, with one hand on the side of his waist, holding his towel up, and taking the cell phone from Jayne abruptly, in the other.

Jayne watched Andrew around the bedroom, watching him get dressed, hiding his cell phone back in his pocket.

"I got to go to work. I'm late. I'll call you tonight, okay?"

"Of course," Jayne answered, a little put out.

There had been a turning point in their relationship. The exchange of text messages between Andrew and Jayne started hot and heavy, multiple times a day, which included photographs, from both of them, in seductive and romantically inclined poses. Now, it was another story. Jayne knew each time Andrew would say he would be in touch later that day, it was a lie. She did her best to not let that feeling of abandonment hurt as much as it did. Jayne told herself that Andrew was the deputy of this town, which was true. She told herself that he was a very busy man who couldn't get to his cell phone as much as she had hoped. She wouldn't usually hear from him for days on end, at times.

Andrew got himself dressed and stood in front of Jayne, maintaining eye contact. He extended his left hand outwards, taking her left hand in his, and squeezed her little finger, twice, in a quick double-pump action, as a smile surfaced to his lips. It was his way of telling her he was thinking of her. He turned and walked out of the master bedroom and down the hallway toward the front door of the house. Jayne was quick to follow. Andrew reached the front door. He turned, again, and leaned in and kissed Jayne deeply and slowly, a moment, before pulling back and opening the door. Jayne stood there, at the entrance of her home, watching the man she was falling in love with running toward his truck. Her eyes pulled off his bulking frame a moment, to a see a single mother pushing a toddler in a pram down her street. The two women exchanged looks, they didn't like one another.

The driver's side door to the truck opened, and Andrew climbed inside. His bulking frame moved from left to right, trying to find that sweet, comfortable position. The door slammed shut. Andrew was sitting behind the steering wheel, staring back at Jayne through his windscreen that was in much need of a clean. There was no hint of a smile on his face. Just concern. The engine to the truck roared to life and slowly backed out of the driveway, and into the traffic in the street, behind him. Andrew looked out at the house one more time before placing his foot on the accelerator and driving to the end of the road. Jayne stood there watching him disappear from her sight.

Jayne stepped slowly backwards, retreating into the rental house she called home for the last eighteen months, give or take. She stepped back a little and closed the door in front of her. Jayne walked around the house. It sounded so quiet. She hated that. She made her way back to the kitchen, standing in the entrance, a moment, looking down at the floor, and at the groceries, she needed to put away. Andrew helped out from time to time, giving her a few extra dollars, now and then.

"Great!" she whispered under her breath sarcastically, before walking in and tending to the groceries, slowly putting them away.

The minutes had passed by. The television set in the living room was now switched on. It was for a bit of noise to fill the house, more than anything. There was some TV drama playing. There was an end in sight, almost reaching the finishing line, as Jayne placed the last of the groceries into the pantry and the refrigerator. The cell phone, her cell phone, on the kitchen counter began to vibrate and make noise. The ringtone was more like a bird chirping. *Chirp. Chirp.* Jayne looked over at her cell phone as she lifted her head out of the refrigerator. The milk went into the refrigerator and the door closed. She reached for the cell phone and pressed a button on the side of the device. The front screen came to life. It was a text message. A smile surfaced to her lips. Jayne immediately thought of Andrew. The ID read *Private Number.* The smile was quick to disappear. Jayne was quick to open the message. The message itself was a photograph. It was a photograph of Jayne standing in her very own kitchen, wearing the very same clothes she was wearing now, putting her groceries away. Her heart thudded. It started to race. She looked up from the cell phone and walked over to the window which overlooked the back yard. There was no one there. She turned to the right, a little, turning her back on the kitchen window. Her heart continued to race. A second text message was received. From the same number. *Private Number.* Jayne opened the message.

"*You fucking slut!*"

In large, black type.

Jayne continued to look at the message. Her index finger of her right hand glided over the message. She felt angry and confused and very aware of her breathing.

"Fuck you! *Whoever* you are!" she whispered.

Peter was Emily's sidekick for the day, at least. He rode shotgun and sat in the front passenger seat as Emily drove to The Watering Hole to scope out the venue for Andrew's birthday party. The radio was blaring. It was playing music, both new and old. And some the two friends remembered from their high school days, and they sang along to the words, as best they could. Peter and Emily couldn't sing to save their own lives. Peter told Emily about his run-in with Jayne in the grocery store. It made her skin crawl.

"What a bitch!" Emily said, just above a whisper, as she concentrated on the road in front of her.

"It's over now," Peter answered, "I won't let her get to me, not as I did in high school."

"Believe me, she isn't worth it."

"I'll just do my best to avoid her at the party."

"Don't let her get to you. You're better than that. Jayne Scott is trash. She was in high school, and she is today. End of story."

The music continued to play on the car radio.

Emily pulled into the car park of The Watering Hole. It was a little after ten in the morning and the car park was practically empty. The engine to her car had died and the two friends climbed out and made their way inside the bar and restaurant.

In the light of day, The Watering Hole looked as though it had passed it's use-by date. There were beer stains on the floor, the curtains, and on the furniture. There were spider webs packed in the rafters. But, with a little elbow grease and some good mood lighting, and some decoration, such as large silver balloons, to distract the eye, the place could be pulled together to look pleasant.

Emily spoke with the manager of the bar, and given the whole five-cent tour of the facility, as she walked from the main bar and into the private dining rooms. Peter wondered around, taking in the sights. He could hear his friend talking with the manager, giving him her list of demands.

"I want warm lighting…" he heard her say. "I will have large silver balloons."

Peter was flashing back to his high school days when Emily ran for class president. That authoritative voice was beginning to shine, once more. Peter chuckled to himself, somewhat.

"Hey," Peter heard a voice. "Can I get you something? A drink, perhaps?"

Peter turned and looked at the bar. And there, standing in front of him, from behind the bar, itself, was a short and stocky man, somewhere in his late thirties to early forties. His arms were muscular and well defined, as was his chest. There were a couple of tattoos on his arms, two, maybe three.

And sported a neatly trimmed dirty blonde beard, with a short haircut, that was shaved on the sides and back of the head.

The man behind the bar wore a simple white t-shirt, which clung tightly to his muscular frame. The t-shirt itself had a moss-green trim around the biceps. It was a very simple, yet classic design.

"Thank you," Peter answered, with an almost nervous smile. "I would. Coke with ice."

"Of course. Coming right up," the barman smiled.

The barman got to work and prepared the drink order. Peter watched on. He was light on his feet and moved around the bar with exact precision. The barman dug the glass into the chilled bucket of ice. The Coke poured, rushing quickly into the glass until it was topped up. And a wedge of lemon, for decoration and added taste. The barman slid the glass across the bar, itself, toward Peter.

"For you," the barman said, just above a whisper and a hint of a smile on his lips. "On the house. My treat."

"You won't get into trouble?"

"I know the manager. We good." he nodded, reassuringly.

"Well, thank you."

Peter took a sip from the glass. It wet his lips and raced down his throat. It was just what he needed. "So, what's going on? Something important, by the looks of it."

"Oh, this? Just a friend from high school. She is organising her boyfriend's birthday party."

"Sounds like fun. Will you be there?"

"Sure."

"Well, I'm here most nights. I'll probably see you around if we are catering to the party."

Peter took a deeper sip from the glass. He wiped his mouth with the back of his left hand. "I look forward to it."

"Me, too," the barman smiled.

"Thank you. For the drink, I mean."

"My pleasure."

Peter slid the near-empty glass back across the bar. The barman took the glass, his hand wrapping around the glass, his index finger of his right hand, touching Peter's left hand, a little, and was quick to place it in the sink, ready to be washed and used again.

The two exchanged pleasantries before Peter walked away from the bar, toward the entrance of one of the private dining rooms. He could hear Emily's voice, again.

"Hey, I didn't even get your name," Peter said, as he turned around one last time, facing the bar. The barman had vanished.

Peter stood there, feeling puzzled. "Everything okay?" Emily called out.

Peter looked at his friend.

"Of course." Forcing a smile, and feeling a little down.

"All good?" Emily smiled.

The day of Andrew's birthday party finally arrived. He started his day waking up from the night before, alone. He was in bed, the bed cover peeled back to his waistline, exposing some of his naked frame underneath. He turned on his side, a little, exposing his right leg and butt cheek from under the cover, as he reached for his cell phone on the nightstand. He pulled it off its charger. The time was a little before seven in the morning, and already there were missed text messages from friends at work, telling him to enjoy his day off, whilst others wished him the best and told him they would see him later this evening at The Watering Hole. There were no text messages from Emily, Jayne, or Peter. Andrew peeled back the rest of the bed cover and climbed to his feet.

The morning progressed a little further. Andrew was dressed for winter. He stood in his front yard. It was a cold and icy start to the morning. Andrew was dressed in a pair of grey sweat pants with navy blue stripes on the outer leg, which ran from the waistline to his ankle. He wore a simple white t-shirt and a dark grey hoodie, which was zipped almost to the top of his chest. He had his headphones plugged into each ear, listening to his music. Andrew was ready to start his morning run.

Andrew arrived home. The morning run took almost a full hour. The television set was switched on. It was the morning news. There was a story breaking about a jealous girlfriend killing her married lover, his wife, and seven-year-old daughter in their sleep. The volume was quite high, enough to travel throughout the house, anyway. The light in the kitchen was switched on. The clothes Andrew had worn on his run were screwed and piled up on the white tiled floor of the bathroom. Andrew had poured himself a hot bath, and lowered himself in, relaxing from the run, feeling his muscles in his legs and lower back unwind. Andrew reached out of the bathtub and grabbed a coffee cup, which sat on the tiled floor of the bathroom. He made himself his first coffee for the morning.

"Happy Birthday to me," he whispered to himself, taking a sip from his coffee.

Andrew placed the coffee cup back on the white tiled floor and retrieved his cell phone, instead. The screen came to life. There was a text message from Peter. Andrew was quick to open it.

"Happy Birthday, A. I hope you have a great time celebrating your special day ahead, and I will see you tonight."

The message read. It brought a smile to Andrew's lips.

There was still no messages from either Emily or Jayne. Andrew placed his cell phone on the floor, close to his coffee cup, before slowly sinking further into the tub. The hot water consumed his chest. His head went under the water. Andrew held his breath and closed his eyes, tightly. And seconds later, he opened them, blinking furiously, getting used to the water. His vision was blurry.

The car park outside The Watering Hole was a little busier now, a little fuller. It was a little past seven in the evening, and the birthday party was in the early stages of getting underway. Peter drove to The Watering Hole alone. Mike was busy at work, stocktake, he said. He also said he would put in an appearance a little later in the evening if he found the time. Peter sat behind the steering wheel of his new sports utility vehicle. It was black, a similar model to his car rental. It was a little something he purchased, with a little help from Robert Prescott. The engine to the truck died, as he sat there a moment longer, his hands gripping the steering wheel at ten and two. Peter climbed out of his truck and slammed the driver's side door to a close. He could hear the music playing from inside the bar. It was like a low, pulsating thump.

Peter stepped inside the bar. It was loud and crowded. The party was in full swing. The lights were switched on, there was music playing from the jukebox, and there were large silver and crimson-red balloons, filled with helium, which decorated the bar and the private dining room, weighted down with bricks, whilst other's escaped, floating to the ceiling. Peter scanned the bar. He couldn't see Emily, nor the birthday boy in question, Andrew. He made his way to the front of the bar, in and amongst the other guests, most, he didn't know, except he had seen them working at the Hillsboro Police Station. The guests were laughing and talking amongst themselves, leaving Peter pretty much to himself. There were some stares from the off-duty officers.

The bar was busy. Peter could see the same barman from a couple of days prior. This evening, he was wearing a simple black t-shirt and denim jeans, just like the rest of the staff. The barman made eye contact with Peter and flashed a hint of a smile. Peter smiled back, with a hint of a wave, as he leaned against the bar.

"Hey, you," the barman smiled, "'it's great to see you again." "And you."

"Have you been here long?"

"I just arrived."

"Well, I hope you and your friends have a fun time, tonight."

"Thank you."

"And don't be shy. I hope you'll head back to the bar and say hi to me this evening." The barman flashed a wink.

Peter was a little taken aback. He smiled, feeling a little nervous.

"What can I get you?" the barman asked, politely, above the sound of the other guests and the music from the jukebox.

"Beer. Whatever you have on tap is fine. Thank you."

"Coming right up. Don't go anywhere."

There was another smile.

The barman returned with the beer. Peter exchanged pleasantries with the barman, again. This time he got his name. It was Blair Holden. And his number.

Peter took his beer, carefully nursing it, as he made his way from the main bar and headed into the private dining room. There was a sign hanging on the front door of The Watering Hole. It read "Closed for Private Function". The private room was alive. A large wooden table stood in the middle of the room, seating close to thirty people. The fireplace roared with fire, keeping the room warm. Peter scanned the room, and there were Emily and Andrew, standing by the fireplace, drinks in hand, and Andrew re-telling a childhood story from a previous birthday party to guests that were hanging onto every word he uttered. Jayne was nowhere to be seen. Peter made eye contact with Andrew and Emily across the room. He lifted his glass, a little, as if to raise a toast.

"Happy birthday!" he mouthed, just above a whisper. Andrew nodded his head in acceptance, smiling.

Emily smiled.

Peter made his way across the room, and over to the fireplace.

The party continued into the evening. The time was getting on, somewhere close to ten, now. And there was still no sign of Mike. Peter checked his cell phone. There were no missed calls or text messages. Peter shrugged his shoulders and gave up. He had been back and forth to the bar, to visit Blair another two times. He switched his choice of drink to soda since he was driving home. The music continued to blare from the jukebox.

The menu this evening consisted of a selection of little beef and chicken sliders, fries, nachos, salad (for the health-conscious), and drinks on tap, to name a few. The far north-east corner of the private room was dedicated to birthday presents. There were wrapped gifts, of all different shapes and sizes.

Andrew excused himself from the crowd a moment, leaving Peter and Emily to talk amongst themselves. He passed his glass of beer to Emily, for her to look after, then gave Peter a somewhat drunken tight hug for turning up to the party, before making his way to the bathroom. Jayne had arrived, fashionably late, she told everyone. The truth was her babysitter had cancelled at the last minute and she found it difficult to find a replacement at such short notice. Jayne sat at the table, with a vodka and lemon, as she listened to a fellow police officer chatting away. She was quickly losing interest and politely excused herself to the bathroom, too. Peter watched, giving Emily a slight nudge. The two friends looked at each other, Emily rolling her eyes, a little.

The door to the men's restroom pushed open. And there, standing in the door frame, was Andrew. He wore a dark-blue-and-black flannel shirt with black jeans and boots. He was neatly dressed. His shirt was tucked in the front, flashing off a large metal belt buckle.

"Is this some kind of fucking joke?" Jayne screamed, waving the picture she received as a text message, labelling her a slut. "This is how you keep me in line? So, I don't say anything? Fuck you!"

"What the actual fuck, Jayne?" Andrew answered, surprised. "What the fuck is going on?"

"You fuck me when you want me when you need something, and abandon me when you go back to Emily and your friends. I won't be played like that any more."

"Calm the fuck down and don't create a scene!" Andrew ordered, just above a whisper. He grabbed Jayne by the shoulders and pushed her backwards, a little, into a tiny hutch, against the wooden walls, out of sight from the other party guests. "I didn't send you no fucking text message." Andrew looked at the photograph, again. His expression didn't change. "It looks like you got yourself an admirer, there. Don't fuck with me and spoil my night. This is my fucking birthday! We will talk about this later. Do I make myself clear?"

"Perfect!"

Jayne looked at Andrew with disdain. She was angry and could feel her heartbeat racing, again. A man she had allowed herself to fall in love with, treated her like *this,* pushing her against a wall, treating her like a dirty little secret. Their eyes still connected until Andrew pulled away, first. He stepped backwards, a little, from out of the tiny hutch, and walked back out to greet the other guests. He forced himself to smile, laughing at the commotion in the dining room.

Jayne stood there, a moment longer, with her back against the wall. Her shaken state was slowly returning to some form of normalcy, although the voice in her head was screaming with rage before her shoulders lowered, and she placed her cell phone back in her pocket. Jayne closed her eyes momentarily, as a mechanism to compose herself. She opened her eyes, again, seconds later.

And a smile surfaced to her lips. Jayne raised her hands, running her fingers through her slicked back ponytail as if to neaten her appearance. She soon followed, giving Andrew a head start, so as not to look suspicious or draw unwanted attention, as she, too, left the restrooms and returned to the party.

The evening progressed. The birthday celebration was reaching its end now. The birthday cake had arrived. The guests gathered and sang Happy Birthday to Andrew. Detective Quinn was in attendance. He arrived late and mingled amongst the other officers. And Peter kept his distance. He felt his eyes on him, from time to time. Peter was polite and nodded in his direction. The conversation was casual and minimal. The birthday cake itself was a two-tier white chocolate sponge cake with a coconut border around the edges. The cake had been sliced and cut into pieces.

Jayne was sitting at the table, alone. The closest person sitting near her, was three seats to her right, another police officer, chatting up another girl, who hung on his every word. Jayne looked at the girl. She was in her early twenties with shoulder-length curly, blonde hair and a petite frame, wearing a simple white sundress and matching heels. Her make-up was simple, as was her jewellery, gold stud earrings and a thin chain around her neck. Jayne rolled her eyes. *Typical*, she thought. Jayne, herself, sat in front of her half-eaten slice of cake with another vodka and lemon, large. The glass was almost empty now. She felt as though she had passed her limit, and was feeling a strong surge of Dutch courage. Her eyes lifted off the cake, scoured the room, and saw Andrew whispering in the ear of Detective Quinn, before she moved to look at Emily, who was quietly talking to Peter on the opposite side of the table, a few chairs down. Jayne pulled herself away from the table, drink in hand, and made her way towards Peter and Emily.

Peter sat to the right of Emily. They had been talking away, reminiscing over high school, Andrew, Hillsboro, drinking away, and sharing a laugh. Peter stopped. He was the first one to look past Emily, raising his eyes a little. The expression on Emily's face changed. It was bare.

"What is it?" Emily asked, a little surprised.

Peter remained silent. He reached out for his glass of soda on the table, nodding forward, a little. Emily turned in her chair, and there in front of her, stood Jayne. She was surprised.

"Jayne, how are you?" she asked, forcing a smile.

"Great," Jayne answered, taking a sip of her drink. "Fun party tonight. Thank you for the invite." There was an awkward silence between the girls.

"Can I talk to you, you know, privately?" Jayne continued.

Emily looked at her a moment, then turned to Peter, and back again.

"Whatever you have to say, Jayne, you can say right here." There was a brief pause. "What is it?"

"I don't want to do *this* here, Emily."

"Cut the shit, Jayne! What are you trying to say, *exactly?"*

Jayne took a moment to process the comment. She finished her drink and placed the glass on the table, before leaning in toward Emily.

"I think you need to keep a leash on Andrew."

"Whatever do you mean, Jayne?"

"Think about it. I couldn't be clearer."

"You're lying," Emily answered, flat and angry, just above a whisper.

"Am I?" Jayne asked. "I could tell you how good your boyfriend's cock feels so good, deep inside me, as a cheap thrill, you know, to fire you up and get you angry." Jayne smiled. "Or I can also tell you, the small idiosyncrasies Andrew has after he cums, such as his incessant need for a shower immediately after sex, because he doesn't like the way he feels all sweaty and out of breath, after having every inch of my body."

Emily smiled, striving for politeness but feeling embarrassed. She stood up from her chair. Jayne watched her carefully, taking a little step backwards.

"Why are you even here, Jayne? I mean, really? Why? I only invited you to be polite. To please Andrew." Emily responded, looking in Andrew's direction a moment. "You're just the same as you were in high school. You're nothing more than the dirty, little poor girl everyone felt sorry for, just because you couldn't afford shit! And look at us now, huh? Nothing has changed." Emily shrugged. "You're like gum on the sidewalk, outside Villa Blanca. You don't belong."

"I may be cheap. But your boyfriend's cock, *does* feel so good, deep inside me. He makes me cum. Every time." Jayne smiled, viciously, almost victoriously, before turning her back on her former high school friends.

"You cunt!" Emily responded, just above a whisper.

"I win," Jayne answered, turning to face Emily, one more time.

"Jayne?"

"Yes?"

"You bitch!" Emily raised her right hand, high above her head, and brought it down with such force and hatred, slapping Jayne hard across the left side of her face. The slap itself, leaving a red welt on her cheek, and just below her eye, knocking her backwards, a little.

"I. Win." Emily continued, holding back the tears welling in her eyes.

She turned, leaning down to collect her personal belongings from the table. She made eye contact with Peter, although very briefly, feeling the most embarrassed she had ever been. Peter looked at his friend, shocked and surprised. His eyes wide open, so, to, was his mouth.

"Emily…" Peter mumbled, just above a whisper.

"Not now." Emily could barely muster the words, ready to break into tears. "I need to get out of here. Excuse me?"

"Of course." Peter nodded.

The fight drew the attention of the other party guests, the ones that stayed on, later into the evening, including Detective Quinn. The music from the jukebox continued to blare, amongst the silence of the party guests. Emily raced around the table, across the private room, and outside, into the bar, before making her way out, into the car park. The front door to The Watering Hole, bounced to a close, behind her. Andrew looked on in horror and surprise. His eyes scanned the room. He looked at Peter sitting helplessly at the table, at Jayne, with her face covered, having fallen into the closest chair she could find, and then at Emily, herself, running out of the bar.

"Shit!" Andrew muttered, just above a whisper. "Fuck!"

Andrew dropped his glass of beer, what little of it that was left, mind you, and raced after Emily, chasing her out into the car park.

The door to The Watering Hole burst open, again. Andrew ran through. He looked around the car park, standing out on the porch. The floodlights were switched on and only did so much. The rest was stepping into darkness. The sound of heels running over gravel grabbed his attention. He could see Emily racing towards her bug, parked on the south side of the car park.

"Emily!" Andrew shouted. There was no answer. "Emily!" he repeated.

Andrew continued the chase. "Wait!"

"Fuck you!" Emily finally responded, as she reached her bug, fumbling for her keys.

Andrew reached her, taking her in his arms, from behind, pushing her forward, a little, toward the car. The gravel scrunched under their feet.

"We are done!" Emily shouted, no longer holding back her

tears. "Done! Go back to your whore, Andrew! I can't do this any more. The lies. The cheating. I officially hate the both of you, okay? You hurt me. You broke me that much, I hate you! So, go back to Jayne… and her kid."

Emily paused a moment, placing her hands over her mouth as if connecting the dots in her head, and realising what the rest of the world knew all along.

"*You're* the father?" the question passed her lips. "No! No! Don't answer. I don't want to know." Emily turned around, pulling herself away from his grip. Andrew pulled his eyes from the gravel. The sombre expression said it all.

"I love you," Andrew said, above a whisper.

"Yeah? You have a funny way of showing it." Emily laughed, with tears in her eyes. "We're over!" She fumbled with her keys to her bug, a little more, before finding the right one, and climbing inside her car. The driver's side car door slammed shut. Andrew stepped back a bit. He looked over his shoulder and saw a few of the guests from the party look on from the porch of the bar. Andrew turned to face Emily, again.

The engine to the bug roared to life. Emily placed her foot on the accelerator and drove out of the car park as fast as her little bug could carry her. Andrew stood there a moment, watching her leave before he turned and raced toward his truck, parked on the other side of the car park.

The party was officially over for the evening. The guests were leaving, in droves. And Jayne stood outside the front door of The Watering Hole, waiting on her taxi cab to take her home for the evening. She had too much to drink to get behind the steering wheel of her car and drive home. She left her car in the car park for the evening. It wasn't the first time, either. Jayne stood out on the porch, with her black blazer hanging neatly over her shoulders and a scarf wrapped loosely around her neck, enough to breathe, anyway. She pulled her cell phone from her purse. There were no missed calls or text messages. The cell phone was stuffed back into the purse, once more, in frustration. The taxi cab soon arrived.

Jayne climbed into the back seat of the taxi cab and slammed the door shut. She made herself comfortable, putting on her seat belt, and leaned forward a little, giving the driver the address and best directions to her home. The taxi cab pulled out of the car park and into the evening traffic. The drive from The Watering Hole took a little over fifteen minutes before the taxi cab pulled into Jayne's street. The street was decorated with lamps, all switched on, and all evenly positioned on either side of the road. The sidewalks were neatly manicured. And the houses, themselves, were mostly single-storey dwellings. The taxi cab pulled up in front of Jayne's house.

The driver turned around to face his passenger, throwing one arm over the seat rest, switching on the small light which was plastered to the roof. The driver had a portly build, and was somewhere in his later forties to early fifties. His hair was chocolate brown, almost black, with a thick, but maintained beard. The driver sported a simple black cotton t-shirt, with a dark grey hoodie, which was unzipped at the chest.

"That will be ten dollars and fifty cents," the driver said, his tone of voice heavy, but polite.

"Here," Jayne answered, digging for spare change from her purse, and her voice a little slurred. "Keep the change."

The driver was quick to count the money. There was enough to cover the fare, plus a so-so tip.

The back-passenger door was pushed open, as far as it could go, on its second attempt. Jayne climbed across the seat and rose to her feet. She stumbled a little, getting out of the car, but was quick to find her balance. The passenger door to the taxi cab slammed with a thud. *Thud.* And Jayne was ready to make her way inside the house. She stumbled, a little more, across the front yard, where the driver of the taxi cab remained, the engine running, watching on, making sure she got inside her house, safely. The front door to the house opened. Jayne was met by the babysitter.

She was a young girl, no older than seventeen, with mousey brown hair, just below the shoulders, and braces.

"Hi, Ms Scott. Glenn was an angel this evening. He is fast asleep. Good night."

"Thank you," Jayne answered, just above a whisper.

The babysitter was quick to run past Jayne and headed for her car parked in the driveway. Jayne made her way inside the house, closing the front door behind her. The taxi cab pulled out from the curb and drove to the end of the street. The babysitter was quick to follow.

The lights in the living room and kitchen were switched on. Jayne made her way deeper inside the house, and down the hallway, to check on her son. She opened the bedroom and peered inside. Glenn was no older than eighteen months. He was lying on his back, neatly wrapped into a cocoon, to keep him warm for the evening. The door to the bedroom closed quietly. The shadow of Jayne's feet, under the door, walked away, down the hallway, and into the kitchen.

Jayne made her way to the end of the hallway, before turning right into the kitchen. The counter was littered with her black jacket and scarf she wore to the party to keep herself warm. There was also her purse. Jayne walked past all of that and went to the refrigerator. The door swung open. The two milk bottles inside clung together, a little. Jayne leaned into the refrigerator and grabbed a handy size bottle of water. She twisted the cap and took a deep sip. The water was refreshingly cold, waking her up, a little. The door leading into the back yard, from the kitchen was closed. The light switched off.

Jayne left the kitchen, taking the bottle of water with her, and headed toward the hallway, again. She walked into the bathroom, the second door on the right, and closed it behind her. The light inside the bathroom flickered on. The water from the shower was quick to turn on. Fade to black.

Fade from black.

Jayne emerged from her bedroom in a simple light pink, cotton t-shirt, which hugged her petite frame well. She sported a grey pair of sweat pants to keep her warm. And her hair was neatly pulled back and rounded into a bun, keeping the wet hair up, and off her neck.

"My cell phone, my cell phone," Jayne whispered to herself, over and over, as she walked down the hallway, barefoot, toward the kitchen.

The light in the kitchen was still switched on. So, were the lights in the living room. There was a hushed voice coming from the television set. It was the late evening news. Jayne got to the kitchen counter and reached for her purse, her concentration on finding her cell phone. She rummaged through, tossing the contents back and forth a little until she found it. A smile surfaced to her lips.

"Yes!" she whispered under her breath, clutching the cell phone tightly in her right hand.

The screen came to life. There were four missed calls. All from Andrew. Jayne rolled her eyes, uninterested in responding so late in the evening. She turned, leaving her purse, her scarf and jacket on the kitchen counter, left behind, and forgotten, as she walked deeper into the house, through the kitchen, and into the living room.

The door leading out into the back yard, by the kitchen, was wide open, now. The open door peered out to the silent and still darkness of the evening. Jayne reached the living room, her nose in her cell phone, checking her social media updates. She walked towards the coffee table, leaning down a little to pick up the remote, pointing, pressing a button, switching off the television set. Jayne stood tall, standing by the side of the coffee table. Her reflection caught in the television set, a moment. And so, too, was that of the clown mask, standing behind her, silent, with a large, sharp kitchen knife gripped tightly in their left hand.

Fade to black.

Chapter Thirteen...

Fade from black.

The events that followed rolled out like a scene from some scary Hollywood movie. Interior.

A close up on the clown mask, itself. The colours of the mask were bright and vibrant. The white. The blues and black. And the crimson red. The mask tilted a little, down and to the left. There was minimal light in the background, only one floodlight sitting on the floor, in the far north-east corner of the room, plugged into a power socket. The light cast shadows across the walls. And the floors were in a state of disrepair, wooden floorboards that were eaten away with time and covered in sand and dirt.

The scary Hollywood movie continued on, as if a camera were pulling away from the mask, to reveal what appeared to be an everyday run-of-the-mill workbench. The surface of the workbench was mahogany, which had seen a few chips and dinks in its time. The surface of the workbench was covered with various items, including a hammer, a kitchen knife, and scalpels, to name a few. The clown mask ran it's left, leather-bound hand over the contents, reaching out for the large, sharp kitchen knife. The clown mask grabbed it, lifting it, clutching the handle, tighter and tighter. The leather glove stretched a little. The clown mask walked over the surface of the decaying floorboards. They bent and cracked under the pressure, splintering and tearing apart.

Fade to black.

We open from the darkness in another room. A second floodlight is switched on. This one, sitting on the floor and plugged into a power socket in the far south-west corner of the room. The light exposed the ageing wall, in all its state of decay. In its day, it had been painted a soft and welcoming beige. And now, nothing more than dirt, debris and rain damage, all accrued over the years.

Jayne was slowly waking from an unconscious state. She had

suffered a minor head wound. The right side of her forehead was bleeding. Her wrists and ankles were bound to tight metal cuffs, which were attached to chains, all part of a large rig and harness. Jayne was strapped up against the wall, standing tall, with both hands held high above her head. Her legs were pulled apart. She was standing there naked, appearing almost like the shape of the letter X. Her head was lowered, down and to the right. Still struggling to reach a state of consciousness. Her hair was ratty looking, pulled forward, almost covering her face. And her wrists and ankles suffering minor contusions brought on by the tight, metal cuffs.

The chains began to rattle, throughout the harness, as Jayne was coming to life. Her left ankle was the first to respond, flinching a little. Followed by her left hand. The toes on her right foot began to move and wriggle, some, barely touching the wooden floorboards beneath her. Jayne was weak and dehydrated. She tilted her head back, a little. She coughed. Her vision was blurry with the floodlight pointed directly at her. Jayne was beginning to shiver now, from the cold.

"Hello?" she called out, barely above a whisper. There was no response.

"Hello, who is there?" she tried again. And, again. No response.

Jayne tried to scream.

Nothing.

The sound of the heavy boots, heavy footsteps could be heard in the near distance growing closer, growing louder. They soon stopped. Jayne peered out into the brightness of the light, itself, trying to look past it. Her eyes were almost closed. Her vision was still blurry. There was nothing but darkness beyond the light. Jayne gave up. Her head sank. She could feel the pain in her muscles, especially around her shoulders grow tighter, over time. Her hands felt cold to the touch.

"You know," the dark and deep, yet familiar, voice started, "you are a very pretty girl, indeed."

"Who is it? Who is there?" Jayne asked, almost begging, her tone of voice was weak.

The clown mask stepped out from the darkness and into the light. It's shadow cast, spraying across the wall behind Jayne.

"I bet you are popular with all the boys and some of the girls," the clown mask continued.

Jayne lifted her head and opened her eyes some more. She saw the large kitchen knife and the mask. Panic began to set in. Jayne screamed again, as loud as her lungs could allow. The clown mask stood there, in front of her, silent.

"What do you want?" Jayne begged, angrily.

"You're a very pretty girl," the clown mask said again, taking a single step forward. "That is why I am going to have some fun with you before you die."

Jayne cried, almost giving up, feeling beaten.

"But, before we get to the main round, how about a small round of question and answer?" the clown mask asked, moving the blade of the kitchen knife, waving it almost.

The tears in Jayne's eyes began to fall now. She was sobbing almost uncontrollably.

"You see, I ask you a question, and you tell me the truth. Failure to comply will result in a very bloody mess. I can guarantee it. Do you understand?"

"Uh-huh," Jayne answered, just above a whisper.

"I can't hear you. Speak up. Do. You. Understand?"

"Yes!" Jayne screamed back, through her hoarse voice and tears.

"Good!"

The blade of the kitchen knife lowered.

"Let's start. Round one. What colour is your hair?"

"Brown," Jayne answered, a little out of breath. "Brown," she repeated, a little louder.

"Yes!" the clown mask answered, very excited. "And what a lovely shade of brown it is."

The clown mask took another step forward, again, closer towards her, taking strands of her hair in its right leather-bound glove, letting it run over and through 'its fingers.

Jayne flinched at the touch.

"And what a shade of mousey brown it is. I can see you dye your hair. Your roots are showing. Very cheap."

"Fuck you!" Jayne shouted back, gathering all the bravado that she could muster.

"Not wise, Jayne!" the clown mask yelled. "I could slice you open and leave you to die a very slow and agonising death. You'd bleed out on the floor right here. And who would care? No one. I mean, where are they? And your sweet, innocent son would grow up without a mother, just like your friend, Peter Harmon. Speaking of which, question two. You were the poor girl growing up in this town, going to school. How did that make you feel when you saw your friends, Emily, Andrew, and Peter?"

"I hated them for it. Everything came so damn easy to them," Jayne answered angrily, and again, just above a whisper in her hoarse voice. "I hate them!" she repeated. "Then, Peter returned to school, shortly after his father was murdered, and he was the goddamn star!"

The mask tilted, again, intrigued by her words.

"I…" Jayne continued, a little out of breath. "I can get to him for you. Peter Harmon. He and his family, especially his mother and grandfather, were nothing but a cancer on this whole damn town! Let me help you. Let me down. Let me go. I will kill him for you. I promise."

The clown mask took another step towards Jayne, the mask tilted, again, as if to ponder the question. The blade of the kitchen knife raised, again.

Jayne could feel her breath catching in her chest.

"You'd sell yourself out, to save yourself, in exchange for another?"

"I'm a mother," Jayne answered, just above a whisper, and out of breath.

Her wrists and ankles were growing tied now. She moved them, as much as she could, anyway. It was painful. The chains rattled some more. The clown mask took a step backwards, taking in a view of the harness, itself. The grand picture of such a horrible state.

"I would do anything to protect my son," Jayne answered. "He needs me. I'm a good mother. Every boy needs his mother!"

"It is life," the clown mask responded. "But this is also a horror movie." Jayne looked at the mask, confused.

"This isn't a movie. This is nothing more than life, itself."

"A life, granted. But you can't pick your genre. This *is* a horror movie. And your role just got cut! Director's cut. Special edition."

The blade of the large, sharp kitchen knife reappeared. It moved at an electric speed as it lifted high in the air, only to come down and slice at the flesh of the young woman's throat. The blood began to pour fast. Jayne's head tilted back, a little. Her eyes welling with tears as she choked, suffocating in a slow and painful death.

The clown mask took another step backwards. Followed by another and another. It stood in front of the floodlight, taking in the view, not only of harness, but also, of the dying, soon-to-be corpse, standing before him. Jayne Scott. Her wrists lowered. Her body slouched forward bent at the knees. Her head fell forward and down and to the left. Her blood poured heavily down her chest, over her breasts and stomach, dripping to the floor below. Jayne Scott was dead.

Fade to black. Fade from black.

It was early morning, a few minutes close to six as a small, compact, four-door car, dark green in colour, with a hatchback, drove along a long and winding road. It reached the top of the hill, pulling into a nearby car park which was splashed with dirt and gravel. The car pulled in and the engine died suddenly. The car park itself was empty and located on the outskirts of Hillsboro. A field of fresh, dark green grass and thick, tall trees decorated the surrounds. It was a popular spot for the health-conscious, the hikers, joggers and bike riders who like to keep fit. There were dirt trails that lead off into the woods, one for the inexperienced and one for the advanced.

A woman, somewhere in her late thirties, emerged from behind the steering wheel of the dark green hatchback. Her hair was blonde and thin, cut short into an uneven bob, just below her ears. The driver's side door slammed to a close. The woman left her car behind and began to walk over toward the start of the walking trails, past the picnic area and restrooms. She paused in her tracks and looked upwards, peering into the trees. A blood-curdling scream broke the morning silence, as it escaped her lungs and passed her lips. It was loud. She screamed, again, falling to her knees. And there in front of her, was a bloodied and tortured corpse. A young female in her early twenties. She was tied and bound high, between two trees. Her naked body was exposed. Her throat was slashed. Her face covered with another clown mask. The blood had dried. Her flesh had turned a light shade of blue and purple. But it was her stomach. It was empty. It was gone. A large, sharp kitchen knife, *the* large, sharp kitchen knife, sliced from the throat, past the breasts and over the rib cage, down the stomach and to the pelvis. Her stomach had been completely hollowed out. Her intestines, her stomach was nowhere to be seen.

The flesh from the knife wound was pulled backwards, pinned to the two trees, themselves. The stomach looked more like the wingspan of a large bird of prey. The blood-curdling scream echoed, quickly flooding the car park and entered the hills. The tears welled in the woman's eyes.

Fade to black.

Chapter Fourteen…

The time was now somewhere close to seven in the morning. The sun was rising over another cold, winter's day in Hillsboro. A truck was parked outside on the curb, outside Emily's home. The engine was dead. The truck belonged to Andrew. The house itself was a single storey sandstone dwelling, with a neatly manicured lawn out front and white picket fence with a porch which ran from the front of the house and down along the right side. It was almost a total cliché.

The curtains in the living room were pulled to a close. There was a stillness about the house. The lights were still switched off. The house itself was three bedrooms and two bathrooms, more than enough space for Emily. The living room was located at the front of the house, with a view that lead out to the porch and front lawn. The room itself was neatly designed, with a large chocolate- brown leather couch, which floated off the wall, with a coffee table in front, and television set.

There was a fireplace opposite the television and framed photographs of Emily, her parents, and friends, hanging on the one side of the wall, all in happier times. There was also a celebrity autobiography sitting on the coffee table.

The living room came off the foyer of the house and lead into the hallway. The hallway was the heart of the house, its veins stretching off into other areas of the home. The master bedroom was located at the far end of the hallway. The door of the master bedroom pushed open to reveal two adult bodies lying under the bed covers, cuddled up to each other, keeping each other warm. The bed cover was peeled back on one side, to the waist. Andrew was naked. His hulking chest and muscular arms were wrapped around Emily, pulling her in and holding her close. Andrew was the big spoon. His clothes from the night before were spread across the floor.

The time on the alarm clock now read seven-sixteen. The nightstand on Andrew's side of the bed was littered with his wallet, keys to his truck and his cell phone. His cell phone began to ring, over and over again, until he woke up. His body was coming to life, with his right arm lifting, and pulling away from Emily. Andrew turned onto his back, a moment, and turned to face the nightstand, reaching for his cell phone.

"Hello?" Andrew answered, just above a whisper.

"It's happened again." Detective Quinn responded. His tone of voice flat. "A woman was about to go jogging this morning and found a body in Quarry Lake Park. Female. Another mask. This doesn't look good. Brutally beaten. We don't have an ID on her yet. She was gutted and completely hollowed out. I need you on this now. Where are you?"

"I'll be there in ten minutes."

"Good!"

The conversation ended and the cell phone call disconnected.

Andrew dropped his cell phone onto his nightstand. He collapsed onto his back, onto the bed. Emily was slowly coming to life, again.

"Shit!" Andrew muttered, as he rubbed the sleep from his eyes.

"What happened?" Emily asked, just above a whisper, as she woke.

"Nothing for you to worry about," Andrew whispered, protecting her from the truth, as he leaned in and cuddling up to her tightly, again. "I love you. Don't give up on me."

Andrew pulled away from Emily. He pushed his side of the bed cover back and climbed to his feet, naked. The floorboards were cool to the touch. His toes wriggled, a little, before hunting for his clothes off the floor. Andrew got dressed in the dark. He grabbed his wallet, keys and cell phone from the nightstand and made his way out of the master bedroom, leaving Emily to get some further sleep.

"I'll call you later," Andrew whispered, as he left the bedroom, pulling the door to a close behind him.

Andrew walked through the house, as quietly as he could, anyway. His large frame carried heavily as he walked across the hardwood floors. He made his way out the front door, and ran across the front yard, over the porch, and toward his truck. He climbed inside and slammed the door shut. Andrew placed the key in the ignition and the engine roared to life, taking a few moments, from the cold winter night before.

"Yes!" Andrew whispered to himself, as the engine roared and the heater kicked in.

Andrew looked in the rear-view mirror a moment, before pulling out from the curb, and into the traffic. He drove to the end of the street, turning left at the stop sign, making his way over to Quarry Lake Park.

The drive this morning came with memories flooding back from the night before. There was, of course, the blow-up at the party. Andrew recalled driving to Emily's, following her, giving her a chance to hear his side, before pulling the plug on their fragile relationship altogether. Andrew arrived at Emily's to find her sitting on the end of her queen-size bed, her legs crossed. She was sobbing, almost rocking back and forth, trying to console herself. Andrew stood in the doorway of the master bedroom. He watched her a moment, before quietly stepping forward, making his way inside. This had ignited a heated exchange of words, on Emily's side, anyway, and rightfully so.

"I just can't trust you, any more. We're done!" Emily said, just above a whisper, too exhausted from the tears and wanting to fight no more.

Andrew closed his eyes tightly, a moment, just a few seconds. He flinched at that memory. He had hated himself in that moment.

The morning progressed. The water in the shower stopped running. The frosted glass door slid open carefully, followed by a large bloom of steam which rushed the bathroom. Peter stepped out of the shower, and grabbed a fresh towel which hung from the wall. He wrapped himself up in the towel, drying himself down, before wrapping it around his waist. His cell phone sat next to the washbasin. Peter rubbed his eyes a moment and leaned in and picked up the cell phone.

The screen came to life. Caller Unknown.

"Hello?" Peter answered his tone of voice a little heavy.

"Turn on the news!" the dark and familiar voice answered, followed by a laugh.

"What do you want?"

"Do as you're told and turn on the news!"

Peter raced from the bathroom, clutching the towel around his waist in one hand, and the cell phone to his ear in the other. He reached the living room, grabbed the remote and turned on the television. He flicked through the channels quickly until he stumbled across a local breaking news story.

Countless police officers were scouring through Quarry Lake Park.

Peter stood there a moment, staring at the television, his cell phone to his left ear.

"You were busy last night," Peter answered, heavily. There was another laugh on the other end of the cell phone.

"Another body has turned up." the dark and familiar voice continued. "And who do you think this town is going to blame, huh? You! With the curfew still in effect, a hopeless detective, the town's people are getting frustrated. They want answers and all you can do is stand back and watch." There was more laughter.

Peter was angry, his expression said everything. "Who?" Peter yelled, demanding to know. "Who is it?"

"Jayne Scott." the voice answered.

Peter felt a punch to his stomach.

"There is no great loss there." the voice continued. "The town slut. People will think she got what she deserved."

"Fuck you!"

"The game will continue, Peter. Remember, I'm coming for you. This. *This* is all because of you and your mother and what you did to this town. It's all your fault!"

Again, another laugh.

Peter disconnected the phone call. "Fuck!" he yelled, out of frustration.

Andrew was quick to arrive at the crime scene. His truck had pulled into the car park at the top of the hill. There were many vehicles already parked. There were members of the media, their trucks set up as mini-television stations, at the ready to report back to their network. There was also members of the Hillsboro Police Department and an ambulance. The engine to the truck had died. Andrew sat there a moment, silent. He peered through the dirty windscreen, a moment, looking out at the crowd of people.

"Shit!" he whispered to himself.

His hulking frame moved from left to right, a little, shifting his weight to climb out of his truck, sliding his cell phone into his jean pocket.

It was busy. And crowded. Andrew walked toward the crime scene slowly, taking it all in. The gravel squished and scratched together under the weight of his black leather boots. He could feel his stomach begin to turn, and felt very aware of his throat. It was tight and dry. The local media crews were already on scene and doing their job, as one of the reporters, and her cameraman, saw Andrew approaching and raced toward him, at a high speed, waving a microphone in his face. Her black leather platform pump with small fringe heels by Gucci scratched against the gravel.

"Deputy Preston. Good morning," the reporter started, "what can you tell us about the latest find? Any clues? Are there any breakthroughs in this story? People want to know. They have every right to know."

"Listen. I just got here!" Andrew answered, biting his tongue, yet wanting to remain as polite and professional as possible. "When we know something, Detective Quinn will make an announcement. But, until then, please, let us do our jobs."

The reporter was in her early to mid-fifties, thin, tall build, with jet-black, straight hair, pulled back into a ponytail. She stopped in her tracks. The microphone dropped by her waist. Her shoulder's slouched. The camera was kept on Andrew, as he walked toward the scene, lifting the police tape, and making his way inside the park.

Andrew made his way past the police tape, the thin yellow line to separate the police department from the local media and any other prying eyes. And, just behind the tape, he walked a further good twenty yards, down a dirt trail, a little, before reaching a large tent-like apparatus, which blocked the view of the crime scene off from the public. He looked around. He watched his colleagues, hard at work. They walked around the crime scene, some whispering amongst themselves, whilst others collected evidence and others took photographs. Andrew made eye contact with the officers. One of the junior officer's pointed in Detective Quinn's direction. Andrew nodded, smiled some and followed the direction.

The crime scene had been closed off to the public, including the media. There was no way of seeing in or out, for that matter, without going through security. The body had been cut down from the trees. Her deceased body had been placed on a waiting stretcher, waiting to be given the go- ahead and taken to the morgue at Hillsboro District Hospital. Detective Quinn was flanked by the coroner.

"You weren't kidding. This is a circus." Andrew said, just above a whisper. Detective Quinn pulled his eyes from the coroner, a moment.

"Good work. Let me know as soon as you can. I want a rush on this as soon as possible."

"Yes, sir," the coroner answered. "Good morning, Deputy."

The coroner made brief eye contact with Andrew, giving him a brief nod of the head, and a hint of a smile, to be polite, as he left the detective and headed toward the deceased body and two ambulance officers, standing near the trees.

"Trutmann."

Deputy Preston focused on Detective Quinn, again. "What have we got?"

"This. This is how you come dressed for work? Where's your uniform?"

"I had a late night."

"Okay. We have hit the fucking jackpot with this one. Some jogger turned up at the park this morning and found a young girl, early twenties, tied, hanging between two trees. Another clown mask. Shit! Her torso completely hollowed out. Her stomach and 'its contents missing. Christ! She looked like fucking Batman, the caped crusader, as the flesh of her stomach was pinned to each tree."

"Fuck! And the mask? Was it removed?"

"Yeah! Forensics has it."

"And the girl?"

Detective Quinn raised his right hand and placed it on Deputy Preston's shoulder a moment as if to console him.

"I have to warn you…" his tone of voice softened, some.

"What? What is it?"

Detective Quinn said nothing.

"Detective. Who is it?"

"Jayne Scott. The girl from your party last night."

Andrew was frozen. He was stunned. He could feel his heart and stomach drop. "Are you sure? I mean, absolutely positive on the ID? I want to see."

"Trust me on this. You don't want to see this. Not this one. Where were you last night?"

"What? Do you think I had something to do with this? Fuck me! If you want to know, I spent the night with Emily. You can call and confirm. I knew Jayne. I've known her since high school. The four of us. Emily. Peter. Jayne. And I. We were a team."

"Well, if you and Emily were together last night, where was Peter?"

"No! Peter had nothing to do with this. Not this! He couldn't. We keep dragging him into this and we keep going round in circles and getting nowhere fast. Peter lived through this, okay? I know him. He is no killer."

"Survivor guilt. Maybe one day, Peter just… snapped. It can happen." "I know. But not Peter."

Peter was at home. He had been awake since five-thirty, starting his day out with another jog around the neighbourhood. He was home, a little after six-thirty, showered, and dressed casually in faded denim blue jeans, barefoot, and a black polo shirt by Lacoste. He was sitting in his office, sitting in front of his laptop computer, typing away on the keyboard, searching the internet. He spent the past half an hour searching the want ads for a job, anything. Something. There was nothing that appealed to him. Not today, anyway. Peter cruised the internet, checking out his favourite movie website before reaching the buzz feed on the latest, breaking news to hit Hillsboro. Peter looked sombre. There was a glass of orange juice sitting by the side of the laptop computer, next to his cell phone. There had been a conversation between Peter and Mike, earlier in the morning, organising a date for the evening. And there had been a back and forth conversation with Andrew, brief as it was. Andrew had arranged to drop by and see Peter. He was on his way.

There was a heavy knock at the front door of the house. Peter lifted his eyes off the screen of his laptop computer, a moment. *Knock. Knock. Knock.* It repeated. Peter reached for his cell phone with his left hand, leaving his computer and orange juice behind in the office. Peter ran to the end of the hallway and down the staircase, again, holding the banister, toward the front door. Peter could see the image of a hulking mass through the frosted glass window. The front door opened with a twist of the door handle. It was Andrew. He was standing outside on the front porch, now in his police uniform and a black coat to keep himself warm.

"Deputy," Peter said, just above a whisper.

Andrew looked at his best friend, sombre, without saying a word.

"Want to come in?"

"Fuck yeah!" Andrew nodded.

Peter stepped to one side, as the front door opened further. Andrew walked into the foyer of the house before the door closed behind him.

The two best friends made their way into the living room. The house was warm. Andrew was sitting on the couch, his black coat slung over the edge of the couch.

"I'd offer you a beer. It looks like you could use one. But coffee is the best I have got right now." Peter walked into the living room and handed Andrew a freshly made coffee. Andrew accepted it and placed it on a coaster on the coffee table in front of him.

"You have no idea how much that beer would feel right about now. But I can't. I'm on duty. Coffee will do. Thank you."

"Of course."

Peter sat opposite Andrew, his cup of coffee warming his hands. "I can't believe this motherfucker got to Jayne. Shit!"

"So, you know it's her. There was a positive ID?"

Andrew nodded slowly, as he was careful to take a sip from his coffee.

"Does Emily know? The fact that we all went to high school together, we're not suspects, are we?" Peter continued to ask.

Andrew lifted his eyes off his coffee and looked at Peter, a moment. He shook his head.

"If you were, you'd know about it. Quinn would be on the front porch with two officers, dragging you down to the station. His hands are tied right now. He is finishing up at the crime scene. Quarry Lake Park."

"How is Emily in all of this? How is she handling the news?" "She goes back and forth," Andrew answered, just above a whisper. "I texted her earlier. I didn't hear anything back."

"Who is doing this, Peter?" Deputy Preston asked, blunt and to the point. "Who is behind these murders? If not one of us, Mike, then who? You can't think of anything, anyone from the past, Petey?"

"Maybe it's Detective Quinn," Peter answered, just as blunt. "A detective with the love for the kill who doesn't want to stop."

"This is serious!" Deputy Preston interrupted. "I am serious."

"You don't think I don't know this? It's my childhood all fucking over again. Only this time, whoever it is, is after my friends. But whoever it is, they will slip up. They always do."

"I wish I had your confidence. And what do we do in the meantime? Watch everyone drop like flies?"

"Speaking as someone who has lived through this, you arm yourself. Be vigilant. Don't let your guard down. You learn to fight back. That's all any of us can do. And hope, that whoever this is, he, she, or whoever, is either brought to justice and brought down."

Andrew looked at Peter with that same sombre expression again. He took a deep sip from his cup of coffee. It felt so warm and inviting, calming his nerves from earlier this morning.

It had been two days now since Peter had seen Mike. Their relationship had gone virtual, whilst Mike worked longer than usual hours in the hardware store with the return to business sale. He was run off his feet. Peter had filled him in on the scene created at Andrew's birthday party, and of course, Jayne, through text message and phone call. Mike got home of an evening and would call Peter and asked him about his day.

Peter kept his word to Andrew and remained vigilant. The window and door alarms were set around the house. If there was another broken window, or if the front or back door were to be forced open, the alarm would trigger, and Peter would hear it.

The lights in the house were switched on. It was warm throughout as the fireplace roared.

The dining table was set for two. Peter ordered take-out from the local Hillsboro Chinese restaurant, including a couple of his favourite dishes, sweet-and-sour pork, special fried rice, without prawns, and satay beef. Mike pushed the food around his plate with his fork, before stabbing the food together and taking a bite. He swallowed it hard with a beer chaser.

The evening progressed to the living room. The television set was switched on, the volume down low. The lights were switched off. An incandescent glow came from the television set, as the light sprayed around the room, reaching the far wall. Mike sat on the far-right corner of the couch, on an angle, with his arms wrapped around Peter's chest, resting on his chest and stomach, a little, and holding him close.

"Thank you for dinner," Mike whispered.

"Anytime."

"Well, next time. It's my place. A home-cooked meal. You'll love it." A hint of a smile surfaced to Peter's lips, a little.

"I was thinking." Mike started. "When work dies down a little, and life gets back to normal, how about you and I get out of Hillsboro for a couple of days? A long weekend, perhaps? We could head into the city, and go to Chicago, maybe?"

"I'd like that. It would be good to get away, even for a couple of days." "Good." Mike smiled. "I'll arrange something."

The two went back to watching the television set. There was nothing important on. It was some late-night sitcom, coupled with bad acting and canned audience laughter.

Mike and Peter retired for the evening and fell asleep in bed. Mike was sleeping on his back, slowly snoring away. The last few days had finally caught up to him. Peter was lying next to him. He awoke from his slumber with another nightmare. Peter was quick to sit up in bed, as the cover rested on his waist. He turned a little and looked down at Mike. He was still fast asleep. Peter rubbed the sleep from his eyes, mostly from frustration before he decided to climb out of bed. He looked down on his nightstand and grabbed his cell phone. The screen came to life. There were no missed calls or text messages. The time was three fifty-eight in the morning. Peter walked out of the master bedroom and down the hallway, as quiet as he could, toward the kitchen for a glass of water. He reached the open door of the master bedroom, before turning around to take another look at Mike, still fast asleep. He turned onto his stomach as his right arm extended out across the sheets, still snoring away.

Peter returned from the kitchen and made his way back to the bed room. He reached the open door, again to find the lamp on the nightstand switched on. Mike was awake, now. He was sitting up in bed. His wallet, keys to his truck and cell phone sat on top of the nightstand. The bed cover had peeled back, also exposing his naked chest.

"What are you doing up so late?" Mike asked, just above a whisper, as he watched Peter standing in the entrance of the master bedroom.

"I couldn't sleep." Peter shrugged with a smile.

"Nightmares?"

"Something like that."

"Oh, shit! Come to bed. Come on. I got you."

Peter looked at Mike a moment as their eyes met. A smile surfaced to Mike's lips as if reassuring him everything was safe, once more. The storms had passed, and the nightmares were over.

Peter walked across the floor of the master bedroom and climbed back into bed. Mike pulled the bed cover over him, snuggling up to him, keeping each other warm. Mike was the big spoon. The lamp on the nightstand switched off.

The time reached a little after six in the morning. The kitchen was alive. The neon light hanging from the ceiling was switched on. The television set in the living room was also on. The volume was raised a little. The morning news was playing. Mike was standing in the kitchen in a pair of grey sweat pants, something he borrowed from Peter's wardrobe, and a plain white, cotton t- shirt. He stood in front of the stove top, preparing a hearty breakfast. It was a breakfast of champions; which included scrambled eggs, two slices of bacon, mushrooms, fried tomatoes and hash brown. There was also toast with freshly made coffee and orange juice.

The water from the faucet in the shower stopped. The frosted glass door slid open cautiously as Peter stepped out onto the white tiled floor and leaned across and grabbed a freshly hanging towel from the wall. He wrapped himself up in it to dry himself off, before wrapping it around his waist loosely. Peter walked toward the basin. He leaned in, and using his left hand, wiped the condensation from the mirror in one downward stroke. The silence in the bathroom broke as the cell phone on the side of the wash basin began to ring. Peter looked down at the screen, a moment. *Unknown Caller.* His stomach turned.

"Good morning Peter," the dark and familiar voice started before laughing.

"Now what?" Peter answered flatly.

"You and Mike looked so peaceful sleeping in your bed last night."

Peter was shocked. His eyes opened further in horror. He could feel his heartbeat racing.

"I could have reached out and sliced you both open, leaving you both there to bleed out, just like your father and stepmother." Another laugh. "But you won't feel the slice of my blade until I am good and ready. Until then, enjoy the show." The phone line disconnected.

Peter clutched his cell phone in his left hand tightly, before holding the side of the towel around his waist with his right. He ran from the bathroom, careful not to slip on the puddles of water across the tiled floor. He opened the bathroom door, turned right and raced to the end of the hallway, down the staircase and toward the alarm panel on the front door. His eyes read the alarm panel, moving left to right, a moment. He turned and faced, deeper into the house, past the foyer and down the hallway and into the kitchen. Mike emerged at the end of the hallway. He was biting down on a piece of toast, smeared in melting butter.

"Hey, what's going on?" Mike asked.

"The alarm is switched off," Peter replied, a little concerned. "When did *you* do that?"

"Last night. After you fell asleep. Why?"

Peter stood there a moment, silent. His face sombre. "Nothing," he answered, eventually.

"If it's nothing, then go upstairs and get dressed. Breakfast will be ready any minute now."

Mike soon left the house, shortly after breakfast. He showered and got changed for work, leaving Peter alone. Peter was standing in front of the alarm system by the front door, again. His left hand lowered, grabbing his cell phone from his pocket. Peter was quick to dial a number. He placed his cell phone to his right ear and waited for the call to be connected. The telephone on Deputy Preston's desk at the Hillsboro Police Department began to ring. Andrew looked around the station a moment, before answering.

"Hello?" he answered, leaning into his desk. His uniform shirt tightened a little around the belly. "Deputy Preston."

"Hey," a somewhat timid voice answered. "It's me. Do you have time to talk?"

"What's up? What's happened?

"I got another call from the killer this morning. He, she or whoever was in my house last night watching me sleep."

"Oh, shit!" Andrew answered, leaning into his desk a little further and rubbing his eyes, some, before leaning back in his chair, looking across the station, into Detective Quinn's office. "What did they say?"

The days passed, inching closer and closer towards Christmas. The body count in Hillsboro had now hit four, after they had found Jayne Scott's corpse hanging between two trees at Quarry Lake Park.

Detective Quinn had fronted the media a second time, making an impassioned plea with the people of Hillsboro to stay vigilant, advising them to report anything they see out of the ordinary, big or small. In the days since the announcement, the phone lines rang off the hook.

The day of Jayne Scott's funeral arrived. It was held on the outskirts of Hillsboro in a small, out-of-the-way funeral parlour, located next door to a locksmith and Don's Carpets. The building itself had aged over the years. But, with a fresh coat of white paint, it stood out to the passing traffic from the side of the road. The walls were painted a fresh white. The window frames and the gutters were aligned in a navy blue. The car park out front was filled with seven or eight cars, total.

The inside of the building was met with staff members, impeccably dressed head to toe in fine dark grey suits and jackets with a crisp white long-sleeved shirt, underneath. The staff were there on hand to welcome all guests and hand out flyers of the deceased. The flyer was basic, at best. It was a picture of Jayne Scott, taken in happier times, smiling, with her hair neatly pulled back, and away from the face. The photograph was black and white. Her name, along with her date of birth and death was written in elegant script in vibrant colours.

The foyer of the building was large. The walls were made of brick and painted in the same shade of white, with navy blue couches strategically positioned around the room, to allow the guests a quiet place to think and reflect. There was a long, stretch table, sitting in the far-left corner of the room, with coffee, tea, cookies, and water on offer to the guests. And there was a condolence book on offer, for guests to sign and write precious memories they once shared with the departed.

Emily and Andrew were the first to arrive. Emily was dressed in a simple black dress which stretched below the knees and a white trench coat that was cinched at the waist with a thick belt that was loosely tied. Andrew followed closely behind, dressed in black trousers and matching shoes, with a white, long-sleeve shirt buttoned one under the neck, with a black leather belt and black trench coat, which he wore open, exposing the white shirt and muscular frame beneath. Emily lead the way, shaking hands with one of the staff members, as she was handed a flyer, before making her way over to the condolence book.

"Thank you," Andrew said, just above a whisper, as he took a flyer for himself, then wandering around the room.

Emily walked over to the condolence book. She picked up the black pen, gripping it tightly and flicking it through her fingers, wondering what to write. She knew what she wanted to say, but that wouldn't be nice. Emily found a fresh, clean page in the condolence book.

Thank you for the memories. Thanks, E.

She wrote.

Emily placed the black pen in the middle of the book, standing tall. She looked down at what she wrote. The bare hint of a smile surfaced to her lips. Emily was content. Her hands reached out, sliding down the inside pages of the book.

Emily turned to see Andrew standing in the left corner of the room, the first to stand, almost hunched, a little, making himself a cup of instant coffee from the urn. He grabbed two sugar-soaked cookies and placed them on the saucer. Her eyes diverted from the bulging mass helping himself to coffee and cookies, and over to the entrance of the building. The staff member was there to greet the guests with a few kind words whilst handing out more flyers. It was Alicia and Todd Scott, Jayne's parents. Alicia was tall, with a thin frame, one gained through a life of powerwalking and a strict diet. Her hair was short, cut just below the ears, with white-and-grey highlights. She was in her early fifties and her frame, from neck to almost the ankles, was covered in a large black cashmere coat, buttoned down the middle, which she reserved for special occasions only. This was one of those occasions. The hint of a white blouse appeared from under the coat. Her eyes were hidden under large, over-sized oval black sunglasses.

Todd Scott was also in his mid-fifties, fifty-four to be exact. He was also tall, just over six feet tall, with a hint of muscle in the biceps and portly belly. He wore a simple black suit for the occasion, to commemorate his deceased daughter, wearing all black: long-sleeved shirt, jacket, tie, trousers and leather shoes.

Todd and Alicia were ushered into the foyer rather quickly. They were approached by the staff and pulled aside privately whilst they quietly exchanged words. Emily left the condolence book and walked over to the table to meet Andrew.

"I hope you're making me a coffee?" Emily asked, just above a whisper.

Andrew turned and looked at her, and in that fleeting moment, the coffee wasn't the concern. The two looked back at Jayne's parents. They ignored them. The memories from high school came flooding back for Emily as she watched two parents in the quiet, private moments of mourning their daughter.

The boyfriend, the latest on Jayne's list of men, was the next to turn up to the service. The two had been seen around Hillsboro for the past eight months. It was the longest Jayne had held onto one man, one that she could truly call her own. Andrew was nothing more than Jayne's side candy. Simple. The boyfriend was also tall, six feet and two inches, almost. He sported fading black jeans, leather boots, and a long-sleeved black shirt that looked as though he'd ripped out from its wrapper just moments ago. There were creases in the sleeves. His eyes were hidden behind black sunglasses. He walked into the foyer, keeping to himself, grabbed a flyer and was quick to sit on the couch in the far corner of the room. His name was Ted. Or Bob. Or Matt. Some one-syllable name.

The list of guests continued. Peter was next to arrive. He was alone. Mike was busy at work, dealing with a pre-Christmas sale on snow tyres. Peter was also dressed in a black jacket, shirt, tie and jeans with leather shoes. He scanned the foyer of the room, making eye contact with Emily and Andrew. A hint of a smile surfaced to Emily's lips. She walked across the room, leaving her stale coffee behind on the table.

"You made it," Emily said, happy to see her friend.

"Of course. Ten o'clock, right?"

"Ten o'clock." she nodded, still sporting that same smile. "So, what have I missed?"

"Jayne's parents are here. They are over there." Emily nodded, trying her best to be inconspicuous. "And of course, the elusive boyfriend is hanging by himself. Andrew and I only arrived five, ten minutes ago. Andrew is hanging around the coffee and cookies, of course. And there is a condolence book available for those who would like to write something nice about Jayne."

Peter looked at Emily, their eyes connected. Their silence said everything, in that fleeting moment. *Thank you for making life so horrible in high school, you fucking bitch!*

Detective Quinn was the last to arrive. He wasn't invited as a friend of the family, he was there performing his civic duty, there to represent the Hillsboro Police Station, and the wider public, in general. Andrew left the remains of his coffee on the table and swallowed the last of his sugar and cream-filled cookie in one go, as he walked across the room to greet Detective Quinn at the entrance of the foyer.

"Hey," Andrew whispered, with a hint of a smile, as he crossed the room, giving Peter a quick squeeze on his right shoulder.

"We will talk later." Peter nodded.

"Of course."

Detective Quinn and Deputy Preston floated across the foyer rather quietly. The two made their way further inside, approaching a member of the staff who was hanging off every word uttered by Alicia Scott. She had removed her sunglasses, exposing her almost fiery-green eyes underneath. The eyes darted between the staff member of the funeral parlour and over to Detective Quinn, who was making his presence known, without actually saying anything to him. The boyfriend watched them gather. He pulled himself off the couch and made his way over. Peter and Emily watched it all play out in front of them, like they were sitting front row, center seats to a TV show or concert.

The conversation was quick to turn. Alicia Scott drew her attention to Detective Quinn and Deputy Preston. She was quick to throw around empty threats and promised she would lodge a civil suit against the local police station for not doing their duty and keeping her daughter safe, keeping her daughter alive. The member of staff working for the funeral parlour defused the situation and took Alicia Scott by the right hand, and commenced the process of ushering her and Todd into the viewing room. Detective Quinn and Deputy Preston were left behind.

"What the fuck just happened? How did that just escalate?" Deputy Preston asked, just above a whisper.

"Fucked if I know. But I do know for sure, I am going to find this motherfucker who is stalking our town, and I am going to put a stop to it, one way or another."

Deputy Preston remained silent. His eyes stayed on his boss, as he made his way into the viewing room.

The viewing room was very basic in its design. The brick walls were painted white, just like the foyer. The carpet on the floor was a rich red, almost crimson in colour, with gold trim. And there were two rows of chairs, each row had ten wooden chairs. The seating capacity was one hundred. The front of the room was decorated with a podium and microphone, and just behind that, in the centre of the room, just behind opened curtains, was Jayne Scott, laid to rest, inside a closed casket. The top of the casket was decorated in white roses. The curtains remained open, as if for the big reveal, the big punch. The member of staff was quick to usher Alicia and Todd Scott to their seats, in the front row, to the left of the casket.

Detective Quinn made his way into the viewing room on his own. The boyfriend followed.

They both sat near each other, behind the grieving parents. Emily, Andrew, and Peter made their way into the service room, together. They sat toward the back of the room, close enough to the family and detective, but not back enough, to make it obvious that they were keeping their distance. Peter sat behind Emily and Andrew. The doors leading into the service room were closed after the final guests made their way into the room, friends and acquaintances. Andrew looked around the room and saw several people, no more than five or six, sitting on the right side of the room, all of which he didn't know. He turned and faced the front of the room, once more.

"Welcome, one and all," a calming voice spoke into the microphone from behind the podium.

It was the staff member who had ushered Alicia and Todd Scott into the service room. The man himself was short and stocky, with a belly that punched past his belt buckle. He was somewhere in his late fifties, possibly early sixties, with a neatly trimmed grey beard.

"Today," the man continued, "we celebrate the life that was Jayne Ellen Scott. She was a student. A mother. A friend. And a daughter. And today, her parents, Todd and Alicia Scott, have invited you to pay your final respects and wishes to the daughter they name Jayne."

The service continued with a reading of a poem, followed by a eulogy, read by Todd Scott. The guests were then welcomed to the front of the room to say a prayer and pay their final respects, as the staff member from the funeral parlour handed small cut flower buds to place on the top of the casket by the white roses. The service ended with a song. It was by the New Kids on the Block, a soft ballad, Jayne's favourite band. The curtains closed on the casket. The show was over. Alicia sobbed, almost uncontrollably, knowing this was the last image she would have of her daughter. She was comforted by her husband, with her eyes now hidden behind her oversized sunglasses

The service was over now. The double doors at the back of the service room opened, again.

The guests stood from their chairs and made their way out into the foyer. The table in the far-left corner was adorned with fresh cookies and other bits and pieces to nosh on, whilst sipping on a cup of coffee or tea. Peter was one of the first to reach the foyer. Emily was quick to catch up, followed by Andrew.

"Hang on!" Emily called out, catching Peter by the cuff of his long-sleeved shirt. "Wait! Where are you going?"

"I just needed some air. The memories, you know?"

"Of course." Emily nodded, reassuringly. "Andrew and I were thinking of grabbing a bite to eat somewhere before he has to head back into work if you care to join?"

Peter looked at Emily, then to his best friend. Andrew smiled. "I'd like that."

"Great," answered Andrew.

Chapter Fifteen...

It had been three days now since Jayne Scott was laid to rest. Alicia and Todd had opted for cremation. It was their way of keeping their daughter close to home, making her feel safe and protected. Alicia already had a place picked out for her daughter. As clichéd as it sounded, it was on top of the fireplace in the living room. She would be there to talk to and catch up with, from time to time, so Alicia and Todd thought.

The front door on the porch opened with a little caution as a cold breeze rushed over the front of the house rather quickly as the snow came down. Peter stood in the doorway. He stepped outside, onto the front porch, in jeans and black leather boots, and a puffer jacket wrapped and zipped up, to keep himself warm, as the snow fell harder this morning. He stepped further out onto the front porch, closing the front door behind him. He stood there a moment, peering out into the front lawn. The front lawn was white, snow white. A good six to eight inches of snow had fallen from the night before.

The road had never looked so icy black. The families across the street, and in the neighbourhood, played in the snow, building snowmen and animals, throwing snowballs, making the most of the impending Christmas season, whilst others salted their walkways and driveways. Peter walked to the letterbox to check for mail. There was nothing today. A day without a bill was always a good day. There was a local newspaper, neatly folded on itself, bundled with a handful of flyers. He grabbed them, turned, and raced to the front porch, again. The front of the house looked peaceful and content.

The inside of the house was warm. Peter stepped deeper into the house, taking a couple of footsteps into the foyer, placing the newspaper and flyers on the small table by the front door before taking off his puffer jacket and hanging it in the closet. He collected them afterwards and made his way into the dining room, where a freshly brewed cup of coffee awaited him, to warm his insides.

The television set was switched on, the volume down low. It was mid-morning television. Peter ignored it. He was just happy for a little noise to fill the house.

The local newspaper unfolded out onto the dining room table. Peter pushed it to one side, as he did with the flyers. A single white envelope slipped out from between the flyers. The front of the envelope, itself, was scrawled in only what could be described as chicken scratch handwriting. The front of the envelope read *"Peter"*. Nothing more. Peter frowned, concerned a little. He was quick to pick it up, flipping it over, and tearing it open. He pulled at the contents. A single sheet of paper unfolded. The paper itself was decorated in letters cut from a magazine and glued on. It looked like nothing more than a ransom letter.

Get out of town!

The letter read.

Peter looked at the message, reading it over and over. It was kids playing a practical joke, nothing more. His eyes peered inside the envelope again and he felt his heart race. There were newspaper clippings. Peter pulled the newspaper clippings out of the envelope, unfolding them and placing them next to the letter, on top of the dining room table. The clippings looked more like a jigsaw puzzle. The articles were of his family, his father, during happier times, and photographs taken from his funeral, his mother, his grandfather, his stepmother, and of course, some of himself.

"Who the fuck is doing this? Whoever this is…" Peter whispered to himself, looking down at the dining room table.

Peter stood there a moment longer, thinking. His hands reached out for the newspaper clippings quickly, as if he had sprung to life, collecting the ransom-like letter, too, and bundling them close to his chest. He ran from the dining room, leaving his cup of coffee behind. He raced to the front door, collecting his keys and wallet on the table in the foyer, and his jacket hanging in the open closet. The front door opened and slammed shut quickly behind.

The double doors which lead into Hillsboro Police Station were pushed open with gusto. The office was busy, for a small country town. A local man, who appeared to be somewhere in his early to mid-fifties, wearing a black and dark blue flannel shirt, with faded black jeans and boots, looked all the worse for wear. He looked as though he was nursing a hangover, after spending the night in the cells. He was in the process of being released. There was also a single mother, sombre and quiet and keeping to herself. She was sitting on a chair, next to her teenage son, minding her own business, and looking more embarrassed than anything else. Her teenage son looked guilty and kept his head lowered, staring at his sneakers.

Peter walked to the front of the customer service counter, his left-hand clutching at the envelope and the contents inside. The officer sitting behind the customer service desk was a bear of a man. He was somewhere in his mid- to late-forties with fine, black hair which was combed to the right side and neat in appearance. He also sported a beard. His uniform shirt stretched around the waistline, the buttons pulled and exposing a hint of a plain, white t-shirt underneath.

"I'd like to see Deputy Preston, please," Peter asked, his voice filled with concern, as he placed the envelope, face-down on the desk, in front of him.

The police officer looked up from his paperwork. The expression on his face showed signs of resistance. Peter picked up on it immediately.

It was then, Andrew Preston appeared from behind the counter, walking across the office. He was dressed in uniform, clutching a handful of manila folders, close to his chest.

"Hey, what are you doing down here?" Andrew asked surprised and delighted to see his best friend. Peter remained silent, staring back.

It took only moments before Peter was ushered inside, deeper into the police station. The officer who worked the customer service desk, continued with his paperwork, but not before lifting his head and watching the scene play out, as Peter was shown to a private office, with Deputy Preston leading the way. The office door closed behind Deputy Preston. The lights flickered on, and Peter took to the closest seat he could reach. Deputy Preston sat opposite him. The envelope remained face-down on the desk. Peter pushed it back and forth, a little, feeling a little nervous.

"You told me once that if I heard from the killer, then I should tell you." Peter started, just above a whisper.

"You did?" Deputy Preston looked concerned, as he leaned into the desk, making himself more comfortable in his chair.

"Yes. No. Not exactly. I don't know." Peter fired.

"So, which is it?"

"You tell me," Peter answered, sombre, as he slid the envelope across the desk. Deputy Preston lowered his eyes to the envelope.

"What's this?" he asked, concerned.

"I got in the mail this morning."

Deputy Preston reached out for the envelope, taking it from Peter. He was quick to open the envelope, himself. The contents poured out on the desk in front of him. Andrew appeared more concerned with the newspaper clippings, as the letter was pushed to one side.

"I'd say it was just kids having fun. But this. These pictures. It's more than that."

"So, what do we do now?"

"I can put another officer on you. The killer has called you. Fuck! They have been in your house. They know where you live. I'm gonna talk to Quinn. I want police protection detail on you, twenty- four, seven. You can trust me. Let me do my job."

Peter leaned back in his chair, sliding down the back of it, a little. He raised his hands and ran his fingers through his hair.

"Fuck!" he answered, just above a whisper. "I got all those *that's him* stares last time. I can't go through that again. Besides, don't you think having official Hillsboro PD protection will only draw the killer out, tease, and taunt them? I can't do that. Someone may get hurt. Or worse. I couldn't live with the guilt of someone innocent getting caught in the middle of all this. If the killer is going to strike, then it's got to be just me and him, whoever this is."

The morning progressed into the evening. Peter had returned home. His cell phone had blown up over the course of the day, receiving text messages from Andrew, pretty much on the hour, checking in and seeing if there was anything he could do, or anything further to report. There must have been almost ten or eleven messages over the course of the day.

The time was somewhere close to ten in the evening now. The lights in the house were switched off. The hallway on the second floor was empty. The doors were closed, all but one. The bedroom door at the end of the hallway, leading into the master bedroom, was wide open. The curtains were pulled open, allowing for some light. A silence fell upon the second storey and throughout the house. And Peter stood alone in the living room. He stood by the front window, peering out onto the front porch. There was no one there. Peter was still dressed in a simple t-shirt and denim jeans and sneakers. He stood there with a thick, metallic torch in his right hand. It was a little something from the hardware store, he picked up when he first met Mike. He also gripped tightly at the large, sharp kitchen knife in his left hand.

"You want me, motherfucker?" Peter mumbled to himself, just above a whisper. "Come and find me!"

The sound of heavy weight ran across the front porch. A shadow quickly followed. Peter stood there in his living room, his eyes widening in horror. He could feel his heartbeat begin to race. He stepped closer to the glass window, his head moving, just inches closer, and closer. His breath held, almost biting his lower lip, hard. A neighbourhood cat raced across the front porch.

"You got to be fucking kidding me," Peter whispered to himself, feeling a sigh of relief. "I hate this shit!" he whispered to himself, again.

Peter slept in the following morning. He didn't crash and fall into bed until way after one in the morning. The time on the alarm clock was almost a quarter past eight. The curtains in the bedroom were wide open, allowing for the light to spray across the walls as a light dusting of snow continued to fall. Peter was showing slow signs of waking up now.

Peter was lying on his back, staring up at the ceiling, wiping the sleep from his eyes. He turned on to his left shoulder, then over onto his stomach, reaching across to the nightstand, grabbing his cell phone, and taking it off the charger. His cell phone had been busy. There were two missed calls, one from Andrew and one from Mike. And there were three text messages, waiting to be read. Peter navigated to the text messages that awaited him. There was one from Mike, Emily, and of course, Andrew. He left them to read later. But, in the meantime, he climbed to his feet and walked naked from the bedroom, down the hallway, and into the bathroom. The bathroom door was pushed to a close.

The neon lights hanging from the bathroom ceiling flickered on. Peter walked across the tiled floor and over to the washbasin as he signed into his cell phone, once more. He navigated to the call history and played the first of his messages, as he switched on the faucet and caught the running cold water in his hands and splashed it across his face, in an attempt to wake up.

"First call. Six thirty-seven this morning. Beep," the robotic phone voice said. "Hey, it's me. It's Andrew."

Peter looked at his reflection in the mirror, as he wiped the beads of water from his face.

"I'm just calling to check in on you. It's the deputy, the papa bear in me, I guess. I hope you're doing okay, and you slept all right. Call me. Let's catch up in the week. Maybe grab a drink somewhere after work. Okay, bye."

Peter was in the shower now. The water was running hot from the faucet. He stretched his hand out, touching the water, before stepping in, stepping further, under the water. Peter poured the liquid soap into his hands next, rubbing it vigorously over his chest, and all over.

"Second call. Seven twenty-three this morning. Beep," the robotic phone voice said, again. "Good morning, babe. It's Mike. God, I miss you. I woke up this morning in an empty bed, wishing you were here with me. I was thinking tonight that maybe we could do something? I still owe you a home-cooked meal, you know. I haven't forgotten. Call me. I miss you."

A hint of a smile surfaced to Peter's lips, a moment.

The shower was over. The faucets switched off. Peter stepped out from the shower cautiously as he slid the frosted glass door open. He was quick to grab another freshly folded towel hanging from the wall, wrap himself in it, grab his cell phone from the washbasin and return to his bedroom, down the hallway. The door leading into the master bedroom closed behind him.

Peter was in the kitchen now, cooking breakfast. Another bacon sandwich as a freshly brewed cup of coffee sat nearby. The bacon sizzled and popped in the cooking oil. The television in the living room was switched on. It was the morning news. A developing story had just broken. It was the reporter, the same one, who had turned up on Peter's front doorstep, not long ago. She was dressed head-to-toe in all white, a shirt dress by Victoria Beckham, which was accented with a large belt, also white in colour, which cinched at the waist. And a matching jacket to keep herself warm, as she held the microphone firmly in her right hand, her jet-black hair, pulled back in a slick ponytail. Peter heard the reporter mention Detective Quinn by name. It was enough for Peter to lift his eyes off the frying pan, switch it off, and walk into the living room. He stared at the television set almost lifelessly.

"This town is reeling, wanting answers," the reporter started. "The people of Hillsboro continue to be on high alert with a nightly curfew still in place. And who is responsible, Detective Wallace Quinn? After local resident, Peter Harmon, chose to return to his home town, a masked killer, resembling a similar pattern to his mother, Sidney Green-Harmon, is stalking their victims, killing them in gruesome, bloody ways, leaving behind what looks like a creepy clown mask, something only seen in a Hollywood slasher film. Detective, please. The people of Hillsboro need answers."

Peter was angry. His face said it all, as he fought the tears welling in his eyes. He reached for the TV remote and switched off the television and stood there, almost lifeless, standing in the middle of the living room. A silence had fallen over the house.

Peter was finished with breakfast. The plates were left soaking in the sink, along with the cutlery and glasses. He was now sitting behind the steering wheel of his sports utility vehicle. The truck pulled out of the driveway and into the traffic. The music from the radio blared as Peter kept his eye on the road, driving through the morning snow. The cell phone began to ring. *Ring. Ring. Ring.* Peter diverted his eyes off the road in front of him, a moment, and onto his cell phone. The screen came to life. It was Emily. Peter turned the volume down on his radio and answered his cell phone, as it sat under the dashboard, attached to a charger.

"Hello?" Peter answered, a little cautiously, as he resumed his eyes on the road and at the oncoming traffic.

"Did you watch the news this morning?" Emily asked, via speakerphone. Her voice sounded grainy, giving out, a little.

"It was a bit hard not to."

"I can't believe the woman. What a bitch! Are you okay?"

Peter took a moment before answering the question as if he had to think about it. "I'm good," he answered, nodding a little.

That was a lie. "What are you up to?"

"Now? I'm out for a drive. I'm running an errand. There was something Andrew said to me the other day, about police protection. It got me thinking."

"Hey, if it makes you feel safe. Go for it, I say."

"Thank you."

The sports utility vehicle was coming to a slow halt, sitting in the middle of the road, indicating, ready to turn right and pull into a nearby car park.

"I'm here now." Peter continued.

"Where's here?" Emily asked, a little concerned.

"I gotta go," Peter answered, dodging the question. "I'll call you later. Don't' forget Christmas."

"Um, okay," Emily answered, feeling a little rushed, thinking that she would have more time with her friend. "Love you. Have a great day! Call me!"

The phone line disconnected.

Peter sat in the car a moment longer. He pulled down the sun visor, staring back at his own reflection in the mirror.

"You got this!" he whispered to himself.

The driver's side door pushed open. Peter reached for his wallet and cell phone, taking the key from the ignition. The wind and the snowfall picked up a little. The door slammed shut and the alarm switched on, as Peter ran towards the main entrance of the gun range and made his way inside the building.

The day progressed into the early evening. The time had just past half-past six, and a black sports utility vehicle was parked in the driveway of Mike's home. It was Peter. From the outside of the home, the light on the front porch was switched off. A thin blanket of snow covered the front yard, and the walkway from the driveway to the porch had been recently salted. The light from the front living room was almost aglow from outside.

The fireplace in the living room was roaring. The inside of the house was nice and warm.

Mike made his way, bouncing from one cupboard to the other, collecting ingredients for this evening's dinner. The menu for this evening was beef stew and vegetables, with a homemade crusty bread roll, cut into chunks, used to soak up the stew. Peter watched on, as music played from the stereo in the living room. The song on the stereo was *"Home"* by *Michael Bublé*. The dining room table was set for two.

The dinner had progressed to late in the evening. The dining room table was cleared away. The glow of the embers from the fireplace had sparked, a little. The music continued to play on the stereo. The volume was now down to a low hum, and Mike held Peter close to him in the centre of the living room, his arms around him, as if they were slow dancing, back and forth, a little.

"I'm sorry life has been chaotic this past couple of weeks," Mike said, just above a whisper. "I promise to make more of an effort, and spend time with you."

Peter lifted his head and looked at Mike. A smile surfaced to his lips, a little. "Life happens when you make plans. It's okay."

"It's not." Mike shook his head, a little. "I can be a better man." Mike leaned in and kissed Peter slowly and passionately.

"I have missed you."

Mike leaned and kissed Peter, again. This time, longer and harder. His hands raised higher up his back as if to support him. The two fell to the floor, in front of the fireplace, kissing passionately. "I love you, Peter Harmon," Mike said, just above a whisper, as he pulled back from the kiss, staring at him longingly.

"I really do." Mike continued.

There was another deep and passionate kiss. Mike dominated Peter, climbing on top of him, as if to pin him down to the floor of the living room, in front of the fireplace. The two tore at each other's clothes, pulling at their shirts and unzipping their jeans. The two were making love. They soon collapsed from exhaustion, Mike wrapping his arms around Peter and pulling him in close to his chest and falling asleep in front of the fireplace.

It was later in the night, somewhere closer to midnight, and somewhere on the other side of Hillsboro. The door leading into the men's restroom swung to a gentle close. The door itself was painted black, that had flecks and chips of paint taken over the years. The restroom was empty.

Almost. A bathroom stall was closed. The door locked. The image of a man stood hunched over the porcelain toilet, his head hovering just above the seat. He was drunk. And coughing heavily, almost violently, as he vomited. The heavy coughing and the vomit began to ease up over time. The image of the man climbed to his feet and flushed the toilet. He turned around, unlocking the door and headed straight for the washbasin.

The water from the washbasin started to run. And fast. The man caught the cold water in his hands, washing his mouth out, and splashing the rest he caught, on his face, to clean up, some. The man stood tall in front of the washbasin, leaning in to catch his reflection in the mirror. It was Detective Quinn.

"Look at you." Detective Quinn whispered to himself. "You're too old for this shit! You should be settled down with a wife and kids, somewhere. Anything but this."

Detective Quinn lowered his head into the washbasin and spat heavily, again, to clear his throat.

It didn't take long before Detective Quinn left the washbasin and the bathroom behind, and stumbled back into the bar. He appeared almost triumphantly, in front of the men's room door, as it swung to a close behind him.

"You messed up my bathroom, again?" asked the man standing behind the bar.

"From the top end only, I promise."

"Eww," the barman answered, with a scowl across his face.

The barman, himself, stood tall at close to six feet and two inches. He sported a white t-shirt with a college football insignia, from one of the southern states, which clung to his beefy and muscular build. His biceps were large, stretching the cotton fabric of the t-shirt, itself. He also wore faded denim blue jeans and black leather boots. His hair was slick, with an almost wet look to it. It was neatly combed back, with a trimmed beard, blonde, with a hint of ginger.

Detective Quinn approached the bar, reaching for his shot of vodka, he had left behind, before going to the bathroom. He lifted the glass and took the shot and caught the alcohol in his mouth. He swirled the vodka in his mouth a little as if to clean it, before swallowing. The shot glass came down on the bar with a hard thud.

"Thank you kindly, sir." Detective Quinn muttered, slurring his words a little.

He left the bar, stumbling a little in his step, as he approached the door. The barman watched him intently as he made his way out of the establishment. Detective Quinn was quick to find his step again.

The bar was close to closing for another evening. There was less than a handful of patrons left, Detective Quinn, included. The front door to the bar, The Pig & Farm, swung open. Detective Quinn made his way outside, onto the pavement. The street was bare, almost empty, except for a few cars parked on either side of the street. The traffic lights at the end of the street had a glow about them this evening, as light snow fell over the country town.

Detective Quinn pulled on his winter coat a little tighter, trying to keep his chest warm, as much as he could. He stumbled down the street, toward his car, a Chevrolet Impala, white in colour, which he was paying off in fortnightly instalments. The cell phone in his trouser pocket began to ring, breaking the silence of a near-empty street. *Ring. Ring. Ring.* Detective Quinn fumbled for his cell phone a little, before answering it.

"Hello?" he muttered.

"Hello," the deep, dark and familiar voice responded.

"Who is this? Who are you calling?" Detective Quinn responded. "What if I said you?"

"Who is this?" Detective Quinn repeated, now a little more annoyed than before.

"I'll give you a moment to catch up."

"It's... you, isn't it? The one behind all this bloodshed?"

"You catch on quick. I can see how you rose through the ranks and made detective." The deep voice laughed, a little.

"So, *who* are you?"

"I'm anyone and everyone. You're the detective. Come and find me." "I will. You can guarantee that!"

"Really? I think differently. I have the upper hand. You have no clues but the crumbs I leave for you."

"And that's it." Detective Quinn answered, almost arrogantly, as he reached his car parked outside the newsagents. "*You're* the crumb. You want to be one of the big boys, huh? Be someone no one will ever forget?

Like Dahmer? Like Gacy? Then, show yourself. Take off that fucking mask!"

"In good time, Detective." There was laughter, again. The telephone line disconnected.

"Shit!" Detective Quinn shouted, in drunken frustration.

The sun rose over another winter Hillsboro morning. The white Chevrolet Impala was parked inside a small garage up a long cement driveway. The apartment building was tall, six storeys high, as each apartment on the front of the building, facing north, all had their own balcony. Detective Quinn lived on the fourth floor of the building, facing south. He, too, had his own balcony. It had a view of the forest lining which sat on the outskirts of town.

The apartment itself was two-bedroom with one bathroom. The living room was close to the front door, which sat near the kitchen. A hallway followed, which led to the bedrooms, bathroom and laundry. And, of course, the balcony. The spare bedroom was used as an office. It was set up with all the mod-cons: a desk, some shelves to store his book collection, and a laptop computer, most for convenience. The master bedroom was located toward the end of the hallway, next to the bathroom. The bedroom door was open, slightly ajar. The couch in the living room also doubled as a pull-out spare bed, used for guests. There weren't that many guests.

The curtains in the master bedroom were pulled open, to allow for the morning sun. A semi- conscious body lay under the covers on the queen-size bed. The bed covers themselves were pulled up high, almost reaching the shoulders of the semi-conscious body. It rolled slowly onto it's back. Its hands raised high, from under the sheets, to rub the sleep from his eyes. It was Detective Quinn. The arms collapsed onto the top of the bed. The light from the morning sun sprayed across the walls of the master bedroom.

Detective Quinn rolled over onto his stomach. He crawled across the surface of his bed, reaching for his cell phone which sat next to his wallet on his nightstand, and pulled it off the charger. He rolled back onto the bed, finding his comfortable spot, again. The screen of the cell phone came to life. There were no missed calls or text messages. Detective Quinn navigated to his call history, the last call received from last night.

The time of the call came in at one twenty-six this morning. The caller ID was blocked.

"Fuck!" Detective Quinn whispered out of frustration and still feeling the end of his hangover from the night before.

The cell phone collapsed onto the bed, resting on his chest.

Detective Quinn pushed the bed cover back, exposing his naked body beneath, as he climbed out of bed and to his feet. His tall, almost lanky and smooth frame, stood by the side of his bed a moment, as he was quick to adjust himself, before walking across the bedroom, out into the hallway, and into the bathroom. The bathroom door closed behind him. The lights to the bathroom switched on. The room itself was small and compact, with a single shower fitted into the far-right corner, sitting next to a bathtub, washbasin and toilet. It was very basic in design. The walls were painted a mild shade of grey with white tiled flooring.

The hot water from the shower was running hard. The steam rose to the ceiling, making its way around the bathroom. The shower curtain was wet and pulled to a close as the air conditioner worked overtime. Detective Quinn stood under the showerhead, his eyes closed, head tilted back, and enjoying the hot water consume his naked body, as he rubbed a bar of soap across his chest.

The water stopped running, now. The shower was over. There were droplets of water falling from the showerhead and splashing on the tiled floor, beneath. Detective Quinn stood hunched over, a little, in front of the washbasin, with a damp towel wrapped loosely around his waist. He was brushing his teeth as he watched his reflection intently in the mirror. His mind raced, thinking of the tone of voice on the other end of the phone call from the early hours of the morning. *A voice modulator to hide the identity of the killer? It could have been anyone.*

Detective Quinn was now back in his master bedroom. He was naked, again. He walked across the bedroom, to and from his bed to the set of mahogany drawers, near his wardrobe, as he opened the top set of drawers, in search of some business socks and underwear. He pulled out a plain pair of black cotton jockey shorts and climbed into them, adjusting himself, a little. He returned to the end of his bed, sitting there, legs crossed, as he pulled on his sock. He stood tall, once more, and walked to the wardrobe to retrieve another long-sleeved shirt and navy-blue tie to wear to work.

The kitchen was alive. The television set in the living room was switched on, just for noise. It was morning television, nothing too exciting. A rock band from the mid-1980s was in the process of being interviewed on some morning news network, announcing their comeback with a new album and tour. Everything that was old was new again. Everything was getting a reboot these days, television and movies included. Detective Quinn didn't pay much attention to it. He concentrated on his breakfast, a single cup of coffee with two slices of toast, lemon spread with melting butter. It hit the spot.

Detective Quinn finished his breakfast. The television set was switched off, as were the lights. He reached for his keys, wallet and cell phone and left his apartment, closing, locking the front door behind him. He made his way out of the apartment building, opting to take the staircase, instead of waiting for the elevator. He passed some of his neighbours, giving them a smile and a quick nod of the head, without actually saying anything, until he reached the entrance of the building, making his way to the garage. Detective Quinn unlocked his car, pulled open the driver's side door, climbing inside a moment, and slamming the door shut. He caught his reflection in the vanity mirror, a moment.

"Who are you?" he asked himself, just above a whisper.

The engine to the car roared to life, as the garage door rolled slowly open.

Peter had woken that morning, finding himself back in bed with Mike. It was a quick start to the morning. Mike had also got himself ready for work and was out the door. Peter followed, grabbing his cell phone, wallet, and car keys and drove home, just after six in the morning. Mike promised he would be in touch, later in the day.

The white Chevrolet Impala pulled into the curb and parked outside Peter's home. The engine died. Detective Quinn kept his hands on the steering wheel a moment longer, turning his head a little, looking up at the two-storey weatherboard home, as he chewed a little on his lower lip. He tilted the weight of his frame from side to side a little, opening the driver's side door, and climbing out of the car. The car door slammed shut behind him. He stood there, surveying the front of the home. The sports utility vehicle was parked in the driveway. The garage door was locked.

And a fine dusting of snow smeared across the front lawn. Detective Quinn made his way towards the house, walking up the pathway, towards the front porch. He reached the front door, as the wooden floorboards cracked under the weight of his feet. He pounded heavily on the front door for a moment. *Pound. Pound. Pound.*

The front door to the house swung open. Peter stood in the entrance of the door. He was surprised and shocked, all in one, to see Detective Quinn standing in front of him, on his front porch, dressed in another suit, unannounced and uninvited.

"Detective, what are you doing here? Am I under arrest?" Peter asked, just above a whisper, and with a little apprehension, as he hid behind his front door, taking a step backwards, a little.

"No, no. Nothing like that," he answered, with a hint of a smile surfacing to his lips. "We need to talk. The killer called me in the early hours of this morning. This is off the record. I promise."

"Why should I help you? I mean, after everything we've been through, the last we saw each other, you had me pinned as the killer."

"You are not the killer!" Detective Quinn answered, raising his voice a little in frustration. Peter looked at the detective, a little curiously.

"How?"

"What?"

"How do you know I am not the killer? If this were a horror movie, this would be the part where I lull you into a false sense of security, before striking and ripping you in half, and see what your insides look like."

Detective Quinn looked genuinely concerned. He shifted his stance, moving his weight and feet, a little. The floorboards on the front porch began to crack under the pressure, again.

"Relax!" Peter answered, reassuringly, with a smile stretched almost from ear to ear.

"The killer called me last night. All joking aside, I need to know everything you can recall. Your childhood growing up with your parents, your grandfather, New York. If I'm going to nail this…" Detective Quinn paused a moment, out of sheer frustration, "…whoever this is, then I need to know it all."

Peter looked at the detective with the same curiosity as before. The front door opened a little more, as he stepped out from hiding.

"Of course, Detective." Peter nodded, with a hint of a smile. "There is a lot to tell. You better come inside."

"Thank you."

Peter stepped to one side to allow Detective Quinn inside his home. The front door closed behind him.

Chapter Sixteen…

Peter invited the detective further inside his home. A silence coursed throughout the house.

Detective Quinn raised his eyes a little, looking up at the staircase, before peering down the hallway, and then made his way into the living room. He was immediately attracted to the framed photographs which hung upon the walls. Detective Quinn gave them the once over before he walked over to the couch and made himself comfortable. The sound of the kettle in the kitchen broke the silence in the house as the water began to boil. Peter fixed himself and his guest a cup of coffee.

"How do you take it? Your coffee, I mean?" Peter called from the kitchen.

"Oh," Detective Quinn answered, a little taken aback. "um, milk and two sugars. Thank you."

Peter soon appeared in the entrance of the living room, carrying a tray with two cups of coffee and a plate of sugary and cream-filled biscuits. He made his way in and placed them down on the coffee table.

"Thank you," Detective Quinn said, accepting his cup of coffee.

"Not a problem," Peter murmured. "Make yourself comfortable. There is a lot to tell."

Peter grabbed his coffee and a cream-filled biscuit and made himself comfortable in the chair opposite the detective.

Peter and Detective Quinn were onto their third cup of coffee before Peter finished with his off-the-record interview. He told him about his childhood, and the years he spent floating between joint custody. It was maddening hell. He told him about the cruel and sadistic abuse he suffered at the hands of his grandfather and mother before he eventually came to live with his father and step- mother full-time. Peter told the detective of the events that transpired in college in New York City, and the events that brought him back to Hillsboro. Peter could see Detective Quinn turn shades of green at certain points during their conversation.

"Thank you again for your time," Detective Quinn said, just above a whisper, as he was being led to the front door.

"Of course," Peter answered, nodding a little. "If there is anything further you need, please, let me know."

"I will. Thank you, again. And for your time, this morning. You were right. There was a lot to tell."

The two reached the front door. Peter leaned in front of the detective a little and opened the front door for him. The snowing had stopped. The sun was shining, but it was still very cold, indeed. Detective Quinn tugged at his suit jacket, a little, trying to keep himself warm, again. Peter stood at the front door, open ajar, as to not allow the heat to escape, too much, as he watched the detective make his way back to his car.

Detective Quinn climbed inside his car. The car door slammed shut and the engine roared to life, once more. He sat there in front of the steering wheel, his hands, at ten and two, ready to pull out from the curb. The car eventually pulled out and drove to the end of the street. Peter stood at the front door watching him leave.

The silence fell upon the house once more. The windows were closed. The front door was locked. And the lights around the house were switched off. Peter found himself driving into town in the early afternoon. The sports utility vehicle raced the streets, hugging the curves of the road, careful to stick to the speed limit. That was a lie. Peter drove a few kilometres over the limit, but nothing scary mind you. The Christmas season was coming into full effect in Hillsboro. The adverts on the television promoting the perfect American Hallmark-like family enjoying another bountiful Christmas was in full swing, reaching regurgitation levels.

The town square was decorated with large, plastic Santa Claus masks, which hung from street lamps, wreaths, and reindeer. The local school children were on break for the next two weeks to enjoy the festivities of the season. The local town square was filled with children, playing in the snow, making snowmen and throwing snowballs at each other, running, laughing and hiding.

Peter found somewhere to park his truck and the engine soon dies. He sat behind the steering wheel, a moment, peering inside a local diner. It was full of patrons. Peter released his grip from the steering wheel and progressed to climb out of his truck, slamming the driver's side door to a close behind him. The alarm switched on as he made his way onto the pavement. He stood there a moment longer, getting his bearings, as he looked around the town square. He reached for his cell phone, in his right trouser pocket. The screen immediately came to life. There were two unread text messages, one from Mike, and the other from Andrew.

Peter lifted his eyes off his cell phone and placed it back in his trouser pocket as he walked past the storefronts, before making his way into a nearby bookstore, to escape the crowds. A small bell chimed as the front door pushed open; it immediately felt incredibly warm inside, with the scent of cinnamon in the air. It was a little real-estate trick, to coax the patrons into buying something they never knew they wanted. The aisles in the bookstore ran deep, and the shelves ran high and hugged the walls. There were two staff members working the counter and cash register, doing their best to get through the long line of customers. The staff members wore matching white cotton t-shirts with a moss-green trim around the neck and biceps. There was printing on the back of the t-shirt. It was the company logo, an open book with the caption which read, *Andrea's Books*, in cursive writing underneath.

Peter surveyed the store and walked down the closest aisle. He past the books, not really looking at the titles. He passed the new release section and made his way over to the autobiographies. They were located in the far-left corner of the store, towards a tiny room for employees, to take their break, and make their way out the back of the store and into the staff parking lot. Peter was deep in thought. His index finger of his left hand glided over the spines of the books. Peter wondered how much the authors could recall of their lives, how much was true, and of course, how much was made up, for the sake of sensationalism.

The patrons in the bookstore became nothing more than a blur. Peter was caught up in his own concentration, the down lights in the ceiling felt as though they began to dim as if the store itself was growing darker and darker. Peter lifted his eyes off the books in the shelf a moment, turning to face the end of the aisle, towards the back of the store, as if in a dream state. And there in front of him, was the image of the clown mask. It stood there ever so silently, as if unseen by the other patrons, staring back. The image of the clown mask gripped a large, sharp kitchen knife tightly in their left hand. It started to pace forward, slowly at first, toward Peter, before growing faster and faster. The large, sharp kitchen knif rose high in the air, above the clown mask's shoulder. The blade came down with such ferocity, slicing through the darkness of the store, ready to strike. Peter raised his arms up in front of him as if to protect himself. A blood-curdling scream followed, as a single hand reached out to him, grasping his left shoulder, squeezing it tightly.

Peter blinked his eyes furiously a moment. He turned around, facing the front of the store. The lights in the bookstore returned to normal. And, there, standing in front of him, was nothing more than a bookstore employee. He was startled. The bookstore was filled with other patrons, all standing around, staring back at him in shock, some whispering amongst themselves. Peter returned his focus to the bookstore employee. He was embarrassed. The bookstore employee was male.

Somewhere in his mid- to late-thirties, clean-shaven with an athletic build and neatly combed hair, black in colour, back and to the sides, with a part a little off-centre.

"Can I help you, sir?" the bookstore employee asked, a little concerned.

Peter looked at the employee, worried. He covered his mouth with his right hand, a moment, as he felt his heartbeat racing wildly in his chest.

"I'm fine," Peter answered, composing himself. "I'll just take these." Peter handed the bookstore employee a handful of autobiographies.

He looked at the book covers.

Peter looked at the employee with a don't-judge-me expression, so clearly marked across his face. "Of course, sir," the employee answered politely. "If you would like to follow me, the cash register is located at the front of the store."

Peter followed the employee to the counter at the front of the store.

"You can come over here," the employee said, "we have a second register."

Peter skipped the majority of the crowd, as he moved to the front of a separate line. He looked at the patrons, continuing to stare back at him. The look looked so familiar.

"It's all your fault!" Peter heard someone whisper.

"Okay, that'll be fifty-nine dollars and eighty cents, including sales tax," the employee said, as he rung up another sale and placed the books in a complimentary, takeaway tote bag.

"Of course." Peter slid a handful of cash across the counter, too embarrassed to count it, but knew that there was more than enough, plus a healthy tip. He just wanted to get out of the store and escape the stares and whispers. Peter grabbed the tote bag and raced out of the bookstore. The patrons, including the employees, stood back and watched him leave. The front door to the bookstore pulled open fast, as the bell rattled.

Peter reached the front of the bookstore. He stepped out onto the crowded footpath, along the town square. The townspeople were walking in different directions, back and forth, and lost himself in the crowd. He still felt embarrassed and shaken, a little.

"Hey, you!" a friendly voice called out.

Peter smiled. It was a familiar voice. It was Emily. "Hey!" Peter answered, surprised.

Emily gave Peter the quick rundown, scanning his latest purchase. She stood there, in front of her high school friend, dressed for the winter season, in a dark brown coat, with a faux fur white fluffy collar, black leather gloves, a scarf, and dark denim jeans with black leather boots, which rested just under her knee.

"It's funny I ran into you here." smiled Emily.

"Yeah? Why's that?"

"I just bought your Christmas present."

Peter laughed, a little.

"Me, too. Yours, I mean. You caught me," he replied, raising the tote bag, a little.

"So... what? Do we exchange now?"

"Not here," Peter answered. "Let's get out of the cold. There is a diner nearby."

"Great!" Emily clapped her leather-gloved hands together, whilst balancing a large purse on her right arm. "Lunch and presents. Could this day get any better?"

Peter forced himself to smile.

The number of patrons in the diner were thinning now. Another small bell chimed as Emily led the way, and pushed the front door opened. It slowly closed behind them as they approached the cash register waiting to be seated. The two friends stood close together, quietly talking amongst themselves, as a large-boned waitress with curly black hair, just below the earlobe, approached the waiting patrons. The waitress wore a pale blue smock with a white apron with red trim. The apron had smears of apple pie down the front. It had been a busy and messy morning.

"Good afternoon," the waitress said, as she leaned into the counter and grabbed two sticky, laminated menus. "Dining in?"

"A table for two?" Emily asked, nodding a little.

The waitress turned her back, ever so slightly, to survey the diner floor. "Of course," she answered, turning back. "Please, follow me."

Emily and Peter followed the waitress. They walked across the floor of the diner. It was filled with other patrons, high school kids, drinking shakes whilst sharing fries, families talking amongst themselves, single people head down, reading their latest book, whilst noshing on something from the kitchen.

The waitress arrived at the table. It was a booth located near the front of the store, with a view of the town square, and the local people passing by. The waitress left the menus on the table. "Thank you," said Emily, politely.

"I'll give you guys a few minutes to decide. I'll be back soon. My name is Kimberly, and I'll be your waitress for the afternoon."

"Thank you," smiled Peter.

Peter was the first to crawl into the booth, sliding across the bright red laminate chair. He sunk into it, a little. The tote bag, filled with books, sat on the table, in front of him, almost obstructing his view.

Emily took a more proper approach as she climbed into the booth and slid across the chair, facing her high school friend. Emily smiled, again.

"What? Peter asked, surprised. "You're looking at me like I left something on my face." The two chuckled.

"I 'didn't, did I?" Peter asked, leaning into the table and feeling a little insecure.

"You're good."

There was a brief pause.

"So, how are you doing?" Emily asked as she made herself a little more comfortable in the booth.

"I'm doing good," Peter answered, releasing a sigh, as his shoulders sank, a little. "I mean, I thought I was."

"What happened?" Emily asked, with genuine concern.

"I was in the bookstore. I must have zoned out or something. I swear I saw the killer. That mask. Cut to me leaving the store and everyone staring at me. It was like high school all over again. And to top it off, I had Detective Quinn turn up on my front porch this morning wanting to know every single detail of my life for the past nine years. The killer called him. I guess he got spooked, or something."

"The killer called Quinn? What did they say?"

"It doesn't matter. It's Christmas. Can't we just take a moment to enjoy this? This moment?"

"Of course," Emily answered, nodding her head almost vigorously. "Absolutely, we can. I can't wait for your Christmas party this year."

"Me, too." Peter nodded. "Something else to focus on, rather than the blatantly obvious. Where are my manners? Presents. Let's do it! Let's exchange!"

Emily chuckled a little, clapping her hands together with excitement, a moment.

"Merry Christmas! Or is it Happy Holidays? I don't know any more. Anyway, I got you this!" Emily fumbled through her bag, a moment, and handed Peter a single, white envelope.

Peter accepted the envelope, almost like a deer caught in the headlights. His eyes were open, stunned almost.

"What is this?" he asked, accepting the envelope.

"It's a little something," Emily answered, shrugging her shoulders, a little. "I know how much you love movies. The Limited is having a Wes Craven movie marathon, early next year. I got two tickets. I thought maybe the two of us could go, you know, together."

"I love Wes Craven," Peter answered, just above a whisper as he opened the envelope and looked at the tickets.

Peter stared at the tickets a moment longer. His eyes blinked heavily.

"What is it?" Emily asked, again, with concern, and a hint of worry in her voice.

"I was just remembering a happy memory, is all," Peter answered, just above a whisper with a smile surfacing to his lips. "Robert and I did a Wes Craven marathon back in New York, a few years ago."

"Oh…" Emily answered.

"It's fine. I love them. Thank you. And of course, you and me. Wes Craven in January." Emily smiled. She clapped her hands again with excitement.

"My turn! My turn!" Emily cheered.

"I know how much you love Andy Cohen and the Real Housewives."

Emily reached across the dining table and pulled the bookstore tote bag toward her. "It's the *Andy Cohen Diaries*."

"I love them. Thank you."

Emily leaned across the dining table and planted a kiss on Peter's right cheek.

Kimberly, the waitress, returned to the table, standing still, with pencil and notepad in hand, ready to take an order.

It was December 23. The day before Christmas Eve. It was the only day, Peter, Mike, Andrew, and Emily could agree upon in order to get together for the Christmas party. The three days of Christmas, Eve, Day, and the day after, were designated to prior family commitments.

Emily was at home. The television set in the living room was set to a low volume. Emily, herself, was toward the back of the house, in her bedroom, deciding on what to wear to the party this evening. She was barefoot and casually dressed in a pair of denim jeans and a simple white cotton T-shirt. The lights in her master bedroom and walk-in wardrobe were switched on. She went through the clothes hanging in front of her, desperate to make a decision. She stopped a moment, pulling her cell phone from her jean pocket to check the time. It was a little past five forty-five in the evening. Sunset was almost half an hour ago. Emily closed her eyes tightly, if only for a moment, giving up on the wardrobe. She sighed a moment as her shoulders slouched, some. Emily turned her back on her clothes and walked out of her bedroom, down the hallway and into the bathroom.

The door leading into the bathroom pushed open. Emily leaned in a little and switched on the light. The neon light hanging from the ceiling flickered on. The bathroom was very neat and spacious. The washbasin was practically empty, except for her toothbrush, toothpaste, and a small travel-size make-up bag. The floor was tiled in a black-and-white mosaic design with white-painted walls. And a frosted-glass shower, which stretched from wall to wall. There was an open window on the side, with a view of the side of the house, which included walkway and fence, plus a few potted plants to add green for colour.

The door leading into the bathroom closed behind Emily. She stepped further into the bathroom, walking towards the shower. She slid open the frosted glass door, leaned into the shower and switched on the faucets. The water ran heavily. The weather outside was starting to turn now. Emily noticed. She pulled her eyes and hand from the shower, as the sound of the rain hit the roof. It sounded like needles smashing against the window on the side of the house. Emily shook the water from her hand, wiping it on the side of her jeans, allowing the water to continue to run, before walking toward the window. She raised her hand, toward the glass. It felt cool to the touch. And, in that fleeting moment, she pulled at the window, opening it a little. The wind was strong. Emily stood back, a little. And, there, on the other side of the window frame, stood the clown mask.

It startled her. The image of the clown mask peering back behind angry, lifeless eyes. Emily gasped, reaching for her chest in shock. She fell backwards, a little, taking a few steps.

Emily fell to the floor, losing her balance. She scurried, pushing and propelling herself forward, to the furthers corner of the room, on her hands and knees. Her right hand buried deep into her pocket, searching for her cell phone. *Ring. Ring. Ring.* The image of the clown mask vanished from the window.

"Hello?" she answered with panic in her voice.

"Welcome to the party, Emily," the dark and familiar voice said, almost angrily.

"What do you mean?" Emily asked, fighting back tears.

"This isn't the *Breakfast Club*, princess. People live. People die. Poor Jayne Scott. She died all because of Peter Harmon. No one mourns for the town slut in a horror movie. But Emily Olsen? The high school "it-girl" who dated the star quarterback, who dabbled in politics, and grew up to be in one messed-up, complicated relationship? There's the real tragedy." The deep and familiar voice laughed.

"Fuck you!" Emily screamed.

"You'll die when I am good and ready, and not a moment before. In the meantime, I hope you are enjoying the show."

Another laugh.

The phone line disconnected.

Emily was physically shaking. She dropped her cell phone to the bathroom floor, as she wiped the tears from her eyes.

There was a heavy pounding coming from the front door. *Knock. Knock. Knock.* Emily screamed, again, pushing herself up against the wall. She climbed to her feet and raced to the bathroom door. The shower continued to run. Another knock. *Knock.* Emily stepped out cautiously from the bathroom. The door opening slowly, as the hinges on the door cracked, a little. Emily held her breath. She held her cell phone out in front of her, close enough to read the screen, but also to use it as a weapon of sorts, if needed. *Knock.*

"Who is it?" she yelled, as she started to dial nine-one-one, and ready to hit the send button. "Who's there?"

"It's me!" Andrew called from the front door.

Emily opened her mouth in surprise. She jammed her cell phone in her jean pocket and raced down the hallway, towards the front door. She reached it, pulling it open. And there, standing in front of her, on the front porch, was Andrew Preston. He was neatly dressed in a pair of denim jeans and red flannel, long-sleeved shirt, which was tucked in at the waist, and black leather boots.

"Are you okay?" Andrew asked, concerned.

"How long have you been here?" Emily asked, just above a whisper.

"I just pulled in. What's wrong?" Andrew asked as his right leather boot stepped forward, inside the house, unannounced.

Emily looked down to the floor and noticed, then back at Andrew, catching his eyes.

"The time must have escaped me." She forced a smile. "I couldn't decide what to wear."

"Let's check it out and see what we can find." Andrew smiled, stepping inside the house and closing the door behind him.

The rain continued to fall as the evening progressed. The front lawn was covered in snow. And an almost glow came from the front living room window, as it sprayed across the front porch. The light above the front door at Peter's home was switched on. The living room was decorated with Christmas. There were tunes playing from the stereo in the living room. It was a combination of traditional Christmas music and current pop hits on the charts. The fireplace was roaring. The Christmas tree itself was in full decoration mode, with a few gifts under the tree.

Mike was in the kitchen. He was neatly dressed in denim jeans, a plain white, cotton t-shirt and long-sleeved, button-down black shirt on top. A bottle of beer, almost half-drunk, sat on the side of the chopping board, as he was preparing dinner for the evening. There was a knock at the front door, and Peter appeared. He also held a bottle of beer in his left hand, with a hint of a smile that surfaced to his lips.

"One second!" Peter called out, as he approached the front door.

Peter could see the image of two bodies standing next to each other through the frosted glass. He leaned in and opened the front door, with his right hand, and there, standing in front of him were Andrew Preston and Emily Olsen. His eyes were immediately drawn to Emily. Her face appeared sombre, almost. She was not her usual, cheerful and happy-go-lucky self. Emily forced a smile and waved briefly, as she stood there in blue denim jeans, a long flowing white blouse and an open black jacket to keep herself warm. She wore sneakers to the party.

"Welcome, welcome," Peter said, standing in the front door with a smile and a beer.

"Merry Christmas, Peter," answered Emily, just above a whisper.

"Please, come on in." Peter stood to one side, opening the front door a little more.

Emily was the first to enter the house. She took the lead and walked past Peter, into the foyer, and deeper into the house.

Peter returned his gaze back to Andrew. He continued to stand in the entrance of the front door, out on the porch. A smile slowly surfaced to Andrew's lips. He took another step forward, leading with his right foot, stepping over the porch and into the foyer of the house. The smile on Andrew's face turned into a cheeky grin and chuckle, as he raised his left hand, moving forward into the house, and giving the host a rub on his belly.

"I send you a text message and you don't even bother to reply? Nice one! You keep me waiting all day for a response?" Andrew chuckled, again.

Peter stood by the front door, pushing it to a close, stunned a little, forgetting his text message.

"I asked you out for a drink after work one day this week, after Christmas, I mean," said Andrew, turning in the foyer of the house to face his best friend.

"Of course," Peter answered, nodding a little. "That would be fun. Let me know when. Feel like a beer?"

"Does a bear shit in the woods?" Andrew chuckled. "Of course I want a beer."

Andrew followed Peter deeper inside the house, past the foyer and down the hallway, and into the kitchen. Emily had made her way into the kitchen, too. Both she and Mike exchanged pleasantries, as she stood back, near the refrigerator, watching Mike bouncing around the kitchen, cooking dinner for the evening. The menu for this evening was a hunk of roast beef, mixed vegetables and mashed potatoes with a hint of wasabi. The kitchen was filled with different aromas. Peter made his way to the refrigerator, opened the door, leaned in and handed a bottle of beer to both Andrew and Emily.

The party continued on through the evening. The dining table, which was once set neatly for four guests, with fine glassware, cutlery, folded tablecloths, was a mess of almost eaten food. The roast beef had been hacked and sliced into, the glasses were filled with beers, wines and spirits, and the plates sported half-eaten food, pushed around the plates with a knife and fork. The guests retreated from the dining table and made their way into the living room. The four friends had exchanged gifts, with the budget of no more than twenty dollars.

"I need to borrow your other half and your best friend," Emily announced, as she stood from the couch in the living room. "Peter, do you have a minute?"

The conversation amongst the group of friends stopped. Peter was immediately drawn to Emily. "Of course," he answered, just above a whisper, and making eye contact with Andrew, then Mike, and back to Emily. "What's up?"

"Walk with me," responded Emily, extending her right hand. Peter reached out for her hand.

The two friends left the living room and started on the twenty-five-cent tour of the property.

Emily led the way. She took Peter out into the hallway, taking a left turn and heading for the staircase in the foyer. Emily climbed the staircase, with Peter in her hand. Andrew and Mike were left behind in the living room. They looked at each other, a little confused, shrugging their shoulders some, as they both took another sip from their glasses of beer.

"What's going on, Emily?" Peter asked, concerned, walking down the hallway of the second storey of the house.

"I need to ask you a question," Emily answered, as her voice was filled with concern and ready to break at a moment's notice. "This is hard, so just bear with me, okay?"

"Of course."

Peter gave her hand a gentle squeeze to let her know he was there for her. He took the lead, pulling her into a spare room he had converted into his office. The light in the office switched on and the two friends took to the couch by the window.

"I need to know about your father." Emily continued, just above a whisper. Peter was drawn in by the statement.

"Your mother. Tell me about her," she continued. Emily appeared confused and worried.

"I need to know about that... mask."

The interrogation was making Peter feel a little uncomfortable. He could feel his stomach turn, but maintained a smile, somewhat, for his friend.

"What's going on, Emily?"

"I think I got a call from the killer this afternoon. I can't forget that mask and that voice. It was just so... dark. And their laugh. It sent chills down my spine."

"Did you tell Andrew? What did he say?"

"Are you kidding me? You're the first person I have told. You know Andrew. I tell him and the police would be everywhere. I am not going to spoil this evening. You've gone to so much trouble."

Peter squeezed Emily's hands, again, as if for reassurance. "What did the voice say?"

"That I'll die by their hands, and in their time, and not a moment before," Emily answered, just above a whisper.

"It was probably just some kids dialling numbers and stumbled across yours by mistake." Peter shrugged, with a smile, as if to assure her everything would be okay. "You know how kids are these days."

"He. She. Or whoever this was. This was no kid." Emily answered. "By the way, you're a terrible liar. But thank you for trying to reassure me."

Peter looked at his high school friend a moment longer. The smile disappeared.

"I remember who my mother was, what she did, and I live with it. It's my burden. It shouldn't have to be anyone else's. In the meantime, stay on your toes. Stay alert. Lock your doors. And most important of all, trust no one. This is life. It gets me by, the good and the bad." There was a brief pause. "Yesterday, I brought myself a gun for protection. No one knows about it, not even Mike. I have lived through this before. This isn't a horror movie. It's life. Stay vigilant."

Emily stared at her friend she had known since high school a moment. A smile rushed to the surface of her lips.

"We have a Christmas party to attend. Let's go. Hey, don't tell Andrew what we talked about, okay?"

"Of course." Peter smiled. "Let's go."

The days progressed. It was Christmas Day. The curtains in the master bedroom were pulled open a little, to allow for the morning light to come through the second storey window. The snow had stopped this morning. The sun was out with a thick layer of snow blanketing the front lawn and the rest of the neighbourhood. Peter was alone in bed. The bed cover was pushed back, exposing his back, as he lay on the bed on his stomach. His scar was visible. He was slowly coming to. His eyes slowly opening. Peter wiped the sleep from his eyes before he reached across the bed and grabbing his cell phone from his nightstand, and pulling it from the charger. Peter rolled onto his back as he looked at the cell phone. There were two text messages already, and it wasn't even seven in the morning. Peter navigated through the cell phone.

Merry Christmas, good buddy! Talk to you soon.

The message from Andrew read.

Merry Christmas! I hope you have a wonderful start to your day. I'm thinking of you. I'll give you a call later on today. Love you.

The second message was from Mike.

Peter lay on the bed, on his back, his eyes diverted from the ceiling and to the screen of his cell phone. It was alive. There were no missed calls. Peter turned a little and placed the cell phone back on the nightstand. He kicked at the bed cover and climbed to the side of the bed, placing his feet on the floor. It was a little cool to the touch. Peter was naked, again. He stood up, adjusting himself, a little, before walking out of the bedroom, down the hallway, and into the bathroom to take a shower and make a start on the day.

The shower was over. Peter found himself in the kitchen. The lights were switched on, so was the television set in the living room, the volume down low, just for noise. The morning news was coming to an end. It was Christmas Day. The news broadcast was hosted by the weekend news hosts.

Peter was dressed for the day. He kept it simple, in a black polo shirt and faded blue denim jeans with sneakers. He was in the kitchen cooking breakfast, also very simple; the first cup of coffee with two slices of toast with melting butter and lemon spread. Peter walked from the kitchen, with cup and plate in hands, balancing, and careful not to drop, and made his way into the living room. He sat on the couch, in front of the television set and coffee table. His eyes drew away from the freshly made breakfast, a moment and to the framed photographs hanging on the wall.

The memories came flooding back. Peter stood up from the couch and walked over to the wall. The photographs were of Peter, his family and friends, during happier times, some photographs in colour, and others in black and white. Peter raised his left hand and touched the glass of the frames. It was a little cold to the touch, at first. He gently ran his fingers over a picture of his father. It was a photograph of the two of them together. Peter was no older than eleven years old. It was a photograph of the two of them on a fishing trip. The two of them laughing at the size of the flounder Peter had caught, which was dragged onto their dingy. Peter smiled at the photograph, fighting to hold back the tears.

"Merry Christmas, Dad," Peter muttered to himself, just above a whisper. "I love you."

Peter turned his back on the photographs on the wall. He walked across the living room, taking only one slice of toast before taking a deep sip from his cup of coffee, and headed towards the front door, grabbing his keys, wallet and cell phone by the door. He walked out of the house, closing, locking the door behind him.

The sports utility vehicle drove through Hillsboro. The roads, for the greater part, were quieter this morning. The vehicle hugged the corners as it took the twists, turns and bends, through the quiet, wintry forest, passing the trees covered in snow. There was music playing from the stereo and a bomber jacket laying in the back seat of the truck. Peter kept his eyes on the road, slowly humming to the tunes on the radio, the ones he knew, anyway.

Peter drove from home to the Hillsboro Cemetery. It was almost a quarter to eight in the morning now, and there were three, maybe four, cars parked in the parking lot. Peter pulled into the parking lot, parking his truck furthest away from the other cars. He didn't like tight spots. The truck pulled in and the engine died. Peter sat there a moment, stuck somewhere in his own thoughts, feeling the warmth from the heater slowly fade, as he stared out into the thick snowfields, and rows of damp, grey headstones. Peter turned in his seat, grabbing his bomber jacket, and climbing out of the truck, slamming the door behind him. The alarm switched on. Peter walked through the snowfields, taking the recently salted walk paths to his father's headstone.

It was cold this morning. The bomber jacket kept Peter's torso warm, but his cheeks were feeling the cold. They were turning a shade of pink. Peter kept his hands buried in his jacket pockets, as he made his way towards his father's burial site. He could see it. It was just a few steps away. The site itself was neatly maintained, although Peter struggled to see it, for the snow everywhere.

"This is better." Peter started, just above a whisper. "Merry Christmas, Dad. I wish you were here. I was in the house, looking at the photographs of us, recalling the happier times, and realised, this is where I needed to be today. The photographs on the wall are a memory, something I can look back on every day. This is where you live now, it's only fitting that I come and visit you."

Peter leaned down, bending at the knees, coming almost to eye level with the headstone. His left hand reached out, touching the lettering of his father's name. Michael.

One of the most festive days of the year had come and gone, for another year, anyway. Peter spent most of the morning talking away, chatting to his father, and catching him up on his life so far, on his move back to Hillsboro, re-connecting with his high school friends, and his love life. The search for a job could wait until the new year. Peter returned home to a quiet house. He switched the volume on the television set up high, just for noise, and touched base with Mike, Andrew and Emily. Well, it was more a case of them touching base with him, checking in on him, making sure he enjoyed the day. Andrew was a little tipsy, to say the least. It was his coping mechanism in dealing with a mother in-law who always disapproved.

Andrew and Peter shared a few laughs and made plans to catch up for lunch at The Watering Hole in the coming days. Mike had promised to pop round later in the day, to take him to dinner, after he finished his stock take. Work never ended, even on holidays.

The town of Hillsboro was returning to some sense of normalcy after Christmas Eve and the day, itself. People were beginning to emerge from their family homes and go about their daily lives, once more, as if nothing had happened. The only real difference was there were a few new haircuts and sweaters being shown around town.

The car park to The Watering Hole was busy, almost to capacity. The sports utility vehicle was parked on the side of the building, in and amongst the other cars and trucks as Peter made his way inside, dressed in the same bomber jacket he wore to the cemetery on Christmas Day. The wood door pushed open. The Watering Hole was alive with people and music. The television set which hung from the corner of the bar was switched on. There was a football game on the tube.

The bar felt warm. Peter tugged at his jacket, popping the buttons open, and exposing his navy-blue polo shirt beneath. It was tucked into the front of his black jeans. Peter surveyed the bar. He couldn't make out Andrew, anywhere. He pulled out his cell phone and navigated through the screens.

I'm at the bar. Where are you?

Peter typed and hit the send button, before stuffing his cell phone in his left pocket.

Peter looked up. He continued to make his way towards the bar. He weaved past the other patrons, waiting for his turn to be served. The cute bartender was back behind the bar, today. The one from Andrew's disastrous birthday party.

"Hey, you." the familiar voice said, with a smile. The barman was dressed in uniform.

"Hi, there," Peter answered, politely.

"I remember you. What can I get you?"

"Coke, please."

"Sure. Coming right up," the barman said, as he tapped the edge of the bar with his index and middle fingers of his right hand.

"Thank you." Peter smiled.

Peter looked around the bar a moment, before keeping his head down. He felt his cell phone in his pocket vibrate. He retrieved it. The screen came to life. It was a text message. Peter opened it.

I'm here. Out back."

The message from Andrew read.

A picture quickly followed. It was a selfie of Andrew, smiling, sticking his tongue into the top of his beer. It still had the head on it. The suds almost touching his nose.

Peter smiled, almost chuckling a little.

You goose. Be right there.

Peter typed and hit the send button, again.

Peter made his way through the bar, out into the beer garden outback. It was catered for the winter season, with heaters positioned around tables, to keep the patrons warm, and a plastic, see- through sheeting which hung from the framed patio, to keep the warmth inside. Peter made his way outside, making eye contact with Andrew. Peter nodded his head with a hint of a smile, carrying his soda, whilst Andrew lifted his beer, as if to cheers him. Andrew had already made a start on the beer. And there, in front of him, was a large basket of fries, enough for two people, and various dipping sauces, to graze on.

"Hey, you," Andrew said with a smile. "Merry Christmas and all that bullshit!" he laughed. Peter chuckled somewhat as he placed his soda on the table.

Andrew stepped closer, giving Peter a tight, bear-hug which lasted several seconds. "How you doing?" he asked.

"I'm doing okay." Peter nodded as if taking a moment to think about the question first. "How are you? Did you survive Christmas?"

"I love Emily, don't get me wrong. It's her mother who is the handful. I'm always a disappointment." Andrew stared at Peter a moment, before breaking out into laughter. "Mrs Olsen. The answer to the question no one asked." Peter laughed.

The afternoon progressed and Peter returned home from The Watering Hole. His truck sat in the driveway, the engine had died. He sat there enjoying the last of the warmth from the heater.

Peter sat behind the steering wheel of his truck, with his hands at ten and two, a moment longer. He recalled some of the conversations he had with his best friend. There was the obligatory conversation about Christmas, of course. There was also talk of a barbeque and firework display at Andrew's home to celebrate New Year's Eve in the coming days, the annual winter carnival coming to town, in mid-January, and of course, Detective Quinn. The curfew was being lifted for the arrival of the winter carnival.

The truck door opened, and Peter climbed out. He slammed the door shut and made his way along the path, to the front porch. The cold of the wooden beams bent and curved under pressure, more so than in the warmer months. Peter walked to the front door, his keys clutched tightly in his left hand, fumbling a little for the right key to unlock the front door. The key slid seamlessly into the lock of the front door. Peter put his right hand on the door handle. He turned around a little, looking over his right shoulder. There was no one there as he looked across the front porch. The afternoon brought about the winter winds. Peter shrugged it off and made his way inside the house.

The house was quiet. The lights in the foyer switched on. Peter dumped his wallet and keys in the bowl on the table and made his way further into the house, hanging his bomber jacket in the closet. The hinges on the closet door scratched a little. In the quiet of the house, it appeared more apparent. The lights in the kitchen and living room switched on. It was still quiet. The sound of the house settling in the winter weather grabbed Peter's attention. He looked up at the ceiling in the hallway, between the kitchen and living room. It was like the sound of a heavy foot walking down a hallway. Peter clutched his cell phone a little tighter in his left hand. The sound eventually disappeared. The grip on the cell phone loosened, a little. Peter let go a deep sigh of relief.

Peter turned. He left the kitchen and the living room and headed for the foyer at the front of the house. He turned again, and took to the banister of the staircase in his left hand, and commenced a slow jog up, towards the second storey of the home. The lights were switched off. The only light came from the windows. Peter reached the top of the staircase. He stood there a moment longer. He looked to the left and the right of him, down either side of the hallway. The sound of the house settling in the winter winds ran through the house, again. Peter turned right, walking down the hallway. His cell phone began to ring, breaking the silence which ran through the house. *Ring. Ring. Ring.*

"Hello?" Peter answered, almost flat.

"Hello, Peter," the dark and familiar voice answered.

"What do you want?"

"It's a little late for Christmas, so what if I said to you…?"

"Enough of this shit! You want me, come and get me!"

"My pleasure!"

Peter's eyes widened in horror, so did his mouth.

The image of the clown mask appeared from behind, out from the darkness of the hallway. The light capturing the white in the mask.

"You're here?"

"Uh-huh!" the clown mask answered, nodding a little.

"Where?" Peter asked, quickly turning around. And there, in front of him, no one. There was nothing there. The hallway was empty.

Peter stood there, between his office and his master bedroom quietly, with his cell phone to his left ear. He peered down the hallway, into the darkness. The weight of his frame leaning forward, a little, causing the wooden floorboards to crack under the pressure. His intuition kicked in.

"You can see me right now?" Peter asked with caution.

"I'm closer than you think!"

Peter was quiet a moment, before answering. He took a step further, back down the hallway, towards the staircase.

"Really? Well, I call your bluff!"

"You do?"

"Uh-huh!" Peter answered, taking another step towards the staircase, at a slow pace, as the floorboards cracked under the pressure. The tension in Peter's face tightened as he tried his best to move without sound. Peter hugged the wall, stepping closer and closer and closer towards the top of the staircase. He was just inches away, hugging the wall tightly, as his back stood against the wall. Peter could hear the sound of the clown mask breathing down the phone line.

"I call your bluff! This ends tonight. No more games. No more calls. No more cops. Just you… and me." Peter answered, just above a whisper.

He stepped out from behind the corner of the wall of the hallway, turning to face the top of the staircase.

The gleam of a blade, of a large, sharp kitchen knife, sliced through the air, stabbing several inches into Peter's left bicep. The pain consumed him immediately. Peter screamed, dropping his cell phone to the floor, falling several steps down the staircase. The blade of the kitchen knife was quick to pull out from the bloody wound. It attacked a second time, slicing at the left bicep. The blood poured heavily from the wound. The image of the clown mask raced down the staircase, past the cell phone, to the foyer, and out the front door, leaving it wide open behind them, as the winter winds blew through the front of the house. Peter collapsed to his knees, covering his bloody wound on his bicep with his right arm, as he tumbled down the staircase, to the foyer beneath. Peter was weak. He was gasping for air, inching across the floor, towards the open door. He was beaten and bloodied.

"Help me!" Peter yelled, just above a whisper.

The image of the clown mask was nowhere to be seen.

The mid-afternoon progressed into the early hours of the evening. The lights in the house were switched on. Peter was conscious. He was upstairs in his bathroom. The door pushed to a close. The light switched on. Peter was standing in front of the washbasin. The basin itself filled with warm, bloodied water. A slow drip came from the faucet. *Drip. Drip. Drip.* Peter had removed his shirt. He stood there, in front of the mirror, hunched over the basin, as best he could, sewing the torn, bloodied flesh of his left bicep together again with needle and thread. Peter used a lighter to cauterise the needle. He flinched and screamed at the pain.

"Fuck!" he yelled, over and over.

Chapter Seventeen...

It was like a scene from a movie. A horror movie. The bathroom door was left wide open and the light switched off. A quiet stillness fell upon the house, peering into the darkness of the bathroom from the empty hallway. The remains of unused thread pinched the surface of the cold, bloodied water as the needle sat at the bottom of the washbasin. The windows were closed and the alarm at the front door was set. Peter was in his bedroom, sitting on his side of the bed, facing the nightstand and the side window, peering out at the night sky. He could see the branches of the nearby trees sway from side to side from the winter winds.

A clean bandage wrapped firmly around his left bicep. A bottle of painkillers, something Peter had left over from his previous trip to the hospital, sat on the nightstand, next to a glass of water. Peter drew his eyes from the window and over to his cell phone, which sat connected to his charger. He reached for his cell phone and dialled a number. He waited patiently. The call went to voicemail.

"This is Andrew Preston. I can't come to the phone right now. You know what to do."

Beep.

"Andrew, it's me." Peter started, his voice just above a whisper and flinching with pain. "The killer dropped by my house this evening. He got me. A flesh wound to the left bicep. I'll be okay. Call me. Where are you?"

Peter disconnected the call and dropped the cell phone back on the nightstand. He turned his back on his cell phone and the nightstand, and climbed into bed, pulling the covers up high, to keep warm.

Peter awoke to the sound of a heavy knocking on his front door. He was asleep in bed, laying on his chest, spread out. The heavy knocking continued. *Knock. Knock. Knock.* Peter was slowly waking up, coming to, showing signs of life, again. His eyes opened and the pain from his bicep coursed through his body. Peter flinched with pain, curling into the foetal position, almost.

"Shit!"

The knocking at the front door continued. *Knock. Knock. Knock.* Peter looked at the time on the alarm clock. It was seven twenty-one in the morning. Peter crawled to the side of the bed and climbed to his feet. He was dressed in a simple white wife-beater and navy-blue boxer shorts. He ran out of the bedroom, down the hallway, and the staircase, towards the front door, wiping the sleep from his eyes. A tall, hulking image appeared through the frosted glass at the front door. Peter stopped in his tracks, catching his breath, a little. He stared at the front door, and the hulking image on the other side of the glass, so early in the morning.

"Who is it?" Peter called. "Who's there?"

"It's me!" a heavy voice called.

Peter's face eased some as he fumbled with the keys and unlocked the door and cancelled the alarm. The front door opened, wide, and standing there, on the front porch, in front of him, was Andrew Preston.

Andrew Preston stood at the front door of the house in his police uniform. He looked tired and worn out. His eyes were bloodshot and his hair a little on the messy side.

"Andrew, what are you doing here?" Peter asked, almost concerned.

"I worked the late shift last night. I got your message this morning as I left the station. The killer was here? What the fuck happened to you?" Andrew leaned in a little, grabbing Peter by the left forearm gently, careful not to squeeze too much. Peter flinched with pain as Andrew inspected the bandage, rotating his arm, a little.

"This scene feels very familiar. I call and you come running. Thank you."

"It's my job."

"Come on in. I'll make you a coffee."

Peter stepped to one side to allow his best friend inside his house. Andrew walked inside, into the foyer of the house. He stood there, a moment, staring up at the staircase. Peter closed the front door behind him.

"You should go to the hospital and get that checked out. You don't want to get an infection." Peter looked down at the bandage. It was still wrapped tight, from the night before, almost.

"Maybe," he shrugged. "Come on. The coffee is in the kitchen."

"You are a lifesaver, you know that? I am beat. Fucking exhausted."
Peter took the lead and Andrew followed his best friend into the kitchen.

Andrew stood by the refrigerator, leaning against it, a little, with his
arms crossed, in front of his chest, as he watched his best friend switch
on the kettle as the water was quick to boil. Peter fumbled a little,
struggling to pull two cups from the cupboard above him. Andrew
stepped forward, bouncing off the balls of his feet, ready to help his friend
before Peter made a comeback and placed the cups on the counter in front
of him. Andrew returned to the refrigerator as his eyes were drawn to the
bandage on his left bicep. His eyes darted again. This time, to his back.
He could see hints of the large scar run down the middle of his back, as it
peeked through the wife-beater which clung tightly to his muscular torso.
Andrew was fraught with concern, chewing on his lower lip a little.

"You're not safe here," Andrew announced.

Peter turned around to face his best friend, whilst in the final stages
of making coffee. A smile surfaced to his lips, before it was quick to fade.

"Excuse me?"

"Look at you," Andrew answered, shrugging his shoulders, as he
propped himself off the refrigerator. "Look at you. Whoever is doing this.
Whoever is terrorising Hillsboro, wants you dead, for whatever reason.
They. Want. You. Dead."

"You think I don't know that, Andrew? What do you want me to do?
Curl up into a ball and disappear? Leave town and disappear off the face
of the Earth?" he shrugged.

"I'm just saying. I care about you, Petey. I always have. I always
will. I am concerned about you. You live in this large house on your own.
Mike is either busy at work or not around."

"I'm not fragile. I'm not glass. I won't break." Peter, interrupted.

"I'm not saying you are. I'm simply saying come spend a couple of
nights at my place. At the very least, until your wound heals a little more.
Lay low. What do you say?"

There was a long pause between the two best friends. "Do I have a
choice?"

"No. And good. And where is my fucking coffee?" Andrew smiled,
chuckling a little.

Peter climbed the staircase and returned to the master bedroom. His right hand ran across the wall as he climbed the steps. Andrew followed. He stood in the doorway as he watched his best friend pack a bag, no larger than a gym bag, with a few clothes he grabbed from a set of drawers and the closet, some t-shirts, jeans, socks and underwear. Andrew gazed around the room some more.

The lights were switched off, but the curtains were pulled open to allow the morning light spray across the walls. The bed was made, almost immaculately.

The hours progressed as the morning turned to afternoon. Peter followed Andrew to the front door of the house, as he locked the front door, and Andrew made his way toward his truck which parked in the driveway. The lights in the house were all switched off. The bag was on the front porch, by his feet. The front door locked, and the alarm was set. Peter kept a firm grip on the door handle, giving it a shake, a little.

"Compound secure," Peter whispered to himself, under his breath.

It didn't mean much. It was a little mantra he repeated to himself, whenever he locked the front door of his house and was going somewhere.

Peter took a couple of steps backwards from the front door as if to get a better look, a bigger picture of the house, as he leaned down and grabbed his bag.

"Okay then," he whispered, again, as a smile surfaced to his lips.

Peter walked from the front porch and made a left turn towards the driveway. Andrew had unlocked his truck and was in the process of climbing inside, shifting his large, muscular, yet heavy frame, onto the seat inside the truck, in front of the steering wheel. The driver's side door was quick to slam shut. The window wound down a little.

"Come on, Hop Along," Andrew said, watching his friend make his way towards his truck, balancing his bag on his right shoulder.

Peter smiled.

The drive to Andrew's home didn't take long, less than ten minutes with traffic. The music from the radio blared. Andrew nodded his head a little to the tunes playing, although he didn't know who it was. Peter entertained himself with his cell phone, texting Mike and telling him where he would be the next couple of nights. There was no answer. Not yet, anyway. The two best friends made it home.

It was Peter's turn to follow. He stood on the front porch as Andrew fumbled with his keys a little, looking for the right key. The bag hung from his right shoulder, again. Peter turned and looked around the porch. There were small signs of neglect. There were spider webs on the outdoor furniture. Nothing major.

"Welcome home," Andrew announced. "Come on in and I will give you the whole twenty-five-cent tour." he chuckled.

Andrew and Peter made their way inside the house. Peter stood there, in front of the door, as Andrew closed it behind him. The lights in the front of the house, the living room, included, switched on. A hallway stretched into darkness, and toward the back of the house.

Here we have the shower." Andrew started, as he made his way down the hallway of the house, and the lights switched on.

"Very picturesque." Andrew laughed. "The bathroom. If nature calls in the night. My office. And of course, a spare room, for guests, from time to time. This is where you'll sleep."

The door to the spare bedroom was open. The room was very basic with minimal design. A double- size bed sat in the middle of the room. The curtains were pulled open to allow for light and there were framed paintings hanging around the room for decoration.

"Thank you," Peter replied, smiling, a little. He made his way inside the bedroom and dumped his bag at the end of the bed.

"Make yourself at home," Andrew said, watching his friend explore the spare bedroom. "And I'm located at the end of the hallway if you need me, or anything for that matter."

"Thank you."

"I am going to go and grab a shower, because," Andrew started as he lifted his left arm and smelt his armpit, "'it's been a ten-hour workday. I stink." Another chuckle.

The police uniform had been taken off and thrown casually on top of the bed in the master bedroom. The underwear, socks and boots were on the floor. The door to the master bedroom was left wide open and the lights switched on. The door to the bathroom was closed. The sound of water pouring from the shower was loud.

The air conditioning system was running at speed. The steam from the hot water rose from the shower and filled the bathroom if it weren't being sucked into the air conditioning system.

Andrew stood under the faucet. The hot water poured quickly, splashing all over him, as he stood with his back to the water, then turning around to face it. Andrew used a bar of soap to lather his chest and body. There was music playing on his cell phone which sat on the side of the washbasin. Andrew closed his eyes, nodded his head, a little, and whistled to the tune some.

Peter made his way out of his one-bedroom accommodation, for the next couple of nights, anyway, and explored the rest of the house. He walked from the bedroom, taking a left to head down the hallway, past Andrew in the shower, and the living room. The room itself was quiet. The television set was switched off. The curtains were pulled open to allow the sunlight from outside. And the walls were decorated in framed photographs, similar to his living room at home. He walked across the room for a closer look. Peter was attracted to one photograph immediately. He raised his left hand, his index finger, reaching out to a black-and-white photograph of the four friends, Andrew, Emily, Jayne, and himself, sitting around a table at The Watering Hole. The photograph wasn't staged. No one was looking at the camera. The photograph, itself, was taken mid- conversation, during happier times, when they were all laughing.

Andrew appeared from the end of the hallway, standing in the entrance of the living room.

He stood there silent, and unnoticed as if spying on his best friend, having just got out of the shower. He stood there standing, his chest and hair still wet from the shower, wearing nothing more than a pair of denim jeans. He was barefoot, with a simple plain, red cotton t-shirt clutched in his hands. He pulled it on, tugging at it, somewhat, at the front of his chest, as it was clinging to his bulging, muscular frame. Andrew took a step inside the living room, leading with his left foot. The weight of his frame caused the hardwood floors of the hallway to bend under the pressure. Peter was unfazed by it all.

"Hey, you," Andrew said, as a smile surfaced to his lips.

Peter turned around, surprised a little by his best friend, to see him standing there behind him.

"Hey," Peter answered, a little sheepishly as if caught with his hand in a cookie jar. His left hand retracted from the photograph very quickly. "I was just checking out the pictures on the wall. So many memories."

"Yeah," Andrew answered, looking down at the floor, as if somewhat embarrassed, and then raising his head to look at Peter and the photographs hanging on the wall. "Some good and some, you know, not so good. It's important to remind ourselves of the bad times, too, I think. It reminds us we're human, that we aren't invisible, even though, I think sometimes, we think we are. Another coffee?"

Peter looked at his best friend a moment. "Sure," He nodded, smiling a little.

The morning progressed a little. The two coffee cups sat empty on the side of the sink, washed out and drying. The living room was empty, so too, was the house. Andrew was asleep in bed. The door to the master bedroom at the end of the hallway was pulled too, not closed completely, but just enough to shield most of the sound from the rest of the house. He had worked the night shift and was exhausted. The pair of denim jeans and a red t-shirt he wore earlier were hanging from a chair in the corner of the room. Andrew was in bed. The cover pulled back some, exposing the definition in his muscular back, exposing his waist, revealing that he slept naked, as he hugged his pillow tightly in his arms, squeezing it a little, as he slept, snoring away.

Peter found himself sitting in the emergency room of the hospital, once more. He had been admitted into one of the rooms, as he sat on the side of the bed, his feet dangling gently, a little, back and forth, back and forth, again. He sat there watching a nurse prepare his workstation to inspect the stitches in his left bicep. A large lamp was moved into position and switched on, shining down on the wound, itself. Peter turned from the glare of the light. In front of the lamp was another metal tray which sat on top of a small, portable table, with medical instruments out on display; including scissors, needles, bandages and gauze. Peter looked away from that, too. He looked at the nurse. The nurse, himself, was somewhere in his early to mid-forties, with dirty blonde hair, a muscular frame, and he was clean-shaven.

"Let's take a look, shall we?" the nurse asked, with a smile, as he dragged his seat closer towards Peter, and adjusting the light, a little.

"Of course," Peter answered, politely.

The nurse started in on the bandage. He snapped at the elastic hooks and gently unwound the bandage from the left bicep. The bandage unravelled quickly, exposing the wound beneath.

He looked at the wound a moment, as a concerned expression fell upon his face. Peter looked down at the wound, himself, then at the nurse. His expression on his face was one of surprise, almost. The wound looked red and sore. There were no signs of infection. Not yet, anyway.

"You did this yourself?" the nurse asked, a little concerned. "The stitches, I mean?"

"Yes, sir," Peter answered, confidently. "I didn't want to waste your time with a minor flesh wound."

"And how did you cause the *minor* flesh wound, if you don't mind my asking?"

"I *do* mind your asking." Peter thought to himself, briefly, but smiled. "This? I was working around the house, installing some lights. I fell from a small ladder."

"Uh-huh," the nurse answered, not believing his story. "You're one lucky man. You didn't cut the veins beneath. But, your stitches, they're gonna have to come out and replace them with all-new, fresh stitches. This might hurt."

"Thank you."

The wound was replaced with fresh stitches, some gauze was used to cover, and a bandage wrapped firmly around the left bicep. There were nine stitches in total. The process took a good part of an hour to finish. Peter emerged from the emergency room, made a right, and walked down the hallway a little, to Emily, who was waiting for him, with her head buried in a celebrity magazine.

Emily looked up from the magazine. Her eyes were drawn to the bandage. Her face was numb, consumed with concern for her high school friend, and a little guilt. This was a reality. It wasn't a movie. This was nothing more than life, itself.

The day progressed further, and it was now into the early evening. The sun was setting over Hillsboro for another day. A blanket of snow covered the front yard of the house, including the steps leading up to the front porch. The truck was parked inside the garage, as the door was pulled down and locked for the evening. The house came to life, again. The lights in the house were all switched on. The gas heater burning. The television set in the living room was on. It was the end of the evening news, but coming up, the premiere of a new sitcom, starring some up and coming comedian. Andrew and Peter didn't pay too much attention to it all. The television was just noise in the background. There were two bottles of beer sitting on the coffee table. Andrew had already drunk one and was onto his second for the evening. Peter was nursing his as he paced the living room, back and forth, on the phone to Mike. Andrew watched him when he wasn't looking at the television set, or consumed with his beer. The front doorbell chimed.

"I'll get it," Andrew said, raising his left hand, a little, as if to ask or answer a question in class, before climbing off the couch and to his feet.

Andrew grabbed the spare cash on the coffee table, by his empty beer bottle, and walked towards the front door, to answer it. Peter continued to pace the living room, watching his best friend answer the front door.

The front door opened. And there, standing under the lights of the front porch, was a local pizza delivery guy. A senior in high school. He couldn't have been more than eighteen years old. A young man with an athletic build, neatly trimmed, mousey brown hair and a serious case of acne.

Andrew exchanged his fist full of cash for one extra-large pizza with sausage, pepperoni, capsicum and onion. There was enough money to cover for the cost of the pizza, plus tip. Andrew retreated from the front door, closing it, and made his way back into the living room, placing the pizza box on the coffee table, then headed for the refrigerator in the kitchen. The door swung open and the light switched on, with an almighty pull. The bottles of beer inside rattled some, as he leaned in and grabbed another two, one for him, and the other for his best friend. Andrew turned and reached for the paper towels on the counter.

"Here you go." Andrew said, leaning down, passing one bottle to his best friend, as he sat on one side of the coffee table. "You look like you could use another."

"Thanks," Peter smiled, nodding a little, reaching for the beer.

"How are you boys doing, by the way?" Andrew asked as he took to the couch, opening the pizza box.

The bottle cap twisted off, as the bubbles rose up the neck of the glass bottle. "We're good," Peter answered, shrugging his shoulders, a little. "I guess."

"Really? Because I didn't buy that for a second. What's going on? Andrew took a deep sip.

"It's hard, I guess, you know, my life, and all. He says he understands, but I don't know. Plus, Mike works all hours in the hardware store." Peter paused a moment, thinking of what he just said. "As the days go on, I feel like I am seeing him less and less. Maybe I should just cut all ties now. For his safety, and mine."

"Mike and I have our differences. We don't always see eye to eye, but that's something only you can decide."

"I guess. I like him. I do. I'm just trying to protect him. What can I say?" Peter asked, just above a whisper, as he leaned in and grabbed his first slice of pizza. "How are you and Emily doing?" Peter asked, changing the subject.

"Good, I guess." Andrew nodded, also grabbing his slice of pizza. "As well as can be expected, I think. We have our days."

The evening progressed on further. The lights in the living room were switched off. The television set was still on, however, the volume was down low. It was the *Shopping Network*. The glow of the television screen highlighted the room, a little, as it sprayed across the walls. The coffee table was a mess with discarded beer bottles and a mostly eaten pizza. There were a couple of movie rentals sitting on the coffee table, too. Andrew was stretched out on the couch, dressed in nothing more than a wife-beater, which clung to his muscular, bulging frame, and grey sweatpants, with the drawstring tied around his waist, loosely. He was slowly drifting in and out of consciousness, as he turned on the couch. He opened his eyes wide and saw Peter asleep, face down on the carpet, on the other side of the coffee table. Andrew wiped the sleep from his eyes, a moment.

"Hey, you awake?" Andrew called out.

Peter slowly came to. He turned on his back, looking back at his best friend on the couch. Andrew pulled himself up from the couch, sitting up. He leaned forward, into the coffee table, helping himself to a cold slice of pizza. He took one bite before dropping the rest of the slice back in the box. "Do you remember when we used to have sleep overs as kids, and we would scare each other silly with ghost stories? Good times." Andrew chuckled, a little.

"Yeah," Peter answered, just above a whisper, and more than a little tired. "I have a scary story for you. It's about a serial killer who stalks their victims in a small country town who wears some creepy-ass clown mask, something my grandfather and mother created years earlier. The question I have for you is, who is doing this? Look around." Peter shrugged his shoulders, a little. "We are dropping like flies around here. Your standard horror movie rules might suggest a horror movie fanatic, or a someone close to the victim's family."

"It could be anyone." Andrew answered, just above a whisper. "Someone out for attention. Someone out to make a name for themselves." Andrew shook his head a moment, as if piecing a puzzle together. "But there is a major plot hole in your theory."

"Yeah? What's that?"

"This isn't a horror movie. This is real life. Period. Killers get caught. Or killers get caught in the line of fire. Either way, we will find whoever is doing this, you have my word. There is always the big reveal or the slip up. They always do."

"Yeah? And when will that be?"

"End credits, I guess."

Peter looked at his best friend, his eyes widened a little.

Peter awoke from his deep sleep somewhere in the early hours of the morning. The bed cover was pulled high, over his shoulders, to keep himself warm. Peter tossed and moved in the bed, raising his arms out from under the cover to wipe the sleep from his eyes. He turned to the right, spread across the bed, a little, and over to the nightstand. The time on the alarm clock was three fifty-seven. Peter rolled back onto the bed, again, facing the ceiling of the spare bedroom. He looked out of the window, and there, in front of him, was nothing more than darkness, itself, as a gentle breeze and sheet of snow blew across the window frame. Peter turned again. He looked across the bedroom. The bedroom door was wide open, leading out to further darkness of the hallway.

The gentle sound of a low humming snore was coming from the master bedroom. It was Andrew. Peter rubbed his eyes again, before kicking the bed cover back, some, and climbing to his feet. He sat there on the edge of the bed a moment in nothing more than a pair of boxer shorts and an old college t-shirt. Peter stood and made his way to the door way entrance, careful not to make too much noise and wake Andrew. He stood there, and leaned forward, a little, peering left then right in the darkness of the hallway.

Still, the darkness consumed the house. Peter turned right, making his way deeper down the hallway, towards the master bedroom. The bedroom door to the master bedroom was wide open, and Peter stood there, in the entrance, unnoticed a moment. He leaned in a little, peering inside the bedroom. And there, in front of him, was Andrew, deep asleep. He was laying on his back, his bulging, muscular frame, naked and entwined in the bed sheets. The snoring grew louder and louder now. Peter turned his back and tiptoed, making his way down the hallway, again.

Peter found himself back in the living room. He stood nearer the far wall, looking at the framed photographs that were taken at different stages of Andrew's life; his childhood, his teen years, as a young adult. There were photographs of Andrew standing next to Emily, smiling and laughing, on camping and fishing trips, and there was a photograph of Andrew, Emily, Jayne, and Peter taken on the outside grounds, at the front of Hillsboro High School. Peter was drawn to the framed photograph. He walked towards it, raising his left hand and touching the glass with his index finger. He couldn't recall the photograph. Peter stared at it concerned, trying desperately to remember it. Nothing.

Peter blinked his eyes a few more times, before turning his back on the photograph hanging on the wall in front of him, and walked back across the living room floor, taking a right turn and walking down the hallway, again, toward his bedroom. He crept down the still darkness of the hallway, stopping again outside the bathroom. The door was wide open. He didn't remember it when he woke up. He peered inside as he did with the master bedroom. The light was switched off. The white tiled floor was dark, and there, in front of him, himself. He caught his reflection in the bathroom mirror. It looked more like a large, shapeless, dark mass, more than anything else. Peter stepped inside the bathroom, turning on his left foot first, as the rest of his body followed. The tiled floor was cool to the touch. Peter stepped inside the bathroom, searching for the light switch, and stepping closer and closer toward the bathroom mirror until he reached the washbasin. The shapeless, dark mass had a figure now. The neon lights flickered on. It was Peter. He caught himself smiling, a moment, feeling more curious than anything, as to what Andrew kept inside his bathroom cabinet. He pulled on the mirror a little until it popped open. His eyes perused the cabinets. There was nothing major to report, except for one blue and one pink toothbrush. Peter assumed it was for Emily when she slept over.

Peter noticed the water dripping from the faucet in the washbasin. He lowered his head and looked down and ran his fingers over the faucet, catching the water some. It beaded through his fingers. It was cold to the touch. Peter turned the faucet right, tighter and tighter until the water stopped dripping. He lifted his head and looked up at the mirror, again. And, with a gentle push, the cabinet closed, as the magnets connected, the image of the hooded clown mask appeared from behind, staring back, silently. The white of the mask almost glowed under the neon lights.

Peter covered his mouth tightly with this left-hand, catching his breath in his throat. Panic consumed him. The clown mask stood there silently, soon to raise its right hand, bound in a black leather glove, reaching for the mask, itself. The mask lifted slowly, as if to give a big reveal. It was his mother, standing there, staring at her son. It was Sidney.

"Welcome home, Peter," Sidney said, just above a whisper.

She stared at her son in the mirror a moment, before releasing a loud, blood-curdling scream. The air escaped her lungs and passed her lips.

Peter screamed. Loud. As he stared in the mirror, staring back at his mother. Andrew appeared at the entrance of the bathroom, seconds later, his reflection caught in the mirror, naked.

"What is it? What happened?" Andrew asked, tired and wired, all in one.

Peter was now alone in the bathroom, screaming. The image of the clown mask, of his mother, gone.

"What do you see?" Andrew asked, as he stepped inside the bathroom, racing toward his best friend and wrapping his arms around him, pulling him close to his chest, as if consoling him. "It's okay to let go. It's okay."

"It was a mistake that I moved back here," Peter answered, out of breath, as the screaming stopped.

"No. No. No. No. No." Andrew answered, just above a whisper.

"I saw my mother and I heard her… voice."

"She is not here. It was just your imagination working overtime, with the murders and all. You're safe. There is no one here but you and me. You're safe, do you hear me? We will get through this together, I promise."

Peter closed his eyes tightly.

Fade to black. Fade from black.

It was morning. A little after nine. The kitchen table, just off the living room, was set. It was a small, round wooden table, something Andrew picked up at a furniture store, on the outskirts of town when he moved into his home. The table was set. There were cotton place mats with a flannel design, one red and white, the other, blue and white. Breakfast was served. On the menu today, it was eggs, sunny side up, toast, hash browns, sautéed mushrooms, and coffee. The television set in the living room was switched on. The volume was down low. It was just noise in the background.

"Last night." Andrew started, just above a whisper, as he took a sip from his coffee mug, "we will keep that between us, okay? I won't say a word. You have *my* word. I promise."

"Thank you," Peter answered. "I'm not crazy, by the way."

"I know you're not. But you did say some out-there stuff… about your mother. She has been dead now for over four years."

"You don't think I don't know that?" Peter answered, his hands wrapped around his coffee mug, keeping them warm. "It was a nightmare. Nothing more. I was tired, not sleeping. End of story. Period."

"Of course." Andrew slowly nodded.

"Don't look at me like I'm stupid or crazy." Peter snapped. "This is what happens. *That* killer, that *mask*, it gets under your skin. This is how I live with my childhood memories. I have nightmares… now and then. Everyone does."

Fade to black. Fade from black.

In the days that followed, Peter found himself back at home. It was now somewhere in the late afternoon, early evening. Peter was dressed very casually. He wore a plain navy-blue t-shirt and grey sweat pants. The bandage on his bicep could be seen under the sleeve of his t-shirt as his arms moved as he walked. The bandage was wrapped firmly around the bicep after another visit to the emergency room for a check-up. Peter was barefoot as he made his way down the staircase, his cell phone in his left hand, as he passed the foyer, and walked into the living room.

The television set in the living room was switched off. Peter leaned in and dropped his cell phone on the coffee table. There were no missed phone calls or text messages from anyone, including Andrew. Peter picked up the TV remote and switched on the television. The evening news was playing. There was a story on the news. That same news reporter who visited the house earlier, was now standing outside the front of what was once Grandfather's house. The reporter was interviewing the same teenage girl who answered the door when Peter visited.

"…he came to our house once, knocking on the door. He looked scared." Peter heard the girl say.

Peter looked at the television screen intently, with anger in his eyes. He was chewing on his lower lip, pointed the remote at the television set, and switched the channel over a few times, looking for anything, something other than *that*.

"Shit!" Peter whispered under his breath. "Shit! Shit! Shit! Shit!" he repeated.

The cell phone on the coffee table began to ring. *Ring. Ring. Ring.* He turned and lowered his eyes and looked down at his cell phone come to life as it sat on the coffee table. He dropped the television remote.

"Hello?" Peter answered, stern and clearing his throat, a little.

"This is your old friend." the dark and familiar voice answered. "You sound almost happy to hear from me. What do you want?"

"You know what I want. What I've always wanted. But not today. What I want to know is, who is Mike Walters? How much do you really know him, huh? I bet you have asked this question, over and over and over again, somewhere in your mind, you know, don't you? I'm sure you have." There was that same laugh.

"Fuck you!"

"Mike says he cares about you. But where is he? The two of you met just days after arriving in Hillsboro. I bet he fed you some line about being an old family friend, am I right?"

Peter listened to the voice, concerned. His eyes almost closed, taking in everything that was said, piecing the conversation together like the pieces of a puzzle.

"Mike…" Peter answered, sheepish almost scared, and just above a whisper. "Is this you?" The voice laughed, loudly, as if winning the fight.

Peter felt angry and embarrassed.

"So, if this isn't you. Then, who are you? Really? What do you want with Mike?"

"I don't want Mike. He is nothing more than a one-dimensional character in a paperback novel. No one turns hundreds of pages or sits through a movie to see if a character like Mike survives. They do it for you. Peter Harmon. A local survivor. A national celebrity. You're the real star, aren't you? You love this notoriety. I *know* you do. I am *sure* you do. You are such an easy target."

"Let's redirect for a moment, shall we? You think you're so original, huh? I've heard this *bullshit* before! If you want me so much, how about you grow some *fucking* balls and come get me!" "Of course I want you. And I will get you. All in good time. But grab a clue! Think about it. All I need to do is pull at your heartstrings and I have you in the palm of my hands."

"What do you mean?"

"Sit back and watch!" the voice laughed, again.

"What?" Peter asked, just above a whisper. "Wait! What?" The phone line disconnected.

Peter pulled the cell phone from his right ear. He looked at the screen. The phone call was dead. He could feel his heartbeat pounding, his hands grow sweaty. He was on the verge of panic. Peter ran from the living room and to the front door of the house, grabbing his wallet and keys on the table on the way. He ran out of the house, slamming the door behind, racing across the front porch, along the walkway, and to his sports utility vehicle parked in the driveway. The alarm unlocked, making that chirping, beeping sound. *Beep.* The door pulled open and Peter climbed inside, slamming the door shut. The engine roared to life, reversing out of the driveway and pulling out onto the traffic. Peter sped to the end of the street, making his way into town. There were children and other neighbours in the street watching the truck race to the end of the street.

The black sports utility vehicle made its way into town. It parked closest to the hardware store. Peter climbed out from behind the steering wheel and raced into the hardware store. The glass door pulled open and the bell above the door began to chime. His feet were cold and dirty from the snow and mud. Peter raced down the closest aisle in front of him, past the hammers and nails, toward the front of the store. And there, in front of him, behind the counter, near the cash register, was Mike and his young assistant. They stood there, talking amongst themselves quietly with a paying customer, an elderly gentleman, who was tall with a thin build, wearing a black flannel shirt and faded denim jeans, tucked at the waist. Mike was the first to pull his eyes away from the customer. He looked over the customer's shoulder at Peter. His eyes opened a little more, almost in horror.

"Hey, you!" Mike said, calling out, with a smile on his face.

Peter stood there in front of him, at the end of the aisle, regaining his composure, his bare feet dirty. "Are you okay?" Mike continued.

"Of course." he nodded, clearing his throat, some. It was a lie.

"Are you sure? You look like you've seen a ghost."

Peter stood there, staring at Mike, their eyes on each other.

The elderly gentleman collected his can of eggshell-white paint and new brushes and made his way out of the store. He made eye contact with Peter as he passed by, nodding a little, to be polite. "Goodbye, Mr Craven," the young assistant called out.

The young assistant busied herself with the pricing gun and stocking packets of nails on the shelf. She looked at her boss, giving him a few minutes to himself. The girl kept herself busy, whilst Peter walked towards the counter, standing in front of Mike. Mike lifted his eyes, a moment, keeping them on his assistant, making sure she was out of earshot. They diverted back to Peter.

"Have you got a minute?" Peter asked, just above a whisper. "Come with me," he answered, a little concerned.

Mike turned his back and walked towards the back of the store, into his office. Peter followed. It was Peter who closed the door behind him, as Mike sat at his desk. The adjustable chair made noise as Mike made himself comfortable. His denim jeans hugged his thick legs. His white cotton t-shirt fit snug to his torso under his sleeveless jacket, to keep his torso warm.

"What's going on?" Mike asked, concerned.

"I got another phone call," Peter answered, as he paced in front of the desk.

"Shit!" Mike answered, just above a whisper, as he buried his head in chest. "What? What did they say?"

"They had a lot to say about *you*."

"Me? What did I do?" Mike answered, resting his right hand on his chest, feeling his heartbeat race. "Maybe we should cool things down, a little. I don't want you getting hurt. This is *my* life. This is serious."

"No," Mike answered flatly.

He pulled himself up from his chair and walked around to the front of his desk, towards Peter. "I'm not going anywhere. Period. Whoever is doing this. They are going to have to get through me to get to you."

"That's what I am worried about," Peter answered, looking at Mike sombre.

Mike simply smiled. He placed his hands, on top of Peter's shoulders and leaned in and gave him a kiss on the lips.

The days continued on. There had been no further phone calls from the killer. No teasing, no taunting. Nothing. Quiet. Peter was sitting in his office, in front of his laptop computer, with a cup of coffee and his cell phone. The cell phone began to chirp. Peter pulled his eyes off the screen and lowered them down onto his cell phone. A text message. Peter was quick to open.

I'm sorry about before. I acted like a dick. I should have known better. I know what you lived through. No one could have lived through what you did and not carry a few scars. Do you forgive me?

The text message from Andrew read. The message brought a smile to Peter's lips. He was quick to reply.

Mike was sitting at the end of the bed in Peter's master bedroom. He sat there, with this legs and torso looming forward. He was watching Peter walk from the hallway, into the master bedroom, having taken a shower, as he wore a damp towel, which hung loosely around his waist, on a slight angle, hanging slightly lower on the left-hand side. Peter entered the bedroom and walked to the set of drawers to retrieve a pair of boxer shorts and socks. He tugged at the damp towel, a little, dropping it to the bedroom floor as he sat next to Mike, naked, a moment, before pulling on his underwear.

"I'm looking forward to tonight," Mike said, politely. "I like Emily. She is a good girl. She complements Andrew, I think. Yeah."

"Don't let Andrew hear you say that; he'll have a fucking heart attack."

"Andrew on the other hand," Mike continued, leaning back on the end of the bed a little, resting his hands on the bed behind him, as Peter leaned forward putting on the last of his socks. "You know when you meet someone new, and no matter what do you, you just can't get along? Have you ever felt like that before?"

"It's because it's the two of you are so practically alike, it's scary." Peter laughed, a little, as he got off the bed and walked over to the wardrobe to pull himself out a pair of denim jeans.

"You think?"

"Why don't you two just end all this hostility towards each other, drop your pants, and see who has the bigger dick? We can then move on." Peter laughed. "You two always like playing the role of the over-protective, bigger brother."

"Shit!" Mike answered, just above a whisper.

Peter was in the final stages of getting dressed for the evening. He wore a blood-red polo shirt with a dark grey hoodie, denim jeans and black leather boots.

Mike continued the role of playing the over-protective, bigger brother, or maybe it was the role of kind sir and a good date and offered to drive Peter to Andrew's home for the evening so they could attend the new year barbeque party, featuring fireworks. The drive didn't take too long. Mike kept his eye on the road, as music played from the radio in his truck. Peter left his hand on Mike's knee as he drove. It felt warm to the touch. Mike liked that. He felt most comfortable when he was in the truck with him, driving somewhere. It was their bond. Peter nodded his head slowly back and forth to the music, as he looked out the window, watching the world pass by. It was a blur of other houses, people in the streets, having parties of their own, and the sounds of fireworks going off in the distance.

Mike had pulled his truck into Andrew's street. The speed was dying now. Peter kept his eye out for Andrew's home. And there it was. The lights in the house were all switched on. And the decorations appeared on the porch from Christmas. The house was almost aglow in the evening, with a clean sheet of snow which covered the front yard.

"Looks busy tonight," Mike said, just above a whisper, parking his truck, finding a place on the curb.

"Yeah," Peter answered.

There were other cars and trucks parked in the driveway, out on the curb, and across the road, in a vacant lot.

The engine to the truck switched off. Peter sat next to Mike a moment longer, in the dark of the truck. He looked out at the other vehicles. He didn't know any of them.

"You ready?" Mike asked, placing his hand on Peter's left knee, and giving it a slight squeeze.

"Let's do this," Peter answered, turning to face him, smiling.

Peter and Mike climbed out of the truck and made their way to the front of the house, following the salted pathway that headed to the front porch. The alarm on the truck was set. Peter was the first to reach the front porch, followed by Mike. The weight of their frames caused the wood panels to bend under pressure. Peter pressed the front doorbell. There was the sound of music, a pop song, playing from the stereo, in the living room. The front door opened. It was Emily. She stood there in tight denim jeans which hugged her petite frame, a simple white blouse and a thick, woollen black scarf, which hung around her neck like a piece of fine jewellery, and boots.

"You guys made it!" Emily announced, smiling, almost from ear to ear. "It is so great to see you, boys. Come in. Come in."

Emily stepped to one side to allow Peter and Mike inside the house.

"Where's Andrew?" Peter asked, leaning in and giving his high school friend a peck on the cheek. "He's out back, somewhere. I'm sure he is hovering over the barbeque, with the burgers and hot dogs."

Peter walked into the house, a little further. He stood in the foyer, turning to watch Mike enter the house, and Emily closes the front door behind them. Mike also greeted Emily with a kiss on the cheek.

Peter stood there, a moment, taking it all in. The living room was alive. A lot more than it was, just days ago, when he spent the night. The television set was switched off. There was music playing from the stereo, there was a handful of people, most, if not all, he did not know, sitting on the couch, quietly talking amongst themselves, as they drank their beer and wine and picked at the selection of nibbles on the coffee table. The three made their way through the house, past the living room, down the hallway, past the kitchen, which looked more like the back end of a liquor store, with a selection of open bottles of liquor, spirits, wine and beers. They made their way out to the back yard.

The back yard was neatly decorated. It took Emily days to put it all together. There were twinkle lights which framed the pergola, with tables and chairs, which spread out across the bricked area. The tables were adorned with bite-sized party foods to nosh on and discarded beer bottles.

Andrew stood over the barbeque, doing his best to keep warm and tending to the burgers and hot dogs, some with cheese.

The other guests in attendance were colleagues from the police station and their respective partners. Detective Quinn was not in sight. Peter got a few more of those *that's him* stares. He shrugged them off, and walked over towards an open esky, and grabbed himself a bottle of beer, as Mike and Emily entertained themselves with mild chatter amongst themselves. Peter leaned down, his right hand working its way through the cold ice and grabbed himself a beer.

"Need a hand?" a voice asked.

Peter looked up. It was Andrew. He was standing in front of the barbeque. Peter could feel the heat from the fire.

"Thanks." Peter smiled.

Andrew took the beer bottle from Peter's hand and used the side of a brick wall to pop the lid off the top of the bottle.

"This looks like a great party." Peter continued, looking around the back yard, and out at the fire pit nearby, as the other guests quietly talked amongst themselves, keeping warm.

"Thanks. It's great to see you made it."

"Of course. I wouldn't miss this for the world." Andrew smiled, happy to see his best friend. "Happy New Year, Petey."

"Happy New Year, good buddy."

The best friends raised a toast with their bottles of beer, and cheered, as the glass bottles scratched against each other. *Clink*. Andrew took a deep sip from his bottle beer, then turned round to tend to the food on the barbeque. Peter watched.

The party continued. Emily played the role of the gracious host to a T. Andrew entertained his guests with jokes he heard around the station, and the most embarrassing stories he had heard people call for an emergency. The audience laughed from time to time. Mike felt at home. He sat around the other guests, talking and laughing. Peter sat around the fire pit, keeping himself warm, as he finished off his second beer for the evening and made his way through a cheeseburger. His cell phone began to ring. *Ring. Ring. Ring*. Peter put his cheeseburger down, next to his beer, and retrieved his cell phone from the left pocket of his hoodie. The front screen of the cell phone came to life. *Unknown Caller*. His face filled with dread.

"Hello?" Peter answered, quite flatly, as he watched his friends enjoy the party.

"Happy New Year, Peter," the dark and familiar voice answered. "It's your best friend, again."

"What do you want now?"

Peter was cautious, as to not draw attention to himself, and made his way inside the house. "You're lucky I have let you live this long. You're mine. But your friends? Will they make it? Tick tock, Peter. Time is running out… for all of you. But who will be next? You can't save them. Sit back and watch the show. It's gonna be a real horror movie for one of them over the coming days. See you soon."

The phone line disconnected. Peter looked concerned. His eyes were filled with rage, fighting the urge to cry. He stood there, in the kitchen, towards the back door of the house, which overlooked the back yard, looking at Mike, Emily and Andrew.

"Shit!" he whispered to himself, under his breath.

"Ten!" Andrew shouted.

"Nine!" the rest of the crowd, continued.

The countdown to the end of the year began. And the fireworks started as the countdown reached zero. Happy New Year.

New Year's Day. The day started just like any other. It was nothing special. But it was special to Peter. The curtains in the master bedroom were pulled open to allow the light from the winter morning to creep inside. The sun sprayed across the walls, creeping higher and higher until it reached the ceiling. The clothes from the party the night before, which lead into the early hours of this morning, lay on the hardwood floor, a mess. Mike and Peter were asleep.

Peter was the first to wake from his deep sleep. His body slowly moved from his stomach, and over onto his back. He wiped the sleep from his eyes and looked at the time on the nightstand. The time was eight twenty. He sat up in bed, a little, looking around the room. The clothes on the floor were still a mess and looked over at Mike. He was slowly coming to.

"Good morning," Mike said, just above a whisper, as he, too, wiped the sleep from his eyes. "What time is it?"

"Almost eight-thirty."

"Jesus! It's late."

Mike opened his eyes, blinking them a little. His vision was still a little blurry. He climbed up in the bed, using the pillows to prop himself up, and leaned across and kissed Peter on the lips.

"Good morning," he repeated.

"Good morning." Peter smiled.

The bed cover pushed back. Peter was the first to climb out of bed. He walked across the hardwood floor of the master bedroom in his boxer shorts, before disappearing down the hallway. The sound of the bathroom door closing soon followed, as did the sound of the light switch flicking on. Mike remained in bed. He leaned over to his side of the nightstand, grabbing his cell phone off the charger. There were no missed calls or messages. The sound of water running from the shower followed next. Mike put his cell phone back down on the nightstand, kicked the bed cover back, and climbed out of bed and stood on his feet, naked. He lifted his arms, stretching his body, before adjusting himself, a little.

The kitchen was alive for the morning. Mike was dressed in the clothes he wore to the barbeque party the night before. He wore a long-sleeve black and white flannel shirt with denim jeans and black leather boots. The flannel shirt was part-way buttoned, exposing his hairy chest, a little, as he worked on preparing breakfast. It was a smaller breakfast than what he had been used to over the years; coffee, scrambled eggs, toast, and bacon. The radio was playing in the background.

Peter arrived downstairs and made his way from the front foyer of the house and into the dining room for breakfast. He has dressed casually in navy blue shorts, a simple white t-shirt and a grey hoodie, open at the chest. The dining table was set for breakfast, with an added glass of orange juice.

"This looks and smells amazing. Thank you." Peter said with a smile, just above a whisper, as he took to his chair at the dining table.

"This?" Mike responded. "It's nothing. A little something, I whipped up whilst you took a shower."

"Well, it looks delicious."

"Eat up!"

Breakfast continued. Both Peter and Mike picked at their food and chatted. Mike told Peter what he thought of the barbeque party to ring in the new year. They traded in a few laughs. And Peter made a point not to mention he received another call from the killer. He did it to protect Mike. Instead, he told him that he would go for another morning run and would make his way into town and assist with another stock take of the store whilst it was a public holiday. Work never stopped for the wicked.

The day progressed. Mike found himself alone in his store. It was the first time in a long time, that it sounded so quiet. He was sitting at his desk in his office. The door was open and the light was switched on. Mike dropped a pen onto the surface of the desk, on top of an open file some paperwork and lifted his head, peering out the open door and into the store. His head tilted a little. It was quiet. He could hear himself breathing. Mike stood up from behind his desk, calling it quits for the day, and made his way to the open door, leaving the pen on top of the open file. He switched off the lights, closing, locking the door to his office behind him, before making his way out of the hardware store for another day. He reached the front door. The bell above him chimed, one final time for the day, as he fumbled through his large collection of keys, which hung from a key ring. A couple of kids, no older than fifteen or sixteen, shot by on bicycles. It made Mike jump, almost out of his skin. The kids laughed and never looked back.

Mike turned and walked down the street a little, heading toward his truck. He pointed the clicker and pressed the button. The alarm disarmed.

Mike saw the lights on the front of his truck flicker. He reached the truck and climbed inside, slamming the door to a close behind him. He sat there a moment, adjusting the rear-view mirror, a little. He leaned across the to the passenger seat of the truck, looking for his cell phone. He found it, amongst his other personal belongings. There were no missed calls or text messages. Mike navigated to his text history.

I hope you are enjoying your day. Thanks again for all your help. Just finished work here and heading home. I'll call you later tonight.

Mike typed and hit the send button. He put the cell phone down on the passenger seat, again, turned, ever so slightly, in his seat, and switched on the ignition. The engine of the truck roared to life. The truck indicated and Mike was cautious on making his way out into the traffic. The truck was quick to pick up speed and raced to the end of the street, stopping at the set of red lights.

It didn't take Mike long to drive home. No more than twenty minutes. The truck pulled into the driveway, parking outside the front of the closed garage doors. The engine died. Mike turned, again, and collected his personal belongings, before climbing out of the truck and walking the pathway to his front porch. The weather appeared eerily quiet. He stopped at the bottom of the front porch and looked over his left shoulder, out at the front yard, a moment. There were kids riding their bikes in the street. Nothing more. He made his way onto the front porch, his cell phone, his wallet, and files from work, bundled in his hands. Mike fumbled for the right key, again, and made his way inside his home, closing the door behind him.

The lights inside the house flickered on and Mike made his way inside the house. He walked the hallway and made his way into his office, to stow the files away for another day. He took his wallet and cell phone with him, walking into the master bedroom next, placing the wallet and the cell phone on the nightstand by the side of his bed. Mike kicked at the heel of each boot, kicking at them, hopping from one foot to the next, pulling them off.

Mike stripped out of his clothes he wore for the majority of the day, and the night before, leaving the clothes on the bedroom floor. He walked out of the master bedroom, naked, and made his way to the bathroom. The door opened. The lights flickered on, again. He walked across the white tiled floor, opened the shower, leaned in and switched on the faucets. The water began to run. Mike watched the water a moment. He could feel the heat from the water, as the steam began to rise. Mike stepped into the water, feeling it splash against him and consume his body. The shower door closed behind him. Mike stood under the hot water, as a bar of soap was pushed from left to right, gliding almost, across his chest, over and under his arms, and all over his body.

The water stopped running. The shower door slid open. And Mike appeared, wet and feeling a lot more relaxed. He walked across the bathroom floor naked, dripping, as he leaned and reached out for a fresh, dry towel that hung on the wall by the bathtub. He wrapped himself in it. The bathroom door opened. Mike stood in the entrance a moment, with the towel wrapped firmly around his waist. He stood there quiet, a moment, turning his head left, looking down the rest of the hallway. It was silent. Eerily, so. Mike shrugged it off and turned right, walking back into the master bedroom. The door closed behind him.

Fade to black. Fade from black.

Mike appeared from the end of the hallway as he made his way into the living room. His black, wet hair, was neatly combed to one side, dressed in a simple black t-shirt and navy-blue shorts, which stopped just above the knee, he wore from time to time when he found the time to go running. He made his way into the living room, switching on the television first, before climbing onto the couch. The evening news was on. Mike made himself comfortable on the couch, stretching from one end to the other.

Fade to black. Fade from black.

The time on the clock face which hung in the living room was eight fifty. Mike was asleep on the couch. The cell phone remained on the nightstand, hooked up to the charger. The phone was fully charged and there were one missed call and a text message on the cell phone.

Fade to black. Fade from black.

Mike continued to sleep on the couch. The television set was still playing. The sound of glass breaking, as if forced open, broke the silence above the low hum of the television set. Mike opened in his eyes. They sprang to life. He sat up on the couch, feeling his heartbeat starting to race in his chest. His left foot, bare, lowered from the couch and touched the living room floor. The hardwood floor cracked under the pressure. Mike closed his eyes tightly, for just a moment. The sound of a door handle shook, for maybe a second or two, somewhere in the back of the house. He looked around the living room, looking for something, anything, that he could use as a weapon.

There was nothing.

"Shit!" he whispered under his breath.

Mike tiptoed to the entrance of the living room, to the edge of the hallway and stood there a moment. He held his breath, placing his right hand over his mouth, careful not to make a sound. The same back door swung open, followed by the steps of someone standing over broken glass and making their way deeper inside the house quickly followed. The sound of the steps made their way from the back of the house and down the hallway, toward the front of the house, toward the living room. Mike removed his hand from his mouth. He let go of his breath, and, leading with his left foot, he stepped out from the living room and into the hallway. His muscular frame turned, and there, standing in front of him was the image of the clown mask. It stood there, looking back at Mike. A wooden baseball bat gripped tightly in their left hand, which rose from behind, rose from the darkness and came down with such a forceful swing. The end of the baseball bat made contact with Mike, hitting him on the left side of his temple and cheekbone. The pressure of the swing of the baseball bat, battered Mike, pushing his stunned body against the side of the wall. The weight of his frame fell fast, almost bouncing back, and hitting the wooden floorboard beneath. Mike was unconscious. A bloody wound began to pour from the side temple. The clown mask stood there, dropping the baseball bat to the floor. It bounced off the wooden floorboards, a little, as the image stepped closer, standing over Mike Walters. The mask tilted, somewhat.

Fade to black.

Chapter Eighteen…

Fade from black.

A cell phone sat on the nightstand, attached to a charger. The screen of the cell phone came to life. An incoming call. The cell phone picked up the ID. Mike Walters. The cell phone continued to ring loudly. *Ring. Ring. Ring.* The sound of loud and heavy footsteps grew louder and louder by the moment. Peter appeared in the entrance of his master bedroom. He raced toward the nightstand, grabbing the cell phone, tearing it from the charger chord. The hint of a smile appeared to the surface of his lips. Peter accepted the call as his left thumb swiped on the green button.

The call connected. It was a FaceTime call and the image on the screen of the cell phone came through. An image appeared from the darkness. The hint of the smile slowly disappeared from the surface of his lips. Peter could feel his heartbeat racing, again. It was the clown mask.

"Hello, Peter," the dark and familiar voice said, just above a whisper, as it raised its left hand, bound in a leather glove, and began to wave, a little.

"What do you want? Where is Mike?" Peter answered, angrily.

"Don't you worry about Mike," the clown mask answered, with a hint of a chuckle. "He is safe…for now."

The clown mask stepped to one side, a little, to reveal Mike, bound to an old, dirty wooden chair, and gagged. His arms, his wrists, his legs and ankles were taped to the chair with duct tape. He was still unconscious. And the blood continued to drip from the left side of his temple.

The lighting of the room was minimal, at best. It was something the clown mask created themselves. There were lamps positioned, from what Peter could see, anyway, in the two corners of the room. The floor appeared to be nothing more than mud and old, decaying floorboards. The walls were dark in colour. There was no paint, nor wallpaper. Somewhere hidden. Somewhere abandoned.

"Let him go!" Peter shouted angrily, as tears welled in his eyes. "Mike never hurt you. He has nothing to do with this!"

"Look at him." the clown mask responded. "He has *everything* to do with this. It is part of the game. Does it remind you of anything? A case of history repeating itself, perhaps? First Robert, now Mike. When you're friends with Peter, or in this case, lovers, you die."

"This is no fucking game!" Peter shouted.

"Of course it is. It always has been.

"Now, I wish I could hang around and chat some more, I do. But, if you call the cops, well, I'm afraid, Mike dies. I guarantee it. In the meantime, we're going to have a little fun."

The clown mask laughed.

The phone call ended, abruptly.

Peter tilted his head back, closing his tear-drenched eyes tightly. "No!" he screamed.

Fade to black. Fade from black.

The clown mask stood there, in the light of the dank room, clutching at the cell phone. They walked forward, and over to a wooden bench, which stood in front of Mike, which was a little off to the side. The surface of the wood bench was littered with various tools; a kitchen knife, an ageing hammer, which showed signs of rust, a scalpel, and a can of gasoline, with a dirty, red cap on the top. Mike began to slowly come to. The clown mask placed the cell phone on the surface of the bench top.

The room itself was like no other. It was not your typical room. It was more like a cell, kept hidden away from the public, somewhere dark and cool, underground somewhere. The cell was fitted with a thick wooden door, maybe seven or eight inches, with rusting iron bars, no more than six inches tall, used as kind of hole to peek through, into the darkness. The wood itself was dark in colour, aged over time, and rotting from the damp.

The clown mask turned 'its back on the table and walked towards Mike. They raised 'its left hand high into the air, high above its head, before it came down again, slapping Mike in the face, heavy and hard. The pressure pushed his almost unconscious body forward, a little. His head raised, a little. Mike could feel the pain on the left side of his neck. The clown mask took several steps backwards, to watch their latest victim come to life, once more.

Mike awoke from his unconscious state with a pounding headache. His tongue moved around the inside of his mouth, at a quick speed, feeling the sharp, jagged edges of broken teeth, and the taste of blood inside his mouth. Mike blinked his eyes several times, in quick succession. His vision was still blurry, but it was coming to. An image appeared in front of him. It was nothing more than black with flecks of bright colours, standing in front of two bright lamps. His vision returned in under a minute. And there, in front of him, was the clown mask. He stared at the image, which looked back at him. Mike blinked his eyes, again. The clown mask took a step closer, as their left hand reached out closer, not to offer assistance in any way, but to reach out for the duct tape, which covered Mike's mouth. The leather glove peeled at the duct tape a moment, until it got a better grip, before tearing at it, hard and fast, pulling it from Mike's mouth.

"Fuck!" Mike screamed.

"Welcome back, Mike," the clown mask responded, quite politely.

Mike turned his head down and to the right, a little, as he spat the blood from the inside of his mouth. There were sharp, jagged edges of some broken teeth, which escaped his mouth, passing his lips, and fell the floor below.

"Wait! Where am I?" Mike asked, just above an angry whisper, as he was starting to feel the full force of the pain consume his head from the bloody wound on the left side of his temple.

"I could tell you. But, at the end of the day, does it matter? Let's just say this, you've reached your final destination, and no matter how hard you try to scream, how hard you try to escape, no one will ever find you. Just like Jayne. I had fun with Jayne before I killed her. And that's what I plan to do with you. I plan to have my *fun* with you before you die!"

"Fuck you!"

"So vulgar! I bet Peter Harmon didn't like that dirty mouth of yours. I'm sure of it."

Mike looked into the lifeless eyes of the mask, a moment. His shoulders relaxed somewhat if all the stress in his life had simply vanished, as if he had been caught with his hand in the cookie jar. A simple, guilty smile followed.

"He liked it when I gave it to him, good and plenty. My *mouth* devoured every inch of that scared, innocent body. What do you know?"

The clown mask tilted their head a little, intrigued, by this not-so-innocent reveal.

"So, you had your fun with him? With Peter?"

"How could I not? Peter Harmon is nothing more than town folklore around these parts. He is an outcast. Someone to gawk at when he passed by. His family history is monumental to this small scab, go nowhere of a town. I knew his father and his mother, back in the day. They were nothing more than a passing acquaintance. Then, one day, *one day,"* Mike repeated, raising his voice, some. "Peter Harmon returns to Hillsboro, out of the blue, and walked through the door of my hardware store. I would have been stupid not to jump all over that!"

"Well, will you look here. Aren't you quite the dirty little bird? Quite the plot twist there, Mike. I must admit. I never saw it coming. Well done. But I'm afraid, you're out!"

"Huh? I can fucking help you. We can kill Peter together. Let me help you!" Mike begged, struggling to ease the binds of the duct tape around his wrists.

The clown mask was quick to notice Mike's arms, and his wrists, struggle.

"I ride alone. Besides, I have seen it all. I was in New York City. I saw this whole game play out years ago."

"Just who the *fuck* are you, anyway?"

"Someone who knows Peter Harmon *very* well," the clown mask responded, leaning in fast and close. "It's people like you that always slip up. You played your cards too early. You revealed yourself before the end of the game. Such the amateur. I was impressed, but you let me down. I was in New York City. I had seen it all. I had seen Peter Harmon during the happier times with Robert Prescott. And let's face it, you're no Robert Prescott, that's for sure. You're nothing more than a one- dimensional, go-nowhere replacement for Peter. A blip. Something to have fun with, to pass the time with, until he grew tired of your sorry-looking ass. Think of me, as just speeding up this process. If this were a novel, no one would turn hundreds of pages to see you two together. If this were a movie, no one would sit through until the end credits to see you two live a happily ever after. They would get excited. They would wet themselves, cream themselves, to see you die a gruesome and bloody death. So, let's give the people what they want, shall we?"

"But this isn't a movie!" Mike shouted as panic consumed his voice.

"It will be. But, in the meantime, let's give the people of Hillsboro just exactly what they are craving for, huh? Some entertainment!"

Mike raised his eyes, looking to the ceiling of the cell. He breathed in deeply, before releasing a blood-curdling scream. The clown mask stood there, laughing as they turned and walked toward the bench top, again.

Fade to black. Fade from black.

Mike watched the image of the clown mask stand before him, behind the dirty wooden bench top. He sat there, bound to the wooden chair. His naked feet were covered in dirt and other debris, as they rubbed against the rotting floorboards.

"And what am I to do with you, huh?" the clown mask asked, standing in front of the bench top, as the gloved left hand floated, almost casually, over the props provided. "A kitchen knife is a classic," the image continued, lifting the kitchen knife from the bench top, as if to inspect it, before placing it back down. "It's the go-to for every serial killer that rises through the ranks. A true classic. But let's go with something a little different, shall we? A scalpel? No. Painful, yes. But, overall, I don't think so. A hammer? Now, there is something that can do some real damage. But no. I see what I am going to use. It's quick. It's effortless. And yes, this is going to hurt, a lot."

The clown mask lifted the can of gasoline from the bench top.

Mike looked at the can of gasoline. His heart raced wildly. There was another scream. His fingers curled, the nails scratching at the wooden chair, as he sat there, bound. Mike shook himself from the chair violently, lasting several seconds, at most, trying his best attempt to escape the tight grip of the duct tape. But nothing. He stopped as if giving up. His shoulders slumped, his head tilted down, and into his chest, feeling defeated.

"Fact." the clown mask started, as he lifted the can of gasoline from the bench top, along with the box of matches and the cell phone. "Peter Harmon could never find happiness with you, not really. Yes, he would for a little while. A year, maybe two, at most. But then, his eyes would start to wander. He would end up resenting you, hating you. And for what? The reality of a go-nowhere life. Peter Harmon is an eagle. He deserves everything in this life. He deserves to soar. You, on the other hand, are nothing more than a simpleton. You may be good in the sack for a quick romp, but after that is all said and done, what does he have left? A life with a blue-collared dullard. So, you do have to die. It's the rules of the game."

The clown mask inched closer and closer towards Mike, slowly. And with each passing step, the image worked on loosening the dirty, red cap from the gasoline can.

The dirty, red cap loosened more until it was free from the gasoline can, itself. The clown mask dropped the cap to the dirty, broken floorboards below. It bounced a little and rolled towards Mike's grubby feet. Mike kicked it away from him as if it were a last-ditch attempt to free himself from the events that were about to unfold. It didn't. The clown mask moved the gasoline can into position, ready to pour.

"What?" Mike asked, just above a whisper, just above a blubbering mess.

The clown mask remained silent. They turned left and started to walk in a clockwise position, around Mike.

The gasoline can moved a little. The clown mask positioned it, lowering it a little, as if ready to point towards the dirty, broken floorboards. The gasoline escaped the can with a jerk here, and a chug there. It escaped the can and splashed on the floorboards, beneath. The gasoline was forming a circle around Mike. The clown mask stood in front of Mike, facing him, once more. They completed their clockwise circle. The marking of the gasoline was etched deep into the floorboards.

"How very original of you," Mike answered, abruptly, angrily, and fighting the tears in his eyes.

"It's quick and efficient. And it does the job very well. I told you this is going to hurt. And believe me, it will. I guarantee it."

The clown mask proceeded to splash Mike with the gasoline, with a jerk here and a chug there, of the can. Mike caught some of the gasoline in his mouth, a little. He spat it out. The taste was horrible. His clothes, his face was quickly consumed in the gasoline. Mike had an almost shine to his skin as he sat there in his damp clothes.

The clown mask stopped throwing the gasoline at Mike. It pulled the gasoline can backwards, up against its chest, almost politely, almost elegantly, as if it had finished what it started. The image stood there, silent, a moment before taking slow, gradual, steps backwards, towards the cell door, pouring the gasoline out of the can once more and in a line, which snaked its way, stretching from Mike to the cell door. The clown mask reached the cell door, opening it, a little, and stepping out, closing it behind them. The image of the mask raised, from the cell door, appearing again through the iron bars.

"And this is where we part ways," the clown mask said, recording the contents of the cell in front of them with the cell phone. "Tick tock. The game is quickly coming to an end for you, Mike Walters. I promised you this was going to hurt, and I always deliver on my word."

The clown mask peered through the iron bars, staring at Mike Walters. A match from the box was lit, tossed through the iron bars of the cell, landing on the dirty floorboards below. The match was quick to ignite the gasoline as it raced along the snake-like line, which stretched from the cell door to Mike Walters. The fire raced, reaching the clockwise circle, which held Mike Walters captive. The fire roared to life, quickly consuming Mike Walters, himself. Mike screamed in panic, in agony, from the touch of the flames. The fire was quick to consume his body, starting at the shoulders and arms, racing down to his fingertips, legs and feet. The fire consumed his face, his screaming only magnified. The clown mask watched on, from behind the lifeless eyes of the resin mask. The light of the fire splashed across the mask, highlighting the red, white and blue. Mike continued to scream.

The fire had consumed his entire body now. Mike Walters was writhing in pain and agony.

His flesh burned from the touch of the fire, exposing the veins and muscle beneath. His clothes were no more. His body was consumed in catastrophic burns, which covered him from head to toe. The screams slowly wilted away until there was nothing more. The fire consumed the room, entirely now. The lights from the lamps exploded. The bench top, and along with the kitchen knife, the scalpel, and the hammer burned.

The clown mask continued to watch on, filming. Mike Walters was dead.

Chapter Nineteen…

The time on the cell phone was now ten fifty-seven in the evening. Peter was sitting on the floor of his bedroom, his back propped up by the side of the bed, his cell phone twirling back and forth between his fingers. The bedroom door was wide open. The only light in the room came from the lamp on the nightstand, just above his head. His knees were arched, close to his chest, visibly shaken.

The cell phone started to vibrate. It startled Peter, a moment. He clutched his cell phone tighter in his hands, as he felt his throat drop and his heartbeat start to race. His nerves were starting to get the better of him, as his palms started to grow sweaty. There was a text message. It was a video file. The caption read *Play Me*. Peter navigated through his cell phone and opened the file.

The video started to play. It looked more like the set of a horror movie than real life. Mike sat in a dark, secluded room somewhere, with minimal lighting, bound to a dirty, wooden chair with duct tape over his mouth. He had a bloody wound from the left side of his temple. It bled profusely.

Peter was fighting back his tears and failing. His index finger of his left hand reached out and touched the screen of the cell phone, touching Mike. The clown mask appeared, stepping into the frame of the homemade video. Peter held his breath in his chest, a moment, frightened to watch any further, yet still wanting to know more. The clown mask stepped closer towards Mike, close enough to tear the duct tape from his lips. Peter flinched in terror as the anger ignited in his eyes. He watched him react to the pain. He watched him spit blood from his mouth. The video paused, as if fading to black. Peter was confused.

"What the fuck?" he muttered to himself under his breath.

The video picked up several seconds later. It jumped in time, as if edited. The video picked up to the clown mask dousing Mike in gasoline. Peter screamed in horror, as the tears welled deep in his eyes. The following seemed like a blur to Peter, the light of the match, the fire igniting, and Mike, tortured as he burnt to death. It was screaming. *His* screaming. Mike screaming, that he couldn't get out of his head. Peter sobbed as the video paused, fading to black, again.

The video began, a third time. The fire was out now. There was nothing more than smoke and the charred remains of a human body, of what was once Mike Walters. Peter watched on, struggling, watching through tears in his eyes.

"Shit! Shit! Shit! Shit!" Peter whispered, muffled under his breath.

The camera work moved quickly as if re-directing for a moment. The camera pulled in for a close up on the clown mask. It's lifeless eyes staring into the camera silent, a moment.

"Poor Mike Walters," the clown mask started. "I'm sorry. But he's out! Mike Walters was always part of the game. He had to be. He was nothing more than a dirty bird who *deserved* to die. There were secrets he took to his grave. Things he only revealed to me. Or did he? So, ask yourself, how well did you know Mike Walters? Or did you even know him at all? First, it was Robert Prescott. Then Jayne Scott. And now Mike Walters. Of course, I had to kill a few more to get your attention, to scare you a little. But look around you. Your so-called friends are dropping around you like flies. You can't save them. All you can do is watch. Tick tock, Peter. Your time is running out. I'm coming for you. Your mother would have been so proud of *me*. See you again, soon."

The clown mask raised their left hand, bound in a black leather glove, waving to the camera.

The video ended. The time was now almost a quarter past eleven.

"Fuck!" Peter shouted angrily.

His hand clutched his cell phone, a little tighter, as he climbed to his feet from the side of his bed. He raced out of his bedroom and down the hallway, in the darkness, towards the top of the staircase. Peter raced down the staircase, using a free hand, sliding down the banister, guiding him, as he ran towards the front door. He grabbed his wallet and car keys, which sat on top of the table in the foyer. Peter fumbled a moment, trying to find the right key to unlock the front door. He found it. Peter ran outside, past the porch and to his truck, parked in the driveway. The truck door opened, slamming shut quickly behind him. The engine roared to life as the lights switched on.

It was a little after half-past eleven now, and Andrew couldn't sleep. He tossed and turned before climbing out of bed. He pulled on a t-shirt and some shorts, grabbing his hoodie from the hanger in the closet and made his way out of the house and to his truck parked in the driveway. The engine came to life and the truck reversed out of the driveway and raced to the end of the street.

Andrew pulled into an all-night parking lot. The engine died. He leaned forward in his seat a little, peering out through the window. The glow of the neon lights touched his face. It was busy.

Andrew was sitting outside his local gymnasium. He could count more than a dozen people inside, working, sweating away. He grabbed his sports bag and made his way inside.

Andrew had been at the gymnasium almost two hours now and worked on the treadmill, a light jog to start with, to build up his steps as well as his heartbeat. He moved onto the bench press next. Andrew was sweating profusely. His chest and arms had a shine to them, from under the neon lights hanging from the ceiling. Andrew was wearing headphones, listening to his favourite music, to help pass the time. He grunted and moaned, a little, as he pushed the weights above his chest.

There was no one there to spot him. He was focused on building his upper-body strength, in an attempt to be taken more seriously at the police station. Andrew could now bench press two hundred and forty-five pounds, a personal best.

Andrew moaned and grunted again, exhausted. He lay there a moment, his hands resting on his chest, feeling the burn in his biceps and pectoral muscles, as he stared up at the ceiling, a moment. The music continued to play on in his headphones. It took a moment for Andrew to catch his breath before attempting to sit up and sit forward, in a comfortable position, on the apparatus. The ache and burn in his upper torso continued as he looked around the gymnasium. His t-shirt was damp from the sweat. It moulded to his sculptured chest like a second skin.

Andrew left the bench press behind him and walked across the floor of the gymnasium, and headed towards the men's locker room. He was still wearing his headphones. The door to the men's locker room was painted dark green. The flecks of paint had chipped and aged over the years and was in much need of another fresh coat of paint. The neon lights in the change room were switched on. There was a mild cool to the air this evening. The room was empty and quiet. Andrew pulled the headphones from his ears, looking around the change room, some, passing the lockers, as he made his way towards the communal shower block. The communal shower block was large and empty.

The floor was tiled in basic white and the walls were painted in a dark shade of grey. There was a fresh stack of neatly folded towels nearby. Andrew grabbed one before making his way closer to the shower.

The shower block was open and spacious. Andrew stood there, a moment, on the outside looking in. He counted twelve shower heads, one next to the other, next to the other, and so on. He looked around, again as an eerie silence set upon the change room. Except for the distant hum of the air conditioning system running inside the gymnasium. There was no one around. Andrew shrugged it off as a brief smile surfaced to his lips, a moment. He dumped the damp towel onto the tiled floor at his feet, took off his headphones, laying them on the wooden bench, as he peeled off his t-shirt, and climbed out of his shorts and underwear. He left his personal belongings behind and walked into the communal shower block, naked. He walked over to the closest shower head, leaned in a little and switched on the water.

The water from the faucet poured from the shower head fast. It was an explosion. The water was very warm, almost hot to the touch. The steam rose. Andrew stepped in closer to the water, feeling it splash against his naked body. It felt ever so relaxing against his aching joints and muscles. The hot water from the shower consumed him. He turned to face the water, a moment. It splashed against his muscular chest, dripping down over him. He reached for the liquid soap, pumping down on the handle, three or four times, before turning his back on the water, again. He closed his eyes as he tilted his head back into the water, soaping up the rest of his body. He stood there alone, under the neon lighting.

The water from the shower head stopped minutes later. Andrew felt refreshed. He walked from the shower block naked, grabbing his towel from the wall, as he wrapped it around his soaking body. Andrew dried himself down, before wrapping the now damp towel loosely around his waist. He collected his personal belongings, his headphones, etc, holding them in a small bundle, close to his chest, as he made his way back to his assigned locker. The key to the locker was attached to what looked like a fluorescent rubber band. Andrew's was red. He wore it around his left wrist.

Andrew reached his locker. The key inserted into the lock, twisting, before the door swung open. And as it did, Andrew caught the glimpse of nothing more than a fast-moving shadow in the corner of his right eye. It startled Andrew a little, catching him off guard. He turned and faced the rest of the lockers. It was enough for him to catch his breath in his chest, a moment. The fast- moving shadow was nothing more than another man. Older. Shorter. And somewhere in his early forties with a chubby build and hairy chest with chocolate-brown hair. The chubby man was also wearing navy blue shorts, which moulded his frame and hung just below his knees and white, cotton tank top. Andrew glared at the man a moment. The two men didn't say a word. They exchanged a glance, and nothing more before Andrew turned his back and returned to his locker. His eyes darted to the contents inside his locker; his cell phone, his clothes, etc. He pulled out his clothes, proceeding to get dressed, as he removed the damp towel from around his waist, dropping it on the wooden bench behind him. He stood there naked and alone.

It didn't take long for Andrew to finish getting dressed. He was wearing denim jeans, white sneakers with a red polo shirt and a grey hoodie, he wore open, exposing the shirt beneath. Andrew reached into the locker, again, retrieving his cell phone. He pressed a button on the side of the device and the main screen came to life. There were two missed text messages. They were both from Peter.

Where are you?

The first message read.

I'm on my way to the police station. The son of a bitch got to Mike.

The second message read.

"Shit!" Andrew whispered to himself, angrily, as he leaned in, burying his head into the locker.

He was quick to grab his personal belongings and stuff them inside his sports bag, before he ran out of the men's change room, out of the gymnasium, past the other clientele, and out toward his truck.

The doors leading into the Hillsboro Police Station pushed open with such force, such intensity, that it broke the silence of the officers on night duty. Eyes shifted away from desks, from processing paperwork, to look up at the commotion that came barrelling through the door. It was Peter Harmon. He made his way over to the customer service counter, with his cell phone gripped tightly in his left hand. The station was rather quiet this evening. There was one officer taking care of a drunken gentleman, somewhere in his early sixties, who found it difficult to maintain his balance and walk in a straight line.

"Come with me," the officer said. "You can sleep it off in the tank and we can talk in the morning." The drunken man, who was dressed in denim overalls and a black and white flannel shirt, stumbled a little more, replying with something inaudible.

The officer was somewhere in his early forties, clean-shaven with neatly trimmed jet-black hair and a husky build. His uniform moulded to his portly frame.

"I'd like to speak with Detective Quinn, please," Peter demanded, slamming his free hand down on the desk of the customer service counter.

"You know, I took the late shift, hoping that it would be a little quieter."

Peter noticed the badge on the police officer behind the counter. It read Campbell. "Now!" Peter shouted.

"Okay." Officer Campbell answered, just above a whisper and with little-to-no interest in his voice. "Let's see what we can do, huh?"

His green-grey eyes pulled away from Peter and down onto his paperwork as he turned in his chair a little.

Peter watched Officer Campbell turn in his chair, looking over his left shoulder, out towards the back of the office, toward the closed offices to the far left of the station. Officer Campbell was pushing his late fifties with thick, greying, curly hair, stubble on his face that hadn't felt a razor blade in the past three days, and a thick, matching grey moustache, which had been there since puberty, and reading glasses. He was a portly man. The shirt of his uniform tented to the mould of his belly.

Detective Quinn emerged from his office. The door opened as he stood there a moment, in the door frame, staring out into the office, behind his reading glasses. He fumbled with his frames a little, before taking them off and walked towards the customer service counter. The other officers on night duty continued with their work in silence.

"What have we got here?" Detective Quinn asked as he approached the counter, standing behind Officer Campbell. "Peter Harmon. I'm seeing a lot of you. What are you doing here this time of night?"

Peter looked at Detective Quinn with anger in his eyes, as he continued to clutch at his cell phone tightly in his hands. Detective Quinn watched him, watched the cell phone turn slowly over and over in his left hand.

"Okay, Campbell." Detective Quinn continued, calmly. "You get back to work. Peter, I'll buzz you through. Come to my office. We can talk there."

Officer Campbell returned to his paperwork, but not before giving Peter another *look*.

Detective Quinn leaned forward and hit the button under the customer service desk to buzz Peter into the office. Detective Quinn made his way around the office, to meet Peter at the door and lead him inside his office. Officer Campbell lifted his head away from his paperwork and watched the young twenty-something disappear behind the closing door of the detective's office.

Andrew was in his truck. There was music playing on the radio loudly. The streets seemed empty and dark, as the floodlights on the front of the truck beamed into nothing but darkness, itself. Andrew leaned forward a little, from behind the steering wheel in his truck, making himself a little more comfortable, as he turned the volume down on the radio a little. He fumbled for his cell phone and dialled. The phone call transferred to voice mail immediately.

"This is Peter Harmon," the voice mail began. "I can't get to the phone right now. Please leave a message."

The annoying, loud beeping noise followed.

"Petey!" Andrew bellowed. "This is me. This is Andrew. I just got your message. Where are you now? I'm on my way to the station. Call me."

The phone call disconnected.

"Shit!" Andrew whispered again, under his breath.

The truck continued to race on down the road, consumed in the darkness of the early hours of the morning. The only light coming from his flood lights on the front of his truck.

The Hillsboro Police Station was quiet once more. The officers on duty busied themselves with paperwork. The sound of fingers typing away on keyboards, and the gentle voices flooding across the office like that of a low chorus. Officer Campbell walked across the office and returned to his position behind the customer service counter, perching himself on top of his chair, as the doors leading into the station burst open, again. This time, it was Deputy Preston. His eyes scanned around the station. He walked immediately toward Officer Campbell. Officer Campbell looked up from his paperwork. A small smile surfaced to his lips, happy to see a friendly colleague.

"Campbell, how's it going?" Andrew asked, leaning into the counter a little, with his voice filled with concern.

"You must have heard about Peter Harmon?" Officer Campbell responded, as his smile retracted a little from his lips.

"Where is he?" Andrew asked as the concern in his voice turned to frustration.

The change in tone of voice caught the attention of some of the other officers on duty. Andrew looked at them a moment. It was almost like a pissing contest. But who could stare the other one down first? Deputy Andrew Preston won. His eyes returned to Officer Campbell.

"What a basket case, huh?" Officer Campbell shrugged with another smile surfacing to his lips. "I mean, *that* family. That *mother*."

"I asked you a question, Officer." Deputy Preston said, just above a whisper, as he leaned further into the counter, grabbing Officer Campbell by the buttons on his shirt, twisting them tightly in his fist.

"Quinn has him in his office!" Officer Campbell responded, pulling back, freeing himself from the deputy's grip, and tidying up his shirt.

"That is my best friend you are talking about. A member of the Hillsboro community. We treat everyone with the same amount of decency and respect. However, after work. You and me, we are going to have words. Okay?"

Officer Campbell showed no interest in the conversation. He lowered his head and returned to his paperwork.

The door which leads into Detective Quinn's office was pushed open gently, careful not to disrupt. Deputy Preston appeared at the door and slowly crept inside.

"I want…" Detective Quinn paused, a moment, as he sat behind his desk, his eyes meeting his deputy's. "Deputy Preston. What are you doing here? Your shift, I believe, doesn't commence for another eight hours."

Peter was the first to respond. He turned in his chair, on the opposite side of the desk, looking over his left shoulder. His eyes also met Andrew's.

"I got a text message from Peter, to meet him at the station, sir." Detective Quinn shifted his glance to Peter.

"It's true," responded Peter, just above a whisper.

"Okay." Detective Quinn nodded his head. "Come on in. Take a seat. And close the door behind you."

"Yes, sir."

Andrew made his way into the office, closing the door behind him before taking to the seat next to his best friend. Andrew turned his head a little to the right, making eye contact with Peter.

"Are you okay?" he mouthed, just above a whisper, like a student sitting in the principal's office, careful not to get caught.

The surface of the desk was neat in presentation. A computer sat on the right corner of the desk. In front of the keyboard, were a handful of manila files, some open, some not, but all had Peter's name written on the outer spine, in capital letters, in black marker. The open files contained newspaper articles and photographs of Peter Harmon, himself, at different ages in his life. There were some of him as a child, no more than three or four, when he was thirteen, and then again at twenty-one. There were photographs of his family, including his mother and father.

The far wall of the office was decorated with a large pin board. And on that pin board, were four A-4 size photographs, which looked more like Hollywood head shots, something actors used to promote their careers. The photographs were of Jane Doe, Dorothy Baeyer, Eleanor Padbury and Jayne Scott. They were the photographs of the victims found in Hillsboro, in chronological order, all tied together to the creepy clown mask. And, underneath the individual photographs, were different coloured Post-It's, with notes scribbled, with dates, times and locations.

"Jayne Doe." Detective Quinn started.

"Sir?" Deputy Preston responded.

Peter sat up in his chair, as if making himself more comfortable, and intrigued by the detective. "Jayne Doe was…" Deputy Preston continued.

"Dorothy Baeyer," Detective Quinn interrupted. "Eleanor Padbury. Jayne Scott."

Deputy Preston and Peter Harmon remained quiet, listening on as the detective continue to talk. "These are the bodies found in Hillsboro, in chronological order. All victims were found in various states. But all were wearing the same clown mask." Deputy Preston jumped in, with a quiet but serious tone to his voice.

"Yes, Deputy," replied Detective Quinn.

"What are you saying, Detective?" Peter asked, concerned, as he shifted in his chair, a little. "You still think whoever is doing this, is me?"

"All I am saying, Mr Harmon," Detective Quinn, responded, with nothing more than a smile, "is that there is someone out there, who is articulate. They bide their time. And they have been very busy."

"You still think this is me, don't you? Shit!" Peter whispered, angrily, as tears welled in his eyes. And what about you, Deputy? Do you think I did *this*? That I am capable of something like *this*?" he asked, turning in his chair to face his best friend.

"No!" Deputy Preston answered, just above a whisper.

"I hate to burst your bubble, Detective," Peter turned in his chair again, facing Detective Quinn, once more, "but, you are going to have to find another suspect."

Peter leaned forward in his chair, into the desk, a little more. Deputy Preston looked on, concerned. Peter slid his cell phone across the surface of the desk.

"You can add Mike Walters name to that list of yours, Detective." Peter continued. "His picture deserves to be up on that wall."

"What's this?" Detective Quinn asked, reaching for the cell phone.

"It's my cell phone, Detective. The killer sent me a video. A video of them torturing Mike Walters." Peter's tone of voice remained quiet, breaking almost.

Andrew flinched in his chair.

"The killer, whoever this is, tortured Mike Walters. He was kidnapped. He was bound and gagged to a chair before the killer took a can of gasoline, dousing him with it, and lighting a single match and throwing it at him. The killer torched Mike Walters. I watched him burn alive. I saw the pain he must have felt. The screaming. His voice I can't get out of my head. Whoever is doing this, is targeting the people I care about, the people I love. Would you like to watch, Detective?"

Detective Quinn looked at the cell phone, for a long second. The intrigue floated to the surface of his eyes.

"Go on, Detective," Peter continued, "pick up the cell phone. Feel it. Play the video. See for yourself."

Detective Quinn reached across the surface of his desk and collected the cell phone in his left hand. "There you go," Peter continued, just above a whisper, "feel it. It's all ready for you. All you need to do is hit the play button. Do it."

Detective Quinn lifted his eyes off the cell phone, a moment, and made contact with Peter. He moved his eyes towards Deputy Preston as if seeking his approval.

"You call yourself a detective. This is part of your job. Press play. Do it."

Detective Quinn swallowed hard, a moment. He looked at Peter Harmon once more. He lowered his eyes to the cell phone and pressed the play button. The video started to play, again. The sound of Mike Walters screaming, burning to death, filled the silence of the office. Detective Quinn flinched in his chair, only lasting several seconds, unable to watch any more of the video. He pressed the stop button, placed the cell phone back on the surface of his desk, and slid it toward Peter. "Enough, already."

"A young man returns to the town of Hillsboro, the town he grew up in as a kid. He returns to the town filled with bloodstained memories of his family. At the very same time, a serial killer strikes the town once more. Enter a detective, a bit long in the tooth, on the hunt for the grand prize: said serial killer. But nothing turns up. A curfew is set in place. Yet, the body count continues to rise. And still, no leads. See, Detective? I couldn't bring myself to do something like that. Not to anyone. I'm no killer."

"I am going to need that video as evidence, Mr Harmon."

"Yes, sir," Peter responded, "of course."

"This sounds like the plot to some scary Hollywood movie." Andrew interrupted.

"But this is life. My *life*." Peter answered, turning in his chair to face his best friend, once more. "If you think this is a movie, then any one of us could be next. The movie wouldn't be over until the big reveal."

"What are you saying, Peter?"

"I'm saying the killer isn't finished yet. The end credits haven't rolled." "How do you know the *movie* hasn't finished?" asked Detective Quinn.

"I'm still alive, aren't I? And besides, you haven't caught the killer. You either catch the killer or…"

"Or?" asked Detective Quinn.

"You kill them."

Molly Harris had been working for Mike Walters in his hardware store for almost two years now. She was a tall and confident young girl, who knew her way around the ins and outs of all things hardware. She was a senior at Hillsboro High School, and would be using every penny saved for her first year at college in Chicago. It would be the first time she would be on her own, fending for herself. She wanted to escape the confines of a sometimes, overbearing mother and the likes of small country town mentality, with dreams of a career in radio broadcasting. The customers also liked her. This morning, she came down the staircase of her parent's home, like she did every morning, and made her way into the kitchen.

The television set was playing in the living room. A soft murmur filled the room. It was the local morning news. Molly was dressed in denim jeans, a white pleather coat, with black boots that rose above the ankle, and a pink-and-grey scarf her grandmother knitted for her the previous Christmas. She made her way into the kitchen and sat at the table. Her mother, Marge, had been awake for the greater part of the last hour, cooking breakfast. She wore a white terry-cloth robe with her chocolate brown hair pulled back into a just-out-of-bed-messy ponytail and without a stitch of make-up.

The kitchen was alive with that smell of home cooking. Molly took to the closest chair at the kitchen table. A glass of orange juice was already awaiting her. Molly took a sip as she watched her mother, in between checking her cell phone. Breakfast was served. Mother turned to face her daughter with a plate in her left hand. It slid across the kitchen table, in front of Molly. It consisted of scrambled eggs, toast, two slices of bacon, extra crispy, and sautéed mushrooms.

"You working today?" asked mother.

"Uh-huh," Molly answered, anticipation in her voice. "Nine to three-thirty, today." Molly shovelled some scrambled eggs onto her fork and took a bite.

"Well, I want you home right after, you hear me? No dilly-dallying. Not today. There is a report of another storm this afternoon. It won't be safe out on those roads."

"Okay, mother."

"Good girl." Mother leaned in and gave her daughter a quick peck on the forehead.

"I gotta go," Molly answered, as she took one hearty sip from her glass of orange juice and stood up from the table.

"But you've hardly touched your breakfast this morning."

"See?" said Molly, taking a crispy piece of bacon and placing it on her slice of toast, for the road. She took a bite if just to please her mother. Mother smiled.

"Thank you."

Molly leaned in close to her mother and returned the kiss on her forehead. "See you this afternoon."

"Be safe out there."

"I will. Bye."

Molly took another bite from her toast, turned her back on her mother, reached for her cell phone on the kitchen table and ran quickly out of the kitchen and toward the front of the house. Mother heard the front door slam shut.

Molly raced from the front door of the house and out into the driveway. Her car was waiting for her. It was a Mini Cooper, 2004 model, silver in colour. She had bought it second-hand out of the back pages of the local newspaper. It did have its problems, but it still got her from point A to point B. Molly unlocked the driver's side door and climbed inside, slamming the door to a close behind her. It was chilly. She tugged a little tighter at the scarf around her neck. Molly made herself comfortable, putting on her seatbelt whilst turning the key in the ignition. The engine came to life. And the music on the radio began to blare. The silver Mini

Cooper reversed out of the driveway and into the neighbourhood traffic behind her. The car raced to the end of the street.

The drive into town didn't take too long, maybe close to twenty minutes, tops. The traffic this morning was a little heavier than usual, with the impending storm front and tree branches down, covering the roads. The council workers were already out in force, starting to clear the roads. Molly was singing to the music on the radio. She drove with caution, as she leaned forward in her seat, clearing the condensation with the palm of her right hand. The heater was on the fritz. It was one of the delights of a second-hand car.

The forest roads leading into town were narrow and wet. Molly applied pressure to the brake pedal as the traffic in front of her was coming to a halt. It was the council workers. They were removing another tree branch. This was thick and heavy, and required chainsaws to cut through.

The Mini Cooper came to a halt. Molly stopped singing, a moment. She leaned forward, a little, and turned the volume on the radio down some. Something grabbed her eye. It was on the side of the road. It was the carcass of a decomposing body. A dog. A golden retriever. There were a handful of crows, maybe three or four, pecking at the remains. And looking at the condition of the carcass, it was mature in age, but difficult to tell if it were male or female, as half of its skull had been crushed and the contents of its stomach were missing. Molly flinched at the sight of the golden retriever. She shook her head a moment, and turned away, focusing on the radio. She turned the volume on the radio up, a little more. Her voice was quiet to start with as if clearing her throat, mouthing the words to the song on the radio, forcing herself to sing, anything to keep her mind off the dog. The traffic was slowly beginning to move, again.

Molly reached the clearing of the fallen tree branch and looked at the council workers, a moment. She could count eight council workers standing on the side of the road, near two parked trucks. They ranged in age, from maybe eighteen to forty-something. It was then her cell phone began to chime. Molly had her hands on the steering wheel, at ten and two, when she looked down at her cell phone on the front passenger seat. It was a text message. Molly diverted her eyes on the road, again, just a moment longer, as she passed the council workers. Molly looked in her rear view mirror a moment, careful not to be seen, and grabbed her cell phone from the passenger seat. She was quick to sign in and navigate through the screens. It was a text message from Mike Walters.

I'm running late. Do you mind opening up the store this morning? See you soon.

The message read.

Molly smiled and shrugged her shoulders, a little, as she tossed her cell phone back on the front passenger chair and focused on the traffic in front of her. The volume of the music from the radio increased, again.

The drive into the town square took just shy of half an hour. Molly made her way into town and parked her car in the employee parking lot behind the store. It was a designated parking area for the other stores in town. The engine of the Mini Cooper died. Molly turned the key in the ignition, again. She sat there a moment, behind the steering wheel of her car, and gazed out the window. The snow had fallen again overnight. The parking lot was covered in a thin blanket of snow. Molly blinked her eyes several times, before a hint of a smile surfaced to her lips. She turned in her seat, a little, turning to grab her personal belongings before climbing out of her car. The driver's side door was quick to slam shut and the sound of the alarm beeped as it set. Molly had her cell phone gripped tightly in her right hand, as she threw her bag over her shoulder, and made her way out of the parking lot and walked down the footpath, towards the store.

Molly made her way closer to the hardware store. She was two, maybe three stores away, when she opened her bag from around her shoulder and retrieved the keys inside. She gripped the keys tightly in her left hand. The curved and jagged edges of the keys felt cold and sharp against the palm of her hand. A married couple, somewhere in their early fifties, walking hand in hand past Molly, smiling briefly, politely. She smiled and nodded, briefly, as she made eye contact, before arriving at the store.

The lights to the hardware store were switched off. Molly stood in front of the door. Her hands fumbled with the keys a little, in the cold of the morning. The key was pushed into the lock of the front door with a little force, before it turned, unlocking, and Molly pushing down on the door handle. The front door opened, and Molly stepped inside the store. Her right hand reached out, sliding up and down the wall, a little, searching for the light switch. She found it. The neon lights hanging from the ceiling flickered on. The doorbell chimed a little with a push of the door. Molly was quick to turn her back to the store, locking the front door, behind her. It was procedure before opening for business for the day.

Molly turned her back, once more, as she made her way to the front of the store. She walked down the closest aisle, past the hammers and nails and glue guns. The sound of her boots scratched along the surface of the floor. The keys jiggled and bounced in her hands. Molly reached the end of the aisle, standing in front of the glass counter and cash register. She stopped in her tracks, dropping the keys to the floor. A blood-curdling scream followed, piercing the silence of the store. And there in front of her, the bloodied, charred remains of Mike Walters, lying on the floor, face-up, in a bloodied heap. The remains of the bloodied and tortured body, was wearing another clown mask.

Molly dropped to her hands and knees, where she stood, releasing a second blood-curdling scream.

Chapter Twenty...

It had been less than half an hour now since Molly arrived at work and the hardware store was now an official crime scene. The front of the hardware store was manned by a police officer, somewhere in his late thirties, with a muscular build, clean-shaven and a buzz-cut with blonde hair. The door leading into the hardware store was propped open but closed off to the general public.

There was yellow police tape used as a temporary police barricade along the footpath of the town square, which stretched to three storefronts in length. There were also a handful of other officers, two directing street traffic, whilst others were controlling the growing, prying crowds.

"There is nothing to see here!" yelled one officer.

"Come on. Move along. Let us get to work. Come on!" yelled another.

The crowds continued to grow. There were almost fifty people, give or take, standing outside the hardware store in huddled masses watching on as the investigation played out. There were kids and adults with their cell phones, taking photographs and recording video, something to sell to the local media outlets or upload to their social media accounts later in the day.

An ambulance sat parked outside the hardware store, nearby. The doors to the back of the ambulance were wide open. Molly was sitting in the back of the ambulance, with a blanket draped over her shoulders, there to keep her warm, as an ambulance officer was in the final stages of checking her over, making sure she was safe to drive home, or at the very least, have her mother come to collect her. A female police officer stood nearby, waiting patiently, there on duty, waiting to ask a string of questions, which would help with the investigation.

The police officer on duty, manning the front of the hardware store, with the muscular build and blonde buzz-cut, looked over his left shoulder a moment, at the crime scene unravelling inside. It was chaotic. There were a lot of warm bodies, other police officers, there on duty, recording evidence and taking photographs. There were Detective Quinn and Deputy Preston quietly talking to each other. The crime scene itself was gory and bloody. It was cold and gruesome. The charred remains of a human body, a male in his forties, of a muscular build, lay on the floor towards the front of the store, facing the ceiling, whilst the remains of his face, were hidden, covered by a hideous clown mask. The fire had done catastrophic damage to the body, burning, breaking the flesh, and exposing the blood, muscles, tendons, and bone beneath. The blood looked almost purple in colour. The clothes worn were torched and blackened, some of the fabric sticking to the flesh beneath.

And the smell. It was like no other. One of the police officers on duty turned his back on the crime scene and made a beeline for the back of the store, unable to stomach the sheer brutality of which the human mind was capable.

"Jesus Christ!" yelled Detective Quinn, as he watched the younger officer race out of the hardware store, clutching his stomach. "Make sure someone goes and checks on the kid, okay?"

"Yes, sir," replied a nearby officer.

"This is a fucking nightmare. Fuck!" Detective Quinn rubbed his eyes, from the stress, redirecting back to Deputy Preston. "You said this, *this* was like the set of some scary Hollywood movie." Deputy Preston slowly nodded his head, a little.

"It's gruesome enough," Detective Quinn continued, "I'll grant you that. I want this guy. He. She. Or whoever this is. I want them. I can fucking taste it in my mouth. I want them in my office now! And if I can't have that, I want a bullet in their head. I mean, who the *fuck* is doing this? If not Peter Harmon, then who?"

"Do you think he still has something to do with it? With *this*?"

Detective Quinn paused a moment. Deputy Preston could see the frustration painted across his face. "Peter Harmon did have a relationship with the deceased, with Mike Walters. They did know each other. Maybe they fought. Maybe his return to Hillsboro was just too much for him to bear. Maybe he just…snapped. It can happen. Maybe he took a can of gasoline and lit the match. Maybe he sent the video to himself from Mike's cell."

"I don't think so," Deputy Preston answered, softly, "not Peter."

"It's always the ones we least suspect."

"Even so. Peter lived through this. I know him. He couldn't bring himself to do this."

"I'm in charge of this investigation!" Detective Quinn snapped.

Deputy Preston looked at the detective, a little shocked. "What do you want me to do?" he asked.

"For the next twenty-four hours, I want the men and women of the Hillsboro Police Station out in force, doing a house to house. I want the main streets in and out of this sleepy little town blocked off. Someone must have seen something, surely. In the meantime, I want you to comb every costume, every dive that sells those creepy looking clown masks. They give me the willies!"

"Yes, sir."

Detective Quinn raised his right hand and placed it over his mouth a moment, as he tilted his head a little, looking up at the ceiling. His eyes raced across the top of the ceiling, coming down on the front door of the hardware store. His hand moved away from his mouth.

"What?" Deputy Preston asked, concerned. "What is it?"

Detective Quinn raced to the front of the store, out past the police officer on duty. Deputy Preston followed. The police officer on duty looked at his senior officers, a moment.

"Someone must have seen something," Detective Quinn repeated under his breath. "The security cameras. There and there." He pointed, down the street, some. "I want the security footage of every access point to this place on my desk within the hour!"

Detective Quinn turned his back on the growing crowd in the street and returned inside the hardware store. Deputy Preston followed. The police officer on duty remained focused on securing the front of the store. Detective Quinn stood a little back from the crime scene, itself, giving the coroner and his assistant enough space to complete their job and make their notes. The coroner was on his knees, his face covered with a light blue surgical mask, inspecting the charred remains up close.

"Whoever did this, knew exactly what they were doing," the coroner said, speaking into a mini voice recorder. "The flames were exacting. The burns were catastrophic. I can see third-degree burns around the neck and upper torso. The lower torso, the inner thighs are burned almost beyond recognition. Almost. The clothes. A polyester blend, or some type, melted to the flesh around the victim. Our victim is wearing another mask, like before. A clown mask."

The coroner pulled back from the charred remains of the deceased, pulling back onto his knees, a little more. He placed the mini recorder in the left pocket of his trousers.

"A scalpel, please," the coroner continued, addressing his assistant.

"Of course."

"Let's take a look and see who we have here, shall we?"

The coroner leaned forward, rocking forward onto his knees, towards the deceased, with a scalpel in his right hand. The sharp tip of the blade from the scalpel sliced under the resin of the clown mask and along the surface of the flesh underneath. The blade pierced the skin, causing what remains of blood to pour from the wound. The coroner flinched, a little, as his face tightened, some. He pulled back on the scalpel and placed his hands on the mask, giving it a slight nudge, and lift, as he removed the mask entirely. The assistant was quick to look over his shoulder, looking away in disgust. Detective Quinn and Deputy Preston watched on, unaffected by it all. Detective Quinn stood there, silent, with his arms crossed over his chest.

The clown mask pulled away from the tortured flesh beneath, exposing the damage, not only to the assistant but to everyone in the store. The surface of the flesh was catastrophically burnt, in some areas, exposing the jawline and dental work beneath. The eye sockets were empty. The right ear was gone. It wasn't missing. The fire consumed the ear to the point where it was simply a burnt mound, solidified to the side of the head.

"Here," the coroner continued, "bag this!"

The coroner was careful to hand the resin clown mask to his assistant. He was on his knees, on the other side of the body, waiting with a large, empty plastic bag, waiting to scoop it up.

"Make your way out the back of the store. I don't want the general public getting their eyes on the mask. You know how gossip spreads in a small, country town."

"Yes, sir."

The assistant climbed to his feet and made his way out the back of the hardware store.

The coroner was next to climb to his feet. He stumbled a little to find his balance. Deputy Preston stepped in to help him out.

"Here, sir, let me help," Deputy Preston said, just above a whisper.

"Thank you, kind sir."

The coroner pulled his plastic gloves from his hands and the surgical mask from his face, before dusting himself down, as the ambulance officers stepped in and placed the charred remains onto the stretcher. The coroner made eye contact with one of the ambulance officers and gave a brief nod. He returned his sight to Detective Quinn.

"We meet again," the coroner said, with a hint of a smile surfacing to his lips.

"What can you tell me about Mike Walters?" Detective Quinn asked, just above a whisper and flat. "You have confirmed the identity already?"

Detective Quinn paused a moment, nodding his head, a little.

"Mike Walters owned this hardware store. The young girl out front worked part-time hours, saving for college.

"Well, Mike. He suffered. Greatly. He would have been in tremendous pain before he died. I found marks consistent with a sharp blade. Puncture wounds. Slicing of the flesh in a manner about the lower stomach, the genitals, and inner thighs. Whoever is doing this, wanted him to suffer before they set him on fire. The fire was just a cover-up. And whoever did this, knows their way around knives and other sharp objects."

Detective Quinn stared back at the coroner. He could feel the stress course through his veins.

The morning had progressed. It was now somewhere in the early hours of the afternoon.

From the outside of the house, it appeared almost abandoned. Almost. The street was quiet, except for the low rustle amongst the trees. The children, who once played in the neighbourhood, were gone. The curtains in the front living room were pulled almost to a close. A thin coat of snow covered the front of the lawn, scattering over the front porch and the street outside. The curtains were open just enough to allow the remaining light of the afternoon to creep inside the house. The clouds were quickly turning a darker shade of grey, as the rain started to fall over the luscious green landscape and the small country town.

The rain fell heavier now. And gusts of wind arced up some, blowing the tops of the trees. It was nothing scary, mind you. It was just enough to make its presence known. Peter hated the winter. He was sitting on the couch in his living room, hunched forward a little, over the coffee table. A freshly brewed cup of coffee sat to his right in front of him, next to his cell phone. The living room itself was lit from the dying outdoor light and three lamps positioned around the room. Peter took his eyes off the open photo albums that spread across the coffee table in front of him and looked up at the ceiling of the living room, a moment, as the winter winds rattled the house, a little.

The pages of the albums were spread open, exposing many photographs, in both colour and black and white, and so many cherished family memories. His eyes began to fall from the ceiling and returned to the photo albums, to the pictures of his mother and father, and his half-sister and grandfather. Peter extended his right hand outwards, onto the pages of the photo album, and running the tips of his fingers over the plastic sleeves which protected the ageing photographs. His eyes diverted to his cell phone, a moment. He picked it up, holding it in his hands, rather tightly. The device came to life with a push of a button. He looked at it a moment, hoping to see a text message, a missed phone call, anything, something from Mike. There was nothing. There were no texts, messages, calls, nothing from Andrew, nor Emily for that matter.

"I can't do this any more, Dad," Peter whispered to himself, as the weight of his shoulders slumped forward.

Tears were beginning to well in his eyes.

A squad car from the Hillsboro Police Department rolled to a slow halt outside a local house, in a random neighbourhood. The engine died. The rain continued to fall, heavier now, with flecks of snow. Deputy Preston sat in the front passenger seat of the squad car. He turned his head and peered through the window. The neighbourhood looked cold and miserable amongst the neatly trimmed and manicured gardens. Deputy Preston shifted the weight of his frame forward a little, pushing the side door open. He climbed to his feet, turning a little, as he surveyed the neighbourhood. A fellow officer climbed out from behind the steering wheel and slammed the door shut.

"What are you thinking, sir?" the officer asked.

"It's cold! It's wet! And there is a fucking killer who seems to be one step ahead of us. Let's do our jobs right and get this shit done, okay?"

"Yes, sir."

The two police officers left the squad car behind and walked up onto the pavement, out the front of the house. Deputy Preston adjusted his raincoat a little, trying his best to stay warm, as he walked toward the front door of the house. The other officer, older, and somewhere in his late thirties, clean-shaven with a robust build, was ahead, already approaching the front porch. Deputy Preston paused in his tracks. He lifted his head a little, looking up at the two-storey weatherboard home, before turning around and surveying the neighbourhood, again.

"Sir?" the officer asked, gently. There was no answer.

"Sir?" the officer asked, again. And, again, there was no answer.

Deputy Preston watched the other officers in the street, next door, and on the other side of the road, on duty walking from house to house, knocking on front doors.

"I hate this shit!" he mumbled.

Emily was in the kitchen. It was quiet. She sat at her kitchen table that was propped up against one side of the wall. The table was set for one. She sat there in front of a bowl of spaghetti, she cooked on the stove top, with a glass of water with three ice cubes, and homemade garlic bread she made with a crusty roll, that she tore into bite-size pieces. The dinner sat upon a plastic place mat with red and white squares spread across the surface. Her cell phone sat near the glass of water. It distracted her, if just for the moment. Emily leaned into the table and reached for it. And there, waiting for her, was nothing. There were no missed calls, text messages, photographs, nothing. Not from Andrew nor Peter. Emily slid the cell phone across the kitchen table, face down, next to her glass of water and resumed eating her dinner in the excruciating quiet. The slow tick of a clock which hung on the kitchen wall, above, was the only thing to break the silence. *Tick. Tick. Tick.*

The door leading into Detective Quinn's office was closed. The neon lights hanging from the ceiling were switched on. And Detective Quinn sat at his desk in front of his laptop computer. He was watching footage taken from the hardware store from the night before. There was nothing to report. The majority of the night the street was empty, except for the occasional kids walking home after leaving the nearby theatre. And a drunken man, somewhere in his late fifties to early sixties, stumbling home, but not before pausing, standing out the front of the hardware store, pulling on his jeans a little, exposing himself to urinate, after a drunken night at a nearby bar. Detective Quinn sat slouched in his chair, his face slumped forward, caught in his hands. The boredom was written over his face.

Detective Quinn lifted his head from his hands and rubbed his eyes, a little. He continued to watch the footage. Still nothing. He leaned in the desk a little, making himself a little more comfortable, before hitting the fast forward button on the keyboard of his laptop computer. The footage sped up. Still nothing. Until a single-crew-cab truck, white in colour, pulled over, parking outside the hardware store. Detective Quinn sat up in his chair, immediately. He could feel his heart start to race, as he leaned in and watched the footage.

"What have we have here, huh?" Detective Quinn whispered to himself. "I got you now you little shit!"

The footage played on. The crew cab truck sat parked outside the hardware store, quiet and alone for almost three minutes, as per the time stamp on the video footage. A hooded figure climbed out from behind the steering wheel of the truck. The image walked from the side of the truck and to the front door of the hardware store. It stood there a moment, searching their pockets, presumably searching for the keys to the store. The hooded figure fumbled with the keys a moment, before unlocking the door and stepping inside a moment, to switch off the alarm. The image of the hooded figure soon emerged from the front of the hardware store, within a couple of minutes. The lights inside the hardware store switched on.

"What are you doing?" Detective Quinn whispered to himself, as he continued to watch the footage.

The image of the hooded figure emerged from the front of the hardware store, finally. It took almost four minutes from the time stamp on the video. The image of the hooded figure walked from the front of the hardware store, took a left, and walked past the truck on the side of the road. The image walked past the truck and toward the security camera in the street. The hooded figure lifted their head from the ground, looking up at the security camera, exposing the clown mask, in all 'its hideous and gruesome glory. The clown mask tilted their head a little to the left as if making eye contact with the camera. Detective Quinn kept his eyes glued to the computer screen. He could feel a cold shiver run down the spine of his back, as he made eye contact with the clown mask.

"There you are," Detective Quinn whispered to himself.

The image of the clown mask returned to the truck, to the back seat of the crew cab. The door to the truck pulled open, and there, the clown mask proceeded to pull, drag the lifeless remains of Mike Walters, hidden in a large black canvas bag. The body bag hit the side of the pavement with a thud, before being dragged inside the hardware store. The clown mask was cautious of their surrounds, keeping an eye out, left and right, for anyone nearby. There was no one. The image of the clown mask disappeared inside the hardware store again, this time dragging the body bag with them. They were in the store for close to ten minutes, before emerging again, setting the alarm, switching off the lights, and locking the front door, before disappearing inside the truck and driving away, racing to the end of the street, out of sight.

"You think you can outsmart me, don't you, you son of a bitch!" Detective Quinn whispered, staring into the screen of the laptop computer, whilst biting down on his lower lip. "People like you eventually slip up, they always do. You gave yourself away, you know that? Or did you leave a cookie behind for me to find? I got your number plate. I got you."

The rain and the snow fell over Hillsboro from the night before as the sun began to rise the following morning. A layer of snow covered the front lawn of Emily's home, as well as her roof and front porch. A single truck was parked in the driveway. It belonged to Andrew. He'd stayed the night with Emily after finishing his shift at work. Her home was closer to the station, which made sense, and Andrew had left some of his personal belongings there; a toothbrush, some shoes, underwear, and clothes.

There was a quiet stir about the house. The lights were switched off, but the curtains in the living room were pulled open, allowing for the morning sun to warm the front of the house. Two wine glasses were sitting on the coffee table in front of the television set, almost empty. Andrew was home in time to watch an episode of *The Late Show with Stephen Colbert*. Both Emily and Andrew loved his style of comedy. From the living room, the house grew darker and darker, progressing further down the hallway. The door to the master bedroom was wide open, and there, in bed, the thick blanket was peeled back, exposing Andrew cuddling up to Emily. He was the bigger spoon. His chest was muscular and bare, and his arms wrapped around Emily, holding her close to his chest. Emily's hair was pulled back into a messy bun and was wearing one of Andrew's favourite football t-shirts, The Chicago Bears. The two were fast asleep.

Peter was wide awake. He had been up and out of bed for a little over an hour now. He turned onto his street, jogging along the pavement, past the other houses, heading toward home.

The street was almost bare. Almost. There was a middle-aged couple, dressed in tracksuits, taking their golden retriever for a walk on a purple lead. The golden retriever was female, old and set in her ways, and held the handle of the lead in her mouth as she casually walked beside her owners at a slow pace. Peter was dressed in grey sweat pants and a black t-shirt with headphones plugged in each ear. His cheeks were a shade of rosy pink as his forehead and chest were sweating. Peter passed the married couple on his morning jog. His eyes were immediately drawn to the golden retriever first, before making eye contact with the couple and giving them a brief nod of the head. The married couple were polite and smiled back.

Peter arrived home from his jog. He reached the driveway and made his way toward the front of the house. He leaned against the front door, a moment, just long enough to retrieve his keys from the pocket of his sweat pants, before unlocking it and disappearing inside the house, as the front door swung to a close behind him. Peter made his way inside the house. He dropped the keys to the house in the bowl on the table, before jogging up the staircase, and making his way towards the bathroom.

The bathroom room door pushed open and the neon lights flickered on as Peter made his way deeper inside. He turned and looked at the open bathroom door a moment, almost shrugging his shoulders, leaving the door ajar. He stood in front of the washbasin, catching his breath a little, and catching his reflection in the bathroom mirror. He noticed the rosy pink in his cheeks and the sweat which consumed his t-shirt. He stood there a moment, leaning into the mirror.

"My God!" he whispered under his breath. "I look almost thirty years old."

Peter stepped back from the bathroom mirror before he peeled his shirt off his muscular and sweaty frame. He tossed it on the floor by the bathtub, then stripped out of his sweat pants and walked over toward the shower. He leaned into the shower and turned the faucets. The water began to run.

Peter stood under the shower head, leaning forward, a little, with his head facing down, and his shoulders hunched forward, some. He felt a little sore from his morning run and he also felt defeated from the events of the past few days as the water splashed over his body. Peter rubbed a bar of soap over his shoulders and chest.

The morning progressed. Andrew woke up, had breakfast and left Emily at home as he made his way back to work. The police station was filled with officers, all going about their business. Some of the phones in the station were ringing off the hook. Other officers were typing away on their computers, completing their paperwork. Deputy Preston followed Detective Quinn across the station, snaking down hallways, and into his office. Detective Quinn was sporting another of his grey suits with a white shirt and navy-blue tie, as Deputy Preston wore his department-issued uniform, which appeared tighter across the chest.

"We have a lead on the case," Detective Quinn said, with a hint of a smile surfacing to his lips.

"You're kidding me? You do? Who is it?" Deputy Preston answered, eagerly.

"Not so fast. I don't have the finer details just yet. But the son of a bitch left us a present when he parked his truck outside the hardware store when I was watching the security footage. The cameras picked up their number plate!"

Deputy Preston's face ignited with anticipation.

"We are running the plates as we speak," Detective Quinn continued. "You think Peter Harmon is still behind this?"

"We will find out soon enough. I should have the information within the hour. Goddamn it! I want everyone on this! This will be our top priority."

"Well, whoever is behind this, I have your back."

"Thank you. I will be planning a raid on the property just as soon as I have an address. I don't want sirens. I want to surprise this son of a bitch! Be ready."

"Yes, sir."

It was almost midday as a handful of squad cars from the Hillsboro Police Station turned onto Wallace Terrace. The neighbourhood seemed nice enough. It wasn't exactly the upper middle class, but the residents got by. Children of about nine or ten were playing in the street, running onto the pavement, out of the car's way, as they clung to their bicycles and held their basketballs, watching it all play out in front of them. It was the most excitement they had seen in a long time.

Detective Quinn sat in the front passenger seat of one of the squad cars, as Deputy Preston was sitting behind the steering wheel, racing towards the end of the street, leading the other cars, and officers, on duty.

"I got the address," Deputy Preston said, with determination in his voice. "Seventeen forty-five Wallace Terrace."

"The vehicle is registered to a Sean Michael Murray. Twenty-nine years old. Does the name ring any bells with you?" asked Detective Quinn.

Deputy Preston thought of the name, taking his time, a moment, before answering. "No, sir," he finally responded. "Nothing. Before my time."

"Well, whoever this guy is, I want as many warm bodies over this as I can get."

"Yes, sir."

The squad cars from the Hillsboro Police Department raced to the end of Wallace Terrace. The houses on the street appeared to grow less and less attractive as they reached the end of the road. Deputy Preston was the first to pull into the driveway of seventeen forty-five Wallace Terrace. The front lawn of the property was neglected and dying. The grass had weathered away, leaving behind mounds of dirt and long stems of grass which had turned a deathly brown in colour. A single weatherboard home sat on the property with an adjoining garage. The state of the house was dilapidated. The red paint on the front door had chipped away over time and sat open, exposing the contents inside. The glass windows in the front of the house were in a state of ruin, chipped, cracked and broken.

Deputy Preston pulled into the driveway, leaving enough distance between himself and the closed garage. The white paint on the garage door was chipped, and the door itself was weather-beaten. The engine to the squad car died. Detective Quinn sat there a moment, shocked and surprised.

"'The fuck?" he muttered, just above a whisper.

The remaining squad cars on duty were quick to find their parking space out the front of the downtrodden property and in the street. The commotion drew the attention of the nearby neighbours. "You're kidding me, yeah?" Deputy Preston asked, surprised.

"This is real? You don't think someone is pulling your chain, sir?"

"I want every inch of this property turned over. I am not leaving here until we have something."

"Yes, sir."

Deputy Preston was the first to climb out from his squad car. He tilted the weight of his frame and stepped out of the car. He stood there a moment, pushing the door shut, staring up at the house a moment, before turning to face the front of the property, and directing, ordering the other officers on duty.

"Fuck!" Detective Quinn shouted in frustration.

The police officers on duty were divided into two separate teams. One team, made up of no more than six officers, took to the rotting remains of the house, with their firearms drawn, and ready to strike, at a moment's notice as they combed each room of the house. The remaining officers formed a semi-circle, with the firearms drawn, pointed at the garage door, also ready to strike on command.

"This can't be it. Surely, not." Detective Quinn said, as approached the other officers in front of the garage, with caution. "Fuck!" he shouted. "I want that garage door open, now. I want to see what we got."

"Yes, sir!" answered Deputy Preston, with a sense of anger in his voice, wanting more than anything, to bring this chapter to a close. "Officer McIntyre, proceed with caution, like your life depended on it, and open that garage door."

"Yes, sir," Officer McIntyre responded, looking over his right shoulder at the deputy, with a sense of delight in his young voice for being selected.

Officer McIntyre was fresh out of the academy and eager to learn. He had been posted to Hillsboro Police Department a little on five months now and was putting a stamp on his career. He was twenty-three years old with a similar build to Deputy Preston. His obsession with building body mass was his way of being taken more seriously within the department. He sported short, cropped hair, black in colour, with a neatly trimmed beard, and a tattoo of a grizzly bear, which stretched from his right shoulder to his wrist. He approached the front of the garage door slow, and with caution, with his firearm drawn. Officer McIntyre was quick to place his firearm back in its holster, using his arms and the strength in his biceps to lift the garage door. The other officers on duty, remained in position with their firearms drawn. The garage door was pushed open with force. It opened in short bursts, fast then slow, then fast again. The rails on the side of the garage door were rusted out. There was no repair here. They were in need of being replaced altogether. The garage was… empty.

"Shit!" Detective Quinn shouted. "I had him. I had that son of a bitch!"

The police officers started to emerge from the front of the house, making their way towards the garage door. The other officers on duty started to lower their firearms.

"Nothing, sir!" shouted the team leader, as he walked towards Detective Quinn. "All clear."

"Fuck!" Detective Quinn shouted.

Deputy Preston looked over his shoulder, out into the neighbourhood. And there, in front of him, were some of the families of the neighbourhood, staring back in horror.

Chapter Twenty-One...

The morning started with an eerie sense of déjà vu. Peter hadn't felt this way in a long time. Not since the day of his father's funeral, what felt like so many years ago now, yet so close, as if it were only yesterday at times. His feelings for his father would likely be forever raw and emotional. Peter was sitting at the dining table. The table was set for one. Breakfast. A simple tablecloth covered the surface of the dining table. It was made of white cotton with dark green boxes embroidered over the top. A plate of scrambled eggs, hash browns and toast sat before him with a glass of freshly squeezed orange juice. He didn't eat much, mostly poking at the food with a fork. He didn't have much of an appetite.

Peter sat at the dining table, still dressed from the night before, in his PJ's; in a simple white cotton tank top and boxer shorts. The boxer shorts were a culmination of colours: black, shades of brown, yellow and grey. The television set in the living room was switched on. It was the morning news. A story about a young girl, no older than six years old, abducted from an apartment in Chicago played out. Her remains found in the trash compactor. The finger was pointed at the super of the building. But Peter's thoughts were elsewhere. As tragic as the news was, he didn't pay too much attention. He looked up at the television screen briefly.

"That poor girl," he whispered to himself.

Peter soon returned to his breakfast. He took a bite from his scrambled eggs and took a sip from his orange juice before he stood up from the table, collecting the plate and glass and returning them to the kitchen. He wiped the plate clean, pushing the remains into the nearby trashcan and washed the plate and glass in the sink. The television set continued to play. Peter left the kitchen and made his way upstairs. He walked down the hallway and turned left, walking into the bathroom. He stepped inside and closed the door behind him. The light flickered on. He stripped out of his clothes, in front of the bathroom mirror, and walked across the floor naked, before stepping in the shower and feeling the warm water consume him.

The door to the master bedroom was left wide open. The lights in the bedroom were switched off. The curtains were open, to allow the morning light to creep inside. Peter appeared in the bedroom doorway. His body was still dripping with beads of water from the shower. A damp towel wrapped loosely around his waist, which sat on an angle, a little. He walked into his bedroom, immediately making his way to the set of drawers at the end of his bed. Peter retrieved some black dress socks from the top drawer, and a pair of boxer shorts from the drawers underneath. He turned and placed them on the end of the bed, before walking over to his walk-in wardrobe and pulling a white, long-sleeved shirt, and black trousers and a simple black tie. The cell phone on the nightstand began to ring. *Ring. Ring. Ring.* It grabbed Peter's attention. He looked over his right shoulder at his cell phone. Peter hung his clothes in the wardrobe again, before turning to answer his cell phone.

Unknown Caller.

"What do you want?" Peter answered, flatly, and not interested in playing in any further games.

"And good morning to you, too." laughed the familiar, deep voice. "It's like déjà vu for you all over again, isn't it? Is this how you felt the day you buried your father? I'm sure it is. I bet it is." There was more laughter.

"Fuck you, you cretin!"

Peter disconnected the phone call, trembling almost, as he clutched his cell phone tightly in his left hand. The cell phone began to ring again, momentarily. *Ring. Ring. Ring.* Peter was more than annoyed.

"What?" Peter screamed.

"Hey, how you doing?" Andrew answered, in a friendlier tone.

"I'm sorry," Peter answered, a little embarrassed. "I just had another call from…"

"Shit!" Andrew answered, interrupting, just above a whisper. "What did they say?"

"He… was talking about my father."

"Sick fuck. Try not to let him get to you. I know it's tough, today and all. I got your back, okay? Wherever you be, I will be."

Peter smiled, a little. He knew his best friend meant well. But it was too late. The killer, whoever it was, had already gotten to him. He had taken Mike away from him. And Robert.

"I'm just about to leave home now." Andrew continued. "Emily and I can swing by and pick you up before the service."

"Thank you. I'd like that."

"Great. We will see you soon."

The phone call disconnected, again. Peter dropped his cell phone on top of his bed. He tilted his head back, a little, staring up at the ceiling, covering his mouth with his right hand, a moment, feeling defeated again.

Peter lowered his head. He stood there, at the side of his bed, a moment, before reaching for his dress socks and underwear. Peter sat on the side of the bed, with the damp towel, still loosely fitted around his waist and pulled on his socks. He tugged at the damp towel and pulled on his underwear next. Peter finished getting himself dressed. It didn't take too long before he found himself back in the kitchen. Peter was now dressed and wearing a black jacket over the top of his long-sleeved white shirt and simple black tie. He also wore black trousers and black leather shoes, lace-ups, he hadn't worn, since his days working in New York City.

Peter was standing in the kitchen finishing off another glass of orange juice when the front doorbell rang. The television set in the living room was now switched off. Peter placed the near- empty glass in the bottom of the sink and made his way towards the front door. He could see the image of two figures standing behind the frosted glass of the front door. Peter leaned in and grabbed his keys and wallet off the table, by the front door. Peter opened the front door.

"Hey, you," Andrew answered, just above a whisper and with a warm smile. Peter smiled back, a little, looking at his best friend and his partner.

Peter sat in the back seat of Emily's car, staring out of the window, watching the world pass by. It was Emily's car, but Andrew was driving. Emily sat in the front passenger seat, her left hand reached out, and rested gently on top of Andrew's knee. He liked that when they drove together. It made him feel more connected to her. The radio was switched off. Andrew was dressed very similar to Peter. They could have almost been twins. Almost. Emily wore a simple dark grey dress which hugged her petite frame under a large black overcoat. Her make-up was simple. And she wore two small diamond stud earrings, which she only wore on special occasions. The earrings were a gift from her parents on her twenty-first birthday.

Peter continued to watch the world pass by. He watched the thick green trees covered in a thin layer of snow flicker past almost, as the car sped along the road. He felt numb. Peter turned his eyes from the window a moment, and looked forward, catching Andrew's eyes in the rear-view mirror. His eyes, Andrew's, seemed so friendly and warm. Peter nodded a little, as his right hand stretched forward, across the back seat of the car, his hand and forearm hugging the ball-shaped urn, which contained Mike's remains.

The car pulled off the road and steadily turned into the car park, just outside Lake Williams. Lake Williams was located not twenty minutes outside the Hillsboro town square. The grass along the lake appeared darker in colour as the morning sun reflected off the ground. A thin layer of snow dusted the grass. The lake itself was still frozen over, with patches showing signs of melting. The engine died. Andrew had pulled the vehicle into the closest parking spot he could find, closest to the lake. There were other cars parked in the parking lot, maybe a dozen, or more. Peter clutched the ball-shaped urn a little tighter a moment, as Emily and Andrew turned slightly, looking over their shoulders, back at their friend. Peter looked at them, as the hint of a smile surfaced to his lips.

"Are you ready, buddy?" Andrew asked softly, just above a whisper.

"Now, is good a time as any, I guess," Peter replied, taking a moment to himself before answering.

"Just know, we are here for you." Emily smiled, reassuringly. "Anything you need."

"Thank you."

Emily was the first to emerge from her car and stretch her legs, a little. She slammed the door behind her. Andrew was the next to climb out of the car, followed by Peter, holding the urn. Andrew peered over the roof of the car itself, looking at Peter, a moment. They didn't look at each other. Peter was hunched forward, a little, his head lowered, looking to the gravel beneath his feet. He lifted his head some, only seconds later, before leading the way, walking from the parking lot and over to the dirt trail which lead to the lake. Andrew joined Emily, taking her hand in his, and followed Peter towards the lake.

Lake Williams was quite busy mid-morning. Parents were pushing their children in strollers, there were people out jogging, and children running, screaming, playing ball in the park. Peter wasn't fazed by the commotion of the screaming children. He walked along the trail by the side of the lake, his eyes were now hidden behind black sunglasses to protect his eyes from the sun's reflection off the lake. There was another guest invited to the service. They were waiting further down the trail, a piece. It was Detective Quinn. He stood there, his eyes also hidden behind sunglasses. He was standing overlooking the lake, dressed in a dark grey suit, with a white shirt and matching grey tie and black leather lace-ups. His arms were resting by his side.

"Thank you for coming," Peter said, just above a whisper, as he cleared his throat a little. Detective Quinn turned to his left, some, making eye contact with Peter, Emily, and Andrew. "Of course," he replied, stretching out his right hand.

Peter looked down at his hand, a moment. He juggled the urn, a little, and shook the detective's hand.

Emily looked on, at the detective, a moment, shifting her eyes off of Peter. She stood there, clutching Andrew's hand a little tighter. Andrew noticed and looked down. He peered over, looking at Emily. They made eye contact, a moment. A smile surfaced to Andrew's lips before Emily returned her gaze to the detective. She was there for emotional support for her high school friend and her partner.

"I'm not the best with words," Peter continued. "So, how about we get to it, huh?"

"Of course." Emily smiled.

"When you're ready, buddy," said Andrew.

Detective Quinn stood there, shifting the weight of his frame over from his right foot to his left.

Emily took the lead. She let go of Andrew's hand and stepped closer toward Peter. She flashed a smile, for emotional support, and placed one hand on his right shoulder, and rested another hand on the small of his back. Emily pulled back. She stood beside him, turning her petite frame, a little, facing the lake. Peter looked back at his high school friend and smiled.

"Thank you," Peter replied, just above a whisper.

Andrew was next. He took his position, standing on the opposite side of Emily, turning to face the lake, too. Detective Quinn stood to Peter's right. The four of them formed one line, spaced out, facing the lake.

"I've known Mike Walters for a little time now," Peter started, "and in that time, he was a good man. Don't get me wrong. He wasn't perfect. No one is. He had his faults. But he did his best to support this community, and help out when he could. And today, I, we, stand here to help celebrate that. I remember Mike telling me once, that Lake Williams was the place he awkwardly kissed his first girlfriend, after school, one day. It was a Friday. Mike remembered the day because he plucked up the courage to ask the girl on a date to the movies for the Saturday. She said yes. Although her father said no, she was too young. That one kiss led them to date for a full two weeks. Lake Williams was the place Mike would come to, to ice skate as a kid, when he would try out for the ice hockey team in high school. And it was also the place where he took me on our first date. So, I thought it was only fitting that we come back here to say our goodbyes."

Peter turned his head, a little, and looked at his friends. Andrew was the first to look back. He nodded his head and flashed the hint of a smile. Emily remained poised, as ever, continuing to look out over the lake. Detective Quinn looked down at the snow on the grass, lost in his thoughts as if paying his respects in his own way. Peter opened the urn. He stood there a moment, before throwing Mike's remains out onto the lake. A moment of silence was followed. Peter stood there, quiet and strong, showing no signs of weakness or breaking down.

Mike Walters was gone. He returned to the town of Hillsboro from which he came. The service, as short as it was, began to break up. Detective Quinn was the first to leave. He paid his respects to Peter, with another handshake and a few kind words, before walking towards Andrew. The detective and the deputy shook hands also, before taking a few steps away from Emily and Peter, to discuss work. Emily could hear a few words mumbled from the detective about the investigation, off in the distance.

The conversation between Detective Quinn and Deputy Preston didn't last too long.

Detective Quinn made his way further down the trail, along the lake. Peter, Emily and Andrew stayed behind, watching him leave. The detective eventually disappeared as he made his way back to the parking lot. The lake seemed busier now. There were more screaming kids and single mothers pushing strollers. And joggers.

"Feel like grabbing a bite to eat?" Andrew asked first, breaking the silence.

"Thank you for the invite," Peter answered, looking at his best friend and his partner. "But I'm good. Honest. I think I will head home and hang around the house. There are a few things I got to get done, anyway."

"Well, you know where we are, if you need anything, day or night. Anything at all. I mean it." Emily responded, reaching out and giving Peter's left bicep a gentle squeeze.

"Thank you." Peter forced himself to smile.

Peter was the next to leave the lake, commencing his walk back to the parking lot, back to the car. "How do you think he's holding up?" Andrew asked Emily, just above a whisper.

"It's hard to tell," replied Emily. "As well as can be expected, I guess. Given the situation. He just said goodbye to another person he loved. Look at his life. Just tragic. He has no family."

"That's not true," Andrew answered, almost interrupting. "He has us!"

"Yes, he does," Emily answered, as she watched Peter walk further and further down the trail.

The day managed to escape Peter. He returned home after the service, with Andrew and Emily giving him a ride. The events of the day were nothing more than just a blur. The suit he wore to the service was back, hanging up in the closet. The jacket, the trousers, and the tie, all neatly packed away. And, so to, were the lace-up, black leather shoes. The long-sleeved white shirt was thrown in the laundry, left on top of the hamper, drenched in sweat, and ready to be washed, again.

Peter was in the living room. The lights and the television were switched off. Peter was stretched out on the couch, fast asleep, dressed in grey sweat pants and a black t-shirt with a print of the band, New Kids on the Block. His cell phone sat on the coffee table, bedside him. There was one missed text message. It was from Andrew. The fire was slowly dying, the embers fading. Peter began to move on the couch as if experiencing the start of a nightmare. He began to toss and turn, slowly at first, on top of the couch. There was the sound scratching, like the blade of a kitchen or hunting knife, tapping and scratching against the glass of a windowpane. The sound grew louder and louder now. A soft, but eerie voice whispered his name.

"Peter," the voice whispered.

Peter awoke from the nightmare, catching his breath in his throat, whilst clutching at his chest. He looked around the living room. The room was dark, except for the dying embers in the fireplace. The sun had set over the town of Hillsboro for another day. Peter sat up on the couch, a moment, still catching his breath. He turned on the couch, placing his feet on the floor. The carpet felt so cool against his bare feet. The sound of a blade scratching against glass started to grow louder and louder, again. Peter looked around the living room. He climbed to his feet and walked cautiously towards the windowpane, overlooking the front porch. It was dark and he was unable to make anything out. Peter raced to the front door. He opened it and stepped out onto the front porch with caution, clutching his door keys tightly in his hand. The sharp, jagged edges protruding through his fingers, like claws, ready to attack at a moment's notice. The light on the front porch switched on. The sound of the blade scratching against the glass continued. Peter stood there still, peering into the darkness, with his keys still in his hands. The sound of the blade scratching now stopped. Silence.

Peter looked confused, a little, for a moment. And there, stepping out of the darkness, appearing at the bottom of the porch, was the clown mask. The image stood there, with the hunting knife, gripped tightly in their left hand.

"What do you want?" Peter screamed. There was no answer.

The image of the clown mask raised their right hand, bound in a black leather glove, high enough to remove the clown mask from the hooded black sweater. The clown mask raised to reveal the face beneath.

"Mother?" Peter asked, just above a whisper.

The image was Sidney Green-Harmon. She stood there silent, the hood of the black sweater pushed back. Her hair tangled and a mess. The clown mask dropped to the front porch. Sidney raised the hunting knife, slowly in front of her, until it reached high above her shoulder. She stood there, standing silent, staring at her son, a moment. Sidney screamed, as loud as she could.

She raced towards Peter, her son, as he shifted the weight of his muscular frame, into an attack position, the sharp, jagged edges of the keys pointed outwards.

Peter awoke, again. He was back on the couch, clutching at his chest tightly, his torso dripped with sweat. He screamed. He screamed before realising where he was. He was safely back in his living room. He looked around the room quickly. The lights and the television set were still switched off. The embers from the fireplace were slowly burning, slowly dying. His hair soaking wet. It was silent, except for the panting of his breath and the tick of the clock which hung on the kitchen wall. *Tick tock. Tick tock. Tick tock.* Peter turned on the couch, placing his feet on the carpet below him. It still felt cool to the touch. His heartbeat was racing wildly, still.

"Shit!" Peter whispered, feeling a little embarrassed and wiping the sleep from his eyes.

He leaned forward, into the coffee table, reaching for his cell phone. The screen came to life. He saw the text message, awaiting him. He opened and read it.

I'm thinking of you, good buddy. Call me, anytime, if you need to talk.

The text message was from Andrew.

"No more nightmares," Peter whispered to himself.

The evening progressed further. It was now a little close to two in the morning. Peter was now in bed, asleep. He tossed and turned from under the bed cover, which was pulled high to his chest, and turned back to the waist. Peter was lying in bed on his back. His body shook quickly, his legs kicking at the bed cover. Peter awoke. He sat up in bed, using his pillow to support his lower back. He turned a little and looked at the time on the alarm clock on the nightstand. It was one forty-eight in the morning.

"Shit!" Peter whispered, again, as he lowered his head. "Fuck!"

Peter climbed out of bed. His feet touched the hardwood floors of the bedroom. He sat on the side of the bed, a moment, before leaning forward and reaching for his cell phone. He pulled it from the phone charger on the nightstand. He grabbed his wallet, too. Peter raced out of the bedroom, in the still of the night, down the hallway, down the staircase, and to the front door. He paused a moment, if only for a brief moment. Peter looked down at the door handle. He gripped it tightly in his hands. His eyes raised off the door handle and peered through the frosted glass. There was nothing there but sheer darkness.

"It was just a stupid nightmare," Peter whispered to himself.

Peter unlocked the front door and pushed heavily down on the door handle. He raced outside, past the front porch and to the garage, dressed only in a navy-blue t-shirt and an old pair of black shorts which were designated for wearing around the house only. Peter had his car keys in his hands. He made his way to his sports utility vehicle and climbed inside. The car door slammed shut behind him. Peter sat in the cold interior of his sports utility vehicle a moment, as he peered outward, and up at the front of his home. The car key turned in the ignition. The engine roared to life. Peter looked over his shoulder and slowly reversed out of the driveway and out on to the street. The sports utility vehicle turned and raced toward the end of the street.

Peter drove in the early hours of the morning, in the pitch darkness. The only light came from the headlights and the street lamps which hugged the corners of the road. Peter drove from his house to Mike's home. It took a little less than ten minutes.

The sports utility vehicle pulled off the road and into the driveway. It crept 'its way up closer to the front of the house before the engine died. The front lawn was manicured and kept clean. A For Sale sign was pitched in the front yard. That was news to Peter. A family member had placed the property on the market for sale only days after the service.

Peter remained seated behind the steering wheel of his sports utility vehicle. He sat there, peering out at the front of the house. The lights on the front of his truck were still switched on. Peter leaned into his steering wheel a little more, making himself comfortable. Peter remembered the good times with Mike. The memories came flooding back. Peter started to laugh, as he fought back his tears. Peter wiped the tears welling in his eyes with the back of his left hand just as quickly as the tears welled in his eyes. He sat there a moment longer, composing himself. He leaned back from the steering wheel now, back into the driver's seat.

"No more tears," Peter whispered to himself, clearing his throat and forcing himself to chuckle, some. "Goodbye, Mike Walters."

Peter leaned forward in his seat, again. He made himself comfortable, switching on the engine. The sports utility vehicle came to life sitting in the driveway. Peter looked over his shoulder once more and reversed out onto the street. Peter placed his foot heavily onto the accelerator and raced to the end of the road and made his way home.

The dawn was breaking over Hillsboro for the start of another day. There was no snow overnight. And what snow remained, was nothing more than a thinning layer which covered the front lawns and rooftops of the local neighbourhoods. However, it was still very chilly. Peter was dressed in his grey sweat pants with a black tank top and matching hoodie, which was zipped up from his waist to sternum. He was out for another jog this morning, still unable to get a full night's sleep. He wore his headphones, listening to his music collection. The street was bare, except for a nearby neighbour, taking their golden retriever for an early morning walk. Peter held his breath tightly in his throat a moment, before letting out one final burst of air, as he ran as fast as he could, along the footpath of his street, making his way up over the front lawn and onto the front porch.

Peter reached the front porch of his home in good time. He could feel his heartbeat racing wildly and the sweat dripping down his back. He collapsed onto the outdoor furniture, staring up at the ceiling, slowly catching his breath, again.

Peter continued to look up at the ceiling of the front porch as his breathing patterns were returning to normal. He used his hands to prop himself up off the furniture and climb to his feet. He could feel the nerve endings in his body ignite and course through his veins. They pulsated as he walked rather light-footed towards the front door. Peter searched for his keys and jiggled with the lock a little, before making his way inside the house. The front door to the house closed behind him. The lights in the foyer switched on. Peter unzipped his hoodie, peeling it from his tired and sweating torso, before dropping it to the floor, behind him. The tank top came next. Peter reached out for the banister, taking leaps in his steps as he climbed the staircase in just his sweat pants. He eventually made it to the second storey of the house, before turning right and making his way down the hallway towards the bathroom.

The door leading into the bathroom was also pushed to a close. The light in the ceiling flickered on. Peter stripped from his sweat pants and headed for the shower. The water ran from the faucet for a good minute or two, before it reached optimum temperature. Peter stepped inside the shower, under the hot water. It felt so inviting against his flesh. Peter leaned in forward toward the shower nozzle, feeling the beads of water splash against his face, his chest. He was feeling beaten after another morning run. The scars over his body, his back, his forehead and his hands, glistened almost under the water.

Peter soon switched the water off at the faucet and stood there a brief moment. He could feel the beads of water drip over his naked body. He turned and made his way out of the shower, grabbing a freshly folded towel from the bathroom wall, unfolding it, and wrapping himself in it.

Peter stood in front of the bathroom mirror, catching his reflection in the mirror, as he dried himself down. He stared at himself a moment, before wrapping the damp towel loosely around his waist.

Peter made his way out of the bathroom and down the hallway toward the master bedroom. The door was wide open. So were the curtains, to allow the light to creep inside the room. The bed was already made. And there was a small black, leather box sitting neatly at the end of the bed. He stood in the doorway of the master bedroom a moment, looking down at that black, leather box, before he made his way inside, toward the bed. He leaned in, picking up the box, opening it. And there, inside, was a gun. A new gun. It was a Ruger LCP. A subcompact pocket pistol. It was just enough to do enough damage if need be. Peter put the black leather box down on the bed, taking the pistol in his hands. It felt good in his hands. Peter gripped the pistol a little tighter. He extended his arms out, pointing the pistol at the wall in front of him.

"What's happening to me?" he muttered under his breath, just above a whisper.

The morning progressed. The gun was stowed and packed away safely, locked away in the bottom drawer of the nightstand next to the bed. Peter got himself dressed and made himself breakfast. He returned to his office and sat in front of his laptop computer, typing away on the keyboard, searching the Internet. He found himself thinking of Robert Prescott, and the days he would find him, sitting in his office, working away on his computer. It brought a fleeting smile to his lips, if just for a moment. The expression on his face soon fell flat. Peter scoured the Internet, typing the name, *Ben Prescott.*

There were newspaper articles and photographs of Ben Prescott from his days in college, in Southampton, enjoying family get-togethers, and of course, the clown mask. The search also brought up related articles, of his family, and of his sister, Carrie, and, of course, of his mother, Anne. Peter could feel his palms grow sweaty and his heartbeat starting to race. There was an article about Robert Prescott, about his remains found electrocuted in a bathtub. A loud, thumping noise came pounding from the front door. It brought Peter back to reality. His eyes shifted off the screen of the laptop computer, and across the office, out into the hallway. He blinked his eyes momentarily. The pounding on the front door continued. *Knock. Knock. Knock.* Peter was quick to close his laptop computer and make his way out of his office, down the hallway and the staircase.

"One second!" Peter called.

The knocking at the front door stopped. But the image standing on the other side of the front door, through the frosted glass, remained.

Peter reached the bottom of the staircase and made his way over to the front door. He leaned in and opened it. And there, standing in front of him, was Andrew. He was dressed in civilian clothing this morning; faded blue denim jeans, with a tear on the left knee and down the right outer leg. Peter didn't know if that was part of the design, or if Andrew needed some new clothes. He also sported a blood-red polo shirt, which hugged his muscular frame well and exposed his hairy chest, beneath.

"Andrew, what are you doing here?" Peter asked, a little concerned and surprised by his best friend. "We're we catching up?"

"You don't remember?" Andrew asked, just above a whisper. "It's the anniversary of your father's passing. I thought we would go and visit his grave site today. That is, of course, if you didn't have other plans?"

Peter was stunned. He stared at his best friend a moment, trying to gather his words and thoughts, and say something.

"You'd do that for me?" Peter asked.

"Of course," Andrew smiled, reassuringly.

Andrew was sitting behind the steering wheel of his truck, driving toward the cemetery.

Peter was sitting next to him. The windows on either side of the truck were cracked, just a little, to allow the cool morning breeze. The music on the radio was down low. It was something new, something topping the charts. Andrew paid little attention to the song. He was tapping his index finger of his left hand on the inside of the truck door. *Tap. Tap. Tap.*

"Thank you for doing this," Peter said, just above a whisper, as he cleared his throat, a little. "I knew it was my father's anniversary. I was going to make my way down to the cemetery later this afternoon."

"Not a problem," Andrew answered, rather upbeat, "my pleasure."

Andrew took his eyes off the road, for just a moment, and turned to look at Peter. There was a hint of a smile. "I always thought you had the coolest dad, growing up."

"You did?" Peter answered, rather surprised, "how so?"

"Uh-huh," Andrew nodded, "he always seemed so friendly, so happy, all the time. You could ask him anything. When you left Hillsboro and went off to make a life for yourself in New York City, I would visit your dad from time to time, when I needed to talk. Or on his anniversary, like today.

"Not every year, mind you. When we were kids, like thirteen or fourteen, he helped me with my own dad. I would talk to him about what it was like to come home from school and find him passed out in the living room or on the kitchen floor, with a bottle of beer spilt across the floor. Your dad was a great man."

Peter looked on in silence. Stunned, almost.

The truck soon pulled off the road and into the parking lot of the cemetery. There weren't that many people there, at a little after ten in the morning. There must have been around a dozen, maybe fifteen or so, cars parked in the lot. The truck pulled into the closest parking bay near the main office. The music on the radio cut out. The engine had died. And the two best friends sat there in the truck, a good minute or two, in silence, staring out at the cemetery in front of them. The layer of snow over the grass was starting to show signs of thinning out.

"Here we are," Andrew said, just above a whisper.

Peter unbuckled his seat belt and turned and faced his best friend. An awkward hint of a smile surfaced to his lips, a little. "This never gets any easier. I thought it would," he shrugged.

"It's your father. You love him. And he loved you. That's never gonna change."

Peter nodded silently.

Andrew was the first to make a move. He unbuckled his seat belt, turned a little and climbed out of the truck. Andrew stretched his legs and twisted from the waist, some. The driver's side truck door slammed shut. Peter was next to follow. He emerged from the front passenger side of the truck and slammed the door to close behind him. He stood there a moment, turning a little, to look back at his best friend, on the other side of the truck, then gaze upon the cemetery grounds.

The morning breeze was showing signs of dying down now and the sun began to burn brightly. Peter left the parking lot and headed toward his father's burial site, with his best friend following behind. Andrew gazed upon all the other burial sites of the local townspeople who had passed away over the years, some elderly, and some quite young, grandmothers, grandfathers, parents and children. They were all here. This was the place for the people of Hillsboro to say their goodbyes and farewells. Andrew walked behind his best friend, his right hand almost floating over the top of the tombstones of the deceased.

"Here we are," Peter said, just above a whisper, as he turned to face Andrew, over his left shoulder. Peter looked down at the tombstone, crouching down some, to run his left hand over the lettering of his father's name, clearing away some of the debris. "Hey, Dad. It's me. It's Peter."

"Hey, Mr Harmon," Andrew said, just above a whisper.

Andrew stood behind Peter, standing there, his hands in his trouser pockets. "I know he can't hear me. I wanted to be polite and say hello. I'll give you some time with your Dad." Andrew turned a little, ready to walk away.

"Wait!" Peter called out. "You can stay."

Andrew paused in his tracks and turned, again, to face Peter. "Are you sure?" he asked.

"Of course," Peter replied. "I mean, he meant a lot to you, too. I don't want to take that away from you."

"Thank you." Andrew smiled.

Peter turned on his best friend and faced his father's tombstone.

"I can't believe it's been nine years already, Dad," Peter started. "I miss you. And need you. So much. Life… just sucks right now. It's happening again. The clown mask. This town. The memories of Mother. You know who she was, what she was capable of. Grandfather, and all. Them. I just wish you were here to help me." Peter stopped a moment, to clear his throat.

Peter returned home from the cemetery. He made his way up to the front porch of his home, as his left hand fished through his jacket pocket, searching for his front door keys. He turned and faced Andrew, one final time, as he sat behind the steering wheel of his truck, parked in the driveway with the motor running. Peter raised his right hand and waved, watching his best friend reverse out of his driveway, and out onto the street. Andrew pressed the horn on his truck a couple of time, two, maybe three, as he raced to the end of the street. Peter turned his back on his best friend and made his way to the front door. He could hear the floorboards under his feet bend, under the pressure.

Peter found the right key and slid it into the lock of the front door, and with a twist of the hand, the key turned and unlocked. He pushed down on the door handle and made his way inside the house, disarming the alarm and closing the front door behind him. The sun from the late morning crept inside the house, along the floorboards inside the foyer, and into the living room. The silence, which consumed the house, broke as the cell phone began to ring. *Ring. Ring. Ring.* Peter searched his other jacket pocket. He retrieved the cell phone from his right pocket.

Caller Unknown.

"What do you want?" Peter answered, annoyed. His tone of voice fell flat.

"Happy anniversary, Peter," the dark and familiar voice answered. "Your mother killed your father nine years ago today. How does it feel?"

"Fuck you!"

"Listen to you, huh?" the dark and familiar voice answered, louder, a little annoyed, a little angrier. "Such a potty mouth! You would have been such a disappointment to your mother if she could have heard you speak like that."

"I had no mother!" Peter snapped, as he walked from the foyer of the front of the house, and into the living room, toward the glass, overlooking the front yard. "My mother was nothing more than a sadistic serial killer. She was just the woman who gave birth to me. That woman was incapable of being a mother. Fuck this! And fuck you! This ends. Now! No cops and no more games. And no more fucking masks! You want me, motherfucker? Come and get me!"

"I'll come for you soon enough. I can promise you that. In the meantime, I think I might play a game with one of your friends. You can't save them all. All you can do is stand back and watch!" the voice started to laugh, almost hysterically.

The phone line disconnected.

Chapter Twenty-Two...

The day crept onward. It was just past midday. Peter was at home, hard at work, in one of the spare, upstairs bedrooms, clearing out the contents he had amassed over the weeks, months and years, which he had carried with him to Hillsboro. The curtains to the bedroom were pulled wide open, allowing the afternoon sun to fill the inside of the room. It felt light and warm. The spare bedroom was filled with boxes, contents he forgot he owned. Peter was on his knees foraging through large, brown cardboard boxes. There were CD's and records, photographs and notebooks, a collection of a life in progress.

"What was I thinking?" Peter whispered to himself, as he looked at some of the album covers, placing them back in the box, upside down, almost embarrassed, laughing to himself.

It was the first time in a while Peter found himself laughing, as small as it was. It was a start.

The cell phone sat by the window, on top of an old desk, something a high school student might use to do their homework. There was music playing on the cell phone. It was loud and it filled the room. It was upbeat and happy. Peter climbed from his knees and onto his feet, as he started to drag the cardboard boxes out of the bedroom. And, over time, the bedroom grew more and more empty as the afternoon progressed. The contents of the boxes were divided into two piles, *keep* and *throw away*.

The spare bedroom was empty now. Well, almost. Peter stood in the middle of the bedroom, his hands supporting his lower back, as he looked around the room. The room was warm, and he developed a thin layer of sweat which covered his forehead and chest, some. The cell phone continued to play music. The surface of the desk was scattered with red push pins, and a clipboard hung from the wall.

"Done," Peter whispered to himself.

Peter collected his cell phone from the desk. The music stopped abruptly, mid song. There were no missed calls or text messages.

It didn't take too long for Peter to freshen up. He left the spare bedroom behind and soon found himself sitting behind the steering wheel of his sports utility vehicle. He left home and was on his way into town. More specifically, to the Hillsboro Community Public Library. The drive took no more than fifteen minutes. Peter pulled his truck into the parking lot. The engine quickly died as he climbed out of the truck, locking the door behind him and setting the alarm, as he made his way inside the building.

The library was filled with residents, there would have been twenty, closer to thirty, spread out, across the spacious desks in the front of the library, reading, studying, and quietly going about their daily lives. Peter made his way inside the library and walked directly over to the information desk. A middle-aged man, somewhere in his mid- to late-forties, with a portly frame, sat in front of a desktop computer, typing away on the keyboard. The man was dressed in a white cotton, long-sleeved shirt that was tucked almost awkwardly into his black trousers. The shirt was buttoned almost to the top, leaving the top button undone, exposing his chest beneath.

"Good afternoon, sir," the man said, just above a whisper, "and how can I assist you today?"

"I am hoping you can assist me. I am looking for some information," Peter replied, lowering his voice to match the man's behind the counter. "I am looking for old newspaper articles from nine years ago."

The man looked at Peter a moment, eyeballing him, his eyes up and down. He then proceeded to adjust his reading frames, a little.

"You will be wanting journals," the man responded. "Over the years, we have done our very best to look after and maintain our microfiche. I can have a colleague show you if you like?"

"Thank you." Peter smiled.

It was only a few minutes before another librarian, a young girl, who didn't look a day over twenty-two, with a petite frame and an almost sleek, long, blonde ponytail pulled back and away from her face, directed Peter around the library and over to the microfiche machine. She pointed out the journals catalogued year by year, before offering him a little privacy, leaving him to his own devices and closing the door behind her. The room itself was plain, to say the least. The walls were painted an off-white colour with basic lighting hanging from the ceiling.

"Great," Peter muttered to himself.

Peter was eager to make a start. He switched on the microfiche machine, before making his way over to the journals. He pulled at the set of mahogany drawers rather gently, cautious not to disturb them more than he wanted. His eyes perused the journals. There were so many records. Peter clutched at a handful of the microfiche and placed them on the desk, by the side of the machine. He searched the records, looking, hoping for an answer. It took a little over fifteen minutes before he found what he was looking for.

"There you are," Peter mumbled to himself. "I found you."

And there it was, staring back at him. It was various pictures of his mother, in various acts of distress. There were photographs of Sidney being taken into custody, under arrest by local law enforcement, and led away in a squad car. There were photographs of her during her days in court. And, of course, photographs of his father, grandfather and the home-made clown mask, something she had created with her father. Peter took the information and made copies.

The drive home seemed faster than it had been to the library. The roads seemed almost bare in the mid-afternoon. Peter drove home with music blaring from the radio, the windows down. A single, manila file sat next to him, on the front passenger seat of the sports utility vehicle. Peter looked down at it from time to time, as he did his best to maintain eye contact on the road in front of him. It didn't take too long for Peter to arrive home. The truck pulled into the driveway, just outside the garage before the engine died. Peter grabbed the manila file and climbed out of the truck, making his way to the front of the house, inside his home.

The front door to the house was quick to close behind him, as Peter made his way back to the top of the staircase, and soon found himself back in the same, near-empty bedroom. The curtains were still pulled open. Peter walked across the room, the floorboards, cracking under pressure, a little, and placed the manila file on top of the desk, standing in front of the clipboard. Peter looked down at the manila file before opening it. He stared at a photocopy of the clown mask. He picked up the single sheet of paper, pulling it in for a closer inspection, looking at the design, the curves of the mask, itself. His eyes grew angry. In the days since Mike's death, it had changed him. Yet again.

The photograph of the clown mask was the first to be pinned to the clipboard. The red pins punched through the A-4 size paper, holding it to the wall. The photocopy of the clown mask took centre stage. The photocopies of the photographs took their turn in being pinned to the clipboard. A photograph of his mother followed next, then his grandfather. A photograph of his father was the last to be pinned on the clipboard. A hint of a smile, as tough as it was, surfaced to Peter's lips. He could feel his heart starting to race, feeling somewhat nervous, again. Peter pinned the photograph of his father upon the clipboard, away from his mother, somewhere to the right side of the clipboard, and away from the clown mask.

"My family tree," Peter whispered under his breath.

He took a step back from the clipboard. It was a collage, a collection of gruesome photographs. The state of newspaper aged over time, allowing the ink to run over the photographs themselves, a little, hiding some of the brutality of the wounds inflicted. At the top of the photographs, above them all, was a quote from Sidney, something she had said during her trial.

"All good children do as they're told. They follow what their parents tell them, without question, without pretence. Just love."

"Who exactly *were* you, Mother?" Peter asked himself.

Chapter Twenty-Three…

The neon lights of the winter carnival glowed against the backdrop of a cool night's sky. It was mid-January and the celebrations into the new year continued with the proud tradition of the Hillsboro Winter Carnival. The winter carnival arrived in Hillsboro during the second week of January and stayed for ten days as had happened for the past thirty-two years and counting. The tradesmen, the men and women who put the carnival together, and put on a show, rented out the rooms of the motel on the outskirts of town during their stay. It brought in much-needed tourist dollars to the sleepy, country town.

The children screamed as the roller coaster roared high into the night' sky. The screams quickly turned into laughter just seconds later. The Winter Carnival was busy. It was opening night. The mayor gave a speech. He was a rotund man in his early fifties who sported a neatly trimmed beard, which was a rich brown, whilst wearing a paperboy hat, which covered his balding scalp. His attire for the evening included a full-length black cashmere coat which hugged his portly frame from neck to ankle, almost, as he waved his hands about, cheering on the crowd. He stood upon his soapbox, welcoming the townspeople in front of the local media, asking them to enjoy taking part in the evening's festivities.

The grounds were packed with children and families, all enjoying the fun and festivities of the night. Andrew, Emily and Peter were there, too. Andrew thought it would be a good distraction for Peter, something to switch his mind off, if only for the evening, and a date night with Emily. It was a win-win situation. Andrew was dressed in a bomber jacket, denim jeans and black leather boots as he held Emily's hand, walking around the park. Emily was dressed quite similarly, in a black puffer jacket to keep her petite frame warm, accompanied with a simple, black knitted scarf, which hung from her shoulders, denim jeans and riding boots, which rose high to her knees. Peter kept it simple, dressed in a leather jacket hoodie, which was zipped from waist to sternum, exposing a simple t-shirt underneath, with jeans and sneakers.

The carnival attractions caught Emily's eye. She was attached to the nearby children, who were all lined up in single formation, holding water guns, racing to fill their balloons the fastest. The fastest won the prize. The entry cost was only three dollars. As the children played the game, their friends and parents stood nearby, some cheering them on, whilst others took delight in the carnival menu of cotton candy, hot dogs on sticks dipped in sauces and soda-pop. Emily clutched at Andrew's right hand a little firmer, pulling him toward the attraction. She peered on as the current game was underway.

"I just love this game," Emily said, unable to hide her smile. "My dad would always let me play when I was a little girl."

Andrew turned his head a little, watching the game.

The sound of a balloon popping filled the air, which was followed by a splash of water falling to the ground. The audience cheered.

"We have a winner!" the game clerk shouted, walking toward a young girl, no older than twelve. "And what would you like, little girl?"

"Ummm," answered the young girl in a light pink dress and matching jacket with chocolate-brown hair in red ribbons. The girl looked over her left shoulder, back at her parents and older brother a moment.

"Go on," said her mother, with a smile, "you won. You get to pick a prize."

A smile came to the young girl's lips. She was quick to turn her back on her mother and face the game clerk, again.

"Ummm," she continued, "I want a giant teddy bear."

"One giant teddy bear for the young girl. Congratulations, kid! Well done!"

The size of the overstuffed teddy bear was too big for the young girl to carry on her own. The game clerk took the teddy bear, which sat in the far-right corner, in front of all the other toys and prizes hanging on the wall, and handed it to the young girl's father.

Peter looked on at the young girl and her family collect the prize. He smiled at the parents, being polite, as the family turned away from the game, and walked away, as they explored other parts of the carnival. The other children playing the game placed their water guns back in their respective holsters and walked away, whilst some of them handed over another three dollars and tried their luck again.

"This looks like fun," Peter said, getting Emily's attention.

She turned and faced her high school friend, with that same friendly smile of hers.

"But I am going to let you guys enjoy your date night, and quit being the third wheel for the evening, and go check out this winter carnival. You know, I can't remember the last one I went to. You guys have fun. I will check in on you later in the evening."

"Are you sure?" asked Andrew, a little concerned.

"Of course. Absolutely. I'm going to walk around and see what this carnival has to offer."

"Thank you," answered Emily.

"I'll check in with you, later on, good buddy," smiled Andrew.

"No worries," answered Peter.

Peter turned and walked off, heading deeper into the carnival, past all the other townspeople.

Emily and Andrew stayed behind. Emily squeezed Andrew's right hand a little tighter, again, as a smile appeared on her face. They turned and watched another game play out. Peter made his way through the crowds, taking in the sights of the carnival, listening to the cheers of the crowd, the laughter, and parts of nearby conversations. The smell of the food filled the air. It reeked of batter and oil. Peter stood in front of the roller coaster. He watched it climb higher and higher into the night's sky before it dropped, plummeting down to Earth again. The laughter followed the screams, again. The queue lining up for the roller coaster was quite long. And at the front of the queue, it had a sign which read, "You Must Be This Tall To Ride This 'Coaster".

A smile surfaced to Peter's lips as quick as it began to fade. He was soon losing interest in the roller coaster and carried on throughout the carnival. A line of children and adults queued for the Gravatron, which was a high-speed ride shaped like a flying saucer. The doors opened, allowing the ticketholders inside. Once inside, each patron ran towards the padded walls and leaned against them. The flying saucer would then start to spin, growing faster and faster, as the neon lights inside flashed. The centrifugal force generated by the speed of the ride held the patrons against the walls, and they screamed and laughed, as they tried their best to climb against the walls as gravity fought against them.

Peter soon found himself leaving behind the flashing neon lights and the cheers and laughter of the winter carnival and headed towards the parking lot, for quiet more than anything else. A group of teens, maybe four or five, and all no older than sixteen or seventeen began to follow. The neon lights seem to grow further and further off in the distance with each passing step towards the parking lot, growing darker and darker. Peter could finally hear himself think.

"Hey!" a young voice called out.

Peter was in his little world, walking further into the parking lot. "You!" the young voice called out, again, "I'm talking to you!"

Peter stopped in his tracks and turned to face the voice. And, there, standing in front of him, were the five teens, all of various shapes and sizes, staring back at him.

"Yes?" Peter asked.

"We know who you are." continued the young voice.

"And?" Peter asked. "You want a prize or something? You're looking in the wrong place. You'll want the carnival for that."

"Listen to the mouth on this one," said another adolescent boy.

"I think he is giving you sass."

"I think you might be right, Randy."

"Look! I don't want any trouble. I am here with some friends, that is all. You go about your business and, like everyone else, have a good time."

A switchblade was quick to appear in the young boy's right hand. The sound of the blade, expelled from its handle flashed, gleaming a little in the night' sky.

"Like I said. I don't want no trouble," Peter continued, as his eyes were drawn to the blade.

"We know all about you and what you mean to this town, faggot! Your mother should have killed you when she had the chance."

There were a few laughs from the other kids, in the background. "Yeah!" some of them agreed.

Peter looked at the young boy with the switchblade gripped tight in his right hand. His face was stone and emotionless.

"Really?"

"Yeah."

"Ah, I see," Peter nodded. "Well, let's see what you're made of, huh? 'Do you think I won't hit a young kid?"

"You can't!" the boy boasted, almost proudly. "I'm a minor. You'll get your faggot-ass thrown in jail."

"Not, in self-defence, you piece of shit!"

"Fuck you!"

The young adolescent who gripped the switchblade charged at Peter rather ferociously, and with great speed. Peter stepped backwards, a little, taking a self-defence stance, keeping his eye on the blade. The other children also charged at Peter, some laughing, but more so just watching on, as it all played out.

The blade of the knife swiped at Peter, a few times, two, maybe three. It cut through the cool, thin air, making no contact. The other children laughed and cheered on their friend.

"Everyone knows you're a faggot!" yelled the boy in anger and frustration. "And they just can't wait to get rid of you."

"Go ahead, if you have the guts!"

The switchblade took another strike at Peter, again. This time, the blade made contact, slicing at his left palm. The flesh tore and the blood poured from the wound rather fast. Peter flinched a little, stepping back further, clutching his hand tightly, doing his best to conceal the wound and the pain.

"Fuck!" Peter shouted.

The bloodstained blade was quick to take another swipe. It missed, again. Peter kept his eye on the switchblade, kicking it from the boy's hand. It fell to the gravel below.

"You fucking cunt!" the kid yelled, "'you'll pay for that."

The boy charged at Peter, again. His friends followed, again. But, this time, the adolescent made further contact. He tightened his left hand and threw a punch. His fist made contact, punching Peter in the jaw. It startled Peter, a little, knocking him off his feet, some. He fell backwards, stumbling, trying to find his balance. He did. Just. And then, there followed another blow. The adolescent kicked at Peter, kicking him in his stomach, and this time, pushing him, knocking him backwards. Peter lost his balance altogether, as he fell to the gravel of the parking lot.

Feeling winded, he clutched at his stomach, with his free hand, whilst gasping for air, feeling the pain course throughout his entire body. Peter released the grip from his bloodied hand. The blood continued to pour. It looked almost purple in the colour of the night.

The adolescent stood over Peter, watching him writhe on the ground in pain and agony. He wiped his nose with the back of his left hand, catching his breath a little. There were beads of sweat glistening on his forehead. His friends stood behind him, almost forming a semi-circle, looking on, watching what would come next.

"Do it!" said one boy.

"Yeah!" said another.

"Where is my knife?" the adolescent demanded, looking over his shoulder.

"What?" asked one of his friends.

"My knife? Where is my fucking knife?"

The friends were quick to search the grounds, in a hurry to find it. They were like scouring animals. The adolescent turned his torso, to the left, ever so slightly, watching his friends scour the darkness of the parking lot, as Peter clutched his stomach tightly, slowly, climbing back to his feet, and gripping his bloodied hand tightly. The pain of the wound was written all over his face. Peter started to laugh, a little, and a little out of breath, as he could feel the sting of the knife.

"You fucking prick!" Peter said, just above a whisper.

The adolescent turned and faced Peter. He was surprised to see him standing on his feet in front of him. He stood a small step back as if to assess his damage.

"You think you are a tough guy, huh?" Peter spat on the ground, as he raced his tongue of two loosened teeth, tasting the blood inside his mouth. "I know what you are, and what you will always be. You're nothing. You're shit!"

"Fuck you!"

"There you go. Shooting off your ugly words. I was right. You're nothing! And always will be." Peter started to laugh, as he stood there in pain.

"Let's finish this."

"Fuck you, you worthless piece of shit!"

The adolescent charged at Peter with such ferocity, screaming angrily, which amalgamated from the bottom of his stomach, rising, and out from his lips. Peter took a step backwards, taking another self-defence stance. He tightened the grip of his right hand, held his breath as chewed on his lower lip, a little, while he threw his punch forward. It connected with the adolescent. Peter felt the bones in his hand crunch against the young boy's jaw. The sound, he couldn't get out of his head. The sound of bone on bone, as if cracking under the pressure.

The adolescent boy fell backwards, clutching his face in pain. He writhed on the gravel of the parking lot. And as angry and hurt as he was, was unable to hide the tears that welled in his eyes. He screamed. Some of his friends raced towards him, helping him climb to his feet, whilst others stood by and watched on in awe.

"It's kids like you that I wish I could wake up from," Peter said, just above a whisper. "It's kids like you that have been my fucking nightmare my entire life. This is it. We are done. I'm not going anywhere. I grew up in this town. You see me in the street, you turn and walk away. You say nothing. Are we clear?"

The kids looked on in shock and horror.

"Are we clear?" Peter asked again, this time raising his voice.

"Yes!" a few nervous voices answered back.

"Good!"

Peter clutched at his stomach tightly, again. He began to limp towards the kids, slowly passing them, walking towards the winter carnival, again, towards the flashing, neon lights, and out of the darkness. He limped slowly, spitting on the ground once more, as he passed the kids. Peter found the switchblade on the ground. The blade of the knife was still bloodied, but dirty from the debris of the gravel. He kicked it with his left foot, to his right, down a small ravine.

"You're shit! And I win!" Peter continued limping slowly.

Andrew and Emily continued with their date. They were standing amongst the other townspeople, outside the fun house. Andrew gazed upon the fun house, almost in awe and amazement, and with a lot of curiosity.

"I hate the look of that thing," Emily said, just above a whisper, as she too, looked at the queue of people, waiting to make their way inside the fun house.

"Really?" Andrew asked, a little surprised. "I think it's fun. Kind of scary, even. A real thrill to get the heart pumping."

"Yeah?" Emily asked, disinterested. "Well, while you go and get your heart pumped, I'll be waiting for you over by the food shack with some cotton candy and a Diet Coke," she laughed.

"Come with me?" Andrew asked, almost pleading with her. "It'll be a blast. Something fun. Something you'll remember for time to come. I promise."

Emily looked at her beau, searching his eyes. She could see the pleading in his eyes. "Fuck no!" she answered. "You're on your own!"

"I thought you were better than that. A fun house? Really?" a voice asked.

"Listen to your girl. They are nothing more than things of nightmares and cheap thrills."

Andrew turned his gaze, past Emily, over her right shoulder. The gazed expression turned to concern and horror.

"What the fuck?" Andrew asked, just above a whisper.

"Fucking kids!" Peter answered, spitting blood from his mouth, again. "What... *happened* to you?" Emily asked, struggling to find her words.

"Let's just say, I gave as good as I got." Peter limped towards his friends in pain.

"Let's get you to a doctor," Andrew shouted, racing towards his friends, helping him balance on his feet.

"No! No!" Peter answered. "Not for me. Just get me out here. Take me home, please."

"Oh shit!" Emily shouted. "You're bleeding!" she cried, watching the blood drip to the ground beneath him, from his left hand.

"It's nothing more than a flesh wound. I'll be fine. Promise."

"Are you sure?" asked Andrew.

"Trust me." Peter forced a smile.

"Let's get you home," Emily said, just above a whisper.

She raced toward Peter, standing on his other side, as they helped him out of the fare ground and back towards the parking lot.

Peter looked over his shoulder, at the fun house. "I hate fun houses.

They are creepy as all fuck!"

The drive home from the winter carnival was done in almost silence. The radio in the car was switched off. The heater was switched on, to battle the cool night air. Peter found himself sitting in the back seat of Emily's car once more, peering out the window, watching the street lamps on the side of the street zip past like a blur. Emily was sitting behind the steering wheel, her eyes focused on the road in front of her. Andrew sat in the front passenger seat. His left hand crept slowly across, towards Emily, resting on her knee, giving it a slight squeeze, to let her know he was thinking of her. Still, she remained focused on the road ahead.

Peter gazed upon the night sky through the passenger window. There was still not much to see, as Emily drove several kilometres faster, over the designated limit. Peter pulled his gaze inside the car. His eyes looked forward, into the rear-view mirror, where he was met by Andrew, staring back at him. His eyes seemed friendly enough. Andrew smiled a little, nodding his head, some.

It didn't take long for Peter to arrive home. Emily pulled into the driveway, leaving the engine running.

"This is me," Peter said, just above a whisper. "Thank you again for the ride."

"Anytime," Emily replied, quite sweetly, as she looked at her high school friend through the rear-view mirror. "I'll call you in a day or two. See how you're doing, you know?"

"Great." Peter smiled.

"Home sweet home, good buddy," said Andrew, as he turned in his seat, looking back at his best friend. "Are you sure you are going to be okay?"

Peter looked at Andrew and saw the smile across his face.

"I will. And thanks again, to you both," said Peter, as he shifted the weight of his frame and climbed out of the back seat of the car.

Emily sat still, behind her steering wheel, with the floodlights of her car switched on, using them more so as a torch, giving Peter light to find his way to the front door of his home. Peter slammed the car door to a close and followed the pathway, up to the front porch, up to the front door, itself, whilst he searched for his keys in his jacket pocket. The lock to the front door jiggled a little before Peter pushed down on the door handle and made his way inside the house. But, not before turning, to face the lights of the car, turning to face his friends, and giving them one last final wave goodbye for the evening. Peter made his way inside, disappearing behind the closed door.

Emily reversed out of the driveway and out on to the street. The floodlights which sprayed across the front of the house, grew smaller and smaller as it made its way out of the driveway.

Peter switched the lights on in the foyer of the house. He made his way up the staircase, before turning and walking down the hallway, towards the bathroom. The door to the bathroom remained open. Peter walked in and switched on the light. It flickered on. He made his way inside, walking up to the washbasin. He emptied his pockets and placed his wallet and cell phone on the side of the washbasin. Peter leaned in and switched on the faucet. The hot water started to run. Peter flinched a little more, as he opened up his left hand some, and pulled at the tissues used to conceal the wound. There were two tissues balled up. Emily gave them to Peter in the car. The white tissues had turned red. The hot water from the faucet continued to run. The water level was increasing now. Peter kept his hand open, as he lowered it into the basin, lowering it beneath the surface of the water. The heat of the water was tremendous. The flesh wound opened some, and the colour of the water was quick to turn shades of red. Peter screamed.

The scream echoed throughout the bathroom, bouncing off the walls, and escaped down the hallway. His eyes rose from the washbasin a moment, catching his reflection, as he turned off the water. The last of the water dripped from the faucet. *Drip. Drip. Drip.* The blood continued to pour from the wound, a little. His fingers on his left hand flinched, some. Peter diverted his eyes off of his reflection and opened the cabinet to retrieve some bandages. Peter placed his supplies on the side of the washbasin, by his wallet and cell phone, closed the cabinet, once more and pulled his hand out of the washbasin. Peter tended to the wound, taking several minutes to plaster it and wrap his left hand firmly in another bandage. He wiggled his fingers on his left hand, just a little, to allow for free circulation. Peter raised his eyes from the bandage around his left hand and caught his reflection, once more. He stood there a moment, taking his time to unzip his jacket and drop it on the surface of the washbasin. Peter removed his t-shirt next. And there, in the reflection, were the starting signs of a growing bruise, across his ribs and stomach. It was tender to the touch. Peter flinched.

"Shit!" he whispered to himself.

It was then, the cell phone on the side of the washbasin began to ring. *Ring. Ring. Ring.* It was an Unknown Caller. Peter looked down at the cell phone. The expression on his face was solemn.

"Hello?" Peter asked, answering the call.

"Hello, Peter," the dark and familiar voice, answered.

"What do you *want*?"

"It's always been you. Peter Harmon is victim royalty, don't you know? The world was first introduced to Peter Harmon as an innocent teenager and his bloodstained family nine years ago. Then, a few more years pass by, and the world catches up with Peter once more as a sophomore in college. And then again, as an adult. You couldn't die... Until now. All things come to an end, Peter Harmon. And that includes you! Your time is coming up. You had to know this day would come? That someone like me would eventually outsmart someone like you?"

"Ah, I see," Peter answered, almost sarcastically. "Fuck you!"

"You're not taking me seriously, are you? There will be consequences for your incompetence. Maybe I should call on one of your little friends? Maybe *they* would like to play with me?"

"You leave them alone. Do you see? I do take you seriously." Peter answered, almost in a panic. "I do!" he repeated. "You want me, then let's end this. Now! Come and get me."

The dark and familiar voice started to laugh.

"Tick, tock Peter, I'll see you soon enough, I can promise you that. But, in the meantime, I might have a little fun with a friend or two. You can't save them. All you can do is see who drops next." The phone line disconnected.

"Fuck!" Peter screamed, again.

The day ended in Hillsboro. The night sky was black as a cold breeze swept over the town, bringing with it, a thin layer of snow. The branches in the trees shook from left to right, a little, as the leaves rustled in the wind. The light from the front living room could be seen from the porch. Andrew was home, alone. He was dressed in civilian attire for the evening, having come off a tiresome day shift. He was dressed in a simple red polo shirt and denim jeans and barefoot.

Andrew was in the living room. The television set was switched on, the volume down low.

And there were copies of movies, three, maybe four, all on Blu-ray, sitting on top of the coffee table. Andrew had a bottle of beer in his right hand. He was slowly nursing it, taking a sip here, and there. The bottle was beading as it thawed from the refrigerator. Andrew walked across the living room, making his way throughout the house, reaching the hallway, and back into the kitchen. The lights in the kitchen were switched on. A wooden bowl sat upon the counter, filled with microwave popcorn, traditional butter flavour, fresh out of the microwave, cooling off a little.

Andrew walked into the kitchen and reached for the bowl, taking another sip of his beer.

The bowl lifted from the kitchen counter when the front doorbell began to buzz. *Buzz. Buzz.*

The bowl filled with popcorn and the bottle of beer was placed back up on the kitchen counter. Andrew peered forward, his face filled with concern, a little. He felt his heart flutter, if just for a moment. A smile soon surfaced to his lips, if just for a moment. Andrew made his way out of the kitchen and toward the front of the house, toward the front door.

Fade to black. Fade from black.

Andrew leaned into the front door of his house, his left hand leaning forward onto the door handle. He squeezed it a little. His warm hand felt the cool of the brass. Andrew turned the door handle, pulling the front door open. And there in front of him, was no one. The front porch was empty. Another concerned expression fell upon his face.

"What the?" he muttered, just above a whisper.

Andrew stepped out onto the front porch, leading with his left foot. His bare feet touched the cool wooden floorboards beneath, as his toes wriggled a little. The light to the front porch switched on. Andrew stepped out further, peering into the darkness of his front yard. There was no one there. The concerned expression quickly dropped, which was followed by a boyish smile. Andrew walked to the end of the front porch, reaching for his cell phone in his denim pocket. He looked at the screen. There were no missed phone calls or text messages.

"Fucking kids these days," Andrew muttered again.

Andrew turned his back, shifting the weight of his frame, and made his way back inside his house. The floorboards of the front porch cracked under the pressure, a little. Andrew reached the front of his house, walking back inside and closing the door behind him. The lights on the front porch switched off.

Fade to black. Fade from black.

Andrew shook his hands, down by his side a little. It was his way of warming up some, and he made his way from the front of the house, down the hallway, and back into the kitchen. The bowl of popcorn and a bottle of beer were still there, untouched. Andrew walked over to the refrigerator, pulled on the door and leaned in for another bottle of beer. There were four remaining on the top shelf. The glass bottles rattled a little, as the refrigerator door pulled open. A second noise broke the silence, this time coming from the ceiling. Andrew lifted his eyes, above the contents of the refrigerator, looking up at the ceiling, a little perturbed.

"Fucking rats! I got you this time, you little motherfuckers!" another mutter.

Andrew stood tall and slammed the refrigerator door to a close. He could hear the beer bottles rattle, again. He walked out of the kitchen and turned right into the hallway, making his way toward the back of the house. He reached the end of the hallway, taking another right, heading toward the laundry. And, there, in front of him, Andrew caught his breath in his chest. The back door to the house was wide open. A cold breeze carried into the house. Andrew stood there staring out into his back yard, his left hand covering his mouth as he felt his heartbeat racing wildly in his chest.

"Fuck!" he muttered, just above a whisper.

Andrew turned, leaving the open back door, untouched. He tiptoed down the hallway and toward the kitchen. The image of the clown mask appeared behind him, unnoticed at the end of the hallway. The white, the blue and the red of the mask almost gleamed under the hallway light, as it stared lifelessly ahead.

Fade to black. Fade from black.

The top kitchen drawer slid open, as quietly as it could. The cutlery rattled some. There were butter knives, spoons, and forks, etc.

"Shit!" Andrew whispered under his breath.

The kitchen drawer slid to a close. Andrew turned in his tracks, searching the kitchen, looking for something, anything he could use to fight back. A large kitchen knife sat by the side of the sink. Andrew reached for it, clutching it tightly in his right hand.

"I got you now, motherfucker!" he whispered again.

Andrew turned his back on the kitchen and made his way to the hallway. He held his breath and closed his eyes tightly, if just for a moment, as he continued to clutch the handle of the kitchen knife. He opened his eyes slowly and leaned forward, a little, and as quiet as he could, peering left and right. There was no one there. Andrew could feel his heartbeat starting to race wildly, again. His palms growing sweaty.

"I hate this shit!" he whispered to himself.

Andrew took a left and made his way down the hallway, toward the front of the house, again. He crept forward. The silence quickly broke. The sound of heavy feet running throughout the house filled the silence, followed by almost childlike laughter.

"Who is it?" Andrew called out loudly. "Who's there?" Andrew called, turning his back on the front door, peering down the hallway.

There was' no answer. Just another laugh.

"Why so shy all of a sudden?" Andrew called out, angrier now, clutching at the kitchen knife, as tight as he could, pointing it out, in front of himself, as he made his way down the hallway and into the living room. "I know you broke into my house. But the joke is on you. Yeah! You broke into the house of the goddamn deputy of this town! One call to the station and this place will be flooded with cops! So, you better leave, I swear!"

"Now, where would be the fun in that?" the clown mask answered, appearing from behind, at the entrance of the living room. "I want to play a game. And you, my dear deputy, are one of the final pieces in my puzzle."

"Fuck you!" Andrew shouted, turning on his feet, and lashing out, lashing forward with the kitchen knife.

"You piece of shit!" the clown mask answered, angrily, kicking the kitchen knife from Andrew's hand.

"What the?"

The clown mask lunged forward, their hands, bound in black leather gloves, reaching forward, gripping, moulding to Andrew's face, as their thumbs gouged at his eyes.

Andrew screamed, as loud as he could, hoping he would draw the attention of someone, a neighbour, anyone.

The clown mask used the weight of their frame, pushing Andrew into the side wall of the living room, by the couch. He was pushed forward, hitting his head. Andrew collapsed to the floor, beneath. He was breathing heavily and fighting to remain conscious. The clown mask stood, almost victoriously, over 'its latest soon-to-be victim, before turning a little and retrieving the kitchen knife from the living room floor. Andrew struggled, fighting to keep his eyes open and retain consciousness. His eyes blinked in quick succession, as he scrambled to his feet.

"I told you I would be back," said the clown mask, "it was just a matter of time."

The clown mask lunged at Andrew, again. This time, the kitchen knife rising high above their left shoulder, before coming down, slicing at Andrew.

The blade of the kitchen knife was stained with blood. It had made contact. The knife sliced at Andrew again, cutting at the flesh across his stomach. The blood was quick to pour from the wound. Andrew fell to his knees, weak, his hands covering the wound, holding back at the blood.

"Welcome to *your* final act!" said the clown mask, as they dropped the kitchen knife to the living room floor, again.

The clown mask took a single step forward, toward Andrew. The black leather boots pressed heavy into the living room carpet as they leaned forward grabbing Andrew, pulling him to his feet, as he gripped him from his head and shoulders. The clown mask was strong. Not superhuman. But, strong, nonetheless. Andrew was fragile. His hair was wet and his face sweating. The blood. The clown mask shifted their weight in their frame once more, throwing Andrew violently forward, sending him crashing into the coffee table and he landed on the floor beneath in a bloody heap.

"Look at you," said the clown mask, just above a whisper, "that blood. You'll soon have no more worries, Mr Preston. You'll bleed out alone. Your rotting corpse found in a day or two."

The clown mask turned their back and raced out of the living room, down the hallway, and out the back of the house, into the back yard, into the darkness of the night.

Andrew was curled up in the foetal position on the floor of the living room, clutching at his stomach tightly, fighting, struggling to remain conscious. His eyes blinked slowly now, rolling into the back of his head.

"Help!" Andrew called, just above a whisper. "Help me!"

Andrew reached into his jean pocket, reaching for his cell phone. He screamed as loudly as he could muster. The pain from the kitchen knife was too strong to bear. His bloodied right hand slowly tugged, pulling at the cell phone in his jean pocket. He pulled it out and slowly began to dial. Nine. One. One.

There was a loud knock at the front door. It burst open. And there, standing in the entrance, was a woman, short with curly black hair, just above her shoulders, and somewhere in her late thirties. She walked deeper into the house, into the living room.

"I heard a horrible noise," she muttered.

"Mrs Flynn," Andrew answered just above a whisper, happy to see his nosy neighbour.

Mrs Flynn stood in the entrance to the living room. Her hazel-coloured eyes scanned the bloodstained horror of the room. The violence. The struggle. She stood there, a moment longer, as a blood-curdling scream escaped her lungs and passed her lips.

Fade to black. Fade from black.

The distant echo of an ambulance wailing grew stronger and stronger in the dark of the night.

Fade to black. Fade from black.

The ambulance turned and pulled into Andrew's street as the siren continued to wail. It was louder now. The lights were aglow in the dark of the night. There were two police squad cars already parked out the front of the house. The house itself had officially become a crime scene. Mrs Flynn was standing on the front porch, being interviewed by one of the police officers there. She found it difficult to listen to the officer's questions as her eyes peered over his shoulders to watch an ambulance officer rush by, pushing a stretcher into the house.

"Is Andrew going to be okay?" Mrs Flynn asked worriedly.

Fade to black.

Chapter Twenty-Four...

The doors in the hospital corridor clattered open violent and Emily and Peter raced to the end of the corridor, towards the nurse's station, just past the waiting area.

"Andrew Preston," Emily demanded, just above a whisper and a little out of breath. "Where is he?" she slammed her left hand down on the surface of the nurse's station. She looked at her dress ring on the middle finger of her hand, clenching her hand into a tight fist.

The nurses behind the desk remained silent and appeared a little confused. They looked at each other, whispering amongst themselves.

"I got a call from the emergency room. You must know something?"

"You made it," a calming, and welcoming voice answered.

Emily turned her back on the nurses.

"Detective Quinn...?" Emily asked, too frightened to finish her question.

"It was touch-and-go there for a little while. But he pulled through. Andrew is a fighter." Detective Quinn answered, with a hint of a smile, across his thin lizard-like lips.

A sudden rush of adrenalin coursed through Emily's veins, as if a weight had been lifted from her shoulders.

"Where is he? Can I see him?"

"Yes." Detective Quinn nodded. "Of course you can. Follow me."

Peter remained silent. He made eye contact with the detective, giving him a brief nod of the head.

Emily was bordering on distraught. She slowly crept inside the hospital room, through the open doors. The curtains were pulled to a close for privacy. Emily peered through the pulled curtains and could see the massive, bulging figure lying on top of the bed. Emily stepped forward. An officer on duty was first to notice, followed by the nurse on duty, tending to Andrew. He was sitting up in bed. The lamp was switched on and hung high, just above him. The bed cover was pulled back neatly, folded on itself, exposing Andrew. His muscular chest was out for all to see. His torso was wrapped in bandages.

Peter stood back, a little. He stood at the end of the bed, in between the curtains and the officer standing at the door. He allowed Emily her private time with her partner, taking it all in. A solemn expression fell upon his face, as if this, all of this, was his fault. Detective Quinn stood to the right side of the bed, stepping out of the way, making room for Emily, as he watched his deputy resting up in bed, and the nurse who catered to him. Emily raced to his side, wanting to take Andrew in her arms and tell him everything was going to be okay, that everything was safe now.

Instead, she stood there, feeling as though she was in the way, awkward, watching the nurse at work.

Andrew was semi-conscious. His eyes flinched a little under the bright light as he looked around the room. He saw Emily standing to the right of him, and Peter standing in the shadows at the end of the bed, peering back at him. A smile surfaced to his lips, sluggish.

"My friends," he mumbled, a little above a whisper.

"Your friend is one lucky man. If the kitchen knife cut him an inch or two deeper, well, let's just say, he is one lucky man," the nurse smiled.

Emily smiled, fighting back her tears. She covered her mouth with her right hand, a moment. "Your friend is going to be sore tomorrow. But, in the meantime, he is floating on cloud nine. He is on Oxycontin to curb the pain."

"Thank you," Emily muttered, nervously.

"Andrew is a little out of it. So, all I can allow is five minutes. Ten, maximum. Then, you'll have to call it a night. You can always come back tomorrow during visiting hours."

The nurse finished up tending to Andrew's bandages and pushed the trolley out of the hospital room. The surface of the trolley was covered with fine scissors, a scalpel, clips, bandages, and gauze, some of it bloodied.

Peter watched the nurse leave the room. Detective Quinn smiled at Andrew, at his deputy, and nodded his head, a little.

"I'll leave you with your loved ones and friends. You rest up and try and get some sleep," he said, just above a whisper. "I'll be back tomorrow with some further questions."

"Yes, boss," Andrew replied, semi-conscious.

Peter watched the detective leave the hospital room, as he pulled the door to a close behind him. "What the actual fuck?" Peter asked, just above a whisper, not wanting to draw the attention of the officer posted at the door, standing in the corridor. "A fucking knife wound? Here you are, getting yourself hurt, again."

"It's a knife wound. Fourteen stitches across the stomach. Pretty cool, huh?" Andrew chuckled to himself, a little.

"This isn't funny!" Emily hissed. "Whoever is doing this, it's dangerous. *This* is dangerous!"

"I'm sorry," Andrew answered, his eyes sombre. "I didn't mean to scare you. I'll be off my feet for a week or two, tops. I'm fine. I promise."

Peter stared at his best friend, in silence.

Emily dragged the closest chair she could find in the room toward the side of the bed, and held Andrew's left hand, tightly. She gripped it, looking at him lovingly. Andrew looked down at her, propped up in bed, and smiled at her, squeezing her hand a little, too.

"It looks like it's my turn to leave next," Peter said, just above a whisper, as he stood at the end of the bed. "Call me, either of you. Day or night. Whatever you need, okay?"

"Of course," Emily answered, with a hint of a smile. "And thank you for the ride to the hospital."

"Anytime. Are you going to be okay getting home?"

Emily nodded. "I'm not going anywhere tonight."

"Okay," Peter smiled.

"Thank you for dropping by," said Andrew.

"You rest up, you hear?"

Andrew and Peter exchanged a glance with a nod of the head. Andrew winked at Peter.

Peter turned his back on his best friend and his partner and made his way out of the hospital room, leaving the two to themselves. He walked out into the corridor, pulling the door to a soft close behind him. The police officer on duty sat in a black plastic chair, slouched forward, a little reading a magazine, off in his own world. Peter looked over toward the nurse's station. There were two nurses on duty now, one male, somewhere in his late forties with neat grey-blonde hair and matching beard, who looked like he spent every spare minute in the gym. And one was female, a short, bubbly type with curly chocolate-brown hair. The two quietly whispered amongst themselves, trading in office gossip, before the bubbly one lifted her eyes from her friend and colleague, making eye contact with Peter, for the briefest of moments. She gave him another one of those *that's him* stares, before forgetting about him and returning to the office gossip.

Peter shrugged off the look and made his way quietly down the corridor. It was peaceful at night. He walked the corridor, past the other patient's rooms, glancing in, just to see who was there. It was hard to see with the lights switched out. Peter reached the elevator and waited for the doors to open, before making his way to the parking lot.

The elevator made 'its way to the ground floor. The doors opened and the sound of a bell chimed. Peter stepped out of the empty elevator, walking forward a little, toward the parking lot. He stopped, for just a moment, and tugged on his jacket, zipping it up from the waist to the chest, to stay warm. A cold breeze blanketed the town of Hillsboro for the evening. It was almost three-thirty in the morning now. The parking lot was fitted with four tall floodlights, one positioned in each corner, for added security. Peter continued, walking forward, towards his sports utility vehicle.

Peter reached into his jacket pocket, on the left side, and pulled out his car keys. He pointed disarming the alarm. The beep of the alarm sounded rather loud in the quiet of the early hours of the morning. His hands were cold as he fumbled with his keys a moment, before opening the driver's side door and climbing in. The door slammed to a close. Peter made himself comfortable and looked over his right shoulder, into the back seat, for just a second, maybe two. It was empty.

The engine of the sports utility vehicle roared to life before making 'its way out of the parking lot.

Peter drove out of the parking lot of the hospital and drove the dark and winding roads home in the early hours of the morning. He switched on the radio, turning the volume up, just a little, just above a whisper, to help keep him awake. He was tired. Peter rubbed his eyes and cracked the driver's side window a little. He could feel the early morning breeze against one side of his face. It felt refreshing. His cell phone began to ring. *Ring. Ring. Ring.* Peter turned the volume down on the radio immediately and looked down on his cell phone which sat face up on the front passenger seat. *Unknown Caller.*

"Hello?" Peter answered, clearing his throat a little.

"Did you like my work?" the dark and familiar voice replied, laughing a little.

"What do you want?" Peter asked, his anger rising in his voice.

"Let's face it. Andrew is a nobody. A kid who grew up, who came from trash, and tried desperately to fit in, somewhere, anywhere. He is nothing more than a minor character you wouldn't think twice about. But, still a *very* important piece in my puzzle. Something to tug at your heartstrings."

Peter remained silent, concentrating on the road in front of him, concentrating on the voice coming from his cell phone.

"Your friend may have survived," the voice continued. "But next time, I will put him in the morgue, just like I did that town slut, Jayne Scott!"

There was more laughter. The phone line disconnected.

The curtains in the master bedroom were pulled open. The morning sun was starting to creep into the bedroom and spray across the walls. Peter was still asleep, slowly coming too, waking up for the day. He was lying in the middle of the bed, on his back, the bed cover turned back a little, exposing some of his muscular chest. His left hand raised slowly from under the bed cover and landed on his face, wiping the sleep from his eyes, a moment. Peter opened his eyes, staring up at the ceiling a moment, before turning on his left shoulder, stretching across the bed, toward the nightstand, reaching out for his cell phone. He pulled it from the charger chord. There was one text message, waiting to be read.

Peter wiped the sleep from his eyes, again, before he signed into his cell phone to read the text message.

"Thank you for stopping by and checking in on me, good buddy. Emily just about lost it after you left last night. Drop by and say hello sometime."

The message was from Andrew.

Peter smiled a little, before navigating out of the text message to read the time on the cell phone. The time was coming on five past eight, in the morning.

"Shit!" Peter whispered to himself. "I can't believe I slept through my alarm."

Peter dropped his cell phone back on top of the nightstand, leaving it off the charger, before he kicked the bed cover back further, exposing the rest of his muscular frame, and climbing out of bed. He sat there a moment, on the side of the bed, in just his jockey shorts, looking around the bedroom, as if getting his bearings. He looked down at the palm of his hands, looking at his scars. He closed his eyes tightly, for maybe a second, or two, as he clenched his hands tightly. Peter stood up and made his way out of the bedroom, down the hallway and into the bathroom to take a shower. The bathroom door was pushed to a close and the water from the shower started to run.

Peter made his way down the staircase of his home and made his way into the living room. He was dressed for the day in a pair of denim jeans and a polo shirt, white in colour. His feet were still bare. He walked into the living room and reached for the TV remote on the couch and switched it on, for noise, more than anything else. A local TV reporter filled the screen. He was a stocky man, somewhere in his early fifties, dressed finely in a dark grey suit, white shirt and blood-red tie. He was clean-shaven, his black hair was slicked back with gel, almost highlighting the salt and pepper look on the side of his temples.

"Resident and town deputy, Andrew Preston, was attacked last night," the reporter started.

Peter clutched the TV remote in his right hand, tightly, as he stared at the television set, watching the news story play out. An angry expression fell upon his face as if he were about to fight back the tears.

"Our sources tell us, this was a case of a home invasion gone wrong. Deputy Preston was stabbed multiple times and rushed to this very hospital. We have to wonder, is the town of Hillsboro safe? And what is Detective Quinn doing to bring whoever is doing this to justice? I'm Will Harris for Channel Three News."

Peter continued to look at the television set. He rolled his eyes, if just for a moment, before switching the channel. It was morning television, more news. Peter switched the television set off. He turned his back on the television set, walking through the living room, dropping the TV remote back on the coffee table, before making his way back to the kitchen.

The light to the kitchen flickered on. Peter lost his appetite. He walked into the kitchen and headed straight for the refrigerator. He leaned in and grabbed himself the carton of orange juice and a doughnut he purchased from the local grocery store. It wasn't the healthiest of breakfasts, but it did the job.

Peter arrived at the hospital, again. He made his way from the parking lot, through the gift shop, rode the elevator to the fourth floor, and walked down the corridor toward the nurse's station. He found himself walking the same corridor he had the night before. The nurses' station seemed a little busier than it was last night. There was a handful of residents, no more than a dozen, of different ages, shapes and sizes, following one of the doctor's on duty. They hung around the nurse's' station whilst the doctor grabbed a patient's file. They stood in the corridor, quietly talking amongst themselves, whilst others referred to their notes. Peter walked past the residents, clutching two magazines that he purchased from the gift store. The magazines were filled with celebrity gossip.

The officer on duty from the night before was gone. The door leading into Andrew's room was open. The lights in the room were dimmed. The small television set which hung from the ceiling was playing. The volume was on mute. It was a mid-morning talk show. Peter stepped inside the room quietly, careful not to disturb Andrew. He peered through the partially closed curtains and could see his best friend wrestling with the bed, trying his best to find a comfortable position.

"Hey, you," Peter said just above a whisper, as he pulled at the curtains around the bed.

"I think I see salvation," Andrew answered, as his eyes came to life, as a smile surfaced to his lips. Andrew propped himself up in bed. Peter dropped the magazines on a chair by the side of the bed and rushed in to help his best friend get comfortable.

"Thank you," Andrew answered, still with the same smile on his face.

Andrew sat up in bed. The two pillows behind him were used to prop him forward from the lower back. The bed cover was folded over on itself, sitting at the waist. His chest was exposed, as his torso was wrapped in bandages.

"You have no idea how good it is to see a friendly face around here." Andrew continued, just above a whisper.

"Enough about me," Peter joked, "how about you? How are you holding up?

"I'll wind up with one mother of a scar, but I'll pull through."

"You're tough."

"I just can't believe that motherfucker made their way inside my house. I felt fucking useless against them."

Peter stood there silent for a moment. He forced himself to smile, to help lighten the mood. "Well, didn't you hear?" Peter asked. "These aren't the days to be a hero, Billy."

"This is serious," replied Andrew.

"Of course it is. You don't think I don't know that? A copycat killer is out there, patterning themselves on my grandfather and mother. I got a call from the killer myself last night when I left the hospital."

"You did?" Andrew asked, worried, "what did they say?"

"You know, the usual." Peter shrugged. "How the next time we meet they want to put me in the morgue."

Peter changed the subject of the conversation he had with the killer, referring to himself, rather than his best friend. It was tact. He was protecting his best friend.

"I want that motherfucker!" Andrew demanded, just above a whisper. "I want to be standing over their lifeless and bloodied corpse after we plough their body full of bullets."

"You're talking about the cops, yeah?"

"Like I said," Andrew shrugged, looking at his best friend, "I want to see that motherfucker dead!"

"So, what did Quinn have to say? Where is Emily?" Peter asked, trying to change the subject.

"I sent Emily home in a cab earlier this morning. She stayed the night but was exhausted. She will drop by later today. Quinn, on the other hand. You know him. That same bullshit. An officer posted out the front of my hospital room door, twenty-four, seven."

"Really? I didn't see anyone on the way in."

"See? Bullshit! Quinn will take a handful of officers and comb the neighbourhood later today."

"That's comforting." Peter shrugged. "Here. Try and get your mind off things. I got you these." Peter handed the magazines to his best friend. Andrew received them, looking at the covers. "Thank you," he answered. "I'm serious. I do mean it. Anything to help pass the time in this place. It's hard enough to get to sleep at night in this place, and have a nurse wake you up in the middle of the night, to stab you with a syringe and draw some blood."

"Nice."

The morning progressed into the afternoon. The clouds raced across the sky as the day passed on, bringing with it, very little rain. The neighbourhood children played in the street, riding around on their bicycles, skipping rope, running, and playing ball. Emily's home remained quiet. Two or three envelopes were sitting in the letterbox. The windows were open, so to, were the curtains, allowing for the light to creep through. The afternoon sun sprayed across the walls. The television set was switched off and the kitchen was quiet. The door leading into the master bedroom, at the end of the hallway, was wide open. Emily was lying on top of the bed, still, in the same clothes, she wore from the day before, fast asleep.

Her unconscious body slowly tossed and turned. The afternoon sun came through the bedroom window, touching her face. It felt warm to the touch, as Emily soon came to, slowly waking up from her deep slumber. Her eyes gently blinked open as she yawned, a little. Emily reached across the side of the bed, over to her nightstand, reaching for her cell phone. The cell phone was hooked up to the charger. Emily pulled the cell phone from the phone charger and the screen came to life. The time was four fifty-eight in the afternoon. Emily dropped her cell phone back down on the nightstand. She covered her eyes from the sunlight, a moment, wiping the sleep from her eyes. There was another yawn. Emily felt embarrassed a little that she had slept so long, as she started to pull herself up, off the bed. She crawled to the side of the bed and sat by the nightstand. Emily checked her cell phone, again. There were no missed calls or text messages. Emily stood up and walked out of the bedroom. She made her way down the hallway, a little, before making her way to the bathroom. The bathroom door closed behind her, the light flickered on, and the water from the shower started to run.

The neon lights which hung from the ceiling in Detective Quinn's office started to flicker a little. Detective Quinn, himself, was sitting at his desk in his office, behind his computer, typing away on his keyboard. He stopped a moment, lifting his reading glasses a little to rub his eyes. The reading glasses fell onto the bridge of his nose. He leaned into his desk, reading his notes on the police report. It was a list of names and incidents of the victims found in Hillsboro over the past few months: Jayne Doe, Mike Walters, Eleanor Padbury, just to name a few. Detective Quinn leaned back in his chair a little, making himself more comfortable, away from his desk now, and placed his hands behind his head. He stared at the computer monitor a little more.

"Give me something more," he whispered to himself, under his breath. "I'll find you." Detective Quinn leaned forward in his chair, again, saving the report and logging off from his computer for another evening.

"It's beer o'clock."

Detective Quinn collected his personal belongings from the surface of his desk; his keys, his cell phone and his wallet, walked across the office floor and reached the door. He opened it, but not before switching off the neon lights, and locking the door behind him. He gave the door handle a slight jiggle, confirming it was locked. Detective Quinn made a mental note to report the flickering lights in his office. It was the third time this week. It was time to call in an electrician.

Detective Quinn turned his back on his office for another evening and walked across the floor of the station, past the other officers on duty, and headed towards the back of the station, towards the parking lot. He walked the corridor, past the interrogation rooms and other offices, as well as the men's change room. The door leading into the men's change room was pushed open as an officer, with a rotund build, clean-shaven, and somewhere in his mid- to late-forties stepped out into the corridor, dressed in civilian attire, carrying a sports bag over his right shoulder.

"'Night, Jackson," Detective Quinn said, with a friendly nod of his head, as he made his way down the corridor.

"'Night, Detective," Jackson replied.

The door leading into the men's change room quietly pulled to a close. But, not before Detective Quinn caught a glimpse inside. There were a number of officers, all in various stages of undress, some in uniform, whilst others were in civilian attire. Other officers were standing by their lockers, sharing in-jokes and office gossip.

Detective Quinn made his way out of the police station. He walked out into the parking lot, toward his car, searching for his keys in his right trouser pocket. The keys jiggled some and knocked together, making that scraping, metal-on-metal sound. The detective clicked on the button to deactivate the car alarm, opened the door and climbed inside, slamming the door to a close. He placed his personal belongings on the front passenger seat before turning, looking over his right shoulder, making sure the back seat was empty. It was. Detective Quinn turned again, this time facing forward. He made himself comfortable, taking off his jacket and tossed it into the backseat of his car. The radio switched on. It was a song by Maroon 5. Detective Quinn loosened his tie and unbuttoned the top two buttons on his shirt with his left hand, whilst his fingers tapped to the music from the radio on the steering wheel with his right hand. The engine to the car ignited. Detective Quinn placed his foot slowly on the accelerator and made his way out of the station parking lot, making his way home for the evening.

Emily pulled her bug into the first vacant parking spot she could find, between a sports utility vehicle and a small truck, in the hospital parking lot. The engine to her small car died. She caught her reflection in the rear-view mirror a moment, struggling to fight back the tears welling in her eyes.

"He didn't die," she whispered to herself, forcing herself to smile. "Andrew will be fine. He will pull through. You'll see." Another smile.

Peter was at home. He was back in the spare bedroom, standing in front of the clipboard he hung on the wall, staring at the pictures of his mother, father and grandfather. Peter leaned into the clipboard, pinning a picture of Andrew to the board, closer to his father. His mind raced with thoughts. The picture of Andrew was just the latest to join the clipboard. There were other pictures on there now, too. There were pictures of the victims found in Hillsboro, in chronological order, found by Detective Quinn and Deputy Preston.

"Who are you?" Peter asked himself, his voice just above a whisper.

The door leading into an apartment opened. The living room of the apartment was bland and simple. The walls were painted an off-white, almost beige. The furniture was minimal at best. There was a black leather couch sitting in front of the television set which hung from the wall and a coffee table in the middle of the room, which was decorated with some outdated magazines.

Detective Quinn unlocked the door to his apartment and made his way inside, closing the door behind him, and placing the keys and his wallet in a bowl on the table, nearby.

Detective Quinn tugged at his tie some more until it loosened from his neck entirely. He threw it over his left shoulder, unbuttoning his shirt some more, exposing his chest and torso beneath. He immediately made his way into the kitchen. The light in the kitchen ceiling switched on. Detective Quinn walked over to the refrigerator, opened the door and leaned in, pulling out a bottle of beer. The lid popped open, rather quickly, as he stood in the middle of the kitchen, in front of the refrigerator, taking a deep sip from his bottle of beer. He next made his way out of the kitchen, walking across the floor of the living room, down the hallway and into the master bedroom, with his bottle of beer in one hand and his cell phone in another.

Detective Quinn placed his bottle of beer on the nightstand, next to his bed, whilst he put his cell phone on the charger. He turned his back on the nightstand and walked to the end of his queen- size bed, pulling at his shirt. He took it off and gave it a quick sniff. His nose wrinkled at the smell of his own body odour. He dropped the shirt on the bedroom floor as he started in on unbuttoning his trousers. He was soon undressed and walking around his bedroom, naked. Detective Quinn walked over to the nightstand, again, and grabbed his beer. He took another deep sip before walking out of the bedroom, down the hallway, a little, and into the bathroom to take a shower.

The door leading into the bathroom was closed. The sound of the water running from the shower sounded heavy. The air conditioner was running, and the near-empty bottle of beer sat on the side of the washbasin. Detective Quinn stood under the shower head, his head tilted back, his eyes closed, consumed in the hot water. He rubbed the liquid soap under his arms and across his chest, soaping himself up.

The water from the shower head stopped now. The glass door of the shower slid open and Detective Quinn was cautious as he stepped out onto the wet tiled floor. He walked over and grabbed himself a fresh towel and wrapped himself up in it, drying himself down, before grabbing the bottle of beer and walking down the hallway and into the master bedroom to get dressed. The damp towel dropped to the bedroom floor as Detective Quinn pulled on a pair of black cotton boxer shorts from the set of drawers, up against the wall, at the end of the bed, and pulled on his old college t-shirt with *Northwestern* printed across the chest.

Fade to black.

Chapter Twenty-Five...

Fade from black.

Detective Quinn walked over to his nightstand and picked up his cell phone. There were no missed calls or text messages. The battery power was at forty-three per cent. He dropped the cell phone back on top of the nightstand and turned to pick up the damp towel off the floor. He emerged from his master bedroom, walking down the hallway, past the bathroom, placing the damp towel in the hamper in the laundry.

The apartment was very quiet. Quinn walked the hallway leaving behind a trail of water from the shower as the weight of his frame pressed down on the hardwood floors. He made his way into the living room, next. The television set switched on, if just for the noise to fill the apartment. The evening news was coming to an end. Update next, the weather report. An overweight man, somewhere in his early fifties, stood in front of a map of the United States of America in a black suit and jacket with a white long-sleeved shirt that was unbuttoned around the neck. His chubby cheeks were a little rosy as he smiled to the camera, moving his hands around a little, excited as the working week ahead was in for some warmer weather. Quinn placed the television remote on the coffee table behind him and made his way into the kitchen. The refrigerator door was pulled open again, and another beer bottle was taken. The lid popped open and he took another deep sip.

"That's the stuff!" he whispered under his breath. "Fuck yeah!"

Quinn pulled out a large bowl from the refrigerator, next. It was leftovers from the past two nights. Spaghetti. He took just enough to fill a smaller bowl that was sitting on the kitchen counter by the microwave, and made himself a small helping. He threw it in the microwave and returned to the couch in the living room and waited for his dinner for one.

The detective looked tired. His eyelids grew heavy as he tried to focus on the television set. It was another B-grade sitcom with canned laughter that the network was trying to pass off as must- watch TV. It wasn't. The countdown on the microwave came to an end with a somewhat annoying beeping sound that seemed to jolt the detective from his near slumber. Detective Quinn looked over his left shoulder, back into the kitchen. He climbed off the couch, adjusting himself a little, and walked over to the microwave. The microwave door popped open. The smell of days-old spaghetti and steam rushed from the inside of the microwave. The cheese sprinkled on top was melting, exposing the meat beneath.

The television set in the living room returned to 'its regularly scheduled programming. The canned laughter cheered on the actors as they delivered their jokes. The light in the living room was minimal. There was a small light switched on above the television set. The coffee table was set for dinner, with a place mat and coaster to catch the bottle of beer. And a single fork used to eat the spaghetti. Quinn was busying himself with dinner. The door handle to the inside of the apartment slowly began to turn, unnoticed. The door itself pushed open, ever so slightly. The laughter from the television set continued. A hand, bound in a black leather glove, grazed over the top of the nearby table, by the front door, picking up the wallet. The wallet opened for inspection, exposing credit cards, some cash, and a driver's licence inside. A photograph of Detective Quinn appeared under the plastic sleeve. Mark Quinn.

A shadow was quick to pass by the table by the front door of the apartment and across the wall. Detective Quinn sat in front of the television set, his eyes glued to the sitcom, his brain set to cruise control, as his fork in his left hand picked at the spaghetti, microwaved to an inch of its life. He picked at his dinner, blowing on it slightly, careful not to burn this inside of his mouth. A sip from his bottle of beer quickly followed. The clown mask walked the hallway, making their way through the apartment, slowly, moving at an almost graceful speed, moving like a shadow.

"Shit!" Quinn muttered to himself, burning the inside of his mouth on the spaghetti, a little. He dropped the fork in the bowl and grabbed his beer bottle.

Detective Quinn stood up from the couch. His eyes slowly pulling away from the television set, as he made his way back into the kitchen. The neon lights which hung from the ceiling were still switched on, giving the kitchen an ambient glow. The remaining leftovers sat on top of the kitchen counter. Quinn darted across the floor and over to the kitchen sink. He leaned in a little, running the faucet and catching the cool water in his hands before taking a sip and washing his mouth out. He gargled the water for a few seconds, four, maybe five, before he spat the water from his mouth and raced his tongue over the inside of his mouth.

"Shit!" he whispered to himself.

He could feel the start of a blister already growing on the inside of his right cheek.

Detective Quinn stood tall and turned to make his way out of the kitchen. The colour in his face quickly faded, as he caught his breath in his chest. He could feel his heart racing.

"What the fuck are you doing here?" he asked, just above a whimper.

The clown mask stood there, in front of him, blocking the entrance into the kitchen. Those black, lifeless eyes, washed with painted blue, stared back.

"I have to say, I'm a little disappointed in you, Detective," the clown mask responded. "You're a detective in this hick town. You're a man of respect. A man who deserves respect, anyway. I thought you would have been on a halfway decent salary instead of which you live in a shit-box of an apartment you call home. Respect doesn't pay the bills."

"Fuck you!" Quinn responded, his voice deepening.

"Quite the potty mouth, Detective." the clown mask answered, shaking their head a little.

A large, sharp kitchen knife appeared, gripped tightly, bound in the left hand of their leather glove. Quinn lowered his eyes, making contact with it. He could feel his heartbeat racing wildly now. The blade of the knife was quick to move. Quinn lifted his hands in front of himself, standing there, shifting the weight in his frame, ready to protect himself. The blade of the kitchen knife sliced through the flesh of the palm on his right hand.

"Fuck!" Quinn screamed.

The blood was quick to pour from the wound. The laughter from the television set continued.

Quinn pulled back, a little. He was fast to clench his right hand tightly, hoping to numb the pain and staunch the loss of blood. He looked down, albeit very briefly, and saw the blood drip from his tight fist and onto the kitchen floor beneath. Mark lifted his left leg and kicked at his assailant.

The clown mask was pushed back a little, losing their balance and dropping the kitchen knife. Quinn raced out of the kitchen. He made his way across the living room floor and down the hallway. The clown mask gathered themselves, finding their balance, and gave chase, picking up the kitchen knife off the kitchen floor, gripping it tighter in their gloved hand.

The clown mask was quick to reach the hallway. They rubbed the handle of the kitchen knife, between their thumb and forefinger of their left hand, readying themselves to strike. The kitchen knife spun furiously, stabbing Mark Quinn in the back, just left of his spine. The blade cut through the cotton fabric of his college t-shirt, piercing the flesh beneath. Mark staggered forward, a little. The pain coursed through his body, throwing him off balance. He fell forward, hitting the left side of his forehead, just above his eyebrow, on the frame of the doorway, leading into the master bedroom. Mark collapsed, unconscious and bleeding. The clown mask walked patiently down the hallway, towards him, only inches away. The assailant leaned forward, tilting their mask, slightly to the right, as if to inspect the remains and pulling the kitchen knife quickly from the wound, but not before twisting the blade, a little. The blood began to pour profusely from the wound.

Fade to black. Fade from black.

The neon light of the bathroom took several seconds to flicker on. The walls were adorned in white tile. The bathroom itself was your everyday basic design. Nothing special. It had a bathtub up against the far wall. A washbasin and wall mirror on the other side of the room, and a shower and toilet facing opposite each other. Some of the tiles were starting to show their age. They were cracked and chipped. Mark Quinn was standing in the middle of the bathroom, slowly coming to, from his unconscious state, held up on his feet, by the clown mask, standing behind him, their reflection caught in the bathroom mirror.

Mark Quinn awoke from his unconscious state with a gasp of air filling his lungs. He could feel the pain in his bloodied forehead and the stab wound in his back, course through his veins. His head was throbbing.

His eyes closed, tightly. Mark opened his eyes as he moved his fingertips of his left hand from above his forehead. He could see the blood rub against his finger tips.

"What the fuck?" he asked, just above a whisper.

"There you are!" the clown mask responded.

Mark could see the image of the mask standing behind him in the bathroom mirror. He was still finding his feet.

"You've been out for quite some time. Do you know how long I have been waiting for this?"

"For what?"

"I waited for you. I waited just long enough for this."

"Waited for what?" Mark shouted again.

"This!"

The bloodstained blade of the kitchen knife appeared once more. It almost gleamed under the neon light of the bathroom. It raised and struck at Mark Quinn, slicing at his throat. The flesh was just as quick to tear open, as the blood poured furiously from the wound. Mark raised his hands to his throat, in an attempt to catch the blood, in an attempt to conceal the wound. His mouth. His mouth opened in horror, attempting to gasp for air. He stood there, slowly losing his balance, slowly suffocating, as the blood coursed over his hands, down his college t-shirt, over his underwear and down his legs to the tiled floor beneath.

"You'll soon have no more worries, Detective," laughed the clown mask.

The grip of the kitchen knife tightened, as the assailant stepped backwards, watching the sheer and utter brutality of their actions playing out.

Mark Quinn stumbling forward, a little, placing his bloodied right hand on the front of the washbasin, to catch his fall. The blood continued to drip into the washbasin and onto the tiled floor. A laugh filled the bathroom, almost echoing off the walls. The laughter was almost hysterical. The blade of the kitchen knife struck at Detective Mark Quinn again, this time, stabbing him in the lower back, on the right side of his spine. Mark screamed. The clown mask pulled on the kitchen knife, retracting the blade from the bloodied wound.

The kitchen knife struck over and over again, striking about the lower stomach, around the intestines and to the side of the stomach, near the love handles. The colour of the blood was turning a darker shade now, almost black. Mark Quinn gasped in horror, fighting for another breath. His eyes opened wide. His pupils dilated. The detective stood in front of the bathroom mirror suffocating in his own blood. Mark Quinn collapsed to the tiled floor of the bathroom, knocking his chin, biting, cracking his two front teeth on the top arch, on the bloodied washbasin. His bloodied, beaten frame collapsed.

"Goodnight, Detective," the clown mask said, just above a whisper.

Detective Mark Quinn lay on the tiled floor of the bathroom, almost in the foetal position, with his eyes open, gasping for his final breath. The image of the clown mask leaned in further, watching the detective's expression. So curious. The last breath escaping his bloodied lips. Detective Mark Quinn was dead.

The sound of the bloodied kitchen knife dropped to the tiled floor of the bathroom. The clown mask stood tall and turned, walking out of the bathroom, leaving the door open, turning right, to walk down the hallway, making their way out of the apartment. The sound of the front door of the apartment was slammed to a close.

Fade to black.

Chapter Twenty-Six...

Four days later.

Andrew was in the final process of being discharged from the hospital. He was dressed for the day, in a pair of blue jeans, sneakers and a loose-fitting Chicago Bears football jersey. The bandages were freshly applied this morning and wrapped firmly around his torso. Emily was on hand, watching Andrew finalise his discharge papers and climb off his bed and into the wheelchair that awaited him, as she stood by and carried his overnight bag. The magazines were left behind, sitting on the side nightstand.

"Let's get you out here then," the male nurse said with a warm smile and friendly demeanour, as he kept a watchful eye on the patient climbing into the wheelchair. "Are you comfortable?"

"Yes, sir," Andrew smiled, "I'm good to go."

The male nurse was somewhere in his early forties, with black hair which was greying on the sides and bright green eyes. He was clean-shaven and had a friendly face. The side of his hair was neatly trimmed, a buzz-cut, which rose high above the ear. It was military inspired. He also had a similar frame to Andrew; he was tall and muscular. His biceps were large as if he spent every spare moment in the gym. There was a hint of a tattoo beneath the white of his shirt uniform, which started from the right side shoulder, and ended at the elbow. It appeared to be a ripped flesh design, with bear fur exposed beneath. Emily remained silent. She smiled politely at the nurse and followed the two out of the hospital room and into the corridor.

The hospital corridor was a little busy, with passing traffic. An elderly gentleman was rushed down the corridor, toward surgery, with an oxygen mask fitted over his mouth. A nurse was calling out the patient's vitals to the doctor on call. The nurses' station was flooded with both doctors, taking the next patient's file, nurses talking amongst themselves, and visitors waiting to hear something, anything on loved ones and friends.

"I think I see salvation!" Andrew whispered under his breath.

He was just feet away from the entrance to the hospital as he was pushed in a wheelchair down the corridor. The morning sun burnt brightly through the clouds. The doors parted open and the male nurse continued to push Andrew in the wheelchair until they reached the curb.

"There's a familiar face!" a voice called out.

Andrew looked to his left. And there was Peter, climbing out of his sports utility vehicle.

"Does someone need a ride home?" Peter asked, almost sarcastically, yet happy to see his friends.

"You have no idea."

Emily dropped Andrew's overnight bag and helped him to his feet as he climbed out of the wheelchair.

"Hey, Peter," said Emily, with a smile on her face.

"You didn't think I would pass up the chance to give you guys a ride home, would you? After everything you have done for me."

Peter raced to the side of his sports utility vehicle and opened the back, passenger door on the driver's side of the truck. Emily raced around the other side of the truck, with a bag in hand, and climbed inside. Peter helped Andrew inside the truck whilst the male nurse pulled the wheelchair back from the side of the curb, turned and made his way back inside the hospital.

Andrew was now sitting inside the truck, with his seatbelt carefully positioned over his chest. Emily sat next to him, clutching his right hand as tight as she could.

"Who is good to go?" Peter asked.

"Get me the fuck out of here, Petey," Andrew replied, his eyes dragging from the rear-view mirror and out the window, out at the hospital.

"You got it."

The engine of the truck roared to life. The music played from the radio, and Peter and his friends pulled out from the curb outside the hospital and carefully into traffic, racing to the end of the street.

Andrew was home now. He had been home for close to two hours. He was still dressed in his Chicago Bears jersey, now barefoot, as he slowly made his way down the hallway, and towards his master bedroom. The dining room table was set for two. The lunch menu for the day was a chicken and salad roll with potato chips on the side with a soda. Emily was bussing the drinks to the table from the kitchen.

Andrew reached the end of the hallway, standing in the entrance to his master bedroom. He stood there a moment, before his left hand raced up the side of the wall, in search of the light switch. The light to the master bedroom switched on. Andrew stood there a moment longer, surveying the room. He shrugged it off and made his way inside. Andrew hobbled over to his side of the bed, over to the nightstand, reaching for the latest paperback novel was reading, *Most Talkative* by Andy Cohen. His cell phone was sitting next to the paperback novel, hooked up to the charger. The cell phone began to ring. *Ring. Ring. Ring.* It broke the silence of the bedroom, startling him a little. Andrew looked down at his cell phone. He dropped the paperback on the nightstand, again, and picked up his cell phone, taking it from the charger. His face dropped. The phone number on the screen looked familiar.

"Preston," Andrew answered, flatly. His face dropped some more. He looked sombre, almost losing colour. "Shit!" he continued, under his breath. "Where? I'm on my way."

Andrew looked up at the ceiling, covering his mouth with his left hand a little, as he gripped his cell phone in the other.

"Fuck!" he muttered, under his breath. "Not again." Fade to black.

Fade from black.

Andrew was sitting behind the steering wheel of his truck, now dressed in his police uniform. The shirt felt a little tighter than usual, as it rubbed up against the bandages wrapped around his torso. He peered through the windscreen, up at the front of his home, his face strained and consumed with worry. He could see Emily standing on the porch, staring back at him. He read the expression on her face. She forced a smile standing there barefoot in jeans and a plain, white cotton t-shirt. Andrew raised his right hand, giving a slight wave and smiling back.

He turned the key in the ignition and the engine roared to life. Andrew looked over his right shoulder and started to reverse out of the driveway. The truck turned and raced to the end of the street, with an almost thunderous echo following him down the empty road. Emily remained standing on the porch a moment longer, lifting her eyes, peering out into the neighbourhood, before making her way inside the house, closing the front door behind her.

The truck sat at the end of the road at the stop sign. The engine purred. Andrew looked left and right for any oncoming traffic, then in his rear-view mirror. There was nothing. He was good. Andrew reached for his cell phone, which sat on the front passenger seat next to him. He buried his head into his cell phone, signing in and navigating to his text history. Andrew starting typing.

It's happened again. The son of a bitch got to Quinn. He's gone.

Andrew finished typing and hit the send button. He dropped the cell phone on the front passenger seat of his truck. The expression on his face was mixed with anger and hurt. He looked left and right for on-coming traffic again, before pressing his foot down on the accelerator and making a left turn.

Fade to black. Fade from black.

Andrew was driving at a high speed now. He was lost in his thoughts as his truck barrelled along the country road towards Detective Quinn's apartment building. He couldn't get the image of the clown mask out of his head. The truck was speeding just above the road limit. There was a conversation coming from the CB radio that was hooked up to the dashboard of the truck. It sounded more like birds chirping. Andrew didn't pay too much attention to it. He maintained eye contact on the road in front him, flashing his headlights sporadically at on-coming traffic, warning them to get out of the way and stay in their lane. The passing traffic tooted on their horns back at the deputy, whilst other local drivers screamed profanity through open windows as they drove past. Andrew didn't pay attention to it. He kept his eyes on the road.

Fade to black. Fade from black.

It took almost fifteen minutes before Andrew arrived. He parked his truck on the curb, outside the front of the apartment building. There was already a handful of squad cars parked out the front, along with an ambulance, and the coroner. There were police officers on duty outside the front of the building, monitoring and controlling the crowd of on-lookers, standing on the opposite side of the road, all curious to know what had happened. There were residents with their cell phones, some taking photographs, whilst others recorded the unfolding, tragic incident, ready to upload to their social media accounts and news outlets later.

The engine to the truck died. Andrew placed his left hand on his torso a moment, feeling a little uncomfortable as he sat behind the steering wheel of his truck. He looked out at the crowd of people standing behind the police barricades, and the officers on duty.

"I hate this fucking shit!" Deputy Preston whispered under his breath, before turning a little in his seat, grabbing his cell phone from the passenger seat.

The driver's side door pushed open. The silence inside the truck was gone and replaced with the conversations on top of each other, of the residents, all demanding to know more.

"Let us do our work and we will be out of here just as soon as we possibly can."

Andrew could hear one of the officers calling out. He looked at the officer in question with a little concern. The ambulance was parked nearby.

Andrew stood by the side of his truck, surveying the commotion of the scene, for just a moment. His cell phone began to vibrate in his hand. He looked down. It was a text message from Peter. He was quick to sign into his cell phone, again and opened the message.

I hope you're holding up okay. Keep me posted.

The message read.

Andrew lifted his eyes off his cell phone. A hint of a smile surfaced to his lips, if for a fleeting moment.

"I hear you, good buddy," he muttered under his breath.

Andrew signed out of his cell phone, gripping it in his right hand a little tighter, for a moment, before turning in his tracks and making his start towards the front of the apartment building. An officer, young in age, who looked like he was only days out of the academy, with a thin frame, clean-shaven, and neatly trimmed black hair burst through the entrance door of the apartment building, along the footpath, towards Deputy Preston.

"You're here," said the officer, "thank God!"

Deputy Preston looked at the officer a little confused. The face wasn't familiar to him. His eyes diverted to his name badge briefly instead.

"Myers." Deputy Preston answered. "What do you mean? What's going on?"

"Excuse me, sir. Can I speak freely?"

Deputy Preston paused again, a moment. He forced a smile. "Go on." he nodded.

"It's a fucking nightmare in there. Like a scene from a fucking horror movie or something. Who the fuck could do such a thing, you know? Officers are walking out of that apartment, losing their lunch."

"That will be all, Myers." Deputy Preston answered, flatly. "Shit!" he whispered under his breath. "Thank you, Officer. Go take a breather. Stay outside. Go keep an eye on the crowd. We don't need them seeing this shit!"

"Thank you, sir."

Officer Myers made his way past Deputy Preston and headed towards the waiting crowd in the street. Deputy Preston looked over his left shoulder a moment, watching the officer walk on by.

Deputy Preston shifted the weight of his frame and focused on the matter ahead. He walked along the footpath of the building and made his way through the entrance door. The foyer of the apartment building was a little old and was in much need of some elbow grease and some tender loving care. The elevator door in the foyer was closed off to public use. The elevator doors remained open and the lights switched off.

Deputy Preston walked from the elevator and over to the mailboxes in the foyer. The information desk just past the entrance door was empty. Andrew could see Mark Quinn's mailbox. He could see his surname written in red marker and in capital letters. The handwriting was barely legible, something just above a chicken scratch. Andrew had visited Mark's apartment in the past, catching up for a beer and a talk, from time to time. He made the start on climbing the stairs of the apartment building.

Deputy Preston was a little out of breath by the time he reached the fourth floor. His shirt clung tightly to his muscular frame as he felt a little sweat drip down his back. It was uncomfortable and moist.

The apartment door leading into Mark Quinn's apartment was wide open. Deputy Preston shifted the weight of his frame forward, as much as his feet ached. He was first to notice another officer standing near the door of the apartment, with a notepad in hand, interviewing what appeared to be a witness. The police officer was reaching his mid-forties, with chocolate-brown hair, stubble on the chin, not having shaved for the good part of the last three days, and sported a 'dad bod''. The woman questioned by the officer was of African American descent. A small frame hunched forward a little, somewhere in her late fifties, with curly, greying hair. Her eyes were filled with grief and horror. Deputy Preston approached the officer and the woman. He tapped the officer on the left shoulder lightly.

"Officer," Deputy Preston nodded, slightly, "this is the witness?" he asked, speaking in a professional tone.

"Deputy Preston," the police officer answered, a little surprised. "Yes, sir," he nodded in response. "This is Laurie Dawson. She is, was, Detective Quinn's cleaning lady, sir. Laurie found the body this morning."

Deputy Preston lifted his eyes and looked at Laurie. He could see first-hand just how distraught she was.

"My condolences, Miss Dawson."

Laurie struggled to hold back her tears.

"Thank you, sir," she responded, just above a whisper.

"I want your notes on my desk as soon as possible, do I make myself clear?"

"Yes, sir. Of course."

Deputy Preston pushed on. He dodged the oncoming human traffic, making his way past the other officers who were quick to make their way outside the front of the building, in search of fresh air, as one officer held his right hand over his mouth, ready to catch whatever was about to come out. He kept his eyes on the officer a moment, before turning again, focusing on what was in front of him, quietly making his way inside the apartment. Deputy Preston advanced to the entrance of the living room, surveying the room. The television set was still switched on.

The living room was in the same shape it was left from the night before; the coffee table was used as dining table. The bowl of spaghetti had grown cold and hardened. A near-empty bottle of beer stood flat. And there were a handful of officers standing around, quietly whispering, talking amongst themselves.

"What are you lot doing?" Deputy Preston asked, raising his voice a little. "Don't you all have something you should be doing? This is Quinn we are dealing with. He was one of us. He wore the badge. Have a little fucking respect!"

The other officers turned and looked at Deputy Preston, some of them nodded and carried on with their work, dispersing from the small group, feeling somewhat embarrassed for being caught out. Deputy Preston moved on. He shifted the weight of his frame once more and made his way past the living room, making his descent down the hallway, toward the bathroom. He lifted his head a moment, taking in the photographs which hung on the walls.

The door leading into the bathroom remained open and was kept clear, for easy access. The neon lights were switched on. They flickered from time to time. Deputy Preston stood in the bathroom doorway a moment, surveying the room. He wanted to turn and run, but stood there, surveying the room. The young officer was right. It looked more like a scene from a horror movie. The bathroom itself was decorated in blood spatter across the walls. The edge of the washbasin was caked in dry blood. A small pool of blood sat at the bottom of the basin. And Mark Quinn lay on the tiled floor, deceased, rotting, stewing in his blood and filth. Deputy Preston stood in the doorway of the bathroom, flinching a little from the smell of the crime scene.

"Deputy," an officer said, quite sombre, making his way out of the bathroom. "Here," he continued, "'you'll need this."

The officer passed a tube of cream to the deputy. Deputy Preston surveyed the room and noticed all the other officers, including the coroner, on the bathroom floor on his hands and knees, all wearing the cream under their nose, to detract from the smell of a decomposed corpse. Deputy Preston turned for a brief moment of privacy, as he applied the cream under his nostrils, a little self-aware of the other officers in the room, who watched on.

"What have we got here?" Deputy Preston asked, turning to face the other officers in the bathroom, raising his voice a little. "Do we know what happened?"

"Deputy Preston," the coroner answered, looking up from the corpse. Detective Mark Quinn was laying on the tiled floor of the bathroom, almost in the foetal position. His hands were just inches away from his throat and mouth. The vicious knife wound, slicing the rotted flesh was open and visible. The colour of his once green eyes was a light shade of grey, and his flesh was doused in blood and was a shade of purple.

"Trutmann," Deputy Preston nodded. "Please, give me something I can use. Something that I can go on."

"It's not good," Coroner Trutmann replied, "there are multiple knife wounds. There are wounds to the neck and there appears to be a further eight stab wounds about the lower back and stomach.

"Detective Quinn died a very painful death. He was found this morning by the cleaning lady. She has her key. She says she went about her daily tasks and walked in on him this morning. His bloodied, corpse, stewing in his blood and filth for the better part of the last three to four days, from my count. I'll know more when I get him to the morgue."

"You do that," Deputy Preston answered, flatly. "But before you do. I want to see him."

"You don't have to. We already have an identification."

"I want to see him!" Deputy Preston repeated himself, raising his voice a little more.

A quiet fell upon the bathroom, itself. Two police officers stepped out of the room, making space for the deputy. They passed him and made their way out into the hallway.

Deputy Preston made his way deeper into the bathroom. He was careful to position his feet as he made his way around the room, stepping on the plastic sheeting. The pain in his torso coursed through his body, but he fought on. He took almost five or six steps into the bathroom, getting himself into position, crouching down in front of Detective Mark Quinn, just inches from his greying eyes and opened, bloodied mouth. The veins that coursed the sides of his temples were visible and ruptured. His teeth stained red, stewing in his blood. Deputy Preston was close enough to make out the small chips in his teeth, on the upper and lower bridges, just left of the middle.

"We will catch the son of a bitch. I promise, Detective," Deputy Preston said, just above a whisper. Deputy Preston climbed to his feet, again. He dusted himself down, straightening out his uniform, a little. "I want you to call me, the moment you have something, Trutmann."

"Yes, sir."

Deputy Preston walked out of the bathroom with a strength in his step, not looking back at the deceased body that lay on the tiled floor, not looking back at a former colleague and friend.

The front doors leading into the Hillsboro Police Station burst open with an almighty force. It was Deputy Preston. He was angry, and his arrival brought about several eyes on him, both from the police department and members of the local community, as he made his way through the office. The office itself was busy again, today. There was a list of the usual suspects, picked up for drink driving and waiting to be processed. Deputy Preston dug his right hand into his uniform trouser pocket to retrieve his swipe card. He buzzed himself in, pushed the door open and walked across the office, heading towards Detective Quinn's office. His right hand sorted through the keys on the chain which held his swipe card, looking for the key to the office. He found it. The key was inserted into the lock and the office door was pushed open. The neon lights in the office flickered on, again. The office smelled of Detective Quinn still. The smell of Old Spice and hard work.

The far wall in the office was decorated with photographs of the Hillsboro victims, including Jayne Scott and the New York victim, Robert Prescott. Deputy Preston made his way deeper into the office, sat behind the desk and booted up the computer. He looked down on the surface of the desk itself, his palms of his hands gently touching the surface of the desk, remembering his colleague and friend, for just a moment. His thoughts quickly turned. He reached for his cell phone in his trouser pocket, signed in, and began to dial. The phone line was connecting.

"Hey," Deputy Preston was the first to talk. "I got some news. It *was* Quinn. He's gone. That fucking clown mask got to him. It was a bloodbath."

"Shit!" Peter answered quietly, under his breath. "So, now what do we do?"

"We catch the son of a bitch. And if that fails, we hunt them down and kill him. Her. Whoever. Stay safe. Stay at home. Lock your doors and windows. I'll post two officers out your front door until we catch this… whoever the fuck this is!"

The day progressed further into the evening. The clouds raced across the sky, bringing with them light rain and a little snow. Peter followed the 'deputy's instruction and stayed home. The light in the kitchen was switched on, as were the lights in the living room. The television set was switched off. A silence filled the house. Peter made his way down the staircase of his home, dressed in blue jeans and a light-grey t-shirt. He was also barefoot. Peter reached the bottom of the staircase and made his way over to the front door. He opened the door and peered outside. There was another squad car parked out the front of the house. Peter could see the two officers, one male, one female. He stared at them a moment longer, his lips opened a little, about to call out. He retracted, pulling back and stepping inside the house, closing the front door. Peter locked the front door, leaving the porch light switched on.

Peter turned his back on the front door and made his way deeper into the house, making his way into the living room. His cell phone began to ring, breaking the silence. It startled him a little. He reached for his cell phone in his jean pocket. He looked down at the cell phone as a smile surfaced to his lips. The caller ID read *Emily*.

"Hey," Peter said, answering the call.

"How are you holding up? Andrew told me about the police officers posted at your front door. That's got to suck! No privacy and all," replied Emily. Her tone of voice was friendly, yet thoughtful.

"I'm holding up. This whole thing feels like déjà vu, you know?"

Peter roamed throughout the house, starting in the living room, talking to Emily. "I feel like a fucking prisoner in my own home."

"Hold tight. *This* will be over soon enough, I promise." The phone line went quiet for a moment.

"Let's change the subject, shall we?" Emily continued. Her tone of voice rejuvenated with a friendly buoyancy about it.

"Please." Peter smiled.

The walking track around the house took Peter back to the foyer of the house. He stood at the bottom of the staircase, his hand on the banister, his head tilted back a little, staring up into the darkness of the second storey of the house.

"What's new?" Peter asked, continuing.

"The movie tickets, of course," Emily answered with a hint of laughter in her voice. "The movie marathon is coming up in a couple of days. You must be excited?"

"I'm looking forward to it. I don't know how I will go with the Hillsboro PD on my back."

"Don't worry about them. You'll have me. We will have a great time, I promise."

"Yes, we will. I can't wait."

"So, I'll talk to you tomorrow, okay?"

"What are you doing?"

"I have a couple of things I need to do around the house. What about you?"

"Andrew is working late this evening. I'll probably crash in front of the television, soon enough."

"He is dedicated."

"To his work? He is." Emily laughed a little. "Sleep well."

"And you."

The phone line disconnected.

Peter continued to look up into the darkness that was the second storey of the house. He gripped the banister and made the climb up the staircase.

Andrew was back behind the steering wheel of his truck. He was still dressed in his police uniform. The time on his watch read nine fifty-eight in the evening. The radio in the truck was switched off. Andrew pulled out of the parking lot of the Hillsboro Police Station and made his way over to the hospital. He received a call from the coroner. It took approximately twenty minutes and change to reach the hospital. There was a lot of traffic on the road this evening. The truck pulled into the parking lot of the hospital and Deputy Preston made his way inside.

The elevator doors opened, and Deputy Preston stepped onto the floor in front of him. He stood there a moment, looking left, then right, reading the directions in front of him, when the elevator doors were quick to close behind him. The hospital corridor was near on empty. He could see an orderly walk the halls on duty, off in the distance. And there were empty stretchers parked in the hallway. There was a sign painted on the wall, offering directions around the basement floor.

Deputy Preston took a right from the elevator and made his way to the end of the corridor.

The neon lights flickered on, as he made his way down the corridor. He reached the end before taking a left. There was a bright light coming from an office, second on the right, and a murmur of voices coming from the room. Deputy Preston made his way further down the corridor. A small black-and-white sign hung from above the office door. It simply read *Morgue*. Deputy Preston stood in the doorway, surveying the room.

The light hanging from the ceiling was bright and Trutmann was sitting at his desk, head down, and typing away on the keyboard of his computer. His assistant was also in the office. She stood in the middle of the room, next to a deceased body, which lay on a metallic slab, naked under a single, white cotton sheet. The office assistant finished pulling the sheet high, over the deceased's head.

"Good evening," the office assistant said, breaking the silence in the office. "Can I help you?" Trutmann stopped typing on the keyboard of his computer and raised his eyes. A smile surfaced to his lips, a moment.

"Good evening, Deputy Preston," Trutmann continued, "please come on in."

"Thank you."

Deputy Preston stepped further into the office. He was very aware of his tongue and could feel his heartbeat racing wildly in his chest. But, to the outside, he did his best to maintain a professional demeanour.

"Thank you for coming down, and so late in the evening. I knew you would want to hear just as soon as I had the results."

"And?"

Deputy Preston moved his eyes from Trutmann a moment and made their way over to the body lying under the large lamp in the middle of the office.

"That's him?"

"Detective Mark Quinn? Yes, sir."

Deputy Preston took another step closer toward the body. He reached the metallic slab and placed his hands on the far edge of the table, closer to the feet. The table felt cool to the touch.

"We found some personal belongings on Mark Quinn. We thought maybe you would want them. I couldn't find any family members."

"Of course," Deputy Preston answered, just above a whisper, staring down at the body that was once his friend and colleague. "You said you had the results. What were your findings, Trutmann?"

"Well," he answered, walking closer toward Mark Quinn, standing next to the deputy. "There were multiple lacerations. The throat."

There was a pause.

"We also found further lacerations around the lower abdomen, including the back, the liver, the stomach and larger intestines. There was a total of thirteen puncture wounds. The depth of the puncture wounds suggests that the stabbings were done at a high ferocity, someone very angry and unable to be reasoned with."

Deputy Preston remained silent, as he continued to stare down at the body. "I want to see him." Deputy Preston murmured.

The office assistant looked up at the deputy, stunned by such a request.

"You don't need that. Like I told you before, we have already made an identification of the body."

"I don't care!" Deputy Preston shouted. "For personal peace of mind. I want to see my friend and colleague."

Trutmann looked at his assistant in silence. Their eyes met each other. The assistant nodded in acceptance.

"Casey, please. If you wouldn't mind."

"Yes, of course."

Deputy Preston raised his eyes and looked at Casey. Their eyes met, only briefly, lasting several seconds at most, before lowering them down again, down on the body that was once his friend and colleague. Casey was a big-boned girl. She was older than Andrew Preston, by six or seven years, at most. Her hair was trimmed short. It was stringy and cropped in places, just below the ear. Casey wore little to no make-up. She stood on the opposite end of the table and pulled back on the single white bed sheet. It was Detective Mark Quinn. His eyes were closed now. It was the first thing Deputy Preston noticed. The tone of his flesh was a shade of purple. The veins about the temple were still visible and ruptured. The blood had been washed away, made presentable for public display, what they were comfortable with showing, that was.

The bed sheet turned back on itself, exposing the detective's remains just under the chin and a little more of the throat. The area was bruised, and the flesh was torn. There was blood. Dried blood. Deputy Preston noticed. He leaned in for a closer inspection.

"What is that?" he asked, just above a mumble.

Trutmann looked at Deputy Preston and then at Casey. "I think that's enough. Casey, if you will…"

"No!" Deputy Preston called out. "I want to see it. I *need* to see it. Casey, please. If you will remove the sheet a little further, please. Lower, please?"

Casey looked to her boss, almost confused. "Go on," Trutmann answered, nodding a little.

"Yes, sir."

The bed sheet was tugged at, pulled on, exposing the knife wound around Mark Quinn's throat.

The slice to the flesh was rough, torn at certain points. The bloodied wound grew more and more brutal, more grotesque, as the flesh peeled back on itself, torn and exposing the muscles beneath.

"Who could do such a thing?" Deputy Preston asked himself, just above a whisper.

He turned away from the body, away from the table, in disgust. He could feel his stomach turn, fighting every urge not to vomit. He wiped his mouth with the back of his right hand and could feel the saliva that emerged to the surface of the lips. Casey was quick to cover Mark Quinn, again. "Thank you." Deputy Preston continued.

He was quick to walk out of the office. "Wait!" Trutmann called out.

He ran toward the door of his office. He turned right to see Deputy Preston move as fast as he could, down the corridor before taking another right.

"But, the personal belongings," Trutmann called out.

A clock sat on top of the nightstand next to the bed. A cell phone sat next to the clock. The time on the alarm clock was six twenty-three in the morning. Andrew was home and fast asleep and alone in bed. He was tossing and turning, a little, trying to make himself as comfortable, as he could. The curtains in the master bedroom were pulled to close. There was just a hint of the morning light through the sliver of a gap in the curtain. The light sprayed across the bedroom floor and crept up onto the bed. Andrew was showing signs of slowly waking up to the start of a new day.

Andrew rolled over onto his back. His ribs felt a little sore. Andrew was in the middle of the bed, his left hand rose from underneath the bed cover to wipe the sleep from his eyes. He was awake now, staring up at the ceiling above. He turned and looked at the time on the alarm clock. It was almost half-past six now. Andrew reached over to his cell phone, pulling it from the charger chord. The screen of the cell phone came to life. Two text messages were waiting for him. Andrew wiped the sleep from his eyes, again. His vision adjusting to the brightness of the screen. Andrew navigated to his conversation history. He opened the text message from Emily first.

I love you.

The message was short but very powerful. The message also ended with a smiley face emoji icon. It brought a smile to his lips. Andrew navigated to the second message waiting for him. It was from Peter.

I hope you're doing okay, good buddy. I'm here if you need to talk.

"Thank you, good buddy," Andrew replied, just above a whisper.

Andrew was in bed for a few more minutes before he peeled the bed cover back, exposing his naked frame beneath. He climbed to the side of the bed, slowly as he could, as not to disturb his torso. Andrew climbed to his feet and stood by the side of the bed a moment, stretching some. He walked out of the master bedroom and made his way down the hallway. The lights in the kitchen switched on. He walked into the kitchen, naked, over to the refrigerator, opened the door and leaned in, pulling out a single bottle of water. Andrew twisted down hard on the lid and took a deep sip.

His head was tilted back, and his eyes were closed. The water was cold to the touch. Andrew took the bottle of water with him from the kitchen and returned to the master bedroom. He placed the bottle on top of the nightstand, near the alarm clock, and climbed back into bed, pulling the bed cover up around his waistline, as he sat up in bed, using his pillows to prop up his lower back.

The cell phone which sat on top of the nightstand began to ring. *Ring. Ring. Ring.* Andrew looked down. His first thought went to Emily, then to the Hillsboro Police Station. The screen of the cell phone came to life. *Unknown Caller.*

"What do you want?" Andrew asked, clearing his throat a little.

"What if I said *you*?" the dark and familiar voice answered, followed by the hint of a laugh. "I told you I would be back. I got rid of Detective Quinn for you. Show some gratitude. Where is the thanks?"

"I never asked you to do anything."

"I know you did. I'm sure you did. You wanted him out of the way, just as much as me. I mean, did you believe Detective Mark Quinn for a moment? He was incompetent. Multiple deaths on his watch, a town in curfew, and not a single clue."

"There were clues."

"I left behind what you wanted to see. And what did you find, huh? Nothing at all." There was another laugh. "And now that Quinn is out of the picture, you and I can have some real fun. The game is in full swing now."

"You're mine. I'm going to *kill* you." There was even more laughter.

"There's the can-do attitude I like to hear," the dark and familiar voice continued, "but, there is one serious fault in your plan."

"Yeah? What's that?"

It's *my* fucking game! And you play by *my* rules. People live. And people are going to die. And I know just how to inflict pain, how to make people hurt, deep down, you know."

The phone call ended with further laughter. The phone call disconnected.

"Shit!" Andrew called out loudly, dropping his cell phone back down on the bed, in front of him. His ribs continued to hurt. "Fuck!" he shouted.

Andrew remained in bed a minute or two longer, before climbing to his feet, again. He left his cell phone behind him on the bed, and walked out of the master bedroom, down the hallway and into the bathroom.

The bathroom door was pushed to a gentle close as the light in the ceiling switched on.

Andrew stood in the middle of the bathroom. He looked up, catching his reflection in the bathroom mirror. He stood there naked, staring at himself. His hands were quick to cover his stomach, placing them over the bandages. Andrew started the slow process of removing the bandages from around his torso. The bandages dropped to the bathroom floor below. Andrew peeled at the surgical tape from his stomach. He flinched at the touch, careful not to cause any further damage to the stitches.

The knife wounds were now exposed. The stitches looked new and the flesh was red and irritated. Andrew touched the stitches gently, as his fingertips ran over them. He looked up at the bathroom mirror, again. His thoughts went to Detective Mark Quinn. He shook his head from left to right, back and forth, several times, and shook off the thought. He turned and walked towards the shower. He leaned and switched on the faucet.

The water was warm to the touch. It felt so inviting. Andrew stepped into the shower, under the water, pulling the shower door to a gentle close behind him. The water splashed at his feet and ankles before he stepped into the shower further, turning his back to the hot water. His head tilted back, a little, and his eyes closed.

The shower was soon over. The flood of water disintegrated to nothing more than a slow drip from the shower head. *Drip. Drip. Drip.* Andrew stepped out from under the shower and stepped across the bathroom floor with caution as he grabbed a fresh cotton towel to wrap himself up in. He walked out of the bathroom, leaning in to open the door and walked down the hallway, toward the kitchen to make himself his first coffee of the morning, with a damp towel wrapped loosely around his waist.

The morning was progressing. The television set in the living room was switched on. A female TV reporter, somewhere in her early forties, with her thick, black hair, pulled back into slick, low ponytail, and wore a black trench coat tied off at the waist over a white blouse and black jeans, stood outside the Hillsboro Cemetery reporting on the story of Detective Mark Quinn's funeral service later in the day. Andrew was back in his bedroom. He finished applying fresh surgical tape over his stitches and wrapped his torso in another bandage. He stood in front of his closet in his jockey shorts, pulling a plain, white long-sleeved shirt from his closet, followed by black trousers, matching tie, and jacket. Andrew got himself dressed, then turned, grabbing his cell phone from the top of the nightstand, again. He placed the cell phone in his left trouser pocket, making his way toward the front door, switching off the television in the living room along the way.

Fade to black. Fade from black.

It was almost eleven o'clock in the morning as a crowd of townspeople gathered on the outside steps of the Hillsboro Catholic

Church. It was a cool and cloudy morning in Hillsboro. The leaves in the nearby trees rattled as a breeze blew by and the clouds raced across the sky, as much as the sun tried to burn through. The local police department was on duty outside the Hillsboro Catholic Church, controlling the small crowds of the local people who stood opposite the historic building, holding placards, protesting for justice for the fallen townsfolk.

A handful of guests to Mark Quinn's funeral service stood on the cement staircase, leading up to the entrance of the church, quietly talking and whispering amongst themselves. Andrew and Emily had already arrived. They stood at the bottom of the staircase, on the footpath. Andrew quietly talked to a handful of colleagues, whilst Emily played the role of the dutiful girlfriend, on hand to provide support and talk amongst the other wives and girlfriends. Peter soon arrived. He walked along the footpath, approaching the church. He felt nervous and a little awkward, kind of like the first day of school. He was dressed in a three-quarter length open black jacket, with a white shirt underneath, black tie, trousers and shoes. Peter made eye contact with Emily as he approached the church. A hint of a smile surfaced to her lips as she gave a small nod of her head. There were two police officers on duty, plain clothed, in the background, watching Peter's every move.

"Good morning," Peter said, just above a whisper, as a hint of a smile surfaced to his lips.

"It's great to see you," Emily replied, leaning in to give her friend a quick kiss on the cheek. "It's nice to see you, even under such circumstances."

"I wasn't going to miss this, as much as people would rather see me hidden away at home."

"Fuck them!" Emily whispered, careful not to draw too much attention to herself and her friend. Peter looked around the crowd of other funeral-goers, some making eye contact, others whispering amongst themselves and shooting *that's him* looks.

"How's the big fella holding up?" Peter asked, nodding towards Andrew.

"You know him, always on duty."

"Ah." Peter nodded.

The front doors to the Catholic church opened. The people standing on the cement staircase quickly noticed and made their way inside the building.

"Here we go," Emily said, her eyes friendly. "Are you ready for this?" "Never," Peter shook his head.

"Well then, let's show them, shall we?" Emily smiled, reassuringly "Let's make our way inside and find our seats."

As the crowd of people slowly made their way up the cement staircase and inside the church, Andrew returned to Emily. He stood in between Emily and Peter, as they made their way inside, taking Emily by the hand, and squeezing it tightly for support.

"Thank you for coming out and supporting me, good buddy," Andrew whispered, leaning into Peter's ear with a smile.

"Any time."

Chapter Twenty-Seven...

The entrance doors to the Hillsboro Catholic Church opened slowly, as the funeral procession made their way down the cement staircase and onto the street, led by the pallbearers carrying Detective Mark Quinn toward a waiting hearse parked on the side of the road. Father William Tierney was a short and stocky man, in his early sixties with snow-white hair and matching beard, that was neatly trimmed. He had been a part of the church for the better part of the last thirty years. He stood atop the cement staircase, greeting the churchgoers. The pallbearers wore their police uniform, in honour of their fallen colleague and friend.

Andrew, Emily and Peter slowly emerged from the entrance of the church, greeted by Father William Tierney. Andrew was the first to shake hands with the Father, followed by Emily. They flashed a quick smile and thanked him for his service. Peter could feel his heartbeat starting to race in his chest. He felt anxious. The memories of his father's funeral came flooding back. Father William Tierney was the first to make eye contact with Peter. His warm eyes were met with a smile which surfaced to his lips as he extended his hand out. He grabbed Peter by the right hand and shook it quickly. Peter could feel his grip tighten around his hand. Peter forced a smile.

"Thank you," Peter said, just above a whisper, and avoiding eye contact.

"If there is anything you need, Peter," Father William Tierney said, still shaking his hand. "You know where my office is. Any time."

"Yes, sir. Thank you."

The crowd of churchgoers was beginning to disperse now. Andrew stood on the side of the footpath, watching Detective Mark Quinn's coffin be loaded into the back of the hearse. He stood there and gazed upon the coffin, fighting back his tears. His mind raced with thoughts, past the brutality of the crime, and finality of death, itself. Emily stood close by, for support. Her hand extended out, taking Andrew's hand in hers and giving it a gentle squeeze.

The coffin was loaded into the back of the hearse. The door slammed shut. And a member of staff and the driver returned to the front of the car. The driver climbed inside, slamming the door to a close. The engine came to life and the hearse was careful to make its way out into the traffic and drive to the end of the street. Andrew watched the hearse reach the end of the street before turning around to face Emily and Peter. A smile slowly raised to the surface of his lips.

"A few of us are heading over to The Watering Hole to have a drink and celebrate Mark's memory. Why don't you come join us?" Andrew asked, looking at his best friend.

Peter thought about the offer before saying anything. "Okay," he nodded. "I'll see you there."

"Great," Andrew answered, still smiling and clapping his hands together, rather heavily.

Peter turned his gaze to Emily. She smiled back with friendly eyes.

Peter left his best friend and his partner behind, turned and walked along the footpath of the outside the church, before making his way to the parking lot. He walked toward his sports utility vehicle, as the gravel squashed under his feet. He tucked his left hand into his jacket pocket, retrieving his keys and unlocked the truck. Peter leaned in and opened the driver's side door and climbed inside, making himself comfortable and closing the door behind him.

Peter sat behind his steering wheel a moment, in silence. He made eye contact with some of the other churchgoers, who attended the service as they sprawled into the parking lot as he peered out the windscreen, before shaking off the somber tone. Peter placed the key into the ignition and the engine roared to life. He sat back in his seat a moment, waiting to make his move. Peter placed his foot on the accelerator and slowly drove out of the parking lot and out into traffic. He made a right turn and drove to the end of the road, increasing in speed.

The radio in the sports utility vehicle was playing. The volume was down low. Peter kept his eyes firmly on the road in front of him as the music played. His cell phone sat atop of the front passenger seat next to him. It started to vibrate. Peter shifted his eyes off the road a moment and looked down at his cell phone. He could see the notification light flashing.

Seconds later, his cell phone vibrated a second time. Concern ravaged his thoughts and face, as he bit his lower lip, a little. Peter shifted his eyes back onto the road in front of him, looking for a place to pull over. The traffic behind him raced past the sports utility vehicle at an almost thunderous speed.

Peter sat behind his steering wheel. He tugged on his seat belt a little, feeling it against his throat. It immediately felt restricting. Peter turned in his chair a little and reached for his cell phone. He pressed the button on the side of the device and the screen came to life. Two text messages were waiting for him. The messages came from a private number. Peter looked at his cell phone. He could feel his heartbeat racing wildly in his chest, again. His palms grew a little sweaty as he stared at his cell phone. Peter switched off the radio and reluctantly opened the first message.

I was so close. I could have reached out and cut someone.

The message read.

"What the fuck?" he whispered to himself, catching his breath in his chest, a moment.

Peter navigated to the second message. This time, it was a picture message. It was a photograph taken from inside the church, during the funeral service. And in the centre of the photograph, was a picture of Andrew, Emily and Peter taken from several rows behind. Peter looked down at the photograph, his mind racing. His cell phone vibrated a third time, startling him, a little. He gasped for air and navigated out of the photograph.

I told you I could have cut someone, Peter. Who will be next, huh? You can't save everyone. Look around you. The townsfolk are dropping like flies.

Peter lifted his eyes off of his cell phone, peering through the windscreen, down the mountainous road ahead. He could feel his cell phone twirling between his fingers a moment as his mind raced, before exploding, dropping the cell phone to the floor.

"Dammit! Fucking goddammit!" he yelled at the top of his lungs, hitting his hands, on top of the steering wheel.

The outburst lasted all of a few seconds before Peter stopped what he was doing and composed himself, once more. He sat there behind his steering wheel, running his left hand down, over his shirt, looking forward out into the road in front of him. He caught his reflection in the rear-view mirror again and smiled at himself. He could see the tears welling in his eyes. Peter took a deep breath. It sounded more like a sigh. He leaned into the dashboard of his truck and turned the volume on the radio up. Way up. He searched the stations for music that was a little more hardcore, a little heavier. He quickly found it. The sports utility vehicle pulled off the side of the road and merged back into the traffic.

The sports utility vehicle was now parked in the parking lot of The Watering Hole. There were several other cars and trucks parked there, too. It was a busy day for the establishment. The private room at The Watering Hole had been booked for Andrew, Peter, Emily, and all the other police officers and their partners, who attended the funeral service. The room held a capacity of fifty-five guests. The guests sat around the tables, quietly talking amongst themselves. Andrew took charge of the room, raising his glass, raising a toast, to a colleague and friend. The guests, including Emily and Peter, cheered him on. Andrew could feel his heartbeat racing whilst he gave his speech.

"Detective Mark Quinn was a character," Andrew started, with a nervous tremor to his voice.

The start of his speech was met with a few laughs and cheers from the audience, as members nodded their heads, a little.

"But you either loved him or hated him," Andrew continued. "There was no in between. But, either way, you knew he had your back. He was there for support, to help you through the good and the bad. I want to ask everyone in the room today, please join me in raising your glass, and raise a toast, to my friend, our colleague, Detective Mark Quinn. We carry you forward in our hearts and we will never forget you. Cheers!"

The audience in the room raised their glasses and cheered to the speech, to their deputy. The guests went about their way, talking amongst themselves, laughing, sharing happy memories. Emily sat in her chair, looking up at Andrew. A smile surfaced to her lips. She couldn't be more proud of her partner, for the kind words he had shared. The two made eye contact, and Emily took a sip from her glass of chardonnay. Peter sat back and surveyed the room. He watched the other police officers, some in uniform, some not, talk amongst themselves. He turned in his seat and looked at Emily and Andrew. The two shared sweet nothings, as Emily smiled, holding Andrew's hand. Peter finished off his glass of soda in one hit, before standing up and stepping away from the table. He walked across the room, toward the restrooms, out toward the balcony, for some fresh air.

Andrew noticed Peter. He couldn't help but pull his eyes away from Emily, at that moment. "If you'll excuse me?" Andrew asked, just above a whisper, as he leaned in close to Emily, to whisper in her left ear.

Emily noticed Peter, too. "Of course," she smiled.

Emily turned to one of the wives or girlfriends sitting next to her.

Andrew grabbed his glass of beer and stood up from the table, following Peter out onto the balcony.

The balcony to The Watering Hole was empty, more or less. There would have been less than half a dozen other officers, standing around, drinking, talking amongst themselves. Andrew could see Peter standing alone, in the far north corner of the balcony, looking out, taking in the view of the surrounding trees. He passed the other officers, giving them brief eye contact, and motioning for them to leave the balcony, to give their deputy and his friend a little private time, alone. The other police officers agreed, with a nod of the head and a smile, and made their way inside the pub.

"Here you are. How are you holding up?" Andrew asked, with a friendly tone to his voice.

"That sounds like a question I should be asking you," Peter responded, turning around to look at his best friend.

His face was rather sombre, losing some of its natural colour. Andrew looked concerned.

"Talk to me." he continued. "What's going on? You definitely know how to make an exit, that's for sure. Emily and I noticed you leave the room back there."

"Look at you," Peter replied, just above a whisper, his voice struggling.

"Look at me? Look at me what? What's going on? Talk to me."
"You've already got hurt."

"Yes. And I survived. Granted, a little sore. But I will pull through. It's going to take a little more than a few stitches to keep me down." Andrew smiled, reassuringly.

"I heard from the killer on the drive over. He. She. Or whoever. They texted me."

Andrew was startled, a little. He could feel his heart race and his palms grew sweaty, again. He took a step back, a moment, wiping the palms of his hands on the sides of his trousers. That reassuring smile vanished.

"What did they say?"

"The killer was at the funeral. They sat just rows behind us. Whoever is doing this, is sneaky. It's someone we may know. I don't know. But whoever it is, managed to talk their way into the detective's funeral service."

"How?"

"I don't fucking know. You're the cop! You sort this out! They sent a picture! Do you see it?" Peter took his cell phone out of his trouser pocket, signed in and flashed him the picture.

"Calm down."

"I am calm. That's all I have ever been for years. Ever since my father, my *fucking* mother and grandfather. Since New York. That's all I ever do. I sit on the side-lines and watch people I care about, people I love, drop like flies whilst I try to remain calm. I want this to end. I want to catch whoever is doing this and put an end to it. I want to stand over their bloodied and beaten body before I put a bullet in their head and end this for good. Are you *hearing* me?"

"I am hearing you," Andrew replied, his tone of voice quiet and soothing. "And we will. I guarantee you. But, until that time arrives, I need you to pull yourself together and stay quiet. Please. Whoever is doing this, gets to you when you let them get under your skin. Don't."

"Yeah? And how do I do that?"

"We catch this motherfucker! You and me. And we kill the son of a bitch!"

"I like the sound of that." Peter forced a smile.

"There's my good buddy, again. I thought for a second there I lost you. Let's keep this talk between us, okay? Don't involve Emily."

"I hear you."

The evening fell upon Hillsboro for another day. Emily was fast asleep in Andrew's bed, the bed cover pulled up high, to her shoulders.

The light in the master bedroom was switched off, and the door left wide open. On the nightstand, her cell phone, hooked up to a charger. And a bottle of sleeping pills, with the cap left off, next to a near-empty glass of water. A light stretched from the hallway.

Andrew was dressed in a loose-fitting tank top and boxer shorts as he made his way around the house. He walked to the end of the hallway and made his way into the kitchen. He peered in, making sure everything was clean and stored away. He walked past the sink and checked the windows. They were locked. He turned his back on the windows and made his way out of the kitchen and into the living room. The television set was switched off. He leaned into the windows, pulling on them a little. They were secure.

Andrew walked out of the living room, switching the lights off at the wall, and made his way over to the front door. His eyes diverted to the bowl on the table, which housed his wallet and a couple of other personal belongings. He made it to the front door and placed his left hand on the door handle, giving it a little jiggle. The door handle was unlocked. It pushed down hard, feeling his heartbeat start to race. The front door opened a little. Andrew leaned forward a little, peering out onto the porch, into the stillness of the night air. The light on the front porch switched on.

He let go of the door handle and stepped outside, and stood under the light of the porch, continuing to peer out into the front yard. The light breeze brushed past the trees, a moment.

"Hello?" Andrew called out into the front yard, his face filled with concern.

He stood there a moment longer. There was no response. Andrew shrugged off his concern and turned his back on the front yard. He stepped off the front porch and made his way inside his home, closing the door behind him. The keys jiggled, again. Andrew gave the door handle another, quick jiggle. The front door was now locked.

Andrew peered through the frosted glass on the front door, again. He couldn't make much out, before he turned his back on the front door, making his way down the hallway, switching the lights off around the house, as he went. As the approached the master bedroom, he tugged at his loose-fitting tank top and removed it, before climbing into bed with Emily, snuggling up close, as much as he could, without hurting the stitches on his stomach.

Peter was at home for the evening, again, after returning from The Watering Hole. He was sitting at his desk in his office, in front of his laptop computer, searching the Internet. He was looking at newspaper articles and pictures from years gone by. The pictures were of his mother, his father, grandfather, and the Prescott family, including Robert, Ben, and Carrie. The photographs of Robert brought a warm smile to his lips, as he fought the tears welling in his eyes. There were also photographs from New York City, from his university years, of himself, Ben, Alison, and Logan, all in happier times. The photographs of the four friends were of happier times; laughing, smiling, and joking around.

The expression on Peter's face changed over time, from the highs of sheer delight, as he looked at his father, and of Robert Prescott, to the deep, terrifying lows, which were of Ben Prescott, and what he brought to his friends and loved ones. Peter was quick to wipe the tears in his eyes and cleared his throat, as he selected the photographs and the news articles that he wanted, and hit the print button. The printer came to life, spitting out the photographs. Peter stood from behind his office desk, collected the photographs and news articles from the printer and made his way out of his office, down the hallway, and into the spare bedroom, to pin them onto the clipboard which hung from the wall.

The photographs, the people, and the news articles, too, were just a snapshot of memories of his life in the past four years and beyond. Peter stood in front of the clipboard, taking several steps backwards, having pinned the last picture of his father to the wall, taking in a larger view of the collage of photographs. His shoulders slouched as he let out a deep sigh.

"This is my life," he whispered to himself.

Peter wiped the remaining tears from his eyes with the back of his right hand, turned his back on the clipboard on the wall, and walked to the open doorway, standing in the hallway. He flicked the spare room light off and turned again, walking towards the master bedroom, at the end of the hallway. Peter stripped from his clothes, leaving them in a messy pile behind him on the floor, as he walked closer toward his bed. He pulled the bed cover back and climbed up on the mattress in his boxer shorts. He sat up in bed, with the bed cover up to his waist, and leaned down to the nightstand. The lamp was switched on. Peter reached for his cell phone, that was attached to the charger. There were no missed calls or text messages. He navigated to his alarm clock, setting the alarm for five-thirty in the morning, wanting to make an early start on the day, starting it out with a two-mile run. He slid under the bed cover, pulling it high up to his shoulders, laying there on his back, staring up at the ceiling a moment before falling asleep.

The quiet of the night filled the house. The time on the alarm clock that sat upon the nightstand read a little after two in the morning now. Peter was fast asleep, slowly snoring away, tossing and turning, a little. A silence filled the house; the hallway was dark, the kitchen was empty, and a glow from the television set came from the living room. The front door handle, on the inside of the house, was still, for a moment, followed by a gentle tremor, as if someone was tapping it from the outside. It lasted all of several seconds, if that. The lock to the front door clicked over, something strong forcing it open. *Click.* The door handle pushed down. The front door to the house opened swiftly and quietly. The clown mask emerged from the front porch, standing in the doorway, before making their way inside the house.

The dark of the night just about consumed its dark clothing, a black hoodie, their leather gloves, their jeans and leather boots. The white of the mask almost glowed in the dark. The mask turned from left to right, as if surveying the room. It looked up at the staircase in front of them. The clown mask made their way deeper inside the house, their right hand, bound in a leather glove, extended outwards, towards the banister, as they climbed the staircase. The clown mask soon reached the top of the staircase, standing on top of the second storey of the house. The mask surveyed the hallway. The clown mask took a right turn, making their way down the hallway, toward the master bedroom.

The sound of the wooden floorboards cracked under the pressure in the quiet, still of the night. The clown mask was now standing in the doorway to the master bedroom, setting its gaze upon an unconscious Peter, fast asleep. They stepped inside the room, quietly, and swiftly, towards the bed. The leather glove, of the left hand, extended outwards, the fingers stretching, towards Peter, inching closer and closer. The leather glove glided up over the bed cover, along the torso, up along the bicep, toward the throat. Peter tossed and turned in bed, a little. The leather glove retracted, pulling backwards quickly, as Peter flinched, awaking from his broken slumber, sitting up in bed, out of breath, and clutching at his throat and chest.

"Shit!" he whispered under his breath to himself. "Fucking nightmares."

Peter looked around the bedroom, there was no one there. He looked down at the time on the alarm clock, it was two twenty-five. He rubbed the sleep from his eyes a moment, feeling a little tired, pushed the bed cover back and climbed out of bed, and to his feet. The floorboards of the bedroom cracked under the pressure. Peter was too tired to notice. He shrugged it off and walked out of the bedroom. He made his way down the hallway, down the staircase, to the foyer of the house.

The light in the kitchen flickered on. Peter stood in the kitchen entrance, rubbing his eyes, again, as they adjusted to the light, a moment. He stepped inside, walking over to the refrigerator. He leaned in and was quick to pull the door open. He stuck his head inside and surveyed the contents, grabbing the jug of water. He turned and grabbed a glass by the sink and poured himself a glass of water. He stood there, tilting his head back a little, drinking. His eyes closed. The image of the clown mask walked past the entrance of the kitchen, behind him, unnoticed. The lock of the front door clicked over, again. Peter's eyes sprang open in surprise. He placed the near-empty glass of water, next to the jug, on the kitchen counter. His eyes were quick to survey the kitchen as he felt his heartbeat race. He reached for a large, sharp kitchen knife, by the chopping board. The light to the kitchen switched off. Peter gripped the handle of the kitchen knife tightly, as he held the knife close to his chest.

Peter hugged the walls of the hallway, making his way through the house, towards the front door. He was stalking his way in the dark. Peter soon reached the front door, the sharp kitchen knife still held tightly in his right hand, as his left, extended forward, slowly out, towards the door handle. Peter held his breath in his chest. He could feel his heartbeat racing wildly, again. Peter closed his eyes tightly, a moment, before holding his breath and giving the door handle a jiggle. The front door was locked, once more. Peter opened his eyes and let out a deep sigh, as he felt the adrenalin course through his veins.

"Shit!" Peter muttered under his breath.

Peter tried his best to shake off the unnerving feeling that consumed his body. He shook his head a moment, his shoulders slouched, again, before he turned and made his way back into the kitchen. He placed the kitchen knife on top of the chopping board, before heading upstairs and returning to bed. He climbed back into bed, pulling the bed cover high again, up to his shoulders.

The morning started a little foggy and cool. The sky was grey and consumed with clouds which raced across the sky. Peter was dressed in his grey sweat pants, running shoes, and a plain white t-shirt that was sweaty and clung to his muscular frame. His forehead was also sweating, and his cheeks had a pinkish hue about them as he continued to jog, turning onto his street, and heading towards the house. He raced forward, along the footpath, and up onto the front yard of the house, before reaching the front porch. The wooden floorboards cracked under the weight of Peter's muscular frame. The cracking sounded more pronounced so early in the morning. Peter paced the front porch a moment, fighting to catch his breath, again. He peered out into the front yard, and the rest of the neighbourhood, as he rested his hands on his hips. It was empty. Peter lowered his left hand from his hip and placed it in the pocket of his sweat pants and retrieved the front door key to the house.

Peter was quick to climb the staircase. He tugged at his damp t-shirt, pulling it off by the time he reached the top of the staircase. Peter walked down the hallway, with his t-shirt hanging low, almost dragging along the floor of the house, in between his fingers of his left hand. He reached the bathroom, pushed the door open, flicked on the light and made his way inside. The bathroom door was pushed to a close, and the water from the shower started to run.

The morning continued. Peter was now sitting behind the steering wheel of his sports utility vehicle. He had left home and made his way into town. He was reaching the traffic lights of the town square, looking ahead, looking to find somewhere to park. The lights at the traffic lights turned green. He spotted an empty parking spot somewhere between a grocery store and newsagents. The engine to the truck died. Peter was quick to unbuckle his seat belt, retrieve his wallet and cell phone from the front passenger seat, and climb out of the truck, slam the driver's side door to a close and set the alarm. Peter made his way onto the footpath and headed towards the diner. The town square was busier than usual, as the residents went about their daily lives.

The door to the diner pulled open. The ring of the bell quickly followed. Peter stood there, at the entrance of the diner, a moment, surveying the restaurant. It was filled with patrons. A hint of a smile surfaced to his lips as the memories of Riley's in New York City came flooding back, for a moment or two. Peter continued to survey the room slowly until his eyes met with Emily, who was sitting in a booth by the window of the diner, which overlooked out onto the town square. She sat there, propping herself up in her chair, a little, raising her right hand, waiving down her high school friend. Their eyes connected and Peter smiled brighter now. He waved back a little, before he ignored the 'wait to be seated' sign by the cash register, and made his way across the diner floor, toward his friend.

"Here you are," Peter said, happy to see Emily.

"You made it. And on time," Emily answered, with a little smile and a quip in her voice.

"Ha. Ha." Peter answered, climbing into the booth.

"I haven't been here long, myself. I ordered you a glass of water. I hope that's okay?"

"Of course." Peter nodded, happily.

"It's great to see you, you know?" Emily responded, nodding her head, a little. "With everything that has happened recently, Quinn, his funeral, Mike." Emily paused a moment. "It's just nice to see you, is what I am trying to say."

"I know." Peter nodded graciously.

"I'm looking forward to the movie marathon." Emily smiled.

"Wes Craven. It should be a fun night. I could use it. Thank you again. And thank you for coming out with me."

"What am I going to do? Andrew is working so hard lately. I hardly see him much these days."

"Wait," Peter said, almost changing the subject. "With all the murders and all and everything happening in this town, do you think two friends going to a horror movie marathon is in poor taste?"

Emily took a sip from her glass of water a moment as if to ponder the deeper meaning behind the question.

"No," she answered, almost bluntly. "I don't. Never let someone else hold you down and stop you from what you love to do. You do that, and you let them win."

"I guess you're right."

The two friends sat opposite each other as one of the waitresses of the diner, approached the table. The waitress was in her late thirties, with a slim build, and long blonde hair pulled back into a curly, messy ponytail.

The door leading into the diner opened, again. The bell chimed as a loud, piercing scream followed. The waitress stopped, mid-order and looked back, over her right shoulder. Peter and Emily followed, peering across the diner. The rest of the patrons also stopped what they were doing to focus their attention on the front door of the diner. And there, standing inches in front of the cash register, just past the wait to be seated sign, was the commotion. It was a thin, haggard figure, leaning forward, a little. The voice of the piercing scream carried an age to it. The image of the figure was average more than anything. It didn't stand out. It was generic. The haggard figure stood there, silent. And wearing the clown mask.

"I'm the mask! I'm the mask!" the heavy and mature voice shouted, over and over again.

Peter looked at the shape wearing the all-too-familiar mask, standing in the middle of the diner. And for the briefest of moments, felt his heart race and his palms grow sweaty. His thoughts returned to his grandfather. He looked over at Emily. He could see the colour drain from her face.

Peter drew his eyes away from his high school friend and land outside the diner, to a bunch of kids, three, maybe four, all no older than sixteen, stand outside, watching on, as their gag played out.

The tired and haggard figure stood in the front of the diner, before lifting their left hand and removing the mask from their face. It was a man. An elderly gentleman who appeared to be confused, somewhere in his early to mid-seventies.

"Do I get my ten dollars now?" he asked, confused.

A tall, muscular, bear of a man, with a neatly trimmed, black beard, with flecks of grey, and thinning hair on top, which was combed back, in a sweaty sleek, slowly crept forward from behind the counter and toward the frightened, elderly man. The muscular man was dressed in chef whites, with a single white apron, which was tied around the front of his waist, with grease marks splashed across the surface, and a plain white t-shirt, which hugged his frame.

"Let's get you something to eat, shall we?" the chef asked, quietly, as if not to scare him away.

Emily raised her left hand to her chest. She could feel her heartbeat pounding heavily in her chest. The colour in the face hadn't returned, not fully, anyway. She reached for a glass of water and took a sip, trying to calm her nerves. Peter returned his gaze upon the kids standing on the other side of the glass window. The kids made eye contact with Peter, one of them flipping him the bird, before they all ran off, away from the scene, all in different directions, laughing. Peter closed his eyes a moment and shook his head.

"Fucking kids," he mumbled quietly under his breath.

It didn't take long before the police were called and arrived at the diner. A squad car from the Hillsboro Police Station was parked outside the front of the diner. The very presence of the car itself drew unwanted attention from the pedestrians from outside, gawking and rubbernecking, checking out what may have happened. There were three police officers present and on duty. One officer was talking to the bear of a chef from behind the counter, the other took the elderly man quietly into custody, ushering him towards the squad car, whilst Deputy Preston stood at the end of the booth, looking down at Emily and Peter.

"It was nothing," Peter was the first to speak. "A sick joke. I saw a bunch of kids in the window watching their ploy play out. They ran away seconds after. It was nothing."

"Some joke, judging by this," Deputy Preston answered, his voice a little heavier, darker, stressed than usual.

"You saw that mask, Peter. It's that same, damn mask. I know what it did to you."

Peter looked at his friend, silent and concerned. He blinked his eyes a moment, as if not to draw too much attention.

"Whoever is doing this. They're not going away until this, *this*, I don't even know what to call it, goes away," Emily continued, her voice sounding more and more strained, as the seconds passed.

"Let's get you out of here." Deputy Preston answered.

Andrew extended his left hand outwards as if to catch Emily coming out of the booth.

Emily shifted her petite frame out from her side of the booth and climbed to her feet. Deputy Preston stood there, next to her. He was acting like the caring boyfriend now, ready to place one arm over her shoulders and escort her out of the diner.

"I want to take you home," Deputy Preston continued, "Peter, are you okay?"

"I'll be fine." Peter nodded, looking at his best friend. "Get Emily home. Make sure she is okay."

"Thanks, good buddy. We will talk soon."

Peter continued to sit on his side of the booth. He reached for his glass of water on the table in front of him, and took a deep sip, as he watched his best friend take his girlfriend home from the diner.

Andrew and Emily made their way out of the diner and out onto the footpath. A slight breeze blew down the street, touching Emily's face. It felt so inviting and relaxing, as she stood there a moment, closing her eyes.

"Come on," Andrew said, just above a whisper. "I've got you. Let's go."

Andrew was quick to usher Emily to the front passenger side of his truck. He unlocked the door, opened it, and ushered Emily inside. He slammed the door to a close. Deputy Preston stood by the side of his truck, a moment longer, peering through the crowd that grew outside the diner, his eyes filled with concern. Emily sat inside the truck. She was quick to turn in her seat and fasten her seat belt. *Click.* Deputy Preston ran around to his side of the truck. The driver's side door opened, and his muscular, heavy frame climbed inside, slamming the door to a close. The engine to the truck roared to life and music started to play from the radio.

Deputy Preston looked at Emily, again, before his eyes returned to the rear-view mirror, to look for any oncoming traffic. There wasn't any. He switched on his indicator and was careful to pull back into the traffic. The truck raced to the end of the street, reaching the traffic lights, within seconds. The drive in the truck was done almost in silence. The music continued to play from the radio, and there were voices sporadically coming from the CB radio, as Deputy Preston kept his eyes on the road in front of him, and occasionally looking to Emily, watching her almost lifeless eyes gaze out of the window, watching the world pass by.

The truck soon pulled up in front of Emily's home. It pulled into the driveway and the engine of the truck died. Emily continued to sit there, silent. She was now staring out the window, to the front of her home. The deputy was officially off the clock. He was just Andrew now, sitting next to his long-time girlfriend, dressed in his police uniform. He turned and looked at her a moment before he pushed the side door open and climbed out of his truck. Andrew was quick to race around to the other side of the truck to meet Emily. He opened the door for her and extended his right hand outwards, ready to take her hand in his, and help her to her feet. Emily climbed out of the truck, leaving the door open behind her. The two walked to the front door of the house.

Emily was in the shower now. The hot water ran from the shower nozzle. Her head was tilted back, her eyes closed, as she felt the water consume her. Andrew was busy in the kitchen. He paced, grabbing a fresh, empty glass from the cupboard, before filling it with water. He returned to the kitchen counter, with a glass of water in one hand, and a prescription bottle for sleeping pills in the other. The glass and the pills sat on the counter in front of him. Andrew popped the lid from the prescription bottle and retrieved two pills. He ground them up, between his thumb and forefinger and stirred them into Emily's water with a spoon, diluting the pills in the water.

The water from the shower stopped running. The frosted glass of the shower door cautiously slid open and Emily emerged to reach for a thick, white cotton towel to wrap herself in. She used the towel to dry herself down, before climbing into a terrycloth robe which hung on the wall, next to the towel. The damp towel fell to the bathroom floor, out from under the robe. Emily felt dry and relaxed now.

Andrew was still standing in the kitchen. He had heard the water from the shower stop and the bathroom door open. Emily walked from the bathroom, taking a left turn, and walked to the end of the hallway, reaching her master bedroom. There were small puddles of water following her every step from the bathroom. Andrew lifted the glass of water from the kitchen counter and made his way to the master bedroom. It didn't take long for him to be standing in the entrance of the open bedroom door, watching Emily climb into bed and pulling the bed cover up high, to her shoulders. She lay there on her back, her pillow gently propping her up, a little.

"Here," Andrew started, just above a whisper, as he walked inside the master bedroom, toward Emily. "I got you this. You had a rough day. It will help you sleep."

"I don't need my sleeping pills," Emily replied, snapping a little.

"You need some rest," Andrew continued, "drink up. Take it."

Emily looked back at Andrew as their eyes met. Emily took the glass of water from Andrew's right hand. The expression on his face had said it all. It was a fight she wasn't going to win. Andrew stood over Emily, watching her down the glass of water, enough for the sleeping pills to take effect. "There," Andrew continued, "'you'll feel so much better after your rest."

Emily climbed in under the bed cover a little further and made herself comfortable. "Sleep now," continued Andrew, "I'll call you later."

Emily lay in bed, staring at Andrew, her eyes growing heavier and heavier with each passing moment. She turned onto her shoulder, her back now facing Andrew. Emily closed her eyes. She was asleep. Andrew stood there, looking down at her. His eyes were drawn to her sleeping pattern. Her back expanded and retracted in a calming rhythm.

The afternoon progressed into the early evening. Andrew was back at work. His shift for the day was coming to an end. He was standing in front of an open locker, inside the men's change room. There were other officers about, all going about their daily lives, and all in various states of dress and undress. Andrew stood in front of his open locker, having just pulled on a pair of jeans.

They were open and unzipped as he turned to face the open locker and pull out a t-shirt. The t-shirt itself was plain, with no logo or print on the front. It was a simple black in colour. Andrew zipped up his jeans and popped in the button, before climbing into his sneakers, grabbing his sports bag, and other personal belongings, including his wallet and his cell phone, and made his way out of the men's change room, down the hallway, and out the back of the police station, into the parking lot.

Andrew walked over to his truck, climbed inside and slid his bag along the front passenger seat, then grabbed his cell phone from his jean pocket. There were no missed calls or texts messages.

Andrew navigated into his conversation history and started to type.

I'm on my way. I'll see you soon.

Andrew hit the send button.

He threw his cell phone on to the front passenger seat, next to his bag, and turned the key in the ignition. The engine roared to life. Andrew looked in the rear-view mirror and cautiously made his way out of the station parking lot and into the traffic.

It didn't take long for Andrew to arrive. The truck pulled into the driveway and the engine died. Andrew sat behind his steering wheel, looking up at Peter's home. It had gone ten past seven in the evening. The sun had set upon Hillsboro for another day, and the lights in the living room, upstairs and the front porch, were all switched on. Andrew pushed on the inside door of his truck and shifted the weight of his frame, before climbing to his feet. Andrew left his sports bag in his truck but remembered to grab his cell phone and wallet. The truck door was quick to slam shut and the alarm was switched on. Andrew made his way up to the front porch and knocked on the front door.

Peter was walking to the bottom of the staircase, as he heard the heavy knock coming from the front door. He reached the foyer and walked across to the door. He leaned in and opened it. And there, standing in front of him, was Andrew Preston. He had a smile surface to his lips, and for the first time, in a long time, looked as relaxed as possible, standing there in his civilian clothes.

"So, are you going to invite me in, or are we going to continue standing here, all awkward like, like some fucking first date?" Andrew asked, jokingly.

Peter laughed. It was the first time in a long while. "Come here. Come on in."

Andrew stepped inside the house, and Peter welcomed him with a hug. The best friends stood there and embraced each other, for a second, or two.

Andrew walked deeper into the house. Peter closed the door behind him.

The evening started with the two friends sitting opposite each other at the dining table in the living room. The lights were switched on. They each were nursing a bottle of beer, slowly. The tone of the evening had changed, to something a little more sombre. Andrew grabbed his cold, sweating bottle of beer from the table and took a deep sip.

"So, what are *we* going to do?" he asked, having swallowed hard.

"You're the cop. I should be asking you the same question. But if it were me. I'd say, we catch the motherfucker and we put an end to this. Put them out of their misery."

"I can think of a few ways," Andrew responded, taking another sip.

"Me, too. Come on. I have something to show you. Grab your beer. You're gonna want it, I promise."

Andrew looked at his best friend, a little surprised. "Lead the way."

Peter stood up from the dining table. Andrew followed, gripping his bottle of beer in his right hand. Peter lead the way, making his way to the foyer of the house, then climbed the staircase. He turned into the hallway and pushed open the door on the spare room. The light switched on. And there, in front of him, was the collage of pictures and newspaper articles. They had grown quite exponentially, past the clipboard. They had taken up most of the wall, now.

"You're shitting me," Andrew said, just above a whisper, surprised. "What is this?"

"This is my life. My memories." Peter responded. "My grandfather and my mother started this, *this*. I don't even know what *this* is. But I am sure as shit going to end *this*."

Andrew walked closer to the wall, with his beer bottle in hand.

"I still miss your dad," Andrew said, just above a whisper as he raised his free hand to touch his face.

"Not as much as me. It's not possible."

Peter's cell phone began to vibrate, breaking the silence in the room. Peter tapped the pockets of his trousers with his free hand, retrieving his cell phone from his left pocket. Andrew turned and looked at his best friend, concerned.

"Who is it?" Andrew asked.

Peter raised his eyes off his cell phone. The caller ID read *Unknown Caller*. Peter turned the cell phone toward Andrew, showing him the screen.

"You tell me," Peter answered, his voice flat, just above a whisper. "Answer it!"

Peter rolled his eyes, a little, hitting the accept button on his cell phone. "Hello?" he answered.

"Look at you two," the deep and familiar voice answered. Andrew's eyes widened in horror.

"Best friends since high school," the voice continued. "Isn't this just deliciously cosy."

"Enough of this shit!" Peter interrupted, shouting. "So? You're here. No more calls. And no more masks. Let's see who is behind this. Why don't you show yourself?"

"Yeah, motherfucker!" Andrew called out.

"Everything comes to those who wait," the voice replied. "And you'll see just who is standing behind the mask. Your mother would have been so proud of me. We are so close to the end of the game. I can promise you that."

The voice laughed.

The phone call disconnected.

Peter and Andrew stood there, standing at each other, dumbfounded.

Chapter Twenty-Eight...

Peter was lying on the couch in the living room, in front of the television set. A small blanket covered him, from toe to shoulders and his head was propped up by a small pillow. Peter was feeling run-down and sneezing. The volume on the television set wasn't too loud. Peter was watching an episode of *The Late Show with Stephen Colbert*. The host of the show was interviewing a new, up-and-coming author, whose debut novel had reached the bestseller's list. The cell phone on the coffee table began to ring. Peter pulled his eyes off the television, reached for the remote and turned the volume down, as he grabbed the cell phone from the coffee table. A hint of a smile surfaced to his lips.

"Hello?" Peter answered, clearing his throat a little.

"I can't believe tonight, of all nights, you had to go and get yourself sick," Emily answered.

"I didn't purposefully go out and get the flu, you know." Peter tried to laugh. "I can still make it. Give me half an hour and I'll be there with bells on."

Emily laughed, chuckling to herself, for a moment.

"You rest up. I guess I have a date with Wes Craven all to myself tonight. Along with one hundred other people."

"Go. Have fun." Peter smiled. "You'll have a great time, I promise. I'll keep the movie ticket. I'll frame it. Tomorrow morning, I want to hear a full report on your night. I want to hear how many times did you jump out of your skin? I want to know how many times you screamed, when the supposedly dead killer came back for one, last scare?"

The two friends laughed.

"Rest up and take care," Emily responded. "I'll talk to you tomorrow. Goodnight."

The phone line disconnected. Peter smiled a little before dropping his cell phone back on the coffee table. He slouched further, deeper into the couch, returning his full attention to *Stephen Colbert*.

Emily was at home, putting the final touches to her outfit, getting ready to go out for the evening to the local cinema in the town square. The lights in the house were all switched on. Emily stood in front of her closet and pulled out a jacket to complete her ensemble. It was a soft-pink suede jacket that sat upon a simple white t-shirt and blue jeans, which hugged her petite frame.

Emily also wore an open toe ankle boot that was black, part of the range by Victoria Beckham. The price tag made her nervous to think about. But she had worked overtime and saved every spare penny to treat herself. Emily stood in front of the floor-to-ceiling mirror of her closet and pulled her hair back into a simple, but sleek ponytail.

"There is nothing wrong with a little *me* time," Emily whispered as she stared at her reflection in the mirror.

Emily dusted down the legs of her jeans and made her way out of her bedroom, down the hallway and to the front door. The lights flickered off as she approached the front door. Emily stood at her front door and took one final look around the house. The light in the kitchen remained on, for added security. Emily let out a deep sigh and walked out the front door confidently, looking forward to a night at the cinema. She pulled the door to a close behind her, jiggling the door handle a little, making sure the front door was locked, and made her way from the front porch and walked along the footpath to her bug that was sitting in the driveway. The alarm deactivated and the driver's side door pulled open. Emily climbed into the bug and slammed the door to a close.

Emily sat behind her steering wheel a moment, catching her reflection in the rear-view mirror. She looked down at her bag that sat on the front passenger seat and hunted for her cell phone. She rummaged through until she clutched tightly in her left hand. Emily navigated to her text history and sent an emoji of a ghost to Peter, which she chuckled to herself, and sent a second message to Andrew.

Don't work too hard tonight. I'm heading out to the movies now. Talk to you later. Love you, Emily typed and hit the send button. She then turned in her seat a little, turned on the ignition, and the engine of the car roared to life. Emily looked over her right shoulder started reversing out of her driveway and pulling into traffic.

The Hillsboro Police Station was busy again, tonight. Deputy Preston had moved desks and was now occupying the office that was once held by Detective Mark Quinn. The door was pulled to a close. Andrew was sitting at his desk, quietly typing away on the keyboard of his computer. His cell phone sat on top of the desk, to his right, next to his bottle of water, unnoticed. A glowing green light flashed from the cell phone, notifying him of an unread text message. The front of the office was busy, too. There was a row of residents, no more than three or four, waiting patiently to report a crime or to post bail for a member of their family, or loved one, who had been picked up for drinking under the influence. A young man, somewhere in his early to mid-twenties, waited patiently in the queue. He was next to be served.

"How can I help you?" Officer Jackson asked, calling the next person in line to the customer service desk.

"I would like to see Deputy Preston, please," the man answered, calmly.

Officer Jackson looked down at the mountainous paperwork he had in front of him, then over to Deputy Preston's office. The door was still closed. Deputy Preston had his head down, typing away at his keyboard. Officer Jackson looked back at the young man in front of him, slightly annoyed. "And you are?" he asked.

"It's important," replied the man.

"The deputy is busy this evening. Give me your name and a message, and I will see to it that he gets it."

"Tell the kind deputy that I dropped by," the man started, "and if he is too important, too busy to talk, then I'll just have to help myself and I will be in touch again, later."

Officer Jackson scrawled the message down on a piece of paper.

"And your name?" Jackson asked, again, as he looked down at the written message. There was no answer.

"Your name?" Officer Jackson repeated.

He looked up to see the man turn and walk out the front of the police station. He walked away wearing a black hoodie, which covered the back of his head, black jeans and black leather boots. Officer Jackson turned and looked at the office door, again. It was still closed. He looked down at the message, shrugged his shoulders and scrunched the piece of paper in his right hand tightly and tossed it in the wastepaper basket, returning to his paperwork.

The engine died. Emily parked her bug one block over from the town square and made her way to the cinema. She climbed out of her car and slammed the door behind her, activated the alarm and made a brisk walk with her bag over her shoulder, clutching it tightly to her right side. There was a cool breeze in the air this evening. Emily felt it against her lips as she walked the footpath.

The neon lights of the movie theatre glowed against the evening sky. Emily walked past the laundry and the diner. The diner was a little busy this evening.

Emily walked into the foyer of the movie theatre and was immediately greeted with the smell of ready-made buttered popcorn. The down lights in the foyer of the cinema shone brightly, giving the place a warm, ambient glow. The movie posters which hung on the walls were framed with light bulbs, as the patrons, all going about their own lives, and were all from different walks of life. Kids were running around the foyer, playing chase, there were also teenagers, some with friends, others on dates, families, and middle-aged couples simply enjoying the night out. Emily made her way to the box office to validate her ticket before heading over to the candy store to purchase one medium soda, small popcorn and a bag of her favourite chocolates to mix with the popcorn. It just boosted the flavours.

The coming attractions hung from the foyer walls. There were pictures made on an extraordinary budget, starring the latest must-see Hollywood A-Listers, to the more modest films, done on a shoestring budget that hung there, garnering media attention during award season. Emily walked past the posters, in search of something that interested her. She balanced her soda and popcorn and candy and looked down at her validated ticket. The first movie for the evening was the 1984 horror, *A Nightmare on Elm Street*. Emily made her way across the foyer and headed over to the young staff member who stood behind a wooden podium, collecting ticket stubs.

"Thank you. Enjoy your movie," the young man said.

It seemed to be on repeat, to all the patrons making their way to their designated movie theatre for the evening. Emily handed over her ticket and received her portion of the stub back. She clutched her soda, her candy and popcorn, close to her chest, and made her way inside the cinema and found her seat.

The Hillsboro Police Station was a little quieter now. The door leading to Deputy Preston's office was wide open. The office itself was empty, the lights were still switched on, but it was empty, nonetheless. Officer Jackson remained seated behind the customer service desk, head down, working his way through his paperwork quietly. The silence of the office was broken by the overpowering frame that was Deputy Preston. He made his way around the office, his uniform clinging to his bulging frame, checking in on the other officers pulling the night shift.

"How's it going this evening, Jackson?" Deputy Preston asked, breaking the young officer's attention.

Officer Jackson placed his pen down on the desk, on top of the paperwork, and looked up to his officer in charge. He rubbed the tired from his eyes, a moment.

"Quiet. Soldiering through."

"Good to hear," Deputy Preston answered, with a hint of a smile, and a soft, gentle pat on the officer's back. "Well, if there is anything you need, just give me a holler."

"Yes, sir."

Deputy Preston started on his left foot and continued his tour around the office. "Deputy!" Officer Jackson called. "You just sparked my memory."

"I did?" he answered, turning around to face the young officer again. "How so?"

"There was a man in the station earlier looking for you."

"Peter Harmon?"

"No, sir. I've never seen this guy before. I didn't get a good look. He was talking as I was writing down a message. I *think* he had an accent."

"What message? What did he look like?"

"All I remember was his voice. He spoke almost… well educated, you know? Very calm, like nothing fazed him. Like he had all the time in the world or something."

"What was he wearing?" Deputy Preston asked, a little more concerned. "Think!"

Officer Jackson shook his head slowly, from left to right, as if to think about it.

"Nothing too out of the ordinary. A black hooded sweater. Black jeans and leather boots. The back of his head was hidden behind an almost over-size hoodie."

"Shit!" Deputy Preston answered, just above a whisper. "What did he say?"

"He said that you were very important, very busy. That he would help himself and be in touch with you later." Officer Jackson shrugged.

"Fuck me!" he whispered, again. "Emily!"

Deputy Preston stood there in front of the junior officer. His hands grew numb. And his heartbeat started to race.

"I want all available squad cars headed over to the town square movie theatre. Now!"

Deputy Preston raced across the floor of the police station, out towards the parking lot at the back of the building. He pushed his way past the other officers and burst through the door of the building and out into the parking lot. He surveyed the darkness of the parking lot a moment and made his way toward his truck. His hands fumbled through his trouser pockets, in search of his keys. The front lights of his truck flashed as the alarm deactivated. Deputy Preston held his breath in his chest a moment as he ran towards his truck. He reached his truck, his hands slamming on the driver's side door, put out in front of him as if to catch his fall. He fumbled with the door before climbing inside. The driver's side door slammed to a close. Deputy Preston could feel his chest exploding, feeling his heartbeat pound. He put his key in the ignition as his eyes widen and his mouth opened in horror. A small piece of paper, no larger than a CD cover, sat under the right-side window wiper. Deputy Preston climbed out of the truck to pull it from the windscreen. The paper tore a little as he flipped it over.

"You can't save her!" The message was scrawled across the paper, in a handwriting that looked more like chicken scratch.

"Fuck!" Deputy Preston shouted. The engine to the truck roared to life.

Fade to black. Fade from black.

The lights in the movie theatre were switched off. The silver screen was aglow. The movie was playing. *A Nightmare on Elm Street*. The audience was drawn into the movie, sitting on the edge of their seat, even after so many years, and seeing the movie countless times, the tension was unrelenting. The tension erupted into a bloody, gory scene of sheer terror. Some moviegoers screamed whilst others laughed. A smile surfaced to Emily's lips as she was engrossed in the film. Her left hand, dove slowly into the popcorn box, grabbing some chocolate and popcorn at the same time. The salty taste was washed from the inside of her mouth with a sip from her soda.

Peter was at home, lying on the couch. The light in the living room was switched off now. The only light was coming from the glow of the television set. Peter climbed off the couch and to his feet, stretching a little, and wiping the sleep from his eyes, some. The television set was playing softly in the background. It was a late-night sitcom, something forgettable. Peter shook his hands by his side, as a way of waking himself up. He walked from the living room and into the kitchen. The light in the kitchen was still switched on. Peter reached the entrance of the kitchen and made his way in. He walked over to the refrigerator and opened the door, to inspect. His cell phone on the kitchen counter started to ring. Peter lifted his eyes off the contents of the refrigerator and over to the kitchen counter. The cell phone continued to ring for a moment. *Ring. Ring. Ring.*

Peter pushed the refrigerator door to a slow close and walked over to the counter and picked it up. *Caller Unknown.* Peter hit the accept button. He held his breath in his throat a moment. The expression on his face turning to anger.

"What do you want?" Peter answered flatly.

"All of these years have passed and you have carried with you the bloodstained memory of coming home from the cinema one night to find your father, stepmother and half-sister murdered, bludgeoned to death at the hand of your very own mother. All these years have passed and we have finally come full circle, you and me. The events in New York City. It's all led up to this. It's like history repeating itself, or something. The night you came home from the movies. Andrew was supposed to join you, but he pulled out at the last minute to spend the evening with Emily instead."

"Emily!" Peter whispered.

"That's right!" the dark and familiar voice laughed. "I know exactly how to inflict pain and cut where it truly hurts. You can't save her. She is just another plaything, to kill and dismember." Another laugh followed.

The phone line disconnected.

"Shit! Shit! Shit!" Peter muttered urgently.

The cell phone vibrated seconds later. Peter clutched his cell phone tightly, almost too scared to open and see what may come next. Peter held his breath in his throat a moment longer and opened his cell phone. It was a picture message. Peter opened. The photograph came from inside the movie theatre. It was a picture of Emily sitting just rows, two, maybe three, in front. The cell phone vibrated, again. Another text message.

No one can save her.

The message read.

Andrew was sitting behind the steering wheel of this truck. He was driving through the narrow, winding country roads at breakneck speed, leaving the police station behind him and headed for the movie theatre. The driver's side window was open a little, to allow the cool evening breeze to rush inside the truck. Andrew had his eyes on the road, his cell phone gripped tightly in his hands, as it balanced on top of the steering wheel. He lifted his cell phone close to his chest, navigating through screens and started to dial Emily's number. The phone call connected and began to ring. *Ring. Ring. Ring.* It continued to ring until it reached voicemail.

"Hi, this is Emily," the call recording started. *"I can't come to the phone right now. Please leave your name, your message and the time you called, and I will get back to you when I can. Thank you. Beep."*

"Emily! Emily!" Andrew shouted in a panic. "It's me," he continued. "Pick up! Please, for the love of God, *pick up!*"

The phone call disconnected. "Fuck!" Andrew shouted.

He continued to speed toward the movie theatre.

Emily sat in her seat inside the movie theatre. Her eyes were glued to the screen. It was the great chase screen, between heroine and villain. The audience was sitting on the edge of their seats, watching on in horror. Emily was clutching at her popcorn box in her right hand, rather hard, as her left hand clutched her soda. She looked down at the soda and gave the cup a little jiggle from left to right. The remaining ice cubes rattled, a little. Emily peeled her eyes away from the silver screen, for just a moment, and took another sip from her cup. The soda was almost gone now. The melting ice inside the cup jiggled a little more. The last of the soda rushed at a high speed through the straw and touched her lips. A sudden rush of cold air followed.

"Shit!" she whispered to herself, as she looked at the amount of popcorn she had left. She hadn't reached the halfway point.

Emily lifted her eyes onto the silver screen again, before discreetly hunching forward in her seat a little, and then made her way outside the movie theatre, slowly dodging the other patrons who were sitting in the same row as her.

"Excuse me," she whispered as she went, "thank you."

Emily reached the end of her row before she made the start, walking along the wall, heading toward the theatre exit and out into the foyer, toward the candy store. The hooded figure followed, silently. The double doors leading into the theatre were painted a heavy red. They had been that way for years and required a touch-up. The double doors pushed open silently. Emily emerged from the theatre, taking a right, as she started to slowly walk down the corridor, toward the candy store, alone. The image of the black hoodie emerged from behind. It was nothing more than an out-of- focus blur. A shapeless figure until a hand, bound in a black leather glove reached out forward, extending, out from behind, covering Emily's mouth tightly. She was pulled backwards quickly, almost knocking her off her feet and making her lose her balance.

"Miss me?" the dark and familiar voice asked, as a hint of the clown mask appeared from behind. The box of chocolates and popcorn fell to the carpeted floor beneath, so too, did the cup of soda. The remains of the drink and the ice cubes sprayed across the royal-red carpet. Emily's eyes widened in horror.

Fade to black. Fade from black.

Emily awoke to blurry vision, at best, for the time being, anyway. Her body a little sluggish before she felt the pain course through her veins and the tension in her wrists. Her eyes were bloodshot. She blinked several times, regaining her vision, some. Her eyes widened in horror, again, as she surveyed the room. A room that was very familiar to her. It was her living room. Her head throbbed with pain. It was like a scene directly out of a horror movie or something. Her mouth was gagged, taped shut. She could taste blood as she ran her tongue over her teeth. Emily was hanging from the ceiling, standing atop a small wooden chair, dragged from the kitchen dining table. Emily was coming to. Her calls for help sounded more like muffled whimpering. Emily screamed louder, angrier. The living room remained empty.

Emily struggled. She rubbed her wrists together, in the hope of breaking free from the tape. It only felt tightened and restricted, with each passing moment. The strain rushed from her wrists, coursed up her arms and to her shoulders. She stopped a moment, trying to catch her breath. It was exhausting. The living room was no longer empty. Her vision was very clear, now. And the image of the clown mask appeared, having walked into the living room from the kitchen, clutching a large, sharp kitchen knife in their left hand. The image did nothing to help. It simply stood there, watching the struggle play out.

"Look at you now," the dark and familiar voice started, "you were always the high school sweetheart, weren't you? And now? Look at you. The popular it-girl with ambition, with confidence, grew up to be a nobody, someone who didn't venture past these city limits and settled on her cheating high-school boyfriend, as the man of her dreams. You became a wallflower, a dullard, a nobody who works in a low-budget, go-nowhere grocery store. You became a side-bitch to your very own cheating boyfriend whilst living with low self-esteem. I'm going to have fun with you before you die. You'll be the crown piece in my game." The kitchen knife raised, pointed at her. "Question time," the voice continued. "In high school, who did you love more, Peter or Andrew? And don't lie! I know when people lie."

Emily continued to struggle as the tears welled in her eyes. The clown mask approached Emily, their right hand extending out, the leather glove, reaching for the gag around her mouth. The leather glove pulled at the tape over the mouth. It tore, some. Emily closed her eyes and tilted her head back, quickly gasping for air.

"Andrew! Andrew! Andrew!" Emily shouted, in quick succession. "In high school, I always loved Andrew! Did you hear me? Are you satisfied?"

"I said *don't lie to me*," the voice answered back, deeper, darker. The clown mask rushed toward Emily, coming face-to-face with her.

"I told you not to lie to me!" the voice repeated.

The kitchen knife appeared, again. It extended outwards, rather quickly, the point of the blade piercing the pink jacket and stabbing at the flesh beneath. The blood poured heavily from the wound. Emily agonised. She screamed.

The blood-stained blade of the kitchen knife retracted, just as fast as it extended. The clown mask took several steps backwards, taking a view of the pain they had inflicted. Emily's legs grew weaker upon the top of the chair. The tears soon dissipated, replaced with a forced smile and laughter from her lips.

"You piece of shit!" Emily laughed through her tears. "You won't get away with this."

"You think so, huh? And what makes you so confident? Because I can tell you, no one knows you're here. You are nothing more than a single, white girl going out on the town on a Saturday night. A single girl who went out for the night on her own, to escape the confines of her local, boring life, and simply disappeared. It happens across the country every day. You're not special. Your claim to fame will be nothing more than a selfie on the side of a milk carton. A poster hanging on the walls of your local post office, the police station. Until everyone will forget about you. You'll become nothing more than a statistic across the United States of fucking America. Tell me, Emily, how does that sound? Am I close?"

Emily fought back the tears. She spat at the mask, at the stranger standing before her. "And now, the game, *my* game, continues." the voice laughed. "The one-time it-girl is going to get her chance to step out from the shadows and become the star she thought she was destined to be. I know the jealousy you harbour towards Peter. It's written all over your face. All that attention he got growing up in this small, scab of a town. The attention he got from teachers, the media. Well, goddamn! Everyone who wanted a piece of him, after his mother pushed him into the limelight, was everything you hated him for. I know it. I'm sure of it."

"Fuck you!"

"Your anger won't change my mind, Emily. You're going to be the star in my little film. Let's begin, shall we?"

Emily screamed again, wildly.

The clown mask stood there, watching. The blade of the kitchen knife raised, again. This time, stabbing at Emily. The blade pierced through her simple shirt beneath her pink jacket. The blade pushed through, tearing at the flesh. The clown mask held the blade of the knife in her stomach a moment longer, gripping the handle. The blade turned on an angle, just a little, mind you, and was just as fast to retract, again, as it pierced the flesh of the stomach. The blade was blood-stained, again. The screaming silenced, somewhat. It became weakened, very quickly, just beneath a moan. The blood rushed from the wound.

The clown mask turned 'its back on Emily hanging from the ceiling. Her legs growing weaker, again. The blood poured from her left arm, down past her stomach. The noose around her neck was growing tighter. The clown mask dialled a number from Emily's cell phone. The phone call connected and started to ring. *Ring. Ring. Ring.* An image of Andrew appeared on the cell phone screen. He switched his eyes between the road in front of him, and the cell phone screen in his hands. Andrew could see the clown mask, up close and personal. Emily hung from the ceiling behind them.

"I told you I would come for you again, Andrew," the clown mask started. "Do I finally have your attention?"

Andrew looked at the screen of his cell phone. His face filled with hatred.

"Now that I have your precious Emily, am I right?" the clown mask continued, "between you and me, Emily and I are going to have some fun."

"You leave her alone, you son of a bitch!" Andrew yelled. "If I'm so important to you, come for me. Leave Emily alone!"

"Andrew!" Emily screamed, wildly.

"Emily!" Andrew replied.

"How sweet!" the clown mask interrupted. "Two lovers reconnecting. I can tell you, it's a real Dear Diary moment. You're giving me chills. Question time, Andrew. Are you ready? I played this game with Emily and she lied to me. And, of course, she paid the penalty. I got a little knife-happy and may have cut her a little."

"I will kill you! I will *fucking* kill you, do you hear me?"

"All you have to do is tell me the truth, and no one gets hurt, any more, that is. Are you ready to play a game?"

"But this isn't a game!" Andrew panicked.

"Of course it is. It always has been. Catch up, Andrew. I don't think the police department was the right career option for you, do you? I bet you joined just because. Just because a short, thin nobody decided to bulk up and demand some respect from the man, from the father he loved, who showed nothing but cold, hard hatred toward his very own son. Ground breaking!"

Andrew looked at the clown mask in quiet anger. He had never been summed up before. Not like that, anyway.

"So," the clown mask continued, "I ask again. Are you ready to play?" Andrew nodded his head, meekly.

"Good!" the clown mask answered with excitement in their voice. "Tell me, Andrew, who did you love more in high school, Emily Olsen or Jayne Scott? You have no idea just how much fun it was to rip her into two."

"Emily! Emily! Emily!" Andrew shouted angrily, fighting the tears in his eyes.

"I'm surprised at you, Andrew. Jayne told me you were the love of her life. That the size of your cock made her melt every time. Every time the two of you made love, every time you forced yourself inside her. She came... every time."

"No! No."

"No?" the clown mask asked, rather confused. "Are you sure? You don't sound so confident now, do you? You look like you just got caught in your lies. And that makes *you* the whore, doesn't it? I'm right! And poor Emily; however, will she cope with the brutal truth that you don't love her? Not really. She was never exciting enough for you. She was the picture of a good wife on paper. But it was Jayne who got your heart and your cock thumping! Maybe Emily doesn't have to cope. I can show her love. I can set her free from the misery of this life you call Hillsboro."

The phone call disconnected.

"I am going to have my fun with you," the clown mask said, as it turned to face a beaten, bloodied and weakened Emily hanging from the ceiling. "You'll love it, I swear. You knew this was coming, didn't you? You had to. That one day, we would eventually meet up like this. That I would exact my revenge. After all, this not about you. It never was. And your "it" days are over."

Emily screamed as loud as she could as the tears fell from her eyes. The clown mask laughed, heinously.

Fade to black. Fade from black.

Emily struggled to open her eyes now. She was growing weaker. The blood continued to pour from her stomach. The air was slowly escaping from her lips. The colour of the blood was turning a darker shade of red, now.

Fade to black. Fade from black.

The white of the clown mask appeared bright under the living room lights in the ceiling. It looked upwards towards Emily, tilting from left to right, a little, watching. Emily appeared like a bloodied and beaten new toy, its batteries showing signs of slowing down.

"How about you wake up, Emily. Let's have some fun!" the clown mask said, just above a whisper. Emily struggled a little more, fighting to keep her eyes open.

The blade of the kitchen knife rose high into the air, high above the left shoulder of the clown mask. The clown mask stepped forward, just a little more, growing closer and closer to Emily. The blade of the kitchen knife came down with tremendous force. It pierced the skin again, just above the stomach, near the ribs on the left side of her body. Emily opened her eyes in horror. She had never felt so much pain course through her body all at the same time. She tilted her head back, a little, screaming. Her eyes closed tightly as the tears welled.

Fade to black. Fade from black.

Emily opened her eyes again, wide. Her mouth opened, too. Gasping. Her lips were dry and the crimson-red lipstick looked old and chipped. The saliva clung to the corner of her lips.

Fade to black. Fade from black.

The blood-stained kitchen knife was pulled from the second stomach wound, hard and rough. It raised into the air, like before, drenched in blood. The kitchen knife came rushing forward again, for a third time, stabbing wildly and repeatedly about her breasts and chest.

Fade to black. Fade from black.

The screams were piercing, agonising and grew weaker by the

moment. The clown mask stood back again, taking in the image of a bloodied and beaten Emily. Emily let out one final, fading scream. Her knees grew weaker and weaker, as they trembled with pain. She lost her balance as the balls of her feet rolled outwards from underneath her, pushing her ankles out. The chair tipped forward, out from underneath her feet. The noose around her neck tightened, again, just enough to choke her bloodied, weakened body. Her body went into violent convulsions. The clown mask dropped the bloodied kitchen knife to the living room floor. It stood there a moment longer, watching the corpse of Emily Olsen hang from the ceiling, before it walked in closer towards her, to inspect her. Emily Olsen was dead.

Fade to black. Fade from black.

Andrew was fast to pull his truck into Emily's driveway. The engine died. Andrew could feel his heartbeat racing wildly in his chest, his palms growing sweaty. He looked up at the house. The lights were all switched on. The front door was pulled to a close. Andrew looked concerned. He looked down at the front passenger seat of his truck, staring down at his cell phone. There was a quiet banter, a conversation floating over the CB radio. His right hand extended, reaching out for the cell phone. He clutched it in his hands and the screen came to life. There were no missed calls or text messages. The last text message was from Peter.

I'm on my way.

The message read.

"Come on, Petey. Where are you?" Andrew whispered, almost nervously to himself as he drew his eyes back to the house.

Fade to black. Fade from black.

The front door to Emily's home pushed open. Andrew stood in the doorway. He stood there, his face drawn of colour, standing there in his police uniform. An eerie silence filled the house.

"Emily?" he called out, his voice shaking. There was no response.

Andrew took a step inside the house. He turned left and made his way, cautiously and quietly down the hallway, toward the kitchen and the living room. Andrew looked over his shoulder down the hallway, towards the master bedroom. The door leading into the master bedroom was left open. The light also switched on. Andrew turned again, making his way to the end of the hallway, creeping forward. He looked right, a moment, into the kitchen. It was empty and it was clean. He proceeded forward, into the living room.

Fade to black. Fade from black.

Andrew stood there in the living room. The colour in his face faded some more as a blood-curdling scream escaped his lips. He fell to his hands and knees as tears welled in his eyes. The bloodied kitchen knife lay on the living room floor, just inches in front of him. His eyes slowly looked up and he could see Emily hanging from the ceiling, bloodied and beaten. Her neck was broken. Her lifeless body hanging from the ceiling with a piece of paper, no larger than a CD cover, pinned to the right side of her waist. The scream continued.

Fade to black. Fade from black.

Andrew used the back of his left hand to wipe the tears from his eyes as he shivered on the living room floor on his knees. He climbed to his feet in a fragile state. His knees felt like jelly, the palms of his hands were cold and trembling. The sound of thunderous footsteps grew louder coming down the hallway. Peter burst into the living room, passing Andrew, as if it were almost a running race, Peter crossing some imaginary line. His back was quick to turn on Emily. Peter covered his mouth with his right hand in horror. He turned his sights to Andrew, instead. Andrew stood there in the living room, staring forward, silently, at Emily, as if caught in some horrible trance. His terrified vulnerability left him a shell of the man Peter knew him to be.

"What is that?" Andrew asked, just above a whisper.

"What's what?" Peter replied, concerned.

"That!" Andrew replied, pointing at Emily. "Pinned to her jacket."

Peter turned to face Emily. It was the first time he had come eye to eye with his beautiful friend, who had been left a bloodied, tortured mess.

"It looks like a note. Who would do such a thing?" Peter lowered his eyes again, shaking his head gently from left to right.

Andrew continued to gaze upon the piece of paper through tear-filled eyes. "I want to see it," Andrew whispered angrily.

"No," Peter answered. "Leave it. Let the cops handle this."

"I *am* the fucking cops!" Andrew shouted back. "I should have paid more attention. I should have done my job! Who the fuck is behind all of this, huh?"

"I don't know." Peter shrugged.

"I'm sick of this shit! I'm tired of hiding, aren't you?"

Peter was stunned by such a question. He stared at his best friend, trying to read the expression on his face, his body language.

Andrew took another step closer toward Emily, keeping his eyes focused on hers. Her eyes were wide open. Her pupils dilated, and the capillaries in her eyes had burst. He lifted his left hand and pulled down the note that was pinned to her waist.

"What does it say?" Peter asked, just above a whisper.

Andrew looked down at the note. He blinked his eyes in quick succession as the tears fell down his face and cleared his throat, a little.

"It says," Andrew started. "*'Peter, doesn't this look familiar?'*" "What?" Peter asked, stunned.

"*Doesn't this look familiar?* What does that mean, Peter? You tell me!"

Peter turned and gazed upon Emily, once more. The expression on her face. The blood on her clothes. The catastrophic knife wounds. Her hair pulled back into a simple, almost sleek ponytail. "It's Mrs Prescott," Peter answered, dumbfounded, feeling almost winded.

"Who? Who is Mrs Prescott?"

Peter could hear the strain in his best friend's voice.

"Ben Prescott's mother. Ben tortured his mother. He murdered her. He hung her lifeless body from the ceiling of their living room in New York City. She was stabbed to death."

"And? So, you think someone is out to duplicate the events of what happened in New York City?"

"No." Peter shook his head slowly, answering just above a whisper. "I think the killer, whoever it is, is ready to reveal themselves."

Fade to black.

Chapter Twenty-Nine...

It had been three days now since Emily Olsen was found hanging from the ceiling in the living room of her own home. The house was now boarded up and officially became yet another crime scene. Coroner Trutmann was working from his office in the morgue of the hospital, picking at Emily's remains, inspecting her bloodied and tortured body further. In the days that followed, Emily's home quickly became the subject of whispers, hearsay and gossip amongst the neighbourhood parents. The home became a haunted house amongst the children. A joke. The children dared each other to run up to the front door, knock three times, then turn and run in the opposite direction.

Andrew was in mourning. He was grief-stricken. He had stayed home from work for the last three days, pacing around his home. He was laying on top of his couch in the living room. The television was switched on. The volume was up, rather loud. He didn't care. A bottle of beer sat on top of the coffee table. Andrew had worked his way through a better part of the bottle, as the cold bottle beaded, marking the coffee table beneath. His cell phone sat next to the beer bottle. The notification light was flashing. There were numerous unread text messages, voicemails from colleagues and friends, including Peter. Andrew stretched out further on the couch, almost out of the foetal position. His right hand reached out for the beer bottle, taking another sip. His eyes were fixed on the television set.

The cell phone began to ring, again. Andrew diverted his eyes from the television set and back to his cell phone. He let it ring. *Ring. Ring. Ring.* The call went directly to voicemail. The cell phone fell silent, once more. The green notification light continued to flash. Andrew placed the beer bottle back on top of the coffee table and reached out for his cell phone. He rolled over onto his back, playing with his cell phone. Andrew navigated to the call history and played the message.

"It's me," the message started.

Andrew blinked his eyes in quick succession. He closed them tightly as he heard the voice play. *"It's me,"* the message continued to play. *"It's Peter. I don't know what to say right now. Shit! There is nothing I can say that will help ease the pain. Just know, I am thinking of you. I'm here for you, day or night, anytime. Call me. Please. Even if it's just to check-in."*

The message finished.

Andrew dropped the cell phone back on top of the coffee table and returned to his bottle of beer and the mindless sitcom playing out on the television set.

The day progressed over the town of Hillsboro. The television set in the living room continued to play. Andrew was up and off the couch. He hadn't showered in the past two days. His hair was a mess. He hadn't shaved. The stubble on his face was showing signs of growth around the chin and cheeks. Andrew continued to pace around his house in an almost haze. He was dressed simply in a white, cotton t-shirt and boxer shorts. His uniform, stained in Emily's blood, lay on top of the hamper in the laundry, in a messy heap. Andrew walked past the kitchen, down the hallway and into his office. He sat at his desk, booted up his computer and collapsed in his chair, a moment. His head tilted back as he closed his eyes.

The computer was going through its updates as the monitor came to life. Andrew opened his eyes, again. He pulled himself together, making himself comfortable in his chair. He was quick to navigate the Internet. He went to his favourite porn site, biting down on his lower lip, a little. He selected a random video. There were one woman and multiple men, three, maybe four. There was an extra set of hands recording the video. Andrew collapsed in his chair, once more. His eyes closed, tilting his head back some. The video played out on the computer screen. The moans, from the woman, and men, filled the room. Andrew slowly ran his hand down, over his chest and stomach, and down, underneath the waistband of his boxer shorts.

Fade to black. Fade from black.

The sun rose over the town of Hillsboro for the start of another morning. The curtains in the master bedroom were pulled to a close, blocking most of the light inside the house. A silence fell upon the house.

The television set in the living room was switched off. Andrew was laying on top of the bed, entwined in the bed cover. His body tossed and turned a little, as he was slowly waking up from a broken slumber. His right arm rose gently and started to wipe the sleep from his eyes.

Andrew looked around the darkened room. He could see the morning light creeping down the hallway, toward the master bedroom.

"Shit!" Andrew whispered to himself.

He leaned over to the nightstand next to his bed and pulled his cell phone from the phone charger.

The cell phone came to life. There was a new text message from Peter, amongst others. Andrew continued to wipe the sleep from his eyes and navigated to the unread text message.

"There is a saying. People say, "I know what you are going through." I think they say it to help calm their own nerves or fears. But I do know what you're going through. You're hurting. You want the world to end, if only for a few days, and hide. The best way I find is to use that pain. Fight back.

Don't let this motherfucker win. We can't."

Andrew dropped his cell phone on the bed, by his waist. He pushed the bed cover back, including the sheets, and crawled to his feet. The bedroom floor felt cool to the touch. Andrew sat there a moment longer, before standing. He was naked. Andrew stretched a little before he walked from the master bedroom, down the hallway, and into the bathroom. The bathroom door was pushed to a close as the light flickered on.

The neon light in the bathroom seemed brighter than usual this morning. Andrew caught his reflection in the bathroom mirror. He stood there, staring back at himself, as he started to unwind the bandage from around his torso. He dropped the bandage on top of the washbasin. The stitches were showing signs of progress and healing now. Andrew turned on his reflection in the mirror and walked towards the shower. He leaned in and slid the door open cautiously. The water from the shower nozzle began to pour. Andrew stepped under the warm water and closed the sliding door behind him.

The shower felt invigorating. Andrew stood under the warm water, with his head tilted back a little, his eyes closed as he cleaned himself up. His mind raced as he felt his body come to life.

Andrew soon turned to face the water, as it splashed against his chest and ran down his naked body. Andrew was soon out of the shower and stood in front of the washbasin with a damp towel wrapped loosely around his waist brushing his teeth. He soon made his way out of the bathroom, taking a right at the hallway, and made his way into the kitchen, for his first cup of coffee for the morning.

Andrew grabbed the remote from the kitchen counter and switched on the television set as the kettle started to boil. It was the morning news.

"I blame the incompetence of the Hillsboro Police Department," a female voice was heard saying. Andrew lifted his eyes to the television set. His face was sombre.

And there, on the television set, being interviewed by a local reporter, was Rose Olsen, Emily's mother. His eyes filled with anger, as tears welled. The kettle continued to boil. It quickly became white noise in the background. Andrew was tightening his grip on the television remote.

"Today is my daughter's funeral. My Emily," Rose continued, talking to the reporter. "She was a young, vibrant, happy-go-lucky type of girl. She had her whole life in front of her. And now, her mother and father are burying their own child. No parent should have to endure this agonising pain. No parent should outlive their child." Rose started to weep.

Andrew lifted the television remote in his left hand and switched it off.

Andrew gave up on the kettle. He turned and walked out of the kitchen, and made his way back to the master bedroom. He walked over to the curtains and pushed them open, with an almost brute force. The plastic rings above his head clashed together. *Clack. Clack. Clack.* The morning light filled the room. Andrew stood there, a moment, and gazed upon the view of his back yard, before he turned his back and got himself dressed for Emily's funeral.

Andrew emerged from his master bedroom. He was dressed for the funeral. He sported a white, long-sleeved cotton shirt that was buttoned to the throat. He added a simple black tie and matching black trousers, with black leather shoes. The jacket hung over a chair that sat around the dining table. The kettle in the kitchen started to boil again, breaking the silence which filled the house. A single coffee cup sat next to the boiling kettle. The coffee was instant. Milk and two sugars. A heavy knock coming from the front door followed. Andrew left the coffee cup on the kitchen counter and diverted his eyes to the front door. The knock continued. *Knock. Knock. Knock.* Andrew headed to the front door. It opened. And there, standing on the porch, was Peter, dressed almost identical. The best friends stared at each other a moment as if reading one another.

"Morning," Andrew said, just above a whisper.

"I tried calling. I sent text messages," Peter answered.

"I know," Andrew nodded slowly. "I got your messages. Come here." Andrew continued. Peter stepped closer. Andrew wrapped his arms around Peter tightly. It was a bear hug.

"I miss her so much," Andrew whispered, fighting back the tears.

"I know, mate. I know."

"I want to kill this son of a bitch. Help me trap them and kill them?"

Peter pulled back from Andrew's embrace. He was stunned. He looked at his best friend, biting down on his lower lip a little. He nodded his head, slightly.

"Come on in," Andrew continued, clearing his throat, a little. I'll make us a coffee. I know I need one. Have you eaten breakfast?"

"I grabbed something to bite before I left the house."

Peter followed Andrew deep inside the house. The front door was pushed to a close.

The day progressed, bleeding deeper into the late morning. The engine to the sports utility vehicle died. Peter sat behind the steering wheel of his truck as he gazed upon the people standing outside the funeral parlour, talking and whispering amongst themselves. The parking lot was full.

"Are you ready for this?" Peter heard himself ask, just above a whisper as he turned to face Andrew, sitting next to him.

"No."

"I got you," Peter nodded with a smile.

The two friends climbed out of the truck and made their way inside.

Andrew and Peter stood in the foyer of the funeral parlour, quietly talking and keeping to themselves. Peter surveyed the room, although only briefly. The foyer was set up almost identical to Jayne's funeral. The guests to the funeral bundled in groups of three, maybe four, all dressed for the occasion. The foyer broke off to a separate service room, which hid behind two closed French doors. A large picture of Emily, taken in happier times, sat upon an easel, out on display.

Rose Olsen and her husband, Jason, moved through the crowded foyer, almost with effortless ease. They made a beeline for Andrew and Peter. Their surviving son, David, no older than sixteen, followed his parents. The guests, some of them, anyway, lifted their eyes from their brewed beverages and gazed upon the grieving parents. The reporter from the news earlier this morning was in attendance. He was a short, portly man, somewhere in his late forties, to early fifties, standing in one corner, watching the stars of their daughter's funeral.

"You know," Rose started, her voice brimming with confidence, yet ready to break at a moment's notice, "the three of you were always very close. You were all best friends throughout high school. That's almost a lifetime ago, now. A lifetime of memories. A lifetime for my daughter, my Emily.

"Look what happened to my Emily! I blame you, Deputy Andrew Preston. This whole town blames you and the incompetent goings-on of the Hillsboro Police Department. All this time, and still no leads? Still nothing? You're shit! You're nothing! I don't know what my Emily ever saw in you, all these years. You're pathetic!"

Andrew maintained eye contact with Rose the entire time. He didn't utter a single word. He watched her collapse in her anger, only to be consoled by her husband, and ushered away to a private room, away from the guests. The remaining guests, some of them at least, including the television reporter, gazed at Andrew and Peter in judgemental silence.

Fade to black.

Chapter Thirty...

We open from the darkness like the set of some scary Hollywood movie. But this wasn't a movie. It was nothing more than life, itself. The time on the alarm clock which sat up on the nightstand read three forty-seven in the morning. The house was asleep. A silence had settled upon it. The living room was neat and kept tidy. The kitchen was clean. Everything was stowed away and kept in place. Almost. A single, empty beer bottle sat alone on top of the kitchen counter, by the side of the sink. The door leading into the master bedroom was left wide open, as an unconscious body lay under the bed cover, gently tossing and turning. It was Andrew. The bed cover had folded back on itself, revealing a plain, grey t-shirt, clung tightly to his torso. Andrew rolled over onto his back, his left arm extended upwards, under the pillow, to help prop his head up, a little. Andrew was snoring away gently.

The latch on the front door turned over and the door handle pushed down with an effortless ease. The front door pushed opened as a cool, gentle breeze blew across the front porch of the house. A dark shadow entered, splashing across the walls of the foyer, as the hulking intruder stepped inside. The front door remained open as the darken, hulking mass lead with their left foot, past the foyer of the front of the house, and down the still darkness of the hallway. The small lights from the appliances in the kitchen caught a glimpse of the hulking figure, if only for a fleeting moment. There were shades of colour. Of white. Of reds. Of blue. The image made their way to the bottom of the hallway and stood in the entrance of the master bedroom as they gripped a large, sharp kitchen knife tightly in their left hand, bound in a leather glove. It was the clown mask. The mask tilted a little, staring at the unconscious body that lay before them, at Andrew. The clown mask took a step inside the bedroom. Andrew continued to snore.

Fade to black. Fade from black.

A cell phone sat upon a nightstand. The device sprang to life. The screen started to light up as it began to ring. *Ring. Ring. Ring.* A heavy hand soon rose from the surface of the bed and landed on top of the cell phone, to muffle, to stop the noise. The cell phone continued to ring as it was pulled from the phone charger. The tired eyes opened reluctantly as the cell phone continued to ring. The call was quickly answered.

The image of the clown mask appeared on the screen. Peter wiped the sleep from his eyes.

"Hello?" Peter asked, quickly waking up.

"Hello, Peter," the clown mask answered.

Peter sat up in bed. He could feel his heart starting to pound. "I told you I was coming for you. Welcome to the final act!"

Behind the clown mask was Andrew. He sat tied and bound to a rickety wooden chair. His torso, this wrists and ankles were wrapped in rope. His mouth was loosely covered with duct tape, enough to allow him to breathe yet muffle his speech and his screams.

"What's the matter?" the clown mask continued. "Does this look familiar? A trusted friend bound and gagged, screaming, begging for your help. Are you experiencing a sense of déjà vu? The plan is very simple. You run, you call the cops, you notify anyone, and Andrew dies. You show up, and he lives. You've lost so many loved ones over the years, Peter, you wouldn't want to lose your best friend, too, would you?"

"How do I know...?"

"How do you know this is real? How do you know this isn't just another nightmare?"

Andrew screamed, as loud as he could.

"Well, I'll tell you, Peter. You run, you ignore me this time, and tomorrow morning, the people of Hillsboro will find parts of Deputy Andrew Preston cut up and carved into tiny, little pieces, scattered all over this scab of a town. Now, do as your told. Wake up. Get out of bed. Get in your truck and I will call you with the directions."

The phone called disconnected.

"Shit! Shit! Shit!" Peter whispered under his breath, as he sat up in bed.

Peter wildly threw the bed cover back. His heartbeat continuing to race in his rib cage. He climbed to his feet, grabbed the t-shirt and jeans he left on the floor of the bedroom, got dressed, and ran to the end of the hallway, down the staircase, and out the front door, grabbing his wallet and keys from the small table that sat nearby.

Peter was sitting behind the steering wheel of his truck, driving along the long and narrow country roads during the early hours of the morning. Peter rubbed his eyes, again, as he focused on the road in front of him. The cell phone started to ring, again. *Ring. Ring. Ring.* Peter hit the accept button on the cell phone.

"I did what you asked, now what?" Peter asked angrily. The clown mask chuckled, a little, in response.

"You take directions very well, Peter. Now, take a right at the end of the road and turn onto Weston. Follow it to the end."

Peter looked into his rear-view mirror, searching for anyone, for any oncoming traffic.

"Pull your truck into the parking lot and wait. You'll hear from me again very soon, I can guarantee it."

The phone line disconnected, again. "Fuck!" Peter whispered.

Peter followed the directions and made a right-hand turn onto Weston. He applied his foot heavier to the accelerator and raced to the end of the street, toward the park. The trees on the side of the road were nothing more than a dark blur, passing by at an accelerated speed. Peter reached the end of the road, his truck slowing in speed as he pulled into the parking lot. It was empty. The headlights of the truck were bright. There was nothing, no-one around. The engine to the truck soon died. Peter sat there, silent. His hands raced up the sides of the steering wheel, until they reached the top, gripping it tightly. He could hear himself breathing. Peter shook the steering wheel in anger and frustration, as brief as it was and screamed. Peter unbuckled his seat belt, turning in his seat a little, pushing the driver's side door open.

The night air was still. The cool breeze was dying down a little, as Peter stepped out from his truck, leaning against the door. He retrieved his cell phone from his jean pocket, navigating through the screens. There were no further text messages or missed calls. He navigated to his torch app, and switched it on, lifting it up in front of him, using it as a guide.

Peter lead with his left foot. He stepped away from the side of his truck, forward, out towards the wooden benches, nearby. The torch was bright. The light moved across the lawn, which was neatly trimmed and cared for. There was still nothing there. Peter lowered his torch, feeling confused, somewhat.

"What the fuck?" Peter muttered under his breath.

The light from the torch moved, lowered down onto the gravel of the parking lot.

The image of the clown mask appeared from behind, out of the darkness, and was quick to make their move. They raised their left hand, bound in a black leather glove. A quick flash of blue light quickly followed. It came and went within seconds, only highlighting the mask itself, and rendering Peter unconscious. The taser dropped to the gravel of the parking lot. Peter went down, dropping his cell phone. The light from the torch app shone upwards. The image of the clown mask stepped forward, into the light further, standing over its prey. They raised their left foot and stepped heavily on top of the cell phone, breaking the screen.

The torch had died.

Fade to black. Fade from black.

Peter was eventually coming to. Slowly. The neon light which hung from the ceiling was switched on. It was nothing more than a white blur for what felt like seconds. Peter raised his hands to his face and rubbed his eyes, a little. His vision was blurry but eventually came round. Peter felt the pain from the taser course through his body. He rolled around a little, not knowing where he was for a moment. He moaned just above a whisper. The pain. Peter blinked his eyes again, in quick succession as his vision returned to normal. He looked around, another body, lay on the floor, bloodied and beaten, just inches away. Peter quickly climbed to his feet, standing there in the kitchen of his very own home.

"Andrew!" Peter gasped, just above a whisper. "Is he...?"

"Dead?" the clown mask asked, standing just inches away. "No. Not yet. I wouldn't dare let you miss out on watching your only friend be brutally butchered, leaving you lost and alone, all over again."

Peter dragged his gaze from Andrew and looked at the clown mask.

"Just who the fuck are you?" Peter asked, almost confused. "You got what you wanted. I'm here. So, now what?"

"I'm someone who knows you so very well," the clown mask answered. "I'm someone who has been there, watching you, stalking you, since New York City."

Peter held his breath in his chest, a moment.

"I guess I won't be needing the mask any more, right?"

The clown mask stood there, pulling at the mask. It peeled away like a second skin and dropped to the kitchen floor. Peter watched the mask drop to the floor and returned his eyes to the man standing in front of him, the man who stood there, dressed head to toe in black. His heartbeat pounded.

"Logan," Peter replied, just above a whisper.

"Surprise, Peter. Have you missed me? Did you even think of me, once? I've thought of you." Peter could feel the tears welling in his eyes a little. He was angry.

"It was you. All along?"

"Uh-huh." Logan nodded slowly. "Pretty fucking amazing, even if I do say so myself."

"Why?"

"How very ground breaking of you. Why? WHY? Peter Harmon wants to know why! Well, how's this for you, huh?"

Andrew slowly started to come round. His hands and feet pushed outwards, across the floor. The flesh of his hands was torn and bloody and sported one nasty cut above his right eyebrow, which looked like it was in need of stitches. Andrew collapsed, again. Still unconscious.

"You and Ben were always so fucking tight!" Logan started, as he took a single step forward, closer toward Peter. Peter watched his every move. "So, close. Then, one day, I got expelled from school and you cut me out of your life for good. Not a phone call. Not a text message. Nothing! You cut me out of your life like I was a fucking cancer or something. Like I was nothing... like I was shit! So, I thought. Why not cut back? Why not cut back where it truly hurts? I got under your skin. I got inside your head. You should have seen the look on your face. My mother always told me I had a purpose in this life. She told me, I could entertain people, or I could make people fear me. I chose fear!"

Andrew was slowly regaining consciousness, again. His eyes opened and he looked around the kitchen. He felt the pain course through his body, as he lay there in a near foetal position. He could see Peter standing just inches away. Andrew bit down on his tongue, tightly, doing his best to muffle the pain, so as not to draw attention. Peter looked down, the two friends locking eyes on one another. "Well, look who's finally awake and decided to join us?" Logan said, sarcastically. "Don't be rude. Don't just lay there. Get up. Go on. Up! Up! Up! We have company. Victim royalty. Peter Harmon, himself," Logan continued, kicking Andrew heavily about the back and stomach. "How are those stitches?"

Andrew writhed in pain on the kitchen floor, in a bloody mess. He slowly climbed to his feet. "Fuck you!" Andrew managed to answer, just above a whisper, before locking eyes on Peter, again. "So, who is this?"

"This is Logan Myers. We went to school together in New York City. He was, sorry, *is*, a failed actor."

Andrew diverted his eyes back to Logan, giving him the eyeball, up and down, a moment. Judging him.

"I can see that," he nodded, "I haven't seen him in anything I would recognise. And he looks like shit!"

"Not wise to mock me when I have a gun in my hand, Deputy. Your girlfriends sure didn't like it when I got a little knife-happy."

Andrew screamed in anger. "That's it! I am going to kill this son of a bitch right now!" Logan lifted his gun, pointing it directly at Andrew, inches away from his chest.

Andrew lowered his eyes a little, looking down the barrel of his police-issue revolver.

"Stop!" Peter shouted. "Stop!" he repeated.

Logan diverted his eyes away from Andrew and back to Peter. "You *were* an actor." Peter continued, calmly.

"I still *am*. I mean, I fooled you, didn't I?"

"Yes, you did. But I was going to say, you *still* look like shit!"

"Ah, really?" Logan asked, looking at Peter, his face stone cold.

Logan pulled the trigger. The revolver fired and Andrew Preston was shot in the stomach. He clutched at his stomach tightly. The pain coursed through his body. The blood poured from the wound like spilt red wine. Andrew collapsed to the floor, unconscious.

Peter screamed.

The revolver moved quickly, now pointing at Peter. Peter caught his breath in his throat.

"Fuck you!" Logan continued. "You know what? You were so easy to tease, know that? To mess with your life, like you messed with mine.

My life was royally *fucked* after I got expelled from school."

"*This*. All of this was because you were expelled from school?"

"Hurts, doesn't it? I was kicked out of school and spent the past four years with nothing, trying anything, something to patch my life back together again, after my parents kicked me out of home with nothing! And who knew what would come next, huh? Ben Fucking Prescott. That was priceless! It was just delicious. Your very own best friend tried to kill you. He almost killed his entire fucking family."

"You really are a piece of shit, aren't you?" Peter replied, as he fought the anger coursing through his veins. "Listen to you. I've heard this shit before! Do you think you're original? Do you think you will get away with this? People like you always get caught."

Logan nodded his head again, slowly.

"I want to get caught," he whispered. "But not like you think. I am going to know fame as I have always dreamed. It's going to be amazing." Logan chuckled to himself. "My social media accounts are going to blow up! I'll be on *The Late Show with Stephen Colbert*, *The Today Show*, all falling over themselves, wanting to hear what I have to say. I am going to be so fucking rich, it'll be amazing. You see, I kill you, and your steroid-induced best friend here, and *I* survive. It's my turn. Can't you taste it? I'm the one who will call the cops and foil *your* plan. You see, Andrew, the deputy over here, was the killer all along. People will be dumb enough to believe that. I'm sure of it. Andrew was jealous of the attention you got, of the life you lived. He was jealous of you for escaping this dump of a town and making it all the way to New. York. City. The NBC Network will be writing my life story within the next six months."

"I see." Peter said, sarcasm dripping.

"Just look at Andrew. My plan is already coming together, Peter. So, you do have to die."

"Really?" Peter questioned, sarcastically, again. "You know why I did what I did? Why I cut you out of my life when you left school? Because it was easier, that's why! You were cancer. You cling to everything. You couldn't let me breathe. Any of us breathe. Alison. Ben. Nothing was ever easy with you. You are just too… *you*."

"I don't need a fucking gun to kill you off, Peter. Your mother and grandfather would have been so proud of me," Logan said, just above a whisper, as he dropped the revolver to the kitchen floor, lunging forward.

"Fuck you!" Peter screamed.

Logan lunged forward at Peter, his leather gloves extended outwards and moving forward at electric speed. The leather gloves gripped onto Peter, at his eyes. Logan pushed down hard, pushing them into their sockets. Peter screamed, again. His hands raised high, above his shoulders, lunging forward at Logan. They gripped at his shoulders tightly, pulling him forward, closer to him. Peter used what strength he had to head-but Logan, knocking his hands from his eyes. Peter maintained his grip on Logan's shoulders and swung him sideways, into the kitchen wall. Logan was tossed forward, hitting the wall, before collapsing under his own feet, to the kitchen floor. Logan was out of breath and barely conscious as he tried to climb to his feet.

Peter tackled Logan to the kitchen floor, again. They wrestled, fighting for dominance. "I'm going to enjoy killing you," Peter said, just above a whisper. "You're right. Everything has been leading to this. Everything comes to an end, Logan. New ending. I kill you, foil your plans and call the cops. And the media interview *me.*"

Logan screamed angrily. He tightened the grip of his left hand and punched Peter in the jaw, knocking him off his balance. Logan was quick to move, climbing on top of him, tightening his grip around his neck, choking him. The colour of Peter's face was quick to turn shades of red and purple, as his eyes almost bulged.

"You think you're so fucking special, don't you?" Logan seethed through angry eyes. "I'm sorry, Peter. But you're not! The world owes you shit! This. All of this was because of me, and I will enjoy the glory. Because let's face it. You're nothing, Peter. You came from a whore of a mother and nothing more."

Logan lunged forward, pushing the weight of his frame, down on Peter, as his hands gripped tighter around his neck. Peter was fighting, struggling to maintain consciousness. His lips turned purple, as the saliva around his mouth turned a thick, milky-white in colour. Logan screamed loudly.

Andrew lay on the kitchen floor, regaining conscious, slowly. He struggled to keep his eyes open. The sound of the screaming, waking him up. Andrew gasped for air. He lifted his left hand from his stomach. He looked down and saw the blood. His bloodied hands were cold to the touch.

The fingers of the left hand, extended outwards, scratching at the tiled floor of the kitchen, as stains of blood were left behind, pulling him forward. Andrew reached out for his revolver which was left behind, just inches away. Andrew cleared his throat, starting to chuckle some.

"You're forgetting one important loophole in your plan," Andrew said, just above a weakened whisper.

"What?" Logan asked confused, looking over his shoulder at Andrew.

"A good cop always comes prepared. Surprise, motherfucker!" Andrew raised his revolver, just higher enough off the kitchen floor, his hands shaking some, and in a weakened state.

Peter gasped for air as the grip around his neck started to loosen. Deputy Preston squeezed the trigger of his revolver. The revolver fired. And a bullet hole, no larger than the size of a single nickel, pierced Logan's face, just below his right eye. The exit wound of the bullet hole shattered the back of his skull. The blood poured quickly. Logan collapsed into a bloody mess on top of the tiled floor. His face was lifeless as the blood rushed down the right side of his face, onto the kitchen floor beneath. His hands, his legs and feet slowly convulsing until it came to a slow halt. Logan Myers was dead.

"Hang in there, Petey," Andrew said, reassuringly, and just above a whisper.

Peter was still gasping for air. His face was still red with shades of purple. Andrew climbed to his knees first, then his feet, and staggered forward a little, before collapsing just inches away from Peter and a lifeless Logan. Andrew rolled onto his back, staring up at the kitchen light. His bullet wound to the stomach was bloodied and exposed.

Fade to black.

Chapter Thirty-One...

Three months later...

The winter season had passed for another year. It was actually warm today. A slight breeze passed through the trees. Peter was standing in front of his father's tombstone, once more. He was dressed very casually, in denim jeans and a red polo shirt, and sneakers. Peter hadn't shaved, not for several days. The stubble was growing about his chin and cheeks.

"Hi Dad," Peter said, looking down at his father's burial plot. "I'm sorry it's been a while. It's over! Finally. That whole business of Mother and Grandfather and that creepy clown mask they created came up again. Andrew Preston, you remember him? He is doing okay. He is taking life one day at a time. After Emily, well, he has his days. Just like me, I guess. I have my ups and downs. I miss Robert Prescott. And you, of course. I try and do my best each day and forgive Mother for what she had done. It's hard. But I guess I can never really forget her completely. She was, is, a part of me.

Just like you. I miss you so much, Dad. I know who Mike Walters is, was. Well, I guess this is it. Bye, for now. I'll come back and visit. And as to what comes next, I don't know. And I'm feeling pretty good about that. I'm catching up with Andrew tomorrow for a drink. Well, bye, Dad."

Peter turned his back on his father's tombstone and made the slow walk through the Hillsboro cemetery. The breeze was light, and the sun felt warm against his skin. Peter closed his eyes, for just a moment and smiled.